Émile Zola

The Assomoir

The Prelude to Nana

Émile Zola

The Assomoir
The Prelude to Nana

ISBN/EAN: 9783743444416

Manufactured in Europe, USA, Canada, Australia, Japa

Cover: Foto ©Andreas Hilbeck / pixelio.de

Manufactured and distributed by brebook publishing software (www.brebook.com)

Émile Zola

The Assomoir

GERVAISE DRIVING NANA OUT OF THE "GRAND HALL OF FOLLY."

p. 366.

THE "ASSOMMOIR."

(THE PRELUDE TO "NANA")

GERVAISE AND COUPEAU AT THE "ASSOMMOIR."   p. 41.

BY EMILE ZOLA.

THE "ASSOMMOIR"

(THE PRELUDE TO "NANA")

A REALISTIC NOVEL.

BY

ÉMILE ZOLA.

TRANSLATED WITHOUT ABRIDGMENT FROM THE 97TH FRENCH EDITION.

Illustrated with Sixteen Page Engravings,

FROM DESIGNS BY BELLENGER, CLAIRIN, ANDRÉ GILL, LELOIR, ROSE, AND VIERGE.

NEW EDITION.

LONDON:

VIZETELLY & CO., 42 CATHERINE STREET, STRAND.

1885.

NOTES UPON THE "ASSOMMOIR."

BY SIGNOR EDMONDO DE AMICIS.[*]

ONCE in a railway carriage, I saw a Frenchman, who was reading a book very attentively, exhibit, from time to time, signs of surprise. Suddenly, whilst I was trying to discover the title upon the cover, he exclaimed, "Oh! this is disgusting!" and put the volume into his valise in the most contemptuous manner. He remained for some moments lost in thought, then re-opened the valise, took up the book again, and began reading. He might have finished a couple of pages, when he suddenly burst out into a hearty laugh, and turning to his companion, said, "Ah! my dear friend, here is the most marvellous description of a wedding dinner!" Then he resumed his reading, showing plainly that he was enjoying it intensely.

The book was the "Assommoir," and that which happened to the Frenchman when perusing it occurs to all who take up the novels of Zola for the first time. You must conquer the first feeling of repugnance; then, whatever may be the final judgment pronounced upon the writer, you are glad to have read his works, and you arrive at the conclusion that you ought to have read them. The first effect produced, particularly after the perusal of other works, is similar to that experienced on coming out of a close and heated theatre, when one feels the first whiff of fresh air in one's face with a keen sense of pleasure, even if it bring with it an odour not altogether agreeable. After reading Zola's novels it seems as though in all others, even in the truest, there were a veil between the reader and the things described, and there is present to our minds the same difference as exists between the representations of human faces on canvas and the reflection of

---

[*] Signor de Amicis is one of the most brilliant and powerful of the present generation of Italian writers.

the same faces in a mirror. It is like finding truth for the first
time. Certain it is, that no matter how strong you may be, and
whether or no you have *le nez solide*, like Gervaise at the hospital,
sometimes you spring back as if from a sudden whiff of foul air.
But even at these points, as at almost every page, though we
may violently protest "This is too much !" there is a devil in us
which laughs and frolics and enjoys himself hugely over our dis-
comfiture. You feel the same pleasure that you would in
hearing a very blunt man talk, even if he were thoroughly vulgar;
a man who expresses, as Othello says, his worst ideas in his worst
language, who describes what he sees, repeats what he hears, says
what he thinks, and tells what he is, without regard for anyone's
feelings, and just as if he were talking to himself—*à la bonne heure!*

From the very first lines you know with whom you are
dealing. Delicate persons withdraw—that is an understood
thing; Zola does not conceal or embellish anything, either
sentiments, thoughts, conversations, acts, or places. He is at
once a judicious romancer, a surgeon, a casuist, a physiologist, and
an expert chancellor of the exchequer, who thus raises every veil,
putting his hands into everything, and calling a spade a spade,
not heeding, but rather being greatly surprised at your
astonishment. Morally, he unveils in his characters those
deepest feelings, which are generally profound secrets,
tremblingly whispered through the grating of the confessional.
Materially, he makes us aware of every odour, every flavour,
and every contact. In language, he scarcely refrains from
those few unspeakable words, which naughty boys stealthily
seek for in the dictionary. No one has ever gone further in
this extreme, and you really do not know whether you ought
most to admire his talent or his courage.

Among the myriads of characters in novels whom we remember, Zola's remain crowded on one side, and are the boldest and
most tangible of all. We have not only seen them pass, and
heard them talk, but have jostled against them, felt their breath,
and become conscious of the odour of their flesh and their garments.
We have seen the blood circulating beneath their skins; know in
what positions they sleep, what they eat, how they dress and un-

dress; we understand the difference between their temperaments and ours, their most secret appetites, the most passionate anger of their language; their gestures, their grimaces, the spots on their linen, the dirt in their nails, &c. And, with characters, he also imprints upon our mind places, because he looks at everything with the keen glance, which embraces all, and which lets nothing escape. In a room already drawn and painted, the light is moved, and he interrupts the story to tell us whither it glides, upon what the ray of the flame falls in its new position, and how the legs of a chair and the hinges of a door gleam in a dark corner. From the description of a shop, he makes us understand that it has just struck twelve, or lacks nearly an hour of sunset. He notes all the shadows, all the spots on the sun; all the shades of colour which succeed each other from hour to hour upon the wall, and presents everything with such marvellous distinctness, that five years after reading, we remember the appearance the upholstery presented about five o'clock in the evening when the curtains had been drawn, and the effect this appearance produced upon the mind of a person seated in the corner of that particular room.

He never forgets anything, and gives life to everything. There is nothing before which his omnipotent pencil stops, neither soiled linen, the manners of drunken men, unclean flesh, or decayed bodies. Among all these things, in all these places—the air of which we breathe, and in which we see and touch everything— moves a varied crowd of women, corrupt to the marrow, foul-mouthed shopkeepers, cunning bankers, knavish priests, prostitutes, dandies, ruffians, and human scum of every kind and shape (among which appears sometimes, like a *rara avis*, a good man). Amongst them all they do a little of everything, swaying to and fro between the prisoner's dock and the hospital, the pawnshop and the tavern, amidst all the passions and brutish tastes, sunk in the mire up to the chin, in a thick and heavy atmosphere, barely freshened from time to time by the breath of a lovely affection, and stirred alternately by plebeian sickness and the heartrending cries of the famished and the dying

Despite all this, it may be resolutely affirmed that Émile Zola is a moral writer. He is one of the most moral novelists of France, and it is really astonishing how any one can doubt this. He makes us note the smell of vice, not its perfume; his nude figures are those of the anatomical table, which do not inspire the slightest immoral thought; there is not one of his books, not even the crudest, that does not leave in the soul, pure, firm, and immutable aversion or scorn for the base passions of which he treats. Brutally, pitilessly, and without hypocrisy, he strips vice naked, and holds it up to ridicule, standing so far off from it that he does not graze it with his garments. Forced by his hand, it is Vice itself that says, "Detest me and pass by!" His novels, he himself says, are really "morals in action." The scandal which comes from them is only for the eyes and ears. And as he holds back, as a man, from the mire in which his pen is dipped, so does he, as a writer, keep completely aloof from the characters which he has created.

There is, perhaps, no other modern author who conceals himself more skilfully in his works. After reading all his novels, one cannot understand who or what he is. He is a profound observer, a powerful painter, and a wonderful writer. Strong, without respect for mankind, brusque, resolute, bold, rather ill-humoured, and little given to benevolence; but you know nothing more of him. Only that, although you do not see his entire face through the pages of his books, you catch a glimpse of his forehead, scored with a straight and deep furrow, and you fancy that he must have seen, at no great distance, a large portion of the misery and vice which he describes. And he seems to be a man who, having been offended by the world, revenges himself by tearing from her her mask, and exhibiting her for the first time as she really is—for the most part odious and disgusting. A thorough conviction guides and strengthens him—that he ought to speak and describe the truth at any risk or any cost, just as it is, boldly, entirely, and without any concealment. . . .

Strength is the pre-eminent gift of Zola, and any one wishing to describe him must say in the first place: "He is powerful!"

Every one of his novels is *"un grand tour de force,"* an enormous weight which he raises from the ground, whilst doing all that in him lies to conceal the effort. After reading the last page, one is forced to exclaim: "Ah, what a hand;" like those three sots in the "Assommoir," when speaking of the Marquis, who had thrown three ruffians to the ground without even taking his gloves off. And the sudden appearance of this novelist in his shirt sleeves, with his hairy chest and rough voice, who in the most impudent manner, and in the open street, says everything to everybody, in the midst of a crowd of novelists in black suits, well educated and smiling, who say a thousand obscene things in a decent fashion in those little romances, *couleur de rose,* which are written for boudoirs and the stage, is in truth an event in literature. Herein lies his greatest merit. He has flung into the air with one kick all the toilet articles of literature, and has washed with a dowlas dish-cloth the bedizened face of Truth.

The publication of the "Assommoir" was originally commenced in the *Bien Public,* but was left off half finished, so many were the protests launched against this "horror" by the subscribers. Then it was printed in a literary journal, and before it was finished those hot polemics commenced, which became so furious after the publication of the work in a volume, and which will be remembered among the fiercest literary battles of the present day.

These polemics gave a powerful impulse to the success of the novel, and it was a noisy, enormous and incredible success. It had been years since so much had been heard about any book. For a long time Paris talked of nothing but the "Assommoir." One heard it loudly discussed in the cafés, theatres, reading-rooms, and even in the shops; and this by its fanatical admirers, who were more in number than its bitter adversaries. The unheard of brutality of the novel seemed a challenge, a slap at Paris, a calumny against the French people; and they called the book—"a dirty thing to be handled with the tongs," "a monstrous abortion," and a "galley offence," and hurled against the author all the abuse

A

that was possible, from the name of "the enemy of his country," to that of "literary sewer," without choosing their
words.   The theatrical "Revues" of the end of the year represented him in the attire of a garbage-gatherer, who goes
about collecting filth with a hook in the streets of Paris.
"It was no longer criticism," he says; "it was downright
slaughter." They denied his talent, originality, style, and even
grammar—there were even those who would not discuss him;
and they came very near to personal challenges in the
streets.   And the most extravagantly odious rumours were circulated respecting him; he was spoken of as a bundle of vice, a
half brute, a man without heart like Lantier, a beast like
Salted-Mouth, and an ugly individual like his father Bazouge,
the mute.

But meanwhile, editions of the "Assommoir" succeeded editions;
the dispassionate gastronomists said in a low voice that the novel
was a masterpiece; the Parisian populace read it largely, because
they found in it their boulevard, buvette, and shop life indel-
ibly depicted with new colours and touches of the brush, in comparison with which all others seemed feeble, and the most
enraged critics were obliged to recognise the fact, that in those
pages which had been such a target, there was something that
eternally blunted the points of their arrows.   The great success
of the "Assommoir" made Zola's other novels sought after, and
one may safely affirm that he became celebrated then.

Through my friend Parodi, I had the honour of meeting
Zola and of passing several hours with him.   In speaking of the
"Assommoir" he said, "The writing of this work was a
torture to me.   It is the book which has cost me the most
trouble in putting together the small details, upon which it
rests.   I intended writing a novel on alcohol.   I did not know
anything further. I had collected a number of notes on the effects
of the abuse of alcohol.   I had determined to make a brute
die the kind of death that Coupeau does.   I did not know,
however, who would be the victim, and before even looking for
him, I went to the hospital of Sainte-Anne to study sickness and

death, like a physician. Then I assigned to Gervaise the occupation of a laundress, and instantly thought of that description of a real wash-house in which I had myself passed many hours. Then, without knowing anything of Goujet, whom I next imagined, I thought of making use of the recollections of the workshop of an ironmonger and blacksmith, where I had passed half holidays at a time when I was a boy. In the same way, before having woven the thread of my romance, I had already prepared the description of a dinner in Gervaise's shop and of the visit to the museum of the Louvre. I had already studied my types of working men, the 'Assommoir' of old Colombe, the shops, the Hôtel Boncœur, everything in fact.

"When all that remained was disposed of, I commenced to occupy myself with that which was to happen, and reasoned thus while writing it. Gervaise comes to Paris with Lantier, her lover. What will follow? Lantier is a *mauvais sujet*, so he leaves her. Then, will you credit it? I came to a standstill here and could not go on for several days. After some delay I took another step. Gervaise thus abandoned, it is natural that she should marry again. She does so, and marries the zinc-worker, Coupeau. This is the man who is to die at Sainte-Anne. But here I was stopped again. In order to put the personages and scenes which I had in my head in their respective places, and to give some sort of a framework to the novel, I needed one more fact, one only, that would connect the two preceding ones. These three facts would be sufficient, the rest was all found, prepared and written out in my mind. But I could not get hold of this third fact. I passed several days quite worried and discontented, when, suddenly one morning, I was seized with an idea. Lantier finds Gervaise again, makes friends with Coupeau, installs himself in the house; and then a family of three is established, such as I have often seen; and ruin follows. I breathe again. The novel is completed."

Saying this Zola opened a box, took out a roll of manuscript and placed it before me. It contained the first studies of the "Assommoir" on so many fly-leaves.

On the first leaves was a sketch of the characters—notes

about the person, temperament, and character. I found the "Miroir Charactéristique" of Gervaise, Coupeau, Mamma Coupeau, the Lorilleux, the Boches, Goujet, and Madame Lerat. All of them were there. The notes seemed like those of the registrar of a court, written in laconic and free language, like that of the novel, and interpolated with short remarks, such as : " Born like this, educated in this manner, he will conduct himself in this way." In one place was written : "What else can a rascal of this kind do?" Among others, I was struck with a sketch of Lantier, composed of nothing but a list of adjectives, each one stronger than the other, such as *grossier, sensuel, brutal, égoïste, polisson.* In some parts was written : " Use such and such a one" (some one known to the author), all written in large, clear characters, and in perfect order.

Then I saw sketches of places, scarcely outlined, but as accurate as the drawing of an engineer. There were a number of them. All the " Assommoir " was drawn, the streets of the quarter in which the plot was laid, with the corners and signs of the shops; the zigzag which Gervaise took to avoid the creditors, the Sunday escapades of Nana, the peregrinations of the set of topers from *bastringue* to *bastringue,* and from *bousingnot* to *bousingnot ;* the hospital and slaughter-house, between which on that terrible evening came and went the poor ironing woman when maddened by hunger. The great house of Marescot was traced minutely—all the upper storey, the landings, windows, the den of the mute, Father Bru's hole—all those dark passages, in which one could hear *un souffle de crevaison,* those walls which resounded like empty vaults, those doors through which were heard the music of blows and the cries of *mioches,* dying from hunger. There was even the plan of Gervaise's shop, room by room, with indications of beds and tables in some places erased and corrected. One could see that Zola had amused himself by the hour, quite forgetting, perhaps, the story, so buried was he in his fiction, as if it were a true record.

With regard to the title of the work, it may be mentioned that "L'Assommoir" was the name given derisively to a tavern at Belleville, which subsequently became noted under that designation. It was then adopted by the proprietor, and has since become the slang term for those low drinking haunts where the common people imbibe adulterated spirits which shorten their existence. The word "Assommoir" literally means a loaded bludgeon, or that weapon ironically termed a life-preserver—in short, anything that will fell, stun, or kill; and, according to M. Alfred Delvau, the author of a French slang dictionary, it is a curious fact that Russian robbers reverse the metaphor, and nick-name a bludgeon, "champagne." It is scarcely necessary to point out that the loaded bludgeon in the hands of a ruffian and the pernicious spirits dispensed at establishments of the above-mentioned character produce a like result.

AUTHOR'S PREFACE.

THE " Rougon-Macquart " series will be composed of about twenty different novels. Ever since 1869, the general plan has been traced, and I have been following it with extreme rigour. The "Assommoir" came at its time; I wrote it as I shall write the others, without deviating for a second from my straight line. That is what constitutes my strength. I have a goal towards which I am advancing.

When the "Assommoir" appeared in a newspaper, it was attacked with unexampled brutality, denounced, accused of every crime. Is it very necessary to explain here in a few lines my intentions as a writer? I have sought to picture the fatal downfall of a family of work-people, in the pestilential surroundings of our faubourgs. After drunkenness and idleness come the loosening of family ties, the filth engendered by progressive forgetfulness of all upright sentiments, and then, as denouement, shame and death. It is simply a lesson in morality.

The "Assommoir" is certainly the most chaste of my works. Often have I had to point to sores far more frightful. The style alone has shocked. Anger has been aroused by the words. My crime consists in having had the literary curiosity of gathering together and running through a highly-worked mould the language of the people. Ah! the style, therein lies the great crime! Yet dictionaries of this language exist, men of letters study it and enjoy its piquancy, and the unpremeditatedness and the strength of its conceptions. It is a treat for burrowing grammarians. Nevertheless, no one has perceived that my wish was to produce a purely philological work, which I believe to be of keen historical and social interest.

I do not seek to defend myself, though. My work will defend me. It is a work of truth, the first novel of the people which does not lie and which possesses the odour of the people. And one must not conclude that all the lower classes are bad, for my characters are not bad, they are only ignorant and spoilt by the surroundings of rough work and misery amidst which they live. Only, it is necessary to read my novels, to understand them, to see them clearly as a whole, before entertaining the grotesque and odious judgments formed beforehand, which are circulating about my person and my works. Ah! if it were only known how my friends laugh at the amazing legend which serves to amuse the crowd! If it were only known that the blood-drinker, the ferocious novelist, is a worthy citizen, a man of study and of art, living discreetly in his corner, and whose sole ambition is to leave behind him a work as vast and lifelike as he can! I contradict no story. I work, and I leave to time and to the good faith of the public the task of unearthing me from beneath the heap of nonsense and abuse that has been piled up.

ÉMILE ZOLA.

THE "ASSOMMOIR."

CHAPTER I.

GERVAISE had waited for Lantier until two in the morning. Then, shivering from having remained in a thin loose jacket, exposed to the fresh air at the window, she had thrown herself across the bed, drowsy, feverish, and her cheeks bathed in tears.

For a week past, on leaving the "Two-Headed Calf," where they took their meals, he had sent her home with the children and never reappeared himself till late at night, alleging he had been in search of work. That evening, while watching for his return, she thought she had seen him enter the dancing-hall of the "Grand-Balcony," the ten blazing windows of which lighted up with the glare of a conflagration the dark expanse of the exterior Boulevards; and, five or six paces behind him, she had caught sight of little Adèle, a burnisher, who dined at their restaurant, swinging her hands, as if she had just quitted his arm so as not to pass together under the dazzling light of the globes at the door.

When, towards five o'clock, Gervaise awoke, stiff and sore, she broke forth into sobs. Lantier had not returned. For the first time he had slept away from home. She remained seated on the edge of the bed, under the strip of faded chintz, which hung from the rod fastened to the ceiling by a piece of string. And, slowly, with her eyes veiled by tears, she glanced round the wretched lodging, furnished with a walnut chest of drawers, minus one drawer, three rush-bottomed chairs, and a little greasy table, on which stood a broken water-jug. There had been added, for the children, an iron bedstead, which prevented any one getting to the chest of drawers, and filled two-thirds of the room. Gervaise's and Lantier's trunk, wide open, in one corner, displayed its emptiness, and a man's old hat right at the bottom almost buried beneath some dirty shirts and socks; whilst, against the walls, above the articles of furniture, hung a shawl full of holes, and a pair of trousers begrimed with mud, the last rags which the dealers in second-hand clothes declined to buy. In the centre of the mantel-piece, lying between two odd zinc candle-sticks, was a bundle of pink pawn-tickets. It was the best room of the hotel, the first floor room, looking on to the Boulevard.

The two children were sleeping side by side, with their heads on the same pillow. Claude, aged eight years, was breathing quietly, with his little hands thrown outside the coverlet; while Étienne, only four years old, was smiling, with one arm round his brother's neck. As the clouded gaze of their mother rested upon them, she broke into a fresh fit of sobbing, and was obliged to press a handkerchief to her mouth, to stifle the faint cries that escaped her. And, bare-footed, without thinking to again put on the old shoes that had fallen on the floor, she resumed her position at the window, her eyes searching the pavements in the distance.

The hotel was situated on the Boulevard de la Chapelle, to the left of the Barrière Poissonnière. It was a building of two stories high, painted a red, of the colour of wine dregs, up to the second floor, and with shutters all rotted by the rain. Over a lamp with starred panes of glass, one could manage to read, between the two windows, the words, " Hôtel Boncœur, kept by Marsoullier," painted in big yellow letters, several pieces of which the mouldering of the plaster had carried away. The lamp preventing her seeing, Gervaise raised herself on tiptoe, still holding the handkerchief to her lips. She looked to the right, towards the Boulevard Rochechouart, where groups of butchers, in aprons smeared with blood, were hanging about in front of the slaughter-houses; and the fresh breeze wafted occasionally a stench of slaughtered beasts. Looking to the left, she scanned a long avenue that ended nearly in front of her, where the white mass of the Lariboisière Hospital was then in course of construction. Slowly, from one end of the horizon to the other, she followed the octroi wall, behind which she sometimes heard, during night time, the shrieks of persons being murdered; and she searchingly looked into the remote angles, the dark corners, black with humidity and filth, fearing to discern there Lantier's body, stabbed to death. When she raised her eyes beyond that grey and interminable wall, which encircled the city with a desert-like belt, she perceived a great light, a sunny dust, already full of the early morning rumbling of awaking Paris. But it was always to the Barrière Poissonnière that she returned, stretching out her neck, and making her head dizzy by watching the uninterrupted flow of men, cattle, and carts, that descended from the heights of Montmartre and La Chapelle, pass between the two low buildings of the octroi. There were the heavy tramp of a drove, a crowd that sudden stoppages formed into groups like puddles in the roadway, an endless procession of labourers going to their work, with loaves of bread under their arms and their tools slung over their shoulders; and this mixed mass was swallowed up by the great city in which it kept on disappearing. Each time Gervaise thought she recognised Lantier among all these people, she leaned out the more, at the risk of falling; then she pressed the handkerchief more firmly to her mouth, as though to repress her grief.

The sound of a young and cheerful voice caused her to leave the window.

" So the old man isn't here, Madame Lantier ? "

" Why, no, Monsieur Coupeau," she replied, trying to smile.

He was a zinc-worker, occupying a mere closet at the top of the house, for ten francs a month. He had his bag slung on his shoulder; and finding the key in the door, he had entered in a neighbourly way.

" You know," he continued, " I'm now working over there at the hospital. What beautiful May weather, isn't it ? The air is rather sharp this morning."

And he looked at Gervaise's face, red with weeping. When he saw that the bed had not been slept in, he shook his head gently; then he went to the children's couch where they were sleeping, looking as rosy as cherubs, and, lowering his voice, he said,

" Come, the old man's not been home, has he ? Don't worry yourself, Madame Lantier. He's very much occupied with politics. The other day, when they elected Eugène Sue, one of the right sort, it appears, he was perfectly crazy. He has very likely spent the night with some friends blackguarding that crapulous Bonaparte."

" No, no," she murmured with an effort. " You don't think that. I know where Lantier is. You see, we have our little troubles like the rest of the world ! "

Coupeau blinked his eyes, to indicate he was not a dupe of this falsehood; and he went off, after offering to fetch her milk, if she did not care to go out : she was a good and cour-

ageous woman, and might count upon him on any day of
trouble.

As soon as he was gone, Gervaise again returned to the
window. At the Barrière, the tramp of the drove still continued
in the cold morning air. You could recognise the locksmiths
by their short blue blouses, the masons by their white overalls,
and the painters by their overcoats, beneath which extended
long blouses. At a distance this throng had the washed-out
appearance of mortar, a neutral tint, in which faded blue and dirty
grey predominated. Now and again, a workman stopped short, to
relight his pipe, while the others around him pressed on, without a laugh, or a word said to a comrade, a cadaverous look on
their cheeks, and their faces turned towards Paris, which
swallowed them, one by one, down the gaping Faubourg-
Poissounière. At both corners of the Rue des Poissonniers,
however, some of the men slackened their pace as they neared
the doors of the two wine-dealers who were taking down their
shutters ; and, before entering, they stood on the edge of the
pavement, looking sideways over Paris, with no strength in
their arms, and already inclined for a day of idleness. Before
the counters, groups of men were standing, treating each other,
wasting their time there as they filled the rooms, coughing,
spitting, and clearing their throats with glasses of neat spirits.
Gervaise was watching old Colombe's wine-shop to the left of
the street, where she thought she had seen Lantier, when a
stout woman, bareheaded and wearing an apron, called to her
from the middle of the roadway :

"I say, Madame Lantier, you're up very early !"

Gervaise leaned out. "Why ! it's you, Madame Boche !—
Oh ! I've a lot of work to-day !"

"Yes, things don't do themselves, do they ?"

And a conversation ensued from the window to the pavement.
Madame Boche was doorkeeper of the building the ground floor of
which was occupied by the restaurant of the "Two-Headed Calf."
Several times Gervaise had waited for Lantier in her room, so
as not to sit down alone among all the men who took their
meals close by. The doorkeeper said she was going a few steps,
to the Rue de la Charbonnière, to catch a clerk in bed, who
owed her husband for the repairing of a frock-coat. Then she
talked of one of her lodgers who had brought a woman home
with him the previous night, and who had prevented everybody
from going to sleep till three o'clock in the morning. But,
whilst chatting, she scrutinized the young woman with piercing

curiosity, and seemed only to have come there and planted herself under the window for the purpose of finding something out.

"Is Monsieur Lantier, then, still in bed?" she asked abruptly.

"Yes, he's asleep," replied Gervaise, who could not avoid blushing.

Madame Boche saw the tears come into her eyes; and, satisfied no doubt, she turned to go, declaring men to be a cursed, lazy set. As she went off, she called back:

"It's this morning you go to the wash-house, isn't it? I've something to wash, too. I'll keep you a place next to me, and we can chat together." Then, as if moved with sudden pity, she added:

"My poor little thing, you had far better not remain there; you'll take harm. You look quite blue with cold."

Gervaise still obstinately remained at the window during two mortal hours, till eight o'clock. The shops had all opened. The flow of men in blouses coming from the heights had ceased; and only a few workmen who were late passed the Barrière with hasty strides. In the wine-shops, the same men standing up continued to drink, cough, and spit. Workwomen had followed the labourers—burnishers, milliners, artificial flower-makers, gathering their thin clothes tightly around them, trotting along the exterior Boulevards; they went in bands of threes and fours, chatting gaily, gently laughing and casting bright glances about them; at long intervals, one all alone, pale-faced and serious-looking, followed the octroi wall, carefully avoiding the filth that lay about there. Then the clerks had passed, blowing on their fingers, and eating their halfpenny rolls as they walked; thin young men in clothes too short, and with a bleared and sleepy look about their eyes; little old men who stumbled along, with sickly countenances, worn out by long office hours, and who kept consulting their watches to regulate their progress to within a few seconds. The Boulevards had assumed their morning calm; the men of leisure of the neighbourhood strolled about in the sunshine; mothers, with heads uncovered, and in dirty skirts, rocked their babies in swaddling clothes, which they changed on the seats; a number of half-naked brats, with dirty noses, jostled each other and rolled upon the ground, amid whining, laughter and tears. Then Gervaise felt herself choking, dizzy with anguish, all hope gone; it seemed to her that everything was ended, even time itself, and that Lantier would return no more. Her eyes vacantly wandered from the old slaughter-houses, foul with butchery and with stench, to the new white hospital, which, through the yawning openings of its ranges of windows, disclosed the naked wards, where death was preparing to mow. In front of her, on the other side of the octroi wall, the bright heavens dazzled her, with the rising sun which rose higher and higher over the vast awaking city.

The young woman was seated on a chair, no longer crying, and with her hands abandoned on her lap, when Lantier quietly entered the room.

"It's you!—it's you!" she cried, rising to throw herself upon his neck.

"Yes, it's me. What of it?" he replied. "You are not going to begin any of your nonsense, I hope!"

He had pushed her aside. Then, with a gesture of ill-humour, he threw his black felt hat on to the chest of drawers. He was a young fellow of twenty-six years of age, short, and very dark, with a handsome figure, and slight moustaches which his hand was always mechanically twirling. He wore a workman's overalls and an old soiled overcoat, which he had made tight at the waist, and he spoke with a strong Provencial accent.

Gervaise, who had fallen back on her chair, gently complained, in short sentences: "I've not had a wink of sleep. I feared some harm had happened to you. Where have you been? Where did you spend the night? For heaven's sake! don't do it again, or I shall go crazy. Tell me, Auguste, where have you been?"

"Where I'd business, of course," he returned, shrugging his shoulders. "At eight o'clock, I was at La Glacière, with my friend, who is to start a hat factory. We sat talking late, so I preferred to sleep there. Now, you know, I don't like being spied upon, so just shut up!"

The young woman recommenced sobbing. The loud voices and the rough movements of Lantier, who upset the chairs, had awakened the children. They sat up in bed, half naked, disentangling their hair with their tiny hands, and, hearing their mother weep, they uttered terrible screams, crying also with their scarcely open eyes.

"Ah! there's the music!" exclaimed Lantier. "I warn you, I'll take my hook! And it will be for good, this time. You won't shut up? Then, good morning! I'll return to the place I've just come from."

He had already taken his hat from off the chest of drawers. But Gervaise threw herself before him, stammering: "No, no!"

And she hushed the little ones' tears with her caresses, smoothed their hair, and soothed them with soft words. The children, suddenly quieted, laughing on their pillow, amused themselves by pinching each other. The father, however, without even taking off his boots, had thrown himself on the bed, looking worn out, his face bearing signs of having been up all night. He did not go to sleep, he lay with his eyes wide open, looking round the room.

"It's clean here!" he muttered. And after observing Gervaise a moment, he malignantly added: "Don't you even wash yourself now?"

Gervaise was only twenty-two years old. She was tall and rather slim, with delicate features already worn by the roughness of her life. Uncombed, and in old shoes, shivering under her thin white jacket all soiled with grease and the dust from the furniture, she seemed aged at least ten years by the hours of anguish and tears she had just gone through. Lantier's words made her throw off her timid and submissive attitude.

"You're not just," said she, spiritedly. "You well know I do all I can. It's not my fault we find ourselves here. I would like to see you, with the two children, in a room where there's not even a stove to heat some water. When we arrived in Paris, instead of squandering your money, you should have made a home for us at once, as you promised."

"I say!" he cried, "you cracked the nut with me; it doesn't become you to sneer at it now!"

But she did not appear to hear him, and she continued: "However, with courage, we can still get right again. I saw Madame Fauconnier, the laundress in the Rue Neuve, yesterday evening; she will take me on Monday. If you get to work again with your friend at La Glacière, we'll have our heads above water again before six months are past, just time enough to get ourselves some clothes and take a place somewhere, that we can call our own. Oh! but we must work, work!"

Lantier turned over towards the wall, looking greatly bored. Then Gervaise lost her temper.

"Yes, that's it, I know the love of work doesn't trouble you much. You're bursting with ambition, you want to be dressed like a gentleman and take out strumpets in silk skirts. You don't think me nice enough, do you, now that you've made me pawn all my dresses? Listen, Auguste, I didn't intend to speak of it, I would have waited a bit longer, but I know where you spent the night; I saw you enter the "Grand-Balcony" with that trollop Adèle. Ah! you choose them well! She's a nice one, she is! she does well to put on the airs of a princess! She's been the mistress of every man who frequents the restaurant."

At a bound Lantier sprang from the bed. His eyes had become as black as ink in his pale face. With this little man, rage blew like a tempest.

"Yes, yes, of every man who frequents the restaurant!" repeated the young woman. "Madame Boche intends to give them notice, she and her long stick of a sister, because they've always a string of men after them on the staircase."

Lantier raised his fists; then, resisting the desire of striking her, he seized hold of her by the arms, shook her violently, and sent her sprawling upon the bed of the children, who recommenced crying. And he lay down again, mumbling, like a man resolving on something that he previously hesitated to do:

"You don't know what you've done Gervaise. You've been wrong; you'll see."

For an instant, the children continued sobbing. Their mother, who remained bending over the bed, held them both in her embrace, and kept repeating these words in a monotonous tone of voice.

"Ah! if you were not there! my poor little ones! If you were not there! If you were not there!"

Stretched out quietly, his eyes raised to the faded strip of chintz, Lantier no longer listened, but seemed to be buried in a fixed idea. He remained thus for nearly an hour, without giving way to sleep, in spite of the fatigue which weighed his eyelids down. When he turned round, raising himself on his arm, with a harsh and determined look upon his face, Gervaise had almost finished tidying the room. She was making the children's bed, they being already up and dressed. He watched her as she swept and dusted about; the room still remained dingy and miserable looking, with its smoky ceiling, its paper peeling off the walls from the damp, its three rickety chairs and its tumble down chest of drawers, to which the dirt obstinately clung and only spread all the more beneath the duster. Then, whilst she washed herself with a great splashing of the water, after doing up her hair in front of a little round hand-glass hung to the window fastening, and which Lantier used to shave himself by, he seemed to examine her bare arms, and throat, and shoulders, the whole of her frame that she exposed, as though his mind was forming a comparison. And he pouted his lips. Gervaise limped with her right leg; but it was scarcely perceptible, excepting on the days when she was tired, when with her hips aching from fatigue she would be careless how she walked. That morning, worn out by the restless night which she had passed, she dragged her leg, and leant against the wall. Silence prevailed ; they had not exchanged another word. He seemed to be waiting for something. She, devouring her grief, trying to assume a look of indifference, hurried over her work. While she was making a bundle of the dirty clothes thrown in a corner, behind the trunk, he at length opened his lips, and asked :

"What are you doing there? Where are you going?"

She did not answer at first. Then, when he furiously repeated his question, she made up her mind, and said :

"I suppose you can see for yourself. I'm going to wash all this. The children can't live in filth."

He let her pick up two or three handkerchiefs. And, after a fresh pause, he resumed : "Have you got any money?"

At these words she stood up and looked him full in the face, without leaving go of the children's dirty shirts, which she held in her hand.

"Money! and where do you think I can have stolen any? You know well enough that I got three francs the day before yesterday on my black skirt. We've lunched twice off it, and money goes quick at the pork-butcher's. No, you may be quite sure I've no money. I've four sous for the wash-house. I don't earn money like some women."

He let this allusion pass. He had moved off the bed, and was passing in review the few rags hanging about the room. He ended by taking up the pair of trousers and the shawl, and searching the drawers, he added two chemises and a woman's loose jacket to the parcel ; then, he threw the whole bundle into Gervaise's arms, saying :

"Here, go and pop this."

"Don't you want me to pop the children as well?" asked she. "Eh! if they lent on children, it would be a fine riddance!"

She went to the pawn-place, however. When she returned at the end of half-an-hour, she laid a hundred sou piece on the mantel-shelf, and added the ticket to the others, between the two candlesticks.

"That's what they gave me," said she. "I wanted six francs, but I couldn't manage it. Oh! they'll never ruin themselves. And there's always such a crowd there!"

Lantier did not pick up the five franc piece directly. He would rather that she got change, so as to leave her some of it. But he decided to slip it into his waistcoat pocket, when he noticed a small piece of ham wrapped up in paper, and the remains of a loaf on the chest of drawers.

"I didn't dare go to the milkwoman's, because we owe her a week," explained Gervaise. "But I shall be back early; you can get some bread and some chops whilst I'm away, and then we'll have lunch. Bring also a bottle of wine."

He did not say no. Their quarrel seemed to be forgotten. The young woman was completing her bundle of dirty clothes. But when she went to take Lantier's shirts and socks from the bottom of the trunk, he called to her to leave them alone.

"Leave my things, d'ye hear! I don't want 'em touched!"

"What's it you don't want touched?" she asked, rising up. "I suppose you don't mean to put these filthy things on again, do you? They must be washed."

And she anxiously scrutinized his handsome face, in which she saw the same harshness, as though nothing would move him ever more. He flew into a passion, and, snatching the things from her hands, threw them back into the trunk.

"Damnation! just obey me for once in a way! I tell you I won't have 'em touched!"

"But why?" she added, turning pale, a terrible suspicion crossing her mind. "You don't want your shirts now, you're not going away. What can it matter to you if I take them?"

He hesitated for an instant, embarrassed by the piercing glance she fixed upon him. "Why—why—" stammered he, "because you go and tell every one that you keep me, that you wash and mend. Well! it worries me, there! Attend to your own business and I'll attend to mine. Washerwomen don't work for dogs."

She supplicated, she protested she had never complained; but he roughly closed the trunk and sat down upon it, saying, "No!" to her face. He could surely do as he liked with what belonged to him! Then, to escape from the inquiring looks she levelled at him, he went and laid down on the bed again, saying that he was sleepy, and requesting her not to make his head ache with any more of her row. This time, indeed, he seemed to fall asleep. Gervaise, for a while, remained undecided. She was tempted to kick the bundle of dirty clothes on one side, and to sit down and sew. But Lantier's regular breathing onded by reassuring her. She took the ball of blue and the piece of soap remaining from her last washing, and going up to the little ones who were quietly playing with some old corks in front of the window, she kissed them, and said in a low voice:

"Be very good, don't make any noise ; papa's asleep."

When she left the room, Claude's and Etienne's gentle laughter alone disturbed the great silence beneath the blackened ceiling. It was ten o'clock. A ray of sunshine entered by the half open window. On the Boulevard, Gervaise turned to the left, and followed the Rue Neuve de la Goutte-d'Or. As she passed Madame Fauconnier's shop, she slightly bowed her head. The wash-house she was bound for was situated towards the middle of the street, at the part where the roadway commenced to ascend. On the top of a flat building three enormous reservoirs of water—zinc tanks strongly riveted—displayed their round grey sides ; whilst, behind, rose up the drying-room, a very lofty second floor, closed on all sides by Venetian shutters, the openings between the laths of which admitted the outer air, and gave a view of clothes drying on brass wire lines. To the right of the reservoirs, the narrow funnel of the steam engine discharged, with a rough and regular respiration, puffs of white smoke. Gervaise, without tucking up her skirts, but like a woman used to moving about amongst puddles, entered the doorway, all encumbered with jars full of some chemical water. She was already acquainted with the mistress of the wash-house, a delicate little woman with sore eyes, who sat in a small glazed closet with account books in front of her, bars of soap on shelves, balls of blue in glass bowls, and pounds of soda done up in packets ; and, as she passed, she asked for her beetle and her scouring-brush, which she had left to be taken care of the last time she had done her washing there. Then, after obtaining her number, she entered the wash-house.

It was an immense shed, with large light windows, and a flat ceiling, showing the beams supported on cast-iron pillars. Pale rays of light passed freely through the hot steam, which remained suspended like a milky fog. Smoke arose from certain corners, spreading about and covering the recesses with a bluish veil. A heavy moisture hung around, impregnated with a soapy odour, a damp insipid smell, continuous though at moments overpowered by the more potent fumes of the chemicals. Along the washing-places, on either side of the central alley, were rows of women, with bare arms and necks, and skirts tucked up, showing coloured stockings and heavy lace-up shoes. They were beating furiously, laughing, leaning back to call out a word

in the midst of the din, or stooping over their tubs, all of them
brutal, ungainly, foul of speech, and soaked as though by a
shower, with their flesh red and reeking.   Around them,
beneath them, was a great flow of water, steaming pailfuls
carried about and emptied at one shoot, high up, taps of cold
water turned on and discharging their contents, the splashings
caused by the beetles, the drippings from the rinsed clothes,
the pools in which the women trod trickling away in streamlets
over the sloping flagstones ; and, in the midst of the cries, of
the cadenced blows, of the murmuring noise of rain, of that
storm-like clamour dying away beneath the saturated ceiling,
the engine on the right, all white with steam, puffed and snorted
unceasingly, the dancing trepidation of its fly-wheel seeming
to regulate the magnitude of the uproar.

Gervaise passed slowly along the alley, looking to the right
and left.   She carried her bundle of clothes on her arm, with
one hip higher than the other, and limping more than usual, in
the passing, backwards and forwards, of the other women who
jostled against her.

"This way, my dear!" cried Madame Boche, in her loud
voice.   Then, when the young woman had joined her, at the
very end on the left, the doorkeeper, who was furiously rubbing
a sock, began to talk incessantly, without leaving off her work.
"Put your things there, I've kept your place.   Oh! I sha'n't
be long over what I've got.   Boche scarcely dirties his things
at all.   And you, you won't be long either, will you ?   Your
bundle's quite a little one.   Before twelve o'clock we shall have
finished, and we can go off to lunch.   I used to send my things to a
laundress in the Rue Poulet, but she destroyed everything with
her chlorine and her brushes ; so now I do the washing myself.
It's so much saved ; it only costs the soap.   I say, you should
have put those shirts to soak.   Those little rascals of children, on
my word ! one would think their bodies were covered with soot."

Gervaise, having undone her bundle, was spreading out the
little ones' shirts, and as Madame Boche advised her to take a
pailful of lye, she answered, "Oh, no ! warm water will do.
I'm used to it."

She had sorted the clothes, and put the few coloured things
on one side.   Then, after filling her tub with four pailfuls of
cold water taken from the tap behind her, she dipped in the
pile of linen, and, tucking up her skirt, drawing it tight between
her legs, she got into a kind of upright box, the sides of which
reached nearly to her waist.

"You're used to it, eh?" repeated Madame Boche. "You were a washerwoman in your native place, weren't you, my dear?"

Gervaise, with her sleeves turned up, displaying her fine fair arms, still young, and scarcely reddened at the elbows, commenced getting the dirt out of her linen. She had spread a chemise over the narrow plank of the washing-place, whitened and eaten away by the wear and tear of the water; she rubbed it over with soap, turned it, and rubbed it on the other side. Before answering, she seized her beetle and began to beat, shouting out her sentences, and punctuating them with rough and regular blows.

"Yes, yes, a washerwoman—When I was ten—That's twelve years ago—We used to go to the river—It smelt nicer there than it does here—You should have seen, there was a nook under the trees, with clear running water—You know, at Plassans—Don't you know Plassans?—It's near Marseilles."

"How she goes at it!" exclaimed Madame Boche, amazed at the strength of her blows. "What a wench it is? She'd flatten out a piece of iron with her little lady-like arms."

The conversation continued in a very high tone. At times, the doorkeeper, not catching what was said, was obliged to lean forward. All the linen was beaten, and with a will! Gervaise plunged it into the tub again, and then took it out once more, each article separately, to rub it over with soap a second time and brush it. With one hand she held the article firmly on to the plank; with the other, which grasped the short couch-grass brush, she extracted from the linen a dirty lather, which fell in long drips. Then, in the slight noise caused by the brush, the two women drew together, and conversed in a more intimate way.

"No, we're not married," resumed Gervaise. "I don't hide it. Lantier isn't so nice for any one to care to be his wife. Ah! if it wasn't for the children. I was fourteen and he eighteen years old when we had our first; the other came four years later. It happened as it always does, you know. I wasn't happy at home. Old Macquart, for a yes or a no, would give me no end of kicks behind; so I preferred to keep away from him. We might have been married, but—I forget why—our parents wouldn't consent."

She shook her hands, which were growing red in the white suds. "The water's awfully hard in Paris," said she.

Madame Boche was now washing only very slowly. She

kept leaving off, making her work last as long as she could, so as to remain there, to listen to that story, which her curiosity had been hankering to know for a fortnight past. Her mouth was half open in the midst of her big, fat face; her eyes, which were almost at the top of her head, were gleaming. She was thinking, with the satisfaction of having guessed right,

"That's it, the little one gossips too much. There's been a row."

Then, she observed out loud, "He isn't nice, then?"

"Don't mention it!" replied Gervaise. "He used to behave very well in the country; but, since we've been in Paris, he's been unbearable. I must tell you that his mother died last year and left him some money—about seventeen hundred francs. He would come to Paris, so, as old Macquart was for ever knocking me about without warning, I consented to come away with him. We made the journey with the two children. He was to set me up as a laundress, and work himself at his trade of a hatter. We should have been very happy; but, you see, Lantier's ambitious and a spendthrift, a fellow who only thinks of amusing himself. In short, he's not worth much. On arriving, we went to the Hôtel Montmartre, in the Rue Montmartre. And then there were dinners, and cabs, and the theatre; a watch for himself and a silk dress for me, for he's not unkind when he's got the money. You understand, he went in for everything, and so well that at the end of two months we were cleaned out. It was then that we came to live at the Hôtel Boncœur, and that this horrible life began."

She interrupted herself. A lump had suddenly risen in her throat, and she could scarcely restrain her tears. She had finished brushing the things.

"I must go and fetch my hot water," she murmured.

But Madame Boche, greatly disappointed at this break off in the disclosures, called to the wash-house boy, who was passing,

"My little Charles, kindly get madame a pail of hot water; she's in a hurry."

The boy took the pail and brought it back filled. Gervaise paid him; it was a sou the pailful. She poured the hot water into the tub, and soaped the things a last time with her hands, leaning over them in a mass of steam, which deposited small beads of grey vapour in her light hair.

"Here, put some soda in, I've got some by me," said the doorkeeper, obligingly.

And she emptied into Gervaise's tub what remained of a bag of soda which she had brought with her. She also offered her some of the chemical water, but the young woman declined it; it was only good for grease and wine stains.

"I think he's rather a loose fellow," resumed Madame Boche, returning to Lantier, but without naming him.

Gervaise, bent almost double, her hands all shrivelled, and thrust in amongst the clothes, merely tossed her head.

"Yes, yes," continued the other, "I've noticed several little things—" But she suddenly interrupted herself, as Gervaise jumped up, with a pale face, and staring wildly at her. Then she exclaimed, "Oh, no! I don't know anything! He likes to laugh a bit, I think, that's all. For instance, you know the two girls who lodge at my place, Adèle and Virginie. Well, he larks about with 'em, but it doesn't go any further, I'm sure."

The young woman standing before her, her face covered with perspiration, the water dripping from her arms, continued to stare at her with a fixed and penetrating look. Then the door-keeper got excited, giving herself a blow on the chest, and pledging her word of honour, she cried,

"I know nothing, I mean it when I say so!"

Then, calming herself, she added in a gentle voice, as if speaking to a person on whom loud protestations would have no effect, "I think he has a frank look about the eyes. He'll marry you, my dear, I'm sure of it!"

Gervaise passed her wet hand over her forehead. She drew another article of clothing from the water, as she again tossed her head. For a while they both remained silent. Peacefulness prevailed around them; eleven o'clock was striking. Half the women, resting one leg on the edges of their tubs, and with open bottles of wine at their feet, were eating sausages between slices of bread. Only the women who had families, and had come there just to wash their little bundles of clothes, hurried over their work as they kept glancing up at the clock which hung above the office. A few beetle strokes were still heard at intervals, in the midst of quiet laughter and conversations, which were drowned in the noise of a glutinous movement of jaws; whilst the steam-engine, ever at work, without truce or repose, seemed to raise its vibrating, snorting voice, until it filled the immense building. But not one of the women noticed it; it was as it were the very breathing of the wash-house—a scorching breath which accumulated, beneath the beams of the ceiling, the mist that incessantly floated about. The heat was becoming unbearable. Rays of sunshine entered through the

tall windows on the left, transforming the smoking vapours
into opaque masses of a pale pink and bluish grey tint; and, as
complaints arose, the boy Charles went from one window to
the other and lowered some coarse blinds; then he crossed to
the other side, the shady one, and opened some of the case-
ments. His movements were greeted with acclamations. There
was a general clapping of hands, a boisterous gaiety passed
over all. Then the last beetles were laid down. The women,
with their mouths full, now only made gestures with the open
knives that they held in their hands. The silence became so
general that one could hear, at regular intervals, the grating of
the stoker's shovel at the further end, as he scooped up the coal
and threw it into the furnace.

Gervaise was washing her coloured things in the hot water
thick with lather, which she had kept for the purpose. When
she had finished, she drew a trestle towards her and hung across
it all the different articles, the drippings from which made
bluish puddles on the floor; and then she commenced rinsing.
Behind her, the cold water tap was set running into a vast tub
fixed to the ground, and across which were two wooden bars
whereon to lay the clothes. High up in the air were two other
bars for the things to finish dripping on.

"We're almost finished, and it's not a pity," said Madame
Boche. "I'll wait and help you wring all that."

"Oh! it's not worth while; I'm much obliged though,"
replied the young woman, who was kneading with her hands
and sousing the coloured things in some clean water. "If I'd
any sheets, it would be another thing."

But she had, however, to accept the doorkeeper's assistance.
They were wringing between them, one at each end, a woollen
skirt of a washed-out chestnut colour, from which dribbled a
yellowish water, when Madame Boche exclaimed:

"Why, there's tall Virginie? What has she come here to
wash, when all her wardrobe that isn't on her would go into a
pocket handkerchief?"

Gervaise quickly raised her head. Virginie was a girl of her
own age, taller than she was, dark and pretty in spite of her
face being rather long. She had on an old black dress with
flounces, and a red ribbon round her neck; and her hair was
done up carefully, the chignon being enclosed in a blue silk
net. She stood an instant, in the middle of the central alley,
screwing up her eyes as though seeking some one; then, when
she caught sight of Gervaise, she passed close to her, erect,

insolent, and with a swinging gait, and took a place in the same row, five tubs away from her.

" There's a freak for you !" continued Madame Boche in a lower tone of voice. " She never even washes a pair of cuffs. Ah ! she's a regular slut, I can tell you ! A needlewoman who doesn't even sew the buttons on her boots ! It's the same with her sister, the burnisher, that trollop Adèle, who's away from the workshop two days out of three ! They know neither their father nor their mother, and they live no one knows how ; and if one cared to talk—What's that she's rubbing there ? Eh ? it's a petticoat ! Isn't it in a filthy state ? It must have seen some fine goings-on, that petticoat !"

Madame Boche was evidently trying to make herself agreeable to Gervaise. The truth was she often took a cup of coffee with Adèle and Virginie, when the girls had any money. Gervaise did not answer, but hurried over her work with feverish hands. She had just prepared her blue in a little tub that stood on three legs. She dipped in the linen things, and shook them an instant at the bottom of the coloured water, the reflection of which had a pinky tinge ; and, after wringing them lightly, she spread them out on the wooden bars, up above. During the time she was occupied with this work, she made a point of turning her back on Virginie. But she heard her chuckles ; she could feel her sidelong glances. Virginie appeared only to have come there to provoke her. At one moment, Gervaise having turned round, they both stared into each other's faces.

" Leave her alone," murmured Madame Boche. " You're not going to pull each other's hair out, I hope. When I tell you there's nothing ! It isn't her, there !"

At this moment, as the young woman was hanging up the last article of clothing, there was a sound of laughter at the door of the wash-house.

" Here are two brats who want their mamma !" cried Charles.

All the women leant forward. Gervaise recognised Claude and Etienne. As soon as they caught sight of her, they ran to her through the puddles, the heels of their unlaced shoes resounding on the flagstones. Claude, the eldest, held his little brother by the hand. The women, as they passed them, uttered little exclamations of affection as they noticed their frightened, though smiling, faces. And they stood there, in front of their mother, without leaving go of each other's hands, and holding their fair heads erect.

" Has papa sent you ?" asked Gervaise.

But as she stooped to tie the laces of Etienne's shoes, she saw the key of their room on one of Claude's fingers, with the brass number hanging from it.

"Why, you've brought the key!" said she, greatly surprised. "What's that for?"

The child, seeing the key which he had forgotten on his finger, appeared to recollect, and exclaimed in his clear voice,

"Papa's gone."

"He's gone to buy the lunch, and told you to come here to fetch me?"

Claude looked at his brother, hesitated, no longer recollecting. Then he resumed all in a breath: "Papa's gone. He jumped off the bed, he put all the things in the box, he carried the box down to a cab. He's gone."

Gervaise, who was squatting down, slowly rose to her feet, her face ghastly pale. She put her hands to her cheeks and temples, as though she felt her head was breaking; and she could find only these words, which she repeated twenty times in the same tone of voice:

"Ah! good heavens!—ah! good heavens!—ah! good heavens!"

Madame Boche, however, also questioned the child, quite delighted at the chance of hearing the whole story.

"Come, little one, you must tell us just what happened. It was he who locked the door and who told you to bring the key, wasn't it?" And, lowering her voice, she whispered in Claude's ear: "Was there a lady in the cab?"

The child again got confused. Then he recommenced his story in a triumphant manner: "He jumped off the bed, he put all the things in the box. He's gone."

Then, when Madame Boche let him go, he drew his brother in front of the tap, and they amused themselves by turning on the water. Gervaise was unable to cry. She was choking, leaning back against her tub, her face still buried in her hands. Slight shivering fits seized her. At times a deep sigh escaped her, whilst she thrust her fists firmer into her eyes, as though to bury herself in the darkness of her abandonment. It was a gloomy abyss to the bottom of which she seemed to fall.

"Come, my dear, pull yourself together!" murmured Madame Boche.

"If you only knew! if you only knew!" said she at length very faintly. "He sent me this morning to pawn my shawl and my shifts to pay for that cab."

And she burst out crying. The recollection of her errand at the pawn-place, fixing in her mind one of the events of the morning, had given an outlet to the sobs which were choking her. That errand was an abomination—the great grief in her despair. The tears ran down on to her chin, which her hands had already wetted, without her even thinking of taking a handkerchief.

"Be reasonable, do be quiet, everyone's looking at you," Madame Boche, who hovered round her, kept repeating. "How can you worry yourself so much on account of a man? You loved him, then, all the same, did you, my poor darling? A little while ago you were saying all sorts of things against him; and now you're crying for him, and almost breaking your heart. Dear me, how silly we all are!"

Then she became quite maternal.

"A pretty little woman like you! can it be possible? One may tell you everything now, I suppose. Well! you recollect when I passed under your window, I already had my suspicions. Just fancy, last night, when Adèle came home, I heard a man's footsteps with hers. So I thought I would see who it was. I looked up the staircase. The fellow was already on the second landing; but I certainly recognised M. Lantier's overcoat. Boche, who was on the watch this morning, saw him coolly come down. It was with Adèle, you understand. Virginie has a gentleman now to whom she goes twice a week. Only it's highly improper all the same, for they've only one room and an alcove, and I can't very well say where Virginie managed to sleep."

She interrupted herself an instant, turned round, and then resumed, subduing her loud voice :

"She's laughing at seeing you cry, that heartless thing over there. I'd stake my life that her washing's all a pretence. She's packed off the other two, and she's come here so as to tell them how you take it."

Gervaise removed her hands from her face and looked. When she beheld Virginie in front of her, amidst three or four women, speaking low and staring at her, she was seized with a mad rage. She thrust out her arms, turned right round as she felt on the ground, trembling in every limb, then walked a few steps, and noticing a bucket full of water, she seized it with both hands and threw the contents with all her might.

"The strumpet!" yelled tall Virginie.

She had stepped back, and her boots alone got wet. The

other women, who for some minutes past had all been greatly
upset by Gervaise's tears, jostled each other in their anxiety to
see the fight. Some, who were finishing their lunch, got on the
tops of their tubs. Others hastened forward, their hands
smothered with soap. A ring was formed.

"Ah! the strumpet!" repeated tall Virginie. "What's the
matter with her? she's mad!"

Gervaise, standing on the defensive, her chin thrust out, her
features convulsed, said nothing, not having yet acquired the
Paris gift of the gab. The other continued :

"Get out! It's tired of wallowing about in the country; it
wasn't twelve years old when it let the soldiers make free with
it; it's left its leg behind in its native place. The leg fell off;
it was rotting away."

The lookers-on burst out laughing. Virginie, seeing her
success, advanced a couple of steps, drawing herself up to her
full height, and yelling louder than ever :

"Here! come a bit nearer, just to see how I'll settle you!
Don't you come annoying us here. Do I even know her, the
hussy? If she'd wetted me, I'd have pretty soon turned up her
skirts, as you'd have seen. Let her just say what I've ever done
to her. Speak, you vixen; what's been done to you?"

"Don't talk so much," stammered Gervaise. "You know
well enough. Some one saw my husband last night. And shut
up, because if you don't I'll most certainly strangle you."

"Her husband! Ah! that's a good joke, that is! Madame's
husband! as if one with such a carcass had husbands! It isn't
my fault if he's chucked you up. You don't suppose I've stolen
him. I'm ready to be searched. I'll tell you why he's gone :
you were infecting the man! He was too nice for you. Did
he have his collar on, though? Who's found madame's husband?
A reward is offered."

The laughter burst forth again. Gervaise contented herself
with continually murmuring in an almost low tone of voice :

"You know well enough, you know well enough. It's your
sister, I'll strangle her—your sister."

"Yes, go and try it on with my sister," resumed Virginie
sneeringly. "Ah! it's my sister! That's very likely. My
sister looks a trifle different to you; but what's that to me?
Can't one come and wash one's clothes in peace now? Just dry
up, d'ye hear, because I've had enough of it!"

But it was she who returned to the attack, after giving five
or six strokes with her beetle, intoxicated by the insults she had

been giving utterance to, and worked up into a passion. She left off and recommenced again, speaking in this way three times :

"Well, yes! it's my sister. There now, does that satisfy you? They adore each other. You should just see them bill and coo! And he's left you with your bastards. Those pretty kids with scabs all over their faces! One of 'em's by a gendarme, isn't he? and you had three others made away with because you didn't want to have to pay for extra luggage on your journey. It's your Lantier who told us that. Ah! he's been telling some fine things ; he'd had enough of you!"

"You dirty jade! you dirty jade! you dirty jade!" yelled Gervaise, beside herself, and again seized with a furious trembling. She turned round, looking once more about the ground ; and only observing the little tub, she seized hold of it by the legs, and flung the whole of the blue water at Virginie's face.

"The cow! she's spoilt my dress!" cried the latter, whose shoulder was sopping wet and whose left hand was dyed blue. "Wait a minute, you walking dungheap!"

In her turn she seized a bucket, and emptied it over the young woman. Then a formidable battle began. They both ran along the rows of tubs, seized hold of the pails that were full, and returned to dash the contents at each other's heads. And each deluge was accompanied by a volley of words. Gervaise herself answered now :

"There! dirty beast! You got it that time. It'll help to cool you."

"Ah! the carrion! That's for your filth. Wash yourself for once in your life."

"Yes, yes, I'll take the shine out of you, you lanky strumpet!"

"Another one! Rinse your teeth, make yourself smart for your watch to-night at the corner of the Rue Belhomme."

They ended by filling the buckets at the taps. And as they waited while these filled, they continued their foul language. The first pailfuls, badly aimed, scarcely touched them; but they soon got the range. It was Virginie who first received one full in the face ; the water entered at the neck of her dress, ran down her back and bosom, and flowed out under her petticoats. She was still quite giddy with the shock, when a second one caught her side-ways, giving her a sharp blow on the left ear and soaking her chignon, which unrolled like a ball of string. Gervaise was first hit in the legs ; the water filled her shoes and rebounded as high as her thighs ; two other pailfuls inundated her hips. Soon, however, it became no longer possible to count the hits. They were both of them dripping from their heads to their heels, the bodies of their dresses were sticking to their shoulders, their skirts clung to their loins, and they appeared thinner, stiffer, and shivering, as the water dropped on all sides as it does off umbrellas during a heavy shower.

"They look jolly funny ! " said the hoarse voice of one of the women.

Every one in the wash-house was highly amused. A good space was left to the combatants, as nobody cared to get splashed. Applause and jokes circulated in the midst of the sluice-like noise of the buckets emptied in rapid succession. On the floor the puddles were running one into another, and the two women were wading in them up to their ankles. Virginie, however, who had been meditating a treacherous move, suddenly seized hold of a pail of boiling lye, which one of her neighbours had left there, and threw it. The same cry arose from all. Every one thought Gervaise was scalded ; but only her left foot had been slightly touched. And, exasperated by the pain, she seized a bucket, without troubling herself to fill it this time, and threw it with all her might at the legs of Virginie, who fell to the ground. All the women spoke together.

"She's broken one of her limbs ! "

"Well, the other tried to cook her ! "

"She's right, after all, the fair one, if her man's been taken from her ! "

Madame Boche held up her arms to heaven, uttering all sorts of exclamations. She had prudently retreated out of the way between two tubs ; and the children, Claude and Etienne, cry-ing, choking, terrified, clung to her dress, with the continuous cry of "Mamma ! mamma ! " broken by their sobs. When she saw Virginie fall she hastened forward, and tried to pull Gervaise away by her skirt, repeating the while,

"Come now, go home ! be reasonable. On my word, it's quite upset me. Never was such a butchery seen before."

But she had to draw back and seek refuge again between the two tubs, with the children. Virginie had just flown at Ger-vaise's throat. She squeezed her round the neck, trying to strangle her. The latter freed herself with a violent jerk, and in her turn hung on to the tail of the other's chignon, as though she was trying to pull her head off. The battle was silently resumed, without a cry, without an insult. They did

not seize each other round the body, they attacked each other's
faces with open hands and clawing fingers, pinching, scratching
whatever they caught hold of. The tall, dark girl's red ribbon
and blue silk hair net were torn off. The body of her dress,
giving way at the neck, displayed a large portion of her
shoulder; whilst the blonde, half stripped, a sleeve gone from
her loose white jacket without her knowing how, had a rent in
her underlinen, which exposed to view the naked line of her
waist. Shreds of stuff flew in all directions. It was from
Gervaise that the first blood was drawn, three long scratches
from the mouth to the chin; and she sought to protect her
eyes, shutting them at every grab the other made for fear of
having them torn out. No blood showed on Virginie as yet.
Gervaise aimed at her ears, maddened at not being able to
reach them. At length she succeeded in seizing hold of one of
the earrings—an imitation pear in yellow glass—when she
pulled and slit the ear, and the blood flowed.

"They're killing each other! Separate them, the vixens!"
exclaimed several voices.

The other women had drawn nearer. They formed themselves into two camps. Some excited the combatants in the
same way as the mob urge on snarling curs, while the others,
more nervous and trembling, turned away their heads, having
had enough of it, and kept repeating that they were sure they
would be ill; and a general battle was on the point of taking
place. The combatants styled each other heartless and good
for nothing; bare arms were thrust out—three slaps were
heard. Madame Boche, meanwhile, was trying to discover
the wash-house boy.

"Charles! Charles! Wherever has he got to?"

And she found him in the front rank, looking on with his
arms folded. He was a big fellow, with an enormous neck.
He was laughing and enjoying the sight of the bits of skin which
the two women displayed. The little blonde was as plump as
a quail. It would be fine if her petticoat slit up.

"Why!" murmured he, winking his eye, "she's got a strawberry mark under the arm."

"What! you're there!" cried Madame Boche, as she caught
sight of him. "Just come and help us separate them. You
can easily separate them, you can!"

"Oh, no! thank you, not if I know it," said he, coolly. "To
get my eye scratched like I did the other day, I suppose! I'm
not here for that sort of thing; I should have too much work

if I was. Don't be afraid, a little bleeding does 'em good ; it'll soften 'em."

The doorkeeper then talked of fetching the police ; but the mistress of the wash-house, the delicate young woman with the sore eyes, would not allow her to do this. She kept saying :

" No, no, I won't ; it'll compromise my establishment."

The struggle on the ground continued. All on a sudden, Virginie raised herself up on her knees. She had just got hold of a beetle and brandished it on high. She had a rattling in her throat, and, in an altered voice, she exclaimed,

" Here's something that'll settle you ! Get your dirty linen ready ! "

Gervaise quickly thrust out her hand, and also seized a beetle, and held it up like a club ; and she too spoke in a choking voice,

" Ah ! you want to wash. Let me get hold of your skin that I may beat it into dish-cloths ! "

For a moment they remained there, on their knees, menacing each other. Their hair all over their faces, their breasts heaving, muddy, swelling with rage, they watched one another, as they waited and took breath. Gervaise gave the first blow. Her beetle glided off Virginie's shoulder, and she at once threw herself on one side to avoid the latter's beetle, which grazed her hip. Then, warming to their work, they struck at each other like washerwomen beating clothes, roughly and in time. Whenever there was a hit, the sound was deadened, so that one might have thought it a blow in a tub full of water. The other women around them no longer laughed. Several had gone off, saying that it quite upset them ; those who remained stretched out their necks, their eyes lighted up with a gleam of cruelty, admiring the pluck displayed. Madame Boche had led Claude and Etienne away, and one could hear at the other end of the building the sound of their sobs, mingled with the sonorous shocks of the two beetles. But Gervaise suddenly yelled. Virginie had caught her a whack with all her might on her bare arm, just above the elbow. A large red mark appeared, the flesh at once began to swell. Then she threw herself upon Virginie, and every one thought she was going to beat her to death.

" Enough ! enough ! " was cried on all sides.

Her face bore such a terrible expression, that no one dared approach her. Her strength seemed to have increased tenfold. She seized Virginie round the waist, bent her down and pressed

THE COMBAT BETWEEN GERVAISE AND VIRGINIE AT THE WASH-HOUSE.

p. 32.

her face against the flagstones; then, in spite of her struggles, she turned up her petticoats, and tore her drawers away. Raising her beetle she commenced beating as she used to beat at Plassans, on the banks of the Viorne, when her mistress washed the clothes of the garrison. The wood seemed to yield to the flesh with a damp sound. At each whack a red weal marked the white skin.

"Oh, oh!" murmured the boy Charles, opening his eyes to their full extent and gloating over the sight.

Laughter again burst forth from the lookers-on, but soon the cry, "Enough! enough!" recommenced. Gervaise heard not, neither did she tire. She examined her work, bent over it, anxious not to leave a dry place. She wanted to see the whole of that skin beaten, covered with contusions. And she talked, seized with a ferocious gaiety, recalling a washerwoman's song,

"Bang! bang! Margot at her tub—Bang! bang! beating rub-a-dub—Bang! bang! tries to wash her heart—Bang! bang! black with grief to part—"

And then she resumed, "That's for you, that's for your sister, that's for Lantier. When you next see them, you can give them that. Attention! I'm going to begin again. That's for Lantier, that's for your sister, that's for you. Bang! bang! Margot at her tub—Bang! bang! beating rub-a-dub—"

The others were obliged to drag Virginie from her. The tall dark girl, her face bathed in tears and purple with shame, picked up her things and hastened away. She was vanquished. Gervaise slipped on the sleeve of her jacket again, and fastened up her petticoats. Her arm pained her a good deal, and she asked Madame Boche to place her bundle of clothes on her shoulder. The doorkeeper referred to the battle, spoke of her emotions, and talked of examining the young woman's person, just to see.

"You may, perhaps, have something broken. I heard a tremendous blow."

But Gervaise wanted to go home. She made no reply to the pitying remarks and the noisy ovation of the other women who surrounded her, erect in their aprons. When she was laden she gained the door, where the children awaited her.

"Two hours, that makes two sous," said the mistress of the wash-house, already back at her post in the glazed closet.

Why two sous? She no longer understood that she was asked to pay for her place there. Then she gave the two sous; and, limping very much beneath the weight of the wet clothes on her shoulder, the water dripping from off her, her elbow black and blue, her cheek covered with blood, she went off, dragging Claude and Etienne with her bare arms, whilst they trotted along on either side of her, still trembling, and their faces besmeared with their tears.

Behind her, the wash-house resumed its great sluice-like noise. The women had eaten their bread and drank their wine, and they beat harder than ever, their faces brightened up, enlivened by the set-to between Gervaise and Virginie. Along the rows of tubs arms were again working furiously, whilst angular, puppet-like profiles, with bent backs and distorted shoulders, kept jerking violently forward as though on hinges. The conversations continued along the different alleys. The voices, the laughter and the indecent remarks mingled with the gurgling sound of the water. The taps were running, the buckets overflowing, and there was quite a little river beneath the washing-places. It was the busiest moment of the afternoon, the pounding of the clothes with the beetles. The vapours floating about the immense building assumed a reddish hue, only broken here and there by orbs of sunshine, golden balls that found admittance through the holes in the blinds. One breathed a stifling, lukewarm atmosphere, charged with soapy odours. All on a sudden the place became filled with a white vapour. The enormous lid of the copper full of boiling lye was rising mechanically on a central toothed rod, and the gaping hole in the midst of the brickwork exhaled volumes of steam savouring of potash. Close by, the wringing machine was in motion. Bundles of wet clothes, inserted between the cast-iron cylinders, yielded forth their water at one turn of the wheel of the panting, smoking machine, which quite shook the building with the continuous working of its arms of steel.

When Gervaise turned into the entry of the Hôtel Boncœur, her tears again mastered her. It was a dark, narrow passage, with a gutter for the dirty water, running alongside the wall; and the stench which she again encountered there caused her to think of the fortnight she had passed in the place with Lantier—a fortnight of misery and quarrels, the recollection of which was now a bitter regret. It seemed to bring her abandonment home to her.

Upstairs the room was bare, in spite of the sunshine which entered through the open window. That blaze of light, that kind of dancing golden dust, exposed the lamentable condition of the blackened ceiling, and of the walls half denuded of paper, all the more. The only thing left hanging in the room was a woman's small neckerchief, twisted like a piece of string. The children's bedstead, drawn into the middle of the apartment, displayed the chest of drawers, the open drawers of which exposed their emptiness. Lantier had washed himself and had used up the last of the pomatum—a penn'orth of pomatum in a playing card; the greasy water from his hands filled the basin. And he had forgotten nothing. The corner which until then had been filled by the trunk seemed to Gervaise an immense empty space. Even the little hand-glass which hung on the window-fastening was gone. When she made this discovery she had a presentiment. She looked on the mantel-piece. Lantier had taken away the paw a tickets; the pink bundle was no longer there, between the two odd zinc candlesticks.

She hung her washing on the back of a chair, and remained standing, turning round, examining the furniture, seized with such a stupor that her tears could no longer flow. One sou alone remained to her out of the four sous she had kept for the wash-house. Hearing Claude and Etienne laughing at the window, feeling already consoled, she went up to them, took their heads under her arms, and forgot for an instant her troubles as she gazed on that grey highway, where she had beheld in the morning the awaking of the labouring classes, of the giant work of Paris. At this hour the pavement, warmed by the labours of the day, kindled a scorching reverberation above the city, behind the octroi wall. It was on that pavement, in that furnace-like atmosphere, that she was cast all alone with her little ones; and her look wandered up and down the exterior Boulevards, to the right and to the left, pausing at either end; and she was seized with a dull fear, as though her life would henceforth hang there, between a slaughter-house and a hospital.

CHAPTER II.

THREE weeks later, towards half-past eleven, one beautiful sun-
shiny day, Gervaise and Coupeau, the zinc-worker, were each par-
taking of a plum preserved in brandy, at the "Assommoir" kept
by old Colombe. Coupeau, who had been smoking a cigarette
on the pavement, had prevailed on her to go inside on her crossing the road as she returned from taking home a customer's
washing; and her big square laundress's basket was on the
floor beside her, behind the little zinc covered table.

Old Colombe's "Assommoir" was situated at the corner of
the Rue des Poissonniers and the Boulevard de Rochechouart.
The inscription outside consisted of the one word "Distillation,"
in tall blue letters, which covered the space from one end to
the other. On either side of the doorway, planted in the two
halves of a cask, were some oleanders covered with dust. The
enormous bar, with its rows of glasses, its filter and its pewter
measures, stretched along to the left on entering; and the vast
apartment was ornamented all round with big barrels painted a
light yellow, shining with varnish, and the hoops and brass taps
of which were dazzling bright. Higher up on shelves, bottles
of liqueurs, glass jars full of preserved fruits, all kinds of phials
neatly arranged covered the walls and reflected in the mirror
placed behind the counter their vivid apple green, pale gold and
delicate crimson tints. But the curiosity of the house was, at
the back, on the other side of an oak barrier, in a glass-covered
courtyard, the distilling apparatus which the customers could
see at work, stills with long necks and worms that went down
into the earth; a regular devil's kitchen before which the
drunken workmen would come and muse.

At this, the luncheon hour, the "Assommoir" was almost
deserted. A stout man of forty, old Colombe, wearing a waistcoat with sleeves, was serving a little girl of about ten with four
sous of brandy in a cup. A blaze of sunshine entered through

the doorway warming the floor ever damp with the saliva of the smokers. And, from the bar, the barrels, the whole place, there arose a spirituous odour, an alcoholic fume, which seemed to thicken and intoxicate the dust floating in the golden sunlight.

Coupeau was making another cigarette. He was very clean, in a short blue linen blouse and cap, and was laughing and showing his white teeth. With a projecting under jaw and a slightly snub nose, he had handsome chestnut eyes, and the face of a jolly dog and thorough good fellow. His coarse curly hair stood erect. His skin still preserved the softness of his twenty-six years. Opposite to him, Gervaise, in a thin black woollen dress, and bareheaded, was finishing her plum which she held by the stalk between the tips of her fingers. They were close to the street, at the first of the four tables placed alongside the barrels facing the bar.

When the zinc-worker had lit his cigarette, he placed his elbows on the table, thrust his face forward, and for an instant looked without speaking at the young woman, whose pretty fair face had that day the milky transparency of china. Then, alluding to a matter known to themselves alone, and already discussed between them, he simply asked in a low voice:

"So it's to be 'no'? you say 'no'?"

"Oh! most decidedly 'no,' Monsieur Coupeau," quietly replied Gervaise with a smile. "I hope you're not going to talk to me about that here. You know you promised me you would be reasonable. Had I known, I wouldn't have let you treat me."

He did not resume speaking, but continued looking at her quite close, with a bold tenderness which seemed to offer itself, especially impassioned as it were by the corners of her lips, little pale rose corners, slightly moist, which showed the vivid red of her mouth when she smiled. She, however, did not draw away from him, but remained placid and fond. At the end of a brief silence she added:

"You can't really mean it. I'm an old woman; I've a big boy eight years old. Whatever could we two do together?"

"Why!" murmured Coupeau winking his eyes, "what the others do, of course!"

But she made a gesture of feeling annoyed. "Oh! do you think it's always amusing? One can very well see you've never lived with any one. No, Monsieur Coupeau, I must think of serious things. Amusing oneself never leads to anything, you know! I've two mouths at home which are never tired of swal-

lowing, I can tell you! How do you suppose I can bring up
my little ones, if I only think of enjoying myself? And listen,
besides that, my misfortune has been a famous lesson to me.
You know, I don't care a bit about men now. They won't catch
me again for a long while."

She explained herself without anger, but with great propriety
and very coldly, as though she had been discussing a question
connected with her work, giving the reasons which prevented
her starching a habit-shirt. One could see that she had thoroughly made up her mind after due reflection.

Coupeau, deeply moved, repeated: "You cause me a great
deal of pain, a great deal of pain."

"Yes, I see I do," resumed she, "and I am sorry for you,
Monsieur Coupeau. But you mustn't take it to heart. If I
had thoughts of amusing myself, well! I would rather do so
with you than with another. You look a good-natured fellow,
you're nice. We might live together, no doubt, and we'd get
along the best way we could. I'm not at all stuck up. I don't
say that it might not have been. Only, where's the use, as I've
no inclination for it? I've been for the last fortnight, now, at
Madame Fauconnier's. The children go to school. I've work,
I'm contented. So the best is to remain as we are, isn't it?"

And she stooped down to take her basket.

"You're making me talk; they must be expecting me at the
shop. You'll easily find some one else prettier than I, Monsieur
Coupeau, and who won't have two brats to drag about with
her."

He looked at the clock inserted in the frame-work of the
mirror, and made her sit down again, exclaiming:

"Don't be in such a hurry! It's only eleven thirty-five. I've
still twenty-five minutes. You can't be afraid I shall do anything foolish; there's the table between us. So you detest me
so much that you won't stay and have a little chat together."

She put her basket down again, so as not to disoblige him;
and they conversed like good friends. She had had her lunch
before taking home the washing; and he, on that day, had
hastily swallowed his soup and his beef, so as to be on the watch
for her. Gervaise, replying complaisantly, looked out of the
window, between the glass jars of preserved fruit, at the commotion in the street which the luncheon hour had filled with an
immense crowd. On both of the narrow foot-pavements there
were hurrying footsteps, swinging arms, and endless elbowings.
The late-comers, the men detained by their work, with looks

sulky through hunger, crossed the road with long strides and entered the baker's opposite; and when they emerged, with a pound of bread under their arm, they went three doors higher up, to the "Two Headed Calf," to partake of an ordinary at six sous a head. Next door to the baker's was a greengrocer, who sold fried potatoes and mussels cooked with parsley; a continuous procession of workwomen, in long aprons, carried off from here potatoes done up in paper and mussels in cups; others, pretty girls with delicate looks, and their hair coquettishly arranged, purchased bunches of radishes. When Gervaise leant forward, she could catch a glimpse of a pork-butcher's shop full of people, out of which came children holding cutlets, sausages, or pieces of hot black-pudding wrapped up in greasy paper in their hands. Along the roadway slippery with black mud, even in fine weather, through the constant treading of the ever moving crowd, some workmen who had already left the eating-houses passed strolling along in bands, and their open hands swinging against their sides, heavy with food, quiet and slow in the midst of the jostling throng.

A group had formed at the doorway of the "Assommoir."

"I say, Bibi-the-Smoker, are you going to stand a go of vitriol?" inquired a hoarse voice.

Five workmen entered and stood before the bar.

"Ah! old Colombe, you thief!" resumed the voice. "You know, you must give us some of the right sort, and not in thimbles, but real glasses!"

Old Colombe quietly served them. Another party of three workmen arrived. Little by little, the men in blouses collected at the corner of the pavement, stood there for a short time, and ended by pushing each other into the dram-shop between the two oleanders grey with dust.

"You're stupid! you only think of dirty things!" Gervaise was saying to Coupeau. "Of course I loved him. Only, after the disgusting way in which he left me—"

They were talking of Lantier. Gervaise had not seen him again; she thought he was living with Virginie's sister, at La Glacière, in the house of that friend who was going to start a hat factory. She had no thought of running after him. At first, his leaving her had caused her great anguish—she had even wanted to drown herself; but, now that she had reasoned with herself, she considered that all was for the best. Perhaps, had she continued with Lantier, she might never have been able to bring up the little ones, for he spent so much money. He

might come and kiss Claude and Etienne, she would not refuse
him admittance.   Only, as far as she herself was concerned, she
would be cut up in pieces before she would let him touch her
with the tips of his fingers.   And she said all these things in
the manner of a woman who was firmly resolved, having perfectly decided on her mode of life, whilst Coupeau, who would
not yield in his desire to possess her, joked and gave an ob·
jectionable meaning to everything, asking her coarse questions
about Lantier so gaily, and showing such white teeth, that she
did not think of taking offence.

  " You used to beat him," said he at length.   " Oh ! you're
not kind !   You whip people."

  She interrupted him with a hearty laugh.   It was true,
though, she had whipped Virginie's tall carcass.   She would
have delighted in strangling some one on that day.   She laughed
louder than ever when Coupeau told her that Virginie, ashamed
at having shown so much of her person, had left the neighbourhood.   Her face, however, preserved an expression of childish
gentleness; she held out her plump hands, saying that she
would not hurt a fly; all she knew of blows was that she had
received plenty in her time.   Then, she talked of her childhood
passed at Plassans.   She wasn't a bit gaddish; the men bored
her; when Lantier took her, at fourteen, she thought it nice,
because he said he was her husband, and she thought they were
playing at being married people.   Her only fault, she asserted,
was that she was too sensitive; she loved every one, and became
attached to those who behaved badly to her.   For instance,
when she loved a man, she had no notions of tomfoolery, all
she dreamed of was their living together for ever and being very
happy.

  And, as Coupeau with a chuckle spoke of her two children,
whom she had certainly not hatched under the bolster, she
tapped his fingers; she added that she was, no doubt, made on
the model of other women; only, men were wrong to think
that women were always rabid after that sort of thing; women
thought of their home, slaved to keep the place clean and tidy,
and went to bed too tired at night not to go to sleep at once.
Besides, she resembled her mother, a stout labouring woman
who died at her work, and who had served as beast of burden
to old Macquart for more than twenty years.   She was still
quite slim, whilst her mother had shoulders broad enough to
demolish the doorways through which she passed; but all the
same, she resembled her by her mania for becoming attached to

people. And if she limped a little, she no doubt owed that to the poor woman, whom old Macquart used to belabour with blows. Hundreds of times had she told her of the nights when the old man, coming home drunk, would indulge in such rough gallantry that he broke her limbs; and she must surely have owed her own existence with her leg all behind hand to his behaviour on one of these occasions.

"Oh! it's scarcely anything, it's hardly perceptible," said Coupeau gallantly.

She shook her head; she knew well enough that it could be seen; at forty she would look broken in two. Then she added gently, with a slight laugh: "It's a funny fancy of yours to fall in love with a cripple."

With his elbows still on the table, he thrust his face closer to hers, and began complimenting her in rather dubious language, as though to intoxicate her with his words. But she continued to shake her head, declining to be tempted, though caressed by his wheedling accents. She listened, gazing out into the street, seemingly again interested by the increasing crowd. The now empty shops were being swept out; the greengrocer withdrew her last panful of fried potatoes from the fire, whilst the pork-butcher put the plates spread over his counter back into their places. Bands of workmen were emerging from all the eating-houses; big fellows with beards pushed and pommelled one another, playing together like children, with their heavy hob-nailed boots grating on the pavement as they slided about; others, with their hands at the bottoms of their pockets, stood musingly smoking, gazing at the sun and blinking their eyes. It was a regular invasion of the foot-pavement, of the roadway and of the kennels, an idle crowd streaming from the open door-ways, stopping in the midst of the vehicles, and forming an endless trail of long and short blouses, and faded and discoloured old overcoats in the bright light which filled the street. The factory bells rang in the distance, yet the workmen did not hurry themselves, but stopped to light their pipes once more; then drawing themselves up, after calling each other from the different wine-shops, they at length slowly bent their steps in the direction of the factories. Gervaise amused herself by watching three workmen, a tall fellow and two short ones, who turned to look back every few yards; they ended by descending the street, and came straight to old Colombe's "Assommoir."

"Ah well!" murmured she, "there're three fellows who don't seem inclined for work!"

"Why!" said Coupeau, "I know the tall one, it's My-Boots, a comrade of mine."

The "Assommoir" was now pretty full. Every one was talking a great deal, and the sharp accents of the shriller voices kept breaking in on the husky murmurs of the hoarser ones. Fists banged down now and again on the bar caused the glasses to jingle. All the customers were standing up, with their hands crossed over their stomachs or clasped behind their backs, and formed little groups pressing close to each other; some parties, over by the barrels, were obliged to wait a quarter of an hour before they had a chance of ordering their drinks of old Colombe.

"Hallo! it's that aristocrat, Young Cassis!" cried My-Boots, bringing his hand down roughly on Coupeau's shoulder. "A fine gentleman, who smokes paper, and wears shirts! So we want to do the grand with our sweetheart; we stand her little treats!"

"Shut up! don't bother me!" replied Coupeau, greatly annoyed.

But the other added, with a chuckle, "Right you are! We know what's what, my boy. Muffs are muffs, that's all!"

He turned his back, after squinting terribly as he looked at Gervaise. The latter drew back, feeling rather frightened. The smoke from the pipes, the strong odour of all those men, ascended in the air, already foul with the fumes of alcohol; and she felt a choking sensation in her throat, and coughed slightly.

"Oh! what a horrible thing it is to drink!" said she, in a low voice.

And she related that formerly, at Plassans, she used to drink aniseed with her mother. But on one occasion it nearly killed her, and that disgusted her with it; now, she could never touch any liqueurs.

"You see," added she, pointing to her glass, "I've eaten my plum; only, I must leave the juice, because it would make me ill."

Coupeau could not understand how people could swallow glassfuls of brandy. A plum now and again was a good thing. As for "vitriol," absinthe, and all such filth, good night! he would have nothing to do with them. In spite of his comrades' chaff, he stood outside when those swiggers entered the boozing-ken. Old Coupeau, who had been a zinc-worker like himself, had cracked his head on the pavement of the Rue Coquenard through falling from the roof of No. 25, one day he had been on the spree; and the constant recollection of that in their minds, caused all the family to keep very steady. Whenever he passed along the Rue Coquenard, and saw the place, he would sooner have swallowed the water of the gutter than have drank a tumbler of wine at the wine-shop, though it were given to him. He concluded with these words:

"In my calling, one must be steady on one's legs."

Gervaise had taken up her basket again. She did not rise from her seat, however, but held the basket on her knees, with a vacant look in her eyes, and lost in thought, as though the young workman's words had awakened within her far-off thoughts of existence. And she said again, slowly, and without any apparent change of manner:

"Well! I'm not ambitious; I don't ask for much. My desire is to work in peace, always to have bread to eat, and a decent place to sleep in, you know; with a bed, a table, and two chairs, nothing more. Ah! I should also like to be able to bring up my children, to make good men of them, if possible. I've still another wish, which is not to be beaten if I ever live with any one again; no, I shouldn't like to be beaten. And that's all, you see, that's all."

She sat thinking, interrogating her desires, unable seemingly to find anything else of consequence which tempted her. After hesitating awhile, she resumed:

"Yes, when one reaches the end, one might wish to die in one's bed. For myself, after having trudged through life, I should like to die in my bed, in my own home."

And she rose from her seat. Coupeau, who cordially approved her wishes, was already standing up, anxious about the time. But they did not leave at once; she had the curiosity to go and take a look at the back, behind the oak barrier, at the big copper still at work beneath the glass roof in the court-yard; and the zinc-worker, who followed her, explained how it operated, pointing out the different pieces of the apparatus, especially the enormous retort, from which a limpid stream of alcohol fell. The still, with its strangely-shaped receivers, its endless coils of pipes, had a sombre look; not the least fume escaped from it; one could just hear a kind of internal breathing, like some rumbling underground; it was as though some midnight labour was being performed in the light of day by a mighty, dumb, and mournful workman.

My-Boots, accompanied by his two comrades, had come and leant over the barrier, whilst waiting until a corner of the bar was free. He had a laugh resembling the noise made by a pulley that wanted greasing, and wagged his head as he looked tenderly at the machine for producing drunkenness. Jove's thunder! it was a pretty invention! There was enough in that big copper arrangement to keep one's throat moist for a week. He would have liked to have had the end of the pipe soldered to his teeth, so as to feel the still hot "vitriol" fill his body, descending downwards to his heels, always, always like a little waterfall. He would never trouble himself about anything else then; it would be a great deal better than having to put up with that ass, old Colombe's thimblefuls! And his comrades chuckled, saying that that animal, My-Boots, was precious funny all the same. The still, slowly, without a flame, without the least brightness in the dull reflection of its copper envelope, continued its work, letting its alcoholic exudation flow like a sluggish and stubborn stream, which, in course of time, was to overrun the whole dram-shop, spread along the exterior Boulevards, and inundate the immense gulf of Paris. Gervaise shiveringly moved away; and she tried to smile, as she murmured:

"It's stupid; but to look at that machine makes me shiver; the thought of drink makes my blood run cold."

Then, returning to the idea she nursed of a perfect happiness, she resumed: "Now, ain't I right? it's much the nicest, isn't it—to have plenty of work, bread to eat, a home of one's own, and to be able to bring up one's children, and to die in one's bed?"

"And never to be beaten," added Coupeau gaily. "But I would never beat you, if you would only try me, Madame Gervaise. You've no cause for fear. I don't drink, and then, I love you too much. Come, shall it be for to-night? we will warm our tootsies at the same fireside."

He had lowered his voice, and was whispering in her ear, whilst she, holding her basket before her, made a way for herself amongst the men. But she still shook her head several times. Yet she looked round, smiled at him, and seemed pleased to know that he did not drink. She would certainly have answered "yes," had she not sworn never again to take up with a man. At length they reached the door, and passed out. Behind them, the "Assommoir" still continued full, and out in the street the hoarse voices of the customers could be plainly heard, whilst the air was impregnated with the spirituous odour of the "vitriol." My-Boots was calling old Colombe a bilk, and accusing him of having only half filled his glass. He was a jolly dog, one of the right sort, a fellow who was all on. The guv'ner might go to blazes, he was not going back to the shed, he had had enough work for that day. And he proposed to his two comrades that they should sheer off to the "Little Old Man with a Cough," a boozing-ken of the Barrière Saint-Denis, where they gave you the right stuff, pure.

"Ah! one can breathe here," said Gervaise, on the pavement outside. "Well! good-bye, and thank you, Monsieur Coupeau. I must hurry back."

And she was about to proceed along the Boulevard. But he had taken her hand, and held it, as he said: "Go round with me by the Rue de la Goutte-d'Or, it won't be much farther for you. I've got to call on my sister before returning to work. We can keep each other company."

She ended by agreeing, and they slowly ascended the Rue des Poissonniers side by side, without taking each other's arms. He talked of his relations. His mother, old Madame Coupeau, used to make waistcoats, but her eyes were failing her, so now she went out charing. She was sixty-two on the third of the previous month. He was the youngest. One of his sisters, Madame Lerat, a widow of thirty-six, worked at artificial flower making, and lived in the Rue des Moines, at Batignolles. The other, aged thirty, had married a gold chain maker, that slyly malicious beggar, Lorilleux. It was on her that he was going to call in the Rue de la Goutte-d'Or. She lived in the big house on the left. Every evening, he dined with the Lorilleux; it was a saving for all three of them. And he was going to tell them not to expect him that evening, as he had been invited by a friend.

Gervaise, who was listening to him, suddenly interrupted him to ask, with a smile: "So you're called 'Young Cassis,' Monsieur Coupeau?"

"Oh!" replied he, "it's a nickname my mates have given me, because I generally drink 'cassis' when they force me to accompany them to the wine-shop. It's no worse to be called Young Cassis than My-Boots, is it?"

"Of course not. Young Cassis isn't an ugly name," observed the young woman.

And she questioned him about his work. He was still working there, behind the octroi wall, at the new hospital. Oh!

there was no want of work, he would not have finished there for a year at least.   There were yards and yards of gutters!

"You know," said he, "I can see the Hôtel Boncœur when I'm up there.   Yesterday, you were at the window, and I waved my arms, but you didn't notice me."

They had already gone about a hundred paces along the Rue de la Goutte-d'Or, when he stood still, and, raising his eyes, said :

"That's the house.   I was born farther on, at No. 22.   But this house is, all the same, a fine block of masonry !   It's as big as a barrack inside !"

Gervaise raised her chin, and examined the frontage.   The house had five storeys looking on the street, and each of them had a row of fifteen windows, the shutters of which, black, and more or less broken, gave an air of ruin to that immense mass of wall.   Down below, four shops occupied the ground floor : to the right of the door was a vast, greasy eating-place ; to the left, a charcoal-dealer's, a linen-draper's, and an umbrella shop. The house appeared all the more colossal through being situated between two little, low, insignificant-looking buildings, which seemed to cling to it; and square in shape, and similar to a block of coarsely-made mortar, rotting and crumbling beneath the rain, it displayed above the neighbouring roofs its enormous rude form, its rough unplastered sides, of the colour of mud, with the interminable bareness of prison walls, and wherein rows of projecting stones looked like so many decayed jaws gaping vacantly.   But Gervaise was more struck by the door—an immense arched door, which rose as high as the second storey, and opened into a deep porch, at the other end of which one could discern the faint light of a large courtyard.   In the centre of this porch, paved like the street, was a gutter, along which flowed some pale pink water.

"Come in," said Coupeau, "no one will eat you."

Gervaise wanted to wait for him in the street.   However, she could not resist going through the porch as far as the door-keeper's room on the right.   And there, on the threshold, she again raised her eyes.   Inside, the façades had six storeys— four regular façades enclosing the vast square of the courtyard. The grey walls, partly eaten away by a kind of yellow léprosy, were streaked by the drippings from the roof, and were perfectly flat from the pavement to the slates, without the slightest piece of moulding · the water-pipes alone curved a little at each floor, where the open sinks were seen, covered with rust. The windows, without shutters, displayed their bare panes, of the greenish hue of cloudy water. At certain windows, mattresses, covered with blue check were hanging out to air; in front of others, clothes were drying on lines, all the washing of the family—the man's shirts, the wife's loose linen jackets, and the children's drawers; at one window, on the third floor, were a baby's soiled napkins. From the top to the bottom, the lodgings, all too small for their occupants, seemed to be bursting, showing scraps of their misery in every crack.

Down below, each frontage had a tall narrow doorway, without any woodwork, merely cut out of the wall, and which gave admittance to a passage, with walls full of crevices, and a muddy staircase, with an iron hand-rail, at the end; there were altogether four of these staircases, distinguised by the first four letters of the alphabet painted on the wall. The ground floors were fitted up as immense workshops, with glass frontages, black with dust; a locksmith's forge was blazing away in one; farther off the sounds of a carpenter's plane could be heard in another; whilst near the entrance, that light pink stream which flowed along the gutter beneath the porch was running from a dyer's laboratory. Dirtied with pools of dyed water, littered with heaps of shavings and cinders, and having tufts of grass growing round its edges in the crevices between the paving stones, the courtyard was lit up by a sharp light, and seemed as though cut in two at the line where the sunshine and the shadow met. On the shady side, around the water tap, which always maintained a certain dampness there, three little hens, their claws all muddy, were pecking the ground, seeking for worms. And Gervaise slowly gazed about, lowering her glance from the sixth floor to the paving stones, then raising it again, surprised at the vastness, feeling, as it were, in the midst of a living organ, in the very heart of a city, and interested in the house, as though it were a giant before her.

"Is madame seeking for any one?" called out the inquisitive doorkeeper, emerging from her room.

The young woman explained that she was waiting for a friend. She returned to the street; then, as Coupeau did not come, she went back to the courtyard, seized with the desire to take another look. She did not think the house ugly. Amongst the rags hanging from the windows she discovered various cheerful touches—a wall-flower blooming in a pot, a cage of chirruping canaries, shaving-glasses shining like stars in the depth of the

shadow.   Down below a carpenter was singing, accompanied by
the regular whistle of his jointing-plane ; whilst, in the locksmith's work-shop, a clatter of hammers beating in time
resembled a silvery peal of bells.   And at almost all the open
windows, against the background of partly seen misery, children
showed their clean and smiling faces, and women sewed, their
placid profiles bent over their work.   It was the resuming of
the task after the mid-day meal, the rooms free of the men, who
were working away from home, the house returning to that
great peacefulness, solely disturbed by the noise of the workmen's tools, by the lullaby of a refrain, ever the same, repeated
for hours together.   Only the yard seemed rather damp.   If
Gervaise had lived there, she would have preferred a lodging at
the further end, on the sunny side.   She had advanced five or
six steps, and was inhaling that unsavoury effluvium pertaining
to the lodgings of the poor—a smell of old dust, of rancid filth ;
but, as the acrid odour of the dyed water predominated, she
thought there was not so great a stench as at the Hôtel
Boncœur.   And she had already chosen her window—a window
up in the left-hand corner, where there was a little flower-box
full of scarlet runners, the slender stems of which had commenced to twine round a little bower of string.

" I'm afraid I've kept you waiting rather a long time," said
Coupeau, whom she suddenly heard close beside her.   "They
always make an awful fuss whenever I don't dine with them,
and it was worse than ever to-day, as my sister had bought
some veal."

And as Gervaise had slightly started with surprise, he continued, glancing around in his turn :

" You were looking at the house.   It's always all let from
the top to the bottom.   There are three hundred lodgers, I
think.   If I had had any furniture, I would have secured a small
room.   One would be comfortable here, don't you think so ?"

" Yes, one would be comfortable," murmured Gervaise.   "In
our street, at Plassans, there weren't near so many people.
Look, that's pretty—that window up on the fifth floor, with the
scarlet runners."

Then he stubbornly asked her again whether she would consent.   As soon as they had a bed, they would try and get a
room there.   But she hastened away, passing hurriedly beneath
the porch, and begging him not to commence his nonsense again.
The house might crumble to pieces, but she would certainly
never sleep in it under the same blanket as he.   Coupeau, how-

ever, as he left her at Madame Fauconnier's door, was able for an instant to hold her hand, which she abandoned to him in all friendliness.

For a month the young woman and the zinc-worker were the best of friends. He admired her courage, when he beheld her half killing herself with work, keeping her children tidy and clean, and yet finding time at night to do a little sewing. There were women who were far from clean, whose looks showed the evil existence they led; but, hang it all! she was nowise like them: she took too serious a view of life! Then she would laugh, and modestly defend herself. It was her misfortune that she had not always been good. And she alluded to her first confinement, when she was only fourteen, and to the quarts of aniseed which she helped her mother to put away in the old days. Experience was correcting her a little—that was all. One was wrong to think she had a strong will. She was, on the contrary, very weak; she let herself go wherever she was pushed, for fear of causing pain to any one. Her dream was to live amongst good people, because bad society, said she, was like the blow of a bludgeon—it cracked one's skull, it would lay a woman on her back in no time. She fell into a cold sweat at the thought of the future, and compared herself to a coin tossed up in the air and coming down head or tail, according to how it struck the ground. All she had already seen, the bad examples spread before her childhood's eyes, had been for her a sharp lesson. But Coupeau chaffed her about her gloomy thoughts, and brought back all her courage by trying to pinch her hips. She pushed him away from her, and slapped his hands, whilst he called out laughingly that, for a weak woman, she was not a very easy capture. He, who always joked about everything, did not trouble himself regarding the future. One day brought another, of course! One could always manage to have a nest and a bit to eat. The neighbourhood was a decent one, excepting for a few drunkards, of whom one might do well to clear the gutters. He was not a bad devil; he sometimes said some very sensible things, was a trifle coquettish, parted his hair carefully on the side, wore pretty neckties and a pair of patent leather shoes on Sundays. With all that, he was as sharp and as impudent as a monkey, full of jokes like most Parisian workmen, and with a tongue ever on the move, which was not so objectionable in a young fellow like him.

They had ended by rendering each other all sorts of services at the Hôtel Boncœur. Coupeau fetched her milk, ran her

errands, carried her bundles of clothes; often of an evening, as
he got home first from work, he took the children for a walk on
the exterior Boulevard.   Gervaise, in return for his polite
attentions, would go up into the narrow room at the top of the
house where he slept, and see to his clothes, sewing buttons
on his blue linen trousers, and mending his linen jackets. A
great familiarity existed between them.   Amused with the
songs he sang and the continual larking of the Paris faubourgs,
all new to her, she was never dull when he was there.   By
constantly rubbing up against her skirts, he became more and
more excited. He was caught, and firmly, too! It ended by
bothering him. He still laughed; but his stomach was so
upset, it felt so oppressed, that it was no longer funny. The
nonsense continued. He could never meet her without asking,
"When's it to be?" She knew what he meant, and she promised her consent when four Thursdays came in the same week.
Then he would tease her, would go to her room with his slippers
in his hand, as though moving in. She also joked with him
about it, and could pass the day without a blush amidst the continual smutty allusions with which he surrounded her life. She
tolerated all so long as he was not rough. She only got angry
on one occasion when he, wishing to snatch a kiss from her, had
pulled out some of her hair.

Towards the end of June, Coupeau lost his liveliness. He
became most peculiar. Gervaise, feeling uneasy at some of his
glances, barricaded herself in at night. Then, after having
sulked ever since the Sunday, he suddenly came on the Tuesday night about eleven o'clock and knocked at her room. She
would not open to him; but his voice was so gentle and so
trembling that she ended by removing the chest of drawers she
had pushed against the door. When he had entered, she
thought he was ill: he looked so pale, his eyes were so red, and
the veins on his face were all swollen. And he stood there,
stuttering and shaking his head. No, no, he was not ill. He
had been crying for two hours, upstairs in his room; he wept
like a child, biting his pillow so as not to be heard by the
neighbours. For three nights past he had been unable to sleep.
It could not go on like that.

"Listen, Madame Gervaise," said he, with a swelling in his
throat, and on the point of bursting out crying again; "we
must end this, mustn't we? We'll go and get married. I'm
willing. I've quite made up my mind."

Gervaise showed great surprise. She was very grave.

"Oh! Monsieur Coupeau," murmured she, "whatever are you thinking of? You know I've never asked you for that. I didn't care about it—that was all. Oh, no, no! it's serious now; think of what you're saying, I beg of you."

But he continued to shake his head, with an air of unalterable resolution. He had already thought it all over. He had come down because he wanted to have a good night. She wasn't going to send him back to weep again, he supposed! As soon as she had said "yes," he would no longer bother her, and she could go quietly to bed. He only wanted to hear her say "yes." They could talk it over on the morrow.

"But I certainly can't say 'yes' like that," resumed Gervaise. "I don't want you to be able to accuse me later on of having incited you to do a foolish thing. You see, Monsieur Coupeau, it's wrong of you to be obstinate. You don't know yourself what your real feelings are for me. If you didn't see me for a week, you'd get all right again, I bet. Men often marry for a night, the first one; and then the nights follow on, the days succeed each other, for the rest of their lives, and they're awfully bothered. Sit down there; I'm willing to talk it over at once."

Then until one in the morning, in the dark room, and by the faint light of a smoky tallow candle which they forgot to snuff, they talked of their marriage, lowering their voices so as not to wake the two children, Claude and Etienne, who were sleeping, breathing gently, their heads on the same pillow. And Gervaise kept alluding to them, showing them to Coupeau. It was a funny dowry for her to bring him; she really could not encumber him with two brats. Then she was seized with shame for him. What would they say in the neighbourhood? They had known her with her lover; they knew her story. It would not be decent for them to see him and her get married two months afterwards. Coupeau replied to all this reasoning by shrugging his shoulders. He did not care what the people of the neighbourhood thought! He did not poke his nose into other people's affairs; to begin with, he would have been too much afraid of dirtying it! Well, yes! she had lived with Lantier before him. What of that? She did not lead an improper life; she would not bring men into her home, like so many women did, and some of the richest. As for the children, they would continue to grow up, and he and she would take care of them, of course! He would never find another woman so courageous, so kind, so full of good qualities. Besides, all that was nothing; she might have rolled about the streets, have been ugly, idle, disgusting, and have had a troop of dirty kids—it would have been nothing in his eyes. He wanted her.

"Yes, I want you," he repeated, bringing his hand down on his knee like a continuous hammering. "You understand, I want you. There's nothing to be said to that, is there?"

Little by little, Gervaise gave way. A cowardliness of the heart and senses seized on her, in the midst of that passionate desire with which she felt herself enveloped. She only ventured on the most timid objections, her hands lying idly in her lap, a look of gentleness on her face. From the outside, through the open window, the beautiful June night wafted in a warm breeze, flickering the candle, the long wick of which was burning as black as a cinder. In the great silence pervading the neighbourhood, now hushed in sleep, one only heard the child-like sobbing of a drunken man, lying flat on his back in the middle of the Boulevard; whilst a very long way off, inside a restaurant, a fiddle was playing a lively quadrille to some belated wedding party—a little crystalline music, clear and sharp like a harmonica. Coupeau, seeing the young woman had exhausted her arguments, and that she was silent and smiling vaguely, seized her hands and drew her towards him. She was in one of those moments of abandonment which she so much dreaded, feeling conquered, and too deeply moved to refuse any-thing and cause pain to anyone. But the zinc-worker did not understand that she was yielding herself to him. He contented himself by roughly grasping her wrists, so as to take posses-sion of her; and they both sighed at this slight pain, which satisfied a little of their love.

"You'll say 'yes,' won't you?" asked he.

"How you worry me!" she murmured. "You wish it? Well then, 'yes.' Ah! we're perhaps doing a very foolish thing."

He jumped up, and, seizing her round the waist, kissed her roughly on the face, at random. Then, as this caress caused a noise, he became anxious, and went softly and looked at Claude and Etienne.

"Hush! we must be good," said he in a whisper, "and not wake the brats. Good-bye till to-morrow."

And he went back to his room. Gervaise, all in a tremble, remained seated on the edge of her bed, without thinking of undressing herself for nearly an hour. She was touched; she considered Coupeau was very honourable; for at one moment

she had really thought it was all over, and that he would sleep
there. The drunkard below, under the window, was now
hoarsely uttering the plaintive cry of some lost animal. The
violin in the distance had left off its saucy tune and was now
silent.

The following days, Coupeau sought to get Gervaise to call
some evening on his sister in the Rue de la Goutte-d'Or; but
the young woman, who was very timid, showed a great dread
of this visit to the Lorilleux. She saw perfectly well that the
zinc-worker was in reality afraid of them. Yet, he was in nowise dependent on his sister who was not the eldest. Mother
Coupeau would freely give her consent, for she never thwarted
her son. Only, the Lorilleux had the reputation among the
family, of earning as much as ten francs a day; and on that
ground they exercised a regular authority. Coupeau would not
have dared to marry without their having accepted his wife
beforehand.

"I have spoken to them of you, they know our plans," explained he to Gervaise. "Come now! what a child you are!
Let's call on them this evening. I've warned you, haven't I?
You'll find my sister rather stiff. Lorilleux, too, isn't always
very amiable. In reality, they are greatly annoyed, because, if
I marry, I shall no longer take my meals with them, and it'll
be an economy the less. But that doesn't matter, they won't
turn you out. Do this for me, it's absolutely necessary."

These words only frightened Gervaise the more. One Saturday evening, however, she gave in. Coupeau came for her at
half-past eight. She had dressed herself in a black dress, a
crâpe shawl with yellow palms, and a white cap trimmed with a
little cheap lace. During the six weeks she had been working,
she had saved the seven francs for the shawl, and the two and
a half francs for the cap; the dress was an old one cleaned and
made up afresh.

"They're expecting you," said Coupeau to her, as they went
round by the Rue des Poissonniers. "Oh! they're beginning
to get used to the idea of my being married. They seem very
nice indeed, to-night. And, you know, if you've never seen gold
chains made, it'll amuse you to watch them. They just happen
to have a pressing order for Monday."

"They've got gold in their rooms?" asked Gervaise.

"I should think so; there's some on the walls, on the floor,
in fact everywhere."

They had passed through the arched doorway and crossed

the courtyard.   The Lorilleux lived on the sixth floor, staircase B.   Coupeau laughingly told her to hold the hand-rail
tight and not to leave go of it.   She looked up, and blinked her
eyes, as she perceived the tall hollow tower of the staircase,
lighted by three gas jets, one on every second landing; the last
one, right up at the top, looked like a star twinkling in a black
sky, whilst the other two cast long flashes of light, of fantastic
shapes, among the interminable windings of the stairs.

 "By Jove!" said the zinc-worker as he reached the first floor
landing, "there's a strong smell of onion soup. Some one's been
having onion soup, I'm sure."

As a matter of fact the grey, dirty, B staircase, with its greasy
hand-rail and stairs, and its scratched walls showing the mortar,
was still filled with a powerful odour of cooking.   On each landing passages branched off sonorous with noise, and yellow painted
doors, blackened near the locks by dirty hands, were opened;
and, on a level with the window, the sink exhaled a fetid humidity, the stench of which mingled with the pungency of the
cooked onions.   One could hear from the ground floor to the
sixth storey the noise of crockery, of saucepans being scoured
out and of pans being scraped with spoons to clean them.   On
the first floor, Gervaise noticed, by a partly open door on which
the word "Draughtsman" was written in big letters, two men
seated before a table covered with American cloth, and from
which the remains of the dinner had just been cleared away,
conversing energetically in the midst of the smoke from their
pipes.   The second and third floors were quieter; through the
chinks in the woodwork one merely heard the sounds of the
rocking of a cradle, of a child's smothered cries, and a woman's
loud voice flowing with the dull murmur of a stream, without
any distinct words being recognisable.   And Gervaise read different names on nailed-up placards : "Madame Gaudron, carder,"
and farther off : "M. Madinier, manufactory of cardboard boxes."
They were fighting on the fourth floor, which shook with the
stamping of feet and the upsetting of furniture, accompanied by
an awful noise of oaths and blows ; all this, however, did not
prevent the neighbours opposite from playing cards, with their
door open, so as to get a little air.

But when Gervaise reached the fifth floor, she had to stop to
take breath ; she was not used to going up so high ; that wall
for ever turning, the glimpses she had of the lodgings following
each other, made her head ache.   Besides, a family blocked up
the landing ; the father was washing some plates on a little

earthenware stove near the sink, whilst the mother, leaning against the handrail, was washing the baby before putting it to bed. Coupeau, however, encouraged the young woman. They were nearly there. And, when he at length reached the sixth landing, he turned round to aid her with a smile. She, with raised head, was trying to find whence proceeded the sound of a voice which she had been listening to from the first stair—a clear, piercing voice, dominating the other noises. It came from a room under the roof, where a little old woman was singing as she dressed dolls at thirteen sous. As a tall girl entered a room close by with a pail of water, Gervaise also saw a tumbled bed on which a man with his coat off lay sprawling, and looking up in the air; when the door was closed, she read written on a card nailed against it: "Mademoiselle Clémence, ironer." Then, right up at the top, feeling short of breath, and with her legs quite worn out, she had the curiosity to lean over the hand-rail. Now, it was the lowest gas-jet which looked like a star at the bottom of the narrow well of the six flights; and the odours and the rumbling caused by the incessant animation of the house, ascended to her as it were in a single breath, scorching her anxious face with a puff of heat, as she paused there as though on the edge of an abyss.

"We're not there yet," said Coupeau. "Oh! it's quite a journey!"

He had gone down a long corridor on the left. He turned twice, the first time also to the left, the second time to the right. The corridor still continued, branching off, contracted, the walls full of crevices, with the plaster peeling off, and lighted at distant intervals by a slender gas-jet; and the doors all alike, succeeding each other the same as the doors of a prison or a convent, and nearly all open, continued to display homes of misery and work, which the hot June evening filled with a reddish mist. At length they reached a small passage in complete darkness.

"We're there," resumed the zinc-worker. "Be careful! keep to the wall; there are three stairs."

And Gervaise carefully took another ten steps in the obscurity. She stumbled, and then counted the three stairs. But at the end of the passage Coupeau had opened a door, without knocking. A brilliant light spread over the tiled floor. They entered.

It was a narrow apartment, and seemed as if it were the continuation of the corridor. A faded woollen curtain, raised up just then by a string, divided the place in two.   The first part contained a bedstead pushed beneath an angle of the attic ceiling, a cast-iron stove still warm from the cooking of the dinner, two chairs, a table and a wardrobe, the cornice of which had had to be sawn off to make it fit in between the door and the bedstead.   The second part was fitted up as the workshop : at the end, a narrow forge with its bellows ; to the right, a vice fixed to the wall beneath some shelves on which pieces of old iron lay scattered ; to the left, near the window, a small workman's bench, encumbered with greasy and very dirty pliers, shears, and microscopical saws.

"It's us !" cried Coupeau, advancing as far as the woollen curtain.

But no one answered at first.   Gervaise, deeply affected, moved especially by the thought that she was about to enter a place full of gold, stood behind the workman, stammering, and venturing upon nods of her head by way of bowing.   The brilliant light, a lamp burning on the bench, a brazier full of coals flaring in the forge, increased her confusion still more.   She ended, however, by distinguishing Madame Lorilleux—little, red-haired and tolerably strong, pulling with all the strength of her short arms, and with the assistance of a big pair of pincers, a thread of black metal which she passed through the holes of a draw-plate fixed to the vice.   Seated in front of the bench, Lorilleux, quite as small of stature, but more slender in the shoulders, worked, with the tips of his pliers, with the vivacity of a monkey, at a labour so minute, that it was impossible to follow it between his scraggy fingers.   It was the husband who the first raised his head—a head with scanty locks, the face of the yellow tinge of old wax, long, and with an ailing expression.

"Ah ! it's you ; well, well !" murmured he.   "We're in a hurry, you know.   Don't come into the workroom, you'd be in our way.   Stay in the bedroom."

And he resumed his minute task, his face again in the reflection of a glass globe full of green-coloured water, through which the lamp shed a circle of bright light over his work.

"Take the chairs !" called out Madame Lorilleux in her turn. "It's that lady, isn't it ?   Very well, very well !"

She had rolled the wire, she carried it to the forge, and then, reviving the fire of the brazier with a large wooden fan, she proceeded to temper the wire before passing it through the last holes of the draw-plate.

Coupeau fetched the two chairs, and seated Gervaise close to

the curtain. The room was so narrow that there was not space
for him to sit beside her. So he placed his chair a little behind
hers, and leant forward to give her explanations of the work.
The young woman, abashed by the strange reception accorded
by the Lorilleux, feeling uneasy beneath their covert glances,
had a singing in her ears which prevented her from hearing.
She thought the woman looked very old for her thirty years,
with her cross-grained manner, her dirty appearance, and her
hair rolled together, looking like a cow's tail as it hung over her
unfastened linen jacket. The husband, only a year his wife's
senior, appeared quite an old man, with his thin wicked-looking
lips, as he sat there in his shirt sleeves and his naked feet in a
pair of old trodden down slippers. But what disheartened her
the most was the smallness of the workroom, the besmeared
walls, the tarnished metal tools, all the black dirt hanging about
there amongst the odds and ends of a dealer in old iron. It
was terribly hot. Beads of perspiration hung about the man's
greenish face, whilst Madame Lorilleux ended by taking off her
loose linen jacket, exposing her bare arms, and her chemise
clinging to her drooping breasts.

"And the gold?" asked Gervaise in a low voice.

Her anxious glances searched the corners, and sought amongst
all that filth for the resplendence she had dreamt of. But Coupeau burst out laughing.

"Gold?" said he; "why, there's some, there's some more,
and there's some at your feet!"

He pointed successively to the fine wire at which his sister
was working, and to another roll of wire, similar to the ordinary
iron wire, hanging against the wall, close to the vice; then,
going down on all fours, he picked up, beneath the wooden
screen which covered the tiled floor of the workroom, a piece
of waste, a tiny fragment resembling the point of a rusty needle.
But Gervaise protested. It could not be gold that black-looking
metal, as ugly as iron! He had to bite it and show her the
shining mark left by his tooth. And he resumed his explanations: the masters supplied the gold in wire, already alloyed;
the workmen first of all passed it through the draw-plate to get
it the required thickness, being careful to temper it five or six
times during the operation, so that it should not break. Oh!
it required a good fist, and practice! His sister would not let
her husband have anything to do with the draw-plates, because
he coughed. She had famous arms; he had seen her draw the
gold as fine as a hair.

Lorilleux, seized with a fit of coughing, almost doubled up on his stool. In the midst of the paroxysm, he spoke, and said in a choking voice, still without looking at Gervaise, as though he was merely mentioning the thing to himself:

"I'm making the herring-bone chain."

Coupeau obliged Gervaise to get up. She might draw nearer and see. The chain-maker consented with a grunt. He wound the wire prepared by his wife round a mandrel, a very thin steel rod. Then he sawed gently, cutting the wire the whole length of the mandrel, each turn forming a link, which he soldered. The links were laid on a large piece of charcoal. He wetted them with a drop of borax, taken from the bottom of a broken glass beside him; and he rapidly made them red-hot at the lamp, beneath the horizontal flame produced by the blow-pipe. Then, when he had soldered about a hundred links, he returned once more to his minute work, pressing against the edge of the block, a small piece of board which the friction of his hands had polished. He bent each link almost double with the pliers, squeezed one end close, inserted it in the last link already in place, and then, with the aid of a point, opened out again the end he had squeezed; and he did this with a continuous regularity, the links joining each other so rapidly that the chain gradually grew beneath Gervaise's gaze, without her being able to follow, or well understand how it was done.

"That's the herring-bone chain," said Coupeau. "There's also the long link, the cable, the plain ring, and the spiral. But that's the herring-bone. Lorilleux only makes the herring-bone chain."

The latter chuckled with satisfaction. He exclaimed, as he continued squeezing the links, invisible between his black finger-nails:

"Listen to me, Young Cassis! I was making a calculation this morning. I commenced work when I was twelve years old, you know. Well! can you guess how long a herring-bone chain I must have made up till to-day?"

He raised his pale face, and blinked his red eye-lids.

"Twenty-six thousand feet, do you hear? Two leagues! That's something! a herring-bone chain two leagues long! It's enough to twist round the necks of all the women of the neighbourhood. And, you know, it's still increasing. I hope to make it long enough to reach from Paris to Versailles."

Gervaise had returned to her seat, disenchanted and thinking everything very ugly. She smiled just to please the Lorilleux.

What most made her feel ill at ease was the silence maintained respecting her marriage, that important matter to her, and but for which she would certainly never have come. The Lorilleux continued to treat her as an unwelcome inquisitive person brought by Coupeau. And the conversation being at length started, it turned solely on the different lodgers of the house. Madame Lorilleux asked her brother if he had heard any fighting as he came upstairs. Those Bénards knocked each other about every day. The husband came home drunk like a pig; the wife also had her faults: she said the most disgusting things.

Then, they talked of the draughtsman of the first floor, that big sponger Baudequin, a fellow who gave himself airs, who owed money right and left, who was always smoking and always having a row with his friends. M. Madinier's cardboard box manufactory was only just managing to jog along. He had only the day before dismissed two more of his workwomen. It would be a blessing if he smashed up, for he squandered everything himself, and let his children go about half-naked. Madame Gaudron carded the wool of her mattresses in a funny manner: she was again in the family way, which was scarcely decent at her age. The landlord had given notice to the Coquets, of the fifth floor; they owed three quarters' rent, besides which, they persisted in lighting their stove on the landing; even the Saturday before, Mademoiselle Remanjou, the old lady of the sixth floor, had only just got down in time to prevent little Linguerlot from being burnt to death, as she was going out to deliver her dolls. As for Mademoiselle Clémence, the ironer, she behaved as she thought proper; but, in spite of all that, one could not deny that she adored animals, and that she had a heart of gold. But what a pity it was such a fine girl should go with all the men! They would certainly finish by meeting her one night walking the streets.

"Look, here's one," said Lorilleux to his wife, giving her the piece of chain he had been working on ever since his lunch. "You can trim it." And he added, with the persistence of a man who does not easily relinquish a joke: "Another four feet and a half. That brings me nearer to Versailles."

Madame Lorilleux, after tempering it again, trimmed it by passing it through the regulating draw-plate. Then she put it in a little copper saucepan with a long handle, full of lye-water, and placed it over the fire of the forge. Gervaise, again pushed forward by Coupeau, had to follow this last operation. When

the chain was thoroughly cleansed, it appeared a dull red colour.
It was finished, and ready to be delivered.

" They're always delivered like that, in their rough state,"
the zinc-worker explained.   " The polishers rub them afterwards
with cloths."

But Gervaise felt her courage failing her.   The heat, more
and more intense, was suffocating her.   They kept the door
shut, because Lorilleux caught cold from the least draught.
Then, as they still did not speak of the marriage, she wanted to
go away, and gently pulled Coupeau's jacket.   He understood.
Besides, he also was beginning to feel ill at ease and vexed at
their affectation of silence.

" Well, we're off," said he.   " We mustn't keep you from
your work."

He moved about for a moment, waiting, hoping for a word,
or some allusion or other.   At length he decided to broach the
subject himself.

" I say, Lorilleux, we're counting on you ; you'll be my wife's
witness."

The chain-maker pretended, with a chuckle, to be greatly
surprised ; whilst his wife, leaving her draw-plates, placed herself in the middle of the workroom.

" So it's serious, then?" murmured he.   " That confounded
Young Cassis, one never knows whether he is joking or not."

" Ah ! yes, madame's the person," said the wife in her turn,
as she stared rudely at Gervaise.   " Well, we've no advice to
give you, we haven't.   It's a funny idea to go and get married,
all the same.   Anyhow, it's your own wish.   When it doesn't
succeed, one's only oneself to blame, that's all.   And it doesn't
often succeed, not often, not often."

She uttered these last words slower and slower, and, shaking
her head, she looked from the young woman's face to her hands,
and then to her feet, as though she had wished to undress her,
and see the very pores of her skin.   She must have found her
better than she expected.

" My brother is perfectly free," she continued more stiffly.
" No doubt, the family might have wished—one always makes
projects.   But things take such funny turns.   For myself, I
don't want to have any unpleasantness.   Had he brought us
the lowest of the low, I should merely have said : ' Marry her
and go to blazes ! '   He was not badly off though, here, with us.
He's fat enough ; one can very well see he didn't fast much ;
and he always found his soup hot, at the very minute.   I say,

Lorilleux, don't you think madame's like Thérèse—you know who I mean, that woman who used to live opposite, and who died of consumption?"

"Yes, there's a certain resemblance," replied the chain-maker.

"And you've got two children, madame? Now, I must admit I said to my brother: 'I can't understand how you can want to marry a woman who's got two children.' You mustn't be offended if I consult his interests; it's only natural. You don't look very strong either. Don't you think, Lorilleux, madame doesn't look very strong?"

"No, no, she's not strong."

They did not mention her leg; but Gervaise understood by their side glances, and the curling of their lips, that they were alluding to it. She stood before them, wrapped in her thin shawl with the yellow palms, replying in monosyllables, as though in the presence of her judges. Coupeau, seeing she was suffering, ended by exclaiming:

"All that's nothing to do with it. What you say and nothing are the same thing. The wedding will take place on Saturday, July 29. I calculated by the almanac. Is it settled? does it suit you?"

"Oh, it's all the same to us," said his sister. "There was no necessity to consult us. I sha'n't prevent Lorilleux being witness. I only want peace and quietness."

Gervaise, hanging her head, not knowing what to do with herself, had put the toe of her boot through one of the openings in the wooden screen which covered the tiled floor of the workroom; then, afraid of having disturbed something when she withdrew it, she stooped down and felt about with her hand. Lorilleux hastily brought the lamp, and he examined her fingers suspiciously.

"You must be careful," said he; "the tiny bits of gold stick to the shoes, and get carried away without one knowing it."

There was quite a fuss. The masters did not allow a milligramme for waste; and he showed the hare's foot, with which he brushed up the particles of gold which remained on the block, and the skin spread over his knees, placed there purposely to receive them. Twice a week the workroom was carefully swept out; they collected all the filth and burnt it, and then sifted the ashes, in which they found every month from twenty-five to thirty francs' worth of gold. Madame Lorilleux did not take her eyes off Gervaise's shoes.

" There's no occasion to get angry," murmured she, with an
amiable smile. " Perhaps madame would not mind looking at
the soles of her shoes."

And Gervaise, turning very red, sat down again, and, holding
up her feet, showed that there was nothing clinging to them.
Coupeau had opened the door exclaiming : "Good-night !" in
an abrupt tone of voice. He called to her from the corridor.
Then she in her turn went off, after stammering a few polite
words : she hoped to see them again, and that they would all
agree well together. But the Lorilleux had already resumed
their work, in the black hole of a workroom, where the little
forge shone, like a final piece of coal coming to a white heat in
the high temperature of a furnace. The wife, with her chemise
slipping from one shoulder, her skin reddened by the reflection
of the brazier, was drawing another wire, each effort swelling
out her neck, the muscles of which were working like strings.
The husband, bending beneath the greenish gleam of the globe
of water, commenced a fresh piece of chain, forming each link
with the pliers, squeezing it at one end, inserting it in the previous one, and then opening out the end again with the aid of
a point, continuously, mechanically, without wasting a movement to wipe the perspiration from his face.

When Gervaise emerged from the corridor on to the landing,
she could not help saying, with tears in her eyes :

".That doesn't promise much happiness."

Coupeau shook his head furiously. He would make Lorilleux
smart for that evening. Had anyone ever seen such a miserly
fellow ? to think that they were going to walk off with two or
three grains of his gold dust ! All the fuss they made was
from pure avarice. His sister thought, perhaps, that he would
never marry, so as to enable her to economise four sous on
her dinner every day. However, it would take place all the
same on July 29. He did not care a hang for them !

But Gervaise, as they went downstairs, felt heavy at heart,
and troubled with a stupid fear, which made her anxiously
examine all the dark shadows of the staircase. At this hour, it
was wrapped in silence, deserted, and only lighted by the gas-
jet of the second-floor landing, the small flame of which looked
down that well of gloom, like the faint glimmer of a night-light.
Behind the closed doors, one could distinguish in the great
silence the heavy slumbers of the workmen who had gone to
bed immediately after their evening meal ; yet a smothered
laugh issued from the ironer's room, whilst a feeble ray of light

shone through Mademoiselle Remanjou's key-hole, as, with the click-click of her scissors, she continued to cut out the dresses of her thirteen-sou dolls. A child continued crying down below, at Madame Gaudron's ; and the sinks emitted a stronger stench in the dark and dumb peacefulness.

Then, down in the courtyard, whilst Coupeau, in a sing-song voice, asked to have the door opened, Gervaise turned round and looked once more at the house. It seemed larger still beneath the moonless sky. The grey façades, as though cleansed of their leprosy and besmeared with shadow, spread out and ascended ; and they now appeared more bare, and completely flat, denuded as they were of the rags, which, in the day-time, hung out to dry in the sun. The closed windows showed no sign of life. Here and there a few vividly lighted up looked like eyes, and gave a squinting appearance to certain corners. Over each entrance, from the bottom to the top, one above the other, the windows of the six landings, whitened with a feeble glimmer, raised a narrow tower of light. A ray from a lamp in the cardboard box manufactory on the second floor spread a yellow trail across the paved courtyard, piercing the darkness which enveloped the work-shops on the ground floor. And in the depths of this darkness, in the damp corner, drops of water fell one by one, with a sonorous noise in the midst of the prevailing silence, from the tap not properly turned off. Then it seemed to Gervaise that the house was upon her, crushing her with its weight, and feeling icy cold against her shoulders. It was only her stupid fear—a childish fancy at which she smiled directly afterwards.

"Take care !" cried Coupeau. And in order to get out, she was obliged to jump over a great pool of water which had flowed from the dyer's. That day the pool was blue, of the deep azure of a summer sky, which the doorkeeper's little night-lamp lighted up with a multitude of stars.

CHAPTER III.

GERVAISE did not want to have any wedding-party. What was the use of spending money? Besides, she still felt somewhat ashamed; it seemed to her quite unnecessary to parade the marriage before the whole neighbourhood. But Coupeau cried out at that. One could not be married without having a feed. He did not care a button for the people of the neighbourhood! Oh! merely something very simple—a little outing in the afternoon, previous to going and having a bite at no matter what eating-house. And no music at dessert, most decidedly; no clarionet to make the ladies dance. Only for the sake of having a few drinks together before going home to by-by, each in his own crib.

The zinc-worker, chaffing and joking, at length got the young woman to consent on promising her that there should be no larks. He would keep his eye on the glasses, to prevent sun-strokes. Then he organised a sort of pic-nic at five francs a head, at the "Silver Windmill," kept by Auguste, on the Boulevard de la Chapelle. He was a small publican, of moderate charges, and had a dancing place in the rear of his back shop, beneath the three acacias in his courtyard. They would be very comfortable on the first floor. During ten days he got hold of guests in the house where his sister lived in the Rue de la Goutte-d'Or—M. Madinier, Mademoiselle Remanjou, Madame Gaudron and her husband. He even ended by getting Gervaise to consent to the presence of two of his comrades—Bibi-the-Smoker and My-Boots. No doubt My-Boots was a boozer; but then he had such a funny appetite that he was always asked to join those sort of gatherings, just for the sight of the caterer's mug when he beheld that bottomless pit swallowing his twelve pounds of bread. The young woman, on her side, promised to bring her employer, Madame Fauconnier, and the Boches, some very agreeable people. On counting, they found there would be

fifteen to sit down to table, which was quite enough. When
there are too many, they always wind up by quarrelling.

Coupeau, however, had no money. Without wishing to do
the grand, he intended to behave handsomely. He borrowed
fifty francs of his employer. Out of that, he first of all purchased the wedding-ring—a twelve franc gold wedding-ring,
which Lorilleux procured for him at the wholesale price of nine
francs. He then bought himself a frock coat, a pair of trousers,
and a waistcoat, at a tailor's in the Rue Myrrha, to whom he
gave merely twenty-five francs on account; his patent leather
shoes and his hat were still good enough. When he had put
by the ten francs for his and Gervaise's share of the feast—the
two children not being charged for—he had exactly six francs
left—the price of a mass at the altar of the poor. He was certainly no friend of the priests, and it almost broke his heart to
take his six francs to those gormandizers, who had no need of
his money to prevent their throats from getting dry. But a
marriage without a mass is, in spite of all one may say, no
marriage at all. He went himself to the church to make a
bargain; and for an hour he argued with a little old priest in a
dirty cassock, and who was as big a thief as a greengrocer. He
felt inclined to pommel him. Then for a joke he asked him if
he could not find in his shop a second-hand mass, not too much
knocked about, and which would still do for an easy-going
couple. The little old priest, grunting that God would have
no pleasure in blessing his union, ended by promising him his
mass for five francs. It was twenty sous saved, and that was
all the money that was left him.

Gervaise also wanted to look decent. As soon as the marriage
was settled, she made her arrangements, worked extra time in
the evenings, and managed to put thirty francs on one side.
She had a great longing for a little silk mantle marked thirteen
francs in the Rue du Faubourg-Poissonnière. She treated herself to it, and then bought for ten francs of the husband of a
washerwoman who had died in Madame Fauconnier's house a
blue woollen dress, which she altered to fit herself. With the
seven francs remaining she procured a pair of cotton gloves, a
rose for her cap, and some shoes for Claude, her eldest boy.
Fortunately the youngsters' blouses were passable. She spent
four nights cleaning everything, and mending the smallest holes
in her stockings and her chemise.

On the Friday night, the eve of the great day, Gervaise and
Coupeau had still a good deal of running about to do up till

E

eleven o'clock, after returning home from their work. Then,
before separating for the night, they spent an hour together in
the young woman's room, happy at being about to be released
from their awkward position. In spite of their resolution not
to trouble themselves about their neighbours, they had ended
by putting their hearts into everything, and thoroughly tiring
themselves out. When they wished each other good night,
they were almost falling asleep where they stood ; but, all the
same, they both heaved a great sigh of relief. Now it was all
settled. Coupeau's witnesses were to be M. Madinier and Bibi-
the-Smoker ; whilst Gervaise was counting on Lorilleux and
Boche. The six of them were to go quietly to the mayor's and
to the church, without lugging a number of other people behind
them. The bridegroom's two sisters had even declared that
they would stay at home, their presence not being at all necessary. Mother Coupeau alone had burst out crying, saying that,
sooner than not be there, she would go before them and hide
herself in a corner ; and so they promised to take her. As for
the general meeting of the wedding party, it was fixed for one
o'clock, at the "Silver Windmill." From there they would go
and get an appetite on the plain of Saint-Denis ; they would
take the train and return on foot along the high road. The
gathering promised to be a very pleasant one ; not a wholesale
booze, but a bit of fun—something nice and respectable.

Whilst dressing himself on the Saturday morning, Coupeau
felt uneasy at having only his twenty sou piece. He had just
recollected that, as a matter of politeness, he ought to offer the
witnesses a glass of wine and a slice of ham whilst waiting for
the dinner hour. Then, perhaps, there would be other unfore-
seen expenses. Twenty sous were decidedly not sufficient. So,
after taking Claude and Etienne to Madame Boche, who was to
bring them to the dinner in the evening, he hastened to the
Rue de la Goutte-d'Or, and boldly went and borrowed ten francs
of Lorilleux. True, he could scarcely get the words out of his
mouth, for he knew the grimace his brother-in-law would make.
The latter grunted, chuckled in an ill-natured way, and finally
lent two five franc pieces. But Coupeau heard his sister mutter
between her teeth that "it was beginning well."

The marriage at the mayor's was to take place at half-past
ten. It was beautiful weather—a storm-presaging sun which
seemed to roast the streets. So as not to be stared at, the
bride and bridegroom, the old mother, and the four witnesses
separated into two bands. Gervaise walked in front with

Lorilleux, who gave her his arm ; whilst M. Madinier followed
with mother Coupeau. Then, twenty steps behind,' on the
opposite side of the way, came Coupeau, Boche, and Bibi-the-
Smoker. These three were in black frock coats, walking erect,
and swinging their arms. Boche had on a pair of yellow
trousers ; Bibi-the-Smoker, buttoned up to his neck, without a
waistcoat, showed only a bit of neckerchief rolled round like a
piece of rope. M. Madinier alone wore a dress coat—a big
dress coat with square cut tails ; and the passers-by stopped to
look at the gentleman escorting fat mother Coupeau, in a green
shawl and a black cap with red ribbons. Gervaise, very gentle
and gay, in her blue dress, her shoulders tightly enveloped in
her scanty little mantle, listened complacently to the chucklings
indulged in by Lorilleux, lost in the midst of an immense overcoat, in spite of the heat ; now and again, at the street corners,
she slightly turned her head, and smiled knowingly at Coupeau,
who felt ill at ease in his new clothes, shining in the sun.

Though they walked very slowly, they arrived at the mayor's
quite half an hour too soon. And as the mayor was late, their
turn was not reached till close upon eleven o'clock. They sat
down on some chairs and waited, in a corner of the apartment,
looking by turns at the high ceiling and the bare walls, talking
low, and over-politely pushing back their chairs, each time that
one of the attendants passed. Yet, among themselves, they
called the mayor a sluggard. He was no doubt at his blonde's,
having his gouty limbs rubbed ; perhaps also he had inad-
vertently swallowed his official sash. But when the magistrate
appeared, they all rose respectfully. They were, however,
motioned back to their seats. Then they assisted at three
marriages, lost amongst three middle-class wedding parties,
with brides dressed in white, little girls with their hair in curls,
young ladies wearing pink sashes, and interminable processions
of ladies and gentlemen all dressed in their Sunday best, and
looking highly respectable.

When at length they were called, they almost missed being
married altogether, Bibi-the-Smoker having disappeared. Boche
discovered him outside smoking his pipe. Well ! they were a
nice lot inside there to humbug people about like that, just
because one hadn't yellow kid gloves to shove under their noses !
And the various formalities—the reading of the Code, the
different questions to be put, the signing of the documents—
were all got through so rapidly that they looked at each other
with an idea that they had been robbed of a good half of the

ceremony. Gervaise, dizzy, her heart full, pressed her handkerchief to her lips. Mother Coupeau wept bitterly. All had
signed the register, writing their names in big straggling letters,
with the exception of the bridegroom, who, not being able to
write, had put his cross. They each gave four sous for the
poor. When an attendant handed Coupeau the marriage
certificate, the latter, prompted by Gervaise, who nudged his
elbow, handed him another five sous.

It was a long walk from the mayor's to the church. On the
way the men had some beer, whilst mother Coupeau and Gervaise took some black currant syrup and water. And they had
to follow a long street down which the sun shone fiercely, without leaving the least bit of shade. The beadle was waiting for
them in the middle of the empty church; he pushed them towards a little chapel, asking them angrily whether it was to
show their contempt for religion that they arrived so late. A
priest looking sulky, his face pale with hunger, advanced with
great strides, preceded by a clerk trotting along in a dirty surplice. The priest hurried through the mass, gobbling up the
Latin phrases, turning about, stooping, spreading out his arms
all in great haste, and with side glances at the bride and bridegroom and their witnesses. In front of the altar, the bride and
bridegroom feeling very ill at ease, not knowing when they had
to kneel, when to stand up, when to sit down, waited for signs
from the clerk. The witnesses, in order to be decent, stood up
all the time, whilst mother Coupeau, again seized with her fit
of weeping, dropped her tears into the open church service
which she had borrowed from a neighbour. However, twelve
o'clock had struck, the last mass had been said, and the church
gradually resounded with the tread of the sacristans' footsteps and
the noise of chairs being put back in their places. The high
altar was evidently being got ready for some grand religious
ceremony, for one could hear the hammers of the upholsterers
who were nailing up the hangings. And in the depths of the
out-of-the-way chapel, amidst the dust caused by the beadle
who was sweeping around, the priest with the sulky look passed
his bony hands over Gervaise's and Coupeau's bent heads, and
seemed to be uniting them in the midst of a removal. When
the wedding party had again signed a register in the vestry,
and were once more out in the sunshine beneath the porch, they
stood there for a moment bewildered and all out of breath at
having been despatched so quickly.

"There!" said Coupeau with an uneasy laugh.

COUPEAU AFFIXING A CROSS TO THE REGISTER OF HIS MARRIAGE
WITH GERVAISE BEFORE THE MAYOR.   p., 68.

He wriggled himself about unable to find something funny to say. However, he added: "Well! it doesn't take long. They do it in double quick time. It's like at the dentist's: you've no time to call out, they marry without pain."

"Yes, yes, it's a fine piece of work," murmured Lorilleux chuckling. "You're joined in five minutes and you can't be undone for the rest of your life. Ah! poor Young Cassis!"

And the four witnesses patted the zinc-worker on the shoulders, whilst he drew himself up. During this time Gervaise smilingly embraced mother Coupeau, her eyes full of tears, however. In answer to the old woman's broken words, she said:

"Don't be afraid, I shall do my best. If anything goes wrong it won't be my fault. No, that's very certain; I long too much to be happy. Anyhow, it's done now, isn't it? It's for him and I to agree together and do our best to help each other."

Then they went straight to the "Silver Windmill." Coupeau had taken his wife's arm. They walked quickly, laughing as though carried away, quite two hundred steps before the others, without noticing the houses, or the passers-by, or the vehicles. The deafening noises of the faubourg sounded like bells in their ears. When they reached the wine-shop, Coupeau at once ordered two bottles of wine, some bread and some slices of ham, to be served in the little glazed closet on the ground floor, without plates or table cloth, simply to have a snack. Then, seeing that Boche and Bibi-the-Smoker appeared to be really hungry, he ordered a third bottle and a piece of Brie cheese. Mother Coupeau had no appetite, she was in too choking a condition to be able to eat. Gervaise, who was dying of thirst, drank several large glasses of water just tinged with wine.

"I'll settle for this," said Coupeau, going at once to the bar, where he paid four francs and five sous.

It was now one o'clock and the other guests began to arrive. Madame Fauconnier, a fat woman, still good looking, first put in an appearance; she wore a chintz dress with a flowery pattern, a pink tie and a cap over-trimmed with flowers. Next came Mademoiselle Remanjou, looking very thin in the eternal black dress which she seemed to keep on even when she went to bed; and the two Gaudrons—the husband, like some heavy animal and almost bursting his brown jacket at the slightest movement, the wife, an enormous woman, whose figure indicated evident signs of an approaching maternity, and whose stiff violet coloured skirt still more increased her rotundity. Coupeau explained that they were not to wait for My-Boots; his comrade would join the party on the Route de Saint-Denis.

"Well!" exclaimed Madame Lerat as she entered, "it'll pour in torrents soon! That'll be pleasant!"

And she called every one to the door of the wine-shop to see the clouds as black as ink which were rising rapidly to the south of Paris. Madame Lerat, the eldest of the Coupeaus, was a tall lean woman of masculine appearance, who talked through her nose, and was slovenly attired in a puce-coloured dress too big for her, the long fringe on which made her resemble a thin poodle just emerged from the water. She handled her parasol like a stick. When she had kissed Gervaise, she resumed:

"You've no idea, it's so stingingly hot in the street. It's just as though fire was being thrown in your face."

Every one then declared that they had felt the storm coming on for a long while. When they came out of church, M. Madinier had seen perfectly well what they had to expect. Lorilleux related that his corns had kept him awake ever since three o'clock in the morning. Besides it could not finish otherwise; the last three days had been really too warm.

"Oh! perhaps it will pass over," repeated Coupeau, standing up in the doorway, anxiously looking at the sky. "We're only waiting for my sister; if she would make haste and come, we might start all the same."

Madame Lorilleux was indeed behind time. Madame Lerat had called in upon her so that they might come together; but, as she found her putting on her stays, they had had a bit of a row. The tall widow added in her brother's ear:

"I just left her there. She's in such a temper! You'll see how she looks!"

And the wedding party had to wait a quarter of an hour longer, walking about the wine-shop, elbowed and jostled in the midst of the men who entered to drink a glass of wine at the bar. Now and again, Boche, or Madame Fauconnier, or Bibi-the-Smoker, left the others, and went to the edge of the pavement, looking up at the sky. The storm was not passing over at all; a darkness was coming on, and puffs of wind sweeping along the ground, raised little clouds of white dust. At the first clap of thunder, Mademoiselle Remanjou made the sign of the cross. All the glances were anxiously directed to the clock over the looking-glass: it was twenty minutes to two.

"Go it!" cried Coupeau. "It's the angels who're weeping."

A gush of rain swept the pavement, along which some women

flew, holding down their skirts with both hands. And it was in the midst of this first shower that Madame Lorilleux at length arrived, furious and out of breath, and struggling on the threshold with her umbrella that would not close.

"Did any one ever see such a thing?" she exclaimed. "It caught me just at the door. I felt inclined to go upstairs again and take my things off. I should have been wise had I done so. Ah! it's a pretty wedding! I said how it would be. I wanted to put it off till next Saturday; and it rains because they wouldn't listen to me! So much the better, so much the better! I wish the sky would burst!"

Coupeau tried to pacify her. But she sent him to the right about. He would not pay for her dress if it were spoilt! She had on a black silk dress, in which she was nearly choking, the body, too tight fitting, was almost bursting the button-holes, and was cutting her across the shoulders; while the skirt only allowed her to take very short steps in walking. Yet, the other ladies of the party looked at her, pursing their lips and seemingly much affected by the gorgeousness of her costume. She did not even appear to see Gervaise seated beside mother Coupeau. She called Lorilleux and asked him for his handkerchief; then, going into a corner of the shop, she carefully wiped off one by one the drops of rain which had fallen on the silk.

The shower had abruptly ceased. The darkness increased, it was almost like night—a livid night rent at times by large flashes of lightning. Bibi-the-Smoker said laughingly that it would certainly rain priests. Then the storm burst forth with extreme violence. For half an hour the rain came down in bucketsful, and the thunder rumbled unceasingly. The men standing up before the door contemplated the grey veil of the downpour, the swollen gutters, the splashes of water caused by the rain beating into the puddles. The women feeling frightened had sat down again, holding their hands before their eyes. They no longer conversed, they were too upset. A jest Boche made about the thunder, saying that Saint Peter was sneezing up there, failed to raise a smile. But, when the thunder-claps became lest frequent and gradually died away in the distance, the wedding guests began to get impatient, enraged against the storm, cursing and shaking their fists at the clouds. A fine and interminable rain now poured down from the sky which had become an ashy grey.

"It's past two o'clock," cried Madame Lorilleux. "We can't stop here though for ever."

Mademoiselle Remanjou having suggested going into the country all the same, even though they went no farther than the moat of the fortifications, the others scouted the idea: the roads would be in a nice state, one would not even be able to sit down on the grass; besides, it did not seem to be all over yet, there might perhaps be another downpour. Coupeau, who had been watching a workman completely soaked, yet quietly walking along in the rain, murmured:

" If that animal My-Boots is waiting for us on the Route de Saint-Denis, he won't catch a sunstroke."

That made some of them laugh; but the general ill-humour increased. It was becoming ludicrous. They must decide on something. They could not possibly intend to look at the whites of each other's eyes, as they were doing, until the dinner hour arrived. Then, for some little while, in face of the obstinate shower, they all puzzled their brains trying to think of something to do. Bibi-the-Smoker proposed a game at cards; Boche, who was of a sly and rather wanton nature, knew a very funny little game, that of playing at confession; Madame Gaudron talked of going and eating some onion tart at a place she knew in the Chaussée Clignancourt; Madame Lerat would have preferred story-telling; Gaudron was not a bit dull, he felt very comfortable there, and merely offered to sit down to dinner at once. And, at each proposal, they wrangled and got more and more angry: it was stupid, it would send them all to sleep, they would be taken for children. Then, as Lorilleux, wishing to put in his word, suggested something very simple, a walk along the exterior Boulevards as far as the Père-Lachaise cemetery, where they might go and see the tomb of Héloïse and Abélard, if there was time, Madame Lorilleux exploded, no longer able to restrain herself. She was off, she was! That's what she was going to do! Were they trying to make a fool of her? She dressed herself, she got wet with the rain, and all that merely to go and stick inside a wine-shop! No, no! she had had enough of a wedding like that, she preferred her own home. Coupeau and Lorilleux had to place themselves in front of the door. She kept repeating:

" Move away from there! I tell you I'm going home!"

Her husband having succeeded in pacifying her, Coupeau went up to Gervaise, who was still quietly sitting in her corner, conversing with her mother-in-law and Madame Fauconnier.

" But you don't suggest anything!" said he, not daring to be very affectionate.

"Oh! anything one likes," she replied, with a laugh. "I'm easy to please. Go out, or stay in, it's all the same to me. I'm very comfortable, I don't ask for anything more."

And, indeed, her face was all beaming with a peaceful joy. Ever since the guests had been there, she had spoken to each in a rather low and tremulous voice in a sensible manner, and without taking part in any of the disputes. During the storm, she had remained with fixed eyes watching the lightning, as though she beheld some serious things very far off in the future by the aid of those sudden flashes.

M. Madinier had, up to this time, not proposed anything. He was leaning against the bar, with the tails of his dress coat thrust apart, while he fully maintained the important air of an employer. He kept on expectorating, and rolled his big eyes about.

"Well!" said he, "one might go to the Museum."

And he stroked his chin, as he blinkingly consulted the other members of the party.

"There are antiquities, pictures, paintings, a whole heap of things. It is very instructive. Perhaps you have never been there. Oh! it is quite worth seeing, at least once in a way."

They looked at each other, interrogatively. No, Gervaise had never been; Madame Fauconnier neither, nor Boche, nor the others. Coupeau thought he had been one Sunday, but he was not sure. They hesitated, however, when Madame Lorilleux, greatly impressed by M. Madinier's importance, thought the suggestion a very worthy and respectable one. As they were wasting the day, and were all dressed, they might as well go somewhere for their own instruction. Every one approved. Then, as it still rained a little, they borrowed some umbrellas of the proprietor of the wine-shop, old blue, green, and brown umbrellas, forgotten by different customers, and started off to the Museum.

The wedding party turned to the right, and descended into Paris along the Faubourg Saint-Denis. Coupeau and Gervaise again took the lead, almost running, and keeping a good distance in front of the others. M. Madinier now gave his arm to Madame Lorilleux, mother Coupeau having remained behind in the wine-shop on account of her old legs. Then came Lorilleux and Madame Lerat, Boche and Madame Fauconnier, Bibi-the-Smoker, and Mademoiselle Remanjou, and finally the two Gaudrons. They were twelve, and made a pretty long procession on the pavement.

"Oh! I assure you we had nothing whatever to do with it," explained Madame Lorilleux to M. Madinier. "We don't know where he picked her up, or rather we know only too well; but it's not for us to say anything, is it? My husband had to buy the wedding-ring. This morning, before we were scarcely out of bed, we were obliged to lend them ten francs, otherwise there would have been nothing done. A bride who doesn't bring a single one of her relations to her wedding! She says she has a sister in Paris, who keeps a pork-butcher's shop. Why didn't she invite her, then?"

She interrupted herself to point to Gervaise, whom the sloping pavement caused to limp a great deal.

"Just look at her! Is it possible? Oh! the hobbler!"

And this word, "Hobbler," passed from mouth to mouth. Lorilleux said, with a chuckle, that they ought to nickname her so. But Madame Fauconnier took Gervaise's part; they were wrong to make fun of her, she was as clean as a newly-coined sou, and could do no end of work when necessary. Madame Lerat, always ready with doubtful allusions, called the little woman's leg a "love skittle;" and, she added, that many men liked them, without being willing to enter into any further explanation.

The wedding party, emerging from the Faubourg Saint-Denis, had to cross the Boulevard. They waited a minute to let the crowd of vehicles pass, then ventured into the roadway, which the storm had transformed into a pool of liquid mud. Another shower was coming on, so they opened the umbrellas, and, beneath the lamentable old ginghams held by the men, the women gathered up their skirts, and the procession spread out in the slush which separated the pavements on either side of the Boulevard. Then a couple of street urchins called out: "What a lot of guys!" The passers-by hastened to obtain a look, whilst the shopmen stood up behind their windows. In the midst of the movement of the crowd, the couples marching in procession presented striking contrasts against the grey wet background of the Boulevards: Gervaise's coarse blue dress, Madame Fauconnier's flowery chintz, Boche's canary yellow trousers; the stiffness common to persons arrayed in their Sunday best, imparted a most ludicrous air to Coupeau's shining frock-coat and M. Madinier's square cut garment; whilst the elegant costume which bedecked Madame Lorilleux, the long fringe worn by Madame Lerat, and Mademoiselle Remanjou's rumpled skirts, mingled the fashions together, and displayed the

tawdry luxury of the poor. But it was more especially the
gentlemen's hats which amused the crowd—old-fashioned hats,
that had been carefully put by, and had become tarnished in
the obscurity of the cupboards; all of them being of the
most comical shapes—tall, broad, pointed, with extraordinary
brims, either turned up or flat, and too broad or too narrow.
And the smiles increased still more when, right in the rear,
forming the close of the spectacle, Madame Gaudron, the carder,
advanced in her stiff violet-coloured dress, with her enormous
stomach protruding in front of her. The wedding guests, however, did not hurry themselves; they were all in the best of
humours, happy at being looked at, and amused by the jocular
remarks passed upon them.

"Hallo! there's the bride!" yelled one of the street urchins,
pointing to Madame Gaudron. "By Jove! what a pip she's
swallowed!"

The whole party burst out laughing. Bibi-the-Smoker, looking back, said that the youngster was precious sharp. The
carder laughed the loudest, and was only too pleased at being
noticed. It was nothing to be ashamed of; on the contrary,
there was more than one lady who had given her a side glance
as she passed, and who would have been only too delighted to
be in a similar condition.

They turned into the Rue de Cléry. Then they took the Rue
du Mail. On reaching the Place des Victoires, there was a halt.
The bride's left shoe lace had come undone, and, as she tied it
up again, at the foot of the statue of Louis XIV., the couples
pressed behind her, waiting, and joking about the bit of the
calf of her leg that she displayed. At length, after passing
down the Rue Croix-des-Petits-Champs, they reached the
Louvre.

M. Madinier politely asked to be their cicerone. It was a big
place, and they might lose themselves; besides, he knew the
best parts, because he had often come there with an artist, a
very intelligent fellow, from whom a large dealer bought drawings to put on his cardboard boxes. Down below, when the
wedding party entered the Assyrian Museum, a slight shiver
passed through it. The deuce! it was not at all warm there; the
hall would have made a capital cellar. And the couples slowly
advanced, their chins raised, their eyes blinking, between the
gigantic stone figures, the black marble gods, dumb in their
hieratic rigidity, and the monstrous beasts, half cats and half
women, with death-like faces, attenuated noses, and swollen

lips. They thought all these things very ugly. The stone carvings of the present day were a great deal better. An inscription in Phœnician characters amazed them. No one could possibly have ever read that scrawl. But M. Madinier, already up on the first landing with Madame Lorilleux, called to them, shouting beneath the vaulted ceiling :

" Come along ! They're nothing, all those things! The things to see are on the first floor ! "

The severe bareness of the staircase made them very grave. An attendant, superbly attired in a red waistcoat and a coat trimmed with gold lace, who seemed to be awaiting them on the landing, increased their emotion. It was with great respect, and treading as softly as possible, that they entered the French Gallery.

Then, without stopping, their eyes occupied with the gilding of the frames, they followed the string of little rooms, glancing at the passing pictures, too numerous to be seen properly. It would have required an hour before each, if they had wanted to understand it. What a number of pictures ! there was no end to them. They must be worth a mint of money. Right at the end, M. Madinier suddenly ordered a halt opposite the " Raft of the Medusa," and he explained the subject to them. All deeply impressed and motionless, they uttered not a word. When they started off again, Boche expressed the general feeling, saying it was marvellous.

In the Apollo Gallery, the inlaid flooring especially astonished the party—a shining floor, as clear as a mirror, and which reflected the legs of the seats. Mademoiselle Remanjou kept her eyes closed, because she could not help thinking that she was walking on water. They called to Madame Gaudron to be careful how she trod on account of her condition. M. Madinier wanted to show them the gilding and paintings of the ceiling ; but it nearly broke their necks to look up above, and they could distinguish nothing. Then, before entering the Square Saloon, he pointed to a window, saying :

"That's the balcony from which Charles IX. fired on the people."

Meanwhile, he kept his eye on the tail of the procession. In the middle of the Square Saloon, he signalled to them to stop. He murmured in a low voice, as though at church, that there were only masterpieces there. They went round the apartment. Gervaise asked to have the " Marriage of Cana " explained to her; it was stupid not to write the subjects of the pictures on the frames. Coupeau stopped before the "Joconde," whom he considered resembled one of his aunts. Boche and Bibi-the-Smoker chuckled to each other every time they discovered a picture of a naked woman; the thighs of "Antiope" especially gave them quite a shock. And, right at the end of the room, the two Gaudrons, the man with his mouth wide open, the woman with her hands folded on her stomach, stood staring with astonishment, deeply moved, and feeling quite stupid, in front of Murillo's "Virgin."

When they had been all round the saloon, M. Madinier wished them to go over it again, it was worth while. He was very attentive to Madame Lorilleux, because of her silk dress; and each time that she questioned him, he answered her gravely, with great assurance. As she was interested in Titian's Mistress, whose yellow hair she thought resembled her own, he stated that the portrait was that of the beautiful Madame Ferronnière, one of Henri IV.'s mistresses, about whom a drama had been written, and performed at the Ambigu Theatre.

Then the wedding party invaded the long gallery occupied by the Italian and Flemish schools. More paintings, always paintings, saints, men and women, with faces which none of them could understand, landscapes that were all black, animals turned yellow, a medley of people and things, the great mixture of the colours of which was beginning to give them all violent headaches. M. Madinier no longer talked as he slowly headed the procession, which followed him in good order, with stretched necks and upcast eyes. Centuries of art passed before their bewildered ignorance, the fine sharpness of the early masters, the splendours of the Venetians, the vigorous life, beautiful with light, of the Dutch painters. But what interested them most were the artists who were copying, with their easels planted amongst the people, painting away unrestrainedly; an old lady, mounted on a pair of high steps, working a big brush over the delicate sky of an immense painting, struck them as something most peculiar. Little by little, however, the news had probably spread that a wedding party was visiting the Louvre; painters, with broad grins on their faces, hastened to the spot; some of the curious secured seats beforehand to witness the procession comfortably; whilst the attendants, repressing their laughter, refrained with difficulty from making some very cutting remarks. And those forming the party, already feeling tired, losing their respect, dragged their hob-nail shoes, and knocked their heels on the sonorous floors, like the stamping of a bewildered

drove of cattle let loose in the midst of the cleanliness and quiet
of the rooms.

M. Madinier was reserving himself to give more effect to a surprise that he had in store.   He went straight to the "Kermesse"
of Rubens; but still he said nothing.   He contented himself
with directing the others' attention to the picture by a sprightly
glance.   The ladies uttered faint cries the moment they had
brought their noses close to the painting.   Then, blushing
deeply, they turned away their heads.   The men, though,
kept them there, cracking jokes, and seeking for the coarser
details.

"Just look!" exclaimed Boche, "it's worth the money.
There's one who's spewing, and another, he's watering the
dandelions; and that one—oh! that one.   Ah, well! they're a
nice clean lot, they are!"

"Let us be off," said M. Madinier, delighted with his success.
"There is nothing more to see here."

They retraced their steps, passing again through the Square
Salon and the Apollo Gallery.   Madame Lerat and Mademoiselle
Remanjou complained, declaring that their legs could scarcely
bear them.   But the cardboard box manufacturer wanted to
show Lorilleux the old jewellery.   It was close by, in a little
room which he could find with his eyes shut.   However, he
made a mistake, and led the wedding party astray through
seven or eight cold, deserted rooms, only ornamented with
severe-looking glass cases, containing numberless broken pots
and hideous little figures.   The party shuddered, and was
beginning to feel awfully bored.   Then, as it was seeking a
door, it came plump upon the drawings.   Now ensued another
long peregrination.   The drawings seemed as though they
would never come to an end.   One room succeeded another,
without anything funny; nothing but sheets of paper scribbled
all over, hanging under glass against the walls.

M. Madinier, losing his head, not willing to admit that he
did not know his way, ascended a flight of stairs, making the
wedding party mount to the next floor.   This time it traversed
the Naval Museum, among models of instruments and cannons,
plans in relief, and vessels as tiny as playthings.   After going
a long way, and walking for a quarter of an hour, it came upon
another staircase; and, having descended this, it found itself
once more surrounded by the drawings.   Then despair took
possession of it.   It wandered through whatever rooms it came
to, all the couples following each other behind M. Madinier,

who was mopping his forehead, almost out of his mind, and furious with the administration, whom he accused of having changed the positions of the doors. The attendants and the visitors, full of astonishment, watched it pass. In less than twenty minutes it was seen again in the Square Saloon, in the French Gallery, and amongst the glass cases, in which slumber the little Eastern gods. Never again would it get out. With aching legs, abandoning itself to fate, the wedding party kicked up an awful row, leaving in its flight Madame Gaudron's protruding stomach a long way in the rear.

"Closing time! closing time!" called out the attendants, in a loud tone of voice.

And the wedding party was nearly shut in. An attendant was obliged to place himself at the head of it, and conduct it to a door. Then, in the courtyard of the Louvre, when it had recovered its umbrellas from the cloak-room, it breathed again. M. Madinier regained his assurance. He had made a mistake in not turning to the left, now he recollected that the jewellery was to the left. The whole party pretended to be very pleased at having seen all they had

Four o'clock was striking. There were still two hours to be employed before the dinner time, so it was decided they should take a stroll, just to occupy the interval. The ladies, who were very tired, would have much preferred to have sat down; but, as no one offered any refreshments, they started off, following the line of quays. There they encountered another shower, and so sharp a one that, in spite of the umbrellas, the ladies' dresses began to get wet. Madame Lorilleux, her heart sinking within her each time a drop fell upon her black silk, proposed that they should shelter themselves under the Pont-Royal; besides, if the others did not accompany her, she threatened to go all by herself. And the procession marched under one of the arches of the bridge. They were very comfortable there. It was, most decidedly, a capital idea! The ladies, spreading their handkerchiefs over the paving-stones, sat down with their knees wide apart, and pulled out the blades of grass that grew between the stones with both hands, whilst they watched the dark flowing water as though they were in the country. The men amused themselves with calling out very loud, so as to awaken the echoes of the arch. One after the other, Boche and Bibi-the-Smoker insulted the vacant space, shouting out "Pig!" with all their might, and laughing heartily each time the echo sent the word back to them; then, their throats getting husky, they picked up some flat stones, and tried to make ducks and drakes with them in the water.

The shower had ceased, but the whole party felt so comfortable that no one thought of moving away. The surface of the Seine was covered with greasy matter, old corks and vegetable parings, heaps of filth which an eddy detained a moment in the restless waters, darkened by the shadow of the arch ; whilst, on the top of the bridge could be heard the rumbling of the passing cabs and omnibuses, all the animation of Paris, of which only the roofs of the houses to the right and the left could be seen, as though from the bottom of some pit. Mademoiselle Remanjou sighed. If there had only been some foliage, it would have reminded her, she said, of a nook on the banks of the Marne, where she used to go, about the year 1817, with a young man for whom she was still mourning.

At last, M. Madinier gave the signal for departure. They passed through the Tuileries gardens, in the midst of a little community of children, whose hoops and balls upset the good order of the couples. Then, as the wedding party on arriving at the Place Vendôme looked up at the column, M. Madinier gallantly offered to treat the ladies to a view from the top. His suggestion was considered extremely amusing. Yes, yes, they would go up ; it would give them something to laugh about for a long time. Besides, it was full of interest for those persons who had never been above their mother earth.

" You make a mistake if you think the Hobbler will venture inside there with her leg all out of place ! " murmured Madame Lorilleux.

" I'll go up with pleasure," said Madame Lerat, " but I won't have any men walking behind me."

And the whole party ascended. In the narrow space afforded by the spiral staircase, the twelve persons crawled up one after the other stumbling against the worn steps, and clinging to the walls. Then, when the obscurity became complete, they almost split their sides with laughing. The ladies screamed. The gentlemen tickled them, pinched their legs ; but they were very stupid to say anything ! The proper plan is to think that it's the mice. Besides, it went no further ; all knew where to leave off for propriety's sake. Then Boche had a funny idea, which the others at once took up. They called out to Madame Gaudron as though she had stuck on the way, and asked her if she was able to get through. Just fancy ! supposing she had become fixed in there, without being able to go up or down,

she would have stopped up the hole, and none of them would
have known how to get out. And they laughed, with a boisterous gaiety which shook the column, at the idea of that woman's
stomach. Afterwards, Boche, who was in quite a merry mood,
declared that they were growing old in that chimney-pot.
Would it never come to an end, were they going right up to
heaven? And he tried to frighten the ladies, by calling out
that he felt it shaking. Coupeau, however, said nothing. He
was behind Gervaise, with his arm round her waist, and felt that
she was abandoning herself to him. When they suddenly
emerged again into daylight, he was just in the act of kissing
her on the neck.

"Well! you're a nice couple; you don't stand on ceremony,"
said Madame Lorilleux with a scandalised air.

Bibi-the-Smoker pretended to be furious. He muttered
between his teeth, "You made such a noise together! I wasn't
even able to count the steps."

But M. Madinier was already up on the platform, pointing out
the different monuments. Neither Madame Fauconnier nor
Mademoiselle Remanjou would on any consideration leave the
staircase. The thought of the pavement below made their
blood curdle, and they contented themselves with glancing out
of the little door. Madame Lerat, who was bolder, went round
the narrow terrace, keeping close to the bronze dome; but, all
the same, it gave one a rude emotion to think that one only had
to slip off. What a somersault, ye gods! The men, rather
pale, looked down on to the Place. One could almost think
oneself up in the air, separated from everything. No, really,
it gave you a chill down the back. M. Madinier, however,
recommended raising the eyes, to look straight in front of one,
far into the distance; it prevented giddiness. And he continued to point out with his finger the Invalides, the Pantheon,
Notre-Dame, the Tour Saint-Jacques, the Buttes Montmartre.
Then Madame Lorilleux thought to inquire whether one could
see, on the Boulevard de la Chapelle, the wine-shop where
they were going to dine, the "Silver Windmill." So, for ten
minutes, they looked about, and even came to quarrelling;
each one placed the wine-shop in a different part. Paris spread
out around them its grey immensity, which in the more distant
parts assumed a bluish tinge, and its deep valleys covered
with a sea of roofs. All the right bank of the river was in
shadow, beneath a vast ragged copper-coloured cloud; and,
from the border of this cloud fringed with gold issued a broad

F

sunbeam, which illumined the thousands of window-panes on the loft bank with a multitude of sparks, causing that corner of the city to stand out against a bright blue sky cleared by the storm.

" It wasn't worth while coming up here to bite each other's noses off," said Boche, angrily, as he turned to descend the staircase.

The wedding party went down, dumb and sulky, awakening no other sound beyond that of shoes clanking on the stone steps. When it reached the bottom, M. Madinier wished to pay ; but Coupeau would not permit him, and hastened to place twenty-four sous into the keeper's hand, two sous each person. It was nearly half-past five, there was just time to get back. So they returned by the Boulevards and the Faubourg Poissonnière. Coupeau, however, considered that their outing could not end like that. He bundled them all into a wine-shop where they took some vermouth.

The repast was ordered for six o'clock. At the " Silver Windmill," they had been waiting for the wedding party a good twenty minutes. Madame Boche, who had got a lady living in the same house to attend to her duties for the evening, was conversing with mother Coupeau in the first floor room, in front of the table, which was all laid out ; and the two youngsters, Claude and Etienne, whom she had brought with her, were playing about beneath the table and amongst the chairs. When Gervaise, on entering, caught sight of the little ones, whom she had not seen all the day, she took them on her knees, and caressed and kissed them.

" Have they been good ?" asked she of Madame Boche. " I hope they haven't worried you too much."

And as the latter related the things those little vermin had said during the afternoon, and which would make one die with laughing, the mother again took them up and pressed them to her breast, seized with an overpowering outburst of maternal affection.

" It's not very pleasant for Coupeau all the same," Madame Lorilleux was saying to the other ladies, at the end of the room.

Gervaise had retained her smiling tranquillity of the morning. Ever since the walk, however, she became at moments quite sad, and watched her husband and the Lorilleux with her pensive and sober-minded air. She found that Coupeau was a coward in his sister's presence. Only the day before he had talked very big, and swore that he would put those vipers back in their places, if they did not treat him properly. But she saw very well that when they were there he was a regular lick-spittle, deferring to them in everything, and almost going out of his mind whenever he thought them angry. And that alone filled the young woman with anxiety for the future.

They were now only waiting for My-Boots, who had not yet put in an appearance.

"Oh! blow him!" cried Coupeau, "let's begin. You'll see, he'll soon turn up, he's got a clear nose, he can scent the grub from afar. I say, he must be amusing himself, if he's still standing like a post on the Route de Saint-Denis!"

Then the wedding party, feeling very lively, sat down making a great noise with the chairs. Gervaise was between Lorilleux and M. Madinier, and Coupeau between Madame Fauconnier and Madame Lorilleux. The other guests seated themselves where they liked, because it always ended with jealousies and quarrels, when one settled their places for them. Boche glided to a seat beside Madame Lerat. Bibi-the-Smoker had for neighbours Mademoiselle Remanjou and Madame Gaudron. As for Madame Boche and mother Coupeau, they were right at the end of the table, looking after the children, cutting up their meat and giving them something to drink, but not much wine.

"Does nobody say grace?" asked Boche, whilst the ladies arranged their skirts under the table-cloth, so as not to get them stained.

But Madame Lorilleux did not like those sort of jokes. And the vermicelli soup, which was nearly cold, was gulped down very quickly, their lips making a hissing noise against the spoons. Two waiters served at table, dressed in little greasy jackets and not over clean white aprons. By the four open windows overlooking the acacias of the courtyard there entered the clear light of the close of a stormy day, with the atmosphere purified thereby though without sufficiently cooling it. The reflection of the trees in this damp corner gave the smoky room a greenish hue, and the shadows of leaves danced over the table-cloth which had a vague musty odour. There were two looking-glasses covered with fly marks, one at either end of the room, which lengthened the table indefinitely, with the coarse white crockery on it fast turning yellow, and in the scratches on which the greasy dish water had left a dark deposit. Each time a waiter returned from the kitchen, the door banged, admitting a strong smell of burning fat.

"Don't all talk at once," said Boche, as every one remained silent with his nose in his plate.

And they were drinking the first glass of wine as their eyes followed two force-meat pies which the waiters were handing round when My-Boots entered the room.

"Well, you're a scurvy lot, you people!" said he. "I've been wearing my pins out for three hours waiting on the high road, and a gendarme even came and asked me for my papers. It isn't right to play such dirty tricks on a friend! You might at least have sent me a growler by a commissionaire. Ah! no, you know, joking apart, it's too bad. And, with all that, it rained so hard that I got my pockets full of water. Honour bright, you might still catch enough fish in 'em for a meal."

The others wriggled with laughter. That animal My-Boots was just a bit on; he had certainly already stowed away his two quarts of wine, merely to prevent his being bothered by all that frog's liquor with which the storm had deluged his giblets.

"Hallo! Count Leg-of-Mutton!" said Coupeau, "just go and sit yourself there, beside Madame Gaudron. You see you were expected."

Oh, he did not mind, he would soon catch the others up; and he asked for three helps of soup, platefuls of vermicelli, in which he soaked enormous slices of bread. Then, when they had attacked the force-meat pies, he became the profound admiration of every one at the table. How he guttled! The bewildered waiters helped each other to pass him bread, thin slices which he swallowed at a mouthful. He ended by losing his temper; he insisted on having a loaf placed on the table beside him. The landlord, very anxious, came for a moment and looked in at the door. The party, which was expecting him, again wriggled with laughter. It seemed to upset the caterer. What a rum card he was, that My-Boots! One day he had eaten a dozen hard boiled eggs and drank a dozen glasses of wine while the clock was striking twelve! There are not many who can do that. And Mademoiselle Remanjou, deeply moved, watched My-Boots chew, whilst M. Madinier, seeking for a word to express his almost respectful astonishment, declared that such a capacity was extraordinary.

There was a brief silence. A waiter had just placed on the table a ragout of rabbits in a vast dish as deep as a salad-bowl. Coupeau, who liked fun, started another joke.

"I say, waiter, that rabbit's from the housetops. It still mows."

And in fact, a faint mew, perfectly imitated, seemed to issue from the dish. It was Coupeau who did that with his throat, without opening his lips; a talent which, at all parties, met with decided success, so much so that he never ordered a dinner abroad without having a rabbit ragout. After that, he purred. The ladies pressed their napkins to their mouths to try and stop their laughter. Madame Fauconnier asked for a head, she only liked that part. Mademoiselle Remanjou had a weakness for the slices of bacon. And as Boche said he preferred the little onions when they were nicely broiled, Madame Lerat screwed up her lips, and murmured:

"I can understand that."

She was as dry as a stick, and led the life of a workwoman immured in her occupations, never having seen the shadow of a man in her home ever since she became a widow, though showing a continual hankering after obscenity, a mania for words of double meaning and dubious allusions so profound, that she alone could understand them. As Boche leant towards her and, in a whisper, asked for an explanation, she resumed:

"Little onions, why of course. That's quite enough, I think."

But the conversation was becoming grave. Each one was talking of his trade. M. Madinier was extolling the manufacture of cardboard boxes; there were real artists at work on that; and he mentioned some boxes for New Year's gifts of which he had seen the models, regular marvels of luxury. Lorilleux, however, chuckled. He was very vain at working gold; he saw a kind of reflection of it on his fingers and all over his person. He said that in olden times jewellers used often to wear swords; and he ignorantly alluded to Bernard Palissy. Coupeau talked of a weather-cock, a work of art that one of his comrades had made; it consisted of a column, above which came a sheaf, then a basket of fruit, and then a flag; the whole was very natural and made with nothing but pieces of zinc soldered together. Madame Lerat showed Bibi-the-Smoker how to make the stalk of an artificial rose, as she turned the handle of her knife between her bony fingers. Meanwhile the voices rose, and mingled. Amidst the hubbub one could hear some words uttered very loud by Madame Fauconnier, who was complaining of her work-girls, especially of a little slattern of an apprentice who, the day before, had let a pair of sheets burn.

"You may talk," cried Lorilleux, banging his fist down on the table, "but gold is gold."

And, in the midst of the silence caused by the statement of

this fact, the only sound heard was Mademoiselle Remanjou's shrill voice continuing :

"Then I turn up the skirt and stitch it inside. I stick a pin in the head to keep the cap on, and that's all ; and they are sold for thirteen sous a-piece."

She was explaining how she dressed her dolls to My-Boots, whose jaws were working slowly like grindstones. He did not listen, though he kept nodding his head, but looked after the waiters to prevent them removing any of the dishes he had not cleaned out. There had been some stewed veal and French beans ; and now they were serving the roast, two skinny chickens lying on a bed of faded watercresses and cooked in the oven. Outside, the sun was setting behind the high branches of the acacias. In the room the greenish reflection was thickening with the fumes that rose from the table, stained all over with wine and gravy, and covered with a pell-mell of crockery, glasses, knives and forks ; and along the wall, dirty plates and empty bottles looked liked so much rubbish swept and shaken from the cloth. It was very warm. The men took off their coats and continued eating in their shirt-sleeves.

"Madame Boche, please don't let them stuff so much," said Gervaise, who spoke but little, and who was watching Claude and Etienne from a distance.

She got up from her seat, and went and talked for a minute behind the little ones' chairs. Children did not reason ; they would eat all day long without refusing a single thing ; and then she herself helped them to some chicken, a little of the breast. But mother Coupeau said they might, just for once in a way, risk an attack of indigestion. Madame Boche, in a low voice, accused Boche of pinching Madame Lerat's knees. Oh, he was a sly dog, and he tippled. She had certainly seen his hand disappear. If he did it again, drat him ! she wouldn't hesitate shying a water-bottle at his head. In the partial silence, M. Madinier was talking politics.

"Their law of May 31 is an abominable one. Now you must reside in a place for two years. Three millions of citizens are struck off the lists. I've been told that Bonaparte is, in reality, very much annoyed, for he loves the people ; he has given them proofs."

He was a republican ; but he admired the prince on account of his uncle, a man the like of whom would never be seen again. Bibi-the-Smoker flew into a passion. He had worked at the Elysée ; he had seen Bonaparte just as he saw My-Boots in front of him over there. Well, that muff of a president was just like a jackass, that was all! It was said that he was going to travel about in the direction of Lyons; it would be a precious good riddance of bad rubbish if he fell into some hole and broke his neck. But, as the discussion was becoming too heated, Coupeau had to interfere.

"Ah, well! how simple you all are to quarrel about politics. Politics are all humbug! Do such things exist for us? Let there be no matter who, a king, an emperor, no one at all, it won't prevent me earning my five francs a day, and eating, and sleeping; isn't that so? No, it's too stupid!"

Lorilleux shook his head. He was born on the same day as the Count de Chambord, the 29th of September, 1820. He was greatly struck with this coincidence, indulging himself in a vague dream, in which he established a connection between the king's return to France and his own private fortunes. He never said exactly what he was expecting, but he led people to suppose that when that time arrived something extraordinarily agreeable would happen to him. So whenever he had a wish too great to be gratified, he would put it off to another time, when the king came back.

"Besides," observed he, "I saw the Count de Chambord one evening."

Every face was turned towards him.

"It's quite true. A stout man, in an overcoat, and with a good-natured air. I was at Péquignot's, one of my friends who deals in furniture in the Grande Rue de la Chapelle. The Count de Chambord had forgotten his umbrella there the day before; so he came in, and just simply said, like this: 'Will you please return me my umbrella?' Well, yes, it was him; Péquignot gave me his word of honour it was."

Not one of the guests suggested the smallest doubt. They had now arrived at the dessert. The waiters were clearing the table with a great clattering of crockery; and Madame Lorilleux, who until then had behaved in a most lady-like manner, allowed a "dirty beast" to escape from her, because one of the waiters had spilt something down her neck as he removed a dish. Her silk dress was most certainly stained. M. Madinier was obliged to look at her back, and he declared there was nothing the matter. Now, in the middle of the table, rose a salad-bowl full of frosted eggs, flanked by two plates of cheese and two plates of fruit. The frosted eggs, with the whites over-cooked and floating on the yellow cream, set every one meditating; they had not been anticipated, so that they produced a very agreeable impression. My-Boots was still eating. He had asked for another loaf. He finished what there was of the cheese ; and, as there was some cream left, he had the salad-bowl passed to him, into which he sliced some large pieces of bread as though for a soup.

"The gentleman is really remarkable," said M. Madinier, again giving way to his admiration.

Then the men rose up to get their pipes. They stood for a moment behind My-Boots, patting him on the back, and asking him if he felt better. Bibi-the-Smoker lifted him up in his chair ; but, Jove's thunder ! the animal had doubled in weight. Coupeau, for a joke, stated that his comrade was only just fairly settling down to work, that he would go on eating like that all through the night. The terrified waiters beat a hasty retreat. Boche, who had just before gone downstairs, came back relating the awful face that the landlord was making over it : he was looking as pale as death behind his bar. His wife, in a state of consternation, had sent out to see if the bakers were still open ; even the cat at the fire-side looked as though ruin was staring it in the face. Really, it was too comic ; it was worth the money of the dinner ; no pic-nic of that sort would be complete without that swallow-all, My-Boots. And the men, smoking their pipes, watched him with jealous looks ; for after all, to be able to eat so much, he must be a precious strong fellow !

"I wouldn't care to be obliged to support you," said Madame Gaudron. "Ah, no ; you may take my word for that !"

"I say, little mother, no jokes," replied My-Boots, casting a side-glance at his neighbour's rotund figure. "You've swallowed more than I have."

The others applauded, shouting "Bravo !"—it was well answered. It was now pitch dark outside, three gas-jets were flaring in the room, diffusing dim rays in the midst of the tobacco-smoke. The waiters, after serving the coffee and the brandy, had removed the last piles of dirty plates. Down below, beneath the three acacias, dancing had commenced, a cornet-a-piston and two fiddles playing very loud, and mingling in the warm night air with the rather hoarse laughter of women.

"We must have a punch !" cried My-Boots ; "two quarts of brandy, lots of lemon, and a little sugar."

But Coupeau, seeing the anxious look on Gervaise's face in front of him, got up from the table, declaring that there should be no more drink. They had emptied twenty-five quarts, a quart and a half to each person, counting the children as grown-up people ; that was already too much. They had had a feed together in good fellowship, and without ceremony, because they esteemed one another, and wished to celebrate the event of the day amongst themselves. All had gone off very pleasantly. They were gay, and they must not go and get beastly drunk if they wished to respect the ladies. In a word, and finally, they had met together to drink the health of the newly-married couple, and not to become regularly scammered. This little speech, spoken in a determined tone of voice by the zinc-worker, who placed his hand on his breast at the end of every sentence, was warmly approved by Lorilleux and M. Madinier. But the others—Boche, Gaudron, Bibi-the-Smoker, and especially My-Boots, all four very much on—only jeered, speaking thick, and feeling a confounded thirst, which they must water at any cost.

"Those who're thirsty are thirsty, and those who aren't thirsty aren't thirsty," remarked My-Boots. "Therefore, we'll order the punch. No one need take offence. The aristocrats can drink sugar-and-water."

And as the zinc-worker commenced another sermon, the other, who had risen on his legs, gave himself a slap, exclaiming :

"Come, let's have no more of that, my boy ! Waiter, two quarts of your best ! "

So Coupeau said very well, only they would settle for the dinner at once. It would prevent any disputes. The well-behaved people did not want to pay for the drunkards ; and it just happened that My-Boots, after searching in his pockets for a long time, could only produce three francs and seven sous. Well, why had they made him wait all that time on the Route de Saint-Denis ? He could not let himself be drowned, and so he had broken into his five-franc piece. It was the fault of the others, that was all ! He ended by giving the three francs, keeping the seven sous for his morrow's tobacco. Coupeau, who was furious, would have knocked him over, had not Gervaise, greatly frightened, pulled him by his coat, and begged him to keep cool. He decided to borrow the two francs of Lorilleux, who, after refusing them, lent them on the sly, for his wife would never have consented to his doing so.

M. Madinier went round with a plate. The spinster and the ladies who were alone—Madame Lerat, Madame Fauconnier, Mademoiselle Remanjou—discreetly placed their five-franc pieces in it the first. Then the gentlemen went to the other

end of the room, and made up the accounts. They were
fifteen; it amounted therefore to seventy-five francs. When
the seventy-five francs were in the plate, each man added five
sous for the waiters. It took a quarter of an hour of
laborious calculations before everything was settled to the
general satisfaction.

But when M. Madinier, who wished to deal direct with the
landlord, had got him to step up, the whole party became lost
in astonishment on hearing him say with a smile that there was
still something due to him. There were some extras; and, as
the word "extras" was greeted with angry exclamations, he
entered into details :—Twenty-five quarts of wine, instead of
twenty, the number agreed upon beforehand; the frosted eggs,
which he had added, as the dessert was rather scanty; finally,
a quarter of a bottle of rum, served with the coffee, in case any
one preferred rum. Then a formidable quarrel ensued. Coupeau,
who was appealed to, protested against everything; he had
never mentioned twenty quarts; as for the frosted eggs, they
were included in the dessert, so much the worse for the landlord
if he chose to add them without being asked to do so. There
remained the rum, a mere nothing, just a mode of increasing
the bill by putting on the table spirits that no one thought anything about.

"It was on the tray with the coffee," he cried; "therefore it
goes with the coffee. Go to the deuce! Take your money,
and never again will we set foot in your den!"

"It's six francs more," repeated the landlord. "Pay me my
six francs; and with all that I haven't counted the four loaves
that gentleman ate!"

The whole party, pressing forward, surrounded him with
furious gestures and a yelping of voices choking with rage.
The women especially threw aside all reserve, and refused to add
another centime. Ah, well, thank you! it was a pretty wedding
party! Mademoiselle Remanjou would never again mix herself up
in anything of the sort! Madame Fauconnier had dined very
badly indeed; at home, for a couple of francs, she could have
had a delicious little meal. Madame Gaudron complained
bitterly of having been placed at the bad end of the table, next
to My-Boots, who had not shown her the least attention. In
short, those sort of parties always wound up badly. When one
wanted to have friends at one's wedding, one should pay all expenses! And Gervaise, who had taken refuge behind mother
Coupeau, in front of one of the windows, said nothing, but was

full of shame, feeling that all those recriminations were directed at her.

M. Madinier ended by going down with the landlord. One could hear them arguing below. Then, when half an hour had gone by, the cardboard box manufacturer returned; he had settled the matter by giving three francs. But the party continued annoyed and exasperated, constantly returning to the question of the extras. And the uproar increased from an act of vigour on Madame Boche's part. She had kept an eye on Boche, and at length detected him squeezing Madame Lerat round the waist in a corner. Then, with all her strength, she flung a water bottle, which smashed against the wall.

"One can easily see that your husband's a tailor, madame," said the tall widow, with a curl of the lip, full of a double meaning. "He's a petticoat measurer, A1. Yet I gave him some pretty hard kicks under the table."

The harmony of the evening was altogether upset. Every one became more and more ill-tempered. M. Madinier suggested some singing, but Bibi-the-Smoker, who had a fine voice, had disappeared some time before; and Mademoiselle Remanjou, who was leaning out of the window, caught sight of him under the acacias, swinging round a big girl who was bare-headed. The cornet-a-piston and the two fiddles were playing the "Mustard Dealer," a quadrille in which every one clapped their hands at the pastourelle. Then, there was a general breaking up of the wedding party: My-Boots and the two Gaudrons went down; Boche himself sneaked off. From the windows, the couples dancing round could be seen through the leaves, to which the lanterns hung amongst the branches gave the formal green-paint hue of scenery on the stage. The night was peaceful, and without a breeze, whilst the heat gave one a feeling of faintness. In the dining-room, M. Madinier and Lorilleux were engaged in serious conversation, whilst the ladies, no longer knowing how to give vent to their ill-humour, were examining their dresses, trying to discover if they had got at all stained.

Madame Lerat's fringe looked as though it had been soused in the coffee. Madame Fauconnier's chintz dress was full of gravy. Mother Coupeau's green shawl, fallen from off a chair, was discovered in a corner, rolled up and trodden upon. But it was Madame Lorilleux especially who became more ill-tempered still. She had a stain on the back of her dress; it was useless for the others to declare that she had not—she felt it.

And, by twisting herself about in front of a looking-glass, she ended by catching a glimpse of it.

"What did I say?" cried she. "It's gravy from the fowl. The waiter shall pay for the dress. I will bring an action against him. Ah! this is a fit ending to such a day. I should have done better to have stayed in bed. To begin with, I'm off. I've had enough of their wretched wedding!"

And she left the room in a rage, causing the staircase to shake beneath her heavy footsteps. Lorilleux ran after her. But all she would consent to was that she would wait five minutes on the pavement outside, if he wanted them to go off together. She ought to have left directly after the storm, as she wished to do. She would make Coupeau smart for that day. When the latter heard she was in such a passion, he seemed quite dismayed; and Gervaise, to save him any unpleasantness, consented to go home at once. Then they all hastily embraced each other. M. Madinier undertook to see mother Coupeau home. For that first night, Madame Boche was to take Claude and Etienne to sleep at her place; their mother might be quite easy, the little ones were sleeping heavily on some chairs with bad stomach-aches from the frosted eggs. As the newly-married couple were starting off with the Lorilleux, leaving the rest of the guests at the wine-shop, a battle commenced down below in the dancing place between their party and another one; Boche and My-Boots, who had kissed a lady, would not give her up to two soldiers to whom she belonged, and threatened to clear out the whole place, amidst the maddening noise of the cornet-a-piston and the two fiddles playing the "Pearl" polka.

It was scarcely eleven o'clock. On the Boulevard de la Chapelle, and in the entire neighbourhood of the Goutte-d'Or, the fortnight's pay, which fell due on that Saturday, produced an enormous drunken uproar. Madame Lorilleux was waiting beneath a gas-lamp about twenty paces from the "Silver Wind-mill." She took her husband's arm, and walked on in front without looking round, at such a rate, that Gervaise and Coupeau got quite out of breath in trying to keep up with them. Now and again they stepped off the pavement to leave room for some drunkard who had fallen there. Lorilleux looked back, endeavouring to make things pleasant.

"We will see you as far as your door," said he.

But Madame Lorilleux, raising her voice, thought it a funny thing to spend one's wedding night in such a filthy hole as the Hôtel Boncœur. Ought they not to have put their marriage off, and have saved a few sous to buy some furniture, so as to have had a home of their own on the first night? Ah! they would be comfortable, right up under the roof, packed into a little closet, at ten francs a month, where there was not even the slightest air.

"I've given notice, we're not going to use the room up at the top of the house," timidly interposed Coupeau. "We keep Gervaise's room, which is larger."

Madame Lorilleux forgot herself, she turned abruptly round.

"That's worse than all!" cried she. "You're going to sleep in the Hobbler's room!"

Gervaise became quite pale. This nickname, which she received full in the face for the first time, fell on her like a blow. And she fully understood, too, her sister-in-law's exclamation: the Hobbler's room was the room in which she had lived for a month with Lantier, where the shreds of her past life still hung about. Coupeau did not understand this, but merely felt hurt at the nickname.

"You do wrong to christen others," replied he angrily. "You don't know, perhaps, that in the neighbourhood they call you Cow's-Tail, because of your hair. There, that doesn't please you, does it? Why should we not keep the room on the first floor? To-night the children won't sleep there, and we shall be very comfortable."

Madame Lorilleux added nothing further, but retired into her dignity, horribly annoyed at being called Cow's-Tail. Coupeau, to console Gervaise, gently squeezed her arm; and he even succeeded in making her smile, by telling her in a whisper that they started on their married life with exactly seven sous—three big ones and a little one, which he shook together in his trouser pocket. When they reached the Hôtel Boncœur, the two couples wished each other good-night, with an angry air; and as Coupeau pushed the two women into each other's arms, calling them a couple of ninnies, a drunken fellow, who seemed to want to go to the right, suddenly slipped to the left and came tumbling between them.

"Why, it's old Bazouge!" said Lorilleux. "He's had his fill to-day."

Gervaise, frightened, squeezed up against the door of the hotel. Old Bazouge, an undertaker's mute of some fifty years of age, had his black trousers all stained with mud, his black cape hooked on to his shoulder, and his black leather hat knocked in by some tumble he had met with.

"Don't be afraid, he isn't spiteful," continued Lorilleux.
" He's a neighbour of ours—the third room in the passage before us. He would find himself in a nice mess if his people
were to see him like this ! "

Old Bazouge, however, felt offended at the young woman's
evident terror.

" Well, what ! " hiccoughed he, " we ain't going to eat any
one. I'm as good as another, any day, my little woman. No
doubt I've had a drop ! When work's plentiful one must
grease the wheels. It's not you, nor your friends, who would
have carried down the stiff'un of forty-seven stone whom I
and a pal brought from the fourth floor to the pavement, and
without smashing him too. I like jolly people."

But Gervaise retreated further into the doorway, seized with
a longing to cry, which spoilt her day of sober-minded joy. She
no longer thought of kissing her sister-in-law, she implored
Coupeau to get rid of the drunkard. Then Bazouge, as he
stumbled about, made a gesture full of philosophical disdain.

" That won't prevent your passing through our hands, my
little woman. You'll perhaps be glad to do so, one of these
days. Yes, I know some women who'd be much obliged if we
did carry 'em off."

And, as Lorilleux led him away, he turned round, and stuttered out a last sentence, between two hiccoughs.

"When one cocks one's toes—listen to this—when one cocks
one's toes, it's for a long time."

CHAPTER IV.

THEN followed four years of hard work. In the neighbourhood, Gervaise and Coupeau had the reputation of being a happy couple, living in retirement, without quarrels, and taking a short walk regularly every Sunday, in the direction of Saint-Ouen. The wife worked twelve hours a day at Madame Fauconnier's, and still found means to keep their lodging as clean and bright as a new coined sou, and to prepare the meals for all her little family, morning and evening. The husband never got drunk, brought his wages home every fortnight, and smoked a pipe at his window in the evening, to get a breath of fresh air before going to bed. They were frequently alluded to on account of their nice, pleasant ways; and, as between them they earned close upon nine francs a day, it was reckoned that they were able to put by a good deal of money.

But, during the earlier days especially, they had to work exceedingly hard to make both ends meet. Their marriage had burdened them with a debt of two hundred francs. Then, too, they abhorred the Hôtel Boncœur. They thought it a disgusting place, full of unpleasant recollections, and they dreamed of having a home of their own, with their own furniture which they could take care of. Twenty times they had reckoned up the sum of money that would be necessary. It amounted in round figures to three hundred and fifty francs, if they wished to have sufficient accommodation for putting their things away, as well as pots and pans handy whenever they required them. They were despairing of being able to save so large a sum in less than two years, when they met with a piece of good luck. An old gentleman of Plassans asked them to let him have Claude, the elder of the little ones, to send to the college there. It was the generous whim of an original, an amateur of paintings, who had been deeply struck by some figures the youngster had sketched in former days. Claude was already costing them

a great deal. When they only had the younger brother,
Etienne, to keep, they were able to put by the three hundred
and fifty francs in seven months and a half. The day when
they bought their furniture at a second-hand dealer's of the
Rue Belhomme, they went for a short walk along the exterior
Boulevards before returning home, their hearts filled with a
great joy. There were a bedstead, a chest of drawers with a
marble top, a wardrobe, a round table with an American cloth
cover, and six chairs, all in old mahogany—without counting
the bedding, the linen, and the kitchen utensils, which were
almost new. It was like a serious and definite entrance into
life with them—something which, in making them owners of
property, gave them a certain importance in the midst of the
well-to-do people of the neighbourhood.

For two months past they had been busy seeking some apartments. At first, they wanted above everything to hire these
in the big house of the Rue de la Goutte-d'Or. But there was
not a single room to let there; so that they had to relinquish
their old dream. To tell the truth, Gervaise was rather glad in
her heart: the neighbourhood of the Lorilleux, almost door to
door, frightened her immensely. Then, they looked about
elsewhere. Coupeau, very properly, did not wish to be far from
Madame Fauconnier's, so that Gervaise could easily run home
at any hour of the day. And at length they met with exactly
what suited them, a large room with a small closet and a kitchen, in the Rue Neuve de la Goutte-d'Or, almost opposite the
laundress's. It was a small house with only a single storey,
reached by a very steep staircase, at the top of which there were
only two lodgings, one to the right and the other to the left;
the ground floor was occupied by a job-master, who had his
stock-in-trade in some stables and coach-houses in a vast courtyard adjoining the street. The delighted young woman almost
fancied herself back again in the country; no neighbours, no
gossip to fear, a little quiet corner which reminded her of an
alley at Plassans, behind the ramparts; and, to crown her good
luck, by stretching her neck, she could see her window from her
ironing table without leaving her work.

They took possession of their new abode at the April quarter.
Gervaise was then eight months pregnant. But she showed
great courage, saying with a laugh that the child helped her
when she worked; she felt its little hands pushing within her
and giving her strength. Ah, well! she just laughed at Coupeau whenever he wanted her to lie down and rest herself! She

would take to her bed when the great pains came on. That would be quite soon enough; for now that there was going to be one more mouth to feed they must not be idle. And it was she who cleaned the place out before helping her husband to put the furniture in its proper places. She had quite a religious regard for the things, dusting them with maternal care, and her heart breaking at the sight of the least scratch. She stood still in a state of dismay, as though she had struck herself, whenever she knocked against them whilst sweeping. The chest of drawers was especially dear to her; she thought it beautiful and solid, and that it had a serious look about it. A dream, of which she dare not speak, was to have a clock to stand in the centre of the marble slab, where it would produce a magnificent effect. Had it not been for the baby that was coming, she would perhaps have risked buying the clock. However, she sighed and put off doing so till later on.

The couple were thoroughly enchanted with their new home. Etienne's bed occupied the small closet, where there was still room to put another child's crib. The kitchen was a very tiny affair and as dark as night, but, by leaving the door wide open, one could just manage to see; besides, Gervaise had not to cook meals for thirty people, all she wanted was room to make her soup. As for the large room, it was their pride. The first thing in the morning, they drew the curtains of the alcove, white calico curtains; and the room was thus transformed into a dining-room, with the table in the centre, and the wardrobe and the chest of drawers facing each other. As the grate burned as much as fifteen sous' worth of coal a day, they closed it up; and a little cast-iron stove, placed on the marble hearthstone, kept them warm during the coldest weather for seven sous. Then, Coupeau decorated the walls as best he could, projecting various embellishments; a tall engraving, representing a marshal of France caracoling with his baton in his hand between a cannon and a heap of cannon-balls, occupied the place of a looking-glass; some family photographs were hung in two rows over the chest of drawers, on either side of a little old gilded china holy-water fount, in which some matches were kept; on the top of the wardrobe, close to the wooden clock, to the ticking of which they seemed to be listening, a bust of Pascal paired with a bust of Béranger, the one looking grave, the other smiling. It was really a pretty room.

"Guess how much we pay here?" Gervaise would ask of every visitor she had.

And whenever they guessed too high a sum, she triumphed and delighted at being so well suited for such a little money, cried :

"One hundred and fifty francs, not a sou more! Isn't it almost like having it for nothing!"

The Rue Neuve de la Goutte-d'Or was itself a good part of the cause of their contentment. Gervaise lived in it, going incessantly backwards and forwards between her home and Madame Fauconnier's. Coupeau would now go down, of an evening, and smoke his pipe on the door-step. The street was a steep uneven one, and without any side pavements. At the top, near the Rue de la Goutte-d'Or, there were some dismal-looking shops with dirty windows, cobblers, coopers, a miserable grocer's, and the establishment of a wine-dealer who had become bankrupt, the shutters of which had been up for weeks and were becoming covered with placards. At the other end, towards Paris, houses of four storeys hid the view of the sky, the ground floors mostly occupied by laundresses, all of a heap, one close to another; one shop-front alone, that of a small barber, painted green and full of delicate-coloured little bottles, enlivened this gloomy corner with the sparkle of its sign—two brass dishes, always shining. But the liveliest part of the street was in the middle, where the buildings, not being so numerous nor so high, admitted the air and the sunshine. The job-master's stables, the manufactory next door where they made seltzer water, the wash-house opposite, gave a large quiet open space in which the smothered voices of the women washing and the regular puffing of the steam-engine seemed to still more increase the peacefulness. Low plots of ground, alleys bordered by black walls, gave the place the appearance of a village. And Coupeau, amused by the rare passers-by who stepped over the constantly flowing stream of soapy water, said that it reminded him of somewhere in the country where one of his uncles had taken him, when he was five years old. Gervaise's joy was a tree planted in a courtyard to the left of her window, an acacia with a single branch, the scanty green foliage of which sufficed for the charm of the entire street.

It was on the last day of April that the young woman was confined. The pains came on in the afternoon, towards four o'clock, as she was ironing a pair of curtains at Madame Fauconnier's. She would not go home at once, but remained there wriggling about on a chair, and continuing her ironing every time the pain allowed her to do so; the curtains were wanted quickly and she obstinately made a point of finishing them. Besides, perhaps after all it was only a colic; it would never do to be frightened by a bit of a stomach-ache. But as she was talking of starting on some shirts, she became quite pale. She was obliged to leave the workshop, and cross the street, doubled in two, holding on to the walls. One of the workwomen offered to accompany her; she declined, but begged her to go instead for the midwife, close by, in the Rue de la Charbonnière. The house was not on fire, there was no need to make a fuss. She would be like that no doubt all through the night. It was not going to prevent her getting Coupeau's dinner ready as soon as she was indoors; then, she might perhaps lie down on the bed a little, but without undressing herself. On the staircase, she was seized with such a violent pain, that she was obliged to sit down on one of the stairs; and she pressed her two fists against her mouth to prevent herself from crying out, for she would have been ashamed to have been found there by any man, had one come up. The pain passed away; she was able to open her door, feeling relieved, and thinking that she had decidedly been mistaken. That evening she was going to make a stew with some neck chops. All went well whilst she peeled the potatoes. The chops were cooking in a saucepan, when the labour pains returned. She mixed the gravy as she stamped about in front of the stove, almost blinded with her tears. If she was going to have a baby, that was no reason why Coupeau should be kept without his dinner. At length the stew began to simmer on a fire covered with cinders. She returned into the room, and thought she would have time to lay the cloth at one end of the table. But she was obliged to put down the bottle of wine very quickly; she no longer had strength to reach the bed; she fell prostrate, and her baby was born on the floor, on a mat. When the midwife arrived, a quarter of an hour later, it was there that she was delivered.

The zinc-worker was still employed at the hospital. Gervaise would not have him disturbed. When he came home at seven o'clock, he found her in bed, well-covered up, looking very pale on the pillow, and the child crying, swathed in a shawl at it's mother's feet.

"Ah, my poor wife!" said Coupeau kissing Gervaise. "And I was joking only an hour ago, whilst you were crying with pain! I say, you don't make much fuss about it—the time to sneeze and it's all over."

She smiled faintly; then she murmured: "It's a girl."

"Exactly!" resumed the zinc-worker, joking so as to enliven her, "I ordered a girl! Well, now I've got what I wanted! You do everything I wish!" And, taking the child up in his arms, he continued: "Let's have a look at you, Miss Malkin! You've got a very black little mug. It'll get whiter, never fear. You must be good, never run about the streets, and grow up sensible like your papa and mamma."

Gervaise looked at her daughter very seriously, with wide open eyes, slowly overshadowed with sadness. She shook her head; she would have preferred a boy, because boys always pull through somehow or other, and do not run so many risks in Paris. The midwife had to take the baby away from Coupeau. She also forbade Gervaise to speak; it was quite bad enough that so much noise was made round about her. Then the zinc-worker said that he must tell the news to mother Coupeau and the Lorilleux, but he was dying with hunger, he must first of all have his dinner. It was a great worry to the invalid to see him have to wait on himself, run to the kitchen for the stew, eat it out of a soup plate, and not be able to find the bread. In spite of being told not to do so, she bewailed her condition, and fidgeted about in her bed. It was stupid of her not to have managed to set the cloth, the colic had laid her on her back like a blow from a bludgeon. Her poor old man would not think it kind of her to be nursing herself up there whilst he was dining so badly. At least, were the potatoes cooked enough? She no longer remembered whether she had put salt to them.

"Keep quiet!" cried the midwife.

"Ah! it's no use your trying to prevent her worrying herself!" said Coupeau with his mouth full. "If you were not there, I'd bet she'd get up to cut my bread. Keep on your back, you big goose! You mustn't move about, otherwise it'll be a fortnight before you'll be able to stand on your legs. Your stew's very good. Madame will eat some with me. Won't you, madame?"

The midwife declined; but she was willing to accept a glass of wine, because it had upset her, said she, to find the wretched woman with the baby on the mat. Coupeau at length went off to tell the news to his relations. Half an hour later he returned with all of them, mother Coupeau, the Lorilleux, and Madame Lerat, whom he had met at the latter's. The Lorilleux, in the face of the couple's prosperity, had become very amiable, making the most flattering remarks about Gervaise, accompanied, however, by little restrictive gestures, nods of the head, and peculiar looks, as though to adjourn their real judgment. In short they knew what they knew; only they would not go against the opinion of the whole neighbourhood.

"I've brought you the whole gang!" cried Coupeau. "It can't be helped! they wanted to see you. Don't open your mouth, it's forbidden. They'll stop there, and look at you, without ceremony, you know. As for me, I'm going to make them some coffee, and some of the right sort!"

He disappeared into the kitchen. Mother Coupeau, after kissing Gervaise, became amazed at the child's size. The two other women also embraced the invalid on her cheeks. And all three, standing before the bed, commented with divers exclamations on the details of the confinement—a most remarkable confinement, just like having a tooth drawn, nothing more. Madame Lerat examined the little one all over, declared that she was well formed, and even added, mysteriously, that she would become a wonderful woman; and, as she considered that her head was too pointed, she began to press it gently, in spite of its cries, so as to make it rounder. Madame Lorilleux in a passion snatched the infant from her: it was sufficient to give a creature every vice imaginable, to mess it about like that, when its skull was so tender. Then, she tried to find who the baby resembled. They nearly all quarrelled over that. Lorilleux, who was stretching his neck in between the women, repeated that the little one was not a bit like Coupeau; perhaps the nose was slightly like his, but only very little! She was nearly the image of her mother, with somebody else's eyes though; those eyes certainly did not belong to their family.

Coupeau, however, had failed to reappear. One could hear him in the kitchen struggling with the grate and the coffee-pot. Gervaise was worrying herself frightfully; it was not the proper thing for a man to make coffee; and she called out and told him what to do, without listening to the midwife's energetic "hush!"

"Here we are!" said Coupeau, entering with the coffee-pot in his hand. "Didn't I just have a bother with it! It all went wrong on purpose! Now we'll drink out of glasses, won't we? because you know, the cups are still at the shop."

They seated themselves round the table, and the zinc-worker insisted on pouring out the coffee himself. It smelt very strong, it was none of that weak stuff. When the midwife had sipped her's up, she went off; everything was going on nicely, she was not required. If the young woman did not pass a good night, they were to send for her on the morrow. She was scarcely down the staircase, when Madame Lorilleux called her a glutton and a good-for-nothing. She put four lumps of sugar in her coffee, and charged fifteen francs for leaving you with your baby all by yourself. But Coupeau took her part; he would willingly fork out the fifteen francs. After all, those sort of women spent their youth in studying, they were right to charge a good price. Then Lorilleux had a dispute with Madame Lerat. He pretended that, to have a boy, you must turn the head of your bedstead towards the north; whilst she shrugged her shoulders, calling it a childish idea, and giving another recipe, which consisted in hiding under the mattress a bundle of green stinging nettles gathered when the sun was upon them, without letting your wife know of it. They had pushed the table close up to the bed, and until ten o'clock, Gervaise, overcome little by little with an immense fatigue, remained smiling and stupid, her head turned sideways on the pillow; she saw, she heard, but she no longer found strength to make a gesture nor to utter a word; she seemed to be dead, of a very gentle death, from the depths of which she felt happy at seeing the others alive. Now and again the little one uttered a faint cry, in the midst of the loud voices, of the interminable opinions on a murder committed the day before in the Rue du Bon-Puits, at the other end of La Chapelle.

Then, as the visitors were thinking of leaving, they spoke of the christening. The Lorilleux had promised to be godfather and godmother; they looked very glum over the matter. However, if they had not been asked to stand they would have felt rather peculiar. Coupeau did not see any need for christening the little one; it certainly would not procure her an income of ten thousand francs, and besides she might catch a cold from it. The less one had to do with priests the better. But mother Coupeau called him a heathen. The Lorilleux, without going and eating consecrated bread in church, plumed themselves on their religious sentiments.

"It shall be next Sunday, if you like," said the chain-maker.

And Gervaise having consented by a nod, every one kissed her and told her to take great care of herself. They also wished the baby good-bye. Each one went and leant over the little trembling body with smiles and loving words as though she were able to understand. They called her Nana, the pet name for Anna, which was her godmother's name.

"Good night, Nana. Come, be a good girl, Nana."

When they had at length gone off, Coupeau drew his chair close up to the bed and finished his pipe, holding Gervaise's hand in his. He smoked slowly, deeply affected, and uttering sentences between the puffs.

"Well, old woman, they've made your head ache, haven't they? You see, I couldn't prevent them coming. After all, it shows their friendship. But we're better alone, aren't we? I wanted to be alone, like this, with you. It has seemed such a long evening to me! Poor little thing, she's had a lot to go through! Those shrimps, when they come into the world, have no idea of the pain they cause. Where is the poor little body, that I may kiss it?"

He gently slid one of his big hands under her back, and drawing her towards him, he kissed the sheet, full of a coarse man's tenderness for that still suffering fecundity. He asked her if he hurt her, he would have wished to have cured her by simply breathing on her aching body. And Gervaise was very happy. She assured him that she was not suffering at all. She was only thinking of getting up as soon as possible, for now it would never do for her to lie there doing nothing. But he tried to reassure her. Wasn't he going to earn all that was necessary for the little one? He would be a contemptible fellow, if he ever left her to provide for the brat. It did not seem to him a wonderful thing to know how to get a child; the merit consisted in feeding it, was it not so?

Coupeau did not sleep much that night. He covered up the fire in the stove. Every hour he had to get up to give the baby spoonfuls of lukewarm sugar and water. That did not prevent his going off to his work in the morning as usual. He even took advantage of his lunch-hour to make a declaration of the birth at the mayor's. During this time Madame Boche, who had been informed of the event, had hastened to go and pass the day with Gervaise. But the latter, after ten hours of sound sleep, bewailed her position, saying that she already felt pains all over her through having been so long in bed. She would become quite ill if they did not let her get up. In the evening, when Coupeau returned home, she told him all her worries : no doubt she had confidence in Madame Boche, only it put her beside herself to see a stranger installed in her room, opening the drawers, and touching her things.

On the morrow the doorkeeper, on returning from some errand, found her up, dressed, sweeping and getting her husband's dinner ready ; and it was impossible to persuade her to go to bed again. They were trying to make a fool of her, perhaps! It was all very well for ladies to pretend to be unable to move. When one was not rich, one had no time for that sort of thing. Three days after her confinement she was ironing petticoats at Madame Fauconnier's, banging her irons, and all in a perspiration from the great heat of the stove.

On the Saturday evening, Madame Lorilleux brought her presents for her godchild—a cap that cost thirty-five sous, and a christening dress, plaited and trimmed with some cheap lace, which she had got for six francs, because it was slightly soiled. On the morrow, Lorilleux, as godfather, gave the mother six pounds of sugar. They did things in a genteel way. Even in the evening, at the feast which was given by the Coupeaus, they did not arrive empty handed. The husband brought a sealed bottle of wine under each arm, whilst the wife carried a big custard bought at a renowned pastry-cook's in the Chaussée Clignancourt. Only, the Lorilleux went and related their grand doings all over the neighbourhood; they had spent close upon twenty francs. Gervaise, on hearing of their gossiping, was greatly incensed, and no longer thought anything of their handsome proceedings.

It was at this christening feast that the Coupeaus ended by becoming intimately acquainted with their neighbours on the opposite side of the landing. The other lodging in the little house was occupied by two persons, mother and son, the Goujets as they were called. Until then, the two families had merely nodded to each other on the stairs and in the street, nothing more; the Coupeaus thought their neighbours seemed rather bearish. Then the mother having carried up a pail of water for Gervaise on the morrow of her confinement, the latter had thought it the proper thing to invite them to the feast, more especially as she considered them very respectable people. And, naturally, they there became well acquainted with each other.

The Goujets came from the Département du Nord. The mother mended lace; the son, a blacksmith, worked at an iron bolt factory. They had lived in their lodging for five years. Behind the quiet peacefulness of their life, a long standing sorrow was hidden. Goujet, the father, one day when furiously drunk at Lille, had beaten a comrade to death with an iron bar, and had afterwards strangled himself in prison with his handkerchief. The widow and child, who had come to Paris after their misfortune, always felt this tragedy hanging over their heads, and atoned for it by a strict honesty, and an unvarying gentleness and courage. There was even a certain pride mingled with their case, for they ended by finding themselves better than others. Madame Goujet, always dressed in black, with her forehead framed in a monachal cap, had the white and calm face of a matron, as though the paleness of the lace, the minuteness of the work performed by her fingers, imparted a reflection of serenity to her. Goujet was a superb-looking giant of twenty-three, with a rosy face, blue eyes, and of herculean strength. His comrades at the factory nicknamed him Golden Mug, on account of his handsome yellow beard.

Gervaise at once felt a great friendship for these people. When she entered their home the first time, she was amazed at the cleanliness of the lodging. There was no denying it, one might blow all about the place without raising a grain of dust; and the tiled floor shone like a mirror. Madame Goujet made her enter her son's room, just to see it. It was pretty and white like the room of a young girl; an iron bedstead with muslin curtains, a table, a washstand, and a narrow bookcase hanging against the wall. Then there were pictures all over the place, figures cut out, coloured engravings nailed up with four tacks, and portraits of all kinds of persons taken from the illustrated papers. Madame Goujet said with a smile that her son was a big baby. In the evenings reading tired him, so he amused himself with looking at his pictures. Gervaise spent an hour with her neighbour, who had returned to her tambour frame, in front of a window. She felt interested in the hundreds of pins which fixed the lace down, happy at being there, breathing the pleasant odour of cleanliness which pervaded the lodging, in which that delicate work induced a thoughtful silence.

The Goujets were worth visiting. They worked long hours, and placed more than a quarter of their fortnight's earnings in the savings-bank. In the neighbourhood every one nodded to them, every one talked of their savings. Goujet never had a hole in his clothes, always went out in a clean short blue blouse, without a stain. He was very polite, and even a trifle timid, in spite of his broad shoulders. The washerwomen at the end of the street laughed to see him hold down his head when he passed them. He did not like their oaths, and thought it disgusting that women should be constantly uttering foul words. One day, however, he came home tipsy. Then Madame Goujet, for sole reproach, held his father's portrait before him, a daub of a painting piously hidden away at the bottom of a drawer; and, ever since that lesson, Goujet never drank more than was good for him, without, however, any hatred of wine, for wine is necessary to the workman. On Sundays he walked out with his mother, who took hold of his arm. He would generally conduct her to Vincennes; at other times they would go to the theatre. His mother remained his passion. He still spoke to her as though he were a little child. Square-headed, his skin toughened by the wielding of the heavy hammer, he somewhat resembled the larger animals: dull of intellect, though good-natured all the same.

In the early days of their acquaintance, Gervaise embarrassed him immensely. Then in a few weeks he became accustomed to her. He watched for her that he might carry up her parcels, treated her as a sister, with an abrupt familiarity, and cut out pictures for her. One morning, however, having opened her door without knocking, he beheld her half undressed, washing her neck; and, for a week, he did not dare to look her in the face, so much so that he ended by making her blush herself.

Young Cassis, with his Parisian cheek, thought Golden Mug a bit of a muff. It was well not to booze, and not to shove your nose into the face of every girl in the street; but all the same, a man should be a man, otherwise he might as well wear petti-coats at once. He would chaff him before Gervaise, accusing him of making eyes at all the women of the neighbourhood; and that drum-major of a Goujet would energetically deny it. This did not prevent the two workmen from being great friends. They called each other in the morning, started off together, and sometimes one of them stood a glass of beer on their way home. Ever since the christening feast they addressed one another quite familiarly. Their friendship had reached this point, when Golden Mug rendered Young Cassis a great service—one of those signal services which a man remembers all his life. It was on the 2nd of December, 1852. The zinc-worker, just for a lark, had had the brilliant idea to go and see the riots. He did not care a hang for the Republic, or Bonaparte, or the rest of them; only, he loved the smell of powder, the firing amused him, and he was on the point of being caught behind a barricade, if the blacksmith had not happened to be there just in time to protect him with his big body, and help him to get away. Goujet, as they ascended the Rue du Faubourg-Poissonnière, walked quickly, with a grave look on his face. He went in for politics, and was a republican, wisely, in the name of justice and of the happiness of all. However, he had not shouldered a musket. And he gave his reasons: the people were tired of drawing the chestnuts out of the fire for the upper classes, and of burning their fingers. February and June were precious lessons, so in future the Faubourgs would leave the city to do what it thought best. Then, when they had reached the high ground, the Rue des Poissonniers, he turned his head, and looked down upon Paris. All the same, they were doing some sorry work there ; one day the people might regret having stood by with their arms folded. But Coupeau jeered, and said they were really too stupid, the asses who were risking their skins just to preserve to the idle beggars of the Chamber their twenty-five francs a day. That evening the Coupeaus invited the Goujets to dinner. During dessert, Young Cassis and Golden Mug kissed each other twice on the cheek. Now their friendship was for life and death.

During three years the existence of the two families went on, on either side of the landing, without an event. Gervaise had managed to bring up the little one without the loss of more than two days' work a week. She was becoming a capital clear starcher, earning as much as three francs a day. Therefore she had decided to send Etienne, who was close upon eight years old, to a little school in the Rue de Chartres, where she paid five francs. The couple, in spite of the expense of bringing up the two children, put twenty or thirty francs every month into the savings-bank. When their savings amounted to the sum of six hundred francs, the young woman, beset with a dream of ambition, was scarcely able to sleep. She wanted to set up in business for herself, to take a small shop, and to have workwomen in her turn. She had calculated everything. In twenty years time, if all went well, they would have a little income, on which they would go and live somewhere in the country. However, she did not dare to run the risk. She pretended to be looking for a shop, so as to give herself time for reflection. The money was in no danger at the savings-bank; on the contrary, it was increasing. In three years she had satisfied only one of her desires—she had bought herself an ornamental clock; and that clock, a clock in a violet ebony case, with twisted columns and a gilded brass pendulum, was to be paid for in a year, by instalments of twenty sous every Monday. She got quite angry, whenever Coupeau talked of winding it up. She alone took off the glass cover, and dusted the columns religiously, as though the marble top of her chest of drawers had become

transformed into a chapel. Under the glass cover, behind the
clock, she hid the savings-bank book ; and often, when she was
dreaming of her shop, she would forget herself, in front of the
dial plate, her eyes fixed on the turning hands, as though she
were awaiting some solemn and particular minute to come to a
decision.

The Coupeaus went out nearly every Sunday with the
Goujets. They were pleasant little excursions, sometimes to
have some fried fish at Saint-Ouen, at others a rabbit at Vincennes, in the garden of some eating-house keeper, without any
grand display. The men drank sufficient to quench their
thirst, and returned home as right as ninepins, giving their
arms to the ladies. In the evening, before going to bed, the
two families made up the accounts, and each paid half the expenses; and there was never the least quarrel about a sou more
or less. The Lorilleux were jealous of the Goujets. They
thought it very funny, all the same, that Young Cassis and the
Hobbler should be for ever going with strangers, when they had
their own relations. Ah, well! they did not seem to care a tinker's
curse for their relations! Ever since they had had a few sous
put by, they gave themselves no end of airs. Madame Lorilleux,
greatly annoyed at seeing her brother avoid her, recommenced
her abuse of Gervaise. Madame Lerat, on the contrary,
took the young woman's part, defended her by telling some
most extraordinary stories—attempts at seduction at night-
time on the Boulevard, from which she made her escape like
the heroine of a drama, slapping the faces of the cowardly
aggressors. As for mother Coupeau, she tried to make them
all friends, that she might be well received by all her children.
Her sight was failing her more and more, she had only one
place left to do the cleaning of, and she was glad to get an
occasional five francs from one or the other.

The very day on which Nana was three years old, Coupeau,
on returning home in the evening, found Gervaise quite upset.
She refused to talk about it ; there was nothing at all the matter
with her, she said. But, as she laid the table all wrong, standing still with the plates in her hands to become absorbed in
deep reflection, her husband insisted upon knowing what was
the matter.

"Well ! this is it," she ended by owning, " the little draper's
shop, in the Rue de la Goutte-d'Or, is to let. I saw it only an
hour ago, when going to buy some cotton. It gave me quite a
turn."

It was a very decent shop, and in that big house where they dreamed of living in former days. There was the shop, a back room, and two other rooms to the right and left ; in short, just what they required. The rooms were rather small, but well placed. Only, she considered they wanted too much ; the land-lord talked of five hundred francs.

"So you've been over the place, and asked the price ?" said Coupeau.

"Oh ! you know, only out of curiosity !" replied she, affect-ing an air of indifference. "One looks about, and goes in wher-ever there's a bill up—that doesn't bind one to anything. But that shop is altogether too dear. Besides, it would perhaps be foolish of me to set up in business."

However, after dinner, she again referred to the draper's shop. She drew a plan of the place on the margin of a newspaper. And, little by little, she talked it over, measuring the corners, arranging the rooms, as though she were going to move all her furniture in there on the morrow. Then Coupeau advised her to take it, seeing how much she wanted to do so ; she would certainly never find anything decent under five hundred francs ; besides, they might perhaps get a reduction. The only objec-tion to it was living in the same house as the Lorilleux, whom she could not bear. But, she protested, she disliked nobody ; in the warmth of her desire she even stood up for the Lorilleux ; they were not spiteful at heart—they would get on very well together. And, when they had gone to bed, Coupeau fell asleep whilst she was still continuing to plan the arrangement of the rooms, without, however, having finally decided to take the place.

On the morrow, when she was alone, she could not resist removing the glass cover from off the clock, and having a peep at the savings-bank book. To think that her shop was there, in those dirty leaves, covered with ugly writing ! Before going off to her work, she consulted Madame Goujet, who highly approved her project of setting up in business for herself ; with a husband like hers, a good fellow who did not drink, she was certain of getting on, and of not having her earnings squan-dered. At the luncheon hour, Gervaise even called on the Loril-leux to ask their advice ; she did not wish to appear to be doing anything unknown to the family. Madame Lorilleux was struck all of a heap. What ! the Hobbler was going in for a shop now ! And, her heart bursting with envy, she stammered, and tried to pretend to be pleased : no doubt the shop was a convenient one—Gervaise was right in taking it. However, when she had somewhat recovered, she and her husband talked of the dampness of the courtyard, of the poor light of the rooms on the ground floor. Oh! it was a good place for rheumatism. Yet, if she had made up her mind to take it, their observations, of course, would not make her alter her decision.

That evening, Gervaise frankly owned, with a laugh, that she would have fallen ill if she had been prevented from having the shop. Nevertheless, before saying " it's done !" she wished to take Coupeau to see the place, and try and obtain a reduction in the rent.

" Very well, then, to-morrow, if you like," said her husband. " You can come and fetch me towards six o'clock at the house where I'm working, in the Rue de la Nation, and we'll call in at the Rue de la Goutte-d'Or on our way home."

Coupeau was then finishing the roofing of a new three-storied house. It so happened that on that day he was to fix the last sheets of zinc. As the roof was almost flat, he had set up his bench on it, a wide shutter supported on two trestles. A beautiful May sun was setting, giving a golden hue to the chimney-pots. And, right up at the top, against the clear sky, the workman was quietly cutting up his zinc with a big pair of shears, leaning over the bench, and looking like a tailor in his shop cutting out a pair of trousers. Close to the wall of the next house, his boy, a youngster of seventeen, thin and fair, was keeping the fire of the chafing dish blazing by the aid of an enormous pair of bellows, each puff of which raised a cloud of sparks.

" Hi ! Zidore, put in the irons !" cried Coupeau.

The boy stuck the soldering irons into the midst of the charcoal, which looked a pale rose colour in the daylight. Then he resumed blowing. Coupeau held the last sheet of zinc. It had to be placed at the edge of the roof, close to the gutter-pipe ; there was an abrupt slant there, and the gaping hollow of the street opened beneath. The zinc-worker, just as though in his own home, wearing list-shoes, advanced, dragging his feet, and whistling the air, " Oh! the little lambs." Arrived in front of the hole, he let himself glide, and then, supporting himself with one knee against the masonry of a chimney-stack, remained halfway from the edge of the roof. One of his legs dangled. When he leant back to call that young viper, Zidore, he held on to a corner of the masonry, on account of the street beneath him.

"You confounded dawdler! Give me the irons! It's no use looking up in the air, you skinny beggar! the larks won't tumble into your mouth already cooked!"

But Zidore did not hurry himself. He was interested in the neighbouring roofs, and in a cloud of smoke which rose from the other side of Paris, close to Grenelle; it was very likely a fire. However, he came and laid down on his stomach, his head over the hole, and he passed the irons to Coupeau. Then the latter commenced to solder the sheet. He squatted, he stretched, always managing to balance himself, sometimes seated on one side, at others standing on the tip of one foot, often only holding on by a finger. He had a confounded assurance, the devil's own cheek, familiar with danger, and braving it. It knew him. It was the street that was afraid, not he. As he kept his pipe in his mouth, he turned round every now and then to spit on to the pavement.

"Hallo! Madame Boche!" cried he, suddenly. "Hi! Madame Boche!"

He had just caught sight of the doorkeeper crossing the road. She raised her head and recognised him, and a conversation ensued between them. She hid her hands under her apron, her nose elevated in the air. He, standing up now, his left arm passed round a chimney-pot, leant over.

"Have you seen my wife?" asked he.

"No, I haven't," replied the doorkeeper. "Is she this way?"

"She's coming to fetch me. And are they all well at home?"

"Why, yes, thanks; I'm the most ill, as you see. I'm going to the Chaussée Clignancourt to buy a small leg of mutton. The butcher near the Moulin-Rouge only charges sixteen sous."

They raised their voices, because a vehicle was passing. In the wide, deserted Rue de la Nation, their words, shouted out with all their might, had only caused a little old woman to come to her window; and this little old woman remained there leaning out, giving herself the treat of a grand emotion by watching that man on the roof over the way, as though she expected to see him fall, from one minute to another.

"Well! good evening," cried Madame Boche. "I won't disturb you."

Coupeau turned round, and took back the iron that Zidore was holding for him. But just as the doorkeeper was moving

off, she caught sight of Gervaise on the other side of the way,
holding Nana by the hand.   She was already raising her head
to tell the zinc-worker, when the young woman closed her mouth
by an energetic gesture, and, in a low voice, so as not to be
heard up there, she told her of her fear : she was afraid, by showing herself suddenly, of giving her husband a shock which might
make him lose his balance.   During four years, she had only
been once to fetch him at his work.   That day was the second
time.   She could not witness it, her blood turned cold when
she beheld her old man between heaven and earth, in places
where even the sparrows would not venture.

" No doubt, it's not pleasant," murmured Madame Boche.
" My husband's a tailor, so I have none of these terrors."

" If you only knew, in the early days," said Gervaise again,
" I had frights from morning to night.   I was always seeing
him on a stretcher, with his head smashed.   Now, I don't think
of it so much.   One gets used to everything.   Bread must be
earned.   All the same, it's a precious dear loaf, for one risks
one's bones more than's fair."

And she left off speaking, hiding Nana in her skirt, fearing a
cry from the little one.   Very pale, she looked up in spite of
herself.   At that moment Coupeau was soldering the extreme
edge of the sheet close to the gutter ; he slid down as far as possible, but without being able to reach the edge.   Then, full
of freedom and heaviness, he risked himself with those slow
movements peculiar to workmen.   For an instant he was immediately over the pavement, no longer holding on, all
absorbed in his work ; and, from below, one could see the little
white flame of the solder frizzling up beneath the carefully
wielded iron.   Gervaise, speechless, her throat contracted with
anguish, had clasped her hands together, and held them up in
a mechanical gesture of prayer.   But she breathed freely as
Coupeau got up and returned back along the roof, without
hurrying himself, and taking the time to spit once more into
the street.

" Ah ! ah ! so you've been playing the spy on me ! " cried he,
gaily, on beholding her.   " She's been making a stupid of herself, oh, Madame Boche? she wouldn't call to me.   Wait a bit,
I shall have finished in ten minutes."

All that remained to do was to fix the top of a chimney—a
mere nothing.   The laundress and the doorkeeper waited on
the pavement, discussing the neighbourhood, and giving an eye
to Nana, to prevent her from dabbling in the gutter, where she

wanted to look for little fishes; and the two women kept glancing up at the roof, smiling and nodding their heads, as though to imply that they were not losing patience. The old woman opposite had not quitted her window, but continued watching the man, and waiting.

"Whatever can she have to look at, that old she-goat?" said Madame Boche. "What a mug she has!"

One could hear the loud voice of the zinc-worker up above singing, "Ah! it's nice to gather strawberries!" Bending over his bench, he was now artistically cutting out his zinc. With his compasses he traced a line, and he detached a large fan-shaped piece with the aid of a pair of curved shears; then he lightly bent this fan with his hammer into the form of a pointed mushroom. Zidore was again blowing the charcoal in the chafing-dish. The sun was setting behind the house in a brilliant rosy light, which was gradually becoming paler, and turning to a delicate lilac. And, at this quiet hour of the day, right up against the sky, the silhouettes of the two workmen, looking inordinately large, with the dark line of the bench, and the strange profile of the bellows, stood out from the limpid background of the atmosphere.

When the capital was got into shape, Coupeau called out: "Zidore! the irons!"

But Zidore had disappeared. The zinc-worker swore, and looked about for him, even calling him through the open skylight of the loft. At length he discovered him on a neighbouring roof, two houses off. The young rogue was taking a walk, exploring the environs, his fair scanty locks blowing in the breeze, his eyes blinking as they beheld the immensity of Paris.

"I say, lazy bones! Do you think you're having a day in the country?" asked Coupeau, in a rage. "You're like Monsieur Béranger, composing verses, perhaps! Will you give me those irons! Did any one ever see such a thing! strolling about on the house-tops! You'd better bring your sweetheart at once, and tell her of your love. Will you give me those irons? you confounded little shirker!"

He finished his soldering, and called to Gervaise: "There, it's done. I'm coming down."

The chimney-pot to which he had to fix the capital was in the middle of the roof. Gervaise, who was no longer uneasy, continued to smile as she followed his movements. Nana, amused all on a sudden by the view of her father, clapped her little hands.   She had seated herself on the pavement to see the better up there.

"Papa! papa!" called she with all her might.   "Papa! just look!"

The zinc-worker wished to lean forward, but his foot slipped. Then suddenly, stupidly, like a cat with its legs entangled, he rolled and descended the slight slope of the roof without being able to save himself.

"Damnation!" said he in a stifled voice.

And he fell.   His body described a gentle curve, turned twice over on itself, and came smashing into the middle of the street with the dull thud of a bundle of clothes thrown from on high.

Gervaise, feeling stupid, her throat rent by one great cry, stood holding up her arms.   Some passers-by hastened to the spot; a crowd soon formed.   Madame Boche, utterly upset, her knees bending under her, took Nana in her arms, to hide her head and prevent her seeing.   Meanwhile, the little old woman opposite quietly closed her window, as though satisfied.

Four men ended by carrying Coupeau into a chemist's, at the corner of the Rue des Poissonniers; and he remained there on a blanket, in the middle of the shop, whilst they sent to the Lariboisière hospital for a stretcher.   He still breathed, but the chemist kept slightly shaking his head.   Now, Gervaise, kneeling on the ground, sobbed continuously, her face bathed in tears, blinded and stupefied.   With a mechanical movement she thrust out her hands and felt her husband's limbs very gently.   Then she drew them back, looking at the chemist, who forbade her to touch him; and a few seconds later she did it again, unable to resist the desire to feel if he were still warm, and thinking she did him good.   When the stretcher at length arrived, and they talked of starting for the hospital, she got up, saying violently:

"No, no, not to the hospital!   We live in the Rue Neuve de la Goutte-d'Or."

It was useless for them to explain to her that the illness would cost her a great deal of money, if she took her husband home.   She obstinately repeated:

"Rue Neuve de la Goutte-d'Or; I will show you the house. What can it matter to you? I've got money.   He's my husband, isn't he?   He's mine, and I will have him."

And they had to take Coupeau to his own home. When the stretcher was carried through the crowd which was crushing up

COUPEAU FALLING FROM THE ROOF OF THE HOUSE IN THE RUE DE LA
NATION.   p. 114

against the chemist's shop, the women of the neighbourhood were excitedly talking of Gervaise. She limped, the jade, but all the same she had some pluck. She would be sure to save her old man; whilst at the hospital the doctors let the patients die who were very bad, so as not to have the bother of curing them. Madame Boche, after taking Nana home with her, returned and gave her account of the accident, with interminable details, and still feeling agitated with the emotion she had passed through.

"I was going to buy a leg of mutton; I was there, I saw him fall," repeated she. "It was all through the little one; he turned to look at her, and bang! Ah! good heavens! I never want to see such a sight again. However, I must be off to get my leg of mutton."

For a week Coupeau was very bad. The family, the neighbours, every one, expected to see him kick the bucket at any moment. The doctor—a very expensive doctor, who charged five francs for each visit—apprehended internal injuries, and these words filled every one with fear. It was said in the neighbourhood that the zinc-worker's heart had been injured by the shock. Gervaise alone, looking pale through her nights of watching, serious and resolute, shrugged her shoulders. Her old man's right leg was broken, every one knew that; it would be set for him, and that was all. As for the rest, the injured heart, that was nothing. She would mend his heart for him. She knew the way to mend hearts—with care, cleanliness, and solid friendship. And she showed a superb conviction, certain of curing him, merely by remaining with him and touching him with her hands in the hours of fever. She did not doubt for a minute. For a whole week she remained up, speaking but little, wrapped up in her obstinacy of saving him, forgetting her children, the street, the entire city. The ninth day—the day on which the doctor at last answered for his patient's recovery —she fell on to a chair, her legs unable longer to support her, her back almost broken, her face bathed in tears. That night she consented to sleep two hours, her head leaning on the foot of the bed.

Coupeau's accident had created quite a commotion in the family. Mother Coupeau passed the nights with Gervaise; but as early as nine o'clock she fell asleep on a chair. Every evening, on returning from work, Madame Lerat went a long round out of her way to inquire how her brother was getting on. At first the Lorilleux had called two or three times a day,

offering to sit up and watch, and even bringing an easy-chair
for Gervaise. Then it was not long before there were disputes
as to the proper way to nurse invalids. Madame Lorilleux
stated that she had saved the lives of enough persons in her
life-time to know how to set about it. She accused the young
woman of behaving roughly to her, of keeping her away from
her brother's bedside. The Hobbler was certainly right in wishing to save Coupeau in spite of everything; for there was no
doubt that if she had not gone and disturbed him in the Rue de
la Nation, he would never have fallen. Only, by the way she
went to work, she was certain to finish him off.

When Gervaise saw that Coupeau was out of danger, she
ceased guarding his bedside with so much jealous fierceness.
Now, they could no longer kill him, and she let people approach
without mistrust. The family invaded the room. The convalescence would be a very long one; the doctor had talked of
four months. Then, during the long hours the zinc-worker
slept, the Lorilleux talked of Gervaise as of a fool. She had
done a smart thing in having her husband at home. At the
hospital they would have cured him twice as quickly. Lorilleux
would have liked to have been ill, to have caught no matter
what, just to show her that he did not hesitate for a moment to
go to Lariboisière. Madame Lorilleux knew a lady who had
just come from there. Well! she had had chicken to eat
morning and night. And the two of them, for the twentieth
time, made the calculation of what the four months' convalescence would cost the little home. First of all, the lost
days of work, then the doctor, the medicine, and later on the
good wine, the juicy underdone meat. If the Coupeaus only
devoured their few sous of savings, they might think themselves
precious lucky; but in all likelihood they would fall into debt.
Oh! that was their business. Anyhow, they must not count on
the family, which was not rich enough to keep an invalid at
home. It was so much the worse for the Hobbler, was it not?
She should do as others did—let her husband go to the hospital.
That would teach her not to be so proud.

One night Madame Lorilleux had the spitefulness to ask her
suddenly:

"Well! and your shop, when are you going to take it?"

"Yes," chuckled Lorilleux, "the landlord's still waiting for
you."

Gervaise stood bursting with anger. She had completely
forgotten the shop; but she saw the wicked joy of those

people, at the thought that she would no longer be able to take
it. From that evening, in fact, they watched for every opportunity to twit her about her hopeless dream. When any one
spoke of some impossible wish, they would say it might be
realised on the day that Gervaise started in business, in a
beautiful shop opening on to the street. And behind her back
they would laugh fit to split their sides. She did not like to
think such an unkind thing; but, really, the Lorilleux now
seemed to be very pleased at Coupeau's accident, as it prevented
her setting up as a laundress in the Rue de la Goutte-d'Or.

Then she also wished to laugh and show them how willingly
she parted with the money for the sake of curing her husband.
Each time that she took the savings-bank book from beneath
the glass clock-cover in their presence, she would say gaily:
"I'm going out; I'm going to take my shop."

She had not been willing to withdraw the money all at once.
She took it out a hundred francs at a time, so as not to keep
such a pile of gold and silver in her drawer; then, too, she
vaguely hoped for some miracle, some sudden recovery, which
would enable them not to part with the entire sum. At each
journey to the savings-bank, on her return home, she added up
on a piece of paper the money they had still left there. It was
merely for the sake of order. In spite of the pile diminishing
more and more, she still kept, in her sensible way and with her
quiet smile, the account of the downfall of their savings. Was
it not already a consolation that the money was being put to
such a good use, to have had it handy at the time of their misfortune? And without a regret she carefully replaced the book
behind the clock, under the glass cover.

The Goujets were very kind to Gervaise during Coupeau's
illness. Madame Goujet was entirely at her disposal. She
never went out without asking her if she wanted any sugar, or
butter, or salt fetched; she always offered her the first plateful
on the evenings when she made any fresh soup; and she even,
when she saw her very busy, looked after her cooking or helped
her to wash-up. Every morning Goujet took the young woman's
pails and filled them at the fountain in the Rue des Poissonniers;
it was a saving of two sous. Then after dinner, when the relations did not invade the room, the Goujets would come and keep
the Coupeaus company. For two hours, up to ten o'clock, the
blacksmith smoked his pipe as he watched Gervaise hovering
round the invalid. He did not utter ten words the whole
evening. With his big fair face set between his giant shoulders,

he was moved at seeing her pour the diet-drink into a cup and
stir up the sugar without making any noise with the spoon.
When she tucked in the bed-clothes, and encouraged Coupeau
with her gentle voice, he felt deeply affected. Never before had
he seen such a plucky little woman. It was no dishonour that
she limped ; it was all the more merit to her that she tired herself out all day waiting on her husband. One could not deny
that she did not even sit down for a quarter of an hour to eat
her meals. She was constantly running to the chemist, poking
her nose into very unpleasant things, working tremendously
hard to keep that room, in which everything was done, neat and
clean ; with all that, she never complained, was always amiable,
even on nights when, from excessive fatigue, she was falling
asleep where she stood, with her eyes open. And the blacksmith, in that atmosphere of devotion, in the midst of those
drugs lying about on the furniture, was seized with a great
affection for Gervaise, as he beheld her loving and nursing
Coupeau with all her heart.

"Well ! old man, you're mended at last," said he one day to
the zinc-worker. "I never thought it would be otherwise ; your
wife is an angel !"

He was going to marry. At least, his mother had found a
very suitable young girl, a lace-mender like herself, whom she
longed to see him take to wife. So as not to grieve her, he had
said "yes," and the wedding had even been settled to take
place early in September. The money to begin the house-
keeping upon had been lying for a long time in the savings-
bank. But he shook his head whenever Gervaise spoke to him
of the marriage, and he murmured in his slow voice :

"All women are not like you, Madame Coupeau. If they
were, one would want to marry ten of them."

At the end of two months, however, Coupeau was able to get
up. He did not go far, only from the bed to the window, and
even then Gervaise had to support him. There he would sit
down in the easy-chair the Lorilleux had brought, with his right
leg stretched out on a stool. This joker, who used to laugh at
the people who slipped down on frosty days, felt greatly put out
by his accident. He had no philosophy. He had spent those
two months in bed, in cursing, and in worrying the people about
him. It was not an existence, really, to pass one's life on one's
back, with a pin all tied up and as stiff as a sausage. Ah ! he
certainly knew the ceiling by heart ; there was a crack, at the
corner of the alcove, that he could have drawn with his eyes

shut. Then when he was made comfortable in the arm-chair, it was another grievance. Would he be fixed there for long, just like a mummy? The street was not so very amusing; no one ever passed there, and it smelt of dirty water and chemicals all day long. No, really, he was growing old there; he would have given ten years of his life just to have had a look at the fortifications. And he was constantly uttering violent accusations against fate. His accident was not just; it ought never to have happened to him—a good workman, not an idle fellow or a drunkard. Had it happened to many others he knew, he could have understood it.

"Papa Coupeau," said he, "broke his neck one day that he'd been boozing. I can't say that it was deserved, but anyhow it was explainable. I had had nothing since my lunch, was perfectly quiet, and without a drop of liquor in my body; and yet I come to grief just because I wanted to turn round to smile at Nana! Don't you think that's too much? If there is a providence, it certainly arranges things in a very peculiar manner. I for one shall never believe in it."

And when at last he was able to use his legs, he retained a secret grudge against work. It was a handicraft full of misfortunes to pass one's days, like the cats, on the roofs of the houses. The employers were no fools! they sent you to your death—being far too cowardly to venture themselves on a ladder—and stopped at home in safety at their fire-sides without caring a hang for the poorer classes; and he got to the point of saying that every one ought to fix the zinc himself on his own house. Well, really! in the name of justice it should be so; if you don't want the water to come in, cover the roof yourself. Then he regretted that he had not learned some other handicraft, something pleasanter and less dangerous; for instance, that of a cabinetmaker. It was all old Coupeau's fault; fathers always had that stupid habit of making their children follow the same trade as themselves.

For another two months Coupeau walked about on crutches. He had first of all managed to get as far as the street, and smoke his pipe in front of the door. Then he had managed to reach the exterior Boulevard, dragging himself along in the sunshine, and remaining for hours on one of the seats. Gaiety returned to him; his infernal tongue got sharper in these long hours of idleness. And with the pleasure of living, he gained there a delight in doing nothing, an indolent feeling took possession of his limbs, and his muscles gradually glided into a very sweet

slumber. It was the slow victory of laziness, which took advantage of his convalesence to obtain possession of his body and un-
nerve him with its tickling. He regained his health, as thorough
a banterer as before, thinking life beautiful, and not seeing why
it should not last for ever. When he was able to lay aside his
crutches, he took longer walks, visited the workshops to see his
comrades again. He would stand with his arms folded in front
of the houses that were being built, chuckling and wagging his
head, and chaffing the workmen who were busying about. He
would hold out his leg to show them the result of exerting oneself. This ridiculing of the labour of others was a sort of satisfaction to his grudge against work. No doubt, he would have
to resume it again, he would be obliged to ; but he would put
off doing so as long as possible. Oh, he had good reason for not
being enthusiastic about it. Besides, it seemed so pleasant to
be able to do nothing for a while !

On the afternoons when Coupeau felt dull, he would call on the
Lorilleux. The latter would pity him immensely, and attract
him with all sorts of amiable attentions. During the first
years following his marriage, he had avoided them, thanks to
Gervaise's influence. Now they regained their sway over him
by twitting him about being afraid of his wife. He was no
man, that was evident ! The Lorilleux, however, showed great
discretion, and were loud in their praise of the laundress's
good qualities. Coupeau, without as yet coming to wrangling,
swore to the latter that his sister adored her, and requested that
she would behave more amiably to her. The first quarrel which
the couple had occurred one evening on account of Etienne. The
zinc-worker had passed the afternoon with the Lorilleux. On
arriving home, as the dinner was not quite ready, and the
children were whining for their soup, he suddenly turned upon
Etienne, and boxed his ears soundly. And during an hour he
did not cease to grumble : the brat was not his ; he did not
know why he allowed him to be in the place ; he would end by
turning him out into the street. Up till then he had tolerated
the youngster without all that fuss. On the morrow he talked
of his dignity. Three days after, he kept kicking the little
fellow behind, morning and evening, so much so, that the child,
whenever he heard him coming, bolted into the Goujets', where
the old lace-mender kept a corner of the table clear for him to
do his lessons.

Gervaise had, for some time past, returned to work. She no
longer had the trouble of looking under the glass cover of the

clock; all the savings were gone; and she had to work hard, work for four, for there were four to feed now. She alone maintained them. Whenever she heard people pitying her, she at once found excuses for Coupeau. Recollect! he had suffered so much; it was not surprising if his disposition had soured! But it would pass off when his health returned. And if any one hinted that Coupeau seemed all right again, that he could very well return to work, she protested: No, no; not yet! She did not want to see him take to his bed again. They would allow her to know best what the doctor said, perhaps! It was she who prevented him returning to work, telling him every morning to take his time and not to force himself. She even slipped twenty sou pieces into his waistcoat pocket. Coupeau accepted this as something perfectly natural. He complained of all sorts of ailments, in order to be pampered up; at the end of six months he was not yet out of his convalescence. On the days when he went to look at the others working, he was always willing to go and have a glass of wine with his pals. One was, all the same, pretty comfortable at the wine-shop; one stayed there joking, just for five minutes. That did not dishonour anybody. It was only fools who stood outside parched with thirst. Those who used to chaff him were quite right, for a glass of wine never yet killed a man. But he slapped his chest as he boasted that he never drank anything but wine; always wine, never brandy; wine prolonged life, made nobody ill, and made nobody drunk. However, on several occasions, after a day of idleness spent in going from workshop to workshop, and from boozing-ken to boozing-ken, he had come home slightly elevated. On those days, Gervaise had kept her door shut, pretending she had a bad headache, so that the Goujets should not hear all the nonsense Coupeau was talking.

Little by little, however, the young woman fell sad. Morning and night she went to the Rue de la Goutte-d'Or to look at the shop, which was still to be let; and she would hide herself as though she were committing some childish prank unworthy of a grown-up person. This shop was beginning to turn her brain. At night-time, when the light was out, she experienced the charm of some forbidden pleasure in thinking of it with her eyes open. She again made her calculations: two hundred and fifty francs for the rent, one hundred and fifty francs for utensils and moving, one hundred francs in hand to keep them going for a fortnight—in all, five hundred francs at the very lowest figure. If

she was not continually talking of it aloud, it was for fear she
should be suspected of regretting the savings swallowed up by
Coupeau's illness. She often became quite pale, having almost
allowed her desire to escape her, and catching back her words quite
confused as though she had been thinking of something wicked.
Now they would have to work for four or five years before they
would succeed in saving such a sum. Her regret was at not
being able to start in business at once; she would have earned
all the home required, without counting on Coupeau, letting
him take months to get into the way of work again; she would
no longer have been uneasy, but certain of the future, and free
from the secret fears which sometimes seized her when he returned
home very gay and singing, and relating some joke of that
animal, My-Boots, whom he had treated to a drink.

One evening, Gervaise being at home alone, Goujet entered,
and did not hurry off again, according to his habit. He
seated himself, and smoked as he watched her. He probably
had something very serious to say; he thought it over, let it
ripen, without being able to put it into suitable words. At
length, after a long silence, he appeared to make up his mind,
and took his pipe out of his mouth to say all in a breath:

"Madame Gervaise, will you allow me to lend you some
money?"

She was leaning over an open drawer, looking for some dish-
cloths. She got up, her face very red. He must have seen
her then, in the morning, standing in ecstasy before the shop for
close upon ten minutes. He was smiling in an embarrassed
way, as though he had made some insulting proposal. But she
hastily refused. Never would she accept money from any one
without knowing when she would be able to return it. Then
also it was a question of too large an amount. And as he
insisted, in a frightened manner, she ended by exclaiming:

"But your marriage? I certainly can't take the money you've
been saving for your marriage!"

"Oh, don't let that bother you," he replied, turning red in
his turn. "I'm not going to be married now. It's an idea of
mine, you know. Really, I would much sooner lend you the
money."

Then they both held down their heads. There was something very pleasant between them to which they did not give
expression. And Gervaise accepted. Goujet had told his
mother. They crossed the landing, and went to see her at
once. The lace-mender was very grave, and looked rather sad

as she bent her face over her tambour-frame. She would not thwart her son, but she no longer approved Gervaise's project; and she plainly told her why. Coupeau was going to the bad; Coupeau would swallow up her shop. She especially could not forgive the zinc-worker for having refused to learn to read during his convalescence. The blacksmith had offered to teach him, but the other had sent him to the right about, saying that learning made people get thin. This had almost caused a quarrel between the two workmen; each went his own way. Madame Goujet, however, seeing her big boy's beseeching glances, behaved very kindly to Gervaise. It was settled that they would lend their neighbours five hundred francs; the latter were to repay the amount by instalments of twenty francs a month; it would last as long as it lasted.

"I say, the blacksmith's sweet on you!" exclaimed Coupeau, laughing, when he heard what had taken place. "Oh, I'm quite easy; he's too big a muff. We'll pay him back his money. But really, if he had to do with some people, he'd find himself pretty well duped."

On the morrow the Coupeaus took the shop. All day long, Gervaise was running from the Rue Neuve to the Rue de la Goutte-d'Or. When the neighbours beheld her pass thus, nimble and delighted to the extent that she no longer limped, they said that she must have undergone some operation.

CHAPTER V.

It so happened that the Boches had left the Rue des Poissonniers at the April quarter, and were now taking charge of the great house in the Rue de la Goutte-d'Or. It was a curious coincidence, all the same! One thing that worried Gervaise, who had lived so quietly in her lodgings in the Rue Neuve, was the thought of returning under the subjection of some unpleasnt person, with whom she would be continually quarrelling, either on account of water spilt in the passage or of a door shut too noisily at night-time. Doorkeepers are such a disagreeable class! But it would be a pleasure to be with the Boches. They knew one another—they would always get on well together. It would be just like members of the same family.

On the day that the Coupeaus went to sign the lease, Gervaise felt her heart swollen with pride as she passed through the high doorway. She was then, at length, going to live in that house as vast as a little town, with its interminable staircases, and passages as long and winding as streets. The grey façades, with the rags hanging out of the windows drying in the sunshine, the dull-lighted courtyard, with its uneven pavement like a street, the hum of work which issued from the walls, caused quite a commotion within her, a joy at being at length on the point of satisfying her ambition, a fear of not succeeding and of finding herself crushed in that enormous struggle against hunger, of which she had a kind of presentiment. It seemed to her that she was doing something very bold, throwing herself into the midst of some machinery in motion, as she listened to the blacksmith's hammers and the cabinetmaker's planes, hammering and hissing in the depths of the workshops on the ground floor. On that day, the water flowing from the dyer's under the entrance porch was a very pale apple green. She smilingly stepped over it; to her the colour was a pleasant omen.

The meeting with the landlord was to take place in the Boches' room. M. Marescot, a wealthy cutler of the Rue de la Paix, had at one time turned a grindstone through the streets. He was now stated to be worth several millions. He was a man of fifty-five, strong, bony, and decorated, with a habit of spreading out his immense labourer's hands; and one of his delights was to get hold of his tenants' knives and scissors, which he would sharpen himself, just for pleasure. He had the reputation of not being proud, because he remained for hours with his doorkeepers, in a secluded corner of their room, overhauling their accounts. It was there that he transacted all the business connected with the house. The Coupeaus found him seated before Madame Boche's greasy table, listening to how the dressmaker on the second floor, staircase A, had refused to pay her rent, making use of a disgusting expression. Then, when the lease was signed, he shook hands with the zinc-worker. He liked workmen. He had had to work precious hard once upon a time. But work was the high road to everything. And, after counting the two hundred and fifty francs for the first two quarters in advance, and dropping them into his capacious pocket, he related the story of his life, and showed his decoration.

Gervaise, however, felt rather ill at ease on account of the Boches' behaviour. They pretended not to know her. They were most assiduous in their attentions to the landlord, bowing down before him, watching for his least words, and nodding their approval of them. Madame Boche suddenly ran out and dispersed a group of children who were paddling about in front of the cistern, the tap of which they had turned full on, causing the water to flow over the pavement; and when she returned, upright and severe in her skirts, crossing the courtyard and glancing slowly up at all the windows, as though to assure herself of the good behaviour of the household, she pursed her lips in a way to show with what authority she was invested, now that she reigned over three hundred tenants. Boche again spoke of the dressmaker on the second floor; he advised that she should be turned out; he reckoned up the number of quarters she owed with the importance of a steward whose management might be compromised. M. Marescot approved the suggestion of turning her out, but he wished to wait till the half quarter. It was hard to turn people out into the street, more especially as it did not put a sou into the landlord's pocket. And Gervaise asked herself with a shudder if she too would be

turned out into the street the day that some misfortune rendered her unable to pay. The smoky room, filled with black
furniture, had the dampness and obscurity of a cellar; what
little light there was fell on to the tailor's board placed in front
of the window, and on which lay an old frock coat sent to be
turned ; whilst Pauline, the Boches' only child, red haired, and
four years old, was seated on the ground, quietly assisting at
the cooking of a piece of veal, delighted, and surrounded by the
strong odour which rose from the stove.

M. Marescot again held out his hand to the zinc-worker, when
the latter spoke of the repairs, recalling to his mind a promise
he had made to talk the matter over later on. But the landlord grew angry, he had never promised anything ; besides, it
was not usual to do any repairs to a shop   However, he consented to go over the place, followed by the Coupeaus and
Boche. The little linendraper had carried off all his shelves
and counters ; the empty shop displayed its blackened ceiling and
its cracked walls, on which hung strips of an old yellow paper.
In the sonorous emptiness of the place, there ensued a heated
discussion. M. Marescot exclaimed that it was the business of
shopkeepers to embellish their shops, for a shopkeeper might
wish to have gold put about everywhere, and he, the landlord,
could not put gold. Then he related that he had spent more
than twenty thousand francs in fitting up his premises in the
Rue de la Paix. Gervaise, with her woman's obstinacy, kept
repeating an argument which she considered unanswerable. He
would repaper a lodging, would he not ? Then, why did he not
treat the shop the same as a lodging ? She did not ask him for
anything else—only to whitewash the ceiling, and put some
fresh paper on the walls.

Boche, all this while, remained dignified and impenetrable ;
he turned about and looked up in the air, without expressing an
opinion. Coupeau winked at him in vain, he affected not to
wish to take advantage of his great influence over the landlord.
He ended, however, by making a slight grimace —a little smile,
accompanied by a nod of the head. Just then, M. Marescot,
exasperated, and seemingly very unhappy, and clutching his
fingers like a miser being despoiled of his gold, was giving way
to Gervaise, promising to do the ceiling and repaper the shop,
on condition that she paid for half of the paper. And he hurried away, declining to discuss anything further.

Then, when Boche was alone with the Coupeaus, he slapped
them on the shoulders, and was awfully jolly and friendly.

Well, the point was carried ! Without him they would never
have got the ceiling whitewashed or the walls repapered. Had
they noticed how the landlord had consulted him out of the
corner of his eye, and how he had suddenly come to a decision
on seeing him smile ? Then, he owned, in confidence, that he
was the real master of the house ; he decided when a notice to
quit should be given, let the rooms when the people suited him,
and received the rents, which he kept for a fortnight together
stowed away in his drawer. That evening, the Coupeaus, by
way of thanking the Boches, thought it only polite to send them
two quarts of wine. What they had done was well worth a
present.

As early as the following Monday, the workmen started doing
up the shop. The purchasing of the paper turned out especially
to be a very big affair. Gervaise wanted a grey paper with blue
flowers, so as to enliven and brighten the walls. Boche offered to
take her to the dealers, so that she might make her own selec-
tion. But the landlord had given him formal instructions not
to go beyond the price of fifteen sous the piece. They were
there an hour. The laundress kept looking in despair at a very
pretty chintz pattern costing eighteen sous the piece, and
thought all the other papers hideous. At length the doorkeeper gave in ; he would arrange the matter, and, if necessary,
would make out there was a piece more used than was really
the case. So, on her way home, Gervaise purchased some tarts
for Pauline. She did not like being behindhand—one always
gained by behaving nicely to her.

The shop was to be ready in four days. The workmen were
there three weeks. At first it was arranged that they should
merely wash the paint. But this paint, originally the colour of
wine lees, was so dirty and so sad-looking, that Gervaise allowed
herself to be tempted to have the whole of the frontage painted
a light blue with yellow mouldings. Then the repairs seemed
as though they would last for ever. Coupeau, who had not yet
returned to work, would arrive the first thing in the morning
to see if things were going on all right. Boche, leaving the coat
or the trousers, the button-holes of which he was mending,
would also come and give an eye to the men. And both of
them, standing in front of the painters, smoking and expectorating with their hands behind their backs, would pass the day
judging each dab of the paint brush. There were interminable
reflections, profound reveries, anent a nail to be pulled out.
The painters, two tall, jolly fellows, would leave their ladders,

and also stand in the middle of the shop, joining in the discussion, and wagging their heads for hours as they looked with a dreamy eye at the commencement of their work. The ceiling was whitewashed pretty rapidly. The painting promised never to be finished. It would not dry. Towards nine o'clock the painters would arrive with their colour pots, and, after putting them in a corner and giving a look round, they would disappear, and would not be seen again. They had gone off to lunch, or else they had had to go and finish a job close by in the Rue Myrrha. On other occasions, Coupeau took the whole gang to have a glass of wine—Boche, the painters, and any comrades who happened to be passing; and that meant another afternoon wasted. Gervaise's patience was thoroughly exhausted, when, suddenly, everything was finished in two days, the paint varnished, the paper hung, and the dirt all cleared away. The workmen had finished it off as though they were playing, whistling away on their ladders, and singing loud enough to deafen the whole neighbourhood.

The moving in took place at once. During the first few days, Gervaise felt as delighted as a child whenever she crossed the road on returning from some errand. She lingered to smile at her home. From a distance her shop appeared light and gay with its pale blue signboard, on which the word "Laundress" was painted in big yellow letters, amidst the dark row of the other frontages. In the window, closed in behind by little muslin curtains, and hung on either side with blue paper to show off the whiteness of the linen, some shirts were displayed, with some women's caps hanging above them on wires. And she thought her shop looked pretty, being the same colour as the heavens. Inside, there was more blue; the paper, in imitation of a Pompadour chintz, represented a trellis overgrown with convolvuli. The work-table, an immense piece of furniture which filled two-thirds of the place, was covered with a thick cloth, and draped round with a piece of cretonne, displaying large blue flowers, so as to hide the trestles on which it stood. Gervaise would seat herself on a stool, breathing contentedly, and delighted with all that beautiful cleanliness, as she devoured her new belongings with her eyes; but her first look was always given to her stove, a cast-iron stove, where ten irons, ranged round the fire on slanting plates, could heat at the same time. She would go down on her knees and look with a constant dread, fearing that her little fool of an apprentice was making the cast-iron crack by stuffing in too much coke.

The lodging at the back of the shop was tolerably decent. The Coupeaus slept in the first room, where they also did the cooking and took their meals; a door at the back opened on to the courtyard of the house. Nana's bed was in the right hand room, which was lighted by a little round window close to the ceiling. As for Etienne, he shared the left hand room with the dirty clothes, enormous bundles of which lay about on the floor. However, there was one disadvantage—the Coupeaus would not admit it at first—but the damp ran down the walls, and it was impossible to see clearly in the place after three o'clock in the afternoon.

In the neighbourhood the new shop produced a great sensation. The Coupeaus were accused of going too fast, and making too much fuss. They had, in fact, spent the five hundred francs lent by the Goujets in fitting up the shop and in moving, without keeping sufficient to live upon for a fortnight, as they had intended doing. The morning that Gervaise took down her shutters for the first time, she had just six francs in her purse. But that did not worry her, customers began to arrive, and things seemed promising. A week later, on the Saturday, before going to bed, she remained two hours making calculations on a piece of paper, and she awoke Coupeau to tell him, with a bright look on her face, that there were hundreds and thousands of francs to be made, if they were only careful.

"Ah, well!" said Madame Lorilleux all over the Rue de la Goutte-d'Or, "my fool of a brother is seeing some funny things! All that was wanting was that the Hobbler should go about on the loose. It becomes her well, doesn't it!"

The Lorilleux had declared war to the knife against Gervaise. To begin with, they had almost died of rage during the time while the repairs were being done to the shop. If they caught sight of the painters from a distance they would walk on the other side of the way, and go up to their rooms with their teeth set. A blue shop for that "nobody," it was enough to discourage all honest, hard-working people! So on the second day, as the apprentice was emptying a basin of starch water in the street just as Madame Lorilleux was going out, the latter drew a crowd round them by accusing her sister-in-law of inciting her workgirls to insult her. And all intercourse was broken off; whenever they met now, they only exchanged the most terrible looks.

"Yes, she leads a pretty life!" Madame Lorilleux kept saying. "We all know where the money came from that she

I

paid for her wretched shop! She earned it with the blacksmith; and he springs from a nice family too! Didn't the
father cut his own throat to save the guillotine the trouble of
doing so? Anyhow, there was something disreputable of the
sort!"

She very plainly accused Gervaise of being Goujet's mistress.
She lied—she pretended she had surprised them together one
night on a seat on the exterior Boulevards. The thought of this
intimacy, of the stolen pleasures that her sister-in-law was no
doubt enjoying, exasperated her still more, because of her own
ugly woman's enforced virtue. Every day the same cry came
from her heart to her lips,

"But whatever is it she has, that wretched cripple, for people
to fall in love with her? Nobody falls in love with me!"

Then there were endless cacklings with the neighbours. She
told the whole story. Ah! she had led them a fine dance on
the wedding-day! Oh! she was not blind, she saw then how
it was going to turn out. Only, later on, the Hobbler had
made herself so pleasant, she was such a hypocrite, that she and
her husband had consented, for Coupeau's sake, to be Nana's
godfather and godmother; and it had cost something, a christening like that. But now, you know, the Hobbler might be at
death's door, and in want of a glass of water, yet she would
certainly never take the trouble to give it to her. She had no
liking for insolent persons, nor hussies, nor harlots. As for
Nana, she would always be welcome whenever she came to see
her godfather and godmother; the little one was not to be
punished for her mother's crimes. Coupeau was in no need of
advice; any other man in his place would have boxed his wife's
ears and given her a ducking. However, that was his business; all they wanted was for him to see that proper respect
was paid to his family. Good heavens! if Lorilleux had caught
her, Madame Lorilleux, in the very act of being unfaithful to
him, it would not have passed off quietly; he would have
stabbed her in the stomach with his shears.

The Boches, however, severe judges of the quarrels of the
house, said that the Lorilleux were in the wrong. The Lorilleux were no doubt respectable persons, quiet, working the
whole day long, and paying their rent regularly. But, really,
jealousy drove them mad. With all that, too, they would have
tried to fleece an egg. Regular misers, there was no other
name for them; people who hid away their bottle of wine whenever anyone called, so as not to have to offer a glass. In short

they were not at all a pleasant couple. One day Gervaise had treated the Boches to some syrup and seltzer water, and they were all drinking it in the doorkeeper's room when Madame Lorilleux passed very stiffly by, and made a point of spitting on the ground before them as she did so; and ever since then, every Saturday when Madame Boche swept down the stairs and passages, she left the dust in front of the chain-maker's door.

"It isn't to be wondered at!" Madame Lorilleux would exclaim, "the Hobbler's for ever stuffing them, the gluttons! Ah! they're all alike; but they had better not annoy me! I'll complain to the landlord. Only yesterday I saw that sly old beast Boche rubbing against Madame Gaudron's skirts. Just fancy! making up to a woman of that age, and who has half a dozen children too; it's positively disgusting! If I catch 'em at anything of the sort again I'll tell Madame Boche, and she'll give her old man a hiding. It'll be something to laugh at!"

Mother Coupeau continued to visit the two homes, saying just what everyone else said, and even managing to get asked oftener to dinner, by complaisantly listening one night to her daughter and the next night to her daughter-in-law. For the time being, Madame Lerat had ceased calling on the Coupeaus, because she had quarrelled with the Hobbler respecting a zouave who had cut his mistress's nose off with a razor. She took the zouave's part, she considered slashing about with a razor a great sign of love, but did not give her reasons; and she had increased her sister's resentment by assuring her that the Hobbler, in the course of conversation before fifteen or twenty persons, had called her Cow's-Tail in the most open manner. Well! yes, the Boches, the neighbours all called her Cow's-Tail now.

In the midst of all this tittle-tattle, Gervaise, quiet and smiling at the door of her shop, greeted her friends with an affectionate little nod of the head. She delighted to come there for a minute during her ironing to laugh at the street, with the pride of a shopkeeper who has a bit of the pavement belonging to her. The Rue de la Goutte-d'Or seemed hers, and the adjacent streets, and the whole neighbourhood. When she stretched out her head, with her loose white jacket on, her arms bare, her fair hair which had come undone in the heat of her work, she would give a glance to the left and another to the right, as far as she could see, so as to take in at once the passers-by, the houses, the pavement, and the sky. To the

left was the Rue de la Goutte-d'Or, quiet and deserted like a
corner in some country town, where women were conversing
in a low voice at their street doors. To the right, a few paces
away, was the Rue des Poissonniers with its noise of passing
vehicles, its continual treading of a crowd which came from all
directions and filled that part with a vulgar mob. Gervaise
loved the street, the bumpings of the heavy carts over the uneven roadway, the jostlings of the people along the narrow,
smooth-flagged side-walks, which were every now and then
broken by a steep sloping pebble pavement. The few yards of
gutter in front of her shop, assumed an enormous importance
in her eyes, became a wide river which she liked to see perfectly
clean—a strange and living river, the waters of which were
capriciously coloured in the midst of the black mud, with the
most delicate tints from the dyer's establishment. Then, too,
she was interested in some of the shops, a vast grocery with its
display of dried fruits protected by some fine netting, a linen-
drapery and hosiery for workpeople, outside which overalls and
blue blouses, hanging with the legs and arms stretched out,
waved in the slightest breeze. At the greengrocer's and the
tripe-seller's, she could see corners of counters on which superb
cats sat quietly purring. Her neighbour, Madame Vigouroux,
the charcoal-dealer, returned her nod. She was a little fat
woman, with bright eyes and a black face, and was idling away
her time laughing with some men, as she leant against her shop
front to which simulated logs of wood painted on a background
the colour of wine lees gave the appearance of a log hut.
Mesdames Cudorge, mother and daughter, her other neighbours,
who kept the umbrella shop, never showed themselves. Their
window always had a sombre look, and their door, ornamented
with two little zinc parasols covered with a thick coat of bright
vermilion, was invariably closed.

But before going in again, Gervaise gave a glance over the
way, to a huge white wall without a window, and in the middle
of which was an immense gateway, through which one could see
the flare of a forge, in a courtyard full of carts and covered
vans standing with their shafts up in the air. On the wall the
word "Farriery" was painted in tall letters, surrounded by a
frame-work of horse-shoes. All day long the hammers resounded on the anvil, and clouds of sparks lighted up the pale
shadows of the courtyard. And at the foot of this wall, in a
hole about the size of a cupboard, between a dealer in old iron
and a fried-potato stall, was a clockmaker, a gentleman in a

frock-coat, looking very clean, who was for ever rummaging inside watches with some very tiny tools, in front of a work-table on which some slender articles reposed under glasses; whilst behind him, the pendulums of two or three dozen little wooden clocks were ticking altogether, amidst the gloomy wretchedness of the street and the cadenced hubbub of the farriery.

The neighbourhood in general thought Gervaise very pretty. There was, it is true, a good deal of scandal related regarding her; but every one admitted that she had large eyes, a small mouth, and beautiful white teeth. In short, she was a pretty blonde, and had it not been for her unfortunate leg, she might have ranked amongst the comeliest. She was now in her twenty-eighth year, and had grown considerably plumper. Her fine features were becoming slightly puffy, and her gestures were assuming a pleasant indolence. At times she occasionally seemed to forget herself on the edge of a chair, whilst she waited for her iron to heat, smiling vaguely and with an expression of greedy joy upon her face. She was becoming fond of good living, everybody said so; but that was not a very grave fault, but rather the contrary. When one earns sufficient to be able to treat oneself to tit-bits, one would be foolish to eat potato parings. All the more so as she continued to work very hard, slaving to please her customers, sitting up late at night after the place was closed, whenever there was anything pressing. She was lucky, as all her neighbours said; everything prospered with her. She did the washing for all the house—M. Madinier, Mademoiselle Remanjou, the Boches. She even secured some of the customers of her old employer, Madame Fauconnier, Parisian ladies living in the Rue du Faubourg-Poissonnière. As early as the third week she was obliged to engage two workwomen, Madame Putois and tall Clémence, the girl who used to live on the sixth floor; counting her apprentice, that little squint-eyed Augustine, who was as ugly as a beggar's breech, that made three persons in her employ. Others would certainly have lost their heads at such a piece of good fortune. It was excusable for her to feast a little on Monday after drudging all through the week. Besides, it was necessary to her. She would have had no courage left, and would have expected to see the shirts iron themselves, if she had not been able to line her stomach with something nice, the desire for which tickled her appetite.

Never before had Gervaise shown so much complaisance. She was as meek as a lamb and as good as bread. Excepting

Madame Lorilleux, whom she called Cow's-Tail, out of revenge,
she detested no one, and found excuses for all. In her slight
gluttonous forgetfulness, when she had lunched well and drank
her coffee, she yielded to the necessity for a general indulgence
all round. Her favourite saying was : "One must forgive one
another, if one does not wish to live like savages." When
people talked of her kindness, she laughed. It would never
have suited her to have been cruel! She protested ; she said
no merit was due to her for being kind. Had not all her dreams
been realised? Had she anything else to wish for in life? She
recalled her dream of bygone days, when she found herself
penniless—to work, have bread to eat, a home to live in, bring
up her children, not to be beaten, and to die in her bed. And
now her dream was more than realised ; she had all, and far
better. As to dying in her bed, added she jokingly, she counted
upon it, only of course at as distant a date as possible.

It was to Coupeau especially that Gervaise behaved nicely.
Never an angry word, never a complaint behind her husband's
back. The zinc-worker had at length resumed work ; and as
the job he was then engaged on was at the other side of Paris,
she gave him every morning forty sous for his luncheon, his
drink, and his tobacco. Only, two days out of every six,
Coupeau would stop on the way, spend the forty sous in drink
with a friend, and return home to lunch, with some cock-and-
bull story. Once even he did not take the trouble to go far ;
he treated himself, My-Boots, and three others to a regular
feast—snails, roast meat, and some sealed bottles of wine—at
the "Capuchin," on the Barrière de la Chapelle. Then, as his
forty sous were not sufficient, he had sent the waiter to his wife
with the bill and the information that he was in pawn. She
laughed and shrugged her shoulders. Where was the harm, if
her old man amused himself a bit? You must give men a long
rein if you want to live peaceably at home. From one word to
another, one soon arrived at blows. It was easy to understand.
Coupeau still suffered from his leg ; besides, he was led astray.
He was obliged to do as the others did, or else he would be
thought a muff. And it was really a matter of no consequence.
If he came home a little bit elevated, he went to bed, and two
hours afterwards he was all right again.

It was now the warm time of the year. One June afternoon,
a Saturday when the work was pressing, Gervaise herself had
piled the coke into the stove, around which ten irons were
heating, whilst a rumbling sound issued from the chimney. At

that hour the sun was shining full on the shop-front, and the pavement reflected an ardent recoil, causing all sorts of quaint shadows to dance over the ceiling ; and that blaze of light, which assumed a bluish tinge from the colour of the paper on the shelves and against the window, was almost blinding in the intensity with which it shone over the ironing-table, like a sunny dust shaken amongst the fine linen. The atmosphere was stifling. The shop door was thrown wide open, but not a breath of air entered ; the clothes, which were hung up on brass wires to dry, steamed, and became as stiff as shavings in less than three quarters of an hour. For some little while past an oppressive silence had reigned in that furnace-like heat, interrupted only by the smothered sound of the banging down of the irons on the thick blanket covered with calico.

"Ah, well!" said Gervaise, "it's enough to melt one ! It's almost impossible to keep a thing on."

She was sitting on the floor, in front of a basin, starching some things. She had on a white petticoat and a loose linen jacket with the sleeves rolled up, showing her bare arms and neck ; and she looked quite rosy, and was perspiring to that extent that little locks of her fair disordered hair were sticking to her skin. She carefully dipped caps, shirt-fronts, entire petticoats, and the trimmings of women's drawers into the milky water. Then she rolled the things up and placed them at the bottom of a square basket, after dipping her hand in a pail and shaking it over the portions of the shirts and drawers which she had not starched.

"This basketful's for you, Madame Putois," she resumed. "Look sharp, now ! It dries at once, and will want doing all over again in an hour."

Madame Putois, a little thin woman of forty-five, was ironing without a drop of perspiration, buttoned up in an old chestnut-coloured dress. She had not even taken her cap off, a black cap trimmed with green ribbons turned partly yellow. And she stood perfectly upright in front of the ironing-table, which was too high for her, sticking out her elbows, and moving her iron with the jerky evolutions of a puppet. On a sudden she exclaimed,

"Ah, no ! Mademoiselle Clémence, you mustn't take your jacket off. You know I don't like indecency. Whilst you're about it, you'd better show everything. There're already three men over the way stopping to look."

Tall Clémence called her an old beast between her teeth.

She was suffocating; she might certainly make herself comfort-able; every one was not gifted with a skin as dry as touchwood. Besides, no one could see anything; and she held up her arms, whilst her fine girl's substantial bosom almost rent her chemise, and her shoulders were bursting through the straps. At the rate she was going, Clémence was not likely to have any marrow left in her bones long before she was thirty years old. The morrow of a night of indulgence she was unable to feel the ground she trod upon, and fell asleep over her work, whilst her head and her stomach seemed as though stuffed full of rags. But she was kept on all the same, for no other workwoman could iron a shirt with her style. Shirts were her specialty.

"It's all my own, you know!" she ended by declaring, as she slapped her bosom. "And it doesn't bite, it hurts nobody."

"Clémence, put your jacket on again," said Gervaise. "Madame Putois is right, it isn't decent. People will begin to take my house for what it isn't."

So tall Clémence dressed herself again, grumbling the while,

"There's prudery for you! As though those fellows had never seen titties before!"

And she vented her rage on the apprentice, that squint-eyed Augustine, who was ironing some stockings and handkerchiefs beside her. She jostled her and pushed her with her elbow; but Augustine, who was of a surly disposition, and slyly spite-ful in the way of an animal and a drudge, spat on the back of the other's dress, just out of revenge, without being seen. Gervaise, during this incident, had commenced a cap belonging to Madame Boche, which she intended to take great pains with. She had prepared some boiled starch to make it look new again. She was gently passing a little iron, rounded at both ends, over the inside of the crown of the cap, when a bony-looking woman entered the shop, her face covered with red blotches and her skirts sopping wet. It was a washerwoman who employed three assistants at the wash-house in the Rue de la Goutte-d'Or.

"You've come too soon, Madame Bijard!" cried Gervaise. "I told you to call this evening. I'm too busy to attend to you now!"

But as the washerwoman began lamenting and fearing that she would not be able to put all the things to soak that day, she consented to give her the dirty clothes at once. They went to fetch the bundles in the left hand room where Etienne slept, and returned with enormous armfuls, which they piled up on the floor at the back of the shop. The sorting lasted a good half hour. Gervaise made heaps all round her, throwing the shirts in one, the chemises in another, the handkerchiefs, the socks, the dish-cloths in others. Whenever she came across anything belonging to a new customer, she marked it with a cross in red cotton, so as to know it again. And from all this dirty linen which they were throwing about there issued an offensive odour in the warm atmosphere.

"Oh, my ! what a stench !" said Clémence holding her nose.

"Of course there is ! If it was clean they wouldn't send it us," quietly explained Gervaise. "It smells as one would expect it to, that's all ! We said fourteen chemises, didn't we, Madame Bijard ? Fifteen, sixteen, seventeen—"

And she continued counting aloud. Used to this kind of thing she evinced no disgust. She thrust her bare, rosy arms into the midst of the soiled chemises, of the dish-cloths stiffened with grease, of the socks rotting with sweat. Yet, in the midst of the strong odour which met her full in the face as she leant over the heaps, a feeling of indifference took possession of her. She was seated on the edge of a stool, almost bent double, slowly stretching her hands out to the right and to the left, as though that human emanation was intoxicating her, whilst she smiled vaguely with a dreamy look in her eyes. And it seemed as if her first tastes for idleness had come from that, from the asphyxia resulting from the dirty clothes, poisoning the air around her. Just as she was shaking out a child's dirty napkin, Coupeau came in.

"By Jove !" he stuttered, "what a sun ! It shines full on your head !"

The zinc-worker caught hold of the ironing-table to save himself from falling. It was the first time he had taken such a dose Until then he had sometimes come home lively, but nothing more. This time, however, he had a black eye, just a friendly slap he had run up against in a playful moment. His curly hair, already slightly streaked with grey, must have dusted a corner in some low wine-shop, for a cobweb was hanging to one of his locks over the back of his neck. He was still as funny as ever, though his features were rather drawn and aged, and his under jaw projected more ; but he was always lively, as he would sometimes say, and his skin was still tender enough to tempt a duchess.

"I'll just tell you," he resumed, addressing Gervaise. "It was Celery-Root, you know him, the bloke with a wooden pin. Well, as he was going back to his native place, he wanted to

treat us. Oh! we were all right, if it hadn't been for that
devil of a sun. In the street everybody's ill. Really, all the
world's boozed!"

And as tall Clémence laughed at his thinking that the people
in the street were drunk, he was himself seized with an intense
fit of gaiety which almost strangled him.

"Look at 'em! the blessed tipplers! Aren't they funny?"
he cried. "But it's not their fault, they've got the sun in their
eyes."

All the shop laughed, even Madame Putois who did not like
drunkards. That squint-eyed Augustine was clucking like a
hen, suffocating with her mouth wide open. Gervaise, however,
suspected Coupeau of not having come straight home, but of
having passed an hour with the Lorilleux, who gave him bad
advice. When he swore that he had not been near them she
laughed also, full of indulgence, and not even reproaching him
with having wasted another day.

"Good heavens! what nonsense he does talk," she murmured.
"How does he manage to say such stupid things?" Then, in
a maternal tone of voice, she added, "Now, go to bed, won't you?
You see we're busy; you're in our way. That makes thirty-
two handkerchiefs, Madame Bijard; and two more, thirty-four."

But Coupeau was not sleepy. He stood there wagging his
body from side to side, like the pendulum of a clock, and
chuckling in an obstinate and teasing manner. Gervaise, who
wished to get rid of Madame Bijard, called Clémence, and made
her count the things whilst she wrote the number down. Then
this tall good-for-nothing made use of some coarse expression,
uttered some foul remark respecting each article; she exposed
the misery of the customers, had workshop jokes to crack upon
every hole and every stain that passed through her hands.
Augustine was as one who did not understand, pricking up
her ears like a vicious little girl. Madame Putois pursed her
lips, and considered it foolish to speak of such things before
Coupeau. There is no need for a man to see the dirty linen;
respectable people avoid such open displays.

Gervaise, serious, and her mind fully occupied with what
she was about, did not seem to hear. As she wrote, she gave a
glance to each article, so as to recognise it as it passed before
her; and she never made a mistake; she guessed the owner's
name just by the look or the colour. Those napkins belonged
to the Goujets, that was evident; they had not been used to
wipe the saucepans with. That pillow-case certainly came from

the Boches, on account of the pomatum with which Madame
Boche always smeared her things. It was not necessary either
to poke one's nose into M. Madinier's woollen undervests to
know that they were his; that man regularly dyed the wool,
his skin was so greasy. And she knew of other peculiarities,
the hidden side of the neighbours who crossed the street in silk
skirts, the number of stockings, handkerchiefs, and chemises,
that they allowed themselves in the week, the way in which
some people tore certain articles always in the same place. She
was also full of anecdotes. Mademoiselle Remanjou's chemises,
for instance, furnished material for interminable comments ;
they were wearing out at the top ; the old maid's shoulder-bones
were probably pointed ; and they were never dirty, even if she
had worn them a fortnight, which showed that at that age one
is like a piece of wood, from which it would be difficult to
extract a drop of moisture of any sort. It was thus that at
every sorting of the dirty linen in the shop, they undressed the
whole neighbourhood of the Goutte-d'Or.

"Here's something luscious !" cried Clémence, opening
another bundle.

Gervaise, suddenly seized with a great repugnance, drew
back.

"Madame Gaudron's bundle ?" said she. "I'll no longer wash
for her, I'll find some excuse. No, I'm not more particular than
another. I've handled some most disgusting linen in my time ;
but, really, that lot I can't stomach. What can the woman do
to get her things into such a state ?"

And she requested Clémence to look sharp. But the girl
continued her remarks, thrusting her fingers through the holes,
with allusions to the things, which she waved like triumphal
banners. Meanwhile, the heaps around Gervaise had grown
higher. Still seated on the edge of the stool, she was now disappearing between the petticoats and chemises. Before her were
sheets, drawers, table-cloths, a complete assortment of uncleanliness ; and there, in the midst of that rising flood, she remained
with her arms and her neck bare, and little locks of her fair hair
sticking to her temples, looking more rosy and languid than
ever. She regained her sedate air, her smile of an attentive
and careful mistress, forgetting Madame Gaudron's dirty linen,
no longer rummaging with one hand amongst the heaps to see
that no mistake had been made. That squint-eyed Augustine,
who delighted in putting shovelfuls of coke into the stove, had
filled it to such an extent that the cast-iron plates were be-

coming red-hot. The sun was shining obliquely on the window; the shop was in a blaze. Then Coupeau, whom the great heat intoxicated all the more, was seized with a sudden fit of tenderness. He advanced towards Gervaise with open arms and deeply moved.

"You're a good woman," he stammered. "I must kiss you."

But he caught his foot in the petticoats which barred the way, and nearly fell.

"What a nuisance you are!" said Gervaise, without getting angry. "Keep still, we've done now."

No, he wanted to kiss her. He must do so because he loved her so much. Whilst he stuttered, he turned the heap of petticoats, and stumbled against the pile of chemises; then, as he obstinately persisted, his feet caught together, and he fell flat, his nose in the midst of the dish-cloths. Gervaise, beginning to lose her temper, pushed him, saying that he was mixing all the things up. But Clémence, and even Madame Putois, maintained that she was wrong. It was very nice of him, after all. He wanted to kiss her. She might very well let herself be kissed.

"You're lucky, you are, Madame Coupeau," said Madame Bijard, whom her drunkard of a husband, a locksmith, was killing with blows every night on returning home. "If my old man was like that, when he's had a drop, it would be a pleasure!"

Gervaise, who had calmed down, was already regretting her hastiness. She helped Coupeau up on his legs again. Then she offered her cheek with a smile. But the zinc-worker, without caring a button for the other people being present, seized her round the waist.

"It's not for the sake of saying so," he murmured; "but your dirty linen stinks tremendously! Still I love you all the same, you know."

"Leave off, you're tickling me," cried she, laughing the louder. "What a great silly you are! How can you be so absurd?"

He had caught hold of her, and would not let her go. She gradually abandoned herself, dizzy from the slight faintness caused by the heap of clothes, and without repugnance for Coupeau's foul-smelling breath. And the big kiss they exchanged on each other's mouths, in the midst of the filth of the laundress's trade, was the first tumble in the slow downfall of their life.

Madame Bijard had commenced to tie the things up in

bundles. She talked of her little girl, two years old, whose name was Eulalie, and who was as sensible as a grown-up woman. You could leave her by herself; she never cried, nor played with the matches. At length she carried off the bundles one by one, her tall body bending beneath the weight, her face streaked with purple blotches.

"It's becoming unbearable, we're roasting," said Gervaise, wiping her face before returning to Madame Boche's cap.

And they talked of boxing Augustine's ears when they saw that the stove was red-hot. The irons, also, were getting in the same condition. She must have the very devil in her body ! One could not turn one's back a moment without her being up to some of her tricks. Now they would have to wait a quarter of an hour before they would be able to use the irons. Gervaise covered the fire with two shovelfuls of cinders. She also had the idea of hanging a pair of sheets, like blinds, on to the wire-lines against the ceiling, so as to allay the heat of the sun. Then they felt pretty comfortable in the shop. The temperature was still tremendously warm ; but one might have thought oneself in an alcove on a clear day, shut in as at one's own home, quite away from the world, though one could hear the people on the other side of the streets walking quickly along the pavement ; and one was able to put oneself at one's ease. Clémence took off her loose cotton jacket. Coupeau still declining to go to bed, he was allowed to remain, but he had to promise to keep quiet in a corner, for they had no time to waste.

"Whatever has that vermin done with my little iron ? " murmured Gervaise, speaking of Augustine.

They were for ever seeking the little iron, which they found in the most out-of-the-way places, where the apprentice, so they said, hid it out of spite. Gervaise at length finished the crown of Madame Boche's cap. She had already done the lace in the rough, pulling it out with her hand and flattening it with a slight touch of the iron. It was a cap with a very ornamental front, consisting of narrow puffs, alternating with embroidered insertions. And she stuck to her work silently, and taking great pains, ironing the puffs and the insertions with an iron of the shape of an egg at the end of a rod fixed in a wooden foot.

Silence reigned around. For a while, one heard nothing but the dull sound of the irons deadened by the thick ironing cloth. On either side of the large square table, the mistress, the two workwomen and the apprentice, stood leaning over at their work, their shoulders rounded, and their arms moving backwards and

forwards without cessation.   Each had her stand on her right,
a flat brick burnt by the hot irons.   In the middle of the table,
a piece of rag and a little brush were soaking on the edge of a
soup-plate full of clear water.   A bunch of large lillies was
blooming in an old glass jar which had formerly contained
cherry-brandy, and which looked like a corner of some royal
garden with its tuft of large flowers, white as snow.   Madame
Putois had started on the basket of linen prepared by Gervaise,
towels, drawers, loose cotton jackets, and pairs of cuffs.   Augustine was dawdling over her stockings and dish-cloths, her nose
up in the air, all engrossed by a big blue bottle that was buzzing
about.   As for tall Clémence, she had reached her thirty-fifth
shirt since the morning.

"Always wine, never spirits !" suddenly said the zinc-worker,
who felt the necessity of making this declaration.   "Spirits
make me drunk, I'll have none of 'em ! "

Clémence took an iron from the stove with her leather holder,
in which a piece of sheet iron was inserted, and held it up to
her cheek, to see how hot it was.   She rubbed it on her brick,
wiped it on a piece of rag hanging from her waist-band, and
started on her thirty-fifth shirt, first of all ironing the shoulders
and the sleeves.

"Bah ! Monsieur Coupeau," said she, after a minute or two,
"a little glass of brandy isn't bad.   It sets me going.   Besides,
the sooner you're merry, the jollier it is.   Oh ! I don't make
any mistake ; I know that I sha'n't make old bones."

" What a nuisance you are with your funereal ideas !" interrupted Madame Putois, who did not like hearing people talk of
anything sad.

Coupeau had risen, and was becoming angry, thinking that
he had been accused of drinking brandy.   He swore on his own
head, and on the heads of his wife and child, that there was not
a drop of brandy in his veins.   And he went up to Clémence
and blew in her face, so that she might smell his breath.   Then,
when he had his nose over her naked shoulders, he began to
chuckle.   Clémence, after having folded the back of the shirt
and ironed it on either side, was now doing the wristbands and
the collar.   But, as he continued pushing up against her, he
caused her to make a crease, and she was obliged to take the
brush from the edge of the soup-plate, to smooth the starch.

"Madame," said she, " do make him leave off bothering me.

"Leave her alone ; it's stupid of you to go on like that,"
quietly observed Gervaise.   " We're in a hurry, do you hear ? "

They were in a hurry, well! what? it was not his fault.
He was doing no harm. He was not touching, he was only
looking. Was it no longer allowed to look at the beautiful
things that God had made? All the same, she had
precious fine arms, that artful Clémence! She might exhibit
herself for two sous, and nobody would regret his money. The
girl allowed him to go on, laughing at these coarse compliments
of a drunken man. And she soon commenced joking with him.
He chaffed her about the shirts. So, she was always doing
shirts? Why, yes, she lived in them. Ah! by Jove! she knew
them well, she knew how they were made. Hundreds and hundreds had passed through her hands! All the fair fellows and
all the dark fellows of the neighbourhood wore her work on their
backs. Yet, she continued her work, her shoulders shaking
with her laughter; she had made five broad flat folds down the
back, by inserting her iron through the opening in the front;
she turned down the fore part and ironed it also in broad
folds.

"That's the banner!" said she, laughing louder than ever.

That squint-eyed Augustine almost. burst, the joke seemed to
her so funny. The others bullied her. There was a brat for
you, who laughed at words she ought not to understand! Clémence handed her her iron; the apprentice finished up the irons
on the stockings and the dish-cloths, when they were no longer
hot enough for the starched things. But she took hold of this
one so clumsily, that she made herself a cuff in the form of a
long burn on the wrist. And she sobbed, and accused Clémence
of having burnt her on purpose. The latter, who had gone to
fetch a very hot iron for the shirt front, consoled her at once by
threatening to iron her two ears, if she did not leave off. Then,
she placed a piece of flannel under the front, and slowly passed
the iron over it, giving the starch time to show up and dry.
The shirt-front became as stiff and as shiny as cardboard.

"By golly!" swore Coupeau, who was treading behind her
with the obstinacy of a drunkard.

He raised himself up, with a laugh that resembled a pulley
in want of grease. Clémence, leaning heavily over the ironing-
table, her wrists turned up, her elbows sticking out and wide
apart, was bending her neck in a last effort; and all her bare
flesh swelled, her shoulders rose with the slow play of the
muscles beating beneath the soft skin, her bosom heaved, wet
with perspiration, in the rosy shadow of the open chemise.
Then Coupeau thrust out his hands to touch her.

"Madame! madame!" cried Clémence, "do make him leave off! I shall go away if it continues. I won't be insulted."

Gervaise had just put Madame Boche's cap on a stand covered with a piece of rag, and was minutely goffering the lace with some goffering-irons. She raised her eyes just as the zinc-worker was thrusting out his hands a second time.

"Really, Coupeau, you're too foolish," said she, with a vexed air, as though she were scolding a child who persisted in eating his jam without bread. "You must come to bed."

"Yes, go to bed Monsieur Coupeau, it will be far better," exclaimed Madame Putois.

"Ah! well," stuttered he, without ceasing to chuckle, "you're all precious particular! So one mustn't amuse oneself now? Women know me, I've never hurt them. One squeezes a lady, you know, but one doesn't go any further; one simply honours the sex. And besides, when one displays one's stock-in-trade, it's that one may make one's choice, isn't it? Why does the tall blonde show all she's got? No, it isn't decent!"

And turning towards Clémence, he added: "You know, my duck, you're wrong to be so strait-laced. If it's because other people are present—"

But he was unable to continue. Gervaise, without any violence, seized hold of him with one hand and placed the other on his mouth. He struggled, just by way of a joke, whilst she pushed him to the back of the shop, towards the room. He got his mouth free, and said that he was willing to go to bed, but that the tall blonde must come and warm his tootsies. Then Gervaise was heard taking his shoes off. She was undressing him, maternally scolding him the while. When she tugged at his trousers he almost died with laughing, and abandoned himself, leaning back, sprawling in the middle of the bed; and he wriggled his legs, and said that she tickled him. At last, she tucked him in carefully, like a child. Was he comfortable, now? But he did not answer, he called to Clémence,

"I say, ducky, I'm here and waiting for you!"

When Gervaise returned to the shop, that squint-eyed Augustine was receiving a sound clout from Clémence. It was on account of a dirty iron, which Madame Putois had taken from the stove. She, not suspecting anything, had blackened the whole of one side of a jacket; and as Clémence, to avoid the imputation of not having cleaned her iron, accused Augustine, and swore by all that was holy that she had not used it, in spite of the dab of burnt starch that was still sticking to it, the apprentice, incensed at such an unjust accusation, had openly spat on the front of her dress. And she had received a good sound clout in consequence. The squint-eyed one kept back her tears, cleaned the iron by scraping it, and then by wiping it after having rubbed a piece of tallow candle over it; but, each time she had occasion to pass behind Clémence, she spat, and laughed inwardly whenever the saliva ran down the tall one's skirt.

Gervaise continued goffering the lace of the cap. And in the sudden calm which ensued, one could hear Coupeau's husky voice issuing from the depths of the back-shop. He was still jolly, and was laughing to himself as he uttered bits of phrases.

"How stupid she is, my wife! How stupid of her to put me to bed! Really! it's too absurd, in the middle of the day, when one isn't sleepy!"

But, all on a sudden, he snored. Then, Gervaise gave a sigh of relief, happy in knowing that he was at length quiet, and sleeping off his intoxication on two good mattresses. And she spoke out in the silence, in a slow and continuous voice, without taking her eyes off the little goffering irons, which she deftly handled.

"You see, he hasn't his reason, one can't be angry. Were I to be harsh with him, it would be of no use. I prefer to say just what he says and get him to bed; then, at least, it's over at once and I'm quiet. Besides, he isn't ill-natured, he loves me very much. You saw just now, he would have gone through fire and water to kiss me. That's very nice of him too; for there are many who, when they are screwed, go and see other women. But he comes straight home here. He jokes with you, but it doesn't go any further. Do you hear, Clémence? you mustn't be offended. You know what men are when they're tipsy; they'd kill father and mother, and not even have the faintest recollection of it afterwards. Oh! I forgive him from the bottom of my heart. He's like all the others, you know!"

She said all this softly, without passion, already used to Coupeau's goings on, and taking to discoursing on his love for her, but no longer seeing any harm in his squeezing the waists of the girls in her employ. When she had finished, silence ensued and was not again broken. Every time she wanted an article, Madame Putois took it from the basket, which she pulled out from under the chintz hanging which adorned the table; then, when she had ironed it, she raised her little arms, and

K

placed it on a shelf. Clémence was finishing folding her thirty-fifth shirt, with the iron. There was no end of work; they had reckoned that they would not get it finished till eleven at night, even with hurrying. Having no longer anything to distract their attention, they now all set to with a will. The bare arms moved to and fro, illuminating the white linen with their ruddy reflection. The stove had been again filled with coke, and as the sun, gliding in between the sheets, shone full upon it, one could perceive the great heat ascending in the ray, an invisible flame which quiveringly agitated the air. The temperature was becoming so stifling beneath the skirts and the table-cloths drying up against the ceiling, that squint-eyed Augustine, having expended all her saliva, allowed a bit of her tongue to hang out at the corner of her mouth. There was a stench from the over-heated stove of sour starch water, of burning from the irons, and of an unsavoury steaming bath-room with which the four workers, almost dislocating their shoulders, mingled the un-pleasant odour of their chignons and their perspiring necks; whilst the bunch of lilies, in the stale greenish water of the glass jar, were fading as they exhaled a very pure and powerful per-fume. And now and again, in the midst of the sound of the irons and the poker grating against the stove, Coupeau's snore rumbled with the regularity of the enormous tick-tack of a clock, regulating the movements of the workers.

On the morrow of his carouses, the zinc-worker always had a headache, a splitting headache which kept him all day with his hair out of curl, whilst his breath was offensive, and his mouth all swollen and askew. He got up late on those days, not shaking the fleas off till about eight o'clock; and he would hang about the shop and expectorate, unable to make up his mind to start off to his work. It was another day lost. In the morning, he would complain that his legs bent like pieces of thread, and would call himself a great fool to guzzle to such an extent, as it broke one's constitution. But one met a host of jolly dogs who would not let one go; so one boozed away in spite of oneself, one got caught in all sorts of traps, and ended by being bowled over, and pretty roughly too! Ah! no, by Jove! that would never happen to him again! he did not in-tend to cock his toes in a boozing-ken in the prime of his life. But, after his lunch, he would deck himself out, and hum! and ha! just to prove to himself that he still had a fine sonorous voice. He would begin to deny the carouse of the day before, he had perhaps had a drop or two, that was all. They no longer made such fellows as he, ever fit, with the devil's own muscle, and able to drink anything without blinking an eye.

Then, for the whole afternoon, he would hang about the place. When he had thoroughly badgered the workwomen, his wife would give him twenty sous to clear out. And off he would go and buy his tobacco at the "Little Civet," in the Rue des Poissonniers, where he generally took a plum in brandy, whenever he met a friend. Then, he spent the rest of the twenty sous at old François's, at the corner of the Rue de la Goutte-d'Or, where there was a famous wine, quite young, which tickled your gullet. It was a boozing-ken of the old style, a dark shop with a low ceiling, and a smoky room at the side in which soup was sold. And he would stop there till night-time, gambling for drink; François supplied him on tick, and had formally promised never to send the bill in to the wife. One must give oneself a rinse out to get rid of the muck of the day before. One glass of wine leads to another. Besides, he was a jolly fellow, who would never do the least harm to the fair sex—a chap who loved a spree, sure enough, and who coloured his nose in his turn, but in a nice manner, full of contempt for those pigs of men who have succumbed to alcohol, and whom one never sees sober! He went home as gay and as gallant as a lark.

"Has your lover been?" he would sometimes ask Gervaise by way of teasing her. "One never sees him now; I must go and rout him out."

The lover was Goujet. He avoided, in fact, calling too often, for fear of being in the way, and also of causing people to talk. Yet, he frequently found a pretext, such as bringing the washing; and he would pass no end of times in front of the shop. There was a corner right at the back in which he liked to sit, without moving for hours, and smoke his short pipe. Once every ten days, in the evening after his dinner, he would venture there and take up his favourite position. And he was no talker; his mouth almost seemed sewn up, as he sat with his eyes fixed on Gervaise, and only removed his pipe to laugh at everything she said. When they were working late on a Saturday, he would stay on, and appeared to amuse himself more than if he had gone to a theatre. At times, the women were ironing up to three o'clock in the morning. A lamp hung by a wire from the ceiling, the shade of it cast a large circle of brilliant light, in which the linen looked as soft and as white as snow. The apprentice put the shutters up at the shop window; but as the July nights were very hot, the street door was left open. And,

as the hour advanced, the women unfastened their things, so as
to be more at their ease.   They had fine skins, which assumed
a golden hue in the lamp light, Gervaise's especially ; she was
quite plump, her fair shoulders had the gloss of silk, her neck
was like a baby's, and had a dimple which Goujet could have
drawn from memory, he knew it so well.   He became oppressed
by the fierce heat from the stove, and by the smell of the clothes
steaming beneath the irons ; and he gradually succumbed to a
slight stupor, his mind slumbered, whilst his eyes became occupied with those women who were hurrying through their work,
swinging their bare arms, spending their night in making their
customers smart on the morrow.   Round about the shop, the
neighbouring houses were slowly becoming wrapped in the great
silence of sleep.   Midnight struck, then one o'clock, then two
o'clock.   The vehicles and the crowd of passers-by had alike
disappeared.   Now, in the dark and deserted street, only the
door showed a ray of light, which looked like a piece of yellow
stuff spread on the ground.   Occasionally a step was heard in
the distance and a man drew near ; and, as he passed, he
stretched his neck, surprised at the noise of the irons which he
heard, and carried away with him a fleeting vision of bare-
breasted women in a ruddy mist.

Goujet, seeing that Gervaise did not know what to do with
Etienne, and wishing to deliver him from Coupeau's kicks, had
engaged him to go and blow the bellows at the factory where
he worked.   The profession of bolt-maker, if not one to be proud
of on account of the dirt of the forge and of the monotony of
constantly hammering on pieces of iron of a similar kind, was
nevertheless a well paid one, at which ten and even twelve francs
a day could be earned.   The youngster, who was then twelve
years old, would soon be able to go in for it, if the calling was
to his liking.   And Etienne had thus become another link between the laundress and the blacksmith.   The latter would
bring the child home and speak of his good conduct.   Every
one laughingly said that Goujet was smitten with Gervaise.
She knew it, and blushed like a young girl, the flush of modesty
colouring her cheeks with the bright tints of the love-apple.
Ah! the poor dear boy, he never embarrassed her!   He had
never spoken to her about it ; nor had he ever made an indecent
gesture, or uttered a rude word.   One did not meet many of
such a virtuous temperament.   And, without admitting it, she
felt a great joy at being thus loved, as though she were a holy
virgin.   Whenever anything bothered her much, she thought

of the blacksmith, and that consoled her. If they found them-selves alone together, they did not feel the least embarrassment; they smilingly looked each other full in the face, without saying what they felt. It was a sensible affection, free from all thought of improper things, because it is ever best to preserve one's peace of mind, when one can manage to do so, and be happy at the same time.

Towards the end of the summer, Nana quite upset the house-hold. She was six years old, and promised to be a thorough good-for-nothing. So as not to have her always under her feet, her mother took her every morning to a little school in the Rue Polonceau, kept by Mademoiselle Josse. She fastened her playfellows' dresses together behind, she filled the school-mistress's snuff-box with ashes, and invented other tricks much less decent, which could not be mentioned. Twice, Mademoiselle Josse expelled her, and then took her back again so as not to lose the six francs a month. Directly lessons were over, Nana avenged herself for having been kept in, by making an infernal noise under the porch and in the courtyard where the ironers, whose ears could not stand her racket sent her to play. There, she would meet Pauline, the Boches' daughter, and Victor, the son of Gervaise's old employer—a big booby of ten. who delighted in playing with very little girls. Madame Fauconnier, who had not quarrelled with the Coupeaus, would herself send her son. In the house, too, there was an extraordinary swarm of brats, flights of children who rolled down the four staircases at all hours of the day, and alighted on the pavement of the court-yard like troops of noisy pillaging sparrows. Madame Gaudron alone contributed nine, both dark and fair, with tangled hair and dirty noses, breeches which almost went up to their eyes, stockings which hung down over their shoes, and torn jackets which showed their white skin under the rags. Another woman, a baker's carrier, contributed seven. Bands issued from nearly every room. And, in this multitude of rosy-faced vermin, who were washed only when it rained, were tall ones looking like pieces of string, stout ones with bellies already as big as men's, and little ones but recently escaped from their cradles, still unsteady on their legs, quite silly, and going on all fours when they wanted to run.

Nana reigned supreme over this host of urchins: she ordered about girls twice her own size, and only deigned to relinquish a little of her power in favour of Pauline and Victor, intimate confidants who enforced her commands. This precious chit was

for ever wanting to play at being mamma, undressing the
smallest ones to dress them again, insisting on examining the
others all over, messing them about and exercising the capri-
cious despotism of a grown-up person with a vicious disposition.
Under her leadership they got up to tricks for which they
should have been well spanked.   The troop paddled in the
coloured water from the dyer's, and emerged from it with legs
stained blue or red as high as the knees; then off it flew to the
locksmith's, where it purloined nails and filings, and started off
again to alight in the midst of the carpenter's shavings, enormous heaps of shavings, which delighted it immensely, and in
which it rolled head over heels.   The courtyard belonged to it,
resounded with the noise of the little shoes scuttling helter-
skelter about, and with the piercing shrieks of the voices which
swelled each time the troop took a fresh flight.   On certain
days even the courtyard did not suffice.   Then the band rushed
down into the cellars, raced up again, climbed to the top of a
flight of stairs, skurried along a passage, ran back into the
courtyard, ascended another staircase, followed another passage,
and kept on at it for hours together without tiring, yelling all
the time, and shaking the colossal house with the gallop of
destructive beasts escaped from every hole and corner.

"Aren't they abominable, those little toads?" cried Madame
Boche.   "Really, people can have but very little to do, to get
so many children.   And yet they complain of having no bread!"

Boche said that children sprouted out of misery like mushrooms on a dungheap.   The doorkeeper was shouting at them
all day, and menacing them with her broom.   She ended by
fastening the door leading to the cellars, because she learnt from
Pauline, to whom she gave a couple of clouts, that Nana had
taken to playing at being the doctor, down there in the dark;
this vicious little thing administered remedies to the others
with sticks.

Well, one afternoon, there was a frightful scene.   It was
bound to have come, sooner or later.   Nana had thought of a
very funny little game.   She had stolen one of Madame Boche's
wooden shoes from outside the doorkeeper's room.   She tied a
string to it, and began dragging it about like a cart.   Victor,
on his side, had had the idea to fill it with potato parings.
Then, a procession was formed.   Nana came first, dragging the
wooden shoe.   Pauline and Victor walked on her right and left.
Then, the entire crowd of urchins followed in order, the big ones
first, the little ones next, jostling one another; a baby in long

skirts, about as tall as a boot, with an old padded cap cocked
on the side of its head, brought up the rear. And the procession chanted something sad, with plenty of ohs! and ahs! Nana
had said that they were going to play at a funeral ; the potato
parings represented the body. When they had gone the round
of the courtyard, they recommenced. They thought it immensely amusing.

"What can they be up to?" murmured Madame Boche,
who emerged from her room to see, ever mistrustful and on the
alert.

And when she understood: "But it's my shoe!" cried she
furiously. "Ah, the rogues!"

She distributed some smacks, clouted Nana on both cheeks,
and administered a kick behind to Pauline, that great goose who
allowed the others to take her mother's shoe. It so happened
that Gervaise was filling a bucket at the tap. When she beheld
Nana, her nose bleeding, and choking with sobs, she almost
sprang at the doorkeeper's chignon. It was not right to hit a
child as though it were an ox. One could have no heart, one
must be the lowest of the low, if one did so. Madame Boche
naturally replied in a similar strain. When one had a beast
of a girl like that, one should keep her locked up. At length,
Boche himself appeared in the doorway, to call to his wife to
come in and not to enter into so many explanations with filth.
There was a regular quarrel.

As a matter of fact, things had not gone on very pleasantly
between the Boches and the Coupeaus for a month past. Gervaise, who was of a very generous nature, was continually be-
stowing wine, broth, oranges, and slices of cake on the Boches.
One night, she had taken the remains of an endive and beetroot
salad to the doorkeeper's room, knowing that the latter would
have done everything for such a treat. But, on the morrow,
she became quite pale with rage on hearing Mademoiselle
Remanjou relate how Madame Boche had thrown the salad
away in the presence of several persons, with an air of disgust,
and under the pretext that she, thank goodness! was not yet
reduced to feeding on things which others had messed about.
And, from that moment, Gervaise put a stop to all the presents:
no more bottles of wine, no more cups of broth, no more oranges,
no more slices of cake, nothing. It was quite a sight to see the
faces the Boches made! It seemed to them like a robbery on
the part of the Coupeaus. Gervaise saw her mistake ; for, if
she had not been so stupid as to stuff them to such an extent,

they would not have got into bad habits, and would have continued to behave nicely. Now, the doorkeeper found nothing
too bad to say about her. At the October quarter, she treated
M. Marescot, the landlord, to no end of slanderous stories, because the laundress, who spent her savings in gormandizing,
was a day behind with her rent; and even M. Marescot, who
was not very polite either, entered the shop, with his hat on
his head, and demanded his money, which by the way was
handed to him at once. Naturally, the Boches had shaken
hands again with the Lorilleux. Now, it was the Lorilleux who
in the midst of the emotions springing from the reconciliation
tippled with the Boches in their room. They would never have
quarrelled had it not been for that Hobbler, who would even
have stirred up strife between mountains. Ah! the Boches
knew her well now, they could understand how much the
Lorilleux must suffer. And whenever she passed beneath the
doorway, they all affected to sneer at her.

One day, however, Gervaise went up to see the Lorilleux. It
was with respect to mother Coupeau, who was then sixty-seven
years old. Mother Coupeau's eyesight was almost completely
gone. Her legs too were no longer what they used to be. She
had been obliged to give up her last place, and now threatened
to die of hunger if assistance were not forthcoming. Gervaise
thought it shameful that a woman of her age, having three
children, should be thus abandoned by heaven and earth. And
as Coupeau refused to speak to the Lorilleux on the subject,
saying that she, Gervaise, could very well go and do so, the
latter went up in a fit of indignation with which her heart was
almost bursting.

When she reached their door, she entered like a tempest, and
without knocking. Nothing had been changed since the night
when the Lorilleux, at their first meeting, had received her so
ungraciously. The same strip of faded woollen stuff separated
the room from the workshop, a lodging like a gun barrel, and
which looked as though it had been built for an eel. Right
at the back, Lorilleux, leaning over his bench, was squeezing
together one by one the links of a piece of chain, whilst Madame
Lorilleux, standing up in front of the vice, was passing a gold
wire through the draw-plate. In the broad daylight the little
forge had a rosy reflection.

"Yes, it's I!" said Gervaise. "I daresay you're surprised
to see me, as we're at daggers drawn. But I've come neither
for you nor for myself, you may be quite sure. It's for mother

Coupeau that I've come. Yes, I have come to see if we're going to let her beg her bread from the charity of others."

"Ah, well, that's a fine way to burst in upon one!" murmured Madame Lorilleux. "One must have a rare cheek."

And she turned her back and resumed drawing her gold wire, affecting to ignore her sister-in-law's presence. But Lorilleux raised his pale face and cried :

"What's that you say?"

Then, as he had heard perfectly well, he continued :

"More back-bitings, eh? She's nice, mother Coupeau, to go and cry starvation everywhere! Yet, only the day before yesterday, she dined here. We do what we can. We haven't got Peru. Only, if she goes about gossiping with others, she had better stay with them, for we don't like spies,"

He took up the piece of chain and turned his back also, adding as though with regret :

"When every one gives five francs a month, we'll give five francs."

Gervaise had calmed down, and felt quite chilled by the wooden looking faces of the Lorilleux. She had never once set foot in their rooms without experiencing a certain uneasiness. With her eyes fixed on the ground, on the holes of the wooden grating, through which the waste gold fell, she now explained herself in a reasonable manner. Mother Coupeau had three children ; if each one gave five francs, it would only make fifteen francs, and really that was not enough, one could not live on it ; they must at least triple the sum. But Lorilleux cried out. Where did she think he could steal fifteen francs a month? It was quite amusing, people thought he was rich, simply because he had gold in his place. Then, he abused mother Coupeau : she would not give up her coffee in the morning, she must have her drop of brandy, she required no end of things just like a person of fortune. Of course everyone liked to take life easy ; but yet, when one had not troubled to save a single sou, one must do as-others did—go without luxuries. Besides, mother Coupeau was not so old as to be unable to work ; she could still manage to see very well when it was a question of getting a tit-bit from the bottom of the dish ; in short, she was an artful old woman, who wanted to be pampered up. Even had he had the means, he would have considered it wrong to support any one in idleness.

Gervaise, however, remained conciliatory, and peaceably argued against all this bad reasoning. She tried to soften the Lorilleux. But the husband ended by no longer answering her. The wife was now at the forge, scouring a piece of chain in the little brass saucepan with the long handle, full of lye-water. She still affectedly turned her back, as though a hundred leagues away. And Gervaise continued speaking, watching them pretending to be absorbed in their labour, in the midst of the black dust of the workshop, their bodies distorted, their clothes patched and greasy, both become stupidly hardened, like old tools, in the pursuit of their narrow mechanical task. Then, suddenly, anger again got the better of her, and she exclaimed:

"Very well, I'd rather it was so; keep your money! I give mother Coupeau a home, do you hear? I picked up a cat the other evening, so I can at least do the same for your mother. And she shall be in want of nothing, she shall have her coffee and her drop of brandy! Good heavens! what a vile family!"

At these words Madame Lorilleux turned round. She brandished the saucepan as though she was about to throw the lye-water in her sister-in-law's face. She stammered with rage:

"Be off, or I shall do you an injury! And don't count on the five francs, because I won't give a radish! no, not a radish! Ah well! yes, five francs! Mamma would be your servant, and you would enjoy yourself with my five francs! If she goes to live with you, tell her this, she may croak, I won't even send her a glass of water. Now, off you go! clear out!"

"What a monster of a woman!" said Gervaise violently slamming the door.

On the morrow, she took mother Coupeau to live with her. She put up her bedstead in the big closet where Nana slept, and which was lighted by a little round window close to the ceiling. The moving did not take long, for all the furniture mother Coupeau possessed, consisted of this bedstead, an old walnut-wardrobe which was placed in the dirty clothes room, a table and two chairs; they sold the table and had the two chairs reseated. And the old woman, on the very evening of her arrival, swept up the crumbs and washed up the dinner things, in fact made herself useful, feeling delighted at having got out of her difficulty. The Lorilleux were bursting with rage, the more so as Madame Lerat had just become reconciled with the Coupeaus. One fine day the two sisters, the artificial flower-maker and the chain-maker, exchanged blows on account

of Gervaise. The first had ventured to approve the last-named's
conduct with respect to their mother; then, through a desire
to tease, seeing that the other was exasperated, she had gone
so far as to say that the laundress had magnificent eyes, eyes
at which one might light pieces of paper; and they ended
by slapping each other's faces and swearing never to meet
again. After that, Madame Lerat spent her evenings in the
shop, where she was inwardly amused by tall Clémence's loose
goings-on.

Three years passed by. There were frequent quarrels and
reconciliations. Gervaise did not care a straw for the Lorilleux,
the Boches and all the others who were not of her way of thinking. If they did not like it, they could do the other thing.
She earned what she wished, that was her principal concern.
The people of the neighbourhood had ended by greatly esteem-
ing her, for one did not find many customers so kind as she
was, paying punctually, never cavilling or higgling. She bought
her bread of Madame Coudeloup, in the Rue des Poissonniers;
her meat of stout Charles, a butcher in the Rue Polonceau; her
grocery at Lehongre's, in the Rue de la Goutte-d'Or, almost
opposite her own shop. François, the wine merchant at the
corner of the street, supplied her with wine in baskets of fifty
bottles. Her neighbour Vigouroux, whose wife's hips must
have been black and blue, the men pinched her so much, sold
coke to her at the same price as the gas company. And, in all
truth, her tradespeople served her faithfully, knowing that there
was everything to gain by treating her well. So, whenever she
went about the neighbourhood, bareheaded and in her slippers,
she was wished good-day on all sides; she was there as though
in her own home, the adjacent streets were like the natural de-
pendencies of her lodging which opened on a level with the
pavement. She would now linger over an errand, happy in
being out of doors in the midst of her acquaintances. The days
when she had not time to cook anything, she went and purchased something all ready, and had a gossip with the eating-
house keeper who occupied the shop on the other side of the
house, a vast apartment with big dusty windows, through the
dirt of which one caught a glimpse of the dull light of the courtyard at the back. Or else, her hands full of plates and basins,
she would stop and talk opposite some ground-floor window,
which gave a view of a cobbler's room, with the bed unmade,
and the floor encumbered with rags, a couple of broken cradles
and the wax-pan full of black water. But the neighbour whom

she still respected the most was the clock-maker opposite, the clean-looking gentleman in the frock coat, who was for ever rummaging watches with dainty little tools; and she often crossed the street to wish him good-day, laughing with pleasure at beholding, in the shop that was as narrow as a cupboard, the gaiety of the little wooden clocks with their pendulums all beating together against time.

CHAPTER VI.

ONE afternoon in the autumn, Gervaise, who had been taking some washing home to a customer in the Rue des Portes-Blanches, found herself at the bottom of the Rue des Poissonniers just as the day was declining. It had rained in the morning, the weather was very mild, and an odour rose from the greasy pavement; and the laundress, burdened with her big basket, was rather out of breath, slow of step, and inclined to take her ease, as she ascended the street with the vague preoccupation of a longing increased by her weariness. She would have liked to have had something nice to eat. Then, on raising her eyes, she beheld the name of the Rue Marcadet, and she suddenly had the idea of going to see Goujet at his forge. He had no end of times told her to look in, any day she was curious to see how iron was wrought. Besides, in presence of the other workmen she would ask for Etienne, and make believe that she had merely called for the youngster.

The manufactory of bolts and rivets was somewhere near there, at that end of the Rue Marcadet, though she did not exactly know where; more especially as the numbers were often missing from the buildings, which were interspersed by vacant plots of land. It was a street in which she would not have lived for all the gold in the world—a wide, dirty street, black from the coal-dust of the neighbouring manufactories, with uneven paving-stones and ruts full of stagnant pools of water. On either side there was a row of sheds, of lofty glazed workshops, of grey unfinished buildings, showing their wooden frameworks, a jumble of tottering masonry, intersected by open spaces, giving a view of the country beyond, and flanked by obscure lodging-houses and low cook-shops. She could only remember that the factory was near an old iron and rag warehouse, a kind of sewer opening on a level with the ground, in which slumbered hundreds of thousands of francs' worth of

goods, according to Goujet. And she tried to find her way
amidst the din of the factories. Slender pipes on the roofs
violently disgorged jets of steam ; at regular intervals, a grating
sound, similar to that produced by a piece of calico being
abruptly torn, issued from a sawmill; button manufactories
shook the ground with the rumbling and ticking of their
machinery. As she was looking towards Montmartre, undecided, and uncertain whether to go any further, a gust
of wind blew the smoke from a tall chimney downward
and infected the street. She closed her eyes, feeling almost
suffocated, when she heard a noise of hammers beating in
time ; without knowing it, she was exactly opposite the place
she was in search of, and she recognised the fact on perceiving
the hole full of rags close by.

Yet she still hesitated, not knowing where to enter. Some
broken palings opened a passage which seemed to lead through
the heaps of rubbish from some buildings recently pulled down.
As a large puddle of muddy water barred the way, two planks
had been thrown across it. She ended by venturing along
them, turned to the left, and found herself lost in the depths of
a strange forest of old carts, standing on end with their shafts
in the air, and of hovels in ruins, the wood-work of which was
still standing. Right at the end, rending the darkness which
blended with a remnant of daylight, a red fire was shining.
The noise of the hammers had ceased. She was advancing carefully, moving in the direction of the light, when a workman,
his face blackened with coal-dust, and wearing a goatee, passed
near her, casting a side-glance with his pale eyes.

"Sir," asked she, "it's here, is it not, that a boy named
Etienne works ? He's my son."

"Etienne, Etienne," repeated the workman, in a hoarse voice,
as he twisted himself about. "Etienne ; no, I don't know him."

His open mouth exhaled that odour of alcohol which comes
from old brandy casks with their bungs out ; and, as the meeting with a woman in that dark corner was beginning to make
him over pleasant, Gervaise drew back, murmuring,

"But yet it's here that Monsieur Goujet works, isn't it ? "

"Ah! Goujet, yes !" said the workman; "I know Goujet !
If you've come for Goujet, go right to the end."

And, turning round, he called out at the top of his voice,
which had a sound of cracked brass,

"I say, Golden-Mug, here's a lady wants you !"

But a clanging of iron drowned the cry. Gervaise went to

the end. She reached a door, and, stretching out her neck, looked in. It opened into a vast apartment in which at first she could distinguish nothing. The forge, as though dead, shone in a corner with the faint glimmer of a star, which rendered the gloom deeper still. Large shadows hung about, and now and again black masses, men inordinately enlarged, whose sinewy limbs could be imagined, passed before the fire, hiding that last gleam of light. Gervaise, not daring to venture in, called from the doorway, in a faint voice,

"Monsieur Goujet! Monsieur Goujet!"

Suddenly all became lighted up. Beneath the puff of the bellows, a jet of white flame had ascended. The shed was seen, enclosed by boarding, with openings roughly plastered round, and corners strengthened with bits of brick wall. The dust that blew from the coal fire had coated the place with a greyish soot. Cobwebs hung from the beams, looking like rags put up there to dry, and heavy with the dirt of years. Around the walls, on shelves, or hanging to nails, or thrown down in the dark corners, was a collection of old iron, of damaged utensils, and of enormous implements, showing, as they lay about, their tarnished, harsh, and broken forms. And the bright white flame continued to blaze away, illuminating as though with a ray of sunshine the trodden ground, on which the shining steel of four anvils, fixed in their blocks, had the reflection of silver streaked with gold.

Then Gervaise recognised Goujet in front of the forge by his beautiful yellow beard. Etienne was blowing the bellows. Two other workmen were there, but she only beheld Goujet, and walked forward and stood before him.

"Why, it's Madame Gervaise!" he exclaimed, with a bright look on his face. "What a pleasant surprise!"

But as his comrades appeared to be rather amused, he pushed Etienne towards his mother and resumed,

"You've come to see the youngster. He behaves himself well, he's beginning to get some strength in his wrists."

"Ah, well!" said she, "it's not easy to get here. I thought myself at the end of the world."

And she told him what a journey she had had. Then she asked him why Etienne's name was not known in the workshop. Goujet laughed, and explained that every one called the boy the little Zouzou, because his hair was cut short like a zouave's. Whilst they were talking together, Etienne left off working the bellows, the flame of the forge gradually lowered, a rosy glimmer was dying away in the middle of the shed, which had once more become dark. The blacksmith, deeply moved, watched the smiling young woman, looking so fresh in that faint light. Then, wrapped in the shadows, as neither continued speaking, he seemed to recollect and broke the silence.

"Excuse me, Madame Gervaise, I've something that has to be finished. You'll stay there, won't you? You're not in anybody's way."

She remained. Etienne returned to the bellows. The forge was soon ablaze again, with a cloud of sparks; the more so as the youngster, to show his mother what he could do, was making the bellows blow a regular hurricane. Goujet, standing up watching a bar of iron heating, was waiting with the tongs in his hand. The bright glare illuminated him without a shadow. His shirt, rolled up at the sleeves, open at the neck, displayed his bare arms and bare chest, a skin as pinky white as a girl's, with little light curly hairs; and, with his head rather low on his enormous shoulders all streaked with muscles, an attentive expression on his face, his pale eyes fixed, without blinking, on the flame, he looked like a giant at rest, calm in the knowledge of his might. When the bar was at white heat, he seized it with the tongs and cut it with a hammer on an anvil, in pieces of equal length, as though he had been gently breaking bits of glass. Then he put the pieces back into the fire, from which he took them one by one to work them into shape. He was forging hexagonal rivets. He placed each piece in a tool-hole of the anvil, beat down the iron that was to form the head, flattened the six sides, and threw the finished rivet, still red hot, on to the black earth, where its bright light gradually died out; and this with a continuous hammering, wielding in his right hand a hammer weighing five pounds, completing a detail at every blow, turning and working the iron with such dexterity that he was able to talk to and look at those about him. The anvil had a silvery ring. Without a drop of perspiration, quite at his ease, he struck in a good-natured sort of way, not appearing to exert himself more than on the evenings when he cut out pictures at home.

"Oh! these are little rivets of twenty millimetres," said he in reply to Gervaise's questions. "A fellow can do his three hundred a day. But it requires practice, for one's arm soon grows rusty."

And when she asked him if his wrist did not feel stiff at the end of the day, he laughed aloud. Did she think him a young lady? His wrist had had plenty of drudgery for fifteen years past; it was now as strong as the iron implements it had been so long in contact with. She was right though; a gentleman who had never forged a rivet or a bolt, and who would try to show off with his five pound hammer, would find himself precious stiff in the course of a couple of hours. It did not seem much, but a few years of it often did for some very strong fellows. During this conversation, the other workmen were also hammering away, all together. Their tall shadows danced about in the light, the red flashes of the iron taken from the fire traversed the gloomy recesses, clouds of sparks darted out from beneath the hammers, and shone like suns on a level with the anvils. And Gervaise, feeling happy and interested in the movement round the forge, did not think of leaving. She was going a long way round to get nearer to Etienne without having her hands burnt, when she saw the dirty and bearded workman, whom she had spoken to outside, enter.

"So you've found him, madame?" asked he in his drunken, bantering way. "You know, Golden-Mug, it's I who told madame where to find you."

He was called Salted-Mouth, otherwise Drink-without-Thirst, the brick of bricks, a dab hand at bolt forging, who wetted his iron every day with a pint and a half of brandy. He had gone out to have a drop, because he felt he wanted greasing to make him last till six o'clock. When he learnt that Zouzou's real name was Etienne, he thought it very funny; and he showed his black teeth as he laughed. Then he recognised Gervaise. Only the day before he had had a glass of wine with Coupeau. You could speak to Coupeau about Salted-Mouth, otherwise Drink-without-Thirst; he would at once say: "He's a jolly dog!" Ah! that joker Coupeau! he was one of the right sort; he stood treat oftener than his turn.

"I'm awfully glad to know you're his missis," added he. "He deserves to have a pretty wife. Eh, Golden-Mug, madame is a fine woman, isn't she?"

He was becoming quite gallant, sidling up towards the laundress, who took hold of her basket and held it in front of her, so as to keep him at a distance. Goujet, annoyed, and seeing that his comrade was joking, because of his friendship for Gervaise, called out to him:

"I say, lazybones, what about the forty millimetre bolts? Do you think you're equal to 'em, now that you've got your gullet full, you confounded guzzler?"

L

The blacksmith was alluding to an order for big bolts which necessitated two beaters at the anvil.

" I'm ready to start at this moment, big baby ! " replied Salted-Mouth, otherwise Drink-without-Thirst.   " It sucks its thumb and thinks itself a man.   In spite of your size, I'm equal to you ! "

" Yes, that's it, at once.   Look sharp, and off we go ! "

" Right you are, my boy ! "

They defied each other, stimulated by Gervaise's presence. Goujet placed the pieces of iron that had been cut beforehand in the fire ; then he fixed a tool-hole of large bore on an anvil.   His comrade had taken from against the wall two sledge-hammers weighing twenty pounds each, the two big sisters of the factory, whom the workmen called Fifine and Dédèle.   And he continued to brag, talking of a half-gross of rivets which he had forged for the Dunkirk lighthouse, regular jewels, things to put in a museum, they were so daintily finished off.   Hang it all, no ! he did not fear competition ; before meeting with another chap like him, you might search every factory in the capital.   They were going to have a laugh ; they would see what they would see.

" Madame shall be judge," said he, turning towards the young woman.

" Enough chattering ! " cried Goujet.   " Now then, Zouzou, show your muscle !   It doesn't heat a bit, my lad."

But Salted-Mouth, otherwise Drink-without-Thirst, asked : " So we strike together ? "

" Not a bit of it ! each his own bolt, my friend ! "

This statement operated as a damper, and Goujet's comrade, on hearing it, remained speechless, in spite of all his boasting. Bolts of forty millimetres fashioned by one man had never before been seen ; the more so as the bolts were to be round-headed, a work of great difficulty, a real masterpiece to achieve. The three other workmen who were present left their work to look on ; a tall, spare fellow wagered a quart that Goujet would be beaten.   The two blacksmiths each took a sledge-hammer with their eyes shut, because Fifine weighed half a pound more than Dédèle.   Salted-Mouth, otherwise Drink-without-Thirst, had the luck to put his hand on Dédèle, so that Fifine fell to Golden-Mug.   And, while waiting till the iron was at a white heat, the first, having recovered his cheek, swaggered about in front of the anvil, casting tender glances at the laundress. He took up his position, stamped on the ground with his foot, like a gentleman fencing, and already made the gesture of swinging Dédèle with all his might. Ah! Jove's thunder! he was in his element; he could have beaten the Vendôme column into a pulp!

"Now then, off you go!" said Goujet, placing one of the pieces of iron, as thick as a girl's wrist, in the tool-hole.

Salted-Mouth, otherwise Drink-without-Thirst, leant back, and swung Dédèle round with both hands. Short, dried-up, with his goatee, and with his wolf-like eyes glaring beneath his unkempt hair, he seemed to snap at each swing of the hammer, springing up from the ground as though carried away by the force he put into the blow. He was a fierce one, who fought with the iron, annoyed at finding it so hard, and he even gave a grunt whenever he thought he had planted a fine stroke. Perhaps brandy did weaken other people's arms, but he needed brandy in his veins, instead of blood. The drop he had taken a little while before had made his carcass as warm as a boiler; he felt he had the power of a steam-engine within him. And the iron seemed to be afraid of him this time; he flattened it more easily than if it had been a quid of tobacco. And it was a sight to see how Dédèle waltzed! She cut such capers, with her tootsies in the air, just like a dollymop of the Elysée Montmartre, who exhibits her under-garments; for it would never do to dawdle, iron is so deceitful, it cools at once just to spite the hammer. With thirty blows, Salted-Mouth, otherwise Drink-without-Thirst, had fashioned the head of his bolt. But he panted, his eyes were half out of his head, and got into a great rage as he felt his arms growing tired. Then, carried away by wrath, jumping about and yelling, he gave two more blows, just out of revenge for his trouble. When he took the bolt from the hole, it was deformed, its head being askew like a hunchback's.

"Come now! isn't that quickly beaten into shape?". said he all the same, with his self-confidence, as he presented his work to Gervaise.

"I'm no judge, sir," replied the laundress, reservedly.

But she saw plainly enough the marks of Dédèle's last two kicks on the bolt, and she was very pleased. She bit her lips so as not to laugh, for now Goujet had every chance of winning.

It was now Golden-Mug's turn. Before commencing, he gave the laundress a look full of confident tenderness. Then he did not hurry himself. He measured his distance, and swung the hammer from on high with all his might and at regular intervals. He had the classic style, accurate, evenly balanced, and supple. Fifine in his hands did not cut capers, like at a dancing-place, cocking her legs above her skirts; she rose and fell in cadence, like a lady of quality solemnly leading some ancient minuet. Fifine's heels beat time gravely, and smote the red-hot iron of the bolt's head with scientific strokes, first flattening the metal in the centre, then modelling it by a series of blows of rhythmical precision. It was certainly not brandy that filled Golden-Mug's veins; it was blood, pure blood, that flowed powerfully even into his hammer, and accomplished the task. It was a magnificent sight to see that fellow at work! The glare of the forge shone full upon him. His short hair curling over his low forehead, his handsome yellow beard with its wavy ringlets, seemed to light up, and illuminated all his face with its golden threads, making it indeed a face of gold. With that he had a neck like a pillar, and as white as a child's; a vast chest, broad enough to bear a woman across it; shoulders and arms which seemed sculptured from those of a giant in some museum. When he took his aim, one could see his muscles rise, mountains of flesh rolling and hardening beneath the skin; his shoulders, his chest, his neck, all swelled; he cast a halo around him; he became beautiful, all-powerful, like a god. He had already brought Fifine down twenty times, his eyes fixed on the iron, taking breath at every stroke, with merely two big drops of perspiration trickling down his temples. He counted: twenty-one, twenty-two, twenty-three. Fifine quietly continued her grand lady's curtseys.

"What affectation!" jeeringly murmured Salted-Mouth, otherwise Drink-without-Thirst.

And Gervaise, standing opposite Golden-Mug, looked on, smiling tenderly. Ah, what fools men are! Were they not each hammering their bolts by way of courting her? Oh, she saw it all: they were fighting for her with their hammers; they were like two big red cocks making up to a little white hen. What devices, eh? All the same, the heart has at times funny ways of declaring itself. Yes, it was for her, that thunder of Dédèle and Fifine beating on the anvil; it was for her, all that crushing of iron; it was for her, that forge in activity, flaring like a conflagration, filled with a shower of fiery sparks. They were forging there a love for her, forging against each other with her as the prize. And, in her heart, this pleased her; for, after all, women love compliments. Golden-Mug's blows especially found an echo in her breast;

GOLDEN-MUG FORGING A BOLT IN THE PRESENCE OF GERVAISE.

p. 165

they resounded there as on the anvil, with a bright music which accompanied the heavy throbbings of her blood. It seems absurd, but she felt that they drove something into her there, something solid, a little of the iron of the bolt. At twilight, before entering the factory, she had experienced a vague desire, as she passed along the wet pavements, to eat something nice; now she felt satisfied, as though the blows Golden-Mug had dealt with his hammer had nourished her. Oh, she had no doubt of his victory. It was to him that she would belong. Salted-Mouth, otherwise Drink-without-Thirst, was too ugly, jumping about like an escaped monkey, in his dirty blouse and overalls. And she waited, looking very red, feeling happy in the stifling heat, however, and taking a delight in being shaken from head to foot by Fifine's final strokes.

Goujet was still counting.

"And twenty-eight!" cried he at length, laying the hammer on the ground. "It's finished; you can look."

The head of the bolt was clean, polished, and without a flaw, regular goldsmith's work, with the roundness of a marble cast in a mould. The other men looked at it and nodded their heads; there was no denying it was lovely enough to be worshipped. Salted-Mouth, otherwise Drink-without-Thirst, tried indeed to chaff; but it was no use, and he ended by returning to his anvil, with his nose put out of joint. Gervaise had squeezed up against Goujet, as though to get a better view. Etienne having let go the bellows, the forge was once more becoming enveloped in shadow, like a brilliant red sunset suddenly giving way to black night. And the blacksmith and the laundress experienced a sweet pleasure in feeling this gloom surround them, in that shed black with soot and filings, and where an odour of old iron prevailed. They could not have thought themselves more alone in the Bois de Vincennes had they met there in the depths of some copse. He took her hand as though he had conquered her.

Outside, they scarcely exchanged a word. All he could find to say was that she might have taken Etienne away with her, had it not been that there was still another half-hour's work to get through. She was at length going off, when he called her back, trying to keep her with him a few minutes longer.

"Come this way; you haven't seen everything. Really, now, it's very curious."

He led her to the right, to another shed, where his employer had set up some machinery. She hesitated at the threshold,

seized with an instinctive fear. The vast apartment shook with
the vibration, and huge shadows, pierced with red fires, hung
about. But he smilingly reassured her, saying that there was
nothing to be afraid of. All she had to do was to be careful
not to let her skirts go near any of the gear. He walked first,
and she followed in the midst of that deafening uproar composed of all sorts of noises, whistling and rumbling, and of those
vapours peopled with vague forms—men black and busy,
machines agitating their arms—which she was unable to distinguish from each other. The passages were very narrow; it
was necessary to step over obstacles, to beware of holes, and to
stand on one side to avoid being jostled. One could not hear
oneself speak. For a time, she saw nothing distinctly; all
danced before her. Then, as she felt the sensation of a great
flapping of wings above her head, she raised her eyes, and
stopped to look at the long straps hanging from the ceiling, like
a gigantic cobweb, each thread of which seemed to be for ever
unwinding without coming to an end; the steam-engine, which
produced the motive-power, was hidden away in a corner behind
a little brick wall; the straps seemed to spin along without any
help, bringing the motion from the depths of the gloom, with
their continuous and regular glide, as gentle as the flight of a
night bird. But she nearly fell, through stumbling against one
of the pipes of the ventilator, which ramified over the trodden
ground, distributing its sharp breath of wind to the little
forges near the machines. And he commenced by showing this
to her, turning the air on to a fire; large fan-shaped flames
spread out on the four sides, forming a dazzling and rugged
collar of fire, slightly tinted with a touch of crimson; the light
was so brilliant that the workmen's little lamps looked like
dark spots on a sun.

Then he raised his voice to give her some explanations, as he
showed her the machinery—the mechanical shears which devoured bars of iron, gobbling a piece at each bite, and spitting
the bits out behind one by one; the bolt and rivet machines,
tall and complicated, which forged the heads with a single
pressure of their powerful screw; the scrapers, with their cast-
iron fly-wheel looking like a ball of cast-iron as it furiously
beat the air round each article, from which they removed the
rough edges; the tappers, worked by women, tapping the bolts
and their nuts, with the tick-tack of their steel wheels that shone
beneath the grease of the machine oil. She could thus follow
the whole fabrication, from the iron in bars leaning up against

the walls to the manufactured bolts and rivets, casefuls of which filled the corners. Then she understood, she smiled as she nodded her head; but all the same she had an oppressive feeling in her throat, uneasy at being so little and so tender amongst those formidable workers in metal, and now and again she turned round, so startled by the dull thud of one of the scrapers that her blood almost froze in her veins. She became accustomed to the gloom, and beheld recesses in which immovable men regulated the breathless dance of the fly-wheels, whenever a fire suddenly shed a flood of light from its collar of flame. And in spite of herself, her eyes wandered back to the roof, to the life, to the very blood of the machines, to the supple flight of the straps, the noiseless and enormous power of which she watched as it passed in the uncertain darkness that hung about the beams and rafters.

Goujet had stopped in front of one of the machines for making rivets. He stood there, wrapped in thought, with bowed head and fixed look. The machine forged rivets of forty millimetres with the quiet ease of a giant. And in truth nothing was simpler. The fireman took the piece of iron from the fire, the striker placed it in the tool-hole, which was moistened by a constant trickling of water to guard against softening the steel, and the thing was done, the screw came down, the rivet jumped to the ground, with its head as round as though it had been cast in a mould. In twelve hours that confounded machine manufactured hundredweights of rivets. Goujet was not spiteful; but, at certain moments, it would have delighted him to have taken Fifine and gone and knocked all that machinery about, in his rage at seeing that it possessed arms more powerful than his own. It caused him great vexation, even when he reasoned with himself, and told himself that flesh could not fight against iron. One day certainly, machinery would kill the workman; wages had already fallen from twelve francs to nine francs a day, and there was a talk of lowering them still more; in short, there was nothing lively in those hulking contrivances which made bolts and rivets just the same as they might have made sausages. He gazed at that one fully three minutes without saying a word; his brow contracted, and his beautiful yellow beard bristled menacingly. Then a look of gentleness and resignation gradually softened the expression of his features. He turned towards Gervaise, who pressed against him, and said with a melancholy smile:

"Eh! it makes one feel precious small! But perhaps it will some day help to insure the prosperity of all of us."

Gervaise did not care a fig for universal prosperity. In her opinion, the machine-made bolts were badly forged.

"You understand what I mean," exclaimed she with warmth; "they are too well done. I like yours better. In them one can at least trace the hand of an artist."

In speaking thus, she gave him very great comfort, because he had feared for a moment that she would despise him, after seeing the machines. For though he was stronger than Salted-Mouth, otherwise Drink-without-Thirst, yet the machines were stronger than he was. When he at length parted from her in the courtyard, he squeezed her wrists almost to the point of breaking them, because of his great joy.

The laundress went every Saturday to the Goujets, to take home their washing. They still lived in the little house in the Rue Neuve de la Goutte-d'Or. During the first year she had regularly repaid them twenty francs a month; so as not to jumble up the accounts, the washing-book was only made up at the end of each month, and then she added to the amount whatever sum was necessary to make the twenty francs, for the Goujets' washing rarely came to more than seven or eight francs during that time. She had therefore paid off nearly half the sum owing, when one quarter day, not knowing what to do, some of her customers not having kept their promises, she had been obliged to go to the Goujets, and borrow from them sufficient for her rent. On two other occasions she had also applied to them for the money to pay her workwomen, so that the debt had increased again to four hundred and twenty-five francs. Now, she no longer gave a halfpenny; she worked off the amount solely by the washing. It was not that she worked less, or that her business was not so prosperous. But something was going wrong in her home; the money seemed to melt away, and she was glad when she was able to make both ends meet. Well! providing one lives, one is not so much to be pitied. She was getting fatter; she gave way to all the little unconstraints of her growing obesity, no longer having the strength to be frightened when she thought of the future. So much the worse! money would always come in, putting it by only made it rusty. Madame Goujet, however, continued to treat Gervaise in a maternal manner. She gently lectured her occasionally, not on account of the money, but because she loved her and feared to see her take the plunge into the mire.

She never even mentioned the debt. In short, she behaved with the utmost delicacy.

The morrow of Gervaise's visit to the forge happened to be the last Saturday of the month. When she reached the Goujets, where she made a point of going herself, her basket had so weighed on her arms that she was quite two minutes before she could get her breath. One would hardly believe how heavy clothes are, especially when there are sheets among them.

"Are you sure you've brought everything?" asked Madame Goujet.

She was very strict on that point. She insisted on having her washing brought home without a single article being kept back, for the sake of order, as she said. She also required the laundress always to come on the day arranged, and at the same hour; in that way there was no time wasted.

"Oh! yes, there's everything," replied Gervaise, smiling. "You know I never keep a thing back."

"That's true," admitted Madame Goujet; "you've got into many bad habits, but you're still free of that one."

And, whilst the laundress emptied her basket, laying the linen on her bed, the old woman praised her: she never burnt the things, nor tore them, like so many others did, neither did she pull the buttons off with the iron; only she used too much blue, and made the shirt fronts too stiff with starch.

"Just look, it's like cardboard," continued she, making one crackle between her fingers. "My son does not complain, but it cuts his neck. To-morrow his neck will be all scratched when we return from Vincennes."

"No, don't say that!" exclaimed Gervaise, quite grieved. "To look nice, shirts must be rather stiff, otherwise it's as though one had a rag on one's body. You should just see how gentlemen have their's done. I do all your things myself. The workwomen never touch them, and I assure you I take great pains—I would if necessary do everything over a dozen times—because it's for you, you know."

She slightly blushed as she stammered out the last words. She was afraid of showing the great pleasure she took in ironing Goujet's shirts. She certainly had no wicked thoughts, but she was none the less a little bit ashamed.

"Oh! I'm not complaining of your work; I know it's perfection," said Madame Goujet. "For instance, you've done this cap splendidly, only you could bring out the embroidery

like that. And the goffering is all so even ! Oh ! I recognise
your hand at once. When you give even a dish-cloth to one
of your workwomen I detect it at once. In future, use a little
less starch, that's all ! Goujet does not care to look like a
gentleman."

She took up the book and ticked off the items with a pen.
Everything was there. When they made up the account, she
saw that Gervaise had charged her six sous for a cap ; she protested against this, but she had to admit that the other things
were charged very low : shirts five sous, women's drawers four
sous, pillow-cases a sou and a half, aprons a sou a piece ; no, it
was really not dear, as many laundresses charged two liards,
and even a sou more for each of those articles. Then, when
Gervaise had called over the dirty linen, which the old woman
wrote down, she put it in the basket ; but, instead of taking
her leave, she remained there in an embarrassed sort of way,
with a request on the tip of her tongue, which she could
scarcely screw up courage to utter.

"Madame Goujet," said she at length, "if it does not inconvenience you, I should like to take the money for this month's
washing."

It so happened that that month was a very heavy one, the
account they had made up together amounting to ten francs
seven sous. Madame Goujet looked at her a moment in a
serious manner, then she replied :

"My child, it shall be as you wish. I will not refuse you
the money, as you are in want of it. Only, it's scarcely the
way to pay off your debt ; I say that for your sake, you know.
Really now, you should be careful."

Gervaise received the lecture with bowed head, and stammering excuses. The ten francs were to make up the amount of a
bill she had given her coke merchant. But on hearing the
word "bill," Madame Goujet became severer still. She gave
herself as an example : she had reduced her expenditure, ever
since Goujet's wages had been lowered from twelve to nine
francs a day. When one was wanting in wisdom whilst young,
one died of hunger in one's old age. Yet, she restrained herself ; she did not tell Gervaise that she merely gave her the
washing to do to enable her to pay off her debt. Previously
she had washed everything herself, and she would do so again
if the washing was going to draw sums like that out of her
pocket. When Gervaise had hold of the ten francs seven sous, she
murmured her thanks and hastened away. And, outside on

the landing, she experienced a sensation of relief; she felt
inclined to dance, for she was already becoming accustomed to
the worries and unpleasantnesses of money matters, retaining of
such vexations only the delight of being free of them, until
the next time.

It was also on that Saturday that Gervaise met with a rather
strange adventure as she descended the Goujets' staircase. She
was obliged to stand up close against the balusters with her
basket, to make way for a tall bare-headed woman who was
coming up, carrying in her hand a very fresh mackerel, with
its gills all bloody, in a piece of paper. And she recognised
Virginie, the girl whose skirts she had turned up at the wash-
house. They looked each other full in the face. Gervaise
shut her eyes, for she thought for a moment that she was going
to receive the mackerel in them. But no, Virginie even smiled
slightly. Then, as her basket was blocking up the staircase,
the laundress wished to show how polite she could be.

"Pray excuse me," said she.

"Most willingly," replied the tall brunette.

And they remained conversing together on the stairs, reconciled at once without having ventured on a single allusion to
the past. Virginie, then twenty-nine years old, had become a
superb woman, of strapping proportions, her face, however,
looking rather long between her two plaits of jet black hair.
She at once began to relate her history just to show off. She
had a husband now; she had married in the spring an ex-journey-
man cabinetmaker, who had recently left the army, and who
had applied to be admitted into the police, because a post of
that kind is more to be depended upon and more respectable.
She had been out to buy the mackerel for him.

"He adores mackerel," said she. "We must spoil them,
those naughty men, mustn't we? But come up. You shall
see our home. We are standing in a draught here."

When Gervaise, after relating in her turn the story of her
own marriage, said that she had lived in the same lodging, and
had even been confined there of a daughter, Virginie pressed
her to come up more than ever. It is always a pleasure to see
the places again where one has been happy. For five years
past she had been residing in the Gros-Caillou district, on the
other side of the water. It was there that she had first known
her husband, who was then in the army. But she was dull;
she longed to return to the neighbourhood of the Goutte-d'Or,
where she knew everybody; and for the last fortnight she had

been living in the lodging facing the Goujets. Oh, all her
things were still in great disorder; they would get straight
little by little.

Then they at length told each other their names on the
landing.

" Madame Coupeau."

" Madame Poisson."

And from that time forth, they called each other on every
possible occasion Madame Poisson and Madame Coupeau, solely
for the pleasure of being madame, they who in former days had
been acquainted when occupying rather questionable positions.
However, Gervaise felt rather mistrustful at heart. Perhaps
the tall brunette had made it up the better to avenge herself
for the beating at the wash-house by concocting some plan
worthy of a spiteful hypocritical creature. Gervaise determined
to be upon her guard. For the time being, as Virginie behaved
so nicely, she would be nice also.

In the room upstairs, Poisson, the husband, a man of thirty-
five, with a cadaverous-looking countenance and carroty moustaches and imperial, was seated working at a table near the window. He was making little boxes. His sole tools consisted of a
penknife, a saw about the size of a finger-nail file, and a pot of
glue. The wood which he used came from old cigar-boxes, thin
strips of unpolished mahogany, which he cut up and embellished
with extraordinary delicacy. All day long, from one end of
the year to the other, he made similar boxes three inches by
two and a quarter. Only, he checkered them, varied the shapes
of the lids, and divided them into compartments. It amused
him and helped to kill time whilst awaiting his appointment in
the police. From his old trade of cabinetmaking, he had only
preserved a mania for constructing little boxes. He did not
sell his work, he distributed it in presents to persons of his
acquaintance.

Poisson rose from his seat and politely bowed to Gervaise,
whom his wife introduced to him as one of her old friends.
But he was no talker; he at once returned to his little saw.
From time to time he merely glanced in the direction of the
mackerel placed on the corner of the chest of drawers. Gervaise
was very pleased to see her old lodging once more. She told
them whereabouts her own furniture stood, and pointed out the
place on the floor where she was confined. What a curious
thing it was ! When they both lost sight of each other in the
old days, they would never have thought of meeting again like

that, and of living one after the other in the same room.
Virginie gave some further information about herself and her
husband. He had inherited a small sum from an aunt. No
doubt he would set her up in business later on; for the time
being, she continued to do needle-work, and occasionally made
up a dress. At length, at the end of a good half-hour, the
laundress took her leave. Poisson scarcely turned round.
Virginie, who escorted her out of the room, promised to return
her visit; besides that, she arranged to give Gervaise her
custom; and as she detained her on the landing, Gervaise
fancied that she wished to speak to her of Lantier, and of her
sister Adèle, the burnisher. She felt quite upset in consequence. But not a word was uttered respecting these unpleasant things; they parted, wishing each other good-bye in a
very amiable manner.

"Good-bye, Madame Coupeau."

"Good-bye, Madame Poisson."

That was the starting-point of a great friendship. A week
later, Virginie never passed Gervaise's shop without going in;
and she remained there gossiping for hours together, to such an
extent, indeed, that Poisson, filled with anxiety, fearing she
had been run over, would come and seek her, with his
expressionless and death-like countenance. Gervaise, seeing
the dressmaker in this way every day of her life, soon became
absorbed in one fixed idea. She could never hear her commence a sentence without thinking she was going to speak of
Lantier; her thoughts reverted to Lantier in spite of herself
all the time the other remained with her. It was as stupid as
could be, for she really did not care a pin for either Lantier or
Adèle, nor for what had become of them; she never asked a
question; in fact, she did not feel the least curiosity to have
news of them. No; it seized upon her, notwithstanding her
determination to the contrary. The thought of them continued
in her head just the same as some bothering chorus sticks to
one's tongue, and declines to be got rid of. She did not bear
Virginie any ill-will, for it was certainly not her fault. She
enjoyed her society very much, and would detain her a dozen
times before letting her go.

Meanwhile, winter had come, the Coupeaus' fourth winter in
the Rue de la Goutte-d'Or. December and January were particularly cold. It froze as hard as it well could. After New
Year's Day, the snow remained three weeks in the street without melting. It did not interfere with work, but the contrary,

for winter is the best season for the ironers. It was very
pleasant inside the shop! There was never any ice on the
window-panes like there was at the grocer's and the hosier's
opposite. The stove, crammed full of coke, maintained the
heat of a bath-room; the clothes steamed away, one could have
thought oneself in the height of summer; and one felt so comfortable with the doors shut, being warm all over, so warm that
one could have fallen asleep with one's eyes open. Gervaise
laughingly said that she fancied herself in the country. And
true enough, the vehicles rolled noiselessly over the snow;
one scarcely heard the footfalls of the passers-by; in the
great silence resulting from the cold, children's voices alone
resounded, the shouts of a troop of youngsters who had made
a big slide along the gutter of the farriery. Now and again
she would go to the door, and, wiping away the steam from one
of the panes of glass, would look out to see how the neighbourhood was getting on in that confounded temperature; but not a
face was to be seen at any of the shops in sight. The neighbours,
wrapped up in snow, seemed to be sulking; and she was only
able to exchange a nod with the charcoal-dealer near by, who
walked about bareheaded, and with her mouth grinning from
ear to ear, ever since the severe frost had set in.

What was especially enjoyable in this awful weather was to
have some nice hot coffee in the middle of the day. The workwomen had no cause for complaint. The mistress made it very
strong and without a grain of chicory. It was quite different
to Madame Fauconnier's coffee, which was like ditch-water.
Only, whenever mother Coupeau undertook to make it, it was
always an interminable time before it was ready, because she
would fall asleep over the kettle. On these occasions, when
the workwomen had finished their lunch, they would do a little
ironing whilst waiting for the coffee.

It so happened that on the morrow of Twelfth-day, half-past
twelve struck, and still the coffee was not ready. It seemed to
persist in declining to pass through the strainer. Mother
Coupeau tapped against the pot with a tea-spoon; and one could
hear the drops falling slowly, one by one, and without hurrying
themselves any the more.

"Leave it alone," said tall Clémence; "you'll make it thick.
To-day there'll certainly be as much to eat as to drink."

Tall Clémence was getting up a shirt, the plaits of which
she separated with her finger-nail. She had caught a cold
sufficient to kill her, her eyes were frightfully swollen, and her

chest was shaken with fits of coughing, which doubled her up beside the work-table. With all that, she had not even a handkerchief round her neck, and she was dressed in some cheap flimsy woollen stuff, in which she shivered. Close by, Madame Putois, wrapped up in flannel, muffled up to her ears, was ironing a petticoat, which she turned round the skirt-board, the narrow end of which rested on the back of a chair ; whilst a sheet laid on the floor prevented the petticoat from getting dirty as it trailed along the tiles. Gervaise alone occupied half the work-table with some embroidered muslin curtains, over which she passed her iron in a straight line, with her arms stretched out to avoid making any creases. All on a sudden, the coffee running through noisily caused her to raise her head. It was that squint-eyed Augustine, who had just given it an outlet by thrusting a spoon through the strainer.

"Leave it alone!" cried Gervaise. "Whatever is the matter with you? It'll be like drinking mud now."

Mother Coupeau had placed five glasses on a corner of the work-table that was free. The women now left their work. The mistress always poured out the coffee herself, after putting two lumps of sugar into each glass. It was the moment that they all looked forward to. On this occasion, as each one took her glass and squatted down on a little stool in front of the stove, the shop-door opened. Virginie entered, shivering all over.

"Ah, my children," said she, "it cuts you in two! I can no longer feel my ears. The cold is something awful!"

"Why, it's Madame Poisson!" exclaimed Gervaise. "Ah, well! you've come at the right time. You must have some coffee with us."

"On my word, I can't say no. One feels the frost in one's bones merely by crossing the street."

There was still some coffee left, luckily. Mother Coupeau went and fetched a sixth glass, and Gervaise let Virginie help herself to sugar, out of politeness. The workwomen drew on one side, and made room near the stove for the new comer. She shivered for a moment, her nose all red, and held her hands stiff with cold round her glass to warm them. She had come from the grocer's, where one froze, merely whilst waiting for a quarter of a pound of Gruyere cheese. And she cried out about the great heat of the shop. Really, it was like entering an oven, it was enough to bring the dead to life again, it filled one's body with such a pleasant sensation. Then, having got

over her numbness, she stretched out her long legs. And all
the six slowly sipped their coffee in the midst of the interrupted
work, in the damp sultriness caused by the steaming clothes.
Only mother Coupeau and Virginie were seated on chairs ; the
others, on their little stools, looked as though they were on the
floor ; and that squint-eyed Augustine had even seized upon a
portion of the sheet beneath the petticoat, so as to sprawl upon
it. No one spoke at first ; all kept their noses in their glasses,
enjoying their coffee.

"It's not bad all the same," declared Clémence.

·But she was seized with a fit of coughing, and almost choked.
She leant her head against the wall to cough with more
force.

"That's a bad cough you've got," said Virginie. "Where-
ever did you catch it ?"

"One never knows !" replied Clémence, wiping her face with
her sleeve. "It must have been the other night. There were
two who were flaying each other outside the 'Grand-Balcony.'
I wanted to see, so I stood there whilst the snow was falling.
Ah, what a drubbing! it was enough to make one die with
laughing. One had her nose almost pulled off; the blood
streamed on the ground. When the other, a great long stick
like me, saw the blood, she slipped away as quick as she could.
And I coughed nearly all night. Besides that, too, men are
so stupid in bed, they don't let you have any clothes over you
half the time."

"Pretty conduct that," murmured Madame Putois. "You're
killing yourself, my girl."

"And if it pleases me to kill myself ! Life isn't so very
amusing. Slaving all the blessed day long to earn fifty-five
sous, cooking one's blood from morning to night in front of the
stove ; no, you know, I've had enough of it ! All the same
though, this cough won't do me the service of making me
croak. It'll go off the same way it came."

A short silence ensued. That good-for-nothing Clémence,
who cocked up her leg the highest and shrieked like a screech-
owl in the low dancing establishments, always saddened every
one with her thoughts of death, whenever she was at the shop.
Gervaise knew her well, and so merely observed,

"You're not lively after you've been on the batter !"

The truth was that Gervaise did not like this talk about
women fighting. Because of the flogging at the wash-house it
annoyed her whenever anyone spoke before her and Virginie of

kicks with wooden shoes and of slaps in the face. It so happened, too, that Virginie was looking at her and smiling.

"Oh!" murmured the tall brunette, "I saw some hair pulled out by the roots yesterday. They were tearing each other to pieces."

"Who?" asked Madame Putois.

"The midwife at the end of the street and her servant, you know, a little blonde. She's a spiteful hussy, that girl! She said to the other, 'Yes, yes, you did the trick for the green-grocer's wife, and I'll go and tell the commissary of police, if you don't pay me.' And she went on about it; you should just have heard her! Then the midwife let fly and gave her one full on the conk. After that the little strumpet flew at her missus, and scratched her face, and pulled out her hair, oh! in grand style. The pork-butcher had to separate them."

The workwomen laughed complacently. Then they all took a sip of coffee, with an air of gluttonous enjoyment.

"Do you believe that about the greengrocer's wife?" asked Clémence.

"Well, it was said so in the neighbourhood," replied Virginie. "I wasn't there, you know. However, it's a part of their trade. They all do it."

"Ah, well!" said Madame Putois, "one's stupid to go to them, and risk being lamed! There's a sovereign way. Every night you must drink a glass of holy water whilst you make the sign of the cross on your stomach three times with your thumb; and it goes off just like wind."

Mother Coupeau, whom the others thought had fallen asleep, protested with a shake of her head. She knew another way, and an infallible one. It consisted in eating a hard boiled egg every two hours, and placing spinach leaves on one's loins. The four other women remained very serious, but that squint-eyed Augustine, whose mirth always got kindled without any-one ever knowing why, gave vent to the cluck-cluck which was her way of laughing. They had forgotten her. Gervaise lifted up the petticoat, and caught sight of her rolling about on the sheet like a young pig, with her legs in the air. She pulled her away, and set her on her legs with a box on the ears. What did she see to laugh at, the fool? She had no business to listen when grown-up people were talking! To begin with, she would just take the washing home to a friend of Madame Lerat's at Batignolles. Whilst speaking, her mistress put the basket on her arm and shoved her towards the door. The

M

squint-eyed one, surly and sobbing, went off dragging her feet
along in the snow.

Meanwhile, mother Coupeau, Madame Putois, and Clémence
were discussing the efficacy of the hard boiled eggs and the
spinach leaves. Then Virginie, who remained thoughtful, with
her glass of coffee in her hand, said, in a very low voice,

"Really, now, one fights and then one makes it up; one
always gets on when one's good-natured."

And, leaning towards Gervaise, she added, with a smile,

"No, truly, I bear you no ill-will. I mean the wash-house
matter, you recollect it?"

The laundress felt dreadfully embarrassed. That was what
she had been fearing. She guessed that the other was about to
speak to her of Lantier and Adèle. The stove roared, an increase of heat issued from the red-hot pipe. In the midst of
the general drowsiness, the workwomen, who made their coffee
last a long while so as to return to their work at the latest
possible moment, watched the snow in the street with greedy
and languishing looks. They were all in a confidential mood;
they related what they would have done if they had had ten
thousand francs a year; they would simply have done nothing
at all, they would have remained like that all day long warming
themselves, spitting at work from a distance. Virginie had
drawn nearer to Gervaise so as not to be heard by the others.
And Gervaise felt herself an awful coward, no doubt because of
the great heat, and so feeble and devoid of courage, that she
could not find strength to turn the conversation; she was even
wanting to hear what the tall brunette had to say, her heart
filled with an emotion which she enjoyed without admitting it.

"I hope I'm not giving you pain," resumed the dressmaker.
"Already it's been twenty times on the tip of my tongue to say
so. However, as we've broached the subject, it's just as well to
talk it over, isn't it? Ah! really now, I don't bear you any ill-
will for what took place. On my word of honour! I bear
you no grudge for it."

She shook the remains of her coffee round in her glass, so as
to get all the sugar, and then drank three drops, making a
slight hissing sound with her lips as she did so. Gervaise, with
a swelling in her throat, still waited, and wondered if Virginie
had really forgiven her the walloping as she pretended she had;
for she noticed some yellow sparks glimmering in her black eyes.
That tall she-devil had probably merely put her rancour into
her pocket and covered it up with her handkerchief.

"It was excusable on your part," continued she. "You had just been treated in a shameful and abominable manner. Oh! I can be just, you know! Had it been me, I'd have taken a knife."

She drank another three drops of her coffee, making the same noise at the edge of the glass. And she dropped her drawling tone of voice, and added quickly, without once stopping:

"And it didn't bring them luck, ah! by Jove, no! very far from it! They went to live, the devil knows where, right away by La Glacière, in a dirty street where there's always mud up to your knees. Two days afterwards, I went off in the morning to lunch with them; it was quite a journey in the omnibus, I can tell you! Well! my dear, I found them already wrangling together. Really, as I entered the room they were coming to blows. There're lovers for you! You know, Adèle isn't worth the rope to hang her. She's my sister, but that doesn't prevent my saying that she's in the skin of a precious dirty strumpet. She's treated me shamefully; it's too long to tell, besides it's a little matter still to be settled between us. As for Lantier, well! you know him, he isn't worth much either. A little gentleman, who pommels you about for a 'yes' or a 'no'! And he has a hard fist when he strikes. So they belaboured each other in all conscience. Whenever one went up the stairs one could hear them knocking each other about. One day, even, the police interfered. Lantier wanted an oil soup, something abominable that they eat in the South; and, as Adèle said it was filthy, they chucked the bottle of oil, the saucepan, the soup-tureen, in fact everything, at one another's heads; in short, there was a row that upset the whole neighbourhood."

She related other awful goings-on that had taken place; there was no end to them; she knew things that would make one's hair stand on end. Gervaise listened to the long story without uttering a word; her face was very pale, and a nervous wrinkle hovered about the corners of her mouth, resembling a faint smile. It was nearly seven years since she had heard any one speak of Lantier. She would never have believed that Lantier's name, whispered thus in her ear, could have caused such a burning sensation in the pit of her stomach. No, she never imagined she had such a curiosity to know what had become of the wretched being who had treated her so shamefully. She could not be jealous of Adèle now; but she laughed inwardly all the same at the couple's squabbles. She could fancy she saw the girl's body covered with bruises, and it avenged her, and amused her. She could have stayed there till the morrow listening to Virginie's reports. She asked no questions, because she would not appear to be interested to that extent. It was as though some one had abruptly filled up a great gap for her; at that moment, her past joined closely on to her present.

Virginie ended by burying her nose in her glass, as she sucked up the sugar, half closing her eyes the while. Then, Gervaise, understanding that she ought to say something, assumed an air of indifference and asked :

"Are they still living at La Glacière ?"

"Oh, no !" replied the other ; "didn't I tell you ? For the last week they've been living apart. One fine morning Adèle went off with her things, and Lantier didn't run after her, I can assure you."

The laundress uttered a faint cry, and said out loud :

"They're no longer living together !"

"Who aren't ?" asked tall Clémence, interrupting her conversation with mother Coupeau and Madame Putois.

"Oh ! nobody you know," said Virginie.

She watched Gervaise, however, and noticed that she looked strangely moved. She drew nearer, and seemed to find a wicked pleasure in resuming her stories. Then, she abruptly asked her what she would do if Lantier were to come hovering about her ; for, after all, men are such queer beings, and Lantier was quite capable of returning to his first love. Gervaise drew herself up, and spoke very clearly and in a very dignified manner. She was married, she would send Lantier to the right about, that was all. There could never again be anything between them, not even a shake of the hands. She would really be the most heartless of women if she ever looked that man in the face.

"I know very well," said she, "that Etienne is his child, there is a tie there that I cannot sever. If Lantier should wish to kiss Etienne, I would send Etienne to him, because it is impossible to prevent a father from loving his child. But as for myself, look you, Madame Poisson, I would let myself be cut up into tiny bits before I would allow him to touch me with his little finger. It's all over."

As she uttered these last words, she made the sign of the cross in the air, as though to seal her oath for evermore. And, desirous of putting an end to the conversation, she seemed to rouse up with a start, and called to the workwomen :

"I say, you there ! do you think the clothes will iron themselves ? What lazybones ! Gee up ! to work !"

The workwomen did not hurry themselves; they were benumbed by a fit of laziness, their arms were lying idly on their laps, whilst with one hand they still held their glasses, in which only the dregs of the coffee remained. They continued conversing.

"It was little Célestine," Clémence was saying. "I knew her. She was mad about cats' hairs. You know, she saw cats' hairs everywhere; she was always turning her tongue about like this, because she thought her mouth was full of them."

"One of my friends," observed Madame Putois, "was a woman who had a worm. Oh! those animals have all sorts of caprices! It used to wriggle about in her stomach if she didn't give it chicken to eat. Just fancy, the husband earned seven francs a day, and all the money went in delicacies for the worm."

"I could have cured her at once, I could," interrupted mother Coupeau. "Why! yes, all one has to do is to swallow a grilled mouse. It poisons the worm on the instant."

Gervaise herself had again lapsed into a happy idleness. But she shook herself and rose to her feet. Ah, well! there was an afternoon wasted in gossip! That would not help to fill her purse! She returned the first to her curtains, but she found them stained with coffee; and before resuming her ironing, she was obliged to rub the stain with a damp rag. The workwomen stretched themselves before the stove, and surlily looked for their iron-holders. The moment Clémence moved, she was seized with another fit of coughing, which almost caused her to vomit her tongue; then she finished her shirt, and pinned the collar and cuffs. Madame Putois had returned to her petticoat.

"Well! good-bye," said Virginie. "I only came out to get a quarter of a pound of Gruyere cheese. Poisson must be thinking that I've got frozen on the way."

But when she had gone a couple of steps along the pavement, she opened the door again to say that she saw Augustine at the end of the street, sliding over the ice with some urchins. It was a good two hours since the young hussy had started on her errand. She came running up, quite red in the face, and all out of breath, with her basket on her arm, and her chignon smothered with a snowball; and she submitted to their scolding with a sly look, excusing herself by saying that it was almost impossible to walk on account of the frost. Some ragamuffin had probably stuffed some bits of ice into her pockets for a joke, for at the end of a quarter of an hour the latter commenced watering the shop like a couple of funnels.

At that period all the afternoons were passed in the same

way. The shop was the refuge of all the chilly people of the
neighbourhood. Every one in the Rue de la Goutte-d'Or knew
that it was warm inside there. It was constantly full of
cackling women, who enjoyed the heat from the stove as they
stood in front of it with their skirts tucked up to their knees.
Gervaise took a certain pride in that generous warmth, and she
attracted the people there, and held receptions, as the Lorilleux
and the Boches spitefully remarked. The truth was that she
was obliging and charitable, to the point of calling in the poor
whenever she saw them shivering outside. She felt an
especial friendship for an old journeyman painter, an old man
of seventy, who lived in one of the lofts of the house, where he
was slowly dying of hunger and cold. He had lost his three
sons in the Crimea, and had been existing as best he could
during the two years that had passed since he had last been
able to hold a paint-brush. The moment Gervaise beheld old
Bru stamping about in the snow to warm himself, she would
call him in, and make a little place for him near the stove; she
even often forced him to eat a piece of bread and cheese. Old
Bru, with his stooping body, his white beard, and his face as
wrinkled as an old apple, would remain there for hours without
uttering a word, listening to the noise made by the burning
coke. Perhaps he was recalling his fifty years of work on
ladders, the half century spent in painting doors and white-
washing ceilings in all quarters of Paris.

"Well! old Bru," the laundress would sometimes ask, "what
are you thinking of?"

"Nothing in particular, all sorts of things," he would reply
with a bewildered air.

The workwomen chaffed him, saying that he was in love.
But he, without hearing them, relapsed into silence, and resumed
his mournful and absorbed attitude.

From that afternoon Virginie frequently spoke to Gervaise of
Lantier. She seemed to find amusement in filling her mind
with ideas of her old lover just for the pleasure of embarrassing
her by making suggestions. One day she related that she had
met him; then, as the laundress took no notice, she said nothing further, and it was only on the morrow that she added he
had spoken about her for a long time, and with a great show of
affection. Gervaise was much upset by these reports, whispered
in her ear in a corner of the shop. The mention of Lantier's
name always caused a burning sensation in the pit of her
stomach. She certainly thought herself strong; she wished to

lead the life of a virtuous woman, because virtue is the half of happiness. So she never considered Coupeau in this matter, having nothing to reproach herself with as regarded her husband, not even in her thoughts. But, with a hesitating and suffering heart, she would think of the blacksmith. It seemed to her that the memory of Lantier—that slow possession which she was resuming—rendered her unfaithful to Goujet, to their unavowed love, sweet as friendship. She passed sad days whenever she felt herself guilty towards her good friend. She would have liked to have had no affection for anyone but him, outside of her family. It was a feeling far above all carnal thoughts, for the signs of which upon her burning face Virginie was ever on the watch.

As soon as spring came, Gervaise went and sought refuge beside Goujet. She could no longer sit musing on a chair without immediately thinking of her first lover; she pictured him leaving Adèle, packing his clothes in the bottom of their old trunk, and returning to her with the trunk outside a cab. The days when she went out, she was seized with the most foolish fears in the street; she was ever thinking she heard Lantier's footsteps behind her. She did not dare turn round, but tremblingly fancied she felt his hands seizing her round the waist. He was, no doubt, spying upon her; he would appear before her some afternoon; and the bare idea threw her into a cold perspiration, because he would to a certainty kiss her on the ear, as he used to do in former days solely to tease her. It was this kiss which frightened her; it rendered her deaf beforehand; it filled her with a buzzing amidst which she could only distinguish the sound of her heart beating violently. So, as soon as these fears seized upon her, the forge was her only shelter; there, under Goujet's protection, she once more became easy and smiling, as his sonorous hammer drove away her disagreeable reflections.

What a happy time! The laundress took particular pains with the washing of her customer in the Rue des Portes-Blanches; she always took it home herself, because that errand, every Friday, was a ready excuse for passing through the Rue Marcadet and looking in at the forge. The moment she turned the corner of the street, she felt light and gay, as though, in the midst of those plots of waste land surrounded by grey factories, she were out in the country; the roadway black with coal-dust, the plumage of steam over the roofs amused her as much as a moss-covered path leading through masses of green foliage

in a wood in the environs; and she loved the dull horizon,
streaked by the tall factory-chimneys, the Montmartre heights,
which hid the heavens from view, the chalky white houses
pierced with the uniform openings of their windows.   She
would slacken her steps as she drew near, jumping over the
pools of water, and finding a pleasure in traversing the deserted
inns and outs of the yard full of old building materials.   Right
at the further end the forge shone with a brilliant light, even
at mid-day.   Her heart leapt with the dance of the hammers.
When she entered, her face turned quite red, the little fair hairs
at the nape of her neck flew about like those of a woman
arriving at some lovers' meeting.   Goujet was expecting her,
his arms and chest bare, whilst he hammered harder on the
anvil on those days so as to make himself heard at a distance.
He divined her presence, and greeted her with a good silent
laugh in his yellow beard.   But she would not let him leave off
his work; she begged him to take up his hammer again,
because she loved him the more when he wielded it with his
big arms swollen with muscles.   She would go and give
Etienne a gentle tap on the cheek, as he hung on to the
bellows, and remain there for an hour, watching the rivets.

The two did not exchange a dozen words.   They could not
have more completely satisfied their love if alone in a room
with the door double-locked.   The chuckles of Salted-Mouth,
otherwise Drink-without-Thirst, did not bother them much, for
they no longer even heard them.   At the end of a quarter of
an hour she would begin to feel slightly oppressed; the heat,
the powerful smell, the ascending smoke, made her dizzy,
whilst the dull thuds of the hammers shook her from the crown
of her head to the soles of her feet.   Then she desired nothing
more; it was her pleasure.   Had Goujet pressed her in his
arms, it would not have procured her so sweet an emotion.   She
drew close to him that she might feel the wind raised by his
hammer beat upon her cheek, and become, as it were, a part of
the blow he struck.   When the sparks made her soft hands
smart, she did not withdraw them; on the contrary, she enjoyed
that rain of fire which stung her skin.   He, for certain, divined
the happiness which she tasted there; he always kept the most
difficult work for the Fridays, so as to pay his court to her with
all his strength and all his skill; he no longer spared himself,
at the risk of splitting the anvils in two, as he panted and his
loins vibrated with the joy he was procuring her.   All one
spring-time their love thus filled the forge with the rumbling of

a storm. It was an idyl amongst giant-like labour, in the midst of the glare of the coal fire, and of the shaking of the shed, the cracking carcass of which was black with soot. All that beaten iron, kneaded like red wax, preserved the rough marks of their love. When, on the Fridays, the laundress parted from Golden-Mug, she slowly reascended the Rue des Poissonniers, contented and tired, her mind and her body alike tranquil.

Little by little, her fear of Lantier diminished; her good sense got the better of her. At that time she would still have led a very happy life, had it not been for Coupeau, who was decidedly going to the bad. One day she just happened to be returning from the forge, when she fancied she recognised Coupeau inside old Colombe's "Assommoir," in the act of treating himself to some goes of "vitriol" in company of My-Boots, Bibi-the-Smoker, and Salted-Mouth, otherwise Drink-without-Thirst. She passed quickly by, so as not to seem to be spying on them. But she glanced back; it was indeed Coupeau who was tossing his little glass of bad brandy down his throat with a gesture already familiar. He lied then; so he went in for brandy now! She returned home in despair; all her old dread of brandy took possession of her. She forgave the wine, because wine nourishes the workman; all kinds of spirit, on the contrary, were filth, poisons which destroyed in the workman the taste for bread. Ah! the government ought to prevent the manufacture of such horrid stuff!

On arriving at the Rue de la Goutte-d'Or, she found the whole house upset. Her workwomen had left the shop, and were in the courtyard looking up above. She questioned Clémence.

"It's old Bijard who's giving his wife a hiding," replied the ironer. "He was in the doorway, as drunk as a trooper, watching for her return from the wash-house. He whacked her up the stairs, and now he's finishing her off up there in their room. Listen, can't you hear her shrieks?"

Gervaise hastened to the spot. She felt some friendship for her washerwoman, Madame Bijard, who was a very courageous woman. She hoped to put a stop to what was going on. Up-stairs, on the sixth floor, the door of the room was wide open, some lodgers were shouting on the landing, whilst Madame Boche, standing in front of the door, was calling out:

"Will you leave off? I shall send for the police; do you hear?"

No one dared to venture inside the room, because it was known that Bijard was like a brute beast when he was drunk. As a matter of fact, he was scarcely ever sober. The rare days on which he worked, he placed a bottle of brandy beside his locksmith's vice, gulping some of it down every half hour. He could not keep himself going any other way. He would have blazed away like a torch if anyone had placed a lighted match close to his mouth.

"But we mustn't let her be murdered!" said Gervaise, all in a tremble.

And she entered. The room, an attic, and very clean, was bare and cold, almost emptied by the drunken habits of the man, who took the very sheets from the bed to turn them into liquor. During the struggle, the table had rolled away to the window, the two chairs knocked over had fallen with their legs in the air. In the middle of the room, on the tiled floor, lay Madame Bijard, all bloody, her skirts still soaked with the water of the wash-house clinging to her thighs, her hair pulled out by the roots. She was breathing heavily, with a rattle in her throat, as she muttered prolonged ohs! each time she received a blow from the heel of Bijard's boot. He had knocked her down with his fists, and now he stamped upon her.

"Ah, strumpet! ah, strumpet! ah, strumpet!" grunted he, in a choking voice, accompanying each blow with the word, taking a delight in repeating it, and striking all the harder the more he found his voice failing him.

Then, when he could no longer speak, he madly continued to kick with a dull sound, rigid in his ragged blue blouse and over-alls, his face turned purple beneath his dirty beard, and his bald forehead streaked with big red blotches. The neighbours on the landing related that he was beating her because she had refused him twenty sous in the morning. Boche's voice was heard at the foot of the staircase. He was calling Madame Boche, saying:

"Come down; let 'em kill each other, it'll be so much scum the less."

Meanwhile, old Bru had followed Gervaise into the room. Between them, they were trying to bring the locksmith to reason, and to get him towards the door. But he turned round, speechless, and foaming at the lips, and in his pale eyes the alcohol was blazing with a murderous glare. The laundress had her wrist injured; the old workman was knocked on to the table. On the floor, Madame Bijard was breathing with greater

BIJARD, THE DRUNKEN LOCKSMITH, MURDERING HIS WIFE.

p. 186.

difficulty, her mouth wide open, her eyes closed. Now, Bijard kept missing her. He had madly returned to the attack, but, blinded by rage, his blows fell on either side, and at times he was taken in by kicks which he sent into space. And, during all this onslaught, Gervaise beheld in a corner of the room little Lalie, then four years old, watching her father murdering her mother. The child held in her arms, as though to protect her, her sister, Henriette, only recently weaned. She was standing up, her head covered with a cotton cap, her face very pale and grave. Her large black eyes gazed with a fixedness full of thought, and were without a tear.

When at length Bijard, encountering a chair, stumbled on to the tiled floor, where they left him snoring, old Bru helped Gervaise to raise up Madame Bijard. The latter was now sobbing bitterly; and Lalie, drawing near, watched her crying, being used to such sights, and already resigned to them. As the laundress descended the stairs, in the silence of the now quieted house, she kept seeing before her that look of this child of four, as grave and courageous as that of a woman.

"Monsieur Coupeau is on the other side of the way," called out Clémence, as soon as she caught sight of her. "He looks awfully screwed."

Coupeau was just then crossing the street. He almost smashed a pane of glass with his shoulder as he missed the door. He was in a state of complete drunkenness, with his teeth clinched and his nose inflamed. And Gervaise at once recognised the "vitriol" of the "Assommoir" in the poisoned blood which paled his skin. She tried to joke and get him to bed, the same as on the days when the wine had made him merry; but he pushed her aside, without opening his lips, and raised his fist in passing as he went to bed of his own accord. He was like the other—the drunkard who was snoring upstairs —tired out by the blows he had struck. A cold shiver passed over her. She thought of the men she knew—of her husband, of Goujet, of Lantier—her heart breaking, despairing of ever being happy.

CHAPTER VII.

GERVAISE'S saint's day fell on the 19th of June. On such occasions, the Coupeaus always made a grand display; they feasted till they were as round as balls, and their stomachs were filled for the rest of the week. There was a complete clear-out of all the money they had. The moment there was a trifle in the house, it went in gorging. They invented saints for those days which the almanac had not provided with any, just for the sake of giving themselves a pretext for gormandizing. Virginie highly commended Gervaise for stuffing herself with all sorts of savoury dishes. When one has a husband who turns all he can lay hands on into drink, it's good to line one's stomach well, and not to let everything go off in liquids. As the money was bound to go, it might just as well go to the butcher as to the publican. And Gervaise, fond of good living, abandoned herself to that excuse. So much the worse! It was Coupeau's fault if they no longer even saved a liard. She had grown fatter still, she limped more than ever, because her leg, swollen with fat, seemed to grow shorter at the same time.

That year, they talked about her saint's day a good month beforehand. They thought of dishes, and smacked their lips in advance. All the shop had a confounded longing to junket. They wanted a merry-making of the right sort—something out of the common, and highly successful. One does not have so many opportunities for enjoyment. What most troubled the laundress was to decide who to invite: she wished to have twelve persons at table, no more, no less. She, her husband, mother Coupeau, and Madame Lerat, already made four members of the family. She would also have the Goujets and the Poissons. Originally, she had decided not to invite her work-women, Madame Putois and Clémence, so as not to make them too familiar; but, as the projected feast was being constantly spoken of in their presence, and their mouths watered, she ended by telling them to come. Four and four, eight, and two made ten. Then, wishing particularly to have twelve, she became reconciled with the Lorilleux, who, for some time past, had been hovering round her; at least, it was agreed that the Lorilleux should come to dinner, and that peace should be made glass in hand. One certainly cannot remain for ever on ill terms with one's relations. Moreover, the thought of the anniversary moved all hearts. It was an opportunity not to be allowed to slip by. Only, when the Boches heard of the projected reconciliation, they at once made up to Gervaise, with a great show of politeness and most obliging smiles, and it became necessary to beg them also to join the festive board. Thus, they would be fourteen, without counting the children. Never before had she given such a dinner; she felt quite scared in the midst of her glory.

The saint's day happened to fall on a Monday. It was a piece of luck. Gervaise counted on the Sunday afternoon to begin the cooking. On the Saturday, whilst the workwomen hurried on their work, there was a long discussion in the shop with the view of finally deciding upon what the feast should consist of. For three weeks past one thing alone had been chosen —a fat roast goose. There was a gluttonous look on every face whenever it was mentioned. The goose was even already bought. Mother Coupeau went and fetched it to let Clémence and Madame Putois feel its weight. And they uttered all kinds of exclamations; it looked such an enormous bird, with its rough skin all swelled out with yellow fat.

"Before that, there will be the pot-au-feu," said Gervaise, "the soup and just a small piece of the boiled beef, it's always good. Then we must have something in the way of a stew."

Tall Clémence suggested rabbit, but they were always having that, everyone was sick of it. Gervaise wanted something more distinguished. Madame Putois having spoken of stewed veal, they looked at one another with an expansive smile. It was a real idea, nothing would look better than a veal stew.

"And after that," resumed Gervaise, "we must have some other dish with a sauce."

Mother Coupeau proposed fish. But the others made a grimace, as they banged down their irons. None of them liked fish, it was not a bit satisfying; and, besides that, it was full of bones. Squint-eyed Augustine having dared to observe that she liked skate, Clémence shut her mouth for her with a good sound clout. At length, the mistress thought of stewed pig's

back and potatoes, which restored the smiles to every countenance, when Virginie entered like a puff of wind, with a strange
look on her face.

" You come just at the right time ! " exclaimed Gervaise.
" Mamma Coupeau, do show her the bird."

And mother Coupeau went a second time and fetched the
goose, which Virginie had to take in her hands. She uttered no
end of exclamations. By Jove ! it was heavy ! But she soon
laid it down on the work-table, between a petticoat and a
bundle of shirts. Her thoughts were elsewhere. She dragged
Gervaise into the back room.

"I say, little one," murmured she rapidly, "I've come to
warn you. You'll never guess who I just met at the corner of
the street. Lantier, my dear ! He's hovering about on the
watch ; so I hastened here at once. It frightened me on your
account, you know."

The laundress turned quite pale. What could the wretched
man want with her ? Coming, too, like that, just in the midst
of the preparations for the feast. She had never had any luck ;
she could not even be allowed to enjoy herself quietly. But
Virginie replied, that she was very foolish to put herself out
about it like that. Why ! if Lantier dared to follow her about,
all she had to do was to call a policeman and have him locked
up. For a month past, ever since her husband had been
admitted into the police force, the tall brunette had assumed
most cavalier ways, and was always talking of having people
arrested. As she raised her voice whilst she uttered the wish
that some one might accost her in the street, to give her the
opportunity of dragging the scoundrel to the station-house and
handing him over to Poisson, Gervaise, by a sign, begged her
to leave off, because the workwomen were listening. The
laundress returned the first to the shop, and resumed, with a
great pretence of calmness :

"After that, there must be a vegetable."

"What do you say to green peas with a little fat bacon ? "
asked Virginie. " That's what I'd have."

"Yes, yes, green peas and bacon ! " approved all the others,
whilst Augustine enthusiastically rammed the poker into the
stove.

By three o'clock on the morrow, Sunday, mother Coupeau
had lighted their two stoves, and also a third one of earthenware which they had borrowed of the Boches. At half-past
three the pot-au-feu was boiling away in an enormous earthen-

ware-pot lent by the eating-house keeper next door, the family pot having been found too small. It had been decided to cook the stewed veal and the pig's back beforehand, because those dishes are best warmed up; only, they would not thicken the sauce for the veal until just at the dinner hour. There would still be quite enough to do on the Monday—the soup, the green peas and bacon, and the goose to roast. The room at the back was quite lighted up by the three fires; brown sauces were simmering in the stew-pans with a strong smell of burnt flour; whilst the enormous earthenware-pot was emitting jets of steam like a boiler, and grave, deep gurglings were shaking its sides. Mother Coupeau and Gervaise, each with a white apron tied in front of her, were all over the room in their haste in picking parsley, in running after pepper and salt, and in stirring the meat about with a wooden spoon. They had turned Coupeau out, so that he should not be in their way. But all the same they had people bothering them throughout the afternoon. The cooking smelt so nice in the house, that the neighbours came down one after the other, looking in under all sorts of pretences, but solely to find out what it consisted of; and they stood waiting there so long that the laundress was obliged to take the lids off the saucepans.

Then, Virginie put in an appearance towards five o'clock. She had again seen Lantier; really, it was impossible to go down the street now without meeting him. Madame Boche also had just caught sight of him standing at the corner of the pavement, with his head thrust forward in an uncommonly sly manner. Then Gervaise, who had at that moment intended going for a sou's worth of burnt onions for the pot-au-feu, began to tremble from head to foot and did not dare leave the house; the more so, as the doorkeeper and the dressmaker put her into a terrible fright by relating horrible stories of men waiting for women with knives and pistols hidden beneath their overcoats. Well, yes! one reads of such things every day in the newspapers. When one of those scoundrels gets his monkey up, on discovering an old love leading a happy life, he becomes capable of everything. Virginie obligingly offered to run and fetch the burnt onions. Women should always help one another, they could not let that little thing be murdered. When she returned, she said that Lantier was no longer there; he had probably gone off on finding he was discovered. In spite of that, though, he was the subject of conversation around the saucepans until night-time. Madame Boche having suggested that Coupeau

should be informed of what was going on, Gervaise was overcome with a great fear and implored her never to say a word
on the subject. Ah! it could only lead to great unpleasantness! Her husband probably already had some suspicions, as,
for some days past, he had taken to swearing and striking his
fist against the wall on getting into bed. Her hands trembled
at the idea that two men might kill each other for her; she
knew Coupeau, he was so jealous, he was capable of attacking
Lantier with his shears. And whilst all four became absorbed
in this drama, the sauces simmered gently on the stoves filled
with coke; each time mother Coupeau took the lids off the
stewed veal and the pig's back, there issued a faint sound, a
discreet murmur; the pot-au-feu continued the noise resembling
the snore of a chorister asleep on his back in the sunshine.
They ended by each having a cupful of the broth, just by way
of tasting it.

At length the Monday arrived. Now that Gervaise was going
to have fourteen persons at table, she began to fear that she would
not be able to find room for them all. She decided that they
should dine in the shop; and the first thing in the morning, she
took measurements so as to settle which way she should
place the table. After that, they had to remove all the clothes,
and take the ironing-table to pieces; the top of this laid on to
some shorter trestles was to be the dining-table. But, just in
the midst of all this moving, a customer appeared and made a
scene because she had been waiting for her washing ever since
the Friday; they were humbugging her, she would have her
things at once. Then, Gervaise tried to excuse herself and lied
boldly; it was not her fault, she was cleaning out her shop,
the workwomen would not be there till the morrow; and she
pacified her customer, and got rid of her by promising to busy
herself with her things at the earliest possible moment. Then,
when this person had gone, she burst out into bad language.
It was true, if one listened to one's customers, one would not
even take sufficient time to eat; one would work oneself to death
just to please them! Yet, one was not a dog chained up!
Ah, well! even if the Grand Turk in person were to bring her a
collar, even if it were a question of earning a hundred thousand
francs, she would not handle an iron on that Monday, because
it was at last her turn to enjoy herself a little.

The entire morning was spent in completing the purchases.
Three times Gervaise went out and returned laden like a mule.
But, just as she was going to order the wine, she noticed that

she had not sufficient money left. She could easily have got it on credit; only, she could not be without money in the house, on account of the thousand little expenses that one is liable to forget. And mother Coupeau and she lamented together in the back-room, as they reckoned that they required at least twenty francs. How could they obtain them, those four pieces of a hundred sous each? Mother Coupeau, who had at one time done the charring for a little actress of the Batignolles theatre, was the first to suggest the pawn-shop. Gervaise laughed with relief. How stupid she was not to have thought of it! She quickly folded her black silk dress up in a towel, which she pinned together. Then she hid the bundle under mother Coupeau's apron, telling her to keep it very flat against her stomach, on account of the neighbours who had no need to know; and she went and watched at the door, to see that the old woman was not followed. But the latter had only gone as far as the charcoal-dealer's, when she called her back.

"Mamma! mamma!"

She made her return to the shop, and, taking her wedding ring off her finger, said:

"Here, put this with it. We shall get all the more."

And when mother Coupeau brought her twenty-five francs, she danced for joy. She would order an extra six bottles of wine, sealed wine to drink with the roast. The Lorilleux would be crushed.

For a fortnight past it had been the Coupeaus' dream to crush the Lorilleux. Was it not true that those sly ones, the man and his wife, a truly pretty couple, shut themselves up whenever they had anything nice to eat, as though they had stolen it? Yes, they covered up the window with a blanket to hide the light, and make believe that they were asleep in bed. Of course that was to prevent people going up and calling on them; and, they stuffed away all alone, they hastened to cram themselves without uttering a word out loud. Even on the morrow, they were too cunning to throw the remains on the dust-heap, because one would have known then what they had had to eat; Madame Lorilleux went to the end of the street and threw them down a sewer opening; one morning Gervaise had caught her there emptying a basket full of oyster-shells. Ah! no, it was quite certain those skinflints were not miserly, and all these artful tricks were indulged in through their mania for wishing to appear poor. Well! one would give them a lesson, and show them that one was not mean. Gervaise

would have laid her table across the street, had she been able
to, just for the sake of inviting each passer-by. Money was not
invented that it should be allowed to grow mouldy, was it? It
is pretty when it shines all new in the sunshine. She resembled
them so little now, that on the days when she had twenty sous
she arranged things to let people think that she had forty.

Mother Coupeau and Gervaise talked of the Lorilleux, whilst
they laid the cloth, as early as three o'clock. They had hung
some big curtains at the windows; but, as it was very warm,
the door was left open, and the whole street passed in front of
the table. The two women did not place a decanter, or a
bottle, or a salt-cellar, without trying to arrange them in such
a way as to annoy the Lorilleux. They had arranged their seats
so as to give them a full view of the superbly laid cloth, and
they had reserved the best crockery for them, well knowing
that the porcelain plates would create a great effect.

"No, no, mamma," cried Gervaise; "don't give them those
napkins! I've two damask ones."

"Ah well!" murmured the old woman; "it'll kill 'em, that's
certain."

And they smiled to each other, as they stood up on either side
of that big white table, on which the fourteen knives and forks,
placed all round, caused them to swell with pride. It had the
appearance of the altar of some chapel in the middle of the
shop.

"That's because they're so stingy themselves!" resumed
Gervaise. "You know, they lied last month, when the woman
went about everywhere saying that she had lost a piece of gold
chain as she was taking the work home. The idea! there's no
fear of her ever losing anything! It was simply a way of making
themselves out very poor, and of not giving you your five
francs."

"As yet, I've only seen my five francs twice," said mother
Coupeau.

"You bet! next month they'll concoct some other story.
That explains why they cover their window up when they have
a rabbit to eat. Don't you see! One would have the right to
say to them: 'As you can afford a rabbit, you can certainly
give five francs to your mother!' Oh! they're full of vice!
What would have become of you if I hadn't taken you to live
with us?"

Mother Coupeau slowly wagged her head. That day she
was all against the Lorilleux, because of the great feast the

Coupeaus were giving. She loved cooking, the little gossipings round the saucepans, the place turned topsy-turvy by the revels of saints' days. Besides, she generally got on pretty well with Gervaise. On other days, when they plagued one another, as happens in all families, the old woman grumbled, saying she was wretchedly unfortunate in thus being at her daughter-in-law's mercy. In point of fact, she probably had some affection for Madame Lorilleux, who, after all, was her daughter.

"Ah!" continued Gervaise, "you wouldn't be so fat, would you, if you were living with them? And no coffee, no snuff, no little luxuries of any sort! Tell me, would they have given you two mattresses to your bed?"

"No, that's very certain," replied mother Coupeau. "When they arrive I shall place myself so as to have a good view of the door, to see the faces they'll make."

The idea of the faces the Lorilleux would make amused them beforehand. But it would not do to stand there looking at the table. The Coupeaus had lunched late, about one o'clock, off something they had had in from the pork-butcher's, because the three stoves were already occupied, and they did not wish to dirty the crockery, all clean for the evening. At four o'clock the two women were at the height of their work. The goose was roasting before a stove placed on the ground against the wall beside the open window; and the bird was so big, they had a difficulty in getting it into the Dutch oven. Squint-eyed Augustine, seated on a foot-stool, and receiving the full reflection of the fire of the stove, was gravely basting the goose with a long-handled spoon. Gervaise was busy with the green peas and bacon. Mother Coupeau, feeling almost crazy in the midst of all these dishes, turned from one to the other as she awaited the time for warming up the pig's back and the stewed veal.

Towards five o'clock the guests began to arrive. First of all came the two workwomen, Clémence and Madame Putois, both in their Sunday best, the former in blue, the latter in black; Clémence carried a geranium, Madame Putois a heliotrope; and Gervaise, whose hands were just then smothered with flour, had to kiss each of them on both cheeks, with her arms behind her back. Then, following close upon their heels, entered Virginie, dressed like a lady in a printed muslin costume with a sash and a bonnet, though she had only a few steps to come. She brought a pot of red carnations. She took the laundress in her big arms and squeezed her tight. At length, Boche

appeared with a pot of pansies, and Madame Boche with a pot
of mignonette; then came Madame Lerat with a balm-mint,
the pot of which had dirtied her violet merino dress. All these
people kissed each other, and gathered together in the back-
room in the midst of the three stoves and the roasting
apparatus, which gave out a stifling heat. The noise from the
saucepans drowned the voices. A dress catching in the Dutch
oven caused quite an emotion. The smell of roast goose was
so strong that it made their mouths water. And Gervaise was
very pleasant, thanking every one for their flowers, without
however letting that interfere with her preparing the thickening for the stewed veal at the bottom of a soup plate. She
had placed the pots in the shop at one end of the table,
without removing the white paper that was round them. A
sweet scent of flowers mingled with the odour of cooking.

"Do you want any assistance?" asked Virginie. "Just
fancy, you've been three days preparing all this feast, and it
will be gobbled up in no time."

"Well! you know," replied Gervaise, "it wouldn't prepare
itself. No, don't dirty your hands. You see, everything's
ready. There's only the soup to warm."

Then they all made themselves at home. The ladies laid
their shawls and their caps on the bed, and pinned up their
skirts, so as not to soil them. Boche, who had sent his wife
back to look after the house until dinner-time, was already
pushing Clémence up into a corner, and asking her if she was
ticklish; whilst Clémence panted and wriggled about, doubling
herself up, her breasts almost bursting through the body of her
dress, for the bare idea of being tickled made her shudder.
The other ladies also came into the shop, so as not to be in the
way of the cooks, and stood up against the wall, looking at the
table; but, as the conversation continued through the open door,
and they were unable to hear each other, they kept returning
back and abruptly invading the room with their loud voices,
surrounding Gervaise, who left off her work to answer them,
with her steaming spoon in her hand. They laughed and said
some rather coarse things. Virginie having stated that she
had eaten nothing for two days, in order to have plenty of
room, that dirty Clémence related something stronger: she
had cleared herself out with a dose of salts, just like the English did. Then Boche gave them a recipe for digesting anything at once, which consisted in squeezing oneself between the
door and the door-post after each plateful; the English also

did that, and it enabled them to gorge for twelve hours at a stretch, without fatiguing their stomachs. Politeness requires one to eat plentifully when one is invited out to dinner. Veal and pork and goose are not put on the table for the cats. Oh! Gervaise could make herself easy; they would clear it all off so cleanly that she would have no need to wash up the crockery on the morrow. And the guests seemed to get up their appetites by sniffing around the saucepans and the Dutch oven. The ladies ended by behaving like little girls; they played at pushing one another about, they ran from one apartment to the other, shaking the floor, stirring up and disseminating the odours of the cooking with their skirts, amidst a deafening uproar, in which their laughter mingled with the noise of mother Coupeau's chopping knife as she minced the bacon.

Just as they were all jumping about and shouting by way of amusement, Goujet appeared. He was so timid he scarcely dared enter, but stood still, holding a tall white rose-tree in his arms, a magnificent plant, with a stem that reached to his face and entangled the flowers in his beard. Gervaise ran to him, her cheeks burning from the heat of the stoves. But he did not know how to get rid of his pot; and, when she had taken it from his hands, he stammered, not daring to kiss her. It was she who was obliged to stand on tip-toe, and place her cheek against his lips; he was so agitated that, even then, he kissed her roughly on the eye, almost blinding her. They both stood trembling.

"Oh! Monsieur Goujet, it's too lovely!" said she, placing the rose-tree beside the other flowers, which it overtopped with the whole of its tuft of foliage.

"Not at all, not at all," repeated he, unable to say anything else.

And, after sighing deeply, he slightly recovered himself, and then stated that she was not to expect his mother; she was suffering from an attack of sciatica. Gervaise was greatly grieved; she talked of putting a piece of the goose on one side, as she particularly wished Madame Goujet to have a taste of the bird. However, no one else was expected. Coupeau was no doubt strolling about in the neighbourhood with Poisson, whom he had called for directly after his lunch; they would be home directly, they had promised to be back punctually at six. Then, as the soup was almost ready, Gervaise called to Madame Lerat, saying that she thought it was time to go and fetch the Lorilleux. Madame Lerat became at once very grave; it was she

who had conducted all the negotiations and who had settled
how everything should pass between the two families. She put
her cap and shawl on again, and went upstairs very stiffly in
her skirts, and looking very stately. Down below, the laundress continued to stir her vermicelli soup without saying a
word. The guests, suddenly become serious, solemnly waited.

It was Madame Lerat who appeared first. She had gone
round by the street, so as to give more pomp to the reconciliation. She held the shop-door wide open, whilst Madame
Lorilleux, wearing a silk dress, stopped at the threshold. All
the guests had risen from their seats; Gervaise went forward,
and, kissing her sister-in-law as had been agreed, said:

"Come in. It's all over, isn't it? We'll both be nice to
each other."

And Madame Lorilleux replied:

"I shall be only too happy if we're so always."

When she had entered, Lorilleux also stopped at the threshold, and he likewise waited to be embraced before penetrating
into the shop. Neither the one nor the other had brought a bouquet. They had decided not to do so, as they thought it would
look too much like giving way to the Hobbler if they carried
flowers with them the first time they set foot in her home.
Gervaise called to Augustine to bring two bottles of wine.
Then, filling some glasses on a corner of the table, she called
every one to her. And each took a glass, and drank to the
good friendship of the family. There was a pause whilst the
guests were drinking, the ladies raising their elbows, and emptying their glasses to the last drop.

"Nothing is better before soup," declared Boche, smacking
his tongue. "It's preferable to a kick behind."

Mother Coupeau had placed herself opposite the door to see
the faces the Lorilleux would make. She pulled Gervaise by
the skirt, and dragged her into the back-room. And as they
both leant over the soup, they conversed rapidly, in a low
voice.

"Eh! what a sight!" said the old woman. "You couldn't
see them; but I was watching. When she caught sight of the
table, her face twisted round like that, the corners of her mouth
almost touched her eyes; and as for him, it nearly choked him,
he coughed, and coughed. Now, just look at them over there;
they've no saliva left in their mouths, they're chewing their lips."

"It's quite painful to see people as jealous as that," murmured
Gervaise.

Really, the Lorilleux had a funny look about them. No one, of course, likes to be crushed; in families, especially, when the one succeeds, the others do not like it; that is only natural. Only, one keeps it in, one does not make an exhibition of oneself. Well! the Lorilleux could not keep it in. It was more than a match for them. They squinted—their mouths were all on one side. In short, it was so apparent, that the other guests looked at them, and asked them if they were unwell. They would never be able to stomach the table, with its fourteen knives and forks, its white tablecloth and napkins, and its slices of bread cut beforehand. One could have thought oneself in a restaurant on the Boulevards. Madame Lorilleux walked right round, holding her head down, so as not to see the flowers, and she slyly felt the big tablecloth, tormented by the thought that it was a new one.

"Everything's ready!" cried Gervaise, as she reappeared, with a smile, her arms bare, and her little fair curls blowing over her temples.

The guests were shuffling about round the table. All were hungry, and they gaped slightly, with a bored air.

"If the governor would only come," resumed the laundress, "we might begin."

"Ah, well!" said Madame Lorilleux, "the soup has time to get cold. Coupeau always forgets. You shouldn't have let him go off."

It was already half-past six. Everything was burning now; the goose would be overdone. Then Gervaise, feeling quite dejected, talked of sending some one to all the wine-shops in the neighbourhood to discover Coupeau. And, as Goujet offered to go, she decided to accompany him. Virginie, anxious about her husband, went also. The three of them, bareheaded, quite blocked up the pavement. The blacksmith, who wore his frock-coat, had Gervaise on his left arm and Virginie on his right: he was doing the two-handled basket, as he said; and it seemed to them such a funny thing to say, that they stopped, unable to move their legs for laughing. They looked at themselves in the pork-butcher's glass, and laughed more than ever. Beside Goujet, all in black, the two women seemed a couple of speckled courtesans—the dressmaker in her muslin costume, sprinkled with pink flowers, the laundress in her white cambric dress, with blue spots, her wrists bare, and wearing round her neck a little grey silk scarf tied in a bow. People turned round to see them pass, looking so fresh and lively, dressed in their Sunday

best on a week day, and jostling the crowd which hung about
the Rue des Poissonniers, on that warm June evening.   But it
was not a question of amusing themselves.   They went straight
to the door of each wine-shop, looked in, and sought amongst
the people standing before the counter.   Had that animal,
Coupeau, gone to the Arc de Triomphe to get his dram?   They
had already done the upper part of the street, looking in at all
the likely places ; at the " Little Civet," renowned for its preserved plums ; at old mother Baquet's, who sold Orleans wine
at eight sous ; at the " Butterfly," the coachmen's house of call,
gentlemen who were not easy to please.   But no Coupeau.
Then, as they were going down towards the Boulevard, Gervaise
uttered a faint cry on passing the eating-house at the corner,
kept by François.

" What's the matter?" asked Goujet.

The laundress no longer laughed.   She was very pale, and
labouring under so great an emotion that she had almost fallen.
Virginie understood it all, as she caught a sight of Lantier,
seated at one of François's tables, quietly dining.   The two
women dragged the blacksmith along.

" My foot twisted," said Gervaise, as soon as she was able to
speak.

At length, they discovered Coupeau and Poisson at the bottom of the street, inside old Colombe's "Assommoir."   They
were standing up, in the midst of a number of men ; Coupeau,
in a grey blouse, was shouting, with furious gestures, and banging his fists down on the counter.   Poisson, not on duty that
day, and buttoned up in an old brown coat, was listening to him
in a dull sort of way, and without uttering a word, bristling his
carroty moustache and imperial the while.   Goujet left the
women on the edge of the pavement, and went and laid his hand
on the zinc-worker's shoulder.   But when the latter caught sight
of Gervaise and Virginie outside, he grew angry   Why was he
badgered with such females as those?   Petticoats had taken to
tracking him about now!   Well! he declined to stir, they
could go and eat their beastly dinner all by themselves.   To
quiet him, Goujet was obliged to accept a drop of something ;
and even then Coupeau took a fiendish delight in dawdling a
good five minutes at the counter.   When he at length came
out, he said to his wife :

" It doesn't suit me.   I'm going to stay where I've business,
do you hear?"

She did not answer.   She was all in a tremble.   She had

probably been talking of Lantier with Virginie, for the latter pushed her husband and Goujet, telling them to walk on in front. Then the two women placed themselves on either side of the zinc-worker, so as to occupy him, and prevent him from seeing. He was only slightly on, more bewildered with having shouted than with drink. As they seemed to wish to go along the left hand pavement, he jostled them, and crossed over to the other side of the street, just for the sake of teasing them. They ran after him in a great fright, and tried to hide the view at François's door. But Coupeau must have known that Lantier was there. Gervaise almost went out of her senses on hearing him grunt:

"Yes, my duck, there's a young fellow of our acquaintance inside there! You mustn't take me for a ninny. Don't let me catch you gallivanting about again with your side glances!"

And he made use of some very coarse expressions. It was not him that she had come to look for, with her bare elbows and her mealy mouth; it was her old beau. Then he was suddenly seized with a mad rage against Lantier. Ah! the brigand! ah! the filthy hound! One or the other of them would have to be left on the pavement, emptied of his guts like a rabbit. Lantier, however, did not appear to notice what was going on, and continued slowly eating some veal and sorrel. A crowd began to form. Virginie led Coupeau away, and he calmed down at once as soon as he had turned the corner of the street. All the same, they returned to the shop far less lively than when they left it.

The guests were waiting round the table with very long faces. The zinc-worker shook hands with them, showing himself off before the ladies. Gervaise, feeling rather dejected, spoke in a low tone, as she directed them to their places. But she suddenly noticed that, Madame Goujet not having come, a seat would remain empty—the one next to Madame Lorilleux.

"We are thirteen!" said she, deeply affected, seeing in that a fresh proof of the misfortune with which she had felt herself threatened for some time past.

The ladies, already seated, rose up, looking anxious and annoyed. Madame Putois offered to retire, because, according to her, it was not a matter to laugh about; besides, she would not touch a thing, the food would do her no good. As to Boche, he chuckled. He would sooner be thirteen than fourteen; the portions would be larger, that was all.

"Wait!" resumed Gervaise. "I can manage it."

And going out on to the pavement, she called old Bru, who was just then crossing the roadway. The old workman entered, stooping and stiff, and his face without expression.

"Seat yourself there, my good fellow," said the laundress. "You won't mind eating with us, will you?"

He simply nodded his head. He was willing; he did not mind.

"As well him as another," continued she, lowering her voice. "He doesn't often eat his fill. He will, at least, enjoy himself once more. We shall feel no remorse in stuffing ourselves now."

Goujet was so moved that the tears came to his eyes. The others pitied the old man, thought it very nice, adding that it would bring luck to them all. However, Madame Lorilleux did not seem pleased at being next to the old fellow; she drew away from him, casting glances at his horny hands, and at his patched and discoloured blouse. Old Bru sat with bowed head, embarrassed above all by the napkin which hid the plate before him. He ended by lifting it off, and placed it gently on the edge of the table, without dreaming of putting it over his knees.

At length, Gervaise served the vermicelli soup; the guests were taking up their spoons, when Virginie remarked that Coupeau had again disappeared. He had perhaps returned to old Colombe's. But the company got angry. This time, so much the worse! one would not run after him; he could stay in the street if he was not hungry; and, as the spoons touched the bottom of the plates, Coupeau reappeared with two pots of flowers, one under each arm, a stock and a balsam. They all clapped their hands. He gallantly placed his pots, one on the right, the other on the left of Gervaise's glass; then, bending over and kissing her, he said:

"I had forgotten you, ducky. But in spite of that, we love each other all the same, on such a day as this."

"Monsieur Coupeau's very nice this evening," murmured Clémence in Boche's ear. "He's just got what he required, sufficient to make him amiable."

The governor's nice behaviour restored the gaiety of the proceedings, which at one moment had been compromised. Gervaise, once more at her ease, was all smiles again. The guests finished their soup. Then the bottles circulated, and they drank their first glass of wine, just a drop, pure, to wash down the vermicelli. One could hear the children quarrelling in the next room. There were Etienne, Pauline, Nana, and little Victor Fauconnier. It had been decided to lay a table

for the four of them, and they had been told to be very good.
That squint-eyed Augustine, who had to look after the stoves,
was to eat off her knees.

"Mamma! mamma!" suddenly screamed Nana, "Augustine
is dipping her bread in the Dutch oven!"

The laundress hastened there and caught the squint-eyed one
in the act of burning her throat, in her attempts to swallow
without loss of time a slice of bread soaked in boiling goose fat.
She boxed her ears, because the young monkey called out that
it was not true. When, after the boiled beef, the stewed veal
appeared, served in a salad-bowl, as they had not got a dish
large enough, the party greeted it with a laugh.

"It's becoming serious," declared Poisson, who spoke but
seldom.

It was half-past seven. They had closed the shop door, so as
not to be spied upon by the whole neighbourhood; the little
clockmaker opposite, especially, was opening his eyes to their
full size, and seemed to take the pieces from their mouths, with
such a gluttonous look, that it almost prevented them from
eating. The curtains hung before the windows admitted a great
white uniform light which bathed the entire table, with its
symmetrical arrangement of knives and forks, and its pots of
flowers enveloped in tall collars of white paper; and this pale
fading light, this slowly approaching dusk, gave to the party
somewhat of an air of distinction. Virginie looked round the
closed apartment hung with muslin, and with a happy criticism
declared it to be pretty. When a cart passed in the street, the
glasses jingled together on the table cloth, and the ladies were
obliged to shout out as loud as the men. But there was not
much conversation; they all behaved very respectably, and
were very attentive to each other. Coupeau alone wore a blouse,
because, as he said, one need not stand on ceremony with
friends, and besides which the blouse was the workman's garb
of honour. The ladies, laced up in their bodices, wore their
hair in plaits greasy with pomatum, in which the daylight was
reflected; whilst the gentlemen, sitting at a distance from the
table, swelled out their chests and kept their elbows wide apart
for fear of staining their frock coats.

Ah! thunder! what a hole they were making in the stewed
veal! If they spoke little, they were chewing in earnest. The
salad-bowl was becoming emptier and emptier, with a spoon
stuck in the midst of the thick sauce—a good yellow sauce
which quivered like a jelly. They fished pieces of veal out of

it, and seemed as though they would never come to the end;
the salad-bowl journeyed from hand to hand, and faces bent
over it as forks picked out the mushrooms. The long loaves
standing against the wall, behind the guests, appeared to melt
away. Between the mouthfuls one could hear the sound of
glasses being replaced on the table. The sauce was a trifle too
salt. It required four quarts to drown that blessed stewed
veal, which went down like cream, but which afterwards lit up
a regular conflagration in one's stomach. And before one had
time to take breath, the pig's back, in the middle of a deep dish,
surrounded by big round potatoes, arrived in the midst of a
cloud of smoke. There was one general cry. By Jove! it was
just the thing! Every one liked it. They would do it justice;
and they followed the dish with a side glance, as they wiped
their knives on their bread, so as to be in readiness. Then, as
soon as they were helped, they nudged one another, and spoke
with their mouths full. Eh! it was just like butter! something sweet and solid which one could feel run through one's
guts right down into one's boots. The potatoes were like sugar.
It was not a bit salt; only, just on account of the potatoes, it
required a wetting every few minutes. Four more quarts were
placed on the table. The plates were wiped so clean that they
also served for the green peas and bacon. Oh! vegetables were
of no consequence. They playfully gulped them down in
spoonfuls. In short, a little greediness, a kind of ladies'
pastime. The best part of the dish was the small pieces of
bacon, just nicely grilled, and smelling like horse's hoof. Two
quarts were sufficient for them.

"Mamma! mamma!" called out Nana suddenly, "Augustine's
putting her fingers in my plate!"

"Don't bother me! give her a slap!" replied Gervaise, in the
act of stuffing herself with green peas.

Nana was at the head of the children in the next room doing
the mistress of the house. She had seated herself beside Victor,
and had placed her brother Etienne next to little Pauline; and
they were playing at being two married couples out for a day's
pleasure. At the beginning Nana had helped her guests very
nicely, with the smiling ways of a grown-up person; but she
had just yielded to her love for bacon, and had kept all the
little pieces for herself. That squint-eyed Augustine, who was
slyly hovering round the children, had taken advantage of the
incident to seize a handful of the bacon, under the pretext of
dividing it properly. Nana, in a rage, bit her wrist.

"Ah! you know," murmured Augustine, "I'll tell your mother that after the veal you asked Victor to kiss you."

But all became quiet again as Gervaise and mother Coupeau went off for the goose. The guests at the big table were leaning back in their chairs taking breath. The men had unbuttoned their waistcoats, the ladies were wiping their faces with their napkins. The repast was, so to say, interrupted ; only one or two persons, unable to keep their jaws still, continued to swallow large mouthfuls of bread, without even knowing that they were doing so. The others were waiting and allowing their food to settle. Night was slowly coming on ; a dirty ashy grey light was gathering behind the curtains. When Augustine brought two lamps and placed one at each end of the table, the general disorder became apparent in the bright glare—the greasy forks and plates, the cloth stained with wine and covered with crumbs. A strong stifling odour pervaded the room. Certain warm fumes, however, attracted all the noses in the direction of the kitchen.

"Can I help you ?" cried Virginie.

She left her chair and passed into the inner room. All the women followed her one by one. They surrounded the Dutch oven, and watched with profound interest Gervaise and mother Coupeau trying to pull the bird out. Then a clamour arose, in the midst of which one could distinguish the shrill voices and the joyful leaps of the children. And there was a triumphal entry. Gervaise carried the goose, her arms stiff, and her perspiring face expanded in one broad silent laugh ; the women walked behind her, laughing in the same way ; whilst Nana, right at the end, raised herself up to see, her eyes open to their full extent. When the enormous golden goose, streaming with gravy, was on the table, they did not attack it at once. It was a wonder, a respectful surprise, which for a moment left every one speechless. They drew one another's attention to it with winks and nods of the head. Golly ! what a lady ! what legs and what a stomach !

"She didn't get fat by licking the walls, I'll bet !" said Boche.

Then they entered into details respecting the bird. Gervaise gave the facts. It was the best she could get at the poulterer's in the Faubourg-Poissonnière ; it weighed twelve pounds and a half in the scales at the charcoal-dealer's ; they had burnt nearly half a bushel of charcoal in cooking it, and it had given three basins full of dripping. Virginie interrupted her to boast

that she had seen the bird raw. One could have eaten it as it
was, she observed, for the skin was so soft and white, a regular
blonde's skin ! All the men laughed in an obscenely gluttonous manner which swelled their lips. Lorilleux and Madame
Lorilleux, however, only bit theirs, and felt ready to choke at
seeing such a goose on the Hobbler's table.

"Well! but we can't eat it whole," the laundress ended by
observing. "Who'll cut it up ? No, no, not me ! It's too
big ; I'm afraid of it."

Coupeau offered his services. Really ! it was very simple.
You caught hold of the limbs, and pulled them off; the pieces
were good all the same. But the others protested ; they
forcibly took possession of the large kitchen knife which the
zinc-worker already held in his hand. Whenever he cut anything up he turned the dish into a regular cemetery. For a
moment they waited for someone to come forward. At length,
Madame Lerat said in a most amiable voice :

"Listen, it should be Monsieur Poisson ; yes, Monsieur
Poisson."

But, as the others did not appear to understand, she added,
in a more flattering manner still :

"Why yes, of course, it should be Monsieur Poisson, who's
accustomed to the use of arms."

And she passed the kitchen knife to the policeman. All
round the table they laughed with pleasure and approval.
Poisson bowed his head with military stiffness, and moved the
goose before him. His neighbours, Gervaise and Madame
Boche, drew further away, so as to leave plenty of room for his
elbows. He carved slowly, with wide gestures, and with his eyes
fixed on the bird, as though to nail it to the dish. When he
thrust the knife into the goose, which cracked, Lorilleux was
seized with an outburst of patriotism.

"Ah ! if it was a Cossack ! " he cried.

"Have you ever fought with Cossacks, Monsieur Poisson ?"
asked Madame Boche.

"No, but I have with Bedouins," replied the policeman, who
was cutting off a wing. "There are no more Cossacks."

A great silence ensued. Necks were stretched out as every
eye followed the knife. Poisson was preparing a surprise.
Suddenly he gave a last cut ; the after part of the bird came
off and stood up on end, the parson's nose in the air : it was
the bishop's mitre. Then admiration burst forth. None were
so agreeable in company as retired soldiers. Meanwhile the

gravy streamed out of the opening in the goose, and Boche smacked his lips.

"I should like it to trickle all that into my mouth," murmured he.

"Oh ! the dirty fellow ! " cried the ladies. "He is dirty !"

"No, I never knew a man more disgusting ! " said Madame Boche, more enraged than the others. "Hold your tongue, will you ? You would disgust an army. You know we're going to eat it ! "

At this moment Clémence persistently repeated in the midst of the noise :

"Monsieur Poisson, listen, Monsieur Poisson. You will save me the parson's nose, won't you ?"

"My dear, the parson's nose is yours by right," said Madame Lerat, in her discreetly smutty way.

However, the goose was now cut up. After letting the party admire the bishop's mitre for some minutes, the policeman laid the pieces down and arranged them round the dish. All was ready to be served ; but the ladies, who were unhooking their dresses, complained of the heat. Coupeau called out that they were at home, that he did not care a button for the neighbours, and he opened the street door wide. The feast continued in the midst of the rumbling of the vehicles and the jostlings of the passers-by. Then, their jaws having had a rest, and some more room being found in their insides, they resumed the dinner, and furiously attacked the goose. Merely waiting and seeing the bird cut up, observed that joker Boche, had sent the stewed veal and the pig's back right down into the calves of his legs.

Then ensued a famous tuck-in ; that is to say, not one of the party recollected ever having before run the risk of such a stomach-ache. Gervaise, looking enormous, her elbows on the table, eat great pieces of the breast, without uttering a word, for fear of losing a mouthful, and merely felt slightly ashamed and annoyed at exhibiting herself thus, as gluttonous as a cat, before Goujet. Goujet, however, was too busy stuffing himself to notice that she was all red with eating. Besides, in spite of her greediness, she remained so nice and good ! She did not speak, but she troubled herself every minute to look after old Bru, and place some dainty bit on his plate. It was even touching to see this glutton take a piece of wing almost from her mouth to give it to the old fellow, who did not appear to be any judge, and who swallowed everything with bowed head, and

bored at having to guttle so much—he whose gizzard had lost
the taste of bread.   The Lorilleux expended their rage on the
roast; they ate enough to last them three days; they would
have stowed away the dish, the table, the very shop, if they
could have ruined the Hobbler by doing so.   All the ladies had
wanted a piece of the breast (the breast is the ladies' part).
Madame Lerat, Madame Boche, Madame Putois, were all picking bones; whilst mother Coupeau, who adored the neck, was
tearing off the flesh with her two last teeth.   Virginie liked the
skin, when it was nicely browned, and the other guests gallantly
passed their's to her; so much so, that Poisson looked at his
wife severely, and bade her stop, because she had had enough
as it was.   Once already, she had been a fortnight in bed, with
her stomach swollen out, through having eaten too much roast
goose.   But Coupeau got angry and helped Virginie to the
upper part of a leg, saying that, by Jove's thunder! if she did
not pick it, she was no woman.   Had roast goose ever done
harm to anybody?   On the contrary, it cured all complaints
of the spleen.   One could eat it without bread, like dessert.
He could go on swallowing it all night without being the least
bit inconvenienced; and, just to show off, he stuffed a whole
drum-stick into his mouth.   Meanwhile, Clémence had got to
the end of her parson's nose, and was sucking it with her lips,
whilst she wriggled with laughter on her chair because Boche
was whispering all sorts of smutty things to her.   Ah, by
Jove! yes, there was a tuck out!   When one's at it, one's at
it, you know; and if one only has the chance now and then,
one would be precious stupid not to stuff oneself up to one's
ears.   Really, one could see their sides puff out by degrees.
The women all looked in the family way.   They were cracking
in their skins, the blessed gormandizers!   With their mouths
open, their chins besmeared with grease, they had such bloated
red faces that one would have said they were bursting with
prosperity.

And the wine, my children! it flowed round the table as
water flows into the Seine.   A regular stream, like when it has
rained and the earth is thirsty.   Coupeau poured it out from
on high to see it froth; and when a bottle was empty, he
turned it upside down, and pressed the neck with the gesture
of a woman milking a cow.   Another dead man with his head
broken!   In a corner of the shop, the heap of dead men
increased, a cemetery of bottles on to which they threw all the
refuse from the table.   Madame Putois, having asked for water,

the zinc-worker indignantly removed all the carafes. Did respectable people drink water? Did she want, then, to breed frogs in her stomach? And tumblerfuls of wine were tossed off; you could hear the liquid shooting down their throats, with the noise of rain-water rushing into the sewers during a storm. It rained a sour wine! a wine which at first had the taste of a stale cask, but to which one soon got accustomed, to such an extent that it ended by having a flavour of nuts.

Ah, ye gods! in spite of what the Jesuits say, grape-juice is, all the same, a famous invention! The guests laughed and applauded; for, after all, the workman could not have lived without wine. Papa Noah must have planted the vine for the zinc-workers, the tailors, and the blacksmiths. Wine cleansed and rested one from work, and put fire into the stomachs of sluggards. Then, when the joker played his tricks on you, well! the king was not your uncle, Paris was yours. With all that, the workman, over-fatigued, penniless, despised by the upper classes, had not many opportunities of enjoying himself, and it was mean to reproach him for an occasional booze, which he went in for merely to get a glimpse of the rosy side of life! At that very moment, for instance, did they care a hang for the Emperor? Perhaps the Emperor himself was also full, but that did not prevent their not caring a hang for him, they defied him to be fuller than they were or to be amusing himself more. To the deuce with the aristocrats! Coupeau sent all the world to blazes. He thought women were prime; he slapped his pocket, in which three sous rattled, laughing as though he had been shovelling up five-franc pieces. Even Goujet, usually so sober, was getting elevated. Boche's eyes were becoming smaller; Lorilleux had a pale look in his; whilst Poisson was rolling glances more and more severe from off his bronzed veteran's face. They were already as drunk as ticks. And the ladies had their touch of it too. Oh, as yet it was but slight, just a glimpse of the wine on their cheeks, with a longing to undress themselves, which caused them to doff their neckerchiefs. Clémence alone was beginning to forget herself. But suddenly Gervaise recollected the six sealed bottles of wine. She had forgotten to put them on the table with the goose; she fetched them, and all the glasses were filled. Then Poisson rose up, and, holding his glass in his hand, said:

"I drink to the health of the missus."

All of them stood up, making a great noise with their chairs

o

as they moved. Holding out their arms, they clinked
in the midst of immense uproar.

"This day fifty years hence!" cried Virginie.

"No, no," replied Gervaise, deeply moved and smiling; "I
shall be too old. Ah! a day comes when one's glad to go."

Through the door, which was wide open, the neighbourhood
was looking on and taking part in the festivities. Passers-by
stopped in the broad ray of light which shone over the pavement, and laughed heartily at seeing all those people stuffing
away so jovially. The coachmen, leaning forward on their
seats, whipping up their jades of horses, glanced in and cracked
a joke as they passed: "I say, aren't you going to stand something? Hallo there! you with the stomach, I'm off for the
midwife!" And the smell of the goose made the whole street
joyful and smiling; the grocer's men fancied they were eating
the bird themselves as they stood on the pavement opposite;
every minute the greengrocer and the tripe-dealer came to
their shop-doors, and sniffed the air as they licked their lips.
The street was positively bursting with indigestion. Mesdames
Cudorge, mother and daughter, who kept the umbrella shop
close by, and, as a rule, were never seen out of doors, crossed
the road one behind the other, casting side-glances, and looking
as red as though they had just been making pancakes. The
little clockmaker, seated at his work-table, could no longer
work, intoxicated with having counted the bottles of wine, and
dreadfully excited in the midst of his merry little clocks.

Yes, the neighbours were devoured with rage and envy! as
Coupeau said. But why should there be any secret made
about the matter? The party, now fairly launched, was no
longer ashamed of being seen at table; on the contrary, it felt
flattered and excited at seeing the crowd gathered there, gaping
with gluttony; it would have liked to have knocked out the
shop-front and dragged the table into the road-way, and there
to have enjoyed the dessert under the very nose of the public,
and amidst the commotion of the thoroughfare. Nothing disgusting was to be seen in them, was there? Then there was
no need to shut themselves in like selfish people. Coupeau,
noticing that the little clockmaker looked very thirsty, held up
a bottle; and, as the other nodded his head, he carried him the
bottle and a glass. A fraternity was established with the
street. They drank to any one who passed. They called in any
chaps who looked the right sort. The feast spread, extending
from one to another, to that degree that the entire neighbour-

hood of the Goutte-d'Or sniffed the grub, and held its stomach, amidst a rumpus worthy of the devil and all his demons. For some minutes, Madame Vigouroux, the charcoal-dealer, had been passing to and fro before the door.

"Hi! Madame Vigouroux! Madame Vigouroux!" yelled the party.

She entered with a broad grin on her washed face, and so fat that the body of her dress was bursting. The men liked pinching her, because they might pinch her all over without ever encountering a bone. Boche made room for her beside him, and at once slyly got hold of her knee beneath the table. But she, being accustomed to that sort of thing, quietly tossed off a glass of wine, and related that all the neighbours were at their windows, and that some of the people of the house were beginning to get angry.

"Oh, that's our business," said Madame Boche. "We're the doorkeepers, aren't we? Well, we're answerable for good order. Let them come and complain to us, we'll receive them in a way they don't expect."

In the backroom there had just been a furious fight between Nana and Augustine, on account of the Dutch oven, which both wanted to scrape out. For a quarter of an hour, the Dutch oven had rebounded over the tiled floor with the noise of an old saucepan. Nana was now nursing little Victor, who had a goose-bone in his throat. She pushed her fingers under his chin, and made him swallow big lumps of sugar by way of a remedy. That did not prevent her keeping an eye on the large table. At every minute she came and asked for wine, bread, or meat, for Etienne and Pauline.

"Here! burst!" her mother would say to her. "Perhaps you'll leave us in peace now!"

The children were scarcely able to swallow any longer, but they continued to stuff all the same, banging their forks down on the table to the tune of a canticle, in order to excite themselves.

In the midst of the noise, however, a conversation was going on between old Bru and mother Coupeau. The old fellow, who was ghastly pale in spite of the wine and the food, was talking of his sons who had died in the Crimea. Ah! if the lads had only lived, he would have had bread to eat every day. But mother Coupeau, speaking thickly, leant towards him and said:

"Ah! one has many worries with children! For instance,

I appear to be happy here, don't I ? Well ! I cry more often than you think. No, don't wish to have children."

Old Bru shook his head.

" I can't get work anywhere," murmured he. " I'm too old. When I enter a workshop the young fellows joke, and ask me if I polished Henri IV.'s boots. Last year, I was still able to earn thirty sous a day at painting a bridge ; I had to remain on my back all the time, with the river flowing beneath. I've coughed ever since then. To-day, it's all over ; they won't have me anywhere."

He looked at his poor stiff hands and added :

" It's easy to understand, I'm no longer good for anything. They're right ; were I in their place I should do the same. You see, the misfortune is that I'm not dead. Yes, it's my fault. One should lie down and croak when one's no longer able to work."

" Really," said Lorilleux, who was listening, " I don't understand why the Government doesn't come to the aid of the invalids of labour. I was reading that in a newspaper the other day."

But Poisson thought it his duty to defend the Government.

" Workmen are not soldiers," declared he. " The Invalides is for soldiers. You must not ask for what is impossible."

The dessert was now served. In the centre of the table was a Savoy cake in the form of a temple, with a dome fluted like a melon ; and this dome was surmounted by an artificial rose, close to which was a silver paper butterfly, fluttering at the end of a wire. Two drops of gum in the centre of the flower imitated dew. Then, to the left, a piece of cream cheese floated in a deep dish ; whilst, in another dish to the right, were piled up some large bruised strawberries, with the juice running from them. However, there was still some salad left, some large coss lettuce leaves soaked with oil.

" Come, Madame Boche," said Gervaise, coaxingly, " a little more salad. I know how fond you are of it."

" No, no, thank you ! I've already had as much as I can manage," replied the doorkeeper.

The laundress turning towards Virginie, the latter put her finger into her mouth, as though to touch the food she had taken.

" Really, I'm full," murmured she. " There's no room left. I couldn't swallow a mouthful."

" Oh ! but if you tried a little," resumed Gervaise with a

smile. "One can always find a tiny corner empty. One doesn't need to be hungry to be able to eat salad. You're surely not going to let this be wasted?"

"You can eat it to-morrow pickled," said Madame Lerat; "it's nicer so."

The ladies puffed as they looked regretfully at the salad-bowl. Clémence related that she had one day eaten three bunches of watercresses at her lunch. Madame Putois could do more than that, she would take a coss lettuce and munch it up with some salt just as it was, without picking it to pieces. They could all have lived on salad, would have treated themselves to tubfuls. And, this conversation aiding, the ladies cleaned out the salad-bowl.

"I could go on all fours in a meadow," observed the door-keeper, with her mouth full.

Then they chuckled together as they eyed the dessert. Dessert did not count. It came rather late, but that did not matter; they would nurse it all the same. Even were they to burst like bomb-shells, they could not allow themselves to be humbugged by cake and strawberries. Besides, there was no hurry; they had plenty of time, all night if they pleased. Meanwhile, they filled their plates with cream cheese and strawberries. The men lit their pipes; and, as the sealed bottles of wine were empty, they returned to the common wine, and drank it as they smoked. But everyone desired that Gervaise should cut the Savoy cake at once. Poisson got up and took the rose, which he very gallantly presented to the lady in whose honour the feast was given, amidst the applause of the whole party. She had to fix it with a pin to the left side of her dress, over her heart. Each movement she made caused the butterfly to flutter about.

"I say!" exclaimed Lorilleux, who had just made a discovery, "but it's your work-table that we're eating off! Ah well! I daresay it's never seen so much work before!"

This malicious joke had a great success. Witty allusions came from all sides. Clémence could not swallow a spoonful of strawberries without saying that it was another shirt ironed; Madame Lerat pretended that the cream cheese smelt of starch; whilst Madame Lorilleux said between her teeth that it was capital fun to gobble up the money so quickly on the very boards on which one had had so much trouble to earn it. There was quite a tempest of shouts and laughter.

But suddenly a loud voice called for silence. It was Boche,

who, standing up in an affected and vulgarly seductive way,
was commencing to sing "The Volcano of Love, or the Seductive Trooper."

"'Tis I, Blavin, seducer of the fair—"

A thunder of applause greeted the first verse. Yes, yes,
they would sing songs! Everyone in turn. It was more
amusing than anything else. And they all put their elbows
on the table, or leant back in their chairs, nodding their heads
at the best parts, and sipping their wine when they came to
the choruses. That rogue Boche had a special gift for comic
songs. He would almost make the water-bottles laugh when
he imitated the raw recruit, with his fingers apart and his hat
on the back of his head. Directly after "The Volcano of
Love," he burst out into "The Baroness de Follebiche," one of
his greatest successes. When he reached the third verse, he
turned towards Clémence and almost murmured in a slow and
voluptuous tone of voice :

> " The baroness had people there,
> Her sisters four, oh ! rare surprise ;
> And three were dark, and one was fair ;
> Between them, eight bewitching eyes. "

Then the whole party, carried away, joined in the chorus.
The men beat time with their heels, whilst the ladies did the
same with their knives against their glasses. All of them
yelled :

> " By Jingo ! who on earth will pay
> A drink to the pa—to the pa—pa—?
> By Jingo ! who on earth will pay
> A drink to the pa—to the pa—tro—o—1 ?"

The panes of glass of the shop-front resounded, the singers'
great volume of breath agitated the muslin curtains. Whilst
all this was going on, Virginie had already twice disappeared,
and each time on returning had leant towards Gervaise's ear to
whisper a piece of information. When she returned the third
time, in the midst of the uproar, she said to her :

"My dear, he's still at François's ; he's pretending to read
the newspaper. He's certainly meditating some evil design."

She was speaking of Lantier. It was him that she had been
watching. At each fresh report, Gervaise became more and
more grave.

" Is he drunk ?" asked she of Virginie.

" No," replied the tall brunette. " He looks as though he

had merely had what he required. It's that especially which
makes me anxious. Eh! why does he remain there if he's
had all he wanted? Good heavens! good heavens! I hope
nothing is going to happen!"

The laundress, greatly upset, begged her to leave off. A
profound silence had suddenly succeeded the clamour. Madame
Putois had just risen, and was about to sing "The Boarding
of the Pirate." The guests, silent and thoughtful, watched her;
even Poisson had laid his pipe down on the edge of the table,
the better to listen to her. She stood up to the full height of
her little figure, with a fierce expression about her, though her
face looked quite pale beneath her black cap; she thrust out
her left fist with a satisfied pride, as she thundered in a voice
bigger than herself:

> " If pirate audacious
> Should o'er the waves chase us,
> The buccaneer slaughter,
> Accord him no quarter.
> To the guns every man,
> And with rum fill each can!
> While these pests of the seas
> Dangle from the cross-trees."

That was something serious. But, by Jove! it gave one a
fine idea of the real thing. Poisson, who had been on board
ship, nodded his head in approval of the description. One
could see too that that song was in accordance with Madame
Putois's own feeling. Coupeau leant forward to relate how one
night in the Rue Poulet, Madame Putois had boxed the ears
of four men who had attempted to insult her.

With the assistance of mother Coupeau, Gervaise was now
serving the coffee, though some of the guests had not yet
finished their Savoy cake. They would not let her sit down
again, but shouted that it was her turn. With a pale face, and
looking very ill at ease, she tried to excuse herself; she seemed
so queer that some one inquired whether the goose had dis-
agreed with her. Then she gave out, "Oh! let me slumber!"
in a sweet and feeble voice. When she reached the chorus,
that wish for a sleep filled with beautiful dreams, her eyelids
partly closed, her rapt gaze lost itself in the darkness of the
street. Directly afterwards, Poisson abruptly saluted the ladies
and commenced a drinking song, the "Wines of France," but
he had a voice like a squirt; only the last verse, the patriotic
one, met with any success, because when alluding to the tri-

colour flag, he raised his glass on high, poised it there a moment, and ended by pouring the contents into his open mouth.

Then came a string of ballads : Madame Boche's barcarolle was all about Venice and the gondoliers ; Madame Lorilleux sang of Seville and the Andalusians in her bolero ; whilst Lorilleux went so far as to allude to the perfumes of Arabia, in reference to the loves of Fatma, the dancer. Around the greasy table, in an atmosphere heavy with the breath of indigestion, horizons of gold opened, across which flitted necks of ivory, jet-black hair, kisses in the moonlight to the accompaniment of guitars, bayaderes scattering pearls and precious stones in their wake ; and the men blissfully smoked their pipes, the ladies smiled unconsciously with enjoyment ; they all fancied themselves there, sniffing delicious odours. When Clémence warbled "Build a Nest," with a shake in the throat, she also caused a great deal of pleasure ; for it recalled the country, the merry birds, the dances beneath the green foliage, the sweet-scented flowers—in short, all that one sees in the Bois de Vincennes on the days when one goes to wring the neck of a rabbit.

But Virginie revived the joking with "My little Drop of Brandy ;" she imitated the sutler's wife, one hand on her hip, the elbow arched, to indicate the little barrel ; and with the other hand she poured out the brandy into space, by turning her fist round. She did it so well that the party then begged mother Coupeau to sing "The Mouse." The old woman refused, vowing that she did not know the smutty thing. Yet, she started off with the remnants of her broken voice ; and her wrinkled face, with its lively little eyes, underlined the allusions, the terrors of Mademoiselle Lise drawing her skirts around her at the sight of a mouse. All the table laughed ; the women could not keep their countenances, and continued casting bright glances at their neighbours ; it was not indecent after all, there were no coarse words in it. To tell the truth, Boche was all the while acting the mouse along the charcoal-dealer's calves. It might have degenerated into something unpleasant, if Goujet had not, on a sign from Gervaise, restored silence and respect with the "Farewell of Abd-el-Kader," which he thundered forth in his bass voice. It was very evident he had a solid wind ! The words came from the midst of his beautiful yellow beard, like from a brass trumpet. When he uttered the cry : " O my noble companion !" alluding to the warrior's black mare, all

hearts beat with him. He was applauded before reaching the end,
for he had shouted so loud.

"Now, old Bru, it's your turn!" said mother Coupeau. "Sing
your song. The old ones are the best, any day!"

And everybody turned towards the old man, pressing him
and encouraging him. He, in a state of torpor, with his immovable mask of tanned skin, looked at them without appearing
to understand. They asked him if he knew the "Five vowels."
He held down his head; he could not recollect it; all the songs
of the good old days were mixed up in his noddle. As they
made up their minds to leave him alone, he seemed to remember, and began to stutter in a cavernous voice:

> " Trou la la, trou la la,
>   Trou la, trou la, trou la la!"

His face assumed an animated expression, this chorus seemed
to awake some far-off gaieties within him, enjoyed by himself
alone, as he listened with a childish delight to his voice which
became more and more hollow.

> "Trou la la, trou la la,
>   Trou la, trou la, trou la la!"

"I say, my dear," Virginie came and whispered in Gervaise's
ear, "I've just been there again, you know. It worried me.
Well! Lantier has disappeared from François's."

"You didn't meet him outside?" asked the laundress.

"No, I walked quick, I didn't think of looking."

But Virginie, who had raised her eyes, interrupted herself and
heaved a smothered sigh.

"Ah! good heavens! He's there, on the pavement opposite;
he's looking this way."

Gervaise, quite beside herself, ventured to glance in the direction indicated. Some persons had collected in the street to hear
the party sing. The grocer's men, the tripe-dealer and the
little clockmaker formed a group, looking as though they were
at the theatre. There were some soldiers, some gentlemen in
frock-coats, and three little girls from five to six years old holding one another by the hand, very grave and lost in amazement.
And Lantier was indeed there in the front row, listening, and
coolly looking on. It was rare cheek, everything considered.
Gervaise felt a chill ascend from her legs to her heart, and she
no longer dared to move, whilst old Bru continued:

> "Trou la la, trou la la,
>   Trou la, trou la, trou la la!".

"Ah well! no, my ancient one, that's enough !" said Coupeau.
"Do you know the whole of it ?   You shall sing it to us another
day, eh ! when we're too lively."

This raised a laugh.   The old fellow stopped short, glanced
round the table with his pale eyes, and resumed his look of a
meditative animal.   The coffee had been all drunk and the zinc-
worker had asked for more wine.   Clémence had just returned
to the strawberries.   For an instant, the singing ceased, they
were talking of a woman who had been found hanged that morning in the house next door.   It was Madame Lerat's turn, but
she required to prepare herself.   She dipped the corner of her
napkin into a glass of water and applied it to her temples,
because she was too hot.   Then, she asked for a thimbleful of
brandy, drank it, and slowly wiped her lips.

"The 'Child of God,' shall it be ?" she murmured, "the
'Child of God.'"

And, tall and masculine-looking, with her bony nose and her
shoulders as square as a grenadier's, she began :

> " The lost child left by its mother alone,
>   Is sure of a home in Heaven above,
> God sees and protects it on earth from His throne.
>   The child that is lost is the child of God's love."

Her voice trembled at certain words, and dwelt on them in
liquid notes ; she looked out of the corner of her eyes to heaven,
whilst her right hand swung before her chest or pressed against
her heart, with an impressive gesture.   Then Gervaise, tortured
by Lantier's presence, could not restrain her tears ; it seemed to
her that the song was relating her own suffering, that she was
the lost child, abandoned by its mother, and whom God was
going to take under His protection.   Clémence, who was very
drunk, suddenly broke into sobs ; and, with her head fallen on
the edge of the table, she stifled her hiccoughs with the cloth.
A silence ensued that made one shudder.   The ladies had produced their handkerchiefs, and were wiping their eyes without
in the least turning away their faces, but thinking their emotion
did them honour.   The men, their heads slightly bent down,
were looking straight before them, blinking their eyelids.
Poisson, choking and grinding his teeth, twice broke a piece off
his pipe, and spat the bits on to the ground, without ceasing to
smoke.   Boche, whose hand remained on the charcoal-dealer's
knee, was seized with a vague remorse and respect, and no longer
pinched her ; whilst two big tears trickled down his cheeks.
Those revellers were as rigid as justice and as tender-hearted

as lambs. The wine was coming out by the way of their eyes, that was all! When the chorus started again, slower and more pathetic, all gave way, all blubbered in their plates, unfastening their clothes, bursting with emotion.

But Gervaise and Virginie could not, in spite of themselves, take their eyes off the pavement opposite. Madame Boche, in her turn, caught sight of Lantier and uttered a faint cry, without ceasing to besmear her face with her tears. Then, all three had very anxious faces as they exchanged involuntary signs. Good heavens! if Coupeau were to turn round, if Coupeau caught sight of the other! What a butchery! what carnage! And they went on to such an extent, that the zinc-worker asked them:

"Whatever are you looking at?"

He leant forward and recognised Lantier.

"Damnation! it's too much," muttered he. "Ah! the dirty scoundrel—ah! the dirty scoundrel. No, it's too much, it must come to an end."

And, as he rose from his seat muttering most atrocious threats, Gervaise in a low voice implored him to keep quiet.

"Listen to me, I implore you. Leave the knife alone. Remain where you are, don't do anything dreadful."

Virginie had to take the knife from him, which he had picked up off the table. But she could not prevent him leaving the shop and going up to Lantier. The party, in its increasing emotion, saw nothing, but wept the more, whilst Madame Lerat sang with an excruciating expression:

> "She had been lost, poor orphan girl,
> And her sad voice was only heard
> By the tall trees and passing bird."

The last line passed like a lamentable breath of the tempest. Madame Putois, who was drinking, was so affected that she spilt her wine all over the table-cloth. Gervaise, meanwhile, remained as one frozen, pressing her hand to her mouth to prevent her from calling out, blinking her eyelids with fright, expecting every second to see one of the two men outside knocked down in the middle of the road. Virginie and Madame Boche, deeply interested, also followed the scene. Coupeau, surprised by the fresh air, had almost plumped down in the gutter, on trying to rush upon Lantier. The latter, with his hands in his pockets, had simply moved on one side. And the two men were now blackguarding each other, the zinc-worker, especially, was making use of some choice expressions, calling the other a sick pig, and talking of eating his tripe. One could hear the

sound of their enraged voices, one could distinguish the furious
gestures they made, as though they were going to screw their
arms off with their numerous blows. Gervaise felt faint and
shut her eyes, because it was lasting too long, and she expected
every minute to see them biting each other's noses off, they
thrust their faces so close together. Then, when she no longer
heard anything, she opened her eyes again and felt quite confused on seeing them quietly conversing together.

Madame Lerat's voice rose again, warbling and tearful, as she
commenced another verse :

> " Next morn exhausted on the ground
> The poor lost child half dead was found."

"Some women are indeed brutes !" said Madame Lorilleux,
amidst general approbation.

Gervaise had exchanged a glance with Madame Boche and
Virginie. Was it going to end amicably then ? Coupeau and
Lantier continued to converse on the edge of the pavement.
They were still abusing each other, but in a friendly way. They
called one another "damned rogue," but in a tone of voice which
had a touch of affection in it. As people were staring at them,
they ended by strolling leisurely side by side past the houses,
turning round again every ten yards or so. A very animated
conversation was now taking place. Suddenly, Coupeau
appeared to become angry again, whilst the other was refusing
something and required to be pressed. And it was the zinc-
worker who pushed Lantier along, and who forced him to cross
the street and enter the shop.

"I tell you you're quite welcome !" shouted he. "You'll
take a glass of wine. Men are men, you know. We ought to
understand one another."

Madame Lerat was finishing the last chorus. The ladies
were singing all together, as they twisted their handkerchiefs :

> " The child that is lost is the child of God's love."

The singer was greatly complimented, and she resumed her
seat, affecting to be quite broken down. She asked for something to drink, because she always put too much feeling into
that song, and she was constantly afraid of straining one of her
nerves. Every one at the table now had their eyes fixed on
Lantier, who, quietly seated beside Coupeau, was devouring the
last piece of Savoy cake which he dipped in his glass of wine.
With the exception of Virginie and Madame Boche, none of the

COUPEAU FORCES LANTIER TO JOIN THE PARTY GIVEN TO CELEBRATE

GERVAISE'S SAINT'S DAY.   p. 220.

guests knew him. The Lorilleux certainly scented some under-hand business, but not knowing what, they merely assumed their most conceited air. Goujet, who had noticed Gervaise's emotion, gave the new-comer a sour look. As an awkward pause ensued, Coupeau simply said :

" A friend of mine."

And turning to his wife, added :

" Come, stir yourself! Perhaps there's still some hot coffee left."

Gervaise, feeling meek and stupid, looked at them one after the other. At first, when her husband pushed her old lover into the shop, she buried her head between her hands, the same as she instinctively did on stormy days at each clap of thunder. She could not believe it possible ; the walls would fall in and crush them all. Then, seeing the two men seated together, without so much as the muslin curtains moving, she suddenly thought it the most natural thing in the world. The goose was disagreeing with her a little ; she had certainly eaten too much of it, and it prevented her from thinking. A happy feeling of langour benumbed her, retained her all in a heap at the edge of the table, with the sole desire of not being bothered. Well ! what is the use of putting oneself out when others do not, and when things arrange themselves to the satisfaction of every-body? She got up to see if there was any coffee left.

In the back room the children had fallen asleep. That squint-eyed Augustine had tyrannised over them all during the dessert, pilfering their strawberries and frightening them with most abominable threats. Now she felt very ill, and was bent double upon a stool, not uttering a word, her face ghastly pale. Fat Pauline had let her head fall against Etienne's shoulder, and he himself was sleeping on the edge of the table. Nana was seated with Victor on the rug beside the bedstead, she had passed her arm round his neck and was drawing him towards her ; and, succumbing to drowsiness her eyes shut, she kept repeating in a feeble voice :

" Oh ! mamma, I'm not well ; oh ! mamma, I'm not well."

" No wonder ! " murmured Augustine, whose head was rolling about on her shoulders, " they're fuddled ; they've been singing like grown-up persons."

Gervaise received another blow on beholding Etienne. She felt as though she would choke when she thought of the youngster's father being there, in the other room, eating cake, and that he had not even expressed a desire to kiss the little fellow. She was on the point of rousing Etienne, and of carrying him there in her arms. Then, she again felt that the quiet way in which matters had been arranged was the best. It would not have been proper to have disturbed the harmony of the end of the dinner. She returned with the coffee-pot and poured out a glass of coffee for Lantier, who, by the way, did not appear to take any notice of her.

"Now, it's my turn," stuttered Coupeau, in a thick voice. "Eh! you've been keeping me for the tit-bit. Well! I'll sing you ' What a piggish child!'"

"Yes, yes, 'What a piggish child!'" cried everyone.

The uproar was beginning again—Lantier was forgotten. The ladies prepared their glasses and their knives for accompanying the chorus. They laughed beforehand, as they looked at the zinc-worker, who steadied himself on his legs as he put on his most vulgar air. Mimicking the hoarse voice of an old woman, he sang:

> " When out of bed each morn I hop,
>   I'm always precious queer ;
> I send him for a little drop
>   To th' drinking-ken that's near.
> A good half hour or more he'll stay,
>   And that makes me so riled,
> He swigs it half upon his way :
>   What a piggish child ! "

And the ladies, striking their glasses, repeated in chorus, in the midst of a formidable gaiety :

> " What a piggish child !
> What a piggish child ! "

Even the Rue de la Goutte-d'Or itself joined in now. The whole neighbourhood was singing "What a piggish child!" Over the way, the little clockmaker, the grocer's men, the tripe-dealer, the greengrocer, who knew the song, took up the chorus, and smacked one another just for a lark. Really, the street was ending by becoming intoxicated ; the festive odour issuing from the Coupeaus' was alone sufficient to make everyone on the pavement more than merry. It is only fair to say that the entire party inside was now awfully drunk. This had come on little by little from the first glass of pure wine after the soup. It was now the climax ; they were all braying and bursting with what they had swallowed, in the reddish haze of the two lamps, which required snuffing. The clamour of this gigantic booze completely drowned the rumbling noise of the last vehicles. Two policemen, thinking there was a riot, hastened to the spot; but, catching sight of Poisson, they just nodded to him, and then slowly moved away, side by side, along the dark houses.

Coupeau was now singing this verse:

" On Sundays at Petite Villette,
Whene'er the weather's fine,
We call on uncle, old Tinette,
Who's in the dustman line.
To feast upon some cherry stones
The young un's almost wild,
And rolls amongst the dust and bones.
What a piggish child!
What a piggish child! '

Then the house almost collapsed, such a yell ascended in the calm warm night air that the shouters applauded themselves, for it was useless their hoping to be able to bawl any louder.

Not one of the party could ever recollect exactly how the carouse terminated. It must have been very late, it's quite certain, for not a cat was to be seen in the 'street. Possibly, too, they had all joined hands and danced round the table. But all was submerged in a yellow mist, in which red faces were jumping about, with mouths slit from ear to ear. They had probably treated themselves to something stronger than wine towards the end, and there was a vague suspicion that some one had played them the trick of putting salt into the glasses. The children must have undressed and put themselves to bed. On the morrow, Madame Boche boasted of having treated Boche to a couple of clouts in a corner, where he was conversing a great deal too close to the charcoal-dealer; but Boche, who recollected nothing, said she must have dreamt it. What everyone agreed was not at all decent, was the behaviour of Clémence, who was most decidedly a girl not to invite again; she had ended by displaying all she had to show, and then was so sick that she quite spoilt one of the muslin curtains. The men had at least the decency to go into the street; Lorilleux and Poisson, feeling their stomachs upset, had stumblingly glided as far as the pork-butcher's shop. It is easy to see when a person has been well brought up. For instance, the ladies, Madame Putois, Madame Lerat, and Virginie, indisposed by the heat, had simply gone into the back room and taken their stays off; Virginie had even desired to lie on the bed for a minute, just to obviate any unpleasant effects. Then the party had seemed to melt away, some disappearing behind the others, all accompanying one another, and being lost sight of in the surrounding darkness, to the accompaniment of a final uproar, a furious quarrel between the Lorilleux, and an obstinate and mournful "trou la la, trou la la," of old Bru's. Gervaise had an idea that Goujet had burst out sobbing when bidding her good-bye; Coupeau was still singing; and as for Lantier, he must have remained till the end. At one moment even she could still feel a breath against her hair, but she was unable to say whether it came from Lantier or if it was the warm night air.

As Madame Lerat refused at that late hour to return to Batignolles, they took a mattress off the bed, and spread it for her in a corner of the shop, after pushing the table on one side. She slept there, amidst the crumbs from the feast. And all the rest of the night, during the heavy sleep of the Coupeaus, digesting all they had swallowed, a neighbour's cat, taking advantage of a window which had been left open, crunched up the goose bones, and finished burying the bird with the little gnawing sound of its sharp teeth.

CHAPTER VIII.

On the following Saturday, Coupeau, who had not come home to dinner, brought Lantier with him towards ten o'clock. They had had some sheep's trotters at Thomas's at Montmartre.

"You mustn't scold, old woman," said the zinc-worker. "We're all right, as you can see. Oh! there's no fear with him; he keeps one in the straight road."

And he related how they happened to meet in the Rue Rochechouart. After dinner, Lantier had declined to have a drink at the "Black Ball," saying that when one was married to a pretty and worthy little woman, one ought not to go liquoring-up at all the wine-shops. Gervaise smiled slightly as she listened. Oh! she was not thinking of scolding; she felt too much embarrassed for that. Ever since the feast, she had been expecting to see her old lover again, one day or other; but, at such an hour, just at bedtime, the sudden arrival of the two men had taken her by surprise; and, with trembling hands, she fastened up her back hair again, which had unrolled down her neck.

"You know," resumed Coupeau, "as he was so polite as to decline a drink outside, you must treat us to one here. Ah! you certainly owe us that!"

The workwomen had been gone a long while. Mother Coupeau and Nana had just got into bed. So Gervaise, who was about to put up the shutters when they appeared, left the shop open, and fetched some glasses and the remains of a bottle of brandy which she placed on a corner of the work-table. Lantier remained standing, and avoided speaking at once to her. However, when she helped him, he exclaimed:

"Only a thimbleful, madame, if you please."

Coupeau looked at them, and then spoke his mind very plainly. They were not going to behave like a couple of geese, he hoped! The past was past, was it not? If people nursed grudges for nine and ten years together, one would end by no

P

longer seeing anybody. No, no, he carried his heart in his hand, he did! First of all, he knew who he had to deal with, a worthy woman and a worthy man—in short, two friends! He felt easy; he knew he could depend upon them.

"Oh! that's certain, quite certain," repeated Gervaise, looking on the ground, and scarcely understanding what she said.

"She is a sister now—nothing but a sister!" murmured Lantier in his turn.

"Damn it all! shake hands," cried Coupeau, "and let those who don't like it go to blazes! When one has proper feelings, one is better off than millionaires. For myself, I prefer friendship before everything, because friendship is friendship, and there's nothing to beat it."

He dealt himself heavy blows in the stomach, and seemed so moved that they had to calm him. They all three silently clinked glasses, and drank their drop of brandy. Gervaise was then able to look at Lantier at her ease; for, on the night of her saint's day, she had only seen him through a mist. He had grown stouter, was fat and round, and his legs and arms appeared heavy on account of his small frame. But his face preserved some handsome features beneath the bloated look of a life of idleness; and as he always took great care of his little moustaches, one would have guessed him just his age—thirty-five years old. That day he wore a grey pair of trousers and a coarse blue overcoat like a gentleman, with a billy-cock hat; he even had a silver watch and chain, from which hung a ring, a keepsake.

"I'm off," said he. "I live no end of a distance from here."

He was already on the pavement, when the zinc-worker called him back to make him promise never to pass the door without looking in to wish them good-day. Meanwhile, Gervaise, who had quietly disappeared, returned pushing Etienne before her. The child, who was in his shirt sleeves, and half asleep, smiled as he rubbed his eyes. But when he beheld Lantier, he stood trembling and embarrassed, and casting anxious glances in the direction of his mother and Coupeau.

"Don't you remember this gentleman?" asked the latter.

The child held down his head without replying. Then he made a slight sign which meant that he did remember the gentleman.

"Well! then, don't stand there like a fool; go and kiss him."

Lantier gravely and quietly waited. When Etienne had made up his mind to approach him, he stooped down, presented both his cheeks, and then kissed the youngster on the forehead himself. At this the latter ventured to look at his father; but all on a sudden he burst out sobbing, and scampered away like a mad creature, with his clothes half falling off him, whilst Coupeau angrily called him a young savage.

"The emotion's too much for him," said Gervaise, pale and agitated herself.

"Oh! he's generally very gentle and nice," exclaimed Coupeau. "I've brought him up famously, as you'll see. He'll get used to you. He must learn to know people. Anyhow, were it only on this youngster's account, we could not always have remained bad friends, could we now? We ought to have made it up for his sake long ago, for I would sooner have my head cut off than prevent a father seeing his child."

Having thus delivered himself, he talked of finishing the bottle of brandy. All three clinked glasses again. Lantier showed no surprise, but remained perfectly calm. By way of repaying the zinc-worker's politeness, he persisted in helping him put up the shutters, before taking his departure. Then, rubbing his hands together to get rid of the dust on them, he wished the couple good-night.

"Sleep well. I shall try and catch the last 'bus. I promise you I'll look in again soon."

After that evening Lantier frequently called at the Rue de la Goutte-d'Or. He came when the zinc-worker was there, inquiring after his health the moment he passed the door, and affecting to have solely called on his account. Then, clean-shaved, his hair nicely combed, and always wearing his over-coat, he would take a seat by the window, and converse politely with the manners of an educated man. It was thus that the Coupeaus learnt little by little the details of his life. During the last eight years he had for a while managed a hat factory; and when they asked him why he had retired from it, he merely alluded to the rascality of a partner, a fellow from his native place, a scoundrel who had squandered all the takings with women. But his former position of employer was apparent all over his person like a title of nobility from which he could not derogate. He was for ever saying that he was on the point of making an admirable arrangement; some wholesale hat manu-facturers were about to set him up in business and trust him with an enormous stock. Meanwhile, he did nothing whatever, but walk about in the sunshine with his hands in his pockets, just like a gentleman possessed of a private income. On the

days when he complained, if any one ventured to tell him of a
factory in want of workmen, he seemed seized with a smiling
pity; he had no desire to die of hunger whilst slaving for
others.

All the same, the fellow, as Coupeau would say, did not live
on air. Oh! he was a cunning blade. He knew how to get
his bread buttered; he had something up his sleeve, for he invariably had such an appearance of prosperity, he must obtain
money somehow to be able always to wear clean white shirts
and neckties worthy of the sons of gentlemen. One morning
the zinc-worker saw him having his boots cleaned on the
Boulevard Montmartre. The real truth was that Lantier, who
was very talkative on the subject of other people, held his
tongue or lied when it was a question of himself. He would not
even say where he lived. No; he was lodging at a friend's, an
awful way off, whilst waiting until his arrangements were completed; and he said it was useless for any one to call on him,
because he was never at home.

"One can find a dozen places when one only wants one," he
would often explain. "Only, it's not worth while entering a
crib where you're certain of not remaining twenty-four hours.
For instance, one Monday, I arrived at Champion's, at Montrouge.
In the evening Champion bothered me about politics; his ideas
were not the same as mine. Well! on the Tuesday morning
off I went, for we're no longer in the days of slavery, and I'm
not going to sell myself for seven francs a day."

It was now the early part of November. Lantier gallantly
brought bunches of violets, which he distributed amongst
Gervaise and the two workwomen. Little by little he multi-
plied his visits, until he came almost every day. He seemed as
though he wished to make a conquest of the household, of the
whole neighbourhood; and he commenced by charming Clémence
and Madame Putois, to whom he was equally most attentive,
notwithstanding the difference in their ages. At the end of a
month the two workwomen positively adored him. The Boches,
whom he flattered enormously in paying them little visits in
their room, were in raptures with his politeness. As for the
Lorilleux, when they learnt who the gentleman was who had
arrived in the midst of the dessert on the day of the feast, they
gave vent to a thousand horrible things against Gervaise, who
dared thus to introduce her old lover into her family. But one
day Lantier called upon them, and made himself so agreeable
whilst ordering a chain for one of his lady friends that they

asked him to sit down, and kept him there an hour, quite charmed with his conversation; they even asked themselves how such a delightful man could ever have lived with the Hobbler. At length the hatter's visits to the Coupeaus no longer made any one indignant, and seemed quite natural, for he had succeeded so well in getting into the good graces of every one in the Rue de la Goutte-d'Or. Goujet alone remained gloomy. If he happened to be there when the other arrived, he at once made for the door, so as not to be obliged to become acquainted with the individual in question.

In the midst, however, of all this extraordinary affection for Lantier, Gervaise, during the first few weeks, lived in a state of great agitation. She felt that burning sensation at the pit of her stomach which affected her on the day when Virginie first alluded to her past life. Her great fear was that she might find herself without strength, if he came upon her all alone one night and took it into his head to kiss her. She thought of him too much; she was for ever full of him. But she gradually became calmer on seeing him behave so well, never looking her in the face, never even touching her with the tips of his fingers when the others' backs were turned. Then Virginie, who seemed to read within her, made her ashamed of all her wicked thoughts. Why did she tremble? One could not hope to come across a nicer man. She certainly had nothing to fear now. And one day the tall brunette manœuvred in such a way as to get them both into a corner, and to turn the conversation to the subject of love. Lantier, choosing his words, declared in a grave voice that his heart was dead, that for the future he wished to consecrate his life solely to his son's happiness. He never alluded to Claude, who was still in the South. He kissed Etienne on the forehead every evening, but never knew what to say to the child if he remained there, and forgetting his presence would turn his attention to Clémence. Then Gervaise, more at ease, felt the past die within her. Lantier's presence obliterated her recollections of Plassans, and of the Hôtel Boncœur. Seeing him constantly, she no longer dreamed of him so much. But she would feel filled with disgust at the thought of their past connection. Oh, it was all over, quite over. If ever he dared to try it on with her again, she would answer him with a couple of smacks; she would sooner tell her husband everything. And again she thought, without remorse, and with extraordinary sweetness, of Goujet's loyal friendship.

One morning, on arriving at the shop, Clémence related that

at eleven o'clock the night before, she had seen M. Lantier with a woman on his arm. In saying this she made use of a great many improper expressions, with a good deal of covert spitefulness too, just to see how her mistress would take it. Yes, M. Lantier was climbing up the Rue Notre-Dame de Lorette. The woman was a blonde, one of those half-dead "cows" of the Boulevard, with nothing to cover her skin but her silk dress. And she had followed them for the fun of the thing. The "cow" had entered a pork-butcher's, and bought some prawns and some ham. Then, in the Rue de La Rochefoucauld, M. Lantier had had to wait on the pavement in front of the house, with his nose in the air, until the little one, who had gone up alone, had signalled to him from the window to join her. But in spite of all the disgusting observations which Clémence appended, Gervaise quietly continued ironing a white dress. Now and again the story brought a slight smile to her lips. Those Southerners, said she, were all mad after women; they must have them in spite of everything; they would even pick them off a rubbish heap with a shovel if they could not get them any other way.

And, in the evening, when the hatter arrived, she amused herself by listening to Clémence teasing him about his blonde. He, too, seemed proud at having been seen. Well, yes, it was an old friend of his whom he saw now and then, when it was not likely to disturb any one. She was a great swell, and had violet ebony furniture; and he mentioned some of her ex-lovers, a viscount, a large china merchant, and the son of a notary. He liked women who had plenty of scent about them. And he was poking his handkerchief, which the little one had scented for him, under Clémence's nose, when Etienne entered. Then he assumed his grave manner, kissed the child, and added that the little amusement would go no further; his heart was dead. Gervaise, bending over her work, nodded her head with approval. Thus it was Clémence who paid the penalty of her spitefulness, for she had already, on two or three occasions, felt Lantier pinching her without seeming to be doing so, and she was bursting with jealousy at not stinking of musk, like the "cow" of the Boulevard.

When the spring-time returned, Lantier, who was now quite one of the family, talked of living in the neighbourhood, so as to be nearer his friends. He wanted a furnished room in a decent house. Madame Boche, and even Gervaise herself, went searching about to find it for him. They explored the neighbouring streets. But he was always too difficult to please; he required a big courtyard, a room on the ground floor; in fact, every luxury imaginable. And then every evening, at the Coupeaus', he seemed to measure the height of the ceilings, study the arrangement of the rooms, and covet a similar lodging. Oh, he would never have asked for anything better, he would willingly have made himself a hole in that warm, quiet corner. Then each time he wound up his inspection with these words:

"By Jove! you are comfortably situated here."

One evening, when he had dined there, and was making the same remark during the dessert, Coupeau, who now treated him most familiarly, suddenly exclaimed:

"You must stay here, old boy, if it suits you. It's easily arranged."

And he explained that the dirty-clothes room, cleaned out, would make a nice apartment. Etienne could sleep in the shop, on a mattress on the ground, that was all.

"No, no," said Lantier, "I cannot accept. It would inconvenience you too much. I know that it's willingly offered, but we should be too warm all jumbled up together. Besides, you know, each one likes his liberty. I should have to go through your room, and that wouldn't be exactly funny."

"Ah, the rogue!" resumed the zinc-worker, choking with laughter, banging his fist down on the table to clear his throat, "he's always thinking of something smutty! But, you joker, we're of an inventive turn of mind! There're two windows in the room, aren't there? Well, we'll knock one out and turn it into a door. Then, you understand, you come in by way of the courtyard, and we can even stop up the other door, if we like. Thus you'll be in your home, and we in ours."

A pause ensued. At length, the hatter murmured:

"Ah, yes, in that manner, perhaps we might. And yet no, I should be too much in your way."

He avoided looking at Gervaise. But he was evidently waiting for a word from her before accepting. She was very much annoyed at her husband's idea; not that the thought of seeing Lantier living with them wounded her feelings, or made her particularly uneasy; but she was wondering where she would be able to keep the dirty clothes. Meanwhile, the zinc-worker began enumerating the advantages of the arrangement. The five-hundred-francs rent had always been rather too much for them. Well, their comrade should pay them twenty francs a month for the furnished room; it would not be too dear for

him, and it would assist them at quarter-day. He added that
he would undertake to knock up a big case under their bed
which would hold all the dirty clothes of the neighbourhood.
Then Gervaise hesitated, and with a glance seemed to consult
mother Coupeau, whom Lantier had won over months before by
bringing her jujubes for her cough.

"You would certainly not be in our way," she ended by saying. "We could so arrange things—"

"No, no, thanks," repeated the hatter. "You're too kind ;
it would be asking too much."

Coupeau could no longer restrain himself. Was he going to
continue making objections when they told him it was freely
offered ? He would be obliging them, there, did he understand ?
Then in an excited tone of voice he yelled :

"Etienne ! Etienne !"

The youngster had fallen asleep on the table. He raised his
head with a start.

"Listen, tell him that you wish it. Yes, that gentleman
there. Tell him as loud as you can : 'I wish it !'"

"I wish it !" stuttered Etienne, his voice thick with sleep.

Everyone laughed. But Lantier soon resumed his grave and
impressive air. He squeezed Coupeau's hand across the table
as he said :

"I accept. It's in all good fellowship on both sides, is it
not ? Yes, I accept for the child's sake."

As early as the morrow—the landlord, M. Marescot, having
come to pass an hour in the Boches' room—Gervaise spoke to
him about the matter. At first he seemed very apprehensive,
refused, and became quite angry, as though she had asked him
to knock down a whole wing of his house. Then, after a minute
inspection of the premises, and when he had gazed up in the
air to see whether the other storeys would be shaken, he ended
by giving the necessary permission, but only on condition that
he should not be called upon to bear any part of the expense ;
and the Coupeaus had to sign a paper in which they undertook
to leave everything as they had found it, at the expiration of
their term. That very evening, the zinc-worker brought some
of his comrades, a mason, a carpenter, a painter—some jolly
dogs who would make the alterations in their spare time, just
to oblige a friend. The putting up of the new door and the
cleaning out of the room, cost nevertheless a hundred francs,
without counting the wine with which the job was watered.
The zinc-worker told his comrades he would pay them later on,

with the first money he received from his tenant. Then, there
was the question of furnishing the room. Gervaise left mother
Coupeau's wardrobe in it; she added a table and two chairs
taken from her own room; then she had to purchase a toilet-
table, and a bedstead and all the bedding, amounting altogether
to a hundred and thirty francs, which she had to pay for at the
rate of ten francs a month. If during the first ten months
Lantier's twenty francs of rent were swallowed up beforehand
by the debts contracted, there would nevertheless be a fine
profit afterwards.

It was during the early days of June that the hatter moved
in. The day before, Coupeau had offered to go with him and
fetch his box, to save him the thirty sous for a cab. But the
other became quite embarrassed, saying that the box was too
heavy, as though he wished up to the last moment to hide the
place where he lodged. He arrived in the afternoon, towards
three o'clock. Coupeau did not happen to be in. And Gervaise,
standing at the shop door, became quite pale, on recognising the
box outside the cab. It was their old box, the one with which
they had journeyed from Plassans, all scratched and broken
now, and held together by cords. She saw it return as she had
often dreamt it would, and it needed no great stretch of imagination to believe that the same cab, that cab in which that
strumpet of a burnisher had played her such a foul trick, had
brought the box back again. Meanwhile, Boche was giving
Lantier a helping hand. The laundress followed them in silence,
and feeling rather dazed. When they had deposited their
burden in the middle of the room, she said for the sake of saying
something:

"Well! that's a good thing finished, isn't it?"

Then, pulling herself together, seeing that Lantier, busy in
undoing the cords, was not even looking at her, she added:

"Monsieur Boche, you must have a drink."

And she went and fetched a quart of wine and some glasses.
Just then Poisson passed along the pavement in uniform.
She signalled to him, winking her eye and smiling. The policeman understood perfectly. When he was on duty, and anyone
winked their eye to him, it meant a glass of wine. He would
even walk for hours up and down before the laundress's, waiting
for a wink. Then, so as not to be seen, he would pass through
the courtyard, and toss off the liquor in secret.

"Ah! ah!" said Lantier when he saw him enter, "it's you,
Badingue!"

He called him Badingue for a joke, just to show how little he cared for the Emperor. Poisson put up with it in his stiff way, without one knowing whether it really annoyed him or not. Besides the two men, though separated by their political convictions, had become very good friends.

"You know that the Emperor was once a policeman in London," said Boche in his turn. "Yes, on my word! he used to take the drunken women to the station-house."

Gervaise had filled three glasses on the table. She would not drink herself, she felt too sick at heart, but she stood there, longing to see what the box contained, and watching Lantier remove the last cords. She recollected that in one corner there used to be a heap of socks, two shirts, and an old hat. Were those things still in it? was she again going to behold the rags and tatters of the past? Before raising the lid, Lantier took his glass and clinked it with the others.

"Good health."

"Same to you," replied Boche and Poisson.

The laundress filled the glasses again. The three men wiped their lips on the backs of their hands. And at last the hatter opened the box. It was full of a jumble of newspapers, books, old clothes, and underlinen, in bundles. He took out successively a saucepan, a pair of boots, a bust of Ledru-Rollin with the nose broken, an embroidered shirt, and a pair of working trousers. And Gervaise, leaning over, inhaled a stench of tobacco, an odour of an unclean individual who only washes the surface, just so much as is seen of his person. No, the old hat was no longer in the left hand corner; but there was a pincushion there which she did not recognise, probably a present from some woman. Then she became calmer; she experienced a vague sadness as she followed the different objects with her eyes, asking herself whether they dated from her time or from the time of the others.

"I say, Badingue, you don't know this, do you?" resumed Lantier.

He thrust under his nose a little book printed at Brussels, "The Amours of Napoleon III.," illustrated with engravings. It related, amongst other anecdotes, how the Emperor had seduced a girl of thirteen, the daughter of a cook; and the picture represented Napoleon III., bare-legged, and only wearing the grand ribbon of the Legion of Honour, pursuing a chit of a girl who was flying from his lust.

"Ah! that's it exactly!" exclaimed Boche, whose slyly

voluptuous instincts felt flattered by the sight. "It always happens like that!"

Poisson was seized with consternation, and he could not find a word to say in the Emperor's defence. It was in a book, so he could not deny it. Then, Lantier continuing to push the picture under his nose in a jeering way, he extended his arms and exclaimed:

. "Well, what next? It's nature, isn't it?"

The answer completely shut up Lantier. He placed his books and his newspapers on a shelf in the wardrobe; and as he seemed to very much regret not having a little bookcase suspended above the table, Gervaise promised to procure him one. He possessed Louis Blanc's "History of Ten Years," with the exception of the first volume, which by the way he had never had; Lamartine's "Girondins," in two sou numbers; Eugène Sue's "Mysteries of Paris" and the "Wandering Jew," besides a number of philosophical and humanitarian works, picked up at second-hand dealers. But he especially looked at his newspapers with tenderness and respect. It was a collection he had been forming for years past. Every time that he chanced to read at a café a successful newspaper article written in accordance with his own ideas, he would purchase the paper and preserve it. He had thus formed an enormous bundle, of all dates and titles, jumbled up anyhow. When he had removed this bundle from the bottom of the box, he slapped it in a friendly way, and said to the other two men:

"You see that? well, it belongs to yours truly, and no one can flatter himself he has anything so good. You've no idea what it contains. That's to say, if half these ideas were carried out, society would be cleansed at once. Yes, your Emperor and all his jackasses would quake in their shoes—"

But he was interrupted by the policeman, whose carroty moustaches and imperial trembled on his pale face.

"And the army, I say, what would you do with it?"

Then Lantier flew into a passion. He banged his fists down on the newspapers as he yelled:

"I require the suppression of militarism, the fraternity of peoples. I require the abolition of privileges, of titles, and of monopolies. I require the equality of salaries, the division of benefits, the glorification of the protectorate. All liberties, do you hear? all of them! And divorce!"

"Yes, yes, divorce, for morality!" insisted Boche.

Poisson had assumed a majestic air.

"Yet, if I won't have your liberties; I'm free to refuse them," he answered.

"If you won't have them—if you won't have them," stuttered Lantier, choking with rage. "No, you're not free! If you won't have them, I'll bundle you off to Cayenne, that's what I'll do! Yes, to Cayenne, with your Emperor and all the pigs who surround him!"

They always quarrelled thus every time they met. Gervaise, who did not like arguments, usually interfered. She roused herself from the torpor into which the sight of the box, full of the stale perfume of her past love, had plunged her, and she drew the three men's attention to the glasses.

"Ah! yes," said Lantier, becoming suddenly calm and taking his glass. "Good health!"

"Good health," replied Boche and Poisson, clinking glasses with him.

Boche, however, was moving nervously about, troubled by an anxiety, as he looked at the policeman out of the corner of his eye.

"All this between ourselves, eh, Monsieur Poisson?" murmured he at length. "We say and show you things—"

But Poisson did not let him finish. He placed his hand upon his heart, as though to explain that all remained buried there. He certainly did not go spying about on his friends. Coupeau arriving, they emptied a second quart. Then the policeman went off by way of the courtyard, and resumed his stiff and measured tread along the pavement.

During the first few days everything was upside down at the laundress's. Lantier true enough had his separate room, his own entrance and his key; but as, at the last moment, they had decided not to fasten up the door communicating between the two rooms, it happened that he generally went through the shop. The dirty clothes too were a great deal in Gervaise's way, for her husband did nothing towards making the big box he had spoken of; and she found herself obliged to put the things everywhere, some few in the corners, but most of them under her bedstead, which was far from pleasant during the summer nights. She was greatly annoyed too at having to make up Etienne's bed every evening in the middle of the shop; when the workwomen were there late, the child would go to sleep on a chair whilst waiting. Then Goujet, having suggested sending Etienne to Lille, where his former employer, a mechanician, was in want of apprentices, she was delighted with the

project, the more so as the youngster, who was not very happy
at home, and longed to be his own master, begged her to consent to his going. Only, she feared a decided refusal from
Lantier. He had come to live with them, solely to be near his
son ; he would not wish to part with him at the end of a fortnight. Yet, when she tremblingly mentioned the matter to
him, he approved the project immensely, saying that young
workmen ought to see plenty of their country. The morning
Etienne left, he made him a little speech about his rights, then
he kissed him and declaimed :

"Remember that the producer is not a slave, but whoever is
not a producer is a drone."

Then things got into shape again, every one calmed down
and fell into the new habits. Gervaise became accustomed to
the dirty clothes lying about, and to Lantier passing to and
fro. The latter was always talking of his large business
matters ; he would sometimes go out with his hair nicely
combed and wearing a clean white shirt, and after disappearing
for a while, perhaps not even coming home to sleep, he would return pretending he was quite worn out, and that his head was
splitting, as though he had been discussing the most weighty
matters for twenty-four hours at a stretch. The truth was
that he was taking life easy. Oh ! there was no fear that he
would ever blister his hands ! He usually rose of a morning
at about ten o'clock, took a stroll in the afternoon if the colour
of the sun pleased him, or, if it was a rainy day, remained in the
shop reading the newspaper. It was his element; he was
nowhere more at his ease than when amongst the skirts, in the
thick of the women, delighting in their coarse language, inciting
them on, all the time speaking in the most choice manner himself; and that explained why he was so fond of sticking so close
to the washerwomen, for they have a knack of calling things by
their true names. Whenever Clémence unburdened herself, he
would sit smiling blandly and twirling his slight moustaches.
The atmosphere of the shop, the perspiring workwomen banging their irons about with their bare arms, that corner resembling an alcove full of the most secret details concerning
all the ladies of the neighbourhood, seemed to him to be the
long-dreamt-of nest, the long-sought haven of idleness and
enjoyment.

At the beginning, Lantier took his meals at François's, at the
corner of the Rue des Poissonniers. But of the seven days in
the week, he dined with the Coupeaus on three or four; so

much so, that he ended by offering to board with them, and to
pay them fifteen francs every Saturday. From that time, he
scarcely ever left the house, but made himself completely at
home there. One would see him from morning till night going
to and fro in his shirt sleeves between the shop and the room
at the back, raising his voice and giving his orders; he even
attended to the customers, he directed everything. François's
wine not being to his liking, he persuaded Gervaise to order her
wine in future of Vigouroux, the charcoal-dealer close by, whose
wife he would go and pinch with Boche, whilst giving the orders.
Then he considered that Coudeloup's bread was not properly
baked, and he sent Augustine to get the bread of Meyer, who
kept the Viennese bakery in the Faubourg Poissonnière. He
also withdrew the custom from Lehongre, the grocer, and only
continued to deal with stout Charles, the butcher of the Rue
Polonceau, because of his political opinions. At the end of a
month, he wished oil to form a part of every dish served at the
table. As Clémence jokingly observed, the oil stain reappeared
on that confounded Southerner in spite of all. He himself
cooked the omelets—omelets turned over on both sides, more
browned than pancakes, and as firm as galettes. He superin-
tended mother Coupeau, insisting on her cooking the beefsteaks
until they became like so much shoe-leather, adding garlic to
everything, and flying into a passion if anyone put herbs into
the salad, horrible weeds, according to him, amongst which
there might easily be something poisonous. But his great
delight was a certain soup, vermicelli, cooked in water, very
thick, into which he poured half a large bottle of oil. Only he
and Gervaise ever ate it, because the others, the Parisians,
having one day ventured to taste it, paid the penalty of almost
depositing their lights and livers on the floor.

Little by little, Lantier also came to mixing himself up in the
affairs of the family. As the Lorilleux always grumbled at having
to part with the five francs for mother Coupeau, he explained that
an action could be brought against them. They must think
that they had a set of fools to deal with! it was ten francs a
month which they ought to give! And he would go up himself for the ten francs, so boldly, and yet so amiably, that the
chainmaker never dared refuse them. Madame Lerat also gave
two five franc pieces now. Mother Coupeau would have kissed
Lantier's hands. He was, moreover, the grand arbiter in all the
quarrels between the old woman and Gervaise. Whenever the
laundress, in a moment of impatience, behaved roughly to her

mother-in-law, and the latter went and cried on her bed, he hustled them about, and made them kiss each other, asking them if they thought themselves amusing with their bad tempers.

And Nana, too : she was being brought up precious badly, according to his idea. In that he was right, for whenever the father spanked the chit, the mother took her part, and if the mother in her turn boxed her ears, the father made a disturbance. Nana, delighted at seeing her parents abuse each other, and knowing that she was forgiven beforehand, was up to all kinds of tricks. Her latest mania was to go and play in the farriery opposite ; she would pass the entire day swinging on the shafts of the carts ; she would hide with bands of urchins in the remotest corners of the grey courtyard, lighted up with the red glare of the forge ; and, suddenly, she would reappear, running and shouting, unkempt and dirty, and followed by the troop of urchins, as though a clash of the hammers had frightened the ragamuffins away. Lantier alone could scold her ; and yet she knew perfectly well how to get over him. This hussy of ten would walk before him like a lady, swinging herself about, and casting side glances at him, her eyes already full of vice. He had ended by undertaking her education : he taught her to dance and to talk patois.

A year passed thus. In the neighbourhood it was thought that Lantier had a private income, for this was the only way to account for the Coupeaus' grand style of living. No doubt, Gervaise continued to earn money ; but now that she had to support two men in doing nothing, the shop certainly could not suffice ; more especially as the shop no longer had so good a reputation, customers were leaving, and the workwomen were tippling from morning till night. The truth was that Lantier paid nothing, neither for rent nor board. During the first months he had paid sums on account, then he had contented himself with speaking of a large amount he had to receive, with which later on he would pay off everything in a lump sum. Gervaise no longer dared ask him for a centime. She had the bread, the wine, the meat, all on credit. The bills increased everywhere at the rate of three and four francs a day. She had not paid a sou to the furniture dealer, nor to the three comrades, the mason, the carpenter, and the painter. All these people commenced to grumble, and she was no longer treated with the same politeness at the shops.

But she was as though intoxicated by a mania for getting

into debt ; she tried to drown her thoughts, ordered the most
expensive things, and gave full freedom to her gluttony now
that she no longer paid for anything ; she remained withal very
honest at heart, dreaming of earning from morning to night
hundreds of francs, though she did not exactly know how, to
enable her to distribute handfuls of five franc pieces to her
tradespeople. In short, she was sinking, and as she sank lower
and lower, she talked of extending her business. Yet, towards
the middle of the summer, tall Clémence had left her, because
there was no longer sufficient work for two women, and because
she had to go for weeks without her money. In the midst of this
downfall, Coupeau and Lantier thoroughly enjoyed themselves.
The fellows gorged till they filled themselves up to their chins,
guttling the shop, fattening on the ruin of the establishment ;
and they stimulated each other to take double helps, and at
dessert playfully slapped one another on the stomach, to help
them digest their food the quicker.

The great subject of conversation in the neighbourhood was
as to whether Lantier had really gone back on his old footing
with Gervaise. On this point opinions were divided. According
to the Lorilleux, the Hobbler was doing all she could to hook
the hatter again, but he would no longer have anything to do
with her, thought her too faded, and had about town some little
women of a very different style. The Boches maintained, on
the contrary, that the very first night the laundress had gone
and joined her old lover directly that noodle, Coupeau, had
commenced to snore. All that, one way or another, was not
very creditable ; but there are so many filthy things in life, and
far worse than this, that people ended by thinking this family
of three quite natural, and even nice, for there was never any
quarrelling, and appearances were respected. It was very certain that if one poked one's nose into some other homes in the
neighbourhood, one would discover something much more disgusting. At the Coupeaus' they were at least a jolly set. All
three attended to their own little cooking, boozed, and slept
together in a friendly way, without interfering with their
neighbours' rest. Besides, the neighbourhood was conquered
by Lantier's pleasant ways. That wheedler shut every gossip's
mouth. Even in the doubt that prevailed as to his relations
with Gervaise, when the greengrocer told the tripe-seller there
was no truth in the reports, the latter seemed to say that it was
really a pity, because, in short, it made the Coupeaus far less
interesting.

Gervaise, however, was quite at her ease in this matter, and not much troubled with these filthy thoughts. Things reached the point that she was accused of being heartless. The family did not understand why she continued to bear a grudge against the hatter. Madame Lerat, who delighted in thrusting herself between lovers, came every evening; and she said that Lantier was an irresistible man, into whose arms the most uppish ladies would end by falling. Madame Boche would never have been sure of her own virtue had she been ten years younger. A secret and continuous conspiracy was formed, gradually inciting Gervaise, as though all the women around her would be satisfying their own desires in giving her a lover. But Gervaise was surprised, and did not consider Lantier particularly seductive. No doubt he had improved : he always wore a coat, and he had acquired some education in the cafés and at political meetings. Only, she knew him well; she could read his very soul through the two holes of his eyes, and she found there a heap of things which made her shudder. In short, if it pleased the others so much, why did they not venture and go in for the gentleman? It was thus that one day she answered Virginie, who was the warmest in the matter. Then, to excite Gervaise, Madame Lerat and Virginie told her of the loves of Lantier and tall Clémence. Yes, she had not noticed anything herself; but, as soon as she went out on an errand, the hatter took the work girl into his room. Now, people met them out together; he probably went to see her at her own place.

"Well," said the laundress, her voice trembling slightly, "what can it matter to me?"

And she looked into Virginie's yellow eyes, in which golden sparks were shining the same as in a cat's. This woman then wished her harm, as she was trying to make her jealous. But the dressmaker put on her stupid air as she replied :

"It can't matter anything to you, of course. Only, you ought to advise him to break off with that girl, who is sure to cause him some unpleasantness."

The worst was that Lantier, feeling himself backed up, changed altogether in his behaviour towards Gervaise. Now, whenever he shook hands with her, he held her fingers for a minute between his own. He tired her with his glance, fixing a bold look upon her, in which she clearly read what it was he asked. If he passed behind her, he dug his knees into her skirts, or breathed upon her neck, as though to send her to sleep. Yet he waited a while before being rough and openly

declaring himself.   But one evening, finding himself alone with
her, he pushed her before him without a word, and pressed her
all trembling against the wall, at the back of the shop, and
there tried to kiss her.   It so chanced that Goujet entered
just at that moment.   Then she struggled and escaped.   And
all three exchanged a few words, as though nothing had
happened.   Goujet, his face deadly pale, looked on the ground,
fancying that he had disturbed them, and that she had merely
struggled so as not to be kissed before a third party.

On the morrow, Gervaise wandered about the shop, feeling
very unhappy, and quite unable even to iron a handkerchief;
she wanted to see Goujet, to explain to him how it was that
Lantier was holding her against the wall.   But since Etienne
had gone to Lille, she no longer dared enter the forge, where
Salted-Mouth, otherwise Drink-without-Thirst, always greeted her
with a sly laugh.   Yet in the afternoon, yielding to her desire,
she took an empty basket and went out under the pretext of
fetching some petticoats from the customer in the Rue des
Portes-Blanches.   Then, when she arrived opposite the bolt
factory in the Rue Marcadet, she slackened her footsteps,
trusting to some chance meeting.   Goujet on his side had no
doubt been expecting her, for she had not been there five
minutes, before he came out just as though by accident.

"What! you've been on an errand?" said he, smiling faintly;
"you're going home?"

He said that for the sake of saying something.   It so happened
that Gervaise was turning her back on the Rue des Poissonniers.   And they made the ascent towards Montmartre side by
side, and without taking one another's arms.   Their only idea
seemed to be to get away from the factory, so as not to appear
to be having meetings just outside the door.   With bowed
heads, they followed the uneven roadway, in the midst of the
hum of the factories.   Then, after proceeding about two hundred yards, they naturally, as though they knew the place,
turned in silence to the left and entered a piece of waste land.
It was a bit of a meadow still green, but with yellow patches
of scorched grass, and situated between a saw-mill and a button
manufactory; a goat, fastened to a stake, kept turning round
and bleating; right at the end, a dead tree was crumbling
away in the fierce sunshine.

"Really!" murmured Gervaise, "it's just like being in the
country."

They went and sat down on the dead tree.   The laundress

placed her basket at her feet. In front of them, the heights
of Montmartre spread out their rows of tall grey and yellow
houses, in the midst of scanty clumps of verdure; and, when
they leant their heads farther back, they beheld the vast
expanse of sky of a dazzling brightness above the town, and
streaked towards the north by a flight of small white clouds.
But the brilliant light dazed them; they lowered their glances
to the distant white buildings of the faubourgs on a level with
the flat horizon, and they especially watched the narrow
chimney of the saw-mill, which kept puffing forth jets of steam.
These great gasps seemed to relieve their oppressed breasts.

"Yes," resumed Gervaise, embarrassed by their mutual
silence, "I was going on an errand, I came out—"

After having so longed for an explanation, she suddenly
found herself unable to say anything. She was seized with a
great shame. And yet she felt that they had come there of
their own accord to talk the matter over; they were indeed
conversing about it, without having the need to utter a word.
The occurrence of the day before remained between them like
a burden which embarrassed them.

Then, seized with an overwhelming sadness, her eyes full of
tears, she gave an account of the last moments of Madame
Bijard, her washerwoman, who had died that morning, after the
most horrible sufferings.

"It was all through Bijard kicking her," said she in a gentle
monotonous voice. "Her stomach swelled up. No doubt, he
had broken something in her inside. Good heavens! in three
days it was all over with her. Ah! there are many scoundrels
in prison who have not done anything so bad as he has. But
justice would have too much to do if it occupied itself about all
the women who have been killed by their husbands. One kick
more or less doesn't count, does it, when one's in the habit of
receiving them all day long? More especially as the poor
woman wished to save her husband from the scaffold, and
stated that she had hurt herself by falling on a tub. She
yelled all through the night before going off."

The blacksmith said nothing, but pulled up the grass with
his trembling fingers.

"It's only a fortnight ago," continued Gervaise, "that she
weaned her last, little Jules; and that's a piece of luck, for
the child won't suffer from it. All the same, there's that
youngster Lalie has got to look after the two little brats.
She's not eight years old yet, but she's as serious and as sen-

sible as a real mother. With that, her father's always beating
her. Ah well! one comes across people who are born to
suffer."

Goujet looked at her and said abruptly, his lips trembling
the while:

"You caused me great pain, yesterday; oh! yes, great pain."

Gervaise, turning pale, clasped her hands. But he continued:

"I know, it was bound to happen. Only, you ought to have
confided in me, have told me the truth about it, so as not to
have let me form ideas—"

He was unable to finish. She rose up when she understood
that Goujet thought she had resumed her old relations with
Lantier, as the whole neighbourhood affirmed was the case.
And, stretching out her arms, she cried,

"No, no, I swear to you. He had pushed me there; he was
trying to kiss me, it's true, but his face did not even touch
mine, and it was the first time that he had tried anything of
the kind. Oh, listen! I swear it on my life, on the lives of my
children, on all that I hold most sacred!"

The blacksmith, however, shook his head. He mistrusted
her, because women always deny. Gervaise then became very
grave, and slowly resumed,

"You know me, Monsieur Goujet, you know I am no liar.
Well! no, it is not so, on my word of honour. And it will
never be so, do you hear? never! The day such a thing were
to happen, I should become the lowest of the low; I should no
longer deserve the friendship of an honest man like you."

And as she spoke, her face was so lovely, so full of truth,
that he took her hand and made her resume her seat. Now he
could breathe freely; he laughed within himself. It was the
first time he had held her hand like that, and he squeezed it in
his own. They both sat without speaking. The little white
clouds moved over the sky with swan-like slowness. In the
corner of the field, the goat turned towards them, looked on,
bleating gently at long, regular intervals. And, without leaving their hold of each other's fingers, their eyes bathed in
tenderness, they looked into the distance at the pale Montmartre slope in the centre of the tall forest of factory chimneys
bordering the horizon, in that desolate suburb of mortar, amidst
which the green arbours of the low pot-houses moved them to
tears.

"Your mother is angry with me, I know she is," resumed

Gervaise in a low voice. "Don't deny it. We owe you so much money!"

But he became violent to induce her to leave off. He shook her hand as though he would break it. He did not wish her to speak of the money. He hesitated, but at length managed to stammer,

"Listen! for a long time past I have been thinking of proposing something to you. You're not happy. My mother assures me that things are going badly for you—"

He stopped a moment; he was almost choking.

"Well! we ought to go off together."

She looked at him, not clearly understanding at first, and surprised by that rough declaration of a love regarding which he had never before opened his lips.

"In what way?" asked she.

"Yes," continued he with bowed head, "we could go off; we could live somewhere together, in Belgium if you like. It's almost my own country. And with both of us working we should soon get comfortable."

Then she became very red. Had he pressed her against him and kissed her, she could not have felt more shame. He was a queer fellow all the same, to propose an elopement to her, just like in novels and in high life. Ah, well! all round about her she saw workmen courting married women; but they did not even take them as far as Saint-Denis; everything occurred on the spot, and openly too.

"Ah! Monsieur Goujet, Monsieur Goujet!" murmured she, without finding anything else to say.

"In short, we should only be our two selves," resumed he. "I can't bear the others, you understand. When I have a fondness for a person, I can't endure seeing that person with others."

But she was recovering herself; she refused now, in a sober-minded way.

"It isn't possible, Monsieur Goujet. It would be very wicked. I'm married, am I not? I've children. I know very well that you have a great friendship for me, and that I cause you pain. Only we should suffer remorse; we should feel no pleasure. I, also, have a great friendship for you. I feel too much to let you do anything foolish. And it would be certainly very foolish indeed. No, listen; we had far better remain as we are. We esteem one another; our sentiments are the same. That is much; the thought of it has sustained me many a time.

When people in our position keep to the right path, they have their reward."

He nodded his head as he listened to her. He approved what she said ; he could not say she was wrong. Suddenly, in the full light of day, he took her in his arms, pressing her almost enough to crush her, and kissed her furiously on the neck, as though he wanted to devour her skin. Then he let go of her without asking anything further, and he did not again speak of their love. She smoothed her things, but showed no anger, feeling that they had both well earned that little pleasure.

The blacksmith, shaking from head to foot with a great trembling, drew away from her, so as not to yield to the desire to seize hold of her again ; and he crawled along on his knees, not knowing how to occupy his hands, picking dandelions which he threw into her basket from a distance. In the midst of the scorched grass there were some superb yellow dandelions. Little by little, this occupation calmed and amused him. He gathered the flowers delicately, with fingers stiffened with wielding the hammer, and threw them one by one, and his kind-looking eyes smiled whenever he did not miss the basket. The laundress, gay and rested, was reclining against the dead tree, and she raised her voice to make herself heard above the panting noise of the saw-mill. When they quitted the waste ground, walking side by side, talking of Etienne, who was very happy at Lille, she carried away her basket full of dandelions.

Gervaise, at heart, did not feel as courageous when with Lantier as she said. She was, indeed, perfectly resolved not to let him touch her, even with the tips of his fingers ; but she was afraid, if ever he should touch her, of her old cowardice, of that feebleness and complacency into which she allowed herself to glide, just to please people. Lantier, however, did not renew his attempt. He several times found himself alone with her and kept quiet. He seemed to be now occupied with the tripe-seller, a woman of forty-five and very well preserved. Gervaise would talk of the tripe-seller in Goujet's presence, so as to set his mind at ease. She would say to Virginie and Madame Lerat, whenever they were ringing the hatter's praises, that he could very well do without her admiration, because all the women of the neighbourhood were smitten with him.

Coupeau went braying about everywhere that Lantier was a friend and a true one. People might jabber about them ; he knew what he knew, and did not care a straw for their gossip, for he had respectability on his side. When they all three went out walking on Sundays, he made his wife and the hatter walk arm-in-arm before him, just by way of swaggering in the street ; and he watched the people, quite prepared to administer a drubbing if any one had ventured on the least joke. No doubt he considered Lantier a trifle stuck up. He accused him of disdaining the "vitriol," and chaffed him because he could read and spoke like a barrister; but, with that exception, he declared he was a jolly good fellow. One could not have found two others like them in all La Chapelle. In short, they understood each other; they had both been made on the same model. Friendship with a man is more steadfast than love with a woman.

There is one thing to be said, Coupeau and Lantier were for ever going out junketting together. Lantier would now borrow money of Gervaise—ten francs, twenty francs at a time, whenever he smelt there was money in the house. Then, on those days, he would keep Coupeau away from his work, talk of some distant errand, and take him with him ; and seated opposite to each other in a corner of some neighbouring eating-house, they would guttle dishes which one cannot get at home, and wash them down with bottles of better class wine. The zinc-worker would have preferred a booze in the hail-fellow-well-met style ; but he was impressed by the aristocratic tastes of the hatter, who would discover on the bill of fare dishes with the most extraordinary names. One could never have imagined a man so delicate and so hard to please. But they are all like that, it seems, in the South. For instance, he would have nothing heating ; he discussed each stew from a sanitary point of view, and had the meat taken away again whenever he thought it too salt or too peppery. It was worse still if there was a draught ; it filled him with a mortal dread ; he abused the whole establishment if a door was left ajar. With all that, he was very stingy, only giving the waiter a couple of sous after a meal costing seven or eight francs.

Nevertheless, people trembled before him, the pair were both well known along the exterior Boulevards, from Batignolles to Belleville. They would go to the Grande Rue des Batignolles to eat tripe cooked in the Caen style, and served on little hot-water plates. At the foot of Montmartre they obtained the best oysters of the neighbourhood at the "Town of Bar-le-Duc." When they ventured to the top of the height, as far as the "Galette Windmill," they had a stewed rabbit. The "Lilacs" in the Rue des Martyrs had a reputation for their calf's head ;

whilst the restaurants of the "Golden Lion" and the "Two Chestnut Trees," in the Chaussée Clignancourt, served them stewed kidneys, which made them lick their lips. But they more often turned to the left towards Belleville, where there was always a table kept for them at the "Vintages of Burgundy," the "Blue Dial," and the "Capuchin," houses to be depended upon, where you could order everything with your eyes shut. They were sly little parties, which they talked of on the morrow in words of hidden meaning, whilst they trifled with Gervaise's fried potatoes. One day even, in one of the arbours of the "Galette Windmill," Lantier brought a woman with whom Coupeau left him at dessert.

One naturally cannot both guttle and work; so that, ever since the hatter had made one of the family, the zinc-worker, who was already pretty lazy, had got to the point of never touching a tool. When, tired of doing nothing, he let himself be prevailed upon to take up a job, his comrade would look him up, and chaff him unmercifully when he found him hanging to his knotty cord like a smoked ham; and he would call to him to come down and have a glass of wine. And that settled it: the zinc-worker would send the job to blazes, and commence a booze which lasted days and weeks. Oh, it was a famous booze, a general review of all the dram-shops of the neighbourhood, the intoxication of the morning slept off by midday and renewed in the evening; the goes of "vitriol" succeeded one another, becoming lost in the depths of the night, like the Venetian lanterns of an illumination, until the last candle disappeared with the last glass! That rogue of a hatter never kept on to the end. He let the other get elevated, then gave him the slip, and returned home smiling in his pleasant way. He coloured his nose decently, without people noticing it. When one got to know him well, one could only tell it by his half-closed eyes and his overbold behaviour to women. The zinc-worker, on the contrary, became quite disgusting, and could no longer drink without putting himself into a beastly state.

Thus, towards the beginning of November, Coupeau went in for a booze which ended in a most dirty manner both for himself and the others. The day before he had been offered a job. This time, Lantier was full of fine sentiments; he lauded work because work ennobles a man. In the morning he even rose before it was light, for he gravely wished to accompany his friend to the workshop, honouring in him the workman really worthy of the name. But when they arrived before the

"Little Civet," which was just opening, they entered to have a plum in brandy, only one, merely to drink together to the firm observance of a good resolution. On a bench opposite the counter, and with his back against the wall, Bibi-the-Smoker was sitting smoking, with a sulky look on his face.

"Hallo! here's Bibi having a snooze," said Coupeau. "Are you down in the dumps, old bloke?"

"No, no," replied the comrade, stretching his arms. "It's the employers who disgust me. I sent mine to the right about yesterday. They're all toads, all scoundrels."

And Bibi-the-Smoker accepted a plum. He was, no doubt, waiting there on that bench for some one to stand him a drink. Lantier, however, took the part of the employers; they often had some very hard times, as he, who had been in business himself, well knew. Workmen were a bad lot! always on the booze, not caring a hang about their work, leaving one in the lurch at some pressing moment, and only putting in an appearance again when their money was all gone. For instance, he had had a little Picardian whose fad was to go driving about; yes, the moment he had got his week's screw, he took cabs for days together. Was that a taste worthy of a worker? Then suddenly Lantier also attacked the employers. Oh, he saw clearly, he would tell every one what he thought of them. A dirty race after all, fellows without the least shame, regular man-eaters. He, thank heaven! could sleep with an easy conscience, for he had always treated his men as friends, and had preferred not to make millions, as others did.

"Let's be off, my boy," said he speaking to Coupeau. "We must be good or we shall be late."

Bibi-the-Smoker followed them, swinging his arms. Outside, the sun was scarcely rising, the pale daylight seemed dirtied by the muddy reflection of the pavement; it had rained the night before, and it was very mild. The gas lamps had just been turned out; the Rue des Poissonniers, in which shreds of night rent by the houses still floated, was gradually filling with the dull tramp of the workmen descending towards Paris. Coupeau, with his zinc-worker's bag slung over his shoulder, walked along in the imposing manner of a fellow on the job, once in a way. He turned round and asked:

"Bibi, are you to be enticed? The governor told me to bring a pal if I could."

"Thanks," answered Bibi-the-Smoker; "I'm purging myself. You should propose that to My-Boots, who was looking out for a crib yesterday. Wait a minute. My-Boots is most likely in there."

And as they reached the bottom of the street, they indeed caught sight of My-Boots inside old Colombe's. In spite of the early hour, the " Assommoir" was flaring, the shutters down, the gas lighted. Lantier stood at the door, telling Coupeau to make haste, because they had only ten minutes left.

"What! you're going to that rascal Bourguignon's ?" yelled My-Boots, when the zinc-worker had spoken to him. "You'll never catch me in his hutch again ! No, I'd rather go till next year with my tongue hanging out of my mouth. But, old fellow, you won't stay there three days, it's I who tell you so."

"Really, now, is it a dirty hole ?" asked Coupeau, anxiously.

"Oh, it's about the dirtiest. You can't move there. The ape's for ever on your back. And such queer ways, too—a missus who always says you're drunk, a shop where you mustn't spit. I sent 'em to the right about the first night, you know."

"Good ; now I'm warned. I sha'n't stop there for ever. I'll just go this morning to see what it's like ; but if the governor bothers me, I'll catch him up and sit him upon his missus, you know, bang together like a pair of soles !"

The zinc-worker shook his comrade's hand to thank him for his warning ; and he was moving off, when My-Boots flew into a rage. Jove's thunder ! was Bourguignon going to prevent them having a drink together ? Were men no longer men, then ? The ape could very well wait for five minutes. And Lantier entering to join in the drink, the four men stood up in front of the bar. My-Boots, with his shoes trodden down at heel, his blouse black with filth, his cap flattened down on the top of his head, yelled at the top of his voice and rolled his eyes as though the whole " Assommoir" belonged to him. He had recently been proclaimed emperor of gormandizers and king of pigs, for having eaten a salad of live cockchafers and bitten a dead cat.

"I say, you Borgia," called he to old Colombe, "give us some of your yellow stuff, your ass's wine, number one."

And when old Colombe, pale and quiet in his blue-knitted waistcoat, had filled the four glasses, these gentlemen tossed them off, so as not to let the liquor get flat.

"That does some good all the same where it passes," murmured Bibi-the-Smoker.

But that animal My-Boots was telling them something awfully comic. He was so drunk on the Friday that his comrades had stuck his pipe in his mouth with a handful of plaster.

Any one else would have died of it; he merely strutted about and arched his back.

"Do you gentlemen require anything more?" asked old Colombe in his oily voice.

"Yes, fill up again," said Lantier. "It's my turn."

Now, they were talking of women. Bibi-the-Smoker had taken his girl to an aunt's at Montrouge on the previous Sunday. Coupeau asked for news of the "Indian Mail," a washerwoman of Chaillot, who was known in the establishment. They were about to drink, when My-Boots loudly called to Goujet and Lorilleux, who were passing by. They came just to the door, but would not enter. The blacksmith did not care to take anything. The chain-maker, pale and shivering, held in his pocket the gold chains he was going to deliver; and he coughed, and asked them to excuse him, saying that the least drop of brandy would nearly make him split his sides.

"There are hypocrites for you!" grunted My-Boots. "I bet they have their drinks on the sly."

And when he had poked his nose in his glass, he attacked old Colombe.

"Vile druggist, you've changed the bottle! You know, it's no good your trying to palm your vitriol off on me!"

The day had advanced; a doubtful sort of light lit up the "Assommoir," where the landlord was turning out the gas. Coupeau, however, found excuses for his brother-in-law, who could not stand drink, which after all was no crime. He even approved Goujet's behaviour, for it was a real blessing never to be thirsty. And he talked of going off to his work, when Lantier, with his grand air of a gentleman, sharply gave him a lesson. One at least stood one's turn before sneaking off; one should not leave one's friends like a mean blackguard, even when going to do one's duty.

"Is he going to badger us much longer about his work?" cried My-Boots.

"So this is your turn, sir?" asked old Colombe of Coupeau.

The latter paid. But when it came to Bibi-the-Smoker's turn, he whispered to the landlord, who refused with a shake of the head. My-Boots understood, and again set to abusing that old Jew Colombe. What! a rascal like him dared to behave in that way to a comrade! Everywhere else one could get drink on tick! It was only in such low boozing-kens that one was insulted! The landlord remained calm, leaning on his big fists on the edge of the counter, and politely said:

"Lend the gentleman some money—that will be far simpler."

"Damnation! yes, I'll lend him some," yelled My-Boots. "Here, Bibi, throw his money in his face, the limb of Satan!"

Then excited, and annoyed at seeing Coupeau with his bag slung over his shoulder, he continued, speaking to the zinc-worker:

"You look like a wet-nurse. Drop your brat. It'll give you a hump-back."

Coupeau hesitated an instant; and then, quietly, as though he had only made up his mind after considerable reflection, he laid his bag on the ground, saying:

"It's too late now. I'll go to Bourguignon's after lunch. I'll tell him that the missus was ill. Listen, old Colombe, I'll leave my tools under this seat, and I'll call for them at twelve o'clock."

Lantier nodded his approval of this arrangement. One must work, no doubt; only, when one is with friends, politeness passes before everything. A desire for tippling had gradually tickled and overcome the four of them, and they stood there with heavy hands consulting each other with a glance. And as soon as they saw they had five hours of idleness before them, they were suddenly seized with a noisy joy, catching each other friendly slaps, and bawling affectionate words in each other's faces. Coupeau especially, feeling relieved and younger, called the others "old bricks!" They had one more round of drinks, and then moved off to the "Sniffing Flea," a low dram-shop possessing a billiard table. The hatter made a grimace at first, for it was not a very clean-looking place; the brandy there cost a franc the litre, ten sous a chopin in two glasses, and the customers had so messed the billiard table that the balls stuck to it. But once the game had begun, Lantier, who was an extraordinarily good player, recovered his grace and his good temper, developing the trunk of his body and accompanying each canon with a swing of the hip.

When lunch time came, Coupeau had an idea. He stamped his feet as he cried:

"We must go and fetch Salted-Mouth. I know where he's working. We'll take him to mother Louis's to have some pettitoes."

The idea was greeted with acclamation. Yes, Salted-Mouth, otherwise Drink-without-Thirst, was no doubt in want of some pettitoes. They started off. The streets had a yellowish look; a fine rain was falling. But they were too warm internally for them to feel the slight watering of their exteriors. Coupeau took them to the bolt factory in the Rue Marcardet. As they arrived a good half hour before the time the workmen came out, the zinc-worker gave a youngster two sous to go in and tell Salted-Mouth that his wife was ill and wanted him at once. The blacksmith made his appearance, waddling in his walk, looking very calm, and scenting a tuck-out.

"Ah! the jokers!" said he, as soon as he caught sight of them hiding in a doorway. "I guessed it. Well! what are we going to eat?"

At mother Louis's, whilst they sucked the little bones of the pettitoes, they again fell to abusing the employers. Salted-Mouth, otherwise Drink-without-Thirst, related that they had a most pressing order to execute at his crib. Oh! the ape was pleasant for the time being. One could be late, and he would say nothing; he no doubt considered himself lucky when any one did turn up. There was no fear that any one would ever dare give Salted-Mouth, otherwise Drink-without-Thirst, the sack, because one could not find many chaps who were his equal. After the pettitoes, they had an omelet. Each drank his quart of wine. Mother Louis had her wine sent from Auvergne—a wine of the colour of blood, and which could almost be cut with a knife. It was beginning to get amusing; the booze was going apace.

"What do you think is the ape's latest idea?" cried Salted-Mouth at dessert. "Why he's been and put a bell up in his shed! A bell! that's good for slaves. Ah well! it can ring to-day! They won't catch me again at the anvil! For five days past I've been sticking there; I may give myself a rest now. If he deducts anything, I'll send him to blazes."

"I," said Coupeau, with an air of importance, "I'm obliged to leave you; I'm off to work. Yes, I promised my wife. Amuse yourselves; my heart, you know, remains with my pals."

The others chaffed him. But he seemed so decided that they all accompanied him, when he talked of going to fetch his tools from old Colombe's. He took his bag from under the seat and laid it on the ground before him whilst they had a final drink. But at one o'clock the party was still standing drinks round. Then Coupeau, with a bored gesture, placed the tools back again under the seat. They were in his way; he could not get near the counter without stumbling against them. It was too absurd; he would go to Bourguignon's on the morrow. The other four, who were quarrelling about the question of salaries,

were not at all surprised when the zinc-worker, without any
explanation, proposed a little stroll on the Boulevard, just to
stretch their legs.   It had left off raining.   The little stroll was
confined to their going a couple of hundred steps all in a row
and swinging their arms ; and, surprised by the fresh air, feeling
bored at being out of doors, they no longer found a word to say
Without even consulting each other with so much as a nudge,
they slowly and instinctively ascended the Rue des Poissonniers,
where they went to François's and had a glass of wine out of
the bottle.   Really, they were in want of that to pull them
together again.   It was too depressing out in the street ; it was
so muddy it would be a shame even to send a policeman out in
it.   Lantier pushed his comrades inside the private room at the
back ; it was a narrow place with only one table in it, and was
separated from the shop by a dull glazed partition.   He usually
preferred to colour his nose in private rooms, because it was
more respectable.   Were they not all very comfortable in
there ?   One could almost think oneself at home, and could
have had a nap without the least trouble.   He called for the
newspaper, spread it out open before him, and looked through
it, frowning the while.   Coupeau and My-Boots had commenced a game at piquet.   Two bottles of wine and five glasses
were scattered about the table.

"Well! what do they say in that rag ? " asked Bibi-the-
Smoker of the hatter.

He did not reply at once.   Then, without raising his eyes,
he said :

"I'm reading the report of the Chamber.   They're no repub-
licans, those lazy scoundrels of the Left !   Do the people elect
them merely for them to swill their sugar and water ?   Here's
one who believes in God, and who's letting himself be cajoled by
those rascally ministers !   If I were elected, I would get into
the tribune and say : 'Excrement !' yes, nothing more, that's
my opinion !"

"You know, Badingue's had a fight with his missus, before
all the court," related Salted-Mouth, otherwise Drink-without-
Thirst.   "I give you my word of honour it's true !   And all
about nothing, just a little wrangle.   Badingue was a bit
boozed."

"Shut up with your politics ! " cried the zinc-worker.
"Read us the murders, they're more amusing."

And returning to his game, he declared a tierce from the
nine and three queens.

"I've a tierce from the sewer and three doves. The crinolines don't forsake me."

They emptied their glasses. Then Lantier read out loud :

"A frightful crime has just spread consternation throughout the Commune of Gaillon, Department of Seine-et-Marne. A son has killed his father with blows from a spade, in order to rob him of thirty sous."

They all uttered a cry of horror. There was a fellow, by Jove! whom they would have taken great pleasure in seeing guillotined! No, the guillotine was not enough; he deserved to be cut into little pieces. The story of an infanticide equally aroused their indignation; but the hatter, highly moral, found excuses for the woman, putting all the wrong on to the back of her seducer; for, after all, if some beast of a man had not put the wretched woman into the way of having a brat, she could not have thrown one down the water-closet. But what really delighted them, were the exploits of the Marquis de T—, who, leaving a ball at two o'clock in the morning, defended himself against three ruffians on the Boulevard des Invalides; without even taking his gloves off, he had rid himself of the first two by butting them in the stomach, and had led the third by the ear to the police station. Ah! what muscle! It was a pity he was an aristocrat.

"Listen to this, now," continued Lantier. "Here's some news of high life: 'A marriage is arranged between the eldest daughter of the Countess de Brétigny and the young Baron de Valançay, aide-de-camp to His Majesty. The wedding trousseau will contain more than three hundred thousand francs' worth of lace.'"

"What's that to us?" interrupted Bibi-the-Smoker. "We don't want to know the colour of her chemise. The girl can have no end of lace, nevertheless she'll see the moon the same way as other people."

As Lantier seemed about to finish his reading, Salted-Mouth, otherwise Drink-without-Thirst, took the newspaper from him, and sat upon it, saying :

"Ah! no, that's enough! Paper's only good for this."

Meanwhile, My-Boots, who had been looking at his hand, triumphantly banged his fist down on the table. He scored ninety-three.

"I've the Revolution," shouted he. "A quint in clubs. That's twenty, isn't it? Then tierce major in diamonds, twenty-three; three kings, twenty-six; three jacks, twenty, nine ; three aces, ninety-two. And I play year one of the Republic, ninety-three."

" You're done for, old boy," cried the others to Coupeau.

They ordered two fresh bottles. The glasses were filled up again as fast as they were emptied, the booze increased. Towards five o'clock, it began to get disgusting, so much so that Lantier kept very quiet, thinking of how to give the others the slip ; brawling and throwing the wine about was no longer his style. Just then Coupeau stood up to make the drunkard's sign of the cross. Touching his head, he pronounced Montpernasse, then Menilmonte as he brought his hand to his right shoulder, La Courtille moving it to his left shoulder, Bagnolet giving himself a blow in the chest, and wound up by saying, stewed rabbit three times as he hit himself in the pit of the stomach. Then, the hatter took advantage of the clamour which greeted the performance of this feat, and quietly made for the door. His comrades did not even notice his departure. He had already had a pretty good dose. But, once outside, he shook himself and regained his self-possession ; and he quietly made for the shop, where he told Gervaise that Coupeau was with some friends.

Two days passed by. The zinc-worker had not returned. He was reeling about the neighbourhood, but no one knew exactly where. Several persons, however, stated that they had seen him at mother Baquet's, at the "Butterfly," and at the "Little Old Man with a Cough." Only, some said that he was alone, whilst others affirmed that he was in the company of seven or eight drunkards like himself. Gervaise shrugged her shoulders in a resigned sort of way. All she had to do was to get used to it. She never ran about after her old man ; she even went out of her way, if she caught sight of him inside a wine-shop, so as not to anger him ; and she waited at home till he returned, listening at night-time to hear if he was snoring outside the door. He would sleep on a rubbish-heap, or on a seat, or in a piece of waste land, or across a gutter. On the morrow, after having only badly slept off his booze of the day before, he would start off again, knocking at the doors of all the consolation dealers, plunging afresh into a furious wandering, in the midst of nips of spirits, glasses of wine, losing his friends and then finding them again, going regular voyages from which he returned in a state of stupor, seeing the streets dance, the night fall, and the day break, without any other thought than to drink and sleep off the effects wherever he happened to be. When in the latter state, the world was ended so far as he was concerned. On the second day, however, Gervaise went to old Colombe's "Assommoir," to find out something about him ; he had been there another five times, they were unable to tell her anything more. All she could do was to take away his tools, which he had left under a seat.

In the evening, Lantier, seeing that the laundress seemed very worried, offered to take her to a music-hall, just by way of passing a pleasant hour or two. She refused at first, she was in no mood for laughing. Otherwise, she would not have said, " no," for the hatter made the proposal in too straightforward a manner for her to feel any mistrust. He seemed to feel for her in quite a paternal way. Never before had Coupeau slept out two nights running. So that, in spite of herself, she would go every ten minutes to the door, with her iron in her hand, and look up and down the street to see if her old man was coming. It made her legs tingle, so she said, in such a way that she could not stand still. Coupeau might very likely get a limb broken, or fall under some vehicle and stay there : it would be a good riddance, and she forbade herself to entertain the least affection in her heart for such a disgusting person as he was. But it was becoming very annoying, never knowing whether he would return or whether he would not. And, when the gas lamps were lighted, as Lantier again proposed the music-hall, she accepted his invitation. After all, she was very stupid to refuse a pleasure, when, for the past three days, her husband had been doing nothing but lead a dog's life. As he did not come home, she too would go out. The place might burn down if it liked. She was ready to set it alight herself, for the troubles of life were beginning to disgust her with everything.

They eat their dinner quickly. Then, when she went off at eight o'clock, arm-in-arm with the hatter, Gervaise told mother Coupeau and Nana to go to bed at once. The shop was shut. She left by the door opening into the courtyard and gave Madame Boche the key, asking her, if her pig came home, to have the kindness to put him to bed. The hatter was waiting for her under the big doorway, arrayed in his best and whistling a tune. She had on her silk dress. They walked slowly along the pavement, keeping close to each other, lighted up by the glare from the shop windows which showed them smiling and talking together in a low voice.

The music-hall was in the Boulevard de Rochechouart, it had

originally been a little café and had been enlarged by means of
a kind of wooden shed erected in the courtyard. At the door,
a string of glass globes formed a luminous porch. Tall posters
pasted on boards stood upon the ground, close to the gutter.

"Here we are," said Lantier. "To-night, first appearance of
Mademoiselle Amanda, serio-comic."

But he caught sight of Bibi-the-Smoker, who was also reading
the poster. Bibi had a black eye; some knock he had run up
against the day before.

"Well! where's Coupeau?" inquired the hatter, looking about.
"Have you, then, lost Coupeau?"

"Oh! long ago, since yesterday," replied the other. "There
was a bit of a mill on leaving mother Baquet's. I don't care for
fisticuffs. We had a row, you know, with mother Baquet's pot-
boy, because he wanted to make us pay for a quart twice over.
Then I sloped. I went and had a bit of a snooze."

He was still gaping; he had slept eighteen hours at a stretch.
He was, moreover, quite sobered, with a stupid look on his face,
and his jacket smothered with fluff; for he had no doubt
tumbled into bed with his clothes on.

"And you don't know where my husband is, sir?" asked the
laundress.

"Well, no, not a bit. It was five o'clock when we left
mother Baquet's. That's all I know about it. Perhaps he
went down the street. Yes, I fancy now that I saw him go to
the 'Butterfly' with a coachman. Oh! how stupid it is!
Really, we deserve to be shot!"

Lantier and Gervaise spent a very pleasant evening at the
music-hall. At eleven o'clock, when the place closed, they
strolled home without hurrying themselves. It was rather
chilly, the spectators went off in parties, and there were some
girls splitting with laughter in the shadow under the trees,
because the men who were with them were larking too familiarly.
Lantier sang one of Mademoiselle Amanda's songs between his
teeth : "It's in the nose that it tickles me." Gervaise, feeling
giddy, as though intoxicated, took up the chorus. She had felt
very warm during the evening. Then the two drinks she had
had, together with the tobacco smoke, and the odour of all those
people crowded together, made her feel sick. But she carried
away with her a very lively impression of Mademoiselle Amanda.
She would never herself have dared to have appeared before the
public in such a state of nudity. But to be just, the lady
had a most delicious skin. And she listened with a sensual

curiosity, whilst Lantier gave some details about the person in question, with the air of a man who had counted her ribs in private.

" Every one's asleep," said Gervaise, after ringing three times, without the Boches opening the door.

At length the door opened, but inside the porch it was very dark, and when she knocked at the window of the doorkeeper's room to ask for her key, the doorkeeper, who was half asleep, called out some rigmarole which she could make nothing of at first. She eventually understood that Poisson, the policeman, had brought Coupeau home in a frightful state, and that the key was no doubt in the lock.

"The deuce!" murmured Lantier, when they had entered, " whatever has he been up to here? The stench is abominable."

When Gervaise, who had been looking for the matches, succeeded in lighting a candle, a pretty sight met their eyes. Coupeau appeared to have disgorged his very inside. Besides that, he had fallen from the bed, where Poisson had probably thrown him, and was snoring on the floor in the midst of the filth like a pig wallowing in the mire, exhaling his foul breath through his open mouth.

" Oh! the pig! the pig!" repeated Gervaise, indignant and exasperated. "He's dirtied everything. No, a dog wouldn't have done that, a dead dog is cleaner."

Never before had the zinc-worker returned home in such a state. The sight was a great shock to the affection his wife still had for him. In the earlier days, when he returned slightly elevated or tipsy, she showed herself kind, and in no way disgusted. But this time it was too much, her stomach turned against it. She would not have taken hold of him with a pair of tongs. The thought alone that that sot's skin would touch her own gave her the same feeling of repugnance as being asked to lie down beside a corpse corrupted by some horrible disease.

"I must, however, get into bed," murmured she. " I can't go and sleep in the street. Oh! I'll tread on him sooner."

She tried to step over the drunkard, but had to catch hold of a corner of the chest of drawers to save herself from slipping. Coupeau completely blocked the way to the bed. Then, Lantier, who laughed to himself on seeing that she certainly would not sleep on her own pillow that night, took hold of her hand, saying in a low and ardent voice :

" Gervaise ; listen, Gervaise."

But she had understood. She freed herself, and in her bewilder-
ment addressed him familiarly as in the old days.

"No, leave me. I implore you, Auguste, go to your own
room. I'll manage to lie at the foot of the bed."

"Come, Gervaise, don't be foolish," resumed he. "It's too
abominable; you can't remain here. Come. What do you fear?
he can't hear us ! "

She struggled, she energetically shook her head. In her confusion, as though to show that she intended to remain there,
she commenced to undress herself, throwing her silk gown on to
a chair, and suddenly appearing all white in her petticoat and
chemise, her throat and arms bare. Her bed was her own, was
it not? she intended to sleep in her bed. Twice again she tried
to find a clear space to enable her to reach it. But Lantier did
not give in, and kept seizing her round the waist, saying all sorts
of things to excite her. Ah ! she was in a pretty position, with
a crapulous husband in front who prevented her getting
respectably under her blanket, and a dirty blackguard of a man
behind, whose only thought was to take advantage of her misfortune to make her his mistress again ! As the hatter raised
his voice, she implored him to keep quiet. And she listened,
with her ear towards the little room occupied by Nana and
mother Coupeau. The child and the old woman were no doubt
asleep, for one could hear a heavy breathing.

"Auguste, leave me, you'll wake them," said she, clasping
her hands. "Be reasonable. Another day, elsewhere. Not
here, not before my child."

He no longer spoke, he stood there smiling ; and he slowly
kissed her on the ear, the same as he used to do to tease and
stupefy her. Then her strength deserted her, she felt a great
buzzing in her ears, a violent tremor passed through her. Yet,
she advanced another step forward. And she was again obliged
to draw back. It was not possible, the disgust was so great.
Coupeau, overpowered by intoxication, lying as comfortably as
though on a bed of down, was sleeping off his booze, without
life in his limbs, and with his mouth all on one side. The
whole street might have entered and kissed his wife without a
hair of his body moving.

"So much the worse," stammered she, "it's his fault, I cannot do it. Ah ! good heavens ! ah ! good heavens ! he drives
me from my bed, I've no longer a bed. No, I cannot, it's his
fault."

LANTIER ENTICING GERVAISE NOT TO REMAIN WITH HER DRUNKEN
HUSBAND.   p. 200.

She trembled, she lost her head. And whilst Lantier pushed her into his room, Nana's head appeared behind one of the panes of the glass door of her little chamber. The child had just awoke, and quietly got up in her night-gown, her face pale with sleep. She looked at her father sprawling in his filth; then, pressing close to the pane, she remained there, waiting till her mother's white petticoat had disappeared inside the other man's room opposite. She was quite grave. Her eyes were opened wide like a vicious child's, and lit up with a sensual curiosity.

CHAPTER IX.

THAT winter, mother Coupeau nearly went off in one of her coughing fits. Each December, she could count on her asthma keeping her on her back for two and three weeks at a time. She was no longer fifteen, she would be seventy-three on Saint-Anthony's day. With that, she was very rickety, getting a rattling in her throat for nothing at all, though she was plump and stout. The doctor said she would go off coughing, just time enough to say: "Good-night, Jeanneton, the candle's out!"

When she was in her bed, mother Coupeau became positively unbearable. It is true though that the little room in which she slept with Nana was not at all gay. Between her bedstead and the child's, there was just room to put a couple of chairs. The wall-paper, an old faded grey one, hung in shreds. The little round window close to the ceiling merely admitted the pale doubtful light of a cellar. One soon grew old in there, especially a person who could scarcely breathe. At night-time, when unable to sleep, she would listen to the child's breathing, and that was some amusement. But, in the day-time, as there was no one to keep her company from morning to night, she grumbled, and cried, and repeated to herself for hours together, as she rolled her head on the pillow:

"Good heavens! what a miserable creature I am! Good heavens! what a miserable creature I am! They'll leave me to die in prison, yes, in prison!"

And as soon as any one called, Virginie or Madame Boche, to ask after her health, she would not reply, but immediately started on her chapter of complaints.

"Ah! the bread which I eat here is dear indeed! No, I could not suffer so much were I amongst strangers! Listen, I wanted a cup of herb tea, well! they brought me a water-jug full, just a way of telling me that I drink too much of it. It's the same with Nana, that child whom I brought up, she goes off bare-footed in the morning, and I don't see her again for the rest of the day. One would think I had something offensive. Yet, at night-time, she sleeps precious sound, and doesn't once wake up to ask me if I'm in pain. In short, I'm in their way, they're waiting for me to croak. Oh! it won't take long. I've no longer a son, that hussy of a laundress has taken him from me. She would beat me, she would finish me off, if she were not afraid of the police."

Gervaise was indeed rather hasty at times. The place was going to the dogs, everyone's temper was getting spoilt, and they sent each other to the right about for the least word. Coupeau, one morning that he had got his hair out of curl, exclaimed : " The old thing's always saying she's going to die, and yet she never does ! " words which struck mother Coupeau to the heart. They reproached her with what she cost, they coolly said that it would be a great saving if she were no longer there. To tell the truth, neither did she behave as she should have done. For instance, whenever she saw her eldest daughter, Madame Lerat, she complained of her poverty-stricken condition, accusing her son and her daughter-in-law of leaving her to starve, and when she had wheedled a twenty sou piece out of her, she would spend it in sweetmeats. She also told the Lorilleux some abominable stories, relating that the laundress spent their ten francs in indulging all sorts of fancies of her own, new caps, cakes eaten in sly corners, and far worse things which one could not mention. On two or three occasions, she almost caused a general fight amongst the family. At one moment she was on this side and the next moment she was on that ; in short, everything was getting into a dreadful mess.

When at her worst, that winter, one afternoon when Madame Lorilleux and Madame Lerat had met at her bedside, mother Coupeau winked her eye as a signal to them to lean over her. She could scarcely speak. She rather hissed than said in a low voice : ·

" It's becoming decent! I heard them last night. Yes, yes, the Hobbler and the hatter. And they were kicking up such a row together ! Coupeau's a nice one. It's becoming decent ! "

And she related, in short sentences, coughing and choking between each, that her son had probably come home dead drunk the night before. Then as she was not asleep, she was easily able to account for all the noises, the Hobbler's bare feet tripping over the tiled floor, the hissing voice of the hatter calling her, the door between the two rooms gently closed, and the

rest. It must have lasted till daylight, she could not tell
the exact time, because, in spite of her efforts, she had ended
by falling into a doze.

"What's most disgusting, is that Nana might have heard,"
continued she. "She was indeed restless all the night, she who
usually sleeps so sound; she tossed about, and kept turning
over, as though there had been some lighted charcoal in her
bed."

The other two women did not seem at all surprised.

"Of course!" murmured Madame Lorilleux "it probably
began the very first night. But as it pleases Coupeau, we've
no business to interfere. All the same, it's not very respectable
for the family."

"If I were there," explained Madame Lerat screwing up her
mouth, "I would give her such a fright, I'd call out something,
no matter what: 'I see you!' or else: 'Police!' A doctor's
servant once told me that her master had said that such a
thing at a certain moment might kill a woman on the spot. If
so, it would serve her right; she would be punished where she
had sinned."

All the neighbourhood soon knew that every night Gervaise
went and joined Lantier. In the neighbours' presence, Madame
Lorilleux was noisily indignant; she pitied her brother, that
noodle who was made drunk by his wife from head to toe; and,
according to her, if she continued to visit such people, it was
solely on account of her poor mother, who was obliged to live
in the midst of these abominations. Then the neighbourhood
fell upon Gervaise. It was she who had seduced the hatter.
You could see it in her eyes. Yes, in spite of the nasty
rumours, that sly blade Lantier remained on his pedestal, because he continued to behave towards every one like a highly
respectable person, walking along the pavement reading his
newspaper, attentive and gallant with the ladies, always having
sweets and flowers to give away. Well! he merely continued
to act his part; a man is a man, one cannot ask him to resist
women who throw themselves at him. But she had no excuse;
she was a disgrace to the Rue de la Goutte-d'Or. And the
Lorilleux, in their capacity of godfather and godmother, enticed
Nana to their rooms for the purpose of obtaining details. When
they questioned her in a round-about way, the child put on her
stupid air, hiding the fire of her eyes with her long soft lashes
as she answered them.

In the midst of this general indignation, Gervaise lived

quietly on, feeling tired out and half asleep. At first, she considered herself very guilty, very dirty, and she felt a disgust for herself. Each time she quitted Lantier's room, she washed her hands, she wetted a dish-cloth and rubbed her shoulders almost till they bled, as though to wipe off the stain. If Coupeau then tried to joke, she would fly into a passion, and run and shiveringly dress herself in the farthest corner of the shop ; neither would she allow the hatter to touch her soon after her husband had kissed her. She would have liked to have changed her skin as she changed the man. But she gradually became accustomed to it. It was too much trouble to wash herself each time. Her idleness was destroying her energy, her wish to be happy made her get all the happiness she could out of these worries. She was accommodating both for herself and for the others, and merely tried to arrange things in such a way that no one should be bothered too much. Providing her husband and her lover were satisfied, that the household went on in its own regular little way, that one amused oneself from morn till night, all of them plump, satisfied with life and taking it easy, there was really nothing to complain of, was there now ?

Then, after all, she could not be doing anything so very wrong, since matters were arranged so easily to the general satisfaction ; one is usually punished if one does what is not right. So her dissoluteness had gradually become a habit. Now, it was as regular an affair as eating and drinking ; each time that Coupeau came home drunk, she retired to Lantier's room, and that happened at least on Monday, Tuesday and Wednesday of every week. She divided her nights. She had even got to the point of leaving the zinc-worker in the middle of his sleep if he merely snored too loud, and going and finishing her by-by on the neighbour's pillow. It was not that she felt any greater affection for the hatter. No, she merely found him cleaner, she rested better in his room, where it was like having a bath. In short, she resembled those she-cats which like to curl themselves up on the clean white clothes.

Mother Coupeau never dared speak of it flatly. But, after a quarrel, when the laundress had bullied her, the old woman was not sparing in her allusions. She would say that she knew men who were precious fools, and women who were precious hussies ; and she would mutter words far more biting, with the sharpness of language pertaining to an old waistcoat-maker. The first time this had occurred Gervaise looked at her straight in the face, without answering. Then, also

avoiding going into details, she began to defend herself with
reasons given in a general sort of way. When a woman had a
drunkard for a husband, a pig who lived in filth, that woman
was to be excused if she sought for cleanliness elsewhere. She
went farther than this; she gave it to be understood that
Lantier was as much her husband as Coupeau, perhaps more
so. Had she not known him from the time she was fourteen
years old? Had she not had two children by him? Well! in such
conditions, everything was excusable, no one had a right to
cast stones at her. She was merely obeying the laws of nature.
Besides, she would not stand being bothered by any one. She
would precious soon give them all a bit of her mind. The Rue
de la Goutte-d'Or was not such a very decent place! Little
Madame Vigouroux was cutting capers from morn till night
amongst her charcoal. Madame Lehongre, the grocer's wife,
was her brother-in-law's mistress, and he was a big driveller
whom no one else would have picked up with a shovel. The
clockmaker opposite, that affected gentleman, had almost been
brought up at the criminal court for a most abominable thing
in connection with his own daughter, a hussy who now rolled
about the Boulevards. And, with a broad gesture, she took
in the whole neighbourhood; it would require an hour merely
to display the dirty linen of all those people—fathers, mothers,
children, all sleeping together in a heap like animals, and
wallowing in their own filth. Ah! she knew all about it;
nastiness was to be found everywhere, it infected the houses
round about! Yes, yes, men and women were something
prime in that corner of Paris, where they are all piled up on the
top of each other, on account of their poverty! Had the two
sexes been put into a mortar, all that one could have obtained
from them would have been something wherewith to manure
the cherry-trees in the plain of Saint-Denis.

"They would do well not to spit in the air, for it only falls
down again on their own noses," she would exclaim, whenever
anybody especially aggravated her. "Every one for himself,
is it not so? They should let other people live in their own
way, if they wish to live in theirs. For myself, I'm agreeable to
everything so long as I'm not dragged through the gutter by
people who have already made the plunge head first."

And mother Coupeau having one day been more pointed in
her observations than usual, she had replied to her, clinching
her teeth:

"You're confined to your bed. and you take advantage of it.

Listen, you're wrong; you see that I behave nicely to you, for I've never thrown your past life into your teeth! Oh! I know all about it! A fine life it was—two and three men at a time, and whilst old Coupeau was alive too. No, don't cough, I've finished what I had to say. It's only to request you to mind your own business, that's all!"

The old woman almost choked. On the morrow, Goujet having called about his mother's washing when Gervaise happened to be out, mother Coupeau called him to her and kept him some time seated beside her bed. She knew all about the blacksmith's friendship, and had noticed that for some time past he had looked dismal and wretched, from a suspicion of the abominable things that were taking place. So, for the sake of gossiping, and out of revenge for the quarrel of the day before, she bluntly told him the truth, weeping and complaining as though Gervaise's wicked behaviour did her some special injury. When Goujet quitted the little room, he leant against the wall, almost stifling with grief. Then, when the laundress returned home, mother Coupeau called to her that Madame Goujet required her to go round with her clothes, ironed or not; and she was so animated that Gervaise, seeing something was wrong, guessed what had taken place, and had a presentiment of the unpleasantness which awaited her.

Very pale, her limbs already trembling, she placed the things in a basket and started off. For years past she had not returned the Goujets a sou of their money. The debt still amounted to four hundred and twenty-five francs. She always spoke of her embarrassments and received the money for the washing. It filled her with shame, because she seemed to be taking advantage of the blacksmith's friendship to make a fool of him. Coupeau, who had now become less scrupulous, would chuckle and say that Goujet had no doubt squeezed her waist in odd corners, and had so paid himself. But she, in spite of the relations she had fallen into with Lantier, would indignantly ask her husband if he already wished to eat of that sort of bread. She would not allow any one to say a word against Goujet in her presence; her affection for the blacksmith remained like a last shred of her honour. Thus, every time she took the washing home to those worthy people, she felt a spasm at her heart the moment she put a foot on their stairs.

"Ah! it's you, at last!" said Madame Goujet sharply, on opening the door to her. "When I'm in want of death, I'll send you to fetch him."

Gervaise entered, greatly embarrassed, not even daring to
mutter an excuse. She was no longer punctual, never came at
the time arranged, and would keep her customer waiting for
days together. Little by little she was giving way to a system
of thorough disorder.

"For a week past I've been expecting you," continued the
lace-mender. "And you tell falsehoods too; you send your
apprentice to me with all sorts of stories : you are then busy
with my things, you will deliver them the same evening, or
else you've had an accident, the bundle's fallen into a pail of
water. Whilst all this is going on, I waste my time, nothing
turns up, and it worries me exceedingly. No, you're most un-
reasonable. Come, what have you in your basket? Is everything there now? Have you brought me the pair of sheets
you've been keeping back for a month past, and the chemise
which was missing the last time you brought home the
washing?"

"Yes, yes," murmured Gervaise, "the chemise is there.
Here it is."

But Madame Goujet cried out. That chemise was not hers,
she would have nothing to do with it. Her things were changed
now; it was too bad! Only the week before, there were two
handkerchiefs which hadn't her mark on them. It was not to
her taste to have clothes coming from no one knew where.
Besides that, she liked to have her own things.

"And the sheets?" she resumed. "They're lost, are they?
Well! young woman, you must see about them, for I insist
upon having them to-morrow morning, do you hear?"

A silence ensued. What completed Gervaise's embarrassment
was the knowledge that, behind her, the door of Goujet's room
was ajar. The blacksmith was no doubt inside, she felt that he
was there ; and how unpleasant, if he was listening to all these
deserved reproaches, to which she could answer nothing! She
became very submissive and gentle, bowing her head as she
placed the clean linen on the bed as quickly as she could. But
matters became worse when Madame Goujet began to look over
the things, one by one. She took hold of them and threw them
down again, saying :

"Ah! you don't get them up nearly so well as you used to
do. One can't compliment you every day now. Yes, you've
taken to mucking your work—doing it in a most slovenly way.
Just look at this shirt-front, it's scorched, there's the mark of
the iron on the plaits ; and the buttons have all been torn off.

I don't know how you manage it, but there's never a button left
on anything. Oh! now, here's a petticoat body which I shall
certainly not pay you for. Look there! The dirt's still on it,
you've simply smoothed it over. So now the things are not
even clean!"

She stopped whilst she counted the different articles. Then
she exclaimed,

"What! this is all you've brought? There are two pairs of
stockings, six towels, a table-cloth, and several dish-cloths
short. You're regularly trifling with me, it seems! I sent
word that you were to bring me everything, ironed or not. If
your apprentice isn't here in an hour with the rest of the
things, we shall fall out, Madame Coupeau, I warn you."

At this moment Goujet coughed in his room. Gervaise
slightly started. How she was treated before him, good
heavens! And she remained standing in the middle of the
room, embarrassed and confused, and waiting for the dirty
clothes; but, after making up the account, Madame Goujet had
quietly returned to her seat near the window, and resumed the
mending of a lace shawl.

"And the dirty things?" timidly inquired the laundress.

"No, thank you," replied the old woman, "there's nothing
this week."

Gervaise turned pale. She was no longer to have the washing. Then she quite lost her head; she was obliged to sit
down on a chair for her legs were giving way under her. And
she did not attempt to vindicate herself. All that she could
find to say was,

"Is Monsieur Goujet ill?"

Yes, he was not well. He had been obliged to come home
instead of returning to the forge, and he had gone to lie down
on his bed to get a rest. Madame Goujet talked gravely,
wearing her black dress as usual, and her white face framed in her
monachal cap. They had again lowered the wages of the bolt-
makers. From nine francs they had fallen to seven, on account
of the machinery which now did almost all the work. And she
explained that they were obliged to economise in everything; in
future, she intended to do her own washing as formerly. It would
naturally have been very acceptable if the Coupeaus had been
able to return her the money lent them by her son; but she
was not going to set the lawyers on them, as they were unable to
pay. Since she commenced speaking of the debt, Gervaise,
with bowed head, seemed to be following the skilful play of her

needle as it gathered up the meshes of the net-work one by
one.

"All the same," continued the lace-mender, "by pinching
yourselves a little you could manage to pay it off. For, really
now, you live very well; you spend a great deal, I'm sure. If
you were only to pay off ten francs a month—"

She was interrupted by the sound of Goujet's voice as he
called,

"Mamma! mamma!"

And when she returned to her seat, which was almost immediately, she changed the conversation. The blacksmith had
doubtless begged her not to ask Gervaise for money; but, in
spite of herself, she again spoke of the debt at the expiration of
five minutes. Oh! she had foreseen what was happening—the
zinc-worker was drinking up the shop, and he would lead his
wife a fine dance. Had her son only listened to her he would
never have lent the five hundred francs. He would have
married, he would not have been bursting with sadness, nor
had the prospect of being miserable for the rest of his life.
She was becoming excited, and likewise very harsh, plainly
accusing Gervaise of having arranged with Coupeau to take
advantage of her foolish child. Yes, there were women who
wore the mask of hypocrisy for years, and whose bad character
in the end was displayed in the light of day.

"Mamma! mamma!" again called Goujet, but louder this
time.

She rose from her seat, and when she returned she said, as
she resumed her lace mending,

"Go in, he wishes to see you."

Gervaise, all in a tremble, left the door open. This scene
filled her with emotion, because it was like an avowal of their
affection before Madame Goujet. She again beheld the quiet
little chamber, with its narrow iron bedstead, and papered all
over with pictures, the whole looking like the room of some lad
of fifteen. Goujet's big body was stretched on the bed. Mother
Coupeau's disclosures seemed to have knocked all the life out of
his limbs. His eyes were red and swollen, his beautiful yellow
beard was still wet. In the first moment of rage he must have
punched away at his pillow with his terrible fists, for the ticking was split and the feathers were coming out.

"Listen, mamma's wrong," said he to the laundress, in a
voice that was scarcely audible. "You owe me nothing, I
won't have it spoken of."

He had raised himself up, and was looking at her. Big tears at once filled his eyes.

"Do you suffer, Monsieur Goujet?" murmured she. "What is the matter with you?—tell me."

"Nothing, thanks. I tired myself too much yesterday. I will sleep a bit."

Then, his heart breaking, he could not restrain this cry,

"Ah, my God! my God! it was never to be—never. You swore it. And now it is—it is! Ah, my God! it pains me too much, leave me!"

And with his hand he gently and imploringly motioned to her to go. She did not draw nearer to the bed. She went off as he requested her to, feeling stupid, unable to say anything to soothe him. When in the other room, she took up her basket; but she did not go home. She stood there trying to find something to say. Madame Goujet continued her mending without raising her head. It was she who at length said,

"Well! good night; send me back my things, we will settle up afterwards."

"Yes, it will be best so—good-night," stammered Gervaise.

She closed the door slowly, giving a last glance at that clean, tidy home, where she seemed to be leaving behind her a part of her respectability. She went back to the shop in the stupid manner of cows returning to their shed, without troubling themselves about the way. Mother Coupeau, who had left her bed for the first time, was seated on a chair beside the big stove. But the laundress did not even utter a single reproach. She was too tired, her bones ached as though she had been beaten. She was thinking that life was indeed too hard, and that one could not tear one's heart out without killing oneself right off.

After this, Gervaise became indifferent to everything. With a vague gesture of her hand she would send everybody about their business. At each fresh worry she buried herself deeper in her only pleasure, which was to have her three meals a day. The shop might have collapsed. So long as she was not beneath it she would have gone off willingly without a chemise to her back. And the shop was collapsing, not suddenly, but little by little, morning and evening. One by one the customers got angry, and sent their washing elsewhere. M. Madinier, Mademoiselle Remanjou, the Boches themselves had returned to Madame Fauconnier, where they could count on greater punctuality. One ends by getting tired of asking for a

pair of stockings for three weeks together, and of putting on
shirts with grease stains dating from the previous Sunday.
Gervaise, without losing a bite, wished them a pleasant journey,
and spoke her mind about them, saying that she was precious glad
she would no longer have to poke her nose into their filth.   Ah,
well! the whole neighbourhood might withdraw its custom, it
would rid her of a fine heap of infection.   Besides that, too, it
would be so much work the less.   Meanwhile, she merely retained the customers who paid badly, the street-walkers, and
the women like Madame Gaudron, whose washing not a laundress of the Rue Neuve would touch.   The shop was done for.
She had had to discharge her last workwoman, Madame Putois;
and she was left alone with her apprentice, that squint-eyed
Augustine, who became all the more stupid the bigger she
grew.   Yet the pair of them had not even then always sufficient
work.   They would sit on their stools doing nothing for entire
afternoons.   In short, it was a regular collapse.   Ruin was
stamped on everything.

Whilst idleness and poverty entered, dirtiness naturally
entered also.   One would never have recognised that beautiful
blue shop, the colour of heaven, which had once been Gervaise's
pride.   Its window-frames and panes, which were never washed,
were covered from top to bottom with the splashes from the
passing vehicles.   On the brass rods in the windows were displayed three grey rags left by customers who had died in the
hospital.   And inside it was more pitiable still; the dampness
of the clothes hung up at the ceiling to dry had loosened all
the wall paper; the Pompadour chintz hung in strips like cobwebs covered with dust; the big stove, broken and in holes
from the rough use of the poker, looked in its corner like the
stock-in-trade of a dealer in old iron; the work-table appeared
as though it had been used by a regiment, covered as it was
with wine and coffee stains, sticky with jam, greasy from the
Monday junkettings.   With all that there prevailed an odour
of stale starch, a stench of mustiness, of burnt fat and of filth.
But Gervaise felt very comfortable in there.   She had not
noticed the shop getting dirty; she abandoned herself to it and
grew used to the torn wall paper, the greasy wood-work, the
same as she got into the way of wearing ragged skirts and of no
longer washing her ears.   To her the dirt even became a warm
nest in which she enjoyed squatting.   To leave things to take
care of themselves, to wait till the dust stopped up all the holes
and covered everything with a coat of velvet, and to feel the

house grow heavy around her in her irresistible laziness, was
indeed a voluptuous pleasure which intoxicated her.

Her own ease was her sole consideration; she did not care a
pin for anything else. The debts, though still increasing, no
longer troubled her. Her probity gradually deserted her;
whether she would be able to pay or not was altogether uncertain, and she preferred not to know. When her credit was
stopped at one shop, she would open an account at some other
close by. She was in debt all over the neighbourhood, she
owed money every few yards. To take merely the Rue de la
Goutte-d'Or, she no longer dared pass in front of the grocer's,
nor the charcoal-dealer's, nor the greengrocer's; and this obliged
her, whenever she required to be at the wash-house, to go round
by the Rue des Poissonniers, which was quite ten minutes out
of her way. The tradespeople came and treated her as a
swindler. One evening, the man who had sold them the furniture for Lantier drew a crowd round the place; he yelled out
that he would turn her skirts up and spank the beast, by way
of paying himself, if she did not fork out his money. Such
scenes, of course, left her all in a tremble; still, she would
shake herself like a cur that had been beaten, and there was an
end of it; she did not dine any the worse afterwards. They
were a lot of insolent scoundrels to come bothering her! She
had no money; she could not make any, could she? Besides,
the tradespeople robbed everyone; they were made to wait.
And she would fall asleep in her hole, trying not to dream of
what was sure to happen one day. She would take the leap, no
doubt; but, until then, she was determined not to be bothered.

Meanwhile mother Coupeau had recovered. For another
year the household jogged along. During the summer months
there was naturally a little more work—the white petticoats.
and the cambric dresses of the dollymops of the exterior Boulevard. The catastrophe was slowly approaching; the home sank
deeper into the mire every week; there were ups and downs,
however —days when one had to rub one's stomach before the
empty cupboard, and others when one eat veal enough to make
one burst. Mother Coupeau was for ever being seen in the
street, hiding bundles under her apron, and strolling in the
direction of the pawn-place in the Rue Polonceau. She strutted
along with the air of a devotée going to mass; for she did not
dislike these errands; haggling about money amused her; this
crying up of her wares like a second-hand dealer tickled her old
woman's fancy. The clerks in the Rue Polonceau knew her

well; they called her mother "Four Francs," because she always asked for four francs when they offered her three on her bundles as big as two sous' worth of butter. Gervaise would have pawned the whole place; she was seized with a mania for putting everything up the spout; she would have had her head shaved, if she could have got anything lent to her on her hair. It was too convenient; one could not help sending there for money when one was in want of a four-pound loaf. Every article of clothing found its way there—the linen, the coats, even the tools and the furniture. At first, she took advantage of the good weeks to get the things out again, even though she had to send them back the week after. Then she gave up caring for her things, and either let the tickets run out, or sold them.

One thing alone gave her a pang—it was having to pawn her clock to pay an acceptance for twenty francs to a bailiff who came to seize her goods. Until then, she had sworn rather to die of hunger than to part with her clock. When mother Coupeau carried it away in a little bonnet-box, she sunk on to a chair, without a particle of strength left in her arms, her eyes full of tears, as though a fortune was being torn from her. But when mother Coupeau reappeared with twenty-five francs, the unexpected loan, the five francs profit consoled her; she at once sent the old woman out again for four sous' worth of brandy in a glass, just to toast the five-franc piece. Often now, whenever they were on good terms together, they would share a drink on a corner of the work-table, generally a mixture, half brandy and half black currant ratafia. Mother Coupeau had a knack for bringing back the glass brimful in the pocket of her apron without spilling a drop. There was no need for the neighbours to know, was there? The truth was that the neighbours knew perfectly well. The greengrocer, the tripe-seller, the grocer's men would say to each other: "Hallo! the old woman's off to uncle's," or else: "Hallo! the old woman's bringing her liquor in her pocket." And that naturally incensed every one against Gervaise. She guttled everything; she would soon have finished up her shanty. Yes, yes, only three or four more mouthfuls, and there would not be a straw left.

In the midst of this general demolishment, Coupeau continued to prosper. The confounded tippler was as well as well could be. The sour wine and the "vitriol" positively fattened him. He eat a great deal, and laughed at that stick Lorilleux,

who accused drink of killing people, and answered him by
slapping himself on the stomach, the skin of which was so
stretched by the fat that it resembled the skin of a drum. He
would play him a tune on it, the glutton's vespers, with rolls
and beats loud enough to have made a quack's fortune. But
Lorilleux, annoyed at having himself no stomach to speak of,
said that it was yellow fat, which was bad. Nevertheless,
Coupeau got more drunk than ever, for the sake of his health.
His pepper and salt hair, waving about his head, dropped off
like the ashes of a fire-brand. His drunkard's face, with its
monkey-shaped jaw, was colouring like a pipe, assuming the
purple tinge of wine. And he remained a child of gaiety; he
behaved roughly to his wife, whenever she took it into her
head to tell him of her embarrassments. Were men made to
have to do with such bothering matters? The store-cupboard
might be in want of bread, that was nothing to him. He
required his fill morning and evening, and he never troubled
himself as to where it came from. When he allowed weeks to
go by without doing a stroke of work, he became more exacting
still. At the same time he continued to give Lantier friendly
slaps on the shoulder. He was certainly ignorant of his wife's
misconduct—at least, many persons, the Boches, the Poissons,
swore by all that was holy that he had not the least suspicion,
and that something dreadful would happen if he ever became
aware of it. But his own sister, Madame Lerat, shook her
head, and related that she knew some husbands who did not at
all object to such a state of things. One night Gervaise herself, who was coming from the hatter's room, shivered with
fright on receiving a knock behind in the dark; but she ended
by reassuring herself, thinking that she had come in contact
with the frame-work of the bedstead. Really, the situation was
too dreadful; her husband could not be amusing himself by
playing jokes upon her.

There was no falling-off in Lantier either. He took great
care of himself, measuring his stomach by the waistband of his
trousers, with the constant dread of having to loosen the buckle
or draw it tighter; he considered himself just right, and out of
coquetry neither desired to grow fatter nor thinner. That made
him hard to please in the matter of food, for he regarded every
dish from the point of view of keeping his waist as it was.
Even when there was not a sou in the house, he required eggs,
cutlets, light and nourishing things. Since he had been sharing
the mistress with the husband, he considered himself entitled

to fully half of everything in the house ; he picked up any
twenty sou pieces which happened to be lying about, made
Gervaise obey his smallest behests, grumbled, yelled, and
seemed more at home than the zinc-worker himself. In short,
it was a crib that had two masters. And the left-hand one,
who was the more cunning, pulled the blanket over himself,
took the best share of everything, of the wife, the food, and the
rest of it. He was skimming the Coupeaus, that was all ! He
no longer took the trouble to churn his butter on the quiet, but
did it in public. Nana continued to be his favourite, because
he liked nice little girls. He bothered himself less and less
about Etienne ; boys, according to him, should know how to
get along by themselves. Whenever any one called and asked
for Coupeau, he was always sure to find the hatter there, in his
slippers and his shirt sleeves, coming out of the back room with
the annoyed look of a husband who has been disturbed ; and
he would answer for Coupeau, saying that it was all the same.

Between these two gentlemen, Gervaise did not laugh every
day. She had nothing to complain of as regards her health,
thank goodness ! She also was growing too fat. But two men
for ever on her back, to coddle and satisfy, was often more than
she could manage. Ah ! good heavens ! one husband is already
too much for a woman ! The worst was that they got on very
well together, the rogues. They never quarrelled ; they would
chuckle in each other's faces, as they sat of an evening after
dinner, their elbows on the table ; they would rub up against
one another all the live-long day, like cats which seek and
cultivate their pleasure. The days when they came home in a
rage, it was on her that they vented it. Go it ! hammer away
at the animal ! She had a good back ; it made them all the
better friends when they yelled together. And it never did for
her to give them tit-for-tat.

At first, when one shouted, she would give the other an
imploring look, to obtain a good word from him. Only, it
seldom succeeded. She bore it meekly now, she bent her fat
shoulders, understanding that it amused them to jostle her
about, she was so round, a regular ball. Coupeau, who was
very foul-mouthed, treated her to some abominable language.
Lantier, on the contrary, chose his insults, getting hold of words
which no one else made use of, and which wounded her far more.
Luckily, one gets accustomed to everything ; the bad words,
the injustice of the two men ended by gliding off her smooth
skin as though it were oil-cloth. She had even reached the

point of preferring them when angry, because, on the occasions when they were nice, they bothered her far more, always after her, not even letting her iron a cap in peace. Then they would ask her for dainty dishes, she was to salt and not to salt, say white and say black, nurse them, and put them to by-by one after the other in cotton wool. At the end of the week her head was splitting, and her limbs could do no more, her brain was in a whirl, and her eyes were like a lunatic's. Such an existence soon wears out a woman.

Yes, Coupeau and Lantier were wearing her out, that was the word; they were burning her at both ends, as one says of a candle. The zinc-worker, sure enough, lacked education; but the hatter had too much, or at least he had education in the same way that dirty people have a white shirt, with uncleanliness underneath it. One night, she dreamt that she was on the edge of a well; Coupeau was knocking her into it with a blow of his fist, whilst Lantier was tickling her in the ribs to make her fall quicker. Well! that resembled her life. Ah! she was at a good school, it was not at all surprising if she fell lower and lower. The people of the neighbourhood were not very just when they reproached her for the bad ways she was getting into, for her misfortune was not of her making. At times, when she lost herself in reflection, a shiver ran through her frame. Then she would think that things might have turned out worse than they had. For instance, it was better having two men to bother her than to lose her two arms. And she would consider that her position was perfectly natural, there were so many others just the same; she tried to get a little happiness out of it for herself. What proved how largely it was becoming a matter of course, was that she did not detest Coupeau any more than she did Lantier. In a play, at the Gaiety, she had seen a strumpet who abhorred her husband, and who poisoned him for the sake of her lover; and it made her angry, because she felt nothing of the sort in her own heart. Was it not more sensible to live all three together in a friendly manner? No, no, none of that nonsense; it upset one's life, which was not very amusing as it was. In short, in spite of the debts, in spite of the poverty which threatened them, she would have admitted herself to be very comfortable, and very content, if the zinc-worker and the hatter had worked her and bullied her a trifle less.

Towards the autumn, unfortunately, things became worse. Lantier pretended he was getting thinner, and pulled a longer

face over the matter every day. He grumbled at everything,
sniffed at the dishes of potatoes—a mess he could not eat, he
would say, without having the colic. The least jangling now
turned to quarrels, in which they accused one another of being
the cause of all their troubles, and it was a devil of a job to
restore harmony before they all retired for the night. When
there is no more bran, the donkeys fight together, do they not?
Lantier scented the coming destitution; it exasperated him to
find that the place was pretty well all eaten up, so completely
cleaned out, that he foresaw the day when he would have to
take his hat and seek for a nest and his pap elsewhere. He
had grown accustomed to his diggings, having fallen into little
habits, and been coddled by everyone; a regular happy land,
the delights of which he would never be able to replace. Well!
one cannot stuff oneself up to one's ears and still have the pieces
on one's plate. He became enraged with his stomach, for, after
all, it was his stomach which had swallowed up everything.
But he did not reason thus; he felt a fierce rancour against the
others for having allowed themselves to be cleared out in two
years. Really, the Coupeaus were not very broad-backed. So
he maintained that Gervaise was not sufficiently economical.
Jove's thunder! what was going to become of them all? His
friends were failing him just as he was on the point of conclud-
ing a fine stroke of business, six thousand francs salary in a
manufactory, sufficient to enable the little family to lead a life
of luxury.

One evening in December they had no dinner at all. There
was not a radish left. Lantier, who was very glum, went out
early, wandering about in search of some other den where the
smell of the kitchen would bring a smile to one's face. He
would now remain for hours beside the stove wrapt in thought.
Then, suddenly, he began to evince a great friendship for the
Poissons. He no longer chaffed the policeman by calling him
Badingue; he even went so far as to admit that the Emperor
was perhaps a decent fellow. He seemed especially to esteem
Virginie, a woman of sense, he would say, and one who would
know perfectly well how to bring her ship home. It was
evident he was getting on the right side of them. It even
seemed that he was trying to arrange to board with them. But
he had something in his head far more complicated than that.
Virginie having acquainted him with her desire to set up in
some sort of business, he agreed with everything she said, and
declared that her idea was a most brilliant one. She was just

the person for trade—tall, engaging, and active. Oh! she
would make as much as she liked. As the money, inherited
from an aunt, had been ready for a long time, she was quite
right to throw up the few dresses she had to do each season,
and start in business; and he mentioned persons who were
making their fortunes: the greengrocer at the corner of the
street, and a little china-dealer on the exterior Boulevard; for
the time was splendid, one might even have sold the sweepings
of the counters. Virginie, however, hesitated; she was looking
for a shop that was to be let, she did not wish to leave the
neighbourhood. Then, Lantier would take her into corners
and converse with her in an undertone for ten minutes at a
time. He seemed to be urging her to do something in spite
of herself; and she no longer said "no," but appeared to
authorise him to act. It was as a secret between them, with
winks and words rapidly exchanged, some mysterious understanding which betrayed itself even in their handshakings.

From this moment, the hatter would covertly watch the
Coupeaus whilst eating their dry bread, and, becoming very
talkative again, would deafen them with his continual
jeremiads. All day long, Gervaise moved in the midst of
that poverty which he so obligingly spread out. He was not
speaking for himself, good heavens! He would starve with his
friends as much as one liked. Only, prudence required that
one should fully understand one's position. They owed at
least five hundred francs in the neighbourhood—to the baker,
the charcoal-dealer, the grocer, and the others. Besides which,
they were two quarters' rent behindhand, which meant two
hundred and fifty francs; the landlord, M. Marescot, even
spoke of having them evicted, if they did not pay him by the
1st of January. Finally, the pawn-place had absorbed everything, one could not have got together three francs' worth of
odds and ends, the clearance had been so complete; the nails
remained in the walls, and that was all, and perhaps there
were two pounds of them at three sous the pound. Gervaise,
thoroughly entangled in it all, her nerves quite upset by this
calculation, would fly into a passion and bang her fists down
upon the table, or else she would end by bursting into tears
like a fool. One night she exclaimed:

"I'll be off to-morrow! I prefer to put the key under the
door and to sleep on the pavement rather than continue to live
in such frights."

"It would be wiser," said Lantier slyly, "to get rid of the

lease, if you could find some one to take it.   When you are
both decided to give up the shop—"

She interrupted him more violently :

" At once, at once ! .Ah ! it'll be a good riddance !".

Then the hatter became very practical.   On giving up the
lease, one would no doubt get the new tenant to be responsible
for the two overdue quarters.   And he ventured to mention
the Poissons, he reminded them that Virginie was looking out
for a shop ; their's would perhaps suit her.   He remembered
that he had heard her say she longed for one just like it.   But,
when Virginie's name was mentioned, the laundress suddenly
regained her composure.   One would see about it ; one always
talked of giving up everything when in a passion, only the
thing did not seem so easy when one took time to consider
about it.

During the following days, it was in vain that Lantier harped
upon the subject.   Gervaise replied that she had seen herself
worse off and had pulled through.   It would be a wonderful
improvement when she no longer had her shop !   It would not
put bread into her mouth.   She would, on the contrary, engage
some fresh workwomen, and work up a fresh connection.   She
said that for the sake of struggling against the hatter's sound
arguments, for he pictured her on the ground, crushed beneath
their debts, and without the least hope of ever getting up again.
But he again made the mistake of pronouncing Virginie's name,
and she then became furiously obstinate.   No, no, never !   She
had always had her doubts of Virginie ; if Virginie coveted the
shop, it was for the purpose of humbling her.   She would
perhaps have given it up to the first woman in the street, but
not to that tall hypocrite who had certainly been waiting for
years to see her take the final leap.   Oh, that explained everything.   She now understood why yellow sparks lighted up the
cat's eyes of that drab.   Yes, Virginie still had the spanking at
the wash-house on her mind ; she was all the while quietly
nursing her rancour.   Well, she would do wisely to put her
spanking under glass, if she did not wish to receive a second one.
And it would not take long ; she could get herself ready for it.

In the face of this flow of unpleasant language, Lantier
began by attacking Gervaise.   He called her wooden-head,
slander-box, mother grumbler, and even went so far as to abuse
Coupeau, accusing him of not knowing how to make his wife
respect his friend.   Then, realizing that passion would compromise everything, he swore that he would never again interest him-

self in other people's affairs, for one always got more kicks than thanks ; and indeed he appeared to have given up all idea of talking them into parting with the lease, but he was really watching for a favourable opportunity of broaching the subject again, and of bringing the laundress round to his views.

January had now arrived ; the weather was horrible, both damp and cold. Mother Coupeau, who had coughed and choked all through December, was obliged to take to her bed after Twelfth-night. It was her annuity, which she looked forward to every winter. But that winter, every one who knew her said that she would only leave her room feet first ; and she had in all truth an awful rattling in her throat, which had the real ring of the coffin about it ; yet for all that she was big and plump, though already blind of one eye, and with half her face contorted. Her children, sure enough, would not have finished her off, only she had been lingering for so long, she was such an encumbrance that they inwardly desired her death as a deliverance for everybody. She herself would be far happier, for she had lasted her time, had she not ? and when one has lasted one's time, one has nothing to regret. The doctor who had been called in once had not even come again. They gave her an infusion, by way of not abandoning her entirely. Every hour some one looked in to see if she were still alive. She no longer spoke, she was suffocating too much ; but with her eye that was still good, clear and full of life, she would look fixedly at the people ; and so many things were reflected in that eye : regret for her youth, sadness at seeing her family so anxious to be rid of her, anger with that vicious Nana, who now openly got up in the night and watched through the glass door in her night-gown.

One Monday evening, Coupeau came home screwed. Ever since his mother was in danger, he had lived in a continual state of deep emotion. When he was in bed, snoring soundly, Gervaise turned about the place for a while. She was in the habit of watching during a part of the night. Nana, however, showed herself very brave, always sleeping beside the old woman, and saying that if she heard her die, she would alarm everyone. That night, as the child was asleep, and the invalid appeared to be dozing peaceably, the laundress ended by yielding to Lantier, who was calling to her from his room, where he advised her to come and get a little rest. They only kept a candle alight, standing on the ground behind the wardrobe. But, towards three o'clock, Gervaise abruptly jumped out of bed, shivering and oppressed with anguish. She had fancied she felt a cold breath pass over her body. The morsel of candle had burnt out; she tied on her petticoats in the dark, all bewildered, and with feverish hands. It was not till she got into the little room, after knocking up against the furniture, that she was able to light a small lamp. In the midst of the oppressive silence of night, the zinc-worker's snores alone sounded as two grave notes. Nana, stretched on her back, was breathing gently between her pouting lips. And Gervaise, holding down the lamp, which caused big shadows to dance about the room, cast the light on mother Coupeau's face, and beheld it all white, the head lying on the shoulder, the eyes wide open. Mother Coupeau was dead.

Gently, without uttering a cry, icy cold yet prudent, the laundress returned to Lantier's room. He had gone to sleep again. She bent over him, and murmured:

"I say, it's all over, she's dead."

Heavy with sleep, only half awake, he grunted at first:

"Leave me alone, get into bed. We can't do her any good if she's dead."

Then, he raised himself up on his elbow, and asked:

"What's the time?"

"Three o'clock."

"Only three o'clock! Get into bed quick. You'll catch cold. When it's daylight, we'll see what's to be done."

But she did not listen to him, she dressed herself completely. Then, he rolled himself up in the blanket, and turned his head to the wall, talking of the confounded obstinacy of women. What need was there of such a hurry to let every one know that there was a death in the house? It was doubly dismal in the middle of the night; and he was exasperated at having his rest broken by unpleasant thoughts. However, when she had removed her things into her own room, even her hair-pins, she sat down and sobbed to her heart's content, no longer fearing being discovered with the hatter. At bottom, she really loved mother Coupeau. She felt a great grief, after having in the first instance only experienced fear and annoyance at her having chosen such an awkward time for going off. And she wept all alone, very bitterly in the silence, without the zinc-worker ceasing his snoring; he heard nothing, she had shaken and called him, then she had decided to let him be, reflecting that it would only be a fresh worry if he did wake up. On re-turning to the body, she found Nana sitting up in bed rubbing her eyes. The child understood, and with her vicious urchin's curiosity, stretched out her neck to get a better view of her grandmother; she said nothing, but she trembled slightly, surprised and satisfied in the presence of this death which she had been promising herself for two days past, like some nasty thing hidden away and forbidden to children; and her young cat-like eyes dilated before that white face all emaciated at the last hiccough by the passion of life, she felt that stiffness in her back which held her behind the glass door when she crept there to spy on what was no concern of chits like her.

"Come, get up," said her mother in a low voice. "You can't remain here."

She regretfully slid out of bed, turning her head round and not taking her eyes off the corpse. Gervaise was much worried about her, not knowing where to put her till day-time. She was about to tell her to dress herself, when Lantier, in his trousers and slippers, rejoined her; he could not get to sleep again, and was rather ashamed of his behaviour. Then, everything was arranged.

"She can sleep in my bed," murmured he. "She'll have plenty of room." .

Nana looked at her mother and Lantier with her big clear eyes, and put on her stupid air, the same as on New Year's day when any one made her a present of a box of chocolate drops. And there was certainly no need for them to hurry her; she trotted off in her night-gown, her bare tootsies scarcely touching the tiled floor; she glided like a snake into the bed which was still quite warm, and she lay stretched out and buried in it, her slim body scarcely raising the counterpane. Each time her mother entered the room, she beheld her with her eyes sparkling in her motionless face, not sleeping, not moving, very red and appearing to reflect on her own affairs.

Lantier assisted Gervaise in dressing mother Coupeau; and it was not an easy matter, for the body weighed heavy. One would never have thought that that old woman was so fat, and so white. They put on her stockings, a white petticoat, a short linen jacket, and a white cap; in short, the best of her linen. Coupeau continued snoring, a high note and a low one, the one sharp, the other flat; one could almost have imagined it to be church music accompanying the Good Friday ceremonies. When the corpse was dressed and properly laid out on the bed, Lantier poured himself out a glass of wine, for he felt quite upset. Gervaise searched the chest of drawers to find a little brass crucifix which she had brought from Plassans; but she recollected that mother Coupeau had in all probability sold it herself. They had lighted the stove; and they passed the rest of the night, half asleep on chairs, finishing the bottle of wine that had been opened, worried and sulking, as though it was their own fault.

Towards seven o'clock, before daylight, Coupeau at length awoke. When he learnt his loss he at first stood still with dry eyes, stuttering, and vaguely thinking that they were playing him some joke. Then, he threw himself on the ground and went and knelt beside the corpse; he kissed it and wept like a calf, with such a copious flow of tears that he quite wetted the sheet with wiping his cheeks. Gervaise had recommenced sobbing, deeply affected by her husband's grief, and the best of friends with him again; yes, he was better at heart than she had thought he was. Coupeau's despair mingled with a violent pain in his head. He passed his fingers through his hair, his mouth was dry like on the morrow of a booze, and he was still a little on in spite of his ten hours sleep. And, clinching his fists, he complained aloud. Damnation! she was gone now, his poor mother whom he loved so much! Ah! what a headache he had, it would settle him! It was like a wig of fire, and now they were tearing out his heart! No, it was not just of fate thus to set itself against a man!

"Come, cheer up, old fellow," said Lantier, raising him from the ground, "you must pull yourself together."

He poured him out a glass of wine, but Coupeau refused to drink.

"What's the matter with me? I've brass in my throat. It's mamma, when I saw her I got a taste of brass in my mouth. Mamma, my God! mamma, mamma!"

And he recommenced crying like a child. All the same he drank the glass of wine, to put out the fire which was burning his chest. Lantier soon went off on the pretext of informing the family and of registering the death at the mayor's. He wanted some fresh air. Therefore he did not hurry himself, but strolled along smoking cigarettes and enjoying the sharp cold of the morning. On leaving Madame Lerat's, he entered one of the Batignolles milk shops and had a good cup of hot coffee. And he stayed there quite an hour wrapt in thought.

Towards nine o'clock, the family was all united in the shop, the shutters of which were kept up. Lorilleux did not cry; moreover, he had some pressing work to attend to, and he re-

turned almost directly to his room, after having stalked about
with a face put on for the occasion. Madame Lorilleux and
Madame Lerat embraced the Coupeaus and wiped their eyes,
from which a few tears were falling. But the first named, after
giving a hasty glance round about the body, suddenly raised
her voice to say that it was unheard of, that one never left a
lighted lamp beside a corpse; there should be a candle, and
Nana was sent to purchase a packet of tall ones. Ah well! it
made one long to die at the Hobbler's, she laid one out in such
a fine fashion! What a fool, not even to know what to do with
a corpse! Had she then never buried any one in her life?
Madame Lerat had to go to the neighbours and borrow a crucifix; she brought one back which was too big, a cross of black
wood with a Christ in painted cardboard fastened to it, which
covered the whole of mother Coupeau's chest, and seemed to
crush her under its weight. Then they tried to obtain some
holy water, but no one had any, and it was again Nana who
was sent to the church to bring some back in a bottle. In time
sufficient to turn round, the tiny room presented quite another appearance; on a little table a candle was burning beside
a glass full of holy water into which a sprig of box was dipped.
Now, if anyone came, it would at least look decent. And they
arranged the chairs in a circle in the shop for receiving people.

Lantier only returned at eleven o'clock. He had been to the
undertaker's for information.

"The coffin is twelve francs," said he. "If you desire a mass,
it will be ten francs more. Then there's the hearse, which is
charged for according to the ornaments."

"Oh! that's quite unnecessary," murmured Madame Lorilleux,
raising her head in a surprised and anxious manner. "We
can't bring mamma to life again, can we! One must do according to one's means."

"Of course, that's just what I think," resumed the hatter.
"I merely asked the prices to guide you. Tell me what you
desire; and after lunch I will give the orders."

They talked in a low voice, in the dim light which entered
the shop through the cracks in the shutters. The door of the
little chamber was kept wide open; and, from that gaping
aperture, issued the great stillness of death. Children's laughter
rose in the courtyard, a troop of urchins were dancing in a ring
in the pale winter sunshine. All on a sudden, one heard Nana,
who had escaped from the Boches', where she had been sent.
She was issuing her commands in her shrill voice, and the heels

heat time on the paving-stones, whilst these words were sung
and ascended in the air like the noise of some chattering birds:

> " Our donkey, our donkey,
>   He has got a bad leg.
>   Madame has had him made
>   A pretty little sock,
>   And some lilac-colour shoes, oes, oes,
>   And some lilac-colour shoes ! "

Gervaise waited to say in her turn :

" We're not rich certainly ; but all the same we wish to act
decently.   If mother Coupeau has left us nothing, it's no reason
for pitching her into the ground like a dog.   No, we must have
a mass, and a hearse with a few ornaments."

" And who will pay for them?" violently inquired Madame
Lorilleux.   " Not we, who lost some money last week ; not you
either, as you're stumped.   Ah ! you ought however to see
where it has led you, this trying to astonish people ! "

Coupeau, when consulted, mumbled something with a gesture
of profound indifference, and then fell asleep again on his chair.
Madame Lerat said that she would pay her share.   She was of
Gervaise's opinion, they should do things decently.   Then, the
two of them fell to making calculations on a piece of paper :
in all, it would amount to about ninety francs, because they
decided, after a long discussion, to have a hearse ornamented
with a narrow scallop.

" We're three," concluded the laundress.   " We'll give thirty
francs a piece.   It won't ruin us."

But Madame Lorilleux broke out in a fury.

" Well !   I refuse, yes, I refuse !   It's not for the thirty
francs.   I'd give a hundred thousand, if I had them, and if it
would bring mamma to life again.   Only, I don't like vain
people.   You've got a shop, you only dream of showing off
before the neighbourhood.   We don't fall in with it, we don't.
We don't try to make ourselves out what we are not.   Oh ! you
can manage it to please yourself.   Put plumes on the hearse if
it amuses you."

" No one asks you for anything," Gervaise ended by answering.   " Even though I should have to sell myself, I'll not have
anything to reproach myself with.   I've fed mother Coupeau
without your help, and I can certainly bury her without your
help also.   I already once before gave you a bit of my mind :
I pick up stray cats, I'm not likely to leave your mother in the
mire."

Then, Madame Lorilleux burst into tears, and Lantier had to prevent her from leaving. The quarrel had become so noisy, that Madame Lerat energetically said "hush!" and thought it her duty to go softly into the little chamber, and give a sorrowful and anxious glance at the dead woman, as though she feared she would find her come to life again, and listening to the discussion going on so near her. At this moment the troop of little girls in the courtyard again broke out with their song, Nana's piercing voice being heard high above the others:

> " Our donkey, our donkey,
> Has got a stomach-ache.
> Madame has had him made
> A nice little waist-band.
> And some lilac-colour shoes, oes, oes,
> And some lilac-colour shoes!"

"Dear me! how those children grate on one's nerves with their singing!" said Gervaise, all upset and on the point of sobbing with impatience and sadness, to the hatter. "Do please make them leave off, and send Nana back to the doorkeeper's with a kick."

Madame Lerat and Madame Lorilleux went away to have their lunch, and promised to return. The Coupeaus sat down to table, and ate some ham, but without any appetite, and not daring to clatter their forks against their plates. They were very much bothered and bewildered with that poor mother Coupeau, who weighed heavily upon their shoulders, and whose presence appeared to them to fill all the rooms. Their life seemed turned topsy-turvy. At first they wandered about unable to find things; they felt stiff like on the morrow of a jollification. Lantier soon made again for the door to return to the undertaker's, taking with him Madame Lerat's thirty francs and sixty francs that Gervaise had gone, bareheaded like a madwoman, and borrowed of Goujet. In the afternoon some visitors called, neighbours devoured by curiosity, who arrived heaving tremendous sighs and rolling tearful eyes; they entered the little room and stared at the corpse, making the sign of the cross and shaking the sprig of box dipped in the holy water; then they sat down in the shop, where they talked interminably of the dear woman, without tiring of repeating the same phrase for hours together. Mademoiselle Remanjou had noticed that her right eye had remained open, Madame Gaudron kept obstinately repeating that she thought she had a beautiful colour for her age, and Madame Fauconnier was stupefied at the recollection of having seen her take her coffee three days before. Really, one went off precious quick; they had better all be making their preparations.

Towards evening the Coupeaus were beginning to have had enough of it. It was too great an affliction for a family to have to keep a corpse so long a time. The government ought to have made a new law on the subject. All through another evening, another night and another morning—no! it would never come to an end. When one no longer weeps, grief turns to irritation; is it not so? One would end by misbehaving one-self. Mother Coupeau, dumb and stiff in the depths of the narrow chamber, was spreading more and more over the lodging and becoming heavy enough to crush the people in it. And the family, in spite of itself, gradually fell into its ordinary mode of life, and lost some portion of its respect.

"You must have a mouthful with us," said Gervaise to Madame Lerat and Madame Lorilleux, when they returned. "We're too sad; we must keep together."

They laid the cloth on the work-table. Each one, on seeing the plates, thought of the feastings they had had on it. Lantier had returned. Lorilleux came down. A pastry-cook had just brought a meat pie, for the laundress was too upset to attend to any cooking. As they were taking their seats, Boche came to say that M. Marescot asked to be admitted, and the landlord appeared, looking very grave, and wearing a broad decoration on his frock-coat. He bowed in silence, and went straight to the little room, where he knelt down. He was very pious; he prayed in the collected manner of a priest, then made the sign of the cross in the air, whilst he sprinkled the body with the sprig of box. All the family, leaving the table, stood up, greatly impressed. M. Marescot, having finished his devotions, passed into the shop and said to the Coupeaus:

"I have called for the two quarters' rent that's overdue. Are you prepared to pay?"

"No, sir, not quite," stammered Gervaise, greatly put out at hearing this mentioned before the Lorilleux. "You see, with the misfortune which has fallen upon us—"

"No doubt, but every one has his troubles," resumed the landlord, spreading out his immense fingers, which indicated the former workman. "I am very sorry, but I cannot wait any longer. If I am not paid by the morning after to-morrow, I shall be obliged to have you put out."

Gervaise, struck dumb, imploringly clasped her hands, her

eyes full of tears. With an energetic shake of his big bony
head, he gave her to understand that supplications were useless.
Besides, the respect due to the dead forbade all discussion. He
discreetly retired, walking backwards.

"A thousand pardons for having disturbed you," murmured
he. "The morning after to-morrow; do not forget."

And as, on withdrawing, he again passed before the little
room, he saluted the corpse a last time, through the wide open
door, by devoutly bending his knee.

They commenced by eating quickly, so as not to appear to
be taking any pleasure in it. But when they reached the
dessert, they lingered, overcome by a desire to take their ease.
Now and again Gervaise, or one of the sisters, went and peeped
into the little room, with her mouth full, and without even laying
down her napkin; and when she regained her seat, finishing
what she was eating, the others looked at her for a second, to
ascertain if everything was going on all right close by. Then
the ladies disturbed themselves less frequently; mother Coupeau
was forgotten. They had made a big bowl of coffee, and very
strong too, so as to keep themselves awake all night. The
Poissons looked in towards eight o'clock. They invited them
to take a glass. Then Lantier, who had been watching
Gervaise's face, seemed to seize an opportunity that he had been
waiting for ever since the morning. In speaking of the
indecency of landlords who entered houses where there was a
corpse to demand their money, he said suddenly:

"He's a Jesuit, the beast, with his air of officiating at a mass!
But, in your place, I'd just chuck up his shop altogether."

Gervaise, quite worn out, and feeling weak and nervous, gave
way and replied:

"Yes, I shall certainly not wait for the bailiffs. Ah! it's
more than I can bear—more than I can bear."

The Lorilleux, delighted at the idea that the Hobbler would
no longer have a shop, approved the plan immensely. One could
hardly conceive the great cost a shop was. If she only earned
three francs working for others, she at least had no expenses;
she did not risk losing large sums of money. They repeated
this argument to Coupeau, urging him on; he drank a great
deal, and remained in a continuous fit of sensibility, weeping all
by himself in his plate. As the laundress seemed to be allowing
herself to be convinced, Lantier looked at the Poissons and
winked. And tall Virginie intervened, making herself most
amiable.

T

"You know, we might arrange the matter between us. I would relieve you of the rest of the lease, and settle your matter with the landlord. In short, you would not be worried nearly so much."

" No thanks," declared Gervaise, shaking herself, as though she felt a shudder pass over her. " I'll work; I've my two arms, thank heaven! to help me out of my difficulties."

" We can talk about it some other time," the hatter hastened to put in. " It's scarcely the thing to do so this evening. Some other time—to-morrow, for instance."

At this moment, Madame Lerat, who had gone into the little room, uttered a faint cry. She had had a fright, because she had found the candle burnt out. They all busied themselves in lighting another; and they shook their heads, saying that it was not a good sign when the light went out beside a corpse.

The wake commenced. Coupeau had gone to lie down, not to sleep, said he, but to think; and five minutes afterwards he was snoring. When they sent Nana off to sleep at the Boches', she cried; she had been looking forward ever since the morning to being nice and warm in her good friend Lantier's big bed. The Poissons stayed till midnight. Some hot wine had been made in a salad-bowl, because the coffee affected the ladies' nerves too much. The conversation became tenderly effusive. Virginie talked of the country: she would like to be buried at the corner of a wood, with wild flowers on her grave. Madame Lerat had already put by in her wardrobe the sheet for her shroud, and she kept it perfumed with a bunch of lavender; she wished always to have a nice smell under her nose when she would be eating the dandelions by the roots. Then, with no sort of transition, the policeman related that he had arrested a fine girl that morning who had been stealing from a pork-butcher's shop; on undressing her at the commissary of police's, they had found ten sausages hanging round her body. And, Madame Lorilleux having remarked, with a look of disgust, that she would not eat any of those sausages, the party burst out into a gentle laugh. The wake became livelier, though not ceasing to preserve appearances.

But just as they were finishing the hot wine, a peculiar noise, a dull trickling sound, issued from the little room. All raised their heads and looked at each other.

"It's nothing," said Lantier quietly, lowering his voice. "She's emptying."

The explanation caused the others to nod their heads in a reassured way, and they replaced their glasses on the table.

At length, the Poissons withdrew. Lantier went off at the same time : he was going to sleep at a friend's, said he, so as to leave his bed for the ladies, who could rest upon it for an hour, each in turn. Lorilleux went off to bed all alone, repeating that such a thing had never happened to him since his marriage. Then, Gervaise and the two sisters, being left with Coupeau, who was sleeping, settled themselves round the stove, on which they kept some warm coffee. They sat there, huddled together, bent double, with their hands under their aprons, their noses over the fire, conversing very low, in the great silence which enveloped the neighbourhood. Madame Lorilleux lamented that she had no black dress, yet she would have liked to avoid having to purchase one, for they were very hard up, very hard up ; and she questioned Gervaise, asking her if mother Coupeau had not left a black skirt, that skirt which was given her on her saint's day. Gervaise was obliged to fetch the skirt. It would do if taken in a little at the waist. But Madame Lorilleux also wanted some old linen, talked of the bed, of the wardrobe, of the two chairs, and looked about for any odds and ends which ought to be divided. There was almost a quarrel. Madame Lerat made peace between them ; she was more just ; the Coupeaus had had the care of the mother, they had well earned the few things she had left. And all three again dozed over the stove, gossiping monotonously.

The night seemed terribly long to them. Now and again they shook themselves, drank some coffee, and stretched their necks in the direction of the little room, where the candle, which was not to be snuffed, was burning with a dull red flame, increased by the black thiefs on the wick. Towards morning, they shivered, in spite of the great heat of the stove. Anguish, and the fatigue of having talked too much, was stifling them, whilst their mouths were parched, and their eyes ached. Madame Lerat threw herself on Lantier's bed, and snored like a man ; whilst the other two, their heads falling forward, and almost touching their knees, slept before the fire. At daybreak, a shudder awoke them. Mother Coupeau's candle had again gone out ; and as, in the obscurity, the dull trickling sound recommenced, Madame Lorilleux gave the explanation of it anew in a loud voice, so as to reassure herself :

" She's emptying," repeated she, lighting another candle.

The funeral was to take place at half-past ten. A nice morning to add to the night and the day before! That is to say, Gervaise, though without a sou, would have given a hundred francs to anybody who would have come and taken mother Coupeau away three hours sooner. No, one may love people, but they are too great a weight when they are dead; and even the more one has loved them, the sooner one would like to be rid of their bodies.

The morning of a funeral is, fortunately, full of diversions. One has all sorts of preparations to make. To begin with, they lunched. Then, it happened to be old Bazouge, the mute, who lived on the sixth floor, who brought the coffin and the sack of bran. He was never sober, the worthy fellow. At eight o'clock that day, he was still lively from the booze of the day before.

"This is for here, isn't it?" asked he.

And he laid down the coffin, which creaked like a new box. But as he was throwing the sack of bran on one side, he stood with a look of amazement in his eyes, his mouth opened wide, on beholding Gervaise before him.

"Beg pardon, excuse me. I've made a mistake," stammered he. "I was told it was for here."

He had already taken up the sack again, and the laundress was obliged to call to him:

"Leave it alone, it's for here."

"Ah! Jove's thunder! let's understand each other!" resumed he, slapping his thigh. "I see, it's the old lady."

Gervaise turned quite pale. Old Bazouge had brought the coffin for her. By way of apology, he tried to be gallant, and continued:

"I'm not to blame, am I? It was said yesterday that some one on the ground floor had cocked their toes. Then I thought— You know, in our business, these things enter by one ear and go out by the other. All the same, allow me to congratulate you. As late as possible, eh? That's best, though life isn't always amusing; ah! no, by Jove!"

She listened to him and drew back, with the fear that he would seize her in his big dirty hands, and carry her away in his box. Once already, on her wedding night, he had told her that he knew women who would thank him if he came to take them away. Well, she had not yet got to that point; it gave her a chill down the back. Her life was spoilt, but she had no wish to go off so soon. Yes, she would rather starve for years, than die the death, just the matter of a second.

"He's abominably drunk," murmured she, with an air of disgust mingled with dread. "They, at least, oughtn't to send us tipplers. We pay dear enough."

Then the mute became insolent, and jeered.

"I say, little woman, it's only put off till another time. I'm entirely at your service, remember! You've only to make me a sign. I'm the ladies' consoler. And don't spit on old Bazouge, because he's held in his arms finer ones than you, who let themselves be tucked in without a murmur, very pleased to continue their by-by in the dark."

"Hold your tongue, old Bazouge!" said Lorilleux, severely, having hastened to the spot on hearing the noise, "such jokes are highly improper. If we complained about you, you would get the sack. Come, be off, as you've no respect for principles."

The mute moved away, but one could hear him stuttering as he dragged along the pavement,

"Well! what? principles! There's no such thing as principles, there's no such thing as principles — there's only honesty!"

At length ten o'clock struck. The hearse was late. There were already several people in the shop, friends and neighbours —M. Madinier, My-Boots, Madame Gaudron, Mademoiselle Remanjou; and every minute, a man's or a woman's head was thrust out of the gaping opening of the door, between the closed shutters, to see if that creeping hearse was in sight. The family, all together in the back room, was shaking hands. Short pauses occurred, interrupted by rapid whisperings, a tiresome and feverish waiting, with sudden rushes of skirts— Madame Lorilleux who had forgotten her handkerchief, or else Madame Lerat who was trying to borrow a prayer-book. Every one on arriving beheld the open coffin in the centre of the little room before the bed; and in spite of oneself, each stood covertly studying it, calculating that plump mother Coupeau would never squeeze into it. They all looked at each other with this thought in their eyes, though without communicating it. But there was a slight pushing at the street door. M. Madinier, extending his arms, came and said, in a low, grave voice,

"Here they are!"

It was not the hearse though. Four mutes entered hastily in single file, with their red faces, their hands all numbed like persons in the habit of moving heavy things, and their rusty black clothes wearing white from constant rubbing against coffins. Old Bazouge walked first, very drunk and very proper.

As soon as he was at work he found his equilibrium. They did
not utter a word, but slightly bowed their heads, already
weighing mother Coupeau with a glance. And they did not
dawdle; the poor old woman was packed in, in the time one
takes to sneeze. The shortest, a young chap who squinted, had
emptied the bran into the coffin, and spread it out, kneading
it as though he wished to make bread. Another, a tall lean
fellow, with a funny look, laid the sheet over it. Then one,
two, off you go! The four of them seized hold of the body and
lifted it up, two at the feet and two at the head. One could
not toss a pancake quicker. The persons who were stretching
their necks might have thought that mother Coupeau had herself jumped into the box. She glided into it as though quite
at home. Oh! a perfect fit, so perfect that one heard her rub
against the new wood. She touched on all sides, a regular
picture in a frame. But anyhow she was in, which fact greatly
surprised the lookers-on. She had surely diminished in size since
the night before.

The mutes were now standing up and waiting; the little one
with a squint took the coffin lid, by way of inviting the family
to bid their last farewell, whilst Bazouge had filled his mouth
with nails and was holding the hammer in readiness. Then
Coupeau, his two sisters, and Gervaise threw themselves on
their knees and kissed the mamma who was going away, weeping bitterly, the hot tears falling on and streaming down the
stiff face cold as ice. There was a prolonged sound of sobbing.
The lid was placed on, and old Bazouge knocked the nails in
with the style of a packer, two blows for each; and they none
of them listened any longer to their own weeping in that din,
which resembled the noise of furniture being repaired. It was
over. The time for starting had arrived.

"What a fuss to make at such a time!" said Madame Lorilleux to her husband as she caught sight of the hearse before
the door.

The hearse was creating quite a revolution in the neighbourhood. The tripe-seller called to the grocer's men, the little
clockmaker came out on to the pavement, the neighbours leant
out of their windows; and all these people talked about the
scallop with its white cotton fringe. Ah! the Coupeaus would
have done better to have paid their debts. But, as the Lorilleux
said, when one is proud it shows itself everywhere and in spite
of everything.

"It's shameful!" repeated Gervaise at the same moment,

speaking of the chain-maker and his wife. "To think that those skinflints have not even brought a bunch of violets for their mother!"

The Lorilleux, true enough, had come empty-handed. Madame Lerat had given a wreath of artificial flowers. And a wreath of immortelles and a bouquet bought by the Coupeaus were also placed on the coffin. The mutes had had to bring all their muscle into play to raise the coffin and get it into the hearse. It was some time before the procession was formed. Coupeau and Lorilleux, in frock coats and with their hats in their hands, were chief mourners; the first, in his emotion, which two glasses of white wine early in the morning had helped to sustain, clung to his brother-in-law's arm, with no strength in his legs and a violent headache. Then followed the other men: M. Madinier, very grave and all in black, My-Boots, wearing a great coat over his blouse, Boche, whose yellow trousers produced the effect of a petard, Lantier, Gaudron, Bibi-the-Smoker, Poisson, and others besides. The ladies came next: in the first row Madame Lorilleux, dragging the deceased's skirt, which she had altered; Madame Lerat, hiding under a shawl her hastily got-up mourning, a gown with lilac trimmings; and following them Virginie, Madame Gaudron, Madame Fauconnier, Mademoiselle Remanjou, and the rest. When the hearse started and slowly descended the Rue de la Goutte-d'Or, amidst signs of the cross and heads bared, the four mutes took the lead, two in front, the two others on the right and left. Gervaise had remained behind to close the shop. She left Nana with Madame Boche, and ran to rejoin the procession, whilst the child, held by the doorkeeper under the porch, watched with a deeply interested gaze her grandmother disappear at the end of the street, in that beautiful carriage.

Just at the moment when the laundress, all out of breath, reached the tail end of the procession, Goujet also joined it. He went with the men; but he looked back and nodded to her, so gently that she felt all on a sudden very wretched and again burst into tears. She was no longer crying for mother Coupeau only; she was bewailing something abominable, which she could not have put into words, and which was stifling her. She kept her handkerchief pressed to her eyes all the way. Madame Lorilleux, with dry and inflamed cheeks, looked at her sideways, with an air of accusing her of doing it all for show.

The ceremony at the church was soon got through. The mass dragged a little though, because the priest was very old.

My-Boots and Bibi-the-Smoker preferred to remain outside, on account of the collection. M. Madinier studied the priests all the while, and communicated his observations to Lantier: those jokers, though so glib with their Latin, did not even know a word of what they were saying; they buried a person just in the same way that they would have baptised or married him; without the least feeling in their heart. Then, M. Madinier blamed all those ceremonies, those lights, those sad voices, and that display before the families. Really, one lost one's relatives twice, at home and at church. And all the men agreed with him; for it was another painful moment, when, the mass over, there was a mumbling of prayers, and the persons present had to pass before the coffin, sprinkling it with holy water.

Happily, the cemetery was not far off, the little cemetery of La Chapelle, a bit of a garden which opened on to the Rue Marcadet. The procession arrived disbanded, with stampings of feet and everybody talking of his own affairs. The hard earth resounded, and many would have liked to have moved about to keep themselves warm. The gaping hole, beside which the coffin was laid, was already frozen over, and looked white and stony, like a plaster quarry; and the followers, grouped round little heaps of gravel, did not find it pleasant standing in such piercing cold, whilst looking at the hole likewise bored them. At length, a priest in a surplice came out of a little cottage; he shivered, and one could see his steaming breath at each *de profundis* that he uttered. At the final sign of the cross he bolted off, without the least desire to go through the service again. The sexton took his shovel, but on account of the frost he was only able to detach large lumps of earth, which beat a fine tune down below, a regular bombardment of the coffin, an enfilade of artillery sufficient to make one think the wood was splitting. One may be a cynic, nevertheless that sort of music soon upsets one's stomach. The weeping recommenced. They moved off, they even got outside, but they still heard the detonations. My-Boots, blowing on his fingers, uttered an observation aloud:

"Ah! Jove's thunder! no! poor mother Coupeau won't feel very warm!"

"Ladies and gentlemen," said the zinc-worker to the few friends who remained in the street with the family, "will you permit us to offer you some refreshments?"

And he was the first to enter a wine-shop in the Rue Marcadet, the "Arrival at the Cemetery." Gervaise, remaining outside, called Goujet, who was moving off, after again nodding to her. Why didn't he accept a glass of wine? He was in a hurry, he was going back to the workshop. Then, they looked at each other a moment without speaking.

"I must ask your pardon for troubling you about the sixty francs," at length murmured the laundress. "I was half crazy, I thought of you—"

"Oh! don't mention it; you're fully forgiven," interrupted the blacksmith. "And you know, I'm quite at your service if any misfortune should overtake you. But don't say anything to mamma, because she has her ideas, and I don't wish to cause her annoyance."

She was still looking at him; and, on beholding him so good, so sad, with his beautiful yellow beard, she was on the point of agreeing to his old proposal, that of going away with him and living happy together somewhere. Then another wicked thought came into her head, which was to borrow of him the money for the two over-due quarters' rent at no matter what cost. She trembled, and resumed in a caressing tone of voice:

"We're not bad friends, are we?"

He shook his head as he answered,

"No, certainly not; we shall never be bad friends. Only, you understand, all is over."

And he went off with long strides, leaving Gervaise bewildered, listening to his last words which rang in her ears with the clang of a big bell. On entering the wine-shop, she seemed to hear a hollow voice within her which said, "All is over, well! all is over; there is nothing more for me to do if all is over!" Sitting down, she swallowed a mouthful of bread and cheese, and emptied a glass full of wine which she found before her.

It was a long, low room on the ground floor, and was furnished with two big tables. Bottles of wine, quarter loaves of bread, and large slices of Brie cheese on three plates were spread out in a row. The party was just having a snack, without either table-cloth or knives. Farther off, beside the roaring stove, the four mutes were finishing their lunch.

"Dear me!" explained M. Madinier, "we each have our turn. The old folks make room for the young ones. Your lodging will seem very empty to you now when you go home."

"Oh! my brother's going to give notice," said Madame Lorilleux quickly. "That shop's ruination."

They had been working upon Coupeau. Every one was urg-

ing him to give up the lease. Madame Lerat herself, who had
been on very good terms with Lantier and Virginie for some
time past, and who was tickled with the idea that they were a
trifle smitten with each other, talked of bankruptcy and prison,
putting on most terrified airs. And, suddenly, the zinc-worker,
already overdosed with liquor, flew into a passion, his emotion
turning to fury.

"Listen," cried he, poking his nose in his wife's face; "I intend that you shall listen to me I Your confounded head will
always have its own way. But, this time, I intend to have
mine, I warn you!"

"Ah I well," said Lantier, "one never yet brought her to
reason by fair words; it wants a mallet to drive it into her
head."

And both fell to abusing her for a while. That did not prevent the jaws from working—the Brie cheese disappeared, the
bottles of wine flowed like fountains. However, Gervaise was
fast giving way before the attack. She answered nothing, but
hurried herself, her mouth ever full, as though she had been
very hungry. When they got tired, she gently raised her head
and said,

"That's enough, isn't it? I don't care a straw for the shop I
I want no more of it. Do you understand? It can go to the
deuce! All is over!"

Then they ordered some more bread and cheese and talked
business. The Poissons took the rest of the lease and agreed
to be answerable for the two quarters' rent overdue. Boche,
moreover, pompously agreed to the arrangement in the landlord's name. He even then and there let a lodging to the
Coupeaus—the vacant one on the sixth floor, in the same passage as the Lorilleux apartment. As for Lantier, well I he
would like to keep his room, if it did not inconvenience the
Poissons. The policeman bowed; it did not inconvenience him
at all; friends always get on together, in spite of any difference
in their political ideas. And Lantier, without mixing himself
up any more in the matter, like a man who has at length settled
his little business, helped himself to an enormous slice of bread
and cheese; he leant back in his chair and eat devoutly, his
blood tingling beneath his skin, his whole body burning with a
sly joy, and he blinked his eyes to peep first at Gervaise and
then at Virginie.

"Hi I old Bazouge I" called Coupeau, "come and have a
drink. We're not proud; we're all workers."

The four mutes who were going off returned to clink glasses with the company. It was no reproach; but the lady they had been handling weighed heavy, and it was well worth a glass of wine. Old Bazouge stared at the laundress, but did not utter an unbecoming word. She rose from her seat, feeling uneasy, and left the men who were all getting tipsy. Coupeau, who was as drunk as a pig, recommenced bellowing and said it was grief.

That evening, when Gervaise found herself at home again, she remained in a stupefied state on a chair. It seemed to her that the rooms were immense and deserted. Really, it would be a good riddance. But it was certainly not only mother Coupeau that she had left at the bottom of the hole in the little garden of the Rue Marcadet. She missed too many things, most likely a part of her life, and her shop, and her pride of being an employer, and other feelings besides, which she had buried on that day. Yes, the walls were bare, and her heart also; it was a complete clear out, a tumble into the pit. And she felt too tired; she would pick herself up again later on if she could.

At ten o'clock, when undressing, Nana cried and stamped. She wanted to sleep in mother Coupeau's bed. Her mother tried to frighten her; but the child was too precocious. Corpses only filled her with a great curiosity; so that, for the sake of peace, she was allowed to lie down in mother Coupeau's place. She liked big beds, the chit; she spread herself out and rolled about. She slept uncommonly well that night in the warm and pleasant feather bed.

CHAPTER X

THE Coupeaus' new lodging was on the sixth floor, staircase E. After passing Mademoiselle Remanjou's door, one followed the passage on the left. Then came another turning. The first door was the Bijards'. Almost opposite, in a hole without air, under a little staircase, which ascended to the roof, old Bru slept. Two lodgings farther on, one came to Bazouge's. Then, next to Bazouge's was the Coupeaus', a room and a closet, looking on to the courtyard. And there were only two more families along the passage before coming to the Lorilleux, who were right at the end.

A room and a closet, no more. The Coupeaus perched there now. And the room was scarcely larger than one's hand. And they had to do everything in there—eat, sleep, and all the rest. Nana's bed just squeezed into the closet; she had to dress in her father and mother's room, and her door was kept open at night-time so that she should not be suffocated. There was such little room, that Gervaise had sold some things to the Poissons when she gave up the shop, not being able to find space for everything. What with the bed, the table, and four chairs, the lodging was about full. With a broken heart, unable to separate herself from her chest of drawers, she had encumbered what little space remained with this great lumbering piece of furniture, which blocked up half the window. One half could never be opened, and but little light and cheerfulness could enter. Whenever she wanted to look down into the courtyard, there was not room for her elbows, as she was growing very stout, and she was obliged to lean out sideways, straining her neck in order to see.

During the first few days, the laundress would continually sit down and cry. It seemed to her too hard, not being able to move about in her home, after having been used to so much room. She felt stifled; she remained at the window for hours, squeezed between the wall and the drawers, and getting a stiff neck. It was only there that she could breathe freely. The courtyard, however, scarcely inspired her with other than sad thoughts. Opposite to her, on the sunny side, she beheld her dream of bygone days, that window on the fifth floor where, every spring, some scarlet runners twined their slender stems over an arbour made of string. Her room was on the shady side, where pots of mignonette would not last a week. Ah! no, life was not taking a pleasant turn, it was scarcely the existence she had hoped for. Instead of spending her old age amidst flowers, she was already floundering in things which were not very clean.

On leaning out one day, Gervaise experienced a peculiar sensation: she fancied she beheld herself down below, near the door keeper's room under the porch, her nose in the air, and examining the house for the first time; and this leap thirteen years backwards caused her heart to throb. The courtyard had not changed, the bare frontages were scarcely blacker or more leprous, a stench still ascended from the sinks rotting with rust; on the lines at the windows, clothes and children's napkins continued to hang out to dry; down below, the uneven pavement was littered with the cinders from the locksmith's and the shavings from the carpenter's; even, in the damp corner near the water-tap, there was a beautiful blue pool that had flowed from the dyer's, a blue as delicate as the blue of other days.' But she herself felt terribly changed and worn. To begin with, she was no longer below, her face raised to heaven, feeling content and courageous, and aspiring to a handsome lodging. She was right up under the roof, among the lousy ones, in the dirtiest hole, the part that never received a ray of sunshine. And that explained her tears; she could scarcely feel enchanted with her fate.

However, when Gervaise had grown somewhat used to it, the early days of the little family in their new home did not pass off so badly. The winter was almost over, and the trifle of money received for the furniture sold to Virginie, helped to make things comfortable. Then, with the fine weather came a piece of luck, Coupeau was engaged to work in the country, at Étampes; and he was there for nearly three months without once getting drunk, cured for a time by the fresh air. One has no idea what a quench it is to the tippler's thirst, to leave Paris where the streets are full of the fumes of wine and brandy. On his return, he was as fresh as a rose, and he

brought back in his pocket four hundred francs, with which
they paid the two overdue quarters' rent of the shop that the
Poissons had become answerable for, and also the most pressing
of their little debts in the neighbourhood.   Gervaise thus
opened two or three streets through which she had not passed
for a long time.   She had naturally become an ironer again at
so much a day.   Madame Fauconnier, a very worthy woman
providing one flattered her, had been willing to re-engage her.
She even paid her three francs, the same as to a first class
workwoman, out of regard for her former position of employer.
Thus it seemed as though the couple would manage to jog
along.· With work and economy, Gervaise even saw the day
when they would be able to pay everyone and arrange an existence that would be supportable.   She promised herself that,
however, in the feverishness arising from the big sum of money
earned by her husband.   When cool, she accepted life as it
came, saying that beautiful things never lasted.

What the Coupeaus most suffered from at that time, was seeing the Poissons take up their abode at their shop.   They were
not naturally of a particularly jealous disposition, but people
aggravated them, purposely expressing amazement in their presence at the embellishments of their successors.   The Boches,
the Lorilleux especially, never tired.   According to them, no
one had ever seen so beautiful a shop.   And they talked of the
dirty state in which the Poissons had found the premises, relating that the cleaning alone had cost thirty francs.   Virginie,
after a great deal of hesitation, had decided to go in for the
nicest part of the grocery business, dealing in such things as
sweetmeats, chocolate, coffee, and tea.   Lantier had warmly
recommended this line to her, saying that enormous sums were
to be made out of dainties.   The shop was painted black, and
relieved with yellow fillets, two genteel colours.   Three carpen-
ters worked eight days at arranging everything—at the pigeon-
holes, the glass-cases and the counter with shelves for the jars,
the same as at a confectioner's.   The little inheritance which
Poisson had in reserve must have been a good deal eaten into;
but Virginie triumphed, and the Lorilleux, assisted by the
doorkeepers, did not spare Gervaise a pigeon-hole, a show-case
or a glass jar, feeling amused whenever they saw her change
countenance.   One may not be envious, but nevertheless one
loses one's· temper when others put on one's boots and crush
one with them.

There was also a question of a man beneath all this.   It was

affirmed that Lantier had broken off with Gervaise. The neighbourhood declared that it was quite right. In short, it gave a
moral tone to the street. And all the honour of the separation
was accorded to the crafty hatter in whom all the ladies continued to believe. Details were given—he had been obliged to
beat the laundress to make her keep quiet, she had such a furious passion for him. Naturally, no one told the real truth ;
those who might have known it, thought it too simple and not
sufficiently interesting. As a matter of fact, Lantier had indeed broken off with Gervaise, in this sense that he no longer
had her day and night at his disposal ; but he certainly went
up to the sixth floor to see her, for Mademoiselle Remanjou met
him coming from the Coupeaus at most peculiar hours. In
short, the connection continued, by hook or by crook, in a "do
as you are bid" manner, without either one or the other feeling
much pleasure ; the remnant of a habit, a few reciprocal com-
placencies, nothing more. Only, what complicated the situation,
was that the neighbourhood now put Lantier and Virginie between the same pair of sheets. There again the neighbourhood
was in too much of a hurry. No doubt, the hatter was making
up to the tall brunette; and that was bound to be, because she
replaced Gervaise in everything and for everything in the lodging.

A good joke was just then going about on the subject: it was
pretended that one night he had gone to seek Gervaise on his
neighbour's pillow, and that he had brought back Virginie instead, and had kept her without recognising her until daybreak,
on account of the obscurity. The story gave rise to much laughter, but Lantier was really not so far advanced, he scarcely ventured to pinch Virginie's hips. The Lorilleux all the same talked
before the laundress of the amours of Lantier and Madame Poisson with a great amount of feeling, hoping thereby to make her
jealous. The Boches also gave out that never before had they
seen so handsome a couple. The funniest part of all this was
that the Rue de la Goutte-d'Or did not seem to take offence at
the new family of three ; no, morality which had been hard for
Gervaise, was mild for Virginie. Perhaps the smiling indulgence of the street came from the fact that the husband was a
policeman.

Luckily, jealousy did not worry Gervaise much. Lantier's in-
fidelities left her very calm, because for a long time her heart
had been as nothing in their relations. She had learnt, without seeking to do so, some very nasty stories, intrigues between

the hatter and all sorts of girls, the first strumpets he came across in the street; and it affected her so little, that she had continued to be obliging, without even feeling sufficient anger to break off the connection. However, she did not accept her lover's new fancy so quietly. With Virginie, it was quite another thing. They had both of them invented that for the sake of annoying her; and if she laughed at trifles, she required to be treated with consideration. So that, whenever Madame Lorilleux or some other spiteful creature made a point of saying in her presence that Poisson could no longer pass under the Porte Saint-Denis, she would turn quite pale, with a gnawing at her heart-strings and a burning sensation in her stomach. She bit her lips, she avoided getting into a passion, not wishing to give such a pleasure to her enemies. But she must have picked a quarrel with Lantier, for one afternoon Mademoiselle Remanjou thought she recognised the sound of a slap; besides, there certainly was some disagreement between them, for Lantier did not speak to her for a fortnight. Then, he was the first to make it up, and everything seemed to jog on as before as though nothing had happened. The laundress preferred to make the best of a bad job, not caring for a general pulling out of hair, and desirous of not making her life worse than it really was. Ah! she was no longer twenty; she no longer loved men to the point of spanking others for their dear sakes, and risking being locked up at the police-station. Only, she added all this on to the rest.

Coupeau laughed. This easy-going husband, who would not see the cuckoldom in his own home, chaffed immensely about Poisson's pair of horns. In his household it did not count; but in others, he thought it a rare joke, and he gave himself no end of pains to watch for those accidents, when the neighbours' wives went and had a look at the wrong side of the leaf. What a noodle he was, that Poisson! and yet he carried a sword, and even allowed himself to jostle people on the footpaths! Then Coupeau had the cheek to chaff Gervaise. Ah well! her lover was indeed chucking her up! She had no luck: the first time, blacksmiths had turned out a failure, and, the second time, it was the hatters who were found wanting. But then, too, she went in for trades that were not at all serious. Why did she not take a mason, a fellow who would stick, who was used to mixing his mortar firm? Of course he merely said these things by way of a joke, but all the same Gervaise would turn quite green with terror, because he pierced her through and through with his little grey eyes, as though he had wished to drive the words into her with a gimlet. When he started on the chapter of abominations she never knew whether he was laughing or not. A man who gets drunk from one end of the year to the other no longer knows what he says, and there are husbands who, very jealous at twenty, at thirty become through drink very easy-going on the question of conjugal fidelity.

It was a sight to see Coupeau swaggering about the Rue de la Goutte-d'Or! He called Poisson the cuckold. That shut up all the gossips' mouths! The cuckold was no longer himself. Oh, he knew what he knew. If he had pretended not to notice anything before, it was apparently because he did not like rows. Each one appears to know what goes on in his own home, and scratches himself where he itches. But it did not make him itch, and he couldn't scratch himself just to please other people. Well! and the policeman, did he notice anything? Yet it was there sure enough this time. The lovers had been seen; it was not a mere bit of scandalous gossip. And he got quite angry. He could not understand how a man, a person in the employ of the Government, could permit such a scandal in his own home. The policeman must have been very fond of other people's leavings, that was all.

On the nights when Coupeau felt dull, all alone with his wife in their hole under the roof, this did not prevent his going down for Lantier and carrying him off by force. He considered the nest a sad place, now that his comrade no longer shared it. He would make him and Gervaise friends again whenever he saw them sulking. Jove's thunder! cannot one send those who are not satisfied to blazes? is it forbidden to amuse oneself as one chooses? He chuckled, broad ideas lit up his drunkard's vacillating eyes, desires to share everything with the hatter, just to beautify life. And it was especially on those evenings that Gervaise was uncertain whether he spoke in jest or in earnest.

In the midst of all this, Lantier put on the most consequential airs. He showed himself both paternal and dignified. On three successive occasions he had prevented a quarrel between the Coupeaus and the Poissons. The good understanding between the two families formed a part of his contentment. Thanks to the tender, though firm, glances with which he watched over Gervaise and Virginie, they always pretended to entertain a great friendship for each other. He reigned over both blonde and brunette with the tranquillity of a pasha, and

U

fattened on his cunning. The rogue was still digesting the
Coupeaus when he already began to devour the Poissons. Oh,
it did not inconvenience him much! as soon as one shop was
swallowed, he started on a second. It is only men of his sort
who ever have any luck.

It was in June of that year that Nana was confirmed. She
was then nearly thirteen years old, as tall as an asparagus shoot
run to seed, and had a bold, impudent air about her. The
year before she had been sent away from the catechism class on
account of her bad behaviour; and the priest had only allowed
her to join it this time, through fear of losing her altogether,
and of casting one more heathen on to the street. Nana danced
for joy as she thought of the white dress. The Lorilleux, being
godfather and godmother, had promised to provide it, and took
care to let every one in the house know of their present.
Madame Lerat was to give the veil and the cap, Virginie the
purse, and Lantier the prayer-book; so that the Coupeaus
looked forward to the ceremony without any great anxiety.
Even the Poissons, wishing to give a house-warming, chose this
occasion, no doubt on the hatter's advice. They invited the
Coupeaus and the Boches, whose little girl was also going to be
confirmed. They provided a leg of mutton and trimmings for
the evening in question.

It so happened that on the evening before, Coupeau returned
home in a most abominable condition, just as Nana was lost in
admiration before the presents spread out on the top of the
chest of drawers. The Paris atmosphere was getting the better
of him again; and he fell foul of his wife and child with
drunken arguments and disgusting language, which no one
should have uttered at such a time. Nana herself was
beginning to get hold of some very bad expressions in the
midst of the filthy conversations she was continually hearing.
On the days when there was a row, she would often call her
mother an old camel and a cow.

"And bread!" yelled the zinc-worker. "I want my soup,
you couple of jades! There're females for you, always thinking
of their finery! I'll sit on the gew-gaws, you know, if I don't
get my soup!"

"He's unbearable when he's screwed!" murmured Gervaise,
out of patience; and, turning towards him, she exclaimed:

"It's warming, don't bother us."

Nana was doing the modest, because she thought it nice on
such a day. She continued to look at the presents on the

chest of drawers, affectedly lowering her eyelids, and pretending not to understand her father's naughty words. But the zinc-worker was an awful plague on the nights when he had had too much. Poking his face right against her neck, he said:

"I'll give you white dresses! Are you going to stuff the body full of paper for titties again, like last Sunday? Yes, yes, wait a bit! I see you wriggling your breech. So fine toys tickle your fancy. They excite your imagination. Just you cut away from there, you ugly little slut! Move your hands about, bundle all that into a drawer, or I'll clean you with it!"

Nana, with bowed head, did not answer a word. She had taken up the little tulle cap, and was asking her mother how much it cost. And as Coupeau thrust out his hand to seize hold of the cap, it was Gervaise who pushed him aside, exclaiming:

"Do leave the child alone! she's very good, she's doing no harm."

Then the zinc-worker let out in real earnest.

"Ah! the strumpets! The mother and daughter, they make the pair. It's a nice thing to go to church just to leer at the men. Dare to say it isn't true, little slattern! I'll dress you in a sack, we'll see if it'll scratch your skin. Yes, in a sack, just to disgust you, you and your priests. I don't want you to be taught anything worse than you know already. Damnation! Just listen to me, both of you!"

At this, Nana turned round in a fury, whilst Gervaise had to spread out her arms to protect the things which Coupeau talked of tearing. The child looked her father straight in the face; then, forgetting the modest bearing inculcated by her confessor, she said, clinching her teeth: "Pig!"

As soon as the zinc-worker had had his soup, he snored. On the morrow, he awoke in a very good humour. He still felt a little of the booze of the day before, but only just sufficient to make him amiable. He assisted at the dressing of the child, deeply affected by the white dress, and finding that a mere nothing gave the little vermin quite a young lady look. And it was something to see Nana's style in her dress that was too short, and she smiling in an embarrassed way like a young bride. When she went downstairs, and caught sight of Pauline, also ready dressed, standing outside the doorkeeper's room, she stopped and examined her with her clear glance, and then became very nice indeed on seeing that her friend did not look as well as herself, and, moreover, had the appearance of a bundle.

The two families started off together for the church. Nana
and Pauline walked first, their prayer-books in their hands, and
holding down their veils on account of the wind ; they did not
speak, but were bursting with delight at seeing the people come
to their shop-doors, and they pouted devoutly every time they
heard any one say as they passed that they looked very nice.
Madame Boche and Madame Lorilleux lagged behind, because
they were interchanging their ideas about the Hobbler, a gobble-
all, whose daughter would never have been confirmed if the
relations had not found everything for her ; yes, everything,
even a new chemise, out of respect for the holy altar. Madame
Lorilleux particularly busied herself with her present, the dress,
crushing Nana with a look, and calling her "big slut" each
time the child got a little dust on her skirt, by going too near
the shop windows.

At church, Coupeau wept all the time. It was stupid, but
he could not help it. It affected him to see the priest holding
out his arms, and all the little girls, looking like angels, pass
before him clasping their hands ; and the music of the organ
stirred up his stomach, and the pleasant smell of the incense
forced him to sniff, the same as though some one had thrust a
bouquet of flowers into his face. In short, he saw everything
cerulean, his heart was touched. There was a canticle especially, something extra sweet, sung whilst the children were
taking the communion, which seemed to run with a shiver down
his neck and his backbone. Round about him, too, all the sensitive people were soaking their pocket handkerchiefs. Really,
it was a bright day, the brightest day of his life. Only, when,
on coming out of church, he went to drink a glass of wine with
Lorilleux, who had kept his own eyes dry, and who chaffed him,
he got in a passion, and accused the rooks of burning the devil's
herbs in their churches in order to unman people. But,
all the same, he made no secret of it, his eyes had melted,
and that merely proved that he had not got a paving-stone
in place of a heart. And he ordered the glasses to be filled
again.

That evening, the Poissons' house-warming was very lively.
Friendship reigned without a hitch from one end of the feast to
the other. When bad times arrive, one thus comes in for some
pleasant evenings, hours during which sworn enemies love each
other. Lantier, with Gervaise on his left and Virginie on his
right, was most amiable to both of them, lavishing little tender
caresses like a cock who desires peace in his poultry-yard.

Opposite to them, Poisson maintained the calm and dignified air of a policeman accustomed to think of nothing, and with a sort of bandage over his eyes during his long wanderings over his beat. But the queens of the feast were the two little ones, Nana and Pauline, who had been allowed to keep on their things; they sat bolt upright, through fear of spilling anything on their white dresses, and at every mouthful they were told to hold up their chins, so as to swallow cleanly. Nana, greatly bored by all this fuss, ended by slabbering her wine over the body of her dress, so it was taken off, and the stains were at once washed out in a glass of water.

Then, at dessert, the children's future careers were gravely discussed. Madame Boche had decided that Pauline should learn the business of a piercer of gold and silver; one could earn from five to six francs a day at it. Gervaise had not made up her mind, Nana showed no vocation for anything. Oh! she ran about the streets, she had a taste for that; but, at everything else, she was butter-fingered.

"In your place," said Madame Lerat, "I would bring her up as an artificial flower-maker. It is a pleasant and clean employment."

"Flower-makers," murmured Lorilleux, "are girls who all follow the first fellow that asks them."

"Well! and I?" retorted the tall widow, biting her lips. "You're not over gallant. You know, I'm not a she-dog. I don't put my paws up in the air whenever anyone whistles!"

But the others made her leave off.

"Madame Lerat! oh! Madame Lerat!"

And they drew her attention with winks to the two young girls who had been confirmed, and who were burying their noses in their glasses, so as not to laugh. Out of decency, the men themselves had up till then all chosen their words. But Madame Lerat would not accept the lesson. What she had just said, she had heard in the very best society. Besides, she flattered herself she knew her mother tongue; she had often been complimented on her way of speaking, even before children, without ever violating the laws of decency.

"There are some very respectable women amongst the artificial flower-makers, just you be pleased to understand!" shouted she. "They're made like other women; they're not all skin, of course. Only, they keep themselves in bounds; they choose with taste when they do what isn't right. Yes, they owe it all to the flowers. It's what preserved me."

"Well!" interrupted Gervaise, "I've no dislike for the artificial flower-making. Only, it must please Nana, that's all I care about; one should never thwart children on the question of a vocation. Come, Nana, don't be stupid; tell me now, would you like to make flowers?"

The child, bending over her plate, was gathering up the cake crumbs with her wet finger, which she afterwards sucked. She did not hurry herself. She grinned in her vicious way.

"Why yes, mamma, I should like to," she ended by declaring.

Then the matter was at once settled. Coupeau was quite willing that Madame Lerat should take the child with her on the morrow to the place where she worked in the Rue du Caire. And they all talked very gravely of the duties of life. Boche said that Nana and Pauline were women now that they had partaken of the communion. Poisson added that for the future they ought to know how to cook, mend socks, and look after a house. Something was even said of their marrying, and of the children they would some day have. The youngsters listened and laughed in their sleeves, rubbing up against one another, red and awkward in their white dresses, their hearts swelling with the pride of being women. But what tickled them most was when Lantier chaffed them, asking them if they had not already got little husbands. And they forced Nana to own that she had a great affection for Victor Fauconnier, the son of the laundress's former mistress.

"Ah well!" said Madame Lorilleux to the Boches, as they were all leaving, "she's our god-daughter, but as they're going to put her into the artificial flower-making, we don't wish to have anything more to do with her. Another drab for the Boulevards. She'll take her hook before six months are over."

On going up to bed, the Coupeaus agreed that everything had passed off well, and that the Poissons were not at all bad people. Gervaise even considered the shop was nicely got up. She was expecting to suffer a great deal in thus spending the evening in her old lodging, where others were strutting about now; and she was surprised at not having felt angry for a single moment. Nana, who was undressing, asked her mother if the dress of the young lady on the second floor who had been married the month before was a muslin one like hers.

But that was their last happy day. Two years passed by, during which they sank deeper and deeper. The winters especially cleared them out. If they had bread to eat during the fine

weather, the rain and cold came accompanied by hunger, by drubbings before the empty cupboard, and by dinner-hours with nothing
to eat in the little Siberia of their larder. That scamp December entered their home under the door, and he brought every
ill imaginable—the closing of the work-shops, the benumbed
idleness engendered by the frost, the black misery of continual
wet weather. The first winter, they still had a fire at times,
huddling round the stove, preferring to be warm rather than
to eat; the second winter, the stove did not even once have the
rust off it, it froze the room with its lugubrious air of a cast-iron
milestone. And what took the life out of their limbs, what
above all utterly crushed them, was the rent. Oh! the January quarter, when there was not a radish in the house and old
Boche came up with the receipt! Then it blew colder, a regular tempest from the north. M. Marescot arrived the following
Saturday, wrapped up in a good warm overcoat, his big hands
hidden in woollen gloves; and he was for ever talking of ejecting
them, whilst the snow continued to fall outside, as though it
were preparing a bed for them on the pavement, with white
sheets. To have paid the quarter's rent they would have sold
their very flesh. It was the rent which emptied the larder and
the stove.

In the entire house, moreover, a general lamentation ascended.
There was weeping on every floor; a music of misfortune
resounded up the staircases and along the passages. Had there
been a corpse in every home, it would not have produced a
more abominable noise of wailing. A regular day of the last
judgment; the end of the end, life rendered utterly impossible,
the annihilation of the poor. The woman on the third floor had
to go and do eight days at the corner of the Rue Belhomme.
A workman, the mason on the fifth floor, had robbed his
employer.

No doubt, the Coupeaus had only themselves to blame.
Life may be a hard fight, but one always pulls through when
one is orderly and economical—witness the Lorilleux, who paid
their rent to the day, the money folded up in bits of dirty
paper; but they, it is true, led a life of starved spiders, which
would disgust one with work. Nana as yet earned nothing at
flower-making; she even cost a good deal for her keep. At
Madame Fauconnier's, Gervaise was beginning to be looked
down upon. She was no longer so expert; she bungled her
work to such an extent that the mistress had reduced her wages
to forty sous a day, the price paid to the clumsiest. With all

that she was very proud and very susceptible, throwing in every one's teeth her former position of a person in business. Some days she never turned up at all, whilst on others she would leave in the midst of her work, simply through a fit of temper; for instance, on one occasion she was so annoyed at Madame Fauconnier's engaging Madame Putois, and at having thus to iron side by side with her former workwoman, that she had gone off and had not returned for a fortnight. When she had recovered her temper, she would be taken back out of charity, which embittered her still more. Naturally, when the end of the week came, she had not much money to receive; and, as she often bitterly observed, it would finish one Saturday by her owing something to her employer.

As for Coupeau, he did perhaps work, but in that case he certainly made a present of his labour to the Government; for since the time he returned from Etampes, Gervaise had never seen the colour of his money. She no longer looked in his hands when he came home on pay-days. He arrived swinging his arms, his pockets empty, and often without his handkerchief; well! yes, he had lost his rag, or else some rascally comrade had sneaked it. At first he rendered accounts; he invented all sorts of lies—ten francs for a subscription, twenty francs fallen through a hole which he showed in his pocket, fifty francs disbursed in paying off imaginary debts. Then he had no longer troubled himself to give any explanations. The money evaporated, that was all! It moved from his pocket into his stomach, and that was a funnier way of bringing it home to his missus. On Madame Boche's advice, the laundress would sometimes go and watch for her husband at the door of the workshop at closing time, so as to secure the coin he had just received. But that did not help her much; some of his comrades would warn Coupeau, and the money would glide into his shoes or some purse dirtier still. Madame Boche was very cunning in this respect, because Boche was in the habit of doing her out of pieces of ten francs, which he hid for the purpose of standing treat to amiable ladies of his acquaintance. She would inspect the smallest corners of his clothes; she generally found the coin that had not answered to the roll-call sewed up in the peak of his cap, between the leather and the cloth. Ah! it was not the zinc-worker who padded his rags with gold! He stuffed it under his flesh. Yet Gervaise could not take her scissors and rip open his stomach.

Yes, it was their fault, if every season found them lower and

lower. But that's the sort of thing one never tells oneself,
especially when one's down in the mire. They accused their
bad luck; they pretended that fate was against them. Their
home had become a regular hell upon earth. They wrangled
the whole day long. However, they had not yet come to blows,
with the exception of a few smacks which somehow flew about
at the height of their quarrels. The saddest part of the business
was that they had opened the cage of affection; all their better
feelings had taken flight like so many canaries. The genial
warmth of father, mother, and child, when united together and
wrapped up in each other, deserted them and left them shivering, each in his or her own corner. The whole three—Coupeau,
Gervaise, and Nana—were ever in the most abominable tempers,
biting each other's noses off for nothing at all, their eyes full of
hatred; and it seemed as though something had broken the
mainspring of the family, the mechanism which, with happy
people, causes all hearts to beat in unison. Ah! it was certain
Gervaise was no longer moved as she used to be when she saw
Coupeau at the edge of a roof, at forty or fifty feet above the
pavement. She would not have pushed him off herself; but if
he had fallen accidentally, in truth! it would have freed the
earth of one who was of but little account. The days when they
were more especially at enmity, she regretted that it seemed he
was never going to be brought home on a stretcher! She was
awaiting it. It would be her happiness they were bringing
back to her. What use was he, that drunkard? To make her
weep, to devour all she possessed, to drive her to sin. Well!
men so useless as he should be thrown as quickly as possible
into the hole, and the polka of deliverance be danced over them.
And when the mother said "Kill!" the daughter responded
"Fell!" Nana read all the reports of accidents in the newspapers, and made reflections that were unnatural for a girl.
Her father had such luck, an omnibus had knocked him down
without even sobering him. Would the beggar never croak?

In the midst of this existence, maddened by misery, Gervaise
suffered also from the hungry groans that she heard around
her. This corner of the house was the lousy one, where three
or four families seemed to have made up their minds not to
have bread every day. Their doors might be open, but there
seldom issued the smell of cooking. Along the passage reigned
the silence of starvation, and the walls gave a hollow sound like
empty stomachs. At times there rose the sound of drubbings,
women weeping, the plaintive cries of hungry brats. It was

only a family devouring themselves to deceive their stomachs.
Cramp in the throat was a general complaint, whilst they were
all gaping through their wide open mouths; and chests contracted merely from breathing that air, in which the flies themselves could not have lived, through want of food.

But what most excited Gervaise's pity was old Bru, in his
hole under the little staircase. He retired into it like a
marmot, and rolled himself up in a ball so as to feel less cold.
He remained for days on a heap of straw without moving.
Hunger no longer drove him out, for it was useless going and
getting up an appetite when nobody had invited him to dinner.
Whenever three or four days passed without his being seen, the
neighbours would push his door open to see if he had come to
an end. No, he lived on all the same; not much, but just a
little—with one eye only. Even death was forgetting him!
Directly Gervaise got hold of some bread she would throw him
a few crusts. If she was becoming bad and detested men, on account of her husband, she always sincerely pitied the animals; and
old Bru, that poor old fellow whom everybody left to die because
he could no longer hold his brush, was like a dog to her, a beast
past service, whose skin and fat even the knackers would not
buy. It was quite a weight on her heart to know of his being
continually there, on the other side of the passage, abandoned
by God and man, nourishing himself solely on himself, returning to the size of a child, shrivelled and dried up like oranges
which become hardened on mantel-pieces.

The laundress also suffered a great deal from the close neighbourhood of Bazouge, the funeral mute. A simple partition,
and a very thin one, separated the two rooms. He could not
put a finger into his mouth without her hearing it. As soon as
he came home of an evening, she listened in spite of herself to
everything he did. His black leather hat laid with a dull thud
on the chest of drawers like a shovelful of earth; the black
cloak hung up and rustling against the wall like the wings of
some night bird; all the black toggery flung into the middle of
the room, and filling it with the trappings of mourning. She
heard him stamping about, felt anxious at the least movement,
and was quite startled if he knocked against the furniture, or
rattled any of his crockery. This confounded drunkard was
her pre-occupation, filling her with a secret fear, mingled with a
desire to know. He, jolly, his belly full every day, his head all
upside down, coughed, spat, sang "Mother Godichon," made
use of many dirty expressions, and fought with the four walls

before finding his bedstead. And she remained quite pale, asking herself whatever he could be up to. She imagined the most atrocious things. She got into her head that he must have brought a corpse home and was stowing it away under his bedstead. Well! the newspapers had related something of the kind—an undertaker's mute who collected the coffins of little children at his home, so as to save himself trouble, and to make only one journey to the cemetery.

For certain, directly Bazouge arrived, a smell of death seemed to permeate the partition. One might have thought oneself lodging against the Père-Lachaise cemetery, in the midst of the kingdom of moles. He was frightful, the animal, continually laughing all by himself, as though his profession enlivened him. Even when he had finished his rumpus and had laid himself on his back, he snored in a manner so extraordinary that it caused the laundress to hold her breath. For hours she listened attentively, with an idea that funerals were passing through her neighbour's room.

Yes, the worst was that, in spite of her terrors, something incited Gervaise to put her ear to the wall, the better to find out what was taking place. Bazouge had the same effect on her as handsome men have on good women: they would like to touch them, but they dare not, their bringing-up restrains them. Well! if fear had not kept her back, Gervaise would have liked to have handled death, to see what it was like. She became so peculiar at times, holding her breath, listening attentively, expecting to unravel the secret through one of Bazouge's movements, that Coupeau would ask her with a chuckle if she had a fancy for the mute next door. She got angry and talked of moving, the close proximity of this neighbour was so distasteful to her ; and yet, in spite of herself, as soon as the old chap arrived, smelling like a cemetery, she became wrapped again in her reflections, with the excited and timorous air of a wife thinking of passing a knife through the marriage contract. Had he not twice offered to pack her up, and carry her off with him to some place where the enjoyment of sleep is so great, that in a moment one forgets all one's wretchedness? Perhaps it was really very pleasant. Little by little the temptation to taste it became stronger. She would have liked to have tried it for a fortnight or a month. Oh! to sleep a month, especially in winter, the month when the rent became due, when the troubles of life were killing her ! But it was not possible—one must sleep for ever, if one commenced to sleep

for an hour; and the thought of this froze her, her desire for
death departed before the eternal and stern friendship which
the earth demanded.

However, one evening in January, she knocked with both
her fists against the partition. She had passed a frightful
week, hustled by every one, without a sou, and utterly dis-
couraged. That evening she was not at all well; she shivered
with fever, and seemed to see flames dancing about her. Then,
instead of throwing herself out of the window, as she had at
one moment thought of doing, she set to knocking and calling:

"Old Bazouge! old Bazouge!"

The mute was taking off his shoes and singing, "There were
three lovely girls." He had probably had a good day, for he
seemed even more maudlin than usual.

"Old Bazouge! old Bazouge!" repeated Gervaise, raising
her voice.

Did he not hear her then? She was ready to give herself
at once; he might come and take her on his neck, and carry
her off to the place where he carried his other women, the poor
and the rich, whom he consoled. It pained her to hear his
song, "There were three lovely girls," because she discerned
in it the disdain of a man who has too many mistresses.

"What is it? what is it?" stuttered Bazouge; "who's unwell? We're coming, little woman!"

But the sound of this husky voice awoke Gervaise as though
from a nightmare. What had she done? she must have been
hammering against the partition. Then she felt as though she
had received a heavy blow across her loins; fright contracted all
the muscles of her body, she drew back, fancying she beheld
the mute's fat hands passing through the wall to seize her by
the hair. No, no, she would not, she was not ready. If she
had knocked, it must have been with her elbow in turning over,
without being aware of it. And a feeling of horror ascended
from her knees to her shoulders at the thought of seeing herself
lugged along in the old fellow's arms, all stiff and her face as
white as a plate.

"Well! is there no one there now?" resumed Bazouge in
the silence. "Wait a bit, we're always ready to oblige the
ladies."

"It's nothing, nothing," said the laundress at length in a
choking voice. "I don't require anything, thanks."

Whilst the mute fell asleep grumbling, she remained anxiously
listening to him, not daring to move for fear he should fancy

that he again heard her knocking. She vowed to be very careful now. She might be dying, she would not ask her neighbour for help. She promised herself this so as to reassure herself, for at certain moments she was still possessed by her horrible fancy, in spite of her fright.

In her corner of misery, in the midst of her cares and the cares of others, Gervaise had, however, a beautiful example of courage in the home of her neighbours, the Bijards. Little Lalie, that youngster of eight, about the size of two sous' worth of butter, looked after everything and kept the place as clean as a grown-up person could have done; and the work was rough, she had the care of two little brats, her brother Jules and her sister Henriette, urchins of three and five years old, whom she had to watch over all day long, even whilst sweeping the place out or washing up the crockery.

Ever since Bijard had killed his wife with a kick in the stomach, Lalie had become the little mother of them all. Without saying a word, and of her own accord, she filled the place of the one who had gone, to the extent that her brute of a father, no doubt to complete the resemblance, now belaboured the daughter as he had formerly belaboured the mother. Whenever he came home drunk, he required women to massacre. He did not even notice that Lalie was quite little; he would not have beaten an old skin harder. With a slap he covered her entire face, and the flesh was still so delicate that the marks of his five fingers remained there for a couple of days. There were most abominable thrashings, kicks for a "yes" or a "no," a regular mad wolf falling on a poor little cat, timid and coaxing, so thin that the sight would make one weep, and who submitted to all this with a resigned look in her beautiful eyes and without a murmur. No, Lalie never rebelled. She bent her neck a little to protect her face; she kept in her cries, so as not to rouse the house. Then, when her father was tired of kicking her about from one corner of the room to another, she waited till she had regained sufficient strength to resume her work, washed her children, made the soup, and did not leave a speck of dust upon the furniture. It was a part of her daily task to be beaten.

Gervaise entertained a great friendship for her little neighbour. She treated her as an equal, as a grown-up woman of experience. It must be said that Lalie had a pale and serious look, with the expression of an old girl. One might have thought her thirty on hearing her speak. She knew very well

how to buy things, mend the clothes, attend to the home, and
she spoke of the children as though she had already gone
through two or three confinements in her time. It made people
smile to hear her talk thus at eight years old ; and then a
lump would rise in their throats, and they would hurry away
so as not to burst out crying. Gervaise drew the child towards
her as much as she could, gave her all she could spare, food
and old clothing. One day as she tried one of Nana's old
dresses on to her, she almost choked with anger on seeing her
back covered with bruises, the skin off her elbow; which was
still bleeding, and all her innocent flesh martyred and sticking
to her bones. Well ! old Bazouge could get his box ready; she
would not last long at that rate ! But the child had begged the
laundress not to say a word. She would not have her father
bothered on her account. She took his part, affirming that he
would not have been so wicked if it had not been for the
drink. He was mad, he did not know what he did. Oh ! she
forgave him, because one ought to forgive madmen everything.

From that time Gervaise watched, and prepared to interfere
directly she heard Bijard coming upstairs. But on most of the
occasions she only caught some whack for her share. When
she entered their room in the day-time, she often found Lalie
tied to the foot of the iron bedstead ; it was an idea of the
locksmith's, before going out, to tie her legs and her body with
some stout rope, without anyone being able to find out why—a
mere whim of a brain diseased by drink, just for the sake, no
doubt, of tyrannising over the child when he was no longer
there. Lalie, as stiff as a stake, with pins and needles in her
legs, remained whole days at the post. She once even passed
a night there, Bijard having forgot to come home. Whenever
Gervaise, carried away by her indignation, talked of unfastening
her, she implored her not to disturb the rope, because her
father became furious if he did not find the knots tied the same
way he had left them. It was really not at all unpleasant, it
rested her ; and she would say that with a smile, whilst her
little cherub-like legs were swollen and lifeless. What grieved
her was that being fastened to the bedstead did not get the
work at all forward, in face of the disorder of the home.
Her father ought certainly to have invented something else.
All the same, she looked after her children, made them obey
her, and called Henriette and Jules to her to have their noses
wiped. As her hands were free she knitted whilst waiting to
be delivered, so as not to waste her time entirely. And she

suffered especially when Bijard untied her. She crawled about a good quarter of an hour on the ground, unable to stand up, because the blood no longer circulated.

The locksmith had also thought of another little game. He heated sous in the frying pan, then placed them on a corner of the mantel-piece; and he called Lalie, and told her to fetch a couple of pounds of bread. The child took up the sous unsuspectingly, uttered a cry, and threw them on the ground, shaking her burnt hand. Then he flew into a fury. Who had saddled him with such a piece of carrion? She lost the money now! And he threatened to beat her to a jelly, if she did not pick the sous up at once. When the child hesitated she received a first warning, a clout of such force that it made her see thirty-six candles. Speechless, and with two big tears in the corners of her eyes, she would pick up the sous and go off, tossing them in the palm of her hand to cool them.

No, one could never imagine the ferocious ideas which may sprout from the depths of a drunkard's brain. One afternoon, for instance, Lalie, having made everything tidy, was playing with her children. The window was open, there was a draught, and the wind blowing along the passage gently shook the door.

"It's Monsieur Hardy," the child was saying. "Come in, Monsieur Hardy. Pray have the kindness to walk in."

And she curtsied before the door, she bowed to the wind. Henriette and Jules, behind her, also bowed, delighted with the game, and splitting their sides with laughing, as though being tickled. She was quite rosy at seeing them so heartily amused, and even found some pleasure in it on her own account, which generally only happened to her on the thirty-sixth day of each month.

"Good day, Monsieur Hardy. How do you do, Monsieur Hardy?"

But a rough hand pushed the door, and Bijard entered. Then the scene changed. Henriette and Jules fell down flat against the wall; whilst Lalie, terrified, remained standing in the very middle of a curtsey. The locksmith held in his hand a big waggoner's whip, quite new, with a long white wooden handle, and a leather thong, terminating with a bit of fine whipcord. He placed this whip in the corner against the bed, and did not give the usual kick to the child, who was already preparing herself by presenting her back. A chuckle exposed his blackened teeth, and he was very lively, very drunk, his phiz lighted up by some idea that amused him immensely.

"What's that?" said he. "You're playing the strumpet, you confounded young hussy! I could hear you dancing about from downstairs. Now then, come here! Nearer, damn you! and full face. I don't want to sniff you behind. Am I touching you, that you tremble like a mass of giblets? Take my shoes off."

Lalie, turned quite pale again, and amazed at not receiving her drubbing, took his shoes off. He had seated himself on the edge of the bed. He lay down with his clothes on, and remained with his eyes open, watching the child move about the room. She busied herself with one thing and another, gradually becoming bewildered beneath his glance, her limbs overcome by such a fright that she ended by breaking a cup. Then, without disturbing himself, he took hold of the whip and showed it to her.

"I say, little calf, look at this. It's a present for you. Yes, it's another fifty sous you've cost me. With this plaything I shall no longer be obliged to run, and it'll be no use you getting into the corners. Will you have a try? Ah! you break the cups! Now then, gee up! Dance away, make your curtsies to Monsieur Hardy!"

He did not even raise himself, but lay sprawling on his back, his head buried in his pillow, making the big whip crack about the room, with the noise of a postillion starting his horses. Then, lowering his arm, he lashed Lalie in the middle of the body, encircling her with the whip, and unwinding it again as though she were a top. She fell, and tried to escape on all fours; but lashing her again, he set her once more on her feet.

"Gee up, gee up!" yelled he. "It's the donkey race! Eh, it'll be fine of a morning in winter. I can lie snug without getting cold or hurting my chilblains, and catch the calves from a distance. In that corner there, a hit, you hussy! And in that other corner, a hit again! And in that one, another hit. Ah! if you crawl under the bed I'll whack you with the handle. Gee up, you jade! gee up! gee up!"

A slight foam came to his lips, his yellow eyes were starting from their black orbits. Lalie, maddened, howling, jumped to the four corners of the room, curled herself up on the floor, and clung to the walls; but the lash at the end of the big whip caught her everywhere, cracking against her ears with the noise of fireworks, streaking her flesh with burning weals. A regular dance of an animal being taught its tricks. This poor little cat waltzed. It was a sight! her heels in the air like little girls playing at skipping, and crying "Faster!" She was all out of breath, rebounding like an india-rubber ball, letting herself be beaten, unable to see, or any longer to seek, a refuge. And her wolf of a father triumphed, calling her strumpet, asking her if she had had enough, and whether she understood sufficiently that she was in future to give up all hope of escaping from him.

But Gervaise suddenly entered the room, attracted by the child's howls. On beholding such a scene she was seized with a furious indignation.

"Ah! the brute of a man!" cried she. "Leave her alone, you brigand! I'll tell the police of you."

Bijard growled like an animal being disturbed, and stuttered,

"I say, Limper, just mind your own business a bit. Perhaps you'd like me to put gloves on when I stir her up. It's merely to warm her, as you can see—simply to show her that I've a long arm."

And he gave a final lash with the whip which caught Lalie across the face. The upper lip was cut, the blood flowed. Gervaise had seized a chair, and was about to fall on the locksmith; but the child held her hands towards her imploringly, saying that it was nothing, and that it was all over. She wiped away the blood with a corner of her apron, and quieted her children, who were sobbing bitterly, as though they had received all the blows.

Whenever Gervaise thought of Lalie, she no longer dared complain. She would have liked to have had the courage of that youngster of eight, who endured in herself alone as much as all the other women of that staircase put together. She had seen her living on nothing but dry bread for three months, not even eating enough crusts to satisfy her hunger, and so thin and weak that she had to cling to the walls when moving about; and when she took her by stealth any bits of meat she had left, she felt her heart melt as she watched her eat, shedding big silent tears the while, and only swallowing very tiny pieces because her contracted throat could scarcely admit the food. Always tender and devoted in spite of that, reasonable beyond her years, she performed her duties of little mother to the point of dying of her maternity, awakened too soon in her child's frail innocence. And Gervaise took an example of suffering and pardon from this dear creature, trying to learn from her how to conceal her martyrdom. Lalie only retained her silent look, her big, black, resigned eyes, in the depths of which one could

divine a night of agony and misery. Never a word, only
her big black eyes opened wide.

In the Coupeaus' home the "vitriol" of the "Assommoir"
was also commencing its ravages. The laundress saw the hour
approaching when her husband would, like Bijard, take a whip
to lead the dance; and the misfortune which threatened her,
naturally enabled her to feel that which had befallen the child
all the more. Yes, Coupeau was spinning a nasty thread. The
time was past when the bad spirit gave him a colour. He
could no longer slap his body and strut about, saying that the
confounded stuff fattened him, for his bad yellow fat of the first
years had melted away, and he was becoming dried up and
scraggy, of a leaden hue variegated with the green tints of a
corpse rotting in a pond. His appetite was also gone. Little
by little he had lost the taste for bread, he had even reached
the point of spurning his meat. One might have placed the
most delicious stew before him, his stomach was barred against
it, his inert teeth refused to chew. To keep himself up he required
his pint of brandy a day. It was his ration, his meat and drink,
the only food he could digest. In the morning, directly he
jumped out of bed, he remained a good quarter of an hour doubled
in two, coughing and cracking his bones, holding his head, and
getting rid of the phlegm, bitter as gall, which swept his throat.
It never missed coming, one might prepare for it beforehand.

Coupeau never got steady on his pins till after his first glass
of consolation, a real remedy, the fire of which cauterised his
bowels; but, during the day, his strength returned. At first,
he would feel a tickling sensation, a sort of pins-and-needles
in his hands and feet; and he would joke, relating that
some one was having a lark with him, that he was sure
his wife put horse-hair between the sheets. Then his legs
would become heavy, the tickling sensation would end by
turning into the most abominable cramps, which gripped his
flesh as though in a vice. That, though, did not amuse him so
much. He no longer laughed, stopped suddenly on the pavement in a bewildered way, with a singing in his ears, and his
eyes blinded with sparks. Everything appeared to him to be
yellow, the houses danced, and he reeled about for three seconds,
with the fear of suddenly finding himself sprawling on the
ground. At other times, while the sun was shining full on his
back, he would shiver, as though iced water had been poured
down his shoulders. What bothered him the most was a slight
trembling of both his hands; the right hand especially must

have been guilty of some crime, it suffered from so many nightmares. Damnation! was he then no longer a man? He was becoming an old woman! He furiously strained his muscles, he seized hold of his glass and bet that he would hold it perfectly steady, as with a hand of marble; but, in spite of his efforts, the glass danced about, jumped to the right, jumped to the left, with a hurried and regular trembling movement. Then, in a fury, he emptied it into his gullet, yelling that he would require dozens like it, and afterwards he undertook to carry a cask without so much as moving a finger. Gervaise, on the other hand, told him to give up drink, if he wished to cease trembling; and he laughed at her, emptying quarts until he experienced the sensation again, flying into a rage, and accusing the passing omnibuses of shaking up his liquor.

In the month of March, Coupeau returned home one evening soaked through. He had come with My-Boots from Montrouge, where they had stuffed themselves full of eel soup, and he had received the full force of the shower all the way from the Barrière des Fourneaux to the Barrière Poissonnière, a good stride. During the night he was seized with a confounded fit of coughing. He was very flushed, suffering from a violent fever, and panting like a broken bellows. When the Boches' doctor saw him in the morning, and listened against his back, he shook his head, and drew Gervaise aside to advise her to have her husband at once taken to the hospital. Coupeau was suffering from inflammation of the lungs.

And Gervaise did not worry herself, you may be sure. At one time she would have been chopped into pieces before trusting her old man with the saw-bones. After the accident in the Rue de la Nation, she had spent their savings in nursing him. But those beautiful sentiments have their day when men take to wallowing in the mire. No, no, she did not intend to embarrass herself like that again. They might take him and never bring him back, she would thank them heartily. Yet, when the litter arrived, and Coupeau was put into it like an article of furniture, she became all pale and bit her lips; and if she grumbled and still said it was a good job, her heart was no longer in her words. Had she but ten francs in her drawer she would not have let him go.

She accompanied him to the Lariboisière hospital, saw the nurses put him to bed at the end of a large apartment, where the patients in a row, looking like corpses, raised themselves up, and followed with their eyes the comrade who had just

been brought in. There was a good deal of death hanging
about in there, a suffocating odour of fever, and a consumptive
music sufficient to make one spit one's lungs out; without
counting that the room had the look of a diminutive Père-
Lachaise cemetery, bordered by its white beds, a regular alley
of tombstones. Then, as Coupeau remained flat on his pillow,
Gervaise went off without finding a word to say, and having
nothing, unfortunately, in her pocket to ease him. Outside, in
front of the hospital, she turned round and gave a last glance
at the edifice. And she thought of former days, when
Coupeau, perched up there on the edge of the gutters, laid his
sheets of zinc whilst he sang in the sunshine. He did not
drink then, he had the skin of a girl. She, from her window at
the Hôtel Boncœur, sought for him, and beheld him right in the
middle of the sky; and they both waved their handkerchiefs,
sending one another kisses by telegraph. Yes, Coupeau had
worked up there, and without the least idea that he was working
for himself. Now he was no longer on the roofs like a jovial and
dissolute sparrow. He was beneath them, he had built his nest
in the hospital, and with his rough hide he had come there to
croak. Ah! how far off their courting days seemed then!

On the day after the morrow, when Gervaise called to obtain
news of him, she found the bed empty. A sister of charity
told her that they had been obliged to remove her husband to
the Asylum of Sainte-Anne, because the day before he had
suddenly gone wild. Oh! a total leave-taking of his senses,
attempts to crack his skull against the wall, howls which prevented the other patients from sleeping. It all came from
drink, it seemed. The drink, which had been brewing in his
body, had taken advantage, the moment the inflammation of
the lungs had laid him on his back without strength, to attack
him and wring his nerves. The laundress returned home in a
state of distraction. Her old man had gone mad now! Life
would become precious queer if they let him out. Nana exclaimed that he ought to be left where he was, because otherwise he would end by murdering them both.

Gervaise was not able to go to Sainte-Anne until the Sunday.
It was a tremendous journey. Fortunately, the omnibus from
the Boulevard Rochechouart to La Glacière passed close to the
asylum. She went down the Rue de la Santé, buying two
oranges on her way, so as not to arrive empty-handed. It was
another monumental building, with grey courtyards, interminable corridors, and a smell of rank medicaments, which did

not exactly inspire liveliness. But when they had admitted her into a cell, she was quite surprised to see Coupeau almost jolly. He was just then seated on the throne, a clean wooden case; and they both laughed at her finding him in this position. Well, one knows what an invalid is. He squatted there like a pope, with his cheek of other days. Oh! he was better as he could do this.

"And the inflammation?" inquired the laundress.

"Done for!" replied he. "They cured it in no time. I still cough a little, but that's all that is left of it."

Then at the moment of leaving the throne to get back into his bed, he joked once more.

And they laughed louder than ever. At heart they felt joyful. It was by way of showing their contentment without a host of phrases that they thus joked together. One must have had to do with patients to know the pleasure one feels at seeing all their functions at work again.

When he was in bed, she gave him the two oranges, and this filled him with emotion. He was becoming quite nice again ever since he had had nothing but infusion to drink. She ended by venturing to speak to him about his violent attack, surprised at hearing him reason like in the good old times.

"Ah, yes," said he, joking at his own expense; "I talked a precious lot of nonsense! Just fancy, I saw rats, and ran about on all fours to put a grain of salt under their tails. And you, you called to me; men were trying to kill you. In short, all sorts of stupid things, ghosts in broad daylight. Oh! I remember it well, my noddle's still solid. Now it's over, I dream a bit when I'm asleep. I have nightmares, but every-one has nightmares."

Gervaise remained with him until the evening. When the house surgeon came, at the six o'clock inspection, he made him spread out his hands; they hardly trembled at all, scarcely a quiver at the tips of the fingers. However, as night approached, Coupeau was little by little seized with uneasiness. He twice sat up in bed, looking on the ground and in the dark corners of the room. Suddenly, he thrust out an arm, and appeared to crush some animal against the wall.

"What is it?" asked Gervaise, frightened.

"The rats! the rats!" murmured he.

Then, after a pause, gliding into sleep, he tossed about, uttering disconnected phrases.

"Damnation! they're tearing my skin!—Oh! the filthy

beasts!—Keep steady! hold your skirts tight round you!
beware of the dirty bloke behind you!—Jove's thunder! she's
down, and the scoundrels laugh!—Scoundrels! blackguards!
brigands!"

He dealt blows into space, caught hold of his blanket, and
rolled it into a bundle against his chest, as though to protect
the latter from the violence of the bearded men whom he
beheld. Then, an attendant having hastened to the spot,
Gervaise withdrew, quite frozen by the scene. But when she
returned, a few days later, she found Coupeau completely cured.
Even the nightmares had left him; he could sleep his ten hours
right off as peacefully as a child and without stirring a limb.
So his wife was allowed to take him away. Only, the house
surgeon gave him the usual good advice on leaving, and advised
him to follow it. If he recommenced drinking, he would again
collapse, and would end by croaking. Yes, it solely depended
upon himself. He had seen how jolly and nice one could become, when one did not get drunk. Well, he must continue
at home the sensible life he had led at Sainte-Anne, fancy himself under lock and key, and that dram-shops no longer existed.

"The gentleman's right," said Gervaise in the omnibus
which was taking them back to the Rue de la Goutte-d'Or.

"Of course, he's right," replied Coupeau.

Then, after thinking a minute, he resumed:

"Oh! you know, a little glass now and again can't kill a
man; it helps digestion."

And that very evening he swallowed a glass of bad spirit,
just to keep his stomach in order. For eight days he was
pretty reasonable. He was a great coward at heart; he had
no desire to end his days in the Bicêtre mad-house. But his
passion got the better of him; the first little glass led him, in
spite of himself, to a second, to a third, and to a fourth; and,
at the end of a fortnight, he had got back to his old ration, a
pint of "vitriol" a day. Gervaise, exasperated, could have
beaten him. To think that she had been stupid enough to
dream once more of leading a worthy life, when she had seen
him at the asylum in full possession of his good sense!
Another joyful hour flown, the last one no doubt! Oh! now,
as nothing could reclaim him, not even the fear of his near
end, she swore she would no longer put herself out; the home
might be all at sixes and sevens, she did not care a hang; and
she talked of also taking her pleasure wherever she found it.

Then the hell upon earth recommenced, a life sinking deeper

into the mire, without a corner of hope opened on to a better season. Nana, whenever her father clouted her, furiously asked why the brute was not at the hospital. She was awaiting the time when she would be earning money, she would say, to treat him to brandy and make him croak quicker. Gervaise, on her side, flew into a passion one day that Coupeau was regretting their marriage. Ah! she had brought him other folks' leavings; ah! she had got herself picked up from the pavement, wheedling him by her virgin ways! Damnation! he had a rare cheek! So many words, so many lies. She did not wish to have anything to do with him, that was the truth. He dragged himself at her feet to make her give way, whilst she was advising him to think well what he was about. And if it was all to come over again, he would hear how she would just say "no!" She would sooner have an arm cut off. Yes, she had seen the moon before him; but a woman who has seen the moon, and who is a worker, is worth more than a sluggard of a man who sullies his honour and that of his family in all the dram-shops. That day, for the first time, the Coupeaus went in for a general drubbing, and they whacked each other so hard that an old umbrella and the broom were broken.

And Gervaise kept her word. She sank lower and lower; she missed going to her work oftener, spent whole days in gossiping, and became as soft as a rag whenever she had a task to perform. If a thing fell from her hands, it might remain on the floor; it was certainly not she who would have stooped to pick it up. She intended to save her bacon. She took her ease about everything, and never handled a broom except when the accumulation of filth almost brought her to the ground. The Lorilleux now made a point of holding something to their noses whenever they passed her room; the stench was poisonous, said they. They slyly lived at the end of the passage, out of the way of all these miseries which filled this corner of the house with whines, locking themselves in so as not to have to lend twenty sou pieces. Oh! kind-hearted folks, neighbours awfully obliging! yes, you may bet! One had only to knock and ask for a light, or a pinch of salt, or a jug of water, one was certain of getting the door banged in one's face. With all that they had vipers' tongues. They cried everywhere that they never occupied themselves with other people, whenever it was a question of assisting their neighbour; but they did so from morning to night, directly they had a chance of pulling any one to pieces. With the door bolted and a rug hung up

to cover the chinks and the key-hole, they would treat themselves to a spiteful gossip, without leaving their gold wire for a
moment.

The fall of the Hobbler especially made them purr the whole
day long, like cats being stroked. What poverty, what a pull-
down, my friends! They watched her when she went market-
ing, and laughed to themselves at the little bit of bread
which she brought back under her apron. They calculated
the days when she had only the empty cupboard to look at.
They knew the thickness of the dust in her home, the number
of dirty plates left lying about, each one of the growing aban-
donments of misery and idleness. And her dresses too, disgusting tatters which even a rag-picker would not have handled!
Oh, ye gods! it was a funny shower that was pouring on this
beautiful blonde's mercery, this dollymop who used once to
give herself such airs in her lovely blue shop. That was where
the love of dissipating, of wantonising, and of gorging brought
one.

Gervaise, who had an idea of the way in which they spoke
of her, would take her shoes off, and place her ear against their
door; but the rug prevented her from hearing. She only
caught them one day calling her "big teats," because no doubt
her frontage was rather developed, in spite of the bad food
which was emptying her skin. She was heartily sick of them;
she continued to speak to them, to avoid remarks, though expecting nothing but unpleasantness from such nasty persons,
but no longer having strength even to give them as much as
they gave her, and to cast them off like a bundle of abuse.
And besides, damn it all! she only wanted her own pleasure,
to sit in a heap twirling her thumbs, and only moving when it
was a question of amusing herself, nothing more.

One Saturday, Coupeau had promised to take her to the
circus. It was well worth while disturbing oneself to see ladies
galloping along on horses and jumping through paper hoops.
Coupeau had just finished a fortnight's work, he could well spare
a couple of francs; and they had also arranged to dine out,
Nana having to work very late that evening at her employer's
because of some pressing order. But at seven o'clock there
was no Coupeau; at eight o'clock it was still the same. Gervaise was furious. Her drunkard was certainly squandering his
earnings with his comrades at the dram-shops of the neighbourhood. She had washed a cap, and had been slaving since the
morning over the holes of an old dress, wishing to look decent.

At last, towards nine o'clock, her stomach empty, her face purple with rage, she decided to go down and look for Coupeau.

"Is it your husband you want?" called Madame Boche, on catching sight of her looking very glum. "He's at old Colombe's. Boche has just been having some cherry brandy with him."

She uttered her thanks, and stalked stiffly along the pavement with the determination of flying at Coupeau's eyes. A fine rain was falling which made the walk more unpleasant still. But when she reached the "Assommoir," the fear of receiving the drubbing herself, if she badgered her old man, suddenly calmed her and made her prudent. The shop was ablaze with the lighted gas, the flames of which were as brilliant as suns, and the bottles and jars illuminated the walls with their coloured glass. She stood there an instant, stretching her neck, her eyes close to the window, between two bottles placed there for show, watching Coupeau who was right at the back; he was sitting with some comrades at a little zinc table, all looking vague and blue in the tobacco smoke; and, as one could not hear them yelling, it created a funny effect to see them gesticulating, with their chins thrust forward and their eyes starting out of their heads. Good heavens! was it really possible that men could leave their wives and their homes to shut themselves up thus in a hole where they were choking?

The rain trickled down her neck; she drew herself up, and went off to the exterior Boulevard, wrapt in thought and not daring to enter. Ah well! Coupeau would have welcomed her in a pleasant way, he who objected to be spied upon! Besides, it really scarcely seemed to her the proper place for a respectable woman. However, beneath the wet trees, a slight shiver passed through her frame, and whilst she still hesitated, she could not help thinking that she was going the right way to catch some serious illness. Twice she went back and stood before the shop window, her eyes again riveted to the glass, annoyed at still beholding those confounded drunkards out of the rain and yelling and drinking. The light of the "Assommoir" was reflected in the puddles on the pavement, which simmered with little bubbles caused by the downpour. She hurried off and floundered about in them, directly the door opened and closed with the clang of its brass facings. At length, she thought she was too foolish, and, pushing open the door, she walked straight up to the table where Coupeau was sitting. After all, it was her husband she came for, was it not? and she was authorized in doing so, because he had promised to take her to the circus that evening. So much the worse! she had no desire to melt like a cake of soap out on the pavement.

"Hallo! it's you, old woman!" exclaimed the zinc-worker, half choking with a chuckle. "Ah! that's a good joke, by Jove! Isn't it a good joke now?"

They all laughed, My-Boots, Bibi-the-Smoker, and Salted-Mouth, otherwise Drink-without-Thirst. Yes, they all thought it a good joke, but they did not explain why. Gervaise remained standing, feeling rather bewildered. Coupeau appeared to her to be in a pleasant humour, so she ventured to say:

"You know we've somewhere to go. We must look sharp. We shall still be in time to see something."

"I can't get up, I'm glued, oh! without joking," resumed Coupeau, who continued laughing. "Try, just to satisfy yourself; pull my arm, with all your strength, damn it! harder than that, tug away, up with it! You see, it's that ass, old Colombe, who's screwed me to his seat."

Gervaise had humoured him at this game; and, when she let go of his arm, the comrades thought the joke so good, that they wriggled up against one another, brawling and rubbing their shoulders like donkeys being thrashed. The zinc-worker's mouth was slit by such a laugh, that you could see right down his throat.

"You great noodle!" said he at length, "you can surely sit down a minute. We're better here than splashing about outside. Well! yes, I didn't come home, I had business to attend to. Though you may pull a long face, it won't alter matters. Make room you others."

"If madame would accept my knees, she would find them softer than the seat," gallantly said My-Boots.

Gervaise, not wishing to attract attention, took a chair and sat down at a short distance from the table. She looked at what the men were drinking, some powerful brandy which shone like gold in the glasses; a little of it had dropped upon the table, and Salted-Mouth, otherwise Drink-without-Thirst, dipped his finger in it, whilst conversing, and wrote a woman's name—"Eulalie," in big letters. She noticed that Bibi-the-Smoker looked shockingly jaded, and thinner than a hundred-weight of nails. My-Boot's nose was in full bloom, a regular purple Burgundy dahlia. They were all four of them very dirty, with their filthy bristly beards which could be smelt from afar, their ragged blouses, and their black paws, the nails of which were all in mourning. But, really, one might all the same be seen in their company, for though they had been lushing ever since six o'clock, they still behaved themselves, and were, in fact, just merry. Gervaise saw two others at the counter having a gargle; they were so screwed, that they tossed the contents of their glasses under their chins and soaked their shirts, fancying all the while they where rinsing their mouths out. Stout old Colombe, thrusting out his enormous arms, the peace-preservers of his establishment, quietly poured out the goes.

The atmosphere was very warm, the smoke from the pipes ascended in the blinding glare of the gas, amidst which it rolled about like dust, drowning the customers in a gradually thickening mist; and from this cloud there issued a deafening and confused uproar, cracked voices, clinking of glasses, oaths and blows sounding like detonations. So Gervaise pulled a very wry face, for such a sight is not funny for a woman, especially when she is not used to it; she was stifling, with a smarting sensation in her eyes, and her head already feeling heavy from the alcoholic fumes exhaled by the whole place. Then, she suddenly experienced the sensation of something more unpleasant still behind her back. She turned round and beheld the still, the machine which manufactured drunkards, working away beneath the glass roof of the narrow courtyard with the profound trepidation of its hellish cookery. Of an evening, the copper parts looked more mournful than ever, lit up only on their rounded surface with one big red star; and the shadow of the apparatus, on the wall at the back, formed most abominable figures, bodies with tails, monsters opening their jaws as though to swallow every one up.

"I say, mother Talk-too-much, don't make any of your grimaces!" cried Coupeau. "To blazes, you know, with all wet blankets! What'll you drink?"

"Nothing, of course," replied the laundress. "I haven't dined yet."

"Well! that's all the more reason for having a glass; a drop of something sustains one."

But, as she still retained her glum expression, My-Boots again did the gallant.

"Madame probably likes sweet things," murmured he.

"I like men who don't get drunk," retorted she getting angry. "Yes, I like a fellow who brings home his earnings, and who keeps his word when he makes a promise."

"Ah! it's that which upsets you?" said the zinc-worker,

without ceasing to chuckle. "You want your share. Then, big goose, why do you refuse a drink? Take it, it's so much to the good."

She looked at him fixedly, in a grave manner, a wrinkle marking her forehead with a black line. And she slowly replied:

"Why, you're right, it's a good idea. That way, we can drink up the coin together."

Bibi-the-Smoker rose from his seat to fetch her a glass of aniseed. She drew her chair up to the table. Whilst she was sipping her aniseed, a recollection suddenly flashed across her mind, she remembered the plum she had taken with Coupeau, near the door, in the old days, when he was courting her. At that time, she used to leave the juice of fruits preserved in brandy. And now, here was she going back to liqueurs. Oh! she knew herself well, she had not two liards of will. One would only have had to have given her a walloping across the back to have made her regularly wallow in drink. The aniseed even seemed to her very good, perhaps rather too sweet and slightly sickening. And she licked her glass, whilst listening to Salted-Mouth, otherwise Drink-without-Thirst, relating his amours with plump Eulalie, she who hawked fish about the streets, a precious cunning woman, a person who scented him in the dram-shops, whilst pushing her truck along the roadway; it was useless for his comrades to warn him and hide him, she often caught him—she had even, only the day before, given him a smack in the face, just to teach him not to miss the workshop. That, at least, was funny.

Bibi-the Smoker and My-Boots, splitting with laughter, were slapping Gervaise's shoulders, whilst she at length laughed, as though being tickled and in spite of herself; and they advised her to take a lesson from plump Eulalie, and to bring her irons and iron Coupeau's ears on the zinc tables of the dram-shops.

"Ah, well! thanks," cried Coupeau, turning upside down the glass his wife had emptied, "you pump it out pretty well. Just look, you fellows, she doesn't take long over it."

"Will madame take another?" asked Salted-Mouth, otherwise Drink-without-Thirst.

No, she had had enough. Yet she hesitated. The aniseed was warming the cockles of her heart. She would rather have taken something stiffer to cure the pain in her stomach. And she cast side glances at the drunkard manufacturing machine behind her. That confounded pot, as round as the stomach of a tinker's fat wife, with its nose that was so long and twisted, sent a shiver down her back, a fear mingled with a desire. Yes, one might have thought it the metal pluck of some big wicked woman, of some witch who was discharging drop by drop the fire of her entrails. A fine source of poison, an operation which should have been hidden away in a cellar, it was so brazen and abominable! But all the same she would have liked to have poked her nose inside it, to have sniffed the odour, have tasted the filth, though the skin might have peeled off her burnt tongue like the rind off an orange.

"What's that you're drinking?" asked she slyly of the men, her eyes lighted up by the beautiful golden colour of their glasses.

"That, old woman," answered Coupeau, "is papa Colombe's camphor. Don't be stupid now, and we'll give you a taste."

And when they had brought her a glass of the "vitriol," and her jaws had contracted at the first mouthful, the zinc-worker resumed, slapping his thighs:

"Eh! it tickles your gullet! Drink it off at a go. Each glassful cheats the doctor of six francs."

At the second glass, Gervaise no longer felt the hunger which had been tormenting her. Now she had made it up with Coupeau, she no longer felt angry with him for not having kept his word. They would go to the circus some other day; it was not so funny to see jugglers galloping about on horses. There was no rain inside old Colombe's, and if the money went in brandy, one at least had it in one's body; one drank it limpid and shining like beautiful liquid gold. Ah! she was ready to send the whole world to blazes! Life was not so pleasant after all; besides, it seemed some consolation to her to have her share in squandering the cash. As she was comfortable, why should she not remain? One might have a discharge of artillery; she did not care to budge, once she had settled down in a heap. She nursed herself in a pleasant warmth, her bodice sticking to her back, overcome by a feeling of comfort which benumbed her limbs. She laughed all to herself, her elbows on the table, a vacant look in her eyes, highly amused by two customers, a fat heavy fellow and a dwarf, seated at a neighbouring table, and kissing each other like loaves of bread, they were so drunk. Yes, she laughed at the "Assommoir," at old Colombe's full moon, a regular bladder of lard, at the customers smoking their short clay pipes, yelling and spitting, and at the big flames of gas which lighted up the looking-glasses and the

bottles of liqueurs. The smell no longer inconvenienced her,
on the contrary, it tickled her nose, and she thought it very
pleasant. Her eyes slightly closed, whilst she breathed very
slowly, without the least feeling of suffocation, tasting the
enjoyment of the gentle slumber which was overcoming her.
Then, after her third glass, she let her chin fall on her hands ;
she could only see Coupeau and his comrades, and she remained
nose to nose with them, quite close, her cheeks warmed by their
breath, looking at their dirty beards as though she had been
counting the hairs. They were very drunk by this time. My-
Boots drivelled, his pipe between his teeth, with the dumb and
grave air of a dozing ox. Bibi-the-Smoker was telling a story—
the manner in which he emptied a bottle at a draught, giving
it such a kiss, that one instantly saw its bottom. Meanwhile
Salted-Mouth, otherwise Drink-without-Thirst, had gone and
fetched the wheel of fortune from the counter, and was playing
with Coupeau for drinks.

"Two hundred ! You're lucky; you get high numbers every
time."

The needle of the wheel grated, and the figure of Fortune, a
big red woman placed under glass, turned round and round
until it looked like a mere spot in the centre, similar to a wine
stain.

"Three hundred and fifty ! You must have been inside it,
you confounded lascar ! Ah ! damn it ! I sha'n't play any
more !"

And Gervaise amused herself with the wheel of fortune. She
was feeling awfully thirsty, and calling My-Boots "my child."
Behind her, the machine for manufacturing drunkards continued
working, with its murmur of an underground stream; and she
despaired of ever stopping it, of exhausting it, filled with a
sullen anger against it, feeling a longing to spring upon the big
still as upon some animal, to kick it with her heels and stave in
its belly. Everything seemed to become confused ; she felt
herself seized by its copper claws, whilst the stream now flowed
through her body.

Then the room danced round, the gas-jets seemed to shoot
like stars. Gervaise was drunk. She heard a furious wrangle
between Salted-Mouth, otherwise Drink-without-Thirst, and
that rascal old Colombe. There was a thief of a landlord who
wanted one to pay for what one had not had ! Yet one was
not at Bondy. Suddenly there was a scuffling, yells were heard,

and tables were upset. It was old Colombe who was turning the party out, without the least hesitation, and in the twinkling of an eye. On the other side of the door they blackguarded him, and called him scoundrel. It still rained, and blew icy cold. Gervaise lost Coupeau, found him, and then lost him again. She wished to go home ; she felt the shops to find her way. This sudden darkness surprised her immensely. At the corner of the Rue des Poissonniers, she sat down in the gutter thinking she was at the wash-house. The water which flowed along, caused her head to swim, and made her very ill. At length she arrived, she passed stiffly before the doorkeepers' room where she perfectly recognised the Lorilleux and the Poissons seated at the table, and who made grimaces of disgust on beholding her in that sorry state.

She never remembered how she had got up the six flights of stairs. Just as she was turning into the passage up at the top, little Lalie, who heard her footstep, hastened to meet her, opening her arms caressingly, and saying with a smile :

"Madame Gervaise, papa has not yet returned ; just come and see my children sleeping. Oh ! they look so pretty."

But, on beholding the laundress's besotted face she tremblingly drew back. She was acquainted with that brandy laden breath, those pale eyes, that convulsed mouth. Then, Gervaise stumbled past without uttering a word, whilst the child, standing on the threshold of her room, followed her with her dark eyes, grave and speechless.

CHAPTER XI.

Nana was growing up and becoming wayward. At fifteen years old she had expanded like a calf, white skinned and very fat, so plump indeed, you might have called her a ball. Yes, such she was—fifteen years old, with all her teeth and no stays. A hussy's phiz, dipped in milk, a skin as soft as peach rind, a funny nose, pink lips and eyes sparkling like tapers, which men would have liked to light their pipes at. Her pile of fair hair, the colour of fresh oats, seemed to have scattered gold dust over her temples, freckle-like, as it were, giving her brow a sunny crown. Ah! a pretty doll, as the Lorilleux said, a dirty nose that needed wiping, with fat shoulders which were as fully rounded and as ripe in smell as those of a full grown woman.

Nana no longer put balls of paper into her bodice. A couple of titties had come to her, a pair of bran new titties too, in white satin. They did not inconvenience her, far from it; she would have liked to have had an armful, and dreamt, in fact, of growing a wet nurse's bubbies, so gluttonous and inconsiderate indeed is youth. What made her particularly tempting was a nasty habit she had of protruding the tip of her tongue between her white teeth. No doubt on seeing herself in the looking-glasses she had thought she was pretty like this; and so all day long she poked her tongue out of her mouth in view of improving her appearance.

"Hide your lying tongue," cried her mother, "make haste and draw that red rag inside again!"

Nana showed herself very coquettish. She did not always wash her feet, but she bought such tight boots that she suffered martyrdom in St. Crispin's prison, and if folks questioned her when she turned purple with pain, she answered that she had the stomach-ache, so as to avoid confessing her coquetry. When bread was lacking at home, it was difficult for her to trick herself out. But she accomplished miracles, brought ribbons back from the workshop, and concocted toilettes—dirty dresses set off with bows and puffs. The summer was the season of her greatest triumphs. With a cambric dress which had cost her six francs, she filled the whole neighbourhood of the Goutte-d'Or with her fair beauty. Yes, she was known from the outer Boulevards to the Fortifications, and from the Chaussée de Clignancourt to the Grande Rue of La Chapelle. Folks called her "the little hen," for she was really as tender and as fresh looking as a chicken.

One dress, especially, suited her to perfection. It was covered with pink spots on a white ground, cut very simply and without any trimmings. The skirt, which was rather short, gave her feet full play. The loose open sleeves allowed her arms to display themselves to the elbows. In a dark corner of the stairs, so as to avoid a box on the ears from father Coupeau, she pinned the upper part of her bodice back heart-wise, in view of showing her snow white neck and shadowy amber bosom. Nothing else, nothing but a pink ribbon tied round her fair hair—a ribbon, the ends of which waved over the nape of her neck. She looked as fresh as a nosegay, dressed like this, exhaling the perfume of youth, the scent which comes from the flesh of a child and a woman.

At this time, Sundays were her great days for meeting the crowd, all the men who passed by and made her advances. She waited the whole week for these occasions, tickled with little longings, stifling, and feeling the need of fresh air, of a stroll in the sunlight among the crowd of the faubourg, rigged out in its Sunday aspect. Early in the morning she began to dress, stopping for hours in her shift in front of the bit of glass hanging over the chest of drawers; but as everyone in the house could see her through the window, her mother oft times grew angry, and asked her if she hadn't pretty nearly finished walking about as naked as a parsnip. But with bare legs and dishevelled hair, with her chemise falling from her shoulders, she quietly continued plastering corkscrew ringlets over her forehead with sugared water, sewing buttons on to her boots or stitching her dress.

Ah! she was just the ticket like that! said father Coupeau sneering and jeering at her, a real Magdalen in despair! She might have turned "savage woman" at a fair, and have shown herself for a penny. Hide your meat, he used to say, and let me eat my bread! In fact she was adorable, white and dainty under her overhanging golden fleece, losing temper to the point

Y

that her skin turned pink, not daring to answer her father, but
cutting her thread with her teeth with a hasty furious jerk
which shook her plump but youthful form.

Then immediately after breakfast she tripped downstairs into
the courtyard. The warm peacefulness of Sunday was sending
the house to sleep, the workshops were closed, the rooms
yawned with open windows, displaying tables already laid for the
evening meal, which awaited households engaged for the nonce
in picking up appetites on the fortifications. One woman on
the third floor was occupying her time in cleaning her room, rolling her bed about, disturbing the furniture and singing the same
song for hours in a soft tearful voice. Then as work was
hushed, in the midst of the empty, echoing courtyard, Nana,
Pauline and other big girls engaged in games of battledore and
shuttlecock. They were five or six who had sprouted together,
and had become the queens of the house, sharing the glances
of the masculine inmates. Whenever a man crossed the courtyard shrill laughter arose, and the rustle of starched skirts
passed by like a gust of wind. Above them flamed the holiday
air, burning and heavy, drowsily lazy as it were, and whitened
by the dust scattered by the promenaders.

But the games were only an excuse for them to make off.
Suddenly stillness fell upon the house. The girls had glided
out into the street and made for the outer Boulevards. Then
linked arm in arm across the full breadth of the pavement, they
went off the whole six of them, clad in light colours with ribbons
tied around their bare heads. With bright eyes, darting
stealthy glances through their partially closed eyelids, they
took note of everything, and constantly threw back their necks
to laugh, displaying the fleshy part of their chins. Their line
became broken in moments of especial gaiety provoked by some
passing hunchback or some old woman waiting for her dog near
the street posts; some of them then remained in the rear and
had to be dragged forward by the others; and meantime they
wriggled their hips, curvetted and pranced in view of attracting
attention, making their dresses crackle under their budding
forms. The street belonged to them; they had grown up in it,
pulling up their skirts alongside the shop-fronts; even now they
trussed themselves up above their knees to re-fasten their
garters. In the midst of the pale and slow-paced crowd, between the stumpy trees of the Boulevard, they straggled hastily
onward from the Barrière Rochechouart to the Barrière Saint-
Denis, pushing against the people they met, winding in zig-zag

fashion through groups of bystanders, turning round and launch-
ing remarks in the midst of their fusee-like laughter.   And
their dresses sped along leaving behind them a trace of the in-
solence of youth ; they displayed themselves in the open air, in
the blaze of light, with blackguard-like coarseness, and yet as
desirable and as tender as virgins returning with moist necks
from the bath.

Nana was in the centre with her pink dress all aglow in the
sunlight.   She gave her arm to Pauline, whose costume, yellow
flowers on a white ground, glared in similar fashion, dotted as
it were with little flames.   As they were the tallest of the band,
the most woman-like and most unblushing, they led the troop
and drew themselves up with breasts well forward whenever
they detected glances or heard complimentary remarks.   The
others, the hussies, extended right and left, puffing themselves
out in order to attract attention.   Nana and Pauline resorted
to the complicated devices of experienced coquettes.   If they
ran till they were out of breath it was in view of shewing their
white stockings and making the ribbons of their chignons wave
in the breeze.   Then when they stopped, pretending to suffocate,
with palpitating breasts thrown back; you might have glanced
around and you would certainly have espied one of their sweet-
hearts, some young blood of the neighbourhood ; then they
walked on with languid steps, whispering laughingly to each
other and watching stealthily from under their eyelids.   They
were especially eager for these chance meetings, among the
jostling throng on the pavement.   Big fellows in Sunday attire,
jackets and felt hats, detained them for a moment at the edge
of the gutter, bantering and striving to squeeze their waists.
Young workmen, just in the twenties, in slovenly grey blouses,
talked slowly to them with crossed arms, puffing the smoke of
their short pipes up their noses.   But all this was of no importance ; these chaps had sprouted up on the pavement at the
same time as themselves.   Still amongst the lot they had
already made their choice.   Pauline was always meeting
Madame Gaudron's son, a seventeen year old carpenter who
treated her to apples ; and Nana distinguished from one end of
the street to the other young Victor Fauconnier, the washerwoman's son, with whom she exchanged kisses in dark corners.
But it did not go any further, they were too vicious to act im-
properly without knowledge.   Only the talk was precious hot.

Then, when the sun set, the great delight of these hussies
was to stop and look at the mountebanks.   Conjurors and

strong men turned up and spread threadbare carpets on the
soil of the avenue.   Loungers collected, and a circle formed,
whilst the mountebank in the centre tried his muscles under
his faded tights.   Nana and Pauline would remain standing for
hours in the thickest of the crowd.   Their pretty fresh dresses
became all creased and tumbled by rubbing against the men's
coats and dirty blouses.   Their bare arms, their bare necks,
their bare heads grew heated amid the foul breathing of the
men, the offensive odour of wine and perspiration combined.
And they laughed in full enjoyment, nowise disgusted, but
rosier rather, as if they had been on their native dunghcap.
Around them filthy words were exchanged in undisguised
indecency—the remarks of drunken men.   But, 'twas their
own language, they knew it well, and they turned round with a
smile, quietly unchaste, without a flush tinging their pallid
satin skins.

The only thing that vexed them was to meet their fathers,
especially when the latter had been drinking.   So they watched
and warned one another.

"I say, Nana," Pauline would suddenly cry out, "here comes
father Coupeau!"

"Eh! he isn't drunk, oh! dear no, not at all!" said Nana,
greatly bothered.   "I'm going to cut and run you know.   I
don't want him to shake my fleas.   Hallo! how he stumbles!
Good Lord, if he could only break his neck!"

At other times, when Coupeau came straight up to her without giving her time to run off, she crouched down, made herself
small and muttered: "Just you hide me, you others.   He's
looking for me, and he promised he'd knock my head off if he
caught me ganging about."

Then, when the drunkard had passed them, she drew herself
up again, and all the others followed her with bursts of
laughter.   He'll find her—he will—he won't!   It was a true
game at hide and seek.   One day, however, Boche had come
after Pauline and caught her by both ears, and Coupeau had
driven Nana home with kicks behind.

When daylight waned, they took a last turn and went home
in the pallid dusk, through the tired crowd.   The dust had
thickened in the atmosphere, attenuating the darkness of the
heavy sky.   The Rue de la Goutte-d'Or might have been a
corner of some provincial town with the housewives gossiping
on the doorsteps, and their bursts of chatter disturbing the
warm silence of the neighbourhood void of vehicles.   The girls

stopped for a minute in the courtyard, took up their battledores and tried to make believe that they hadn't budged from the spot. Then they went upstairs concocting some story which they were often dispensed from repeating, as, for instance, when they found their parents absorbed in cuffing one another, because the soup was over salted, or not hot enough.

Nana was now a workgirl, and earned forty sous a day at Titreville's place in the Rue du Caire, where she had served as apprentice. The Coupeaus had kept her there, so that she might remain under the eye of Madame Lerat, who had been forewoman in the workroom for ten years. Of a morning, when her mother looked at the cuckoo clock, off she went by herself, looking very pretty with her shoulders tightly confined in her old black dress, which was both too narrow and too short; and Madame Lerat had to note the hour of her arrival and tell it to Gervaise. She was allowed twenty minutes to go from the Rue de la Goutte-d'Or to the Rue du Caire, and it was enough, for these young hussies have stag's legs. At times she arrived to the minute, but so red and so out of breath that she certainly had sped from the Barrière in ten minutes, after dawdling on the road beforehand. More usually, however, she was seven or eight minutes late; and then she showed herself most coaxing towards her aunt till night time, looking at her with supplicating eyes and thus trying to touch her and induce her not to tell her father. Madame Lerat who understood youthful vagaries, did not tell the Coupeaus the truth, but she rebuked Nana with interminable chatter, talking of her responsibility and of the dangers a young girl was exposed to in the streets of Paris. Ah! good heavens! wasn't she followed about herself? She gazed at her niece with eyes bright with constantly recurring unchaste ideas, and her senses kindled at the thought of preserving this poor little kitten's virtue warm on the hob.

"Do you see," she repeated, "you must tell me everything. I'm so fond of you that if any misfortune happened to you, I should go and throw myself into the Seine. Do you hear, my little puss? If men talk to you, you must repeat everything to me without omitting a word—eh? Haven't they said anything to you as yet? Will you swear it?"

Nana thereupon laughed, twisting her mouth in a funny manner. No, no, men didn't talk to her. She walked too fast, and besides what could they have had to say to her? She had nothing to do with them; and assuming a simpleton's expression, she explained how it happened that she was often late;

she had stopped to look at some pictures in the shop windows, or else she had accompanied Pauline to hear a story she knew. Folks could follow her, if they did not believe her: she always kept to the pavement on the left hand side; and sped along like a vehicle, overtaking all the other girls and passing them by. To tell the truth, Madame Lerat had one day surprised her with her nose tilted upwards in the Rue du Petit-Carreau, while she was laughing with three other hussies of her own class, at a man who was shaving himself at a window; but when her aunt reproached her, she turned angry and swore that she had just been into the baker's at the corner to buy a ha'penny roll.

"Oh! I watch, you needn't fear," said the widow to the Coupeaus. "I will answer to you for her as I would answer for myself. And rather than let a blackguard squeeze her, why I'd step between them."

The workroom at Titreville's was a large apartment on the first floor with a broad work-table standing on trestles in the centre. Round the four walls, the plaster of which was visible in parts where the dirty yellowish grey paper was torn away, there were several stands covered with old cardboard boxes, parcels, and discarded patterns, under a thick coating of dust. The gas had left what appeared to be like a daub of soot on the ceiling. The two windows opened so wide, that without leaving the work-table, the girls could see the people walking past on the pavement over the way.

Madame Lerat arrived the first, in view of setting an example. Then for a quarter of an hour the door swayed to and fro, and all the workgirls straggled in, perspiring, with tumbled hair. One July morning Nana arrived the last, as very often happened. "Ah me!" she said, "it won't be a pity when I have a carriage of my own." And without even taking off her hat, one which she was weary of patching up, she approached the window, and leant out, looking to the right and the left to see what was going on in the street.

"What are you looking at?" asked Madame Lerat, suspiciously. "Did your father come with you?"

"No, you may be sure of that," answered Nana coolly. "I'm looking at nothing—I'm looking—that it's awfully hot. It's enough to make anyone ill to make them run like that."

It was a stifling hot morning. The workgirls had drawn down the Venetian blinds, between which they could spy out into the street; and they had at last begun working on either side of the table, at the upper end of which sat Madame Lerat.

They were eight in number, each with her pot of glue, pincers, tools, and curling stand in front of her. On the work-table lay a mass of wire, reels, cotton wool, green and brown paper, leaves and petals cut out of silk, satin, or velvet. In the centre, in the neck of a large decanter, one flower-girl had thrust a little penny nosegay which had been fading on her breast since the day before.

"Ah! do you know," said Léonie, a pretty girl with dark hair, as she leant over her stand curling the petals of a rose, "it seems that poor Caroline is awfully miserable with that fellow who used to wait for her every evening."

Nana, who was engaged in cutting narrow bands of green paper, declared that this news in nowise surprised her, for the fellow in question was constantly unfaithful; only she did not say unfaithful, a disgusting expression fell from her lips instead.

An undercurrent of gaiety spread through the workroom, and Madame Lerat found it needful to make a show of severity. She screwed up her nose, muttering: "You are chaste, my dear, and no mistake; you use nice language. I shall tell your father of it, and we'll see if he's pleased."

Nana puffed out her cheeks as if to avoid bursting into laughter. Her father, indeed! Why, he used worse language himself. But suddenly Léonie swiftly whispered: "Eh! take care; here comes madame!"

And indeed Madame Titreville, a tall withered looking woman, now entered the workroom. As a rule she remained down-stairs in the shop. The workgirls lived in fear of her, for she never joked. She went slowly round the work-table, over which every one now remained stooping, silent and active. She called one workgirl a blockhead, and made her begin a daisy over again. Then she went off, as stiffly as she had come.

"Bow! wow!" repeated Nana in the midst of a general growl.

"Young ladies, really, young ladies!" said Madame Lerat, striving to assume an air of severity. "You will compel me to adopt measures—"

But she was not listened to, for she was scarcely feared. She showed herself too tolerant, titillated as it were by associating with those girls whose eyes were full of merriment, taking them aside to question them about their lovers, and telling them their fortunes with cards when an end of the work-table happened to be unencumbered. Her hard skin, her gendarme's carcass, vibrated with a gossip's salutary joy when any doubtful subject was broached. The only thing she objected to was plain words; but providing plain words were not used, anything might be insinuated.

To tell the truth, Nana perfected her education in nice style in the workroom ! No doubt she was already inclined to go wrong. But this was the finishing stroke—associating with a lot of girls who were already worn out with misery and vice. They all hobnobbed and rotted together, just the story of the baskets of apples when there are rotten ones among them. No doubt there was a make believe at decency in the presence of strangers ; the girls avoided disgusting expressions, and pretended to be well-brought up young people. Only, nasty remarks were exchanged in corners, in one another's ears, as fast as could be managed. Two of them could not remain together without at once wriggling with laughter as they related something improper. Then in the evening they saw each other home; and confidential revelations were exchanged—stories calculated to set the hair on end, which delayed the girls on the pavement, and made them burn with desire in the midst of the elbowing crowd. For those who had so far remained virgins like Nana, the workroom had a pernicious atmosphere replete with the odour of low music-halls and sleepless nights, brought there by the more vicious girls, in their slovenly fastened hair and their tumbled skirts—so tumbled indeed that the wearers seemed to have gone to bed in them. Over the work-table among the bright fragile artificial flowers, there passed a perverted breath typified by the idle languor which follows nights of vice, and by the dark circles around the hussies' eyes—the stamp of love as Madame Lerat was wont to say. Nana sniffed and intoxicated herself as it were when she was beside some girl who had already seen "the wolf." For a long while she had sat next to big Lisa, who was said to be in an interesting condition ; and she was ever casting glowing glances at her neighbour as though she expected to see her suddenly expand and burst. As for learning anything new, that was a difficult matter. The little hussy knew everything, had learnt everything on the pavement of the Rue de la Goutte-d'Or. In the workroom however, she saw precept carried into practice, and by degrees there came to her a longing with cheek enough to do the same in her turn.

"It's hot enough to make one stifle," she said, approaching a window as if to draw the blind farther down ; but she leant forward and again looked out both to the right and left.

At the same moment Léonie, who was watching a man

stationed on the foot pavement over the way, exclaimed, "What's that old fellow about? He's been spying here for the last quarter of an hour."

"Some tom cat," said Madame Lerat. "Nana, just come and sit down! I forbade your remaining at the window."

Nana took up the stems of some violets she was rolling, and the whole workroom turned its attention to the man in question. He was a well-dressed individual with a frock coat on, and he looked about fifty years old. He had a pale face, very serious and dignified in expression, framed round with a well trimmed grey beard. He remained for an hour in front of a herborist's shop with his eyes fixed on the Venetian blinds of the workroom. The flower-girls indulged in little bursts of laughter which died away amid the noise of the street, and while leaning forward, to all appearance busy with their work, they glanced askance so as not to lose sight of the gentleman.

"Ah!" remarked Léonie, "he wears glasses. He's a swell. He's waiting for Augustine, no doubt."

But Augustine, a tall, ugly, fair-haired girl, sourly answered that she did not like old men; whereupon Madame Lerat, jerking her head, answered with a smile full of underhand meaning, "That is a great mistake on your part, my dear; the old ones are more tender."

At this moment Léonie's neighbour, a plump little body, whispered something in her ear, and Léonie suddenly threw herself back on her chair, seized with a fit of noisy laughter, wriggling, looking at the gentleman and then laughing all the louder. "That's it. Oh! that's it," she stammered. "How dirty that Sophie is!"

"What did she say? What did she say?" asked the whole workroom, aglow with curiosity.

Léonie wiped the tears from her eyes without answering. When she became somewhat calmer, she began curling her flowers again and declared, "It can't be repeated."

The others insisted, but she shook her head, seized again with a gust of gaiety. Thereupon Augustine, her left-hand neighbour, besought her to whisper it to her; and finally Léonie consented to do so, with her lips close to Augustine's ear. Augustine threw herself back and wriggled with convulsive laughter in her turn. Then she repeated the phrase to a girl next to her, and from ear to ear it travelled round the room amid exclamations and stifled laughter. When they were all of them acquainted with Sophie's disgusting remark, they looked at one another and

burst out laughing together, although a little flushed and confused. Madame Lerat alone was not in the secret and she felt
extremely vexed.

"That's very impolite behaviour on your part, young ladies,"
said she. "It is not right to whisper when other people are
present. Something indecent, no doubt! Ah! that's becoming!"

However, she did not venture to ask what it was that Sophie
had said, despite her furious longing to learn it. But, for a
moment, looking dignified, with her nose pointed downwards,
she regaled herself with the chatter of the workgirls. None of
them could make a remark, the most innocent one in the world,
about her work, for instance, without the others interpreting it
maliciously; they distorted its meaning, and gave it a nasty
signification. And they connected everything with the gentleman who was waiting over the way—they always contrived to
associate him with their allusions. Ah! his ears must have
tingled, and no mistake! They ended by saying some very
stupid things in their anxiety to be witty. Still, this did not
prevent them from finding the pastime an amusing one, and
excited, with sparkling eyes, they indulged in hotter remarks
than ever. Madame Lerat had no occasion to scold, for no plain
words were spoken.

You should have seen how Nana enjoyed all this merriment.
No word with a double meaning escaped her. She, herself,
launched some very stiff ones, underscoring them with a movement of the chin, sitting back, and feeling superlatively delighted. She was at home in vice, like a fish is at home in
water. And meantime, whilst she wriggled on her chair, she
kept on preparing her violet stems with wonderful ease, and in
less time than you might have rolled a cigarette. One movement to take a strip of green paper, and then, presto! the paper
glided round the wire; next a drop of gum on the top so as to
affix the flower, and it was done—a fresh delicate bit of green,
fit to be placed on a lady's bosom. The dexterity was in her
fingers, her hussy's fingers, which were nimble and supple,
double-jointed, as it were. This was all she had been able to
learn of the profession, and all the stems of the workroom were
entrusted to her, so skilfully did she prepare them.

However, the gentleman over the way had gone off. The
room grew calmer, and work was carried on in the sultry heat.
When twelve o'clock struck—meal-time—they all shook themselves. Nana, who had hastened to the window again, volun-

teered to do the errands if they liked. And Léonie ordered a penn'orth of shrimps, Augustine a screw of fried potatoes, Lisa a bunch of radishes, Sophie a sausage. Then as Nana was going downstairs, Madame Lerat, who found her partiality for the window that morning rather curious, overtook her with her long legs.

"Wait a bit," she said. "I'll go with you. I want to buy something too."

But in the passage below she perceived the gentleman, stuck there like a candle, and exchanging glances with Nana. The girl flushed very red, whereupon her aunt at once caught her by the arm and made her trot over the pavement, whilst the individual followed behind. Ah! so the tom cat had come for Nana. Well, that *was* nice! At fifteen years and a half old, to drag men about after her skirts! And then Madame Lerat hastily began to question her. Oh! really, Nana didn't know; he had only been following her for five days, but she could not poke her nose out of doors without stumbling on him. She believed he was in business; yes, a manufacturer of bone buttons. Madame Lerat was greatly impressed. She turned round and glanced at the gentleman out of the corner of her eye.

"One can see he's got a long purse," she muttered. "Listen to me, pussy; you must tell me everything. You have nothing more to fear now."

Whilst speaking, they hastened from shop to shop—to the pork butcher's, the fruiterer's, the cook-shop; and the errands in greasy paper were piled up in their hands. Still they remained amiable, curvetting and casting bright glances behind them with gusts of gay laughter. Madame Lerat herself tried the graceful, acting the young girl, on account of the button manufacturer who was still following them.

"He is very distinguished looking," she declared as they returned into the passage. "If he only had honourable views."

Then as they were going upstairs she suddenly seemed to remember something. "By the way, tell me what the girls were whispering to each other—you know, what Sophie said?"

Nana did not make any ceremony. Only she caught Madame Lerat by the neck and caused her to descend a couple of steps, for, really, the remark in question could not be repeated aloud, even on a staircase. And then she whispered it. Hot as it was, her aunt merely jerked her head, opening her eyes and twisting her mouth. At all events, she knew what it was now, and no longer itched with curiosity.

The flower-girls eat off their knees, so as not to mess the work-table.   They hastily bolted their food, for eating bothered them, and they preferred to spend the hour they were allowed for their meal in watching the passers-by out of the window, or indulging in confidential chit-chat in the corners.   On that day they tried to find out what had become of the gentleman who had waited over the way during the morning, but he had alto-gether disappeared.   Madame Lerat and Nana glanced at each other, but kept their mouths shut.   It was already ten minutes past one, and the girls did not seem at all in a hurry to take up their pliers again—when Léonie suddenly articulated "*prr-rout*," like house-painters do to call each other, in view of signalling the mistress's approach.   At once they all seated themselves on their chairs again, with their noses bent over their work.   The next moment Madame Titreville came in and severely made the round.

From this day forth Madame Lerat regaled herself with her niece's first love adventure.   She no longer left her, but ac-companied her morning and evening, bringing her responsibility well to the fore.   This somewhat annoyed Nana, but all the same she expanded with pride at seeing herself guarded like a treasure ; and the talk she and her aunt indulged in, in the street, with the button manufacturer behind them, inflamed her and rather quickened her desire to take the jump.   Oh ! her aunt understood the feelings of the heart ; she even com-passionated the button manufacturer, this elderly gentleman, who looked so respectable, for after all, sentimental feelings are more deeply rooted among people of a certain age.   Still she watched.   And yes, he would have to pass over her body be-fore reaching her niece.

One evening she approached the gentleman, and told him, as straight as a bullet, that his conduct was most improper.   He bowed to her politely, without answering, like an old satyr who was accustomed to hear parents tell him to go about his business.   She really could not be cross with him, he was too well mannered.   Then came practical advice on love, allusions to dirty blackguards of men, and all sorts of stories about hussies who had repented of their frailty, which left Nana in a state of languor, with eyes gleaming brightly in her pale face.

One day, however, in the Rue du Faubourg-Poissonnière, the button manufacturer ventured to poke his nose between the aunt and the niece in view of muttering things which ought not to have been said.   Thereupon Madame Lerat was so frightened that she declared she no longer felt safe on her own account, and she told the whole business to her brother. Then came another row. There were some pretty rumpuses in the Coupeaus' rooms. To begin with, the zinc-worker gave Nana a hiding. What was that he learnt? The hussy gallivanted with old men. All right. Only let her be caught philandering out of doors again, she'd be done for ; he, her father, would cut off her head in a jiffy. Had the like ever been seen before ! A dirty nose who thought of dishonouring her family ! Thereupon he shook her, declaring in God's name that she'd have to walk straight, for he'd watch her himself in future. As soon as she came home he searched her, and looked her well in the face to see if she had a little mark on the eye, one of those little kisses which steal there noiselessly. He smelt her and turned her round. One evening she received another hiding on account of his having found a black spot on her neck. The hussy dared to say that it wasn't a sucking mark ! Yes, she called it a bruise—a bruise which Léonie had made in playing. He'd give her bruises indeed ; he'd prevent her gallivanting even if he had to break her skittles. On other occasions, when he was in a good humour, he bantered her and made fun of her. Really now ! She was a nice bit for a man to make up to—as flat as a sole, with salt cellars above her chest big enough to shove a fist into ! Nana, beaten for what she had not done, exposed to all the crudity of her father's abominable charges, showed the cunning infuriated submission of a hunted animal.

"Why don't you leave her alone?" repeated Gervaise, who was more reasonable. "You will end by making her wish to do what she oughtn't by talking to her about it so much."

Ah ! yes, indeed, she did wish to do it. She itched all over, longing to break loose and go the whole hog, as father Coupeau said. He insisted so much on the subject that even an honest girl would have fired up. Even, when he was abusing her, he taught her things she did not know as yet, which, to say the least, was astonishing. Then, little by little, she acquired some singular habits. One morning he noticed her rummaging in a paper bag and rubbing something on her face. It was rice powder, which she plastered on her delicate satin-like skin with perverse taste. He caught up the paper bag and rubbed it over her face, violently enough to graze her skin, and called her a miller's daughter. On another occasion she brought some red ribbons home, to do up her old black hat which she was so ashamed of. And he asked her in a furious voice where she had

got those ribbons from. Eh? She had earned them immorally,
or else she had bagged them! A hussy or a thief, and perhaps
both together. On various occasions he caught her with something pretty in her hands—a cornelian ring, a pair of cuffs with
lace edges, one of those silver-gilt heart-shaped lockets called
" Come and feel," which girls hang between their titties.
Coupeau wanted to destroy everything; but she defended her
property frantically. It was her's; a lady had given it to her,
or else she had obtained it from a girl at the workroom in exchange for something else. As for the locket, she had found it in
the Rue d'Aboukir. When her father crushed it with his heel, she
remained erect and pale, with clinched hands, whilst a feeling
of revolt came over her, inciting her to spring upon him and
tear something off him. For a couple of years she had dreamed
of having that locket, and there he had gone and flattened it.
No, she found that too strong; there must be an end of it!

However, Coupeau was more worrying than judicious in the
manner he ruled Nana. He was often in the wrong, and his
injustice exasperated the girl. She at last left off attending the
workshop, and then when the zinc-worker gave her a hiding, she
declared she would not return to Titreville's again, for she was
always placed next to Augustine, who must have swallowed her
feet to have such a foul breath. Then Coupeau took her himself to the Rue du Caire, and requested the mistress of the
establishment to place her always next to Augustine, by way of
punishment. Every morning for a fortnight he took the trouble
to come down from the Barrière Poissonnière to escort Nana to
the door of the flower shop. And he remained for five minutes
on the footway, to make sure that she had gone in. But one
morning, while he was drinking a glass with a friend in a wine-
shop in the Rue Saint-Denis, he perceived the hussy darting
down the street. For a fortnight she had been deceiving him;
instead of going into the workroom, she climbed a storey higher,
and sat down on the stairs, waiting till he had gone off. When
Coupeau began casting the blame on Madame Lerat, the latter
flatly replied that she would not accept it. She had told her
niece all she ought to tell her, to keep her on her guard against
men, and it was not her fault if the girl still had a liking for the
nasty beasts. Now, she washed her hands of the whole business; she swore she would not mix up in it, for she knew what
she knew. Scandal-mongering in the family; yes, folks who
charged her with debauching Nana, and taking a wicked
pleasure in witnessing her immorality. On the other hand,

Coupeau learned from the mistress that Nana was led astray by another workgirl, that little camel Léonie, who had just abandoned flower-making to lead an immoral life. No doubt, the girl, merely gluttonous of pastry and gadding about in the streets, might yet have married with a wreath of orange blossom on her head. But dash it! One must make haste if she was to be given to a husband, clean, intact, and complete like young ladies who respect themselves.

In the house in the Rue de la Goutte-d'Or, Nana's old fellow was talked about as a gentleman everyone was acquainted with. Oh! he remained very polite, even a little timid, but awfully obstinate and patient, following her ten paces behind like an obedient poodle. Sometimes, indeed, he ventured into the courtyard. One evening Madame Gaudron met him on the second floor landing, and he glided down alongside the balusters with his nose lowered, and looking as if on fire, but frightened. And the Lorilleux threatened to move if their rag of a niece brought any more men into the house behind her, for it was becoming disgusting, the staircase was full of them, and one could no longer go down without meeting some fellow or another on every step, sniffing and waiting; indeed, one might have thought there was some dog on heat in the house. The Boches pitied the fate of this poor gentleman, such a respectable individual, who had fallen in love with a little hussy. After all, he was in business, they had seen his button manufactory on the Boulevard de la Villette, and he might have given a woman a position if he had come across an honest girl. Thanks to the particulars communicated by the doorkeepers, all the people of the neighbourhood, even the Lorilleux themselves, showed the greatest respect for the old fellow, when he passed by at Nana's heels, with hanging lips, a pale face, and a framework of grey beard becomingly cropped.

For the first month Nana was greatly amused with her old fellow. You should have seen him always dogging her—a perfect dip-in-the-pot who felt her skirts behind, in the crowd, without seeming to do so. And his legs! regular lucifers. No more moss on his pate, only four straight hairs falling on his neck, so that she was always tempted to ask him where his hairdresser lived. Ah! what an old gaffer, he was comical and no mistake.

Then, on finding him always behind her, she no longer thought him so funny. She became afraid of him, and would have called out if he had approached her. Often, when she

stopped in front of a jeweller's shop, she heard him stammering
something behind her. And what he said was true; she would
have liked to have had a cross with a velvet neck-band, or a
pair of coral earrings, so small, you would have thought they
were drops of blood. Indeed, without aspiring to jewellery she
could not remain a rag, she was tired of decking herself with
such refuse as she could pick up in the workrooms of the Rue
du Caire, and especially she had had enough of her hat, the
"caloquet," on which the flowers cribbed at Titreville's hung.
Trotting along in the mud, splashed by the vehicles, dazed by
the display in the shop windows, she had longings which twisted
her chest—longings to be well dressed, to eat in the restaurants,
to go to the theatre, to have a room of her own with handsome
furniture. She paused, pale with desire, she felt a heat mount
within her from the pavement of Paris, she was seized with a
ferocious appetite to partake of the enjoyment which she
elbowed in the crowd on the footways. And it never missed;
just at those very moments the old fellow whispered his pro-
posals into her ear. Ah! how she would have shaken hands
with him in token of assent, if she had not been afraid of him,
if she had not experienced a sensation of revolt which strengthened her in her refusals and made her furious and disgusted
with man, and the unknown, despite all her vice.

However, when the winter arrived, life became impossible at
home. Nana had her hiding every night. When her father
was tired of beating her, her mother smacked her to teach her
how to behave. And very often it was a general set-to; as
soon as one of them began to beat her, the other took her part,
so that all three of them ended by rolling on the tiled floor in
the midst of the broken crockery. And with all this, there
were short commons and they shivered with cold. Whenever
the girl bought anything pretty, a bow or a pair of sleeve-links,
her parents confiscated the purchase and drank what they
could get for it. She had nothing of her own, excepting her
allowance of blows, before coiling herself up between the rags
of a sheet, where she shivered under her little black skirt,
which she stretched out by way of a blanket. No, that cursed
life could not continue; she was not going to leave her skin
in it. Her father had long since ceased to count for her; when
a father gets drunk like her's did, he isn't a father, but a dirty
beast one longs to get rid of. And now, too, her mother was
going down the hill in her esteem. She drank as well. She
liked to go and fetch her husband at old Colombe's, so as to be

treated; and she willingly sat down, with none of the air of disgust that she had assumed on the first occasion, draining glasses indeed at one gulp, dragging her elbows over the tables for hours, and leaving the place with her eyes starting out of her head.

When Nana passed in front of the "Assommoir" and saw her mother inside, with her nose in her glass, fuddled in the midst of the disputing men, she was seized with anger; for youth, which has other dainty thoughts uppermost, does not understand drink. On these evenings it was a pretty sight. Father drunk, mother drunk, a hell of a home that stunk with liquor, and where there was no bread. To tell the truth, a saint would not have stayed in the place. So much the worse if she took French leave one of these days; her parents might say their *mea culpa*, and own that they had forced her out of the house.

One Saturday when Nana came home she found her father and her mother in a lamentable condition. Coupeau, who had fallen across the bed, was snoring. Gervaise, crouching on a chair, was swaying her head, with her eyes vaguely and threateningly staring into vacancy. She had forgotten to warm the dinner, the remains of a stew. A tallow dip which she neglected to snuff revealed the shameful misery of the room.

"It's you, caterpillar?" stammered Gervaise. "Ah well, your father will give you a dance."

Nana did not answer, but remained pale, looking at the cold stove, the table on which no plates were laid, the lugubrious hovel which this pair of drunkards invested with the pale horror of their callousness. She did not take off her hat, but walked round the room; then, with her teeth tightly set, she opened the door and went out.

"You are going down again?" asked her mother, who was unable even to turn her head.

"Yes; I've forgotten something. I shall come up again. Good evening."

And she did not return. On the morrow when the Coupeaus were sobered they fought together, reproaching each other with being the cause of Nana's flight. Ah! she was far away if she were running still! As children are told of sparrows, her parents might set a pinch of salt on her tail, and then perhaps they would catch her. It was a great blow, and crushed Gervaise, for, despite the impairment of her faculties, she realised perfectly well that her daughter's misconduct lowered her still more; she was alone now, with no child to respect, able to let herself sink as low as she could fall. Yes, this heartless creature had carried the last remnants of her mother's reputation away in her dirty skirts. And Gervaise drank furiously for three days, with clinched fists and her mouth swollen with abominable words respecting her hussy of a daughter. Coupeau, after rolling round the outer Boulevards, and looking at all the harlots who passed by, as if trying to find Nana among them, took to smoking his pipe again quietly enough; only, when he was sitting at table at meal-time, he often sprang to his feet, raising his arms in the air with a knife in his hand, and crying out that he was dishonoured, and then he sat down again to finish his soup.

In the house, where girls flew off every month like canaries whose cages are left open, no one was astonished to hear of the Coupeaus' mishap. But the Lorilleux were triumphant. Ah! they had predicted that the girl would reward her parents in this fashion. It was deserved; all artificial flower-girls went wrong. The Boches and the Poissons also sneered, with an extraordinary display and outlay of virtue. Lantier alone covertly defended Nana. Good Lord! said he, with his puritanical air, no doubt a girl who went on the town offended against every law; but, with a gleam in the corner of his eyes, he added that, dash it! the girl was, after all, too pretty to lead such a life of misery at her age.

"Do you know," cried Madame Lorilleux, one day in the Boches' room, where the party were taking coffee, "well, as sure as this is daylight, the Hobbler sold her daughter! Yes, she sold her, and I have proof of it! The old fellow who was always on the stairs morning and night, went up to pay something on account. It stared one in the face. And, yesterday, too! Why, they were seen together at the Ambigu Theatre—the tabby and her tom. 'Pon my word of honour, they're together, so you see it was so."

The gossips discussed the subject whilst finishing their coffee. After all, it was possible; stranger things than that had happened. And in the neighbourhood the most respectable folks ended by repeating that Gervaise had sold her daughter.

Gervaise now shuffled along in her slippers, without caring a rap for any one. You might have called her a thief in the street, she wouldn't have turned round. For a month past she hadn't looked at Madame Fauconnier's; the latter had had to turn her out of the place to avoid disputes. In a few weeks' time she had successively entered the service of eight washer-women; she did two or three days' work in each place, and then she got the sack, so badly did she iron the things entrusted to her, careless and dirty, and losing her head to such a point that she quite forgot her calling. At last, realising her own inca-pacity, she abandoned ironing, and went out washing by the day at the wash-house in the Rue Neuve, where she still jogged on, floundering about in the water, fighting with filth, reduced to the roughest but easiest work, a bit lower on the down-hill slope. However, the wash-house scarcely beautified her. A real mud-splashed dog when she came out of it, soaked, and showing her blue skin. At the same time, she grew stouter and stouter, despite her frequent dances before the empty sideboard, and her leg became so crooked, that she could no longer walk beside any one without the risk of knocking him over, so great indeed was her lameness.

Naturally enough, when a woman falls to this point, all her pride leaves her. Gervaise had divested herself of all her old self-respect, coquetry, and need of sentiment, propriety, and politeness. You might have kicked her no matter where, she did not feel kicks, for she had become too fat and flabby. Lan-tier had altogether turned her up; he no longer squeezed her, even for form's sake; and she did not seem to notice this finish of a long connection, slowly spun out, and ending in mutual lassitude. It was work the less for her. Even Lantier's inti-macy with Virginie left her quite calm, so great was her indif-ference now for all the fondling that had once been so much to her taste. Everyone was aware that the hatter and the grocer were playing a fine game. They really had too much facility, for every two days the luckless Poisson had to turn out on night-duty, and shiver on the deserted pavement whilst his wife and his neighbour kept their feet warm at home. Oh! they didn't disturb themselves, they heard his step resound as he went slowly past the shop in the dark empty street, without as much as poking their noses above the counterpane. A police-man only knows his duty, of course, and they remained together till daybreak tampering with his belongings, whilst the stern fellow watched over other people's. The whole neighbourhood of the Rue de la Goutte-d'Or laughed at this good joke. They thought it capital fun that a representative of authority should be thus disgraced. Besides, Lantier had conquered the corner. The shop and the shopwoman went together. He had recently eaten a washerwoman out of doors; now he was nibbling a grocer up; and if he chose to turn to the dressmakers and the feminine drapers and stationers, he had jaws wide enough to swallow them all in turn.

No, never had a man been seen who rolled about in sweetmeats as he did. Lantier had thought of himself when he advised Virginie to deal in dainties. He was too much of a Provincial not to adore sugared things; and, in fact, he would have lived off sugar candy, lozenges, pastilles, sugar plums, and chocolate. Sugared almonds especially left a little froth on his lips, so keenly did they tickle his palate. For a year he had been living only on sweetmeats. He opened the drawers and stuffed himself, whenever Virginie asked him to mind the shop. Often, when he was talking in presence of five or six people, he would take the lid off a jar on the counter, dip his hand into it, and begin to nibble at something sweet; the glass jar remained open, and its contents diminished. People ceased paying attention to it, it was a mania of his, so he had declared. Besides, he had devised a perpetual cold, an irritation of the throat, which he always talked of calming.

He still did no work, for he had more and more important schemes than ever in view. He was contriving a superb invention—the umbrella-hat, a hat which transformed itself into a gingham on your head as soon as a shower commenced to fall; and he promised Poisson half shares in the profits of it, and even borrowed twenty franc pieces of him to defray the cost of experiments. Meanwhile, the shop melted away on his tongue. All the stock-in-trade followed suit, down to the chocolate cigars and pipes in pink caramel. Whenever he was stuffed with sweetmeats, and seized with a fit of tenderness, he paid himself with a last lick on the groceress in a corner, who found him all sugar, with lips which tasted like burnt almonds. Such a delightful man to kiss! He was positively becoming all honey. The Boches said he merely had to dip a finger into his coffee to sweeten it.

Softened by this perpetual dessert, Lantier showed himself paternal towards Gervaise. He gave her advice and scolded her because she no longer liked work. The deuce, indeed! a woman of her age ought to know how to turn herself round. And he accused her of having always been a glutton. Nevertheless, as one ought to hold out a helping hand, even to folks who don't deserve it, he tried to find her a little work. Thus he had prevailed upon Virginie to let Gervaise come once a week to scrub the shop and the rooms. That was the sort of

GERVAISE REDUCED TO CLEANING OUT THE SHOP OF HER OLD
ENEMY VIRGINIE   p. 357.

thing she understood, and on each occasion she earned her thirty sous. Gervaise arrived on the Saturday morning with a pail and a scrubbing brush, without seeming to suffer in the least at having to perform a dirty, humble duty, a charwoman's work, in the dwelling-place where she had reigned as the beautiful fair-haired mistress. It was a last humiliation, the end of her pride.

One Saturday she had a hard job of it. It had rained for three days, and the customers seemed to have brought all the mud of the neighbourhood into the shop on the soles of their boots. Virginie was at the counter, doing the grand, with her hair well combed, and wearing a little white collar and a pair of lace cuffs. Beside her, on the narrow seat covered with red American cloth, Lantier did the dandy, looking for all the world as if he were at home, as if he were the real master of the place, and from time to time he carelessly dipped his hand into a jar of peppermint drops, just to nibble something sweet according to his habit.

"I say, Madame Coupeau!" cried Virginie, who was watching the scrubbing with compressed lips, "you have left some dirt over there in that corner. Scrub that rather better, please."

Gervaise obeyed. She returned to the corner and began to scrub again. She bent double on her knees in the midst of the dirty water, with her shoulders prominent, her arms full stretched and purple with cold. Her old skirt, fairly soaked, stuck to her figure. And there, on the floor, she looked a dirty, ill-combed drab, the rents in her jacket showing her puffy form, her fat, flabby flesh which heaved, swayed, and floundered about whenever she was roughly shaken by her work; and all the while she perspired to such a point that from her moist face big drops of sweat fell on to the floor.

"The more elbow grease one uses the more it shines," said Lantier, sententiously, with his mouth full of peppermint drops.

Virginie, who sat back with the demeanour of a princess, her eyes but partly open, was still watching the scrubbing, and indulging in remarks. "A little more on the right there. Take care of the wainscot. You know I was not very well pleased last Saturday. The stains remained."

And both together, the hatter and the grocer assumed a more important air, as if they had been on a throne whilst Gervaise dragged herself through the black mud at their feet. Virginie must have enjoyed herself, for a yellowish flame darted from her cat's eyes, and she looked at Lantier with an insidious smile. At last she was revenged for that hiding she had received at the wash-house, and which she had never forgotten !

However, whenever Gervaise ceased scrubbing, a sound of sawing came from the back room. Through the open doorway, Poisson's profile stood out against the pale light of the court-yard. He was on leave that day, and was profiting by his leisure time, to indulge in his mania for making little boxes. He was seated at a table, and was cutting out arabesques in a cigar box with extraordinary care.

"I say, Badingue !" cried Lantier, who had given him this surname, again, out of friendship, "I shall want that box of yours as a present for a young lady."

Virginie pinched the hatter, but without ceasing to smile ; he repaid evil with good, gallantly caressing her knee under the counter ; and he drew his hand up quite naturally, when the husband at last raised his head, showing his red moustaches and imperial bristling on his mud-coloured face.

"Quite so," said the policeman. "I was working for you, Auguste, in view of presenting you with a token of friendship."

"Ah ! if that's the case, I'll keep your little affair !" rejoined Lantier laughing. "I'll hang it round my neck with a ribbon."

Then, suddenly, as if this thought brought another one to his memory, "By the way," he cried, "I met Nana last night."

This news caused Gervaise such emotion, that she sunk down in the dirty water which covered the floor of the shop. She sat there perspiring, and out of breath, with her scrubbing brush in her hand.

"Ah !" she muttered.

"Yes ; as I was going down the Rue des Martyrs, I caught sight of a girl who was wriggling on the arm of an old fellow in front of me, and I said to myself: I know that mug ? I stepped out and sure enough found myself face to face with Nana. There's no need to pity her, she looked deuced happy, with a pretty woollen dress on her back, a gold cross, and an awfully pert expression."

"Ah !" repeated Gervaise in a huskier voice.

Lantier who had finished the pastilles, took some barley-sugar out of another jar.

"She's vicious the hussy," he resumed. "Do you know she made a sign to me to follow her, with wonderful composure. Then she left her old fellow somewhere in a café—oh, a wonderful chap, the old bloke, quite used up !—and she came and joined me under a doorway. A perfect little serpent, pretty, and doing the grand, and licking you like a little dog. Yes, she kissed me, and wanted to have news of every one—I was very pleased to meet her."

"Ah!" said Gervaise, for the third time. She drew herself together, and still waited. Hadn't her daughter had a word for her then. In the silence Poisson's saw could be heard again. Lantier, who felt gay, was sucking his barley-sugar, and smacking his lips.

"Well, if *I* saw her, I should go over to the other side of the street," interposed Virginie who had just pinched the hatter again most ferociously. "Yes, I should blush to be recognised in public by one of those drabs. It isn't because you are there. Madame Coupeau, but your daughter is a rotten baggage. Why, Poisson runs in girls who are no better than she is, every day."

Gervaise said nothing, nor did she move; her eyes were fixed on vacancy. She ended by jerking her head to and fro, as if in answer to her thoughts, whilst the hatter with a gluttonous mien, muttered :

"As for being rotten, a fellow would willingly stuff himself with such rottenness. It's as tender as chicken."

But the grocer gave him such a terrible look, that he had to pause and quiet her with some delicate attention. He watched the policeman, and perceiving that he had his nose lowered over his little box again, he profited of the opportunity to shove the barley-sugar into Virginie's mouth. Thereupon she laughed at him good naturedly, and turned all her anger against the charwoman."

"Just make haste, eh? The work doesn't advance, whilst you remain stuck there like a street post. Come, look alive, I don't want to flounder about in the water till night time."

And she added, hatefully, in a lower tone. "It isn't my fault, if her daughter's gone on the town."

No doubt, Gervaise did not hear. She had begun to scrub the floor again, with her back bent, and dragging herself along with a frog-like motion. With both hands tightly clutching hold of the brush, she pushed back the black flood which splashed her with mud, even to the hair. Then after sweeping the dirty water into the gutter, it only remained for her to rinse the floor.

However after a pause Lantier, who felt bored, raised his voice again, "Do you know, Badingue," he cried, "I met your boss yesterday in the Rue de Rivoli. He looked awfully down

in the mouth He hasn't six months' life left in his body. Ah !
after all with the life he leads—"

He was talking of the Emperor. The policeman did not
raise his eyes, but curtly answered, " If you were the Government you wouldn't be so fat."

"Oh, my dear fellow, if I were the Government," rejoined the
hatter, suddenly affecting an air of gravity, " things would go
on rather better, I give you my word for it. Thus, their foreign
policy, why for some time past it has been enough to make a
fellow sweat. If I—I who speak to you—only knew a journalist
to inspire him with my ideas."

He was growing animated, and as he had finished crunching
his barley-sugar, he opened a drawer from which he took a
number of jujubes which he swallowed, gesticulating,

" It's quite simple. Before anything else I should give Poland
her independence again, and I should establish a great Scandin-
avian state to keep the Giant of the North at bay. Then I
should make a republic out of all the little German states. As
for England, she's scarcely to be feared ; if she budged ever so
little, I should send a hundred thousand men to India. Add
to that I should send the Sultan back to Mecca and the Pope
to Jerusalem, belabouring their backs with the butt end of a
rifle. Eh ? Europe would soon be clean. Come, Badingue, just
look here."

He paused to take five or six jujubes in his hand. " Why it
wouldn't take longer than to swallow these."

And he threw one jujube after the other into his open mouth.

" The Emperor has another plan," said the policeman, after
reflecting for a couple of minutes.

" Oh leave me alone ! " rejoined the hatter. " We know what
his plan is ? Europe doesn't care a curse for us. Every day
the Tuileries footmen pick your boss up under the table between
a couple of high life drabs."

But Poisson had risen to his feet. He came forward and
placed his hand on his heart, saying ; " You hurt me, Auguste.
Discuss, but don't indulge in personalities."

Thereupon Virginie intervened, bidding them stop their row.
She didn't care a fig for Europe. How could two men, who
shared everything else, always be disputing about politics? For
a minute they mumbled some indistinct words. Then the
policeman, in view of showing that he harboured no spite, produced the cover of his little box which he had just finished ; it
bore the inscription in marquetry: " To Auguste, a token of

friendship." Lantier, feeling exceedingly flattered, lounged back and spread himself out so that he almost sat upon Virginie. And the husband viewed the scene, with his face the colour of an old wall, and his bleared eyes fairly expressionless; but all the same at moments the red hairs of his moustaches stood up on end of their own accord in a very singular fashion, which would have alarmed any man who was less sure of his business than the hatter.

This beast of a Lantier had the quiet cheek which pleases ladies. As Poisson turned his back he was seized with the idea of printing a kiss on Madame Poisson's left eye. As a rule he was stealthily prudent, but when he had been disputing about politics he risked everything so as to show the wife his superiority. These gloating caresses, cheekily stolen behind the policeman's back, revenged him on the Empire which had turned France into a house of ill-fame. Only on this occasion he had forgotten Gervaise's presence. She had just finished rinsing and wiping the shop, and she stood near the counter waiting for her thirty sous. However the kiss on Virginie's eye left her perfectly calm, as being quite natural, and as part of a business she had no right to mix herself up in. Virginie seemed rather vexed. She threw the thirty sous on to the counter in front of Gervaise. The latter did not budge, but stood there waiting, still palpitating with the effort she had made in scrubbing, and looking as soaked and as ugly as a dog fished out of a sewer.

" Then she didn't tell you anything?" she asked the hatter at last.

" Who?" he cried. "Ah, yes, you mean Nana. No, nothing else. What a mouth she has, the little hussy! real strawberry jam."

And Gervaise went off with her thirty sous in her hand. The holes in her shoes spat water forth like pumps, they were real musical shoes, and played a tune as they left moist traces of their broad soles along the pavement.

In the neighbourhood, the feminine bibbers of her own class now related that she drank to console herself for her daughter's misconduct. She herself, when she gulped down her dram of spirits on the counter, assumed a dramatic air, and tossed the liquor into her mouth, wishing it would "do" for her. And on the days when she came home boozed, she stammered that it was all through grief. But honest folks shrugged their shoulders; they knew what that meant: ascribing the effects of the peppery fire of the "Assommoir" to grief, indeed; at

all events, she ought to have called it bottled grief. No doubt,
at the beginning, she couldn't digest Nana's flight. All the
honest feelings remaining in her revolted at the thought; and
besides, as a rule, a mother doesn't like to have to think that
her daughter, at that very moment perhaps, is being familiarly
addressed by the first chance comer. But Gervaise was already
too stultified, with a sick head and a crushed heart, to think of
the shame for long. With her it came and went. She remained
sometimes for a week together without thinking of her hussy;
and then suddenly a tender or an angry feeling seized hold of
her, sometimes when she had her stomach empty, at others
when it was full, a furious longing to catch Nana in some
corner, where she would perhaps have kissed her, or perhaps
have beaten her, according to her fancy of the moment. She
ended by having a very confused idea of what was right and
what was wrong. Only Nana belonged to her, of course; and
no one likes to see his belongings evaporate.

Whenever these thoughts came over her, Gervaise looked on
all sides in the streets with a bobby's eyes. Ah, if she had
only seen her baggage, how quickly she would have brought
her home again! The neighbourhood was being turned topsy-
turvy that year. The Boulevard Magenta and the Boulevard
Ornano were being pierced; they were doing away with the old
Barrière Poissonnière, and cutting right through the outer Boulevard. The district could not be recognised. The whole of one
side of the Rue des Poissonniers had been pulled down. From
the Rue de la Goutte-d'Or a large clearing could now be seen,
a dash of sunlight and open air; and in place of the gloomy
buildings which had hidden the view in this direction, there
rose up, on the Boulevard Ornano, a perfect monument, a six-
storeyed house, carved all over like a church, with clear
windows, which with their embroidered curtains seemed
symbolical of wealth. This white house, standing just in front
of the street, illuminated it with a jet of light as it were, and
every day it caused discussions between Lantier and Poisson.

The hatter was never tired of talking about the demolitions
of Paris. He accused the Emperor of setting palaces everywhere, so as to drive the working classes into the provinces;
and the policeman, pale with concentrated anger, replied that
on the contrary, the Emperor thought of the working classes
before aught else, and that he would raze Paris to the ground
if needs be, with the sole object of procuring employment for
them. Gervaise was also extremely annoyed by these embellish-

ments, which disturbed the dark corner of the faubourg she was accustomed to. Her vexation came from the fact that the neighbourhood was being embellished just as she was going downhill to ruin. When a person is in the gutter, he doesn't care to have a sunray dart upon his head ; and so, on the days when Gervaise was looking for Nana, she preferred to stride over the building materials, flounder about on the unfinished footways, and knock against the palings. The fine house on the Boulevard Ornano was too much for her patience. Such houses as that were only for drabs like Nana.

. However, she had several times had tidings of the girl. There are always ready tongues anxious to pay you a sorry compliment. Yes, she had been told that the hussy had turned up her old protector, just like the inexperienced girl she was. She had got on capitally with this old fellow, petted, adored, and free too, if she had only known how to set to work. But youth is foolish, and she had no doubt gone off with some stripling, no one knew exactly where. What seemed certain was that one afternoon she had left her old protector on the Place de la Bastille, just for half a minute, and the old fellow was still waiting for her. Other persons swore they had seen her since kicking up her heels at the "Grand Hall of Folly," in the Rue de la Chapelle. Then it was that Gervaise took it into her head to frequent all the dancing places of the neighbourhood. She did not pass in front of a public ball-room without going in. Coupeau accompanied her. At first they merely made the round of the room, looking at the drabs who were jumping about. But one evening, as they had some coin, they sat down and ordered a large bowl of hot wine in view of regaling themselves and waiting to see if Nana would turn up. At the end of a month or so, they had forgotten her, but they frequented the balls for their own pleasure, liking to look at the dancers. They would remain for hours without exchanging a word, resting their elbows on the table, stultified amidst the quaking of the floor, and yet no doubt amusing themselves as they stared with pale eyes at the Barrière hussies, in the stifling atmosphere and ruddy glow of the hall.

It happened one November evening that they went into the "Grand Hall of Folly" to warm themselves. Out of doors a sharp wind cut you across the face. But the hall was crammed. There was a thundering big swarm inside ; people at all the tables, people in the middle, people up above, any amount of meat. Yes, those who cared for tripes could enjoy themselves.

When they had made the round twice without finding a vacant
table, they decided to remain standing and wait till somebody
went off.   Coupeau was wagging on his legs, in a dirty blouse,
with an old cloth cap which had lost its peak flattened down on
his head.   And as he intercepted the way, he saw a scraggy
young fellow who was wiping his coat-sleeve after elbowing him.

"I say!" cried Coupeau in a fury, as he took his pipe out of
his black mouth.   "Can't you apologise?   And you play the
disgusted, eh? because a fellow wears a blouse!"

The young man turned round and looked at the zinc-worker
from head to foot.

"I'll just teach you, you scraggy young scamp," continued
Coupeau, "that the blouse is the finest garment out; yes! the
garment of work.   I'll wipe you if you like with my fists.   Did
one ever hear of such a thing—a ne'er-do-well insulting a
workman!"

Gervaise tried to calm him, but in vain.   He drew himself
up in his rags, in full view, and struck his blouse, roaring:
"There's a man's chest under that!"

Thereupon the young man dived into the midst of the crowd,
muttering: "What a dirty blackguard!"

Coupeau wanted to follow and catch him.   He wasn't going
to let himself be insulted by a fellow with a coat on.   That one
wasn't even paid for!   Some second-hand toggery to impose
upon a girl with, without having to fork out a centime.   If he
caught the chap again, he'd bring him down on his knees and
make him bow to the blouse.   But the crush was too great;
there was no means of walking.   He and Gervaise turned slowly
round the dancers; there were three rows of sightseers packed
close together, whose faces lighted up whenever a man sprawled
or a woman cocked her legs up in the air; and as Coupeau and
Gervaise were both short, they raised themselves up on tiptoe,
trying to see something at all events—the chignons and hats
that were bobbing about.   The cracked brass instruments of
the orchestra were furiously thundering a quadrille, a perfect
tempest which made the ball shake; while the dancers, striking
the floor with their feet, raised a cloud of dust which dimmed
the brightness of the gas.   The heat was unbearable.

"Look there," said Gervaise suddenly.

"Look at what?"

"Why, at that velvet hat over there."

. They raised themselves up on tiptoe.   On the left hand there
was an old black velvet hat trimmed with ragged feathers

bobbing about—regular hearse's plumes. It was dancing a
devil of a dance, this hat—curvetting and whirling round,
diving down and then springing up again. Coupeau and
Gervaise lost sight of it as the people round about moved their
heads, but then suddenly they saw it again, swaying farther off
with such droll effrontery that folks laughed merely at the sight
of this dancing hat, without knowing what was underneath it.

"Well?" asked Coupeau.

"Don't you recognise that chignon?" muttered Gervaise
in a stifled voice. "May my head be cut off if it isn't
her."

With one shove the zinc-worker made his way through the
crowd. By the name of heaven, yes, it was Nana! And in a
nice pickle too! She had nothing on her back but an old silk
dress, all stained and sticky from having wiped the tables of
boozing dens, and with its flounces so torn that they fell in
tatters round about. Not even a bit of a shawl over her
shoulders; no, she openly displayed her bare bodice with its
torn buttonholes. And to think that the hussy had had such
an attentive old protector, and had yet fallen to this condition,
merely for the sake of following some bully who beat her no
doubt! Nevertheless she had remained fresh and tempting,
with her hair as frizzly as a poodle's, and her mouth bright pink
under that rascally hat of hers.

"Wait a bit, I'll make her dance!" resumed Coupeau.

Naturally enough, Nana was not on her guard. You should
have seen how she wriggled about! She twisted to the right
and to the left, bending double as if she were going to break
herself in two, and darting her feet into her partner's face as if
she meant to split herself! There was a crowd round her; she
was applauded, and she caught up her skirts as high as her
knees and, quivering with the movement of the dance, spun
round and round like a whipping top, falling on to the floor
with her legs wide apart; then she indulged in a modest little
dance, with her breast and her hips undulating in wonderful
style. It made you positively long to carry her off into a
corner and cover her with kisses.

However, as Coupeau fell into the midst of the pastourelle
he disarranged the figure, and was cuffed by the bystanders.

"I tell you it's my daughter!" he cried; "let me pass."

Nana was just going backwards, sweeping the floor with her
flounces, rounding her figure and wriggling it, so as to look all
the nicer. She received a masterly kick just in the right

place, raised herself up, and turned quite pale on recognising
her father and mother. Bad luck and no mistake.

"Turn him out!" howled the dancers.

But Coupeau, who had just recognised his daughter's cavalier
as the scraggy young man in the coat, did not care a fig for
what people said.

"Yes, it's us," he roared. "Eh? you didn't expect it. So
we catch you here, and with a whipper-snapper, too, who insulted me a little while ago!"

Gervaise, whose teeth were tight set, pushed him aside, exclaiming, "Shut up. There's no need of so much explanation."

And, stepping forward, she dealt Nana a couple of cuffs,
something nice. The first knocked the feathered hat on one
side, and the second left a red mark on the girl's white cheek.
Nana was too stupefied either to cry or resist. The orchestra
continued playing, the crowd grew angry and repeated savagely,
"Turn them out! Turn them out!"

"Come, make haste!" resumed Gervaise. "Just walk in
front, and don't try to run off. You shall sleep in prison if
you do."

The scraggy young man had prudently disappeared. Nana
walked ahead, very stiff and still stupefied by her bad luck.
Whenever she showed the least unwillingness, a cuff from
behind brought her back to the direction of the door. And
thus they went out, all three of them, amid the jeers and
banter of the spectators, whilst the orchestra finished playing
the pastourelle with such thunder that the trombones seemed
to be spitting bullets.

The old life began again. After sleeping for twelve hours in
her closet, Nana behaved very well for a week or so. She had
concocted herself a modest little dress, and wore a cap with
the strings tied under her chignon. Seized indeed with remarkable fervour, she declared she would work at home, where
one could earn what one liked without hearing any nasty workroom talk; and she procured some work and installed herself
at a table, getting up at five o'clock in the morning on the first
few days to roll her violet stems. But when she had delivered a
few gross, she stretched her arms and yawned over her work,
with her hands cramped, for she had lost her knack of stem-
rolling, and suffocated, shut up like this at home after allowing
herself so much open air freedom during the last six months.
Then the glue dried the petals and the green paper got stained-

with grease, and the flower-dealer came three times in person
to make a row and claim his spoiled materials.

Nana jogged on, constantly getting a hiding from her father,
and wrangling with her mother morning and night—quarrels
in which the two women flung horrible words at each other's
head.　It couldn't last; the twelfth day the hussy took herself
off, with no more luggage than her modest dress on her back
and her cap on her ears.　The Lorilleux, who had pursed their
lips on hearing of her return and repentance, nearly died of
laughter now.　Second performance, eclipse number two, young
ladies for the reformatory take the train!　No, it was really
too comical.　Nana took herself off in such an amusing style.
Well, if the Coupeaus wanted to keep her in future they must
shut her up in a cage.

In presence of other people the Coupeaus pretended they were
very glad to be rid of the girl, though in reality they were enraged.　However rage can't last forever, and soon they heard
without even blinking that Nana was stalking the neighbourhood.　Gervaise who accused her of doing it to disgrace them,
set herself above scandal; she might meet her baggage on the
street, she said, she wouldn't even dirty her hand to cuff her;
yes, it was all over, she might have seen her kicking the bucket
on the ground, lying naked on the pavement, and she would
have passed by without even thinking this cub had been littered
by her.

Nana, meanwhile was enlivening the dancing halls of the
neighbourhood.　She was known from the "Ball of Queen
Blanche" to the "Great Hall of Folly."　When she entered the
"Elysée-Montmartre," folks climbed on to the tables to see her
do the "sniffing crawfish," during the figure of the pastourelle.
As she had twice been turned out of the "Château Rouge" ball,
she walked outside the door waiting for some one she knew to
escort her inside.　The "Black Ball" on the outer Boulevard
and the "Grand Turk" in the Rue des Poissonniers, were respectable places where she only went when she had clean petticoats on.　Of all the jumping places of the neighbourhood, however,
those she most preferred were the "Hermitage Ball" in a damp
courtyard and "Robert's Ball" in the Impasse du Cadran, two
corrupt little halls, lighted up with half-a-dozen oil lamps, and
kept paternally, everyone pleased and everyone free, so much
so that the men and their girls kissed each other at their ease,
in the corners, without being disturbed.　And meanwhile Nana
had ups and downs, perfect transformations, now tricked out

like a stylish woman and now all dirt like a slut. Ah ! she had
a fine life.

On several occasions the Coupeaus fancied they saw their
daughter in some dirty den. They turned their backs and de-
camped in another direction so as not to be obliged to recognise
her. They didn't care to be laughed at by a whole dancing
hall again for the sake of bringing such a drab home. One
night as they were going to bed, however, someone knocked at
the door. It was Nana who quietly came to ask for a bed; and
in what a state, good heavens ! her head bare, her dress in
tatters, and her boots full of holes—such a toilet as might have
led the police to run her in, and take her off to the Dépôt.
Naturally enough she received a hiding, and then she gluttonously fell on to a crust of stale bread and went to sleep, worn
out, with the last mouthful between her teeth. Then this sort
of life continued. When the girl picked up a bit, she took herself off. Neither seen nor known. The bird had flown. And
weeks and months elapsed and she seemed lost, when suddenly
up she turned again without even saying where she came from,
sometimes in such a filthy state you wouldn't have taken hold
of her with a pair of tongs, and scratched from top to bottom,
at others well-dressed but so weakened and emptied by riotous
living that she could no longer stand on her legs. Her parents had to accustom themselves to it. Hidings were of no
good. They stamped on her, but it didn't prevent her from
looking on home as an inn, where she could lodge by the week.
She knew she should pay for her lodging with a hiding, so she
considered and came to receive it, if she thought it likely to be
profitable. Besides one grows tired of striking, and the Coupeaus ended by letting Nana do as she liked. She came home
or stayed away ; providing she didn't leave the door open, that
sufficed. After all, habit wears out self-respect like it wears
out everything else.

There was only one thing that really worried Gervaise. This
was to see her daughter come home in a dress with a train and
a hat covered with feathers. No, she couldn't stomach this
display. Nana might indulge in riotous living if she chose,
but when she came home to her mother's she ought to dress
like a workgirl. The dresses with trains caused quite a revolution in the house: the Lorilleux sneered ; Lantier, whose mouth
watered, turned the girl round to sniff how nice she smelt ; the
Boches had forbidden Pauline to associate with this baggage in
her frippery. And Gervaise was also angered by Nana's ex-

hausted slumber, when after one of her fugues, she slept till
noon, with her breast bare, her chignon undone and still full
of hair pins, looking so white and breathing so feebly that she
seemed to be dead. Her mother shook her five or six times in the
course of the morning, threatening to throw a jugfull of water
over her. The sight of this handsome lazy girl, half-naked and
fat with vice, exasperated her, as she saw her lying there, sleeping off the debauchery which puffed her out, and unable even
to wake up. Nana opened an eye, closed it again, and then
stretched herself out all the more.

One day, after reproaching her with the life she led, Gervaise
put her threat into execution by shaking her dripping hand over
Nana's body. Quite infuriated, the girl rolled herself up in the
sheet, and cried out :

"That's enough, mamma. It would be better not to talk
about men. You did what you liked and now I do what I like."

"What ! what !" stammered the mother.

"Yes, I never spoke to you about it, for it didn't concern
me ; but you didn't put yourself out at all ; I often saw you
walking about in your shift down-stairs when papa was snoring.
You don't care for it now, but others do. So just shut up ; you
shouldn't have set me the example."

Gervaise remained pale, with trembling hands, turning round
without knowing what she was about, whilst Nana, flattened
on her breast, embraced her pillow with both arms and subsided into the torpor of her leaden slumber.

Coupeau growled, no longer sane enough to think of launch-
ing out a backhander. He was altogether losing his mind.
And really there was no occasion to call him an unprincipled
father, for liquor deprived him of all consciousness of good and
evil.

Now it was a settled thing. He wasn't sober once in six
months ; then he was laid up and had to go into the Sainte-
Anne hospital ; a pleasure trip for him. The Lorilleux said
that the Duke of Bowel-Twister had gone to visit his estates.
At the end of a few weeks he left the asylum, repaired and set
together again, and then he began to pull himself to bits once
more, till he was down on his back and needed another mending. In three years he went seven times to Sainte-Anne in this
fashion. The neighbourhood said that his cell was kept ready
for him. But the worst of the matter was that this obstinate
bibber demolished himself more and more each time, so that
from relapse to relapse one could foresee the final tumble, the

last cracking of this shaky cask, all the hoops of which were
breaking away, one after the other.

At the same time, he forgot to improve in appearance; a
perfect ghost to look at ! The poison was having terrible effects.
By dint of imbibing alcohol, his body shrunk up like the foeti
displayed in glass jars in chemical laboratories. When he approached a window you could see through his ribs, so skinny
had he become. With sunken cheeks, and dripping eyes from
which enough wax for a set of cathedral tapers exuded, he only
kept his truffle nose fine and red and flowery, like a pink in the
midst of his ravaged face. Those who knew his age, only forty
years just gone, shuddered when he passed by, bent and unsteady, looking as old as the streets themselves. And the
trembling of his hands increased, the right one danced to such
an extent, that sometimes he had to take his glass between both
fists to carry it to his lips. Oh I that cursed trembling ! it was
the only thing that worried his addled brains. You could hear
him growling ferocious insults against those hands of his. On
other occasions you could see him contemplating them for
hours, watching them dance like frogs, without saying a word,
no longer angry, but looking rather as if he were trying to think
what internal mechanism was making them bob up and down
like that; and one evening Gervaise had found him like this,
with two big tears dripping down his drunkard's scorched
cheeks.

The last summer, during which Nana came home to spend
such of her nights as remained, after she had finished knocking
about, was especially bad for Coupeau. His voice changed entirely as if liquor had set a new music in his throat. He became deaf of one ear. Then in a few days his sight grew dim,
and he had to clutch hold of the balusters to prevent himself
from falling. As for his health, he had abominable headaches
and dizziness. All on a sudden he was seized with acute pains
in his arms and legs; he turned pale; was obliged to sit down,
and remained on a chair witless for hours; indeed, after one
such attack, his arm remained paralysed for the whole day.
He took to his bed several times; he rolled himself up and hid
himself under the sheet, breathing hard and continuously like
a suffering animal. Then the strange scenes of Sainte-Anne
began again. Suspicious and nervous, worried with a burning
fever, he rolled about in a mad rage, tearing his blouse and
biting the furniture with his convulsed jaws; or else he sank
into a great state of emotion, complaining like a child, sobbing

and lamenting because nobody loved him. One night when Gervaise and Nana returned home together they were surprised not to find him in his bed. He had laid the bolster in his place. And when they discovered him, hiding between the bed and the wall, his teeth were chattering, and he related that some men had come to murder him. The two women were obliged to put him to bed again and quiet him like a child.

Coupeau only knew one remedy, to screw a pint of spirits inside him, a whack in his stomach, which set him up right again. This was how he doctored his gripes of a morning. His memory had left him long ago, his brain was empty; and he no sooner found himself on his feet than he poked fun at illness. He had never been ill. Yes, he had got to the point when a fellow kicks the bucket declaring that he's quite well. And his wits were going a-wool-gathering in other respects too. When Nana came home after gadding about for six weeks or so, he seemed to fancy she had returned from doing some errand in the neighbourhood. Often when she was hanging on an acquaintance's arm she met him and laughed at him without his recognising her. In short, he no longer counted for anything; she might have sat down on him if she had been at a loss for a chair.

When the first frosts came Nana took herself off once more, under the pretence of going to the fruiterer's to see if there were any baked pears. She scented winter and didn't care to let her teeth chatter in front of the fireless stove. The Coupeaus simply called her a strumpet because they had waited for the pears. No doubt she would come back again. The other winter she had stayed away three weeks to fetch her father a penn'orth of tobacco. But the months went by, and the girl did not show herself. This time she must have indulged in a hard gallop. When June arrived, she did not even turn up with the sunshine. Evidently it was all over, she had found new bread somewhere or other. One day when the Coupeaus were hard-up they sold the girl's iron bedstead for six francs down, which they drank together at Saint-Ouen. The bedstead had been in their way.

One morning in July Virginie called to Gervaise, who was passing by, and asked her to lend a hand in washing up, for Lantier had entertained a couple of friends on the day before. And while Gervaise was cleaning up the plates and dishes, greasy with the traces of the spread, the hatter, who was still digesting in the shop, suddenly called out:

"I say, do you know I saw Nana the other day."

Virginie, who was seated at the counter looking very care-
worn in front of the jars and drawers, which were already three
parts emptied, jerked her head furiously. She restrained herself so as not to say too much, but really it smelt very strong.
Lantier met Nana too often. Oh! she was by no means sure
of him, he was a man to do even worse things than that when
a petticoat fancy came into his head. Madame Lerat, very
intimate just then with Virginie who confided in her, had that
moment entered the shop; and hearing Lantier's remark she
pouted suggestively, and asked:

"In what sense did you see her?"

"Oh, in the proper sense," answered the hatter, who felt
highly flattered, and began to laugh and twirl his moustaches.
"She was in a vehicle; and I was floundering on the pavement.
Really it was so, I swear it! If it had been otherwise there
would be no occasion to disown it, for the young fellows of
position who are on intimate terms with her are devilish lucky!"

His eyes had brightened, and he turned towards Gervaise who
was standing in the rear of the shop, wiping a dish.

"Yes, she was in a carriage, and wore such a stylish dress!
I didn't recognise her, she looked so much like a lady of the
upper set, with her white teeth in her mug which was as fresh
as a flower. It was she who waved her glove to me. She has
raised a viscount I believe. Oh! she's launched for good!
She can afford to do without any of us; she's head over heels in
happiness, the little beggar! What a love of a little kitten!
no, you've no idea what a little kitten she is!"

Gervaise was still wiping her plate, although it had long
since been clean and shiny. Virginie was reflecting, anxious
about a couple of bills which fell due on the morrow, and which
she didn't know how to pay; whilst Lantier stout and fat, perspiring the sugar he fed off, ventured his enthusiasm for well-
dressed little hussies in the centre of the shop, which was
already three parts eaten up, and smelt of ruin. Yes, there
were only a few more burnt almonds to nibble, a little more
barley-sugar to suck, to clean the Poissons' business out.
Suddenly, on the pavement over the way, he perceived the
policeman, who was on duty, pass by, buttoned up, with his
sword dangling by his side. And this made him all the gayer.
He compelled Virginie to look at her husband.

"Dear me," he muttered, "Badingue looks fine this morning!
Be careful, see how stiff he walks. He must have stuck a glass
eye in his back to catch his criminals unawares."

When Gervaise went upstairs at home, she found Coupeau seated on the bed, in the torpid state induced by one of his attacks. He was looking at the window-panes with his dim expressionless eyes. She sat herself down on a chair, tired out, her hands hanging beside her dirty skirts; and for a quarter of an hour she remained in front of him without saying a word.

"I've had some news," she muttered at last. "Your daughter's been seen. Yes, your daughter's precious stylish and hasn't any more need of you. She's awfully happy she is! Ah! God of heaven! I'd give a great deal to be in her place."

Coupeau was still staring at the window-pane. But suddenly he raised his ravaged face, and stammered with an idiotic laugh:

"Come, my duck, I don't detain you. You're not yet so bad looking when you wash yourself. As folks say, however old a pot may be, it ends by finding its lid. And, after all, if it only buttered our bread!"

CHAPTER XII.

It must have been the Saturday after quarter day, something like the 12th or 13th January—Gervaise didn't quite know. She was losing her wits, for it was centuries since she had had anything warm in her stomach. Ah! what an infernal week! A complete clear out. Two loaves of four pounds each on Tuesday, which had lasted till the Thursday; then a dry crust found the night before, and finally not a crumb for thirty-six hours, a real dance before the cupboard! What she did know, by the way, what she felt on her back, was the frightful cold, a black cold, a sky as grimy as a frying-pan, thick with snow which obstinately refused to fall. When winter and hunger are both together in your tripes, you may tighten your belt as much as you like, it hardly feeds you.

Perhaps Coupeau would bring back some money in the evening. He said that he was working. Everything is possible, eh? And Gervaise, although she had been caught many and many a time, had ended by relying on this coin. After all sorts of troubles, she herself couldn't find as much as a duster to wash in the whole neighbourhood; and even an old lady, whose rooms she did, had just given her the sack, charging her with swilling her liqueurs. No one would engage her, it was too hot for her everywhere; and this secretly suited her, for she had fallen to that state of indifference, when one prefers to croak rather than move one's fingers. At all events, if Coupeau brought his pay home they would have something warm to eat. And meanwhile, as it wasn't yet noon, she remained stretched on the mattress, for one doesn't feel so cold or so hungry when one is lying down.

Gervaise called it a mattress; but to tell the truth it was only a heap of straw in the corner. By degrees the sleeping accommodation had found its way to the second-hand furniture dealers in the neighbourhood. First of all, on days when they

were hard up, she had unsewn the mattress, and taken out
handfuls of wool which she hid in her apron and sold for ten sous
a pound in the Rue Belhomme. Then when the mattress was
emptied, she had obtained thirty sous for the ticking, so as to
treat herself to some coffee one morning. The pillows had
followed, and then the bolster. There remained the wooden
framework of the bed, which she couldn't put under her arm on
account of the Boches, who would have called every one in the
house to the spot if they had seen the landlord's guarantee
going off.

And yet, one evening with Coupeau's assistance, she watched
the Boches who were feeding, and quietly removed the bedstead,
bit by bit, the sides, the back, and the framework at the bottom.
With the ten francs they thus procured, they fed for three days.
Didn't the straw mattress suffice? Even its ticking had joined
that of the woollen one, and so thus they had finished eating up
their sleeping accommodation, allowing themselves an indigestion
of dry bread after a twenty-four hours' starve. The straw was
swept aside with a broom, the dust was always turned over, and
it wasn't dirtier than anything else.

Gervaise bent herself like a gun-trigger on the heap of straw,
with her clothes on, and her feet drawn up under her rag of a skirt,
so as to keep them warm. And huddled up, with her eyes wide
open, she turned some scarcely amusing ideas over in her mind
that morning. Ah! no, dash it all, she couldn't continue living
without food. She no longer felt her hunger, only she had a
weight on her chest, and her brain seemed empty. Certainly,
there was nothing gay to look at in the four corners of the
hovel. A perfect kennel, now, where greyhounds, who wear
wrappers in the streets, would not even have lived in effigy.
Her pale eyes stared at the bare walls. Everything had long
since gone to "uncle's." All that remained were the chest of
drawers, the table, and a chair. Even the marble top of the
chest of drawers, and the drawers themselves, had evaporated
in the same direction as the bedstead. A fire could not have
cleaned them out more completely; the little nick-nacks had
melted, beginning with the ticker, a twelve franc watch, down to
the family photos, the frames of which had been bought by a
woman keeping a second-hand store; a very obliging woman,
by the way, to whom Gervaise carried a saucepan, an iron, a
comb, and who gave her five, three, or two sous in exchange,
according to the article; enough, at all events, to go upstairs
again with a bit of bread. But now there only remained a

broken pair of snuffers, which the woman refused to give her
even a sou for.

Oh ! if she could only have sold the rubbish and refuse, the
dust and the dirt, how speedily she would have opened shop,
for the room was filthy to behold ! She only saw cobwebs in
the corners, and although cobwebs are perhaps good for cuts,
there are, so far, no merchants who buy them. Then, turning
her head, abandoning the idea of doing a bit of trade, Gervaise
gathered herself together more closely on her straw, preferring
to stare through the window at the snow-laden sky, at the dreary
daylight, which froze the marrow in her bones.

What a lot of worry ! Though, after all, what was the use
of putting herself in such a state, and puzzling her brains ? If
she had only been able to have a snooze. But her hole of a
home wouldn't go out of her mind. M. Marescot, the landlord,
had come in person the day before to tell them that he should
turn them out into the street if the two quarters' rent now overdue were not paid during the ensuing week. Well, so he might,
they certainly couldn't be worse off on the pavement ! Fancy
this ape, in his overcoat and his woollen gloves, coming upstairs
to talk to them about rent, as if they had had a treasure hidden
somewhere ! By Jove ! instead of tightening her throat, she
would have begun by shoving something into her stomach !
Really, now, she found this glutton altogether too provoking,
and she wished him somewhere else.

Just the same with that brute of a Coupeau, who couldn't
come home now without beating her; she wished him in the
same place as the landlord. She sent them all there, wishing
to rid herself of everyone, and of life too. She was becoming a
real storehouse for blows. Coupeau had a cudgel, which he
called his ass's fan, and he fanned his old woman. You should
just have seen him giving her abominable sweatings, which
made her perspire all over. She was no better herself, for she
bit and scratched him. Then they stamped about in the empty
room, and gave each other such drubbings as were likely to
ease them of all taste for bread for good. But Gervaise ended
by not caring a fig for these thwacks, not more than she did for
anything else. Coupeau might celebrate Saint Monday for
weeks together, go off on the spree for months at a time, come
home mad with liquor, and seek to sharpen her as he said, she
had grown accustomed to it, she thought him plaguy, but
nothing more. It was on these occasions that she wished him
somewhere. Yes, somewhere, her beast of a man, and the Loril-

leux, the Boches, and the Poissons too ; in fact, the whole
neighbourhood, which she had such contempt for. She sent all
Paris there with a gesture of supreme carelessness, and yet
pleased to be able to revenge herself in this style.

Unfortunately, although people may accustom themselves to
a good many things, no one has yet acquired the habit of doing
without food. And it was merely this that irritated Gervaise.
She didn't care a fig whether she were the lowest of the low,
fairly in the gutter ; it was all the same to her if folks wiped
themselves when she passed near them. Bad manners no
longer worried her, but hunger was always griping at her
bowels. Oh ! she had bidden tit-bits good-bye, she had fallen
to devouring whatever she could get. On high days, now, she
bought parings and scraps of meat at the butchers, at the rate
of four sous a pound, meat which was tired of lying about, and
blackening on a plate, and she cooked this in a saucepan with a
mess of potatoes. Or else she fried a bullock's heart, a dish
that made her lick her lips.

On other occasions, when she had some wine, she treated herself to a sop, a true parrot's pottage. Two sous' worth of Italian
cheese, bushels of white apples, quarts of dry beans, cooked in
their own juice, these also were dainties she was not often able
to indulge in now. She came down to "arlequins," in low
eating dens, where, for a sou, she had a pile of fish bones, mixed
with the parings of mouldy roast meat. She fell even lower,
she begged a charitable eating-house keeper to give her his customers' dry crusts, and she made herself a bread sop, letting the
crusts simmer as long as possible on a neighbour's fire. On the
days when there was nothing to hope, she searched about with
the dogs, to see what might be lying outside the tradespeople's
doors before the dustmen went by ; and thus, at times, she
came across rich men's food, rotten melons, stinking mackerel,
and chops, which she carefully inspected, for fear of maggots.

Yes, she had come to this. The idea may be a repugnant
one to delicate-minded folks, but if they hadn't chewed anything
for three days running, we should hardly see them quarrelling
with their stomachs ; they would go down on all fours and eat
filth like other people. Ah ! the death of the poor, the empty
entrails, howling hunger, the animal appetite, that leads one
with chattering teeth to fill one's stomach with beastly refuse
in this great Paris, so bright and golden ! And to think that
Gervaise had filled her belly with fat goose ! Now, she might
wipe her nose with what was left of it. One day, when Coupeau

bagged two bread tickets from her to go and sell them and get
some liquor, she nearly killed him with the blow of a shovel,
so hungered and so enraged was she by this theft of a bit of
bread.

However, after a long contemplation of the pale sky, she had
fallen into a painful doze.   She dreamt that the snow loading
the sky was falling on her, so cruelly did the cold pinch.   Suddenly she sprang to her feet, awakened with a start by a shudder
of anguish.   Good heavens ! was she going to die ?   Shivering
and haggard she perceived that it was still daylight.   Wouldn't
the night come then ?   How long the time seems when the
stomach is empty !   Her's was waking up in its turn, and beginning to torture her.   Sinking on to the chair, with her head
bent and her hands between her legs to warm them, she began
to think what they would have for dinner, as soon as Coupeau
brought the money home : a loaf, a quart of wine, and two platefuls of tripe in the Lyonnese fashion.   Three o'clock struck by
father Bazouge's clock.   Yes, it was only three o'clock.   Then
she began to cry,   She would never have strength enough to
wait till seven.   Her body swayed backwards and forwards, she
oscillated like a child nursing some sharp pain, bending herself
double and crushing her stomach, so as not to feel it.   Ah ! an
accouchement is less painful than hunger !   And unable to ease
herself, seized with rage, she rose and stamped about, hoping to
send her hunger to sleep, by walking it to and fro like an infant.
For half an hour or so, she knocked against the four corners of
the empty room.   Then, suddenly, she paused with a fixed stare.
So much the worse !   They might say what they liked ; she
would lick their feet if needs be, but she would go and ask the
Lorilleux to lend her ten sous.

At winter time, up these stairs of the house, the paupers'
stairs, there was a constant borrowing of ten sous and twenty
sous, petty services which these hungry beggars rendered each
other.   Only they would rather have died than have applied to
the Lorilleux, for they knew they were too hard-fisted.   Thus
Gervaise displayed remarkable courage in going to knock at
their door.   She felt so frightened in the passage, that she experienced the sudden relief of people who ring a dentist's bell.

"Come in ! " cried the chain-maker in a sour voice.

How warm and nice it was inside.   The forge was blazing, its
white flame lighting up the narrow workroom, whilst Madame
Lorilleux set a coil of gold wire to heat.   Lorilleux, in front of
his worktable, was perspiring with the warmth as he soldered

the links of a chain together. And it smelt nice ; some cabbage soup was simmering on the stove, exhaling a steam
which turned Gervaise's heart topsy turvy, and almost made
her faint.

"Ah ! it's you," growled Madame Lorilleux, without even
asking her to sit down. "What do you want ?"

Gervaise did not answer. She was not on such very bad
terms with the Lorilleux that week. But the request for the
ten sous stuck in her throat at sight of Boche seated at his ease
near the stove, talking scandal. He looked as if he didn't care
a curse for any one, the animal ! He laughed like a fool, with
his mouth curved and his cheeks so puffed out that they hid his
nose.

"What do you want ?" repeated Lorilleux.

"You haven't seen Coupeau ?" Gervaise finished by stammering at last. "I thought he was here."

The chain-makers and the doorkeeper sneered. No, for certain,
they hadn't seen Coupeau. They didn't stand treat often
enough to see Coupeau like that. Gervaise made an effort and
resumed, stuttering :

"It's because he promised to come home. Yes, he's to bring
me some money. And as I have absolute need of something—"

Silence followed. Madame Lorilleux was roughly fanning the
fire of the stove ; Lorilleux had lowered his nose over the bit of
chain between his fingers, while Boche continued laughing,
puffing out his face till it looked like the full moon.

"If I only had ten sous," muttered Gervaise in a low voice.

The silence persisted.

"Couldn't you lend me ten sous ? Oh ! I would return them
to you this evening !"

Madame Lorilleux turned round and stared at her. Here was
a wheedler trying to get round them. To-day she asked them
for ten sous, to-morrow it would be for twenty, and there would
be no reason to stop. No, indeed ; it would be warm if they
lent her anything.

"But, my dear," cried Madame Lorilleux. "You know very
well that we haven't any money ! Look ! there's the lining of
my pocket. You can search us. If we could, it would be with
a willing heart, of course."

"The heart's always there," growled Lorilleux. "Only when
one can't, one can't."

Gervaise looked very humble, and nodded her head ap-
provingly. However, she did not take herself off. She squinted

at the gold, at the gold tied together hanging on the walls, at
the gold wire the wife was drawing out with all the strength of
her little arms, at the gold links lying in a heap under the
husband's knotty fingers. And she thought that the least bit
of this ugly black metal would suffice to buy her a good dinner.
The workroom was as dirty as ever, full of old iron, coal dust,
and sticky oil stains half wiped away ; but now, as Gervaise saw
it, it seemed resplendent with treasure, like a money-changer's
shop. And so she ventured to repeat softly : "I would return
them to you, return them without fail. Ten sous wouldn't
inconvenience you."

Her heart was swelling with the effort she made not to own
that she had had nothing to eat since the day before. Then she
felt her legs give way ; she was frightened that she might burst
into tears, and she still stammered :

"It would be so kind of you! You don't know. Yes, I'm
reduced to that, good Lord—reduced to that!"

Thereupon the Lorilleux pursed their lips, and exchanged
covert glances. So the Hobbler was begging now! Well, the
fall was complete. But they did not care for that kind of thing
by any means! If they had known, they would have barricaded
the door, for people should always be on their guard against
beggars, folks who make their way into apartments under a
pretext, and carry precious objects away with them ; and
especially so in this place, as there was something worth while
stealing. One might lay one's fingers no matter where, and
carry off thirty or forty francs by merely closing the hands.
They had felt suspicious several times already on noticing how
strange Gervaise looked when she stuck herself in front of the
gold. This time, however, they meant to watch her. And as
she approached nearer, with her feet on the board, the chain-
maker roughly called out, without giving any further answer to
her question : "Look out, pest—take care ; you'll be carrying
some scraps of gold away on the soles of your shoes. One
would think you had greased them on purpose to make the
gold stick to them."

Gervaise slowly drew back. For a moment she leant against
a rack, and seeing that Madame Lorilleux was looking at
her hands, she opened them and showed them, saying softly,
without the least anger, like a fallen woman who accepts everything,

"I have taken nothing, you can look."

And then she went off, because the strong smell of the

cabbage soup, and the warmth of the workroom, made her feel too ill.

Ah! the Lorilleux did not detain her. Good riddance; the deuce if they opened the door to her again. They had seen enough of her face. They didn't want other people's misery in their rooms, especially when that misery was so well deserved. They revelled in their selfish delight at being seated so cosily in a warm room, with a dainty soup preparing for them. Boche also stretched himself, puffing with his cheeks still more and more, so much, indeed, that his laugh really became indecent. They were all nicely revenged on the Hobbler, for her former manners, her blue shop, her spreads, and all the rest. It was too satisfactory, it showed where the love of good living led one. That's what became of women who were gluttonous and idle, and immoral!

"So that is the style now? Begging for ten sous," cried Madame Lorilleux behind Gervaise's back. "Wait a bit; I'll lend her ten sous, and no mistake, to go and get drunk with."

Gervaise shuffled along the passage in her slippers, bending her back and feeling heavy. On reaching her door she did not open it—her room frightened her. It would be better to walk about, she would learn patience. As she passed by she stretched out her neck, peering into father Bru's kennel under the stairs. There, for instance, was another one who must have a fine appetite, for he had breakfasted and dined by heart during the last three days. However, he wasn't at home, there was only his hole, and Gervaise felt somewhat jealous, thinking that perhaps he had been invited somewhere. Then, as she reached the Bijards', she heard some one complaining, and, as the key was in the lock as usual, she opened the door and went in.

"What is the matter?" she asked.

The room was very clean. One could see that Lalie had carefully swept it, and arranged everything during the morning. Misery might blow into the room as much as it liked, carry off the chattels and spread all its dirt and refuse about. Lalie, however, came behind and tidied everything, imparting, at least, some appearance of comfort within. She might not be rich, but you realised that there was a housewife in the place. That afternoon her two little ones, Henriette and Jules, had found some old pictures which they were cutting out in a corner. But Gervaise was greatly surprised to see Lalie herself in bed, looking very pale, with the sheet drawn up to her chin. In bed, indeed, then she must be seriously ill!

"What is the matter with you?" repeated Gervaise, feeling anxious.

Lalie no longer complained. She slowly raised her white eyelids, and tried to compel her lips to smile, although they were convulsed by a shudder.

"There's nothing the matter with me," she whispered very softly. "Really nothing at all."

Then, closing her eyes again, she added with an effort, "I was too tired during the last few days, and so I'm doing the idle; I'm nursing myself, as you see."

But her childish face, streaked with livid stains, assumed such an expression of anguish that Gervaise, forgetting her own agony, joined her hands and fell on her knees near the bed. For the last month she had seen the girl clinging to the walls for support when she went about, bent double, indeed, by a cough which seemed to presage a coffin. Now the poor child could not even cough. She had a hiccough, and drops of blood oozed from the corners of her mouth.

"It isn't my fault if I hardly feel strong," she murmured, as if relieved. "I've tired myself to-day trying to put things to rights. It's pretty tidy, isn't it? And I wanted to clean the windows as well, but my legs failed me. How stupid! However, when one has finished one can go to bed."

She paused to say, "Pray see if my little ones are not cutting themselves with their scissors."

And then she relapsed into silence, trembling and listening to a heavy footfall which was approaching up the stairs. Suddenly father Bijard brutally opened the door. As usual he was far gone, and his eyes shone with the furious madness imparted by the "vitriol" he had swallowed. When he perceived Lalie in bed, he tapped on his thighs with a sneer, and took the whip from where it hung.

"Ah! by blazes, that's too strong," he growled, "we'll just have a laugh. So the cows lie down on their straw at noon, now! Are you poking fun at me, you lazy beggar? Come, quick now, up you get."

And he already cracked the whip over the bed. But the child beggingly replied,

"Pray, papa, don't—don't strike me. I swear to you you would regret it. Don't strike!"

"Will you jump up?" he roared still louder, "or else I'll tickle your ribs! Jump up, you little hound!"

GERVAISE INTERFERES TO PROTECT LALIE FROM BIJARD'S BRUTALITY.

p. 391.

Then she softly said, "I can't—do you understand? I'm going to die."

Gervaise had sprung upon Bijard and torn the whip away from him. He stood bewildered in front of the bed. What was the dirty nose talking about? Do girls die so young without even having been ill? Some excuse to get sugar out of him no doubt. Ah! he'd make inquiries, and if she lied let her look out!

"You will see, it's the truth," she continued. "As long as I could I avoided worrying you; but be kind now, and bid me good-bye, papa."

Bijard wriggled his nose as if he fancied she was deceiving him. And yet it was true she had a singular look, the serious mien of a grown up person. The breath of death which passed through the room in some measure sobered him. He gazed around like a man awakened from a long sleep, saw the room so tidy, the two children clean, playing and laughing. And then he sank on to a chair stammering, "Our little mother, our little mother."

These were the only words he could find to say, and yet they were very tender ones for Lalie, who had never been so much spoiled. She consoled her father. What especially worried her was to go off like this without having completely brought her little ones up. He would take care of them, would he not? With her dying breath she told him how they ought to be cared for and kept clean. But stultified, with the fumes of drink seizing hold of him again, he wagged his head, watching her pass away with an uncertain stare. All kinds of things were touched in him, but he could find no more to say, and he was too utterly burnt with liquor to shed a tear.

"Listen," resumed Lalie, after a pause. "We owe four francs and seven sous to the baker; you must pay that. Madame Gaudron has an iron of ours, which you must get from her. I wasn't able to make any soup this evening, but there's some bread left, and you can put some potatoes to warm."

Till her last rattle, the poor kitten still remained "the little mother." Surely she could never be replaced! She was dying because she had had, at her age, a true mother's reason, because her breast was too small and weak for so much maternity. And if her ferocious beast of a father lost this treasure, it was his own fault. After kicking the mother to death, hadn't he murdered the daughter as well? The two good angels would lie in the pauper's grave, and all that could be in store for him was to kick the bucket like a dog in the gutter.

However, Gervaise restrained herself not to burst out sobbing.
She extended her hands, desirous of easing the child, and as the
shred of a sheet was falling, she wished to tuck it in and arrange
the bed.   Then the dying girl's poor little body was seen.   Ah !
Lord, what misery ! what woe ! Stones would have wept.
Lalie was bare, with only the remnants of a jacket on her
shoulders by way of chemise ; yes, bare, with the grievous,
bleeding nudity of a martyr.   She had no flesh left ; her bones
seemed to protrude through her skin.   From her ribs to her
thighs there extended a number of violet stripes—the marks of
the whip forcibly imprinted on her.   A livid bruise, moreover,
encircled her left arm, as if the tender limb, scarcely larger than
a lucifer, had been crushed in a vice.   There was also an im-
perfectly closed wound on her right leg, left there by some ugly
blow, and which opened again and again of a morning, when she
went about doing her errands.   From head to foot, indeed, she
was but one bruise !   Oh ! this murdering of childhood ; those
heavy hands crushing this lovely girl ; how abominable that
such weakness should have such a weighty cross to bear !
Again did Gervaise crouch down, no longer thinking of tucking
in the sheet, but overwhelmed by the pitiful sight of this
martyrdom ; and her trembling lips seemed to be seeking for
words of prayer.

"Madame Coupeau," murmured the child, "I beg you—"
With her little arms she tried to draw up the sheet again,
ashamed as it were for her father.   Bijard, as stultified as ever,
with his eyes on the corpse which was his own work, still
wagged his head, but more slowly, like a worried animal
might do.

When she had covered Lalie up again, Gervaise felt she could
not remain there any longer.   The dying girl was growing
weaker and ceased speaking ; all that was left to her was her
gaze—the dark look she had had as a resigned and thoughtful
child, and which she now fixed on her two little ones who were
still cutting out their pictures.   The room was growing gloomy,
and Bijard was working off his liquor while the poor girl was in
her death agonies.   No, no, life was too abominable !   How
frightful it was ! how frightful !   And Gervaise took herself
off, and went down the stairs unwittingly, her head wandering
and so full of disgust that she would willingly have thrown herself under the wheels of an omnibus to have finished with her
own existence.

As she hastened on, growling against cursed fate, she suddenly

GERVAISE WAITING IN COMPANY WITH OTHER WORKMEN'S WIVES
AT THE FACTORY DOOR ON A PAY-DAY.   p. 385.

found herself in front of the place where Coupeau pretended
that he worked. Her legs had taken her there, and now her
stomach began singing its song again, the complaint of hunger
in ninety verses—a complaint she knew by heart. However,
if she caught Coupeau as he left, she would be able to pounce
upon the coin at once, and buy some grub. A short hour's
waiting at the utmost; she could surely stay that out, though
she had sucked her thumbs since the day before.

It was in the Rue de la Charbonnière, at the corner of the
Rue de Chartres, an open space where the wind played at hide
and seek. Dash it all! stalking the pavement didn't warm
one. It would have been better if one had only had a fur
mantle. The sky retained its ugly leaden hue, and the snow,
amassed above, covered the neighbourhood with an icy cap.
Nothing fell, but the air was profoundly still, presaging a complete disguise for Paris by-and-by—a pretty ball dress, quite
white and new. Gervaise raised her nose, begging Providence
not to let the muslin fall yet awhile. She stamped her feet,
looked at a grocer's shop over the way, and then turned on her
heels, as it was not worth while sharpening her appetite by the
contemplation of good things. There was nothing amusing
round about. The few passers-by strode rapidly along, wrapped
up in comforters; naturally enough one does not care to tarry
when the cold is griping one's hindquarters. However,
Gervaise perceived four or five women who were mounting
guard like herself outside the door of the zinc-works; unfortunate creatures of course—wives watching for the pay to
prevent it going to the dram-shop. There was a tall creature
with a gendarme's face stuck against the wall, ready to spring
on her husband as soon as he showed himself. A dark little
woman with a delicate humble air was walking about on the
other side of the way. Another one, a fat creature, had brought
her two kids with her, and was dragging them along, one on
either hand, and both of them shivering and sobbing. And
all these women, Gervaise like the others, passed and repassed,
exchanging glances, but without speaking to one another. A
pleasant meeting and no mistake. They didn't need to make
friends to learn what number they lived at. They could all
hang out the same signboard, "Misery & Co." It seemed to
make one feel even colder, to see them walk about in silence,
passing each other in this terrible January weather.

However, nobody as yet left the zinc-works. But presently
one workman appeared, then two, and then three, but these

were no doubt decent fellows who took their pay home regularly, for they jerked their heads significantly as they saw the shadows wandering up and down. The tall creature stuck closer than ever to the side of the door, and suddenly fell upon a pale little man, who was prudently poking his head out. Oh! it was soon settled! She searched him and collared his coin. Caught, no more money, not even enough to pay for a dram! Then the little man, looking very vexed and cast down, followed his gendarme, weeping like a child. The workmen were still coming out; and as the fat mother with the two kids approached the door, a tall fellow, with a cunning look, who noticed her, went hastily inside again to warn her husband; and when the latter arrived he had stuffed a couple of cart wheels away, two beautiful new five franc pieces, one in each of his shoes. He took one of the kids on his arm, and went off telling crams to his old woman, who was complaining. There were other workmen also, mournful-looking fellows, who carried in their clinched fists the pay for the three or five days' work they had done during a fortnight, who reproached themselves with their own laziness, and took drunkards' oaths. But the saddest thing of all was the grief of the dark little woman, with the humble, delicate look; her husband, a handsome fellow, took himself off under her very nose, and so brutally indeed that he almost knocked her down, and she went home alone, stumbling past the shops and weeping all the tears in her body.

At last the defile finished. Gervaise, who stood erect in the middle of the street, was still watching the door. The look-out seemed a bad one. A couple of workmen who were late appeared on the threshold, but there were still no signs of Coupeau. And when she asked the workmen if Coupeau wasn't coming, they answered her, being up to snuff, that he had just gone off by the back-door with Lantimêche. Gervaise understood what this meant. Another of Coupeau's lies; she could whistle for him if she liked. Then, shuffling along in her worn-out shoes, she went slowly down the Rue de la Charbonnière. Her dinner was going off in front of her, and she shuddered as she saw it running away in the yellow twilight. This time it was all over. Not a copper, not a hope, nothing but night and hunger. Ah! a fine night to kick the bucket, this dirty night which was falling over her shoulders!

She was walking heavily up the Rue des Poissonniers when she suddenly heard Coupeau's voice. Yes, he was there, in the

"Little Civet," letting My-Boots treat him. That comical chap, My-Boots, had been cunning enough at the end of last summer to espouse in authentic fashion a lady who, although rather advanced in years, had still preserved considerable traces of beauty. She was a lady of the Rue des Martyrs, none of your Barrière hussies. And you should have seen this fortunate mortal, living like a man of means, with his hands in his pockets, well clad and well fed. He could hardly be recognised, so fat had he grown. His comrades said that his wife had as much work as she liked among the gentlemen of her acquaintance. A wife like that and a country-house is all one can wish for to embellish one's life. And so Coupeau squinted admiringly at My-Boots. Why, the lucky dog even had a gold ring on his little finger!

Gervaise touched Coupeau on the shoulder just as he was coming out of the "Little Civet."

"I say, I'm waiting; I'm hungry. Is that all you stand?"

But he silenced her in a capital style. "You're hungry, eh? Well, eat your hand, and keep t'other for to-morrow."

He considered it highly improper to do the dramatic in other people's presence. What, he hadn't worked, and yet the bakers kneaded bread all the same. Did she take him for a fool, to come and try and frighten him with her stories?

"Do you want me to turn thief?" she muttered, in a husky voice.

My-Boots stroked his chin in conciliatory fashion. "No, that's forbidden," said he. "But when a woman knows how to manage—"

And Coupeau interrupted him to call out "Bravo!" Yes, a woman always ought to know how to manage. But his wife had always been a helpless thing. It would be her fault if they died on the straw. Then he relapsed into his admiration for My-Boots. How awfully fine he looked! A regular landlord; with clean linen and swell shoes! They were no common stuff! His wife, at all events, knew how to row the boat!

The two men walked towards the outer Boulevard, and Gervaise followed them. After a pause, she resumed, talking behind Coupeau's back: "I'm hungry; you know, I relied on you. You must find me something to nibble."

He did not answer, and she repeated, in a tone of despairing agony: "Is that all you stand?"

"But, dash it all, I've got no coin," he roared, turning round in a fury. "Just leave me alone, eh? or else I'll hit you."

He was already raising his fist. She drew back, and seemed
to make up her mind. "All right, I'll leave you. I shall always
be able to find a man."

The zinc-worker laughed at this. He pretended to make a
joke of the matter, and strengthened her purpose without seeming to do so. That was a fine idea of her's, and no mistake !
In the evening, by gaslight, she might still make some conquests.
If she got hold of a man, he recommended her to try the
"Capuchin" restaurant, where capital fare was to be had in the
private rooms. And as she went off along the Boulevard, looking pale and furious, he called out after her : "I say, just
listen, bring me back some dessert. I like cakes ; and if your
gentleman's well dressed, ask him for an old overcoat. I should
like to have one."

With these words ringing in her ears, Gervaise walked softly
away. But when she found herself alone in the midst of the
crowd, she slackened her pace. She was quite resolute.
Between thieving and doing *that*, she preferred *that*, for at all
events she wouldn't harm any one. She would only dispose of
herself. No doubt, it wasn't proper. But what was proper and
what was improper were sorely muddled together in her brain.
When you are dying of hunger, you don't philosophize, you eat
whatever bread turns up. She had gone along as far as the
Chaussée-Clignancourt. It seemed as if the night would never
come. However, she followed the Boulevards like a lady who
is taking a stroll before dinner. The neighbourhood in which
she felt so ashamed, so greatly was it being embellished, was
now full of fresh air. The Boulevard Magenta, coming from
the heart of Paris, and the Boulevard Ornano going off into the
country, had pierced through the old Barrière, levelling a large
number of houses ; and at the flanks of the two long avenues,
still white with plaster, one could see the Faubourg-Poissonnière
and the Rue des Poissonniers, dark, dingy, and crooked. The
demolition of the octroi wall had long since widened the outer
Boulevard, allowing space for two paved roads, with a central
foot-walk planted with four rows of scrubby plane trees. The
view stretched as far as the horizon, along the broad highways
crowded with people, and ending in a chaos of half-built houses.
But among the lofty new buildings there remained many tottering hovels. Between the carved façades there were a number
of black dens, standing back, perfect kennels, with rags hanging
from their windows. Amid the rising luxury of Paris, the

misery of the faubourg was apparent, surrounding the hastily erected new piles with dirt.

' Lost in the crowd on the broad footway, walking past the little plane trees, Gervaise felt alone and abandoned. The vistas of the avenues seemed to empty her stomach all the more. And to think that among this flood of people there were many in easy circumstances, and yet not a Christian who could guess her position, and slip a ten sous piece into her hand! Yes, it was too great and too beautiful; her head swam, and her legs tottered under this broad expanse of grey sky stretched over so vast a space. The twilight had the dirty-yellowish tinge of Parisian evenings, a tint that gives you a longing to die at once, so ugly does street life seem. The horizon was growing indistinct, assuming a mud-coloured tinge as it were. Gervaise, who was already weary, met all the workpeople returning home. At this hour of the day the ladies in bonnets, the well-dressed gentlemen living in the new houses, mingled with the people, with files of men and women still pale from inhaling the tainted atmosphere of workshops and workrooms. From the Boulevard Magenta and the Rue du Faubourg-Poissonnière, came bands of people, rendered breathless by their uphill walk. As the omnibuses and the cabs rolled by less noiselessly among the vans and trucks returning home empty at a gallop, an ever-increasing swarm of blouses and blue vests, covered the pavement. Commissionaires returned with their crotchets on their backs. Two workmen, stepping out, took long strides side by side, talking to each other in loud voices, with any amount of gesticulation, but without looking at one another; others who were alone, in overcoats and caps, walked along the curbstones with lowered noses; others, again, came in parties of five or six, following each other, with pale eyes and their hands in their pockets, and not exchanging a word. Some still had their pipes, which had gone out, between their teeth. Four masons poked their white faces out of the windows of a cab which they had hired between them, and on the roof of which their mortar-troughs rocked to and fro. House-painters were swinging their pots; a zinc-worker was returning laden with a long ladder, with which he almost poked people's eyes out; whilst a belated dealer in filter-taps, with his box on his back, played the tune of "The Good King Dagobert" on his little trumpet. Ah! the sad music, a fitting accompaniment to the tread of the flock, the tread of the weary beasts of burden.

Another day's work over! Really worktime was too long

and came too often. Hardly time to fill one's stomach, and
digest one's food; and it would be daylight again, and the
collar of misery must be resumed. But, nevertheless, the
plucky ones whistled, stamping on the pavement, and darting
along, erect, with their mouths turned supper-wards. And
Gervaise let the crowd flow past her, careless of being knocked
against, elbowed to the right, and elbowed to the left, and still
carried onward by the tide. Men haven't the time to indulge
in gallantry when they are bent double with fatigue, and
pinched by hunger.

. Suddenly on raising her eyes she noticed the old Hôtel
Boncœur in front of her. After being an ill-famed café, which
the police had shut up, the little house was now abandoned;
the shutters were covered with posters, the lantern was broken,
and the whole building was rotting and crumbling away from
top to bottom, with its smudgy claret coloured paint, quite
mouldy. The stationer's and the tobacconist's were still there.
In the rear, over some low buildings, you could see the leprous
façades of several five-storeyed houses rearing their tumble-
down outlines against the sky. The "Grand Balcony" dancing
hall, alone, no longer existed; some sugar-cutting works, which
hissed continually, had been installed in the hall with the ten
flaming windows. And yet it was here, in this den—the Hôtel
Boncœur—that the whole cursed life had commenced. Gervaise remained looking at the window of the first floor, from
which hung a broken shutter, and recalled to mind her youth
with Lantier, their first rows and the ignoble way in which he
had abandoned her. Never mind, she was young then, and it
all seemed gay to her, seen from a distance. Only twenty
years, good Lord! and yet she had fallen to the pavement.
Then the sight of the lodging house oppressed her and she
walked up the Boulevard in the direction of Montmartre.

The night was gathering, but children were still playing on
the heaps of sand between the benches. The march past continued, the work-girls went by, trotting along and hurrying to
make up for the time they had lost in looking in at the shop
windows; one tall girl who had stopped, left her hand in that
of a big fellow, who had accompanied her, three doors off from
her home; others, as they parted from each other, made ap-
pointments for the night at the "Grand Hall of Folly" or the
"Black Ball." In the midst of the groups, piece-workmen
went by, carrying their clothes folded under their arms. A
plumber, harnessed with leather braces, was drawing a truck

along, and nearly got himself crushed by an omnibus, owing to
his carelessness. Among the crowd which was now growing
scantier, there were several women running with bare heads;
after lighting the fire, they had come down stairs again, and
were hastily making their purchases for dinner; they jostled
the people they met, darted into the bakers' and the pork
butchers', and went off again with all despatch, their provisions in
their hands. There were little girls of eight years old, who had
been sent out on errands, and who went along past the shops,
pressing long loaves of four pounds' weight, as tall as they were
themselves, against their breasts, as if these loaves had been
beautiful yellow dolls; at times these little ones forgot themselves for five minutes or so, in front of some pictures in a shop
window, and rested their cheeks against the bread. Then the
flow subsided, the groups became fewer and farther between,
the working classes had gone home; and as the gas blazed now
that the day's toil was over, idleness and amusement seemed to
wake up.

Ah! yes, Gervaise had finished her day! She was wearier even
than all this mob of toilers who had jostled her as they went
by. She might lie down there and croak, for work would have
nothing more to do with her, and she had toiled enough during
her life to say: "Whose turn now? I've had enough." At present everyone was eating. It was really the end, the sun had
blown out its candle, the night would be a long one. Good
Lord! To stretch oneself at one's ease and never get up again,
to think one had put one's tools by for good, and that one could
lie lazy for ever! That's what is good, after tiring oneself out
for twenty years! And Gervaise, as hunger twisted her stomach,
thought in spite of herself of the fête days, the spreads and the
revelry of her life. Of one occasion especially, an awfully cold
day, a mid-Lent Thursday. She had enjoyed herself wonderfully
well. She was very pretty, fair-haired and fresh looking at
that time. Her wash-house in the Rue Neuve had chosen her
as queen in spite of her leg. And then they had had an outing
on the Boulevards in vehicles decked with green stuff, in the
midst of stylish people who ogled her. Real gentlemen put up
their glasses as if she had been a true queen. In the evening
there was a wonderful spread, and then they had danced till
daylight. Queen, yes Queen! with a crown and a sash for
twenty-four hours—twice round the clock! And now oppressed
by hunger, she loooked on the ground, as if she were seeking
for the gutter in which she had let her fallen majesty tumble.

She raised her eyes again.   She was in front of the slaughter-
houses which were being pulled down; through the gaps in the
façade one could see the dark, stinking courtyards still damp
with blood.   And when she had gone down the Boulevard again,
she also saw the Lariboisière Hospital, with its long grey wall,
above which she could distinguish the mournful fan-like wings
pierced with windows at even distances.   A door in the wall
terrified the neighbourhood ; it was the door of the dead in
solid oak, and without a crack, as stern and as silent as a tomb-
stone.   Then to escape her thoughts, she hurried further down
till she reached the railway bridge.   The high parapets of
riveted sheet iron hid the line from view ; she could only distinguish a corner of the station standing out against the
luminous horizon of Paris, with a vast roof black with coal dust.
Through the clear space she could hear the engines whistling
and the trucks being shunted, in token of colossal hidden
activity.   Then a train passed by, leaving Paris, with puffing
breath and a growing rumble.   And all she perceived of this
train was a white plume, a sudden gust of steam which rose
above the parapet and then evaporated.   But the bridge had
shaken, and she herself seemed impressed by this departure at
full speed.   She turned round as if to follow the invisible
engine, the noise of which was dying away.   In this direction
she divined the existence of the country and fresh air, far away
beyond a cutting with tall isolated houses to the right and left,
erected without order, now showing their fronts, and now unplastered side-walls, with others painted over with giant
advertisements, and all of them dirtied by the smoke from the
engines with the same yellowish tinge.   Ah ! if she had only
been able to go off like that, far from these abodes of misery and
suffering.   Perhaps she might then have begun her life over
again.   Then she found herself stupidly reading the bills posted
on the sheet-iron parapet.   They were of every tint.   One of
them—a little one, of a pretty shade of blue—promised fifty
francs reward for a bitch which had been lost.   That animal
had been loved, plainly enough.

Gervaise slowly resumed her walk.   In the smoky-shaded
fog which was falling, the gas lamps were being lighted up ;
and the long avenues, which had grown black and indistinct,
suddenly showed themselves plainly again, sparkling to their
full length and piercing through the night, even to the vague
darkness of the horizon.   A great gust swept by ; the widened
spaces were lighted up with girdles of little flames, shining under

the far-stretching moonless sky. It was the hour when from
one end of the Boulevard to the other the dram-shops and the
dancing halls flamed gaily as the first glasses were merrily
drunk and the first dance began. It was the great fortnightly
pay-day, and the pavement was crowded with jostling revellers
on the spree. There was a breath of merrymaking in the air
—deuced fine revelry, but not objectionable so far. Fellows
were filling themselves in the eating-houses; through the
lighted windows you could see people feeding, with their mouths
full, and laughing without taking the trouble to swallow.
Drunkards were already installed in the wine-shops, squabbling
and gesticulating. And there was a cursed noise on all sides,
voices shouting amid the constant clatter of feet on the pavement.

"I say! are you coming to sip?" "Make haste, old man;
I'll pay for a glass of bottled wine." "Hallo! here's Pauline!
Sha'n't we just laugh!" The doors swung to and fro, letting a
smell of wine and a sound of cornet playing escape into the
open air. There was a gathering in front of old Colombe's
"Assommoir," which was lighted up like a cathedral for high mass;
and, dash it all! you would have said a real ceremony was going
on, for several capital fellows with rounded paunches and
swollen cheeks, looking for all the world like professional
choristers, were singing inside. They were celebrating Saint-
Pay, of course—a very amiable saint who no doubt keeps the
cash-box in Paradise. Only, on seeing how gaily the evening
began, the retired petty tradesmen who had taken their wives
out for a stroll wagged their heads and repeated that there
would be any number of drunken men in Paris that night.
And the night stretched very dark, dead-like and icy above
this revelry, perforated only with lines of gas-lamps extending
to the four corners of heaven.

Gervaise stood in front of the "Assommoir," thinking that if she
had had a couple of sous she could have gone inside and drunk
a dram. No doubt a dram would have quieted her hunger. Ah!
what a number of drams she had drunk in her time! Liquor
seemed good stuff to her after all. And from outside she
watched the fuddling machine, realising that her misfortune was
due to it, and yet dreaming of finishing herself off with brandy
on the day she had some coin. But a shudder passed through
her hair, as she saw that it was now almost dark. Well, the
night time was approaching. She must have some pluck and
show herself coaxing if she didn't wish to kick the bucket in the
midst of the general revelry. Looking at other people gorging

themselves didn't precisely fill her own stomach. She slackened
her pace again, and looked around her. There was a darker
shade under the trees. Few people passed along, only folks in
a hurry who swiftly crossed the Boulevards. And on the broad,
dark, deserted footway, where the sound of the revelry died
away, women were standing and waiting. They remained for
long intervals, motionless, patient, and as stiff-looking as the
scrubby little plane trees; then they slowly began to move,
dragging their slippers over the frozen soil, taking ten steps or
so and then waiting again, rooted as it were to the ground.
There was one of them with a huge body and insect-like arms
and legs, wearing a black silk rag, with a yellow scarf over her
head; there was another one, tall and bony, who was bareheaded and wore a servant's apron; and others, too—old ones
plastered up, and young ones so dirty that a rag-picker would
not have picked them up. However, Gervaise tried to learn the
trade by imitating them; girlish-like emotion tightened her
throat; she was hardly aware whether she felt ashamed or not
—she seemed to be living in a horrible dream. For a quarter
of an hour she remained standing erect. Men hurried by without even turning their heads. Then she moved about in her
turn, and venturing to accost a man who was whistling with
his hands in his pockets, she murmured in a strangled voice :
  " Sir, just listen."
  The man gave her a side glance and then went off, whistling
all the louder.
  Gervaise grew bolder, and, with her stomach empty, she became
absorbed in this chase, fiercely rushing after her dinner, which
was still running away. She walked about for a long while,
without thinking of the flight of time or of the direction she took.
Around her the dark mute women went to and fro under the
trees like wild beasts in a cage. They stepped out of the shade
like apparitions, and passed under the light of a gas lamp with
their pale faces fully apparent; then they grew vague again as
they went off into the darkness, with a white strip of petticoat
swaying to and fro. Men let themselves be stopped at times,
talked jokingly, and then started off again, laughing. Others
discreetly went away ten paces behind a woman. There was a
deal of muttering, quarrelling in an undertone, and furious
bargaining, which suddenly subsided into profound silence.
And as far as Gervaise went she saw these women standing like
sentinels in the fight; they seemed to be placed along the
whole length of the Boulevard. As soon as she met one, she

GERVAISE IMPORTUNING THE PASSERS-BY AT NIGHT TIME.

p. 394

saw another twenty paces further on, and the file stretched out
unceasingly. Entire Paris was guarded. She grew enraged on
finding herself disdained, and, changing her place, she now per-
ambulated between the Chaussée de Clignancourt and the
Grande Rue of La Chapelle.

"Sir, just listen."

But the men passed by. She started from the slaughter-
houses, which stunk of blood. She glanced on her way at the
old Hôtel Boncœur, now closed. She passed in front of the
Lariboisière hospital, and mechanically counted the number of
windows that were illuminated with a pale quiet glimmer, like
that of night-lights at the bedside of some agonising sufferers.
She crossed the railway bridge as the trains rushed by with a
noisy rumble, rending the air in twain with their shrill
whistling! Ah! how sad everything seemed at night-time!
Then she turned on her heels again, and filled her eyes with
the sight of the same houses, doing this ten and twenty times
without pausing, without resting for a minute on a bench. No;
no one would have anything to do with her. Her shame
seemed to be increased by this contempt. She went down
towards the hospital again, and then returned towards the
slaughter-houses. It was her last promenade—from the blood-
stained courtyards, where animals were stricken low, down to
the pale hospital wards, where death stiffened the patients
stretched between the sheets. It was between these two establishments that she had passed her life.

"Sir, just listen."

But suddenly she perceived her shadow on the ground.
When she approached a gas-lamp it gradually became less
vague, till it stood out at last in full force—an enormous
shadow it was, positively grotesque, so portly had she become.
Her stomach, breast, and hips, all equally flabby, jostled
together as it were. She walked so lame that the shadow
bobbed almost topsy-turvy at every step she took; it looked
like a real Punch! Then as she left the street lamp behind her,
the Punch grew taller, becoming in fact gigantic, filling the
whole Boulevard, bobbing to and fro in such style that it
seemed fated to smash its nose against the trees or the houses.
Good Lord! how frightful she was! She had never realised her
disfigurement so thoroughly. And she could not help looking at
her shadow; indeed, she waited for the gas lamps, still watching
the Punch as it bobbed about. Ah! she had a pretty companion beside her! What a figure! It ought to attract men

at once! And at the thought of her unsightliness, she lowered her
voice, and only just dared to stammer behind the passers-by:

"Sir, just listen."

However, it must have been very late. Matters were growing bad in the neighbourhood. The eating-houses had shut
up, and voices, gruff with drink, could be heard disputing in
the wineshops. Revelry was turning to quarrelling and fisticuffs. A big ragged chap roared out, "I'll knock yer to bits;
just number yer bones." A loose woman had quarrelled with a
fellow outside a dancing place, and was calling him "dirty
blackguard" and "sick pig," whilst he on his side kept on
repeating, "How about your sister?" as if he could think of
nothing else. Drink seemed to have imparted a fierce desire
to indulge in blows, and the passers-by, who were now less
numerous, had pale contracted faces. There was a battle at
last; one drunken fellow came down on his back, with all fours
raised in the air, whilst his comrade, thinking he had done
for him, ran off with his heavy shoes clattering over the
pavement.

There were bands of fellows braying beastly songs, then a deep
silence came, interrupted only by the hiccoughs and the falls of
drunkards. The fortnightly merriment always finished like
this; so much wine had flowed since six o'clock, that now it was
about to stroll over the pavement. Such a mess on the very
middle of the footways, for belated people with delicate minds
to step over, if they did not care to walk through it. The
neighbourhood was really clean! If a foreigner had visited it
before the matutinal sweeping, he would have gone away with
a very nice opinion indeed. But the drunkards were at home,
and they didn't care a rap for Europe. By Jove! knives slipped
out, and the little fête ended in bloodshed. Women walked
hastily along, men prowled round with wolves' eyes, the night
grew thicker, swollen with abomination.

Gervaise still hobbled about, going up and down, with the
idea of walking for ever. At times, she felt drowsy, and went
to sleep, rocked, as it were, by her lame leg; then she looked
round her with a start, and noticed she had walked a hundred
paces unconsciously. Her feet were swelling in her ragged
shoes. The last clear thought that occupied her mind was that
her hussy of a daughter was perhaps eating oysters at that very
moment. Then everything became cloudy; and, albeit, she
remained with open eyes, it required too great an effort for her
to think. And the only sensation that remained to her, in her

utter annihilation, was that it was frightfully cold, so sharply, mortally cold, she had never known the like before. Why, even dead people could not feel so cold in their graves. With an effort she raised her head, and something seemed to lash her face. It was the snow, which had at last decided to fall from the smoky sky—fine thick snow, which the breeze swept round and round. For three days it had been expected. It fell just at the right time.

Woke up by the first gusts, Gervaise began to walk faster. Eager to get home, men were running along, with their shoulders already white. And, as she suddenly saw one who, on the contrary, was coming slowly towards her under the trees, she approached him, and again said : " Sir, just listen—"

The man had stopped. But he did not seem to have heard her. He held out his hand, and muttered in a low voice: " Charity, if you please ! "

They looked at one another. Ah ! good Lord ! They were reduced to this—father Bru begging, Madame Coupeau on the town ! They remained stupefied in front of each other. They could shake hands now. The old workman had prowled about the whole evening, not daring to stop anyone, and the first person he accosted was as hungry as himself. Lord, was it not pitiful ! To have toiled for fifty years, and be obliged to beg ! To have been one of the most prosperous washerwomen in the Rue de la Goutte-d'Or, and to end beside the gutter ! They still looked at one another. Then, without saying a word, they went off in different directions under the lashing snow.

It was a perfect tempest. On these heights, in the midst of this open space, the fine snow revolved round and round, as if the wind came from the four corners of heaven. You could not see ten paces off, everything was confused in the midst of this flying dust. The surroundings had disappeared, the Boulevard seemed to be dead, as if the storm had stretched the silence of its white sheet over the hiccoughs of the last drunkards. Gervaise still went on, blinded, lost. She felt her way by touching the trees. As she advanced, the gas lamps shone out amidst the whiteness like torches. Then, suddenly, whenever she crossed an open space, these lights failed her ; she was enveloped in the whirling snow, unable to distinguish anything to guide her. Below stretched the ground, vaguely white; grey walls surrounded her, and when she paused, hesitating, and turning her head, she divined that behind this icy veil extended the

immense avenues with interminable vistas of gas-lamps—the
black and deserted Infinite of Paris asleep.

She was standing where the outer Boulevard meets the Boulevards Magenta and Ornano, thinking of lying down on the
ground, when suddenly she heard a footfall. She began to run,
but the snow blinded her, and the footsteps went off, without
her being able to tell whether it was to the right or to the left.
At last, however, she perceived a man's broad shoulders, a dark
form which was disappearing amid the snow. Oh ! she'd have
that one, he shouldn't escape her ! And she ran on all the
faster, reached him, and caught him by the blouse : "Sir, sir,
just listen—."

The man turned round. It was Goujet.

So now she accosted Golden-Mug ! But what had she done
on earth to be tortured like this by Providence ? It was the
crowning blow—to stumble against Goujet, and be seen by him,
pale and begging, like a Barrière drab. And it happened just
under a gas-lamp ; she could see her deformed shadow swaying
on the snow like a real caricature. You would have said she
was drunk. Good Lord ! not to have a crust of bread, or a drop
of wine in her body, and to be taken for a drunken woman ! It
was her own fault, why did she booze ? Goujet no doubt
thought she had been drinking, and that she was up to some
nasty pranks.

However he looked at her while the snow scattered daisies
over his beautiful yellow beard. Then as she lowered her head
and stepped back he detained her.

"Come," said he.

And he walked on first. She followed him. They both
crossed the silent district, gliding noiselessly along the walls.
Poor Madame Goujet had died of rheumatism in the month of
October. Goujet still resided in the little house in the Rue
Neuve, living gloomily alone. On this occasion he was belated
because he had sat up nursing a wounded comrade. When he
had opened the door and lighted a lamp, he turned towards
Gervaise, who had remained humbly on the threshold. Then,
in a low voice, as if he were afraid his mother could still hear
him, he exclaimed, "Come in."

The first room, Madame Goujet's, was piously preserved in
the state she had left it. On a chair near the window lay the
tambour by the side of the large arm-chair, which seemed to be
waiting for the old lace-worker. The bed was made, and she
could have stretched herself beneath the sheets if she had left

the cemetery to come and spend the evening with her child.
There was something solemn, a perfume of honesty and goodness about the room.

"Come in," repeated the blacksmith in a louder tone.

She went in, half frightened, like a disreputable girl gliding
into a respectable place. He was quite pale, and trembled at
the thought of ushering a woman like this into his dead mother's
home. They crossed the room on tiptoe, as if they were
ashamed to be heard. Then when he had pushed Gervaise into
his own room he closed the door. Here he was at home. It
was the narrow closet she was acquainted with ; a schoolboy's
room, with a little iron bedstead hung with white curtains. On
the walls the engravings cut out of illustrated newspapers had
gathered and spread, and they now reached to the ceiling.
The room looked so pure that Gervaise did not dare to advance,
but retreated as far as she could from the lamp. Then without
a word, in a transport as it were, he tried to seize hold of her
and press her in his arms. But her strength was giving way,
and she murmured : "Oh, my God ! oh, my God !"

The fire in the stove, having been covered with coke-dust,
was still alight, and the remains of a stew which Goujet had put
to warm, thinking he should return to dinner, was smoking in
front of the cinders. Gervaise, who felt her numbness leave her in
the warmth of this room, would have gone down on all fours to eat
out of the saucepan. Her hunger was stronger than her will ;
her stomach seemed rent in two ; and she stooped down with a
sigh. But Goujet had realised the truth. He placed the stew on
the table, cut some bread, and poured her out a glass of wine.

"Thanks ! thanks !" said she. "Oh, how kind you are !
Thanks !"

She stammered ; she could hardly articulate. When she
caught hold of her fork she began to tremble so acutely that she
let it fall again. The hunger that possessed her made her wag
her head. She carried the food to her mouth with her
fingers. As she stuffed the first potato into her mouth, she
burst out sobbing. Big tears coursed down her cheeks and fell
on to her bread. She still cat, gluttonously devouring this
bread thus moistened by her tears, and breathing very hard all
the while. Goujet compelled her to drink to prevent her from
stifling, and her glass chinked, as it were, against her teeth.

"Will you have some more bread ?" he asked in an undertone.

She cried, she said "no," she said "yes," she didn't know.

Ah, Lord! how nice and yet how sad it is to eat when one
is starving.

And standing in front of her, he looked at her all the while;
under the bright light cast by the lamp-shade he could see her
well. How aged and altered she seemed! The heat was melting the snow on her hair and clothes, and she was dripping.
Her poor wagging head was quite grey; there were any number
of grey locks which the wind had disarranged. Her neck sank
into her shoulders, as it were, and she had become so fat and
ugly, you might have cried on noticing the change. And he
recollected their love, when she was quite rosy, working with
her irons, and showing the child-like plait which set such a
charming necklace round her throat. In those times he had
watched her for hours, glad to look at her. Later on she had
come to the forge, and there they had enjoyed themselves whilst
he beat the iron, and she stood by watching his hammer dance.
Ah! in those days, how often he had bit his pillow of a night-
time, longing to have her in his room! Oh! he would have
crushed her, had he taken hold of her then, so great was his
desire. And now she was his—he could take her! She was
finishing her bread, soaking it in her tears which had fallen
into the saucepan, her big silent tears which still rolled down
on to her food.

Gervaise rose; she had finished. She remained for a moment
with her head lowered, and ill at ease. Then, thinking she detected a gleam in his eyes, she raised her hand to her jacket
and unfastened the top button. But Goujet had fallen on his
knees, and taking hold of her hands he exclaimed softly,

"I love you, Madame Gervaise; oh! I love you still and in
spite of everything, I swear it to you."

"Don't say that, Monsieur Goujet!" she cried, maddened to
see him like this at her feet. "No, don't say that; you grieve
me too much."

And as he repeated that he could never love twice in his life,
she became yet more despairing.

"No, no, I am too ashamed. For the love of God get up.
It is my place to be on the ground."

He rose, he trembled all over and stammered, "Will you
allow me to kiss you?"

Overcome with surprise and emotion she could not speak, but
she assented with a nod of the head. After all, she was his;
he could do what he chose with her. But he merely protruded
his lips.

"That suffices between us, Madame Gervaise," he muttered.
"It is all our friendship, is it not?"

He kissed her on the forehead on a lock of her grey hair.
He had not kissed any one since his mother's death. His sweetheart Gervaise alone remained to him in life. And then when
he had kissed her with so much respect, he fell back across his
bed with sobs rising in his throat. And Gervaise could not remain there any longer. It was too sad and too abominable to
meet again under such circumstances when one loved. "I love
you, Monsieur Goujet," she exclaimed. "I love you dearly also.
Oh! it isn't possible, I understand it. Good-bye, good-bye, it
would stifle us both."

And she darted through Madame Goujet's room and found
herself outside on the pavement again. When she recovered
her senses, she had rung at the door in the Rue de la Goutte-
d'Or, and Boche was pulling the string. The house was quite
dark, and in the black night, the yawning, dilapidated porch
looked like an open mouth. To think that she had been ambitious of having a corner in this barracks! Had her ears been
stopped up then, that she had not heard the cursed music of
despair which sounded behind the walls? Since she had set foot
in the place she had begun to go downhill. Yes, it must bring
bad luck to shut oneself up in these big workmen's houses; the
cholera of misery was contagious there. That night everyone
seemed to have kicked the bucket. She only heard the Boches
snoring on the right-hand side; while Lantier and Virginie on
the left were purring like a couple of cats who are not asleep,
but have their eyes closed and feel warm. In the courtyard she
fancied she was in a perfect cemetery; the snow paved the ground
with white; the high frontages, livid grey in tint, rose up un-
lighted like ruined walls, and not a sigh could be heard; it
seemed as if a whole village, stiffened with cold and hunger,
were buried here. She had to step over a black gutter—water
from the dye-works—which smoked and streaked the whiteness
of the snow with its muddy course. It was the colour of her
thoughts. The beautiful light blue and light pink waters had
long since flowed away!

Then, whilst ascending the six flights in the dark, she could
not prevent herself from laughing; an ugly laugh, which hurt
her. She recalled her ideal of former days: to work quietly,
always have bread to eat and a tidy home to sleep in, to bring
up her children, not to be beaten, and to die in her bed. No,
really, it was comical how all that was becoming realised! She

no longer worked, she no longer eat, she slept on filth, her
daughter frequented all sorts of bad places, and her husband
drubbed her at all hours of the day ; all that was left for her to
do, was to die on the pavement, and it would not take long, if on
getting into her room she could only pluck up courage to fling
herself out of the window. Was it not enough to make one think
that she had asked heaven for thirty thousand francs a year
and no end of respect ? Ah ! really, in this life it is no use
being modest, one only gets sat upon ! Not even pap and a
nest, that is the common lot.

What increased her ugly laugh was the recollection of her
grand hope of retiring into the country after twenty years
passed in ironing. Well ! she was on her way to the country.
She was going to have her green corner in the Père-Lachaise
cemetery.

When she entered the passage, she was like a madwoman.
Her poor head was whirling round. At heart, her great grief
was at having bid the blacksmith an eternal farewell. All was
ended between them, they would never see each other more.
Then, besides that, all her other thoughts of misfortune pressed
upon her and almost caused her head to split. As she passed,
she poked her nose in at the Bijards' and beheld Lalie dead,
with a look of contentment on her face at having at last cocked
her toes, and slumbering for ever. Ah well ! children were
luckier than grown up people ! And, as a glimmer of light
passed under old Bazouge's door, she walked boldly in, seized
with a mania for going off on the same journey as the little one.

That old joker Bazouge had come home that night in an extraordinary state of gaiety. He had had such a booze, that he
was snoring on the ground, in spite of the temperature ; and
that no doubt did not prevent him from dreaming something
pleasant, for he seemed to be laughing from his stomach as he
slept. The candle, which he had not put out, lighted up his
old garments, his black cloak which he had drawn over his
knees, as though it had been a rug.

On beholding him Gervaise uttered such a deep wailing, that
he awoke.

"Damnation ! shut the door ! It's so cold !. Ah ! it's you !
What's the mattter ? what do you want ? "

Then Gervaise, stretching out her arms, no longer knowing
what she stuttered, began passionately to implore him.

"Oh ! take me away, I've had enough ; I want to go off. You
mustn't bear me any grudge. I didn't know, good heavens ! One

never knows until one's ready. Oh! yes, one's glad to go one day! Take me away, take me away, and I shall thank you."

And she fell on her knees, all shaken with a desire which caused her to turn ghastly pale. Never before had she thus dragged herself at a man's feet. Old Bazouge's mug, with his mouth all on one side and his hide begrimed with the dust of funerals, seemed to her as beautiful and resplendent as a sun. The old fellow, who was scarcely awake, thought, however, that it was some practical joke.

"I say now," murmured he, " no jokes!"

"Take me away," repeated Gervaise, more ardently still. " You remember, I knocked one evening against the partition; then I said that it wasn't true, because I was still a fool. But see! give me your hands, I'm no longer frightened. Take me away to by-by; you'll see how still I'll be. Oh! that's all I care for. Oh! I'll love you so much!"

Bazouge, ever gallant, thought that he ought not to be hasty with a lady who appeared to have taken such a fancy to him. She was falling to pieces, but all the same what remained was very fine, especially when she was excited.

"What you say's very true," said he in a convinced manner. " I packed up three more to-day, who would only have been too glad to have given me something for myself, could they but have got their hands to their pockets. But, little woman, it's not so easily settled as all that—"

"Take me away, take me away," continued Gervaise, " I want to go off—"

"Ah! but there's a little operation to be gone through beforehand—you know, conic!"

And he made a noise in his throat, as though swallowing his tongue. Then, thinking it a good joke, he chuckled.

Gervaise slowly rose to her feet. So he too could do nothing for her. She went to her room and threw herself on her straw, feeling stupid, and regretting she had eaten. Ah! no indeed, misery did not kill quick enough.

CHAPTER XIII

THAT night, Coupeau went on the batter. Next day, Gervaise received ten francs from her son Etienne, who was an engineer on some railway. The youngster sent her a few francs from time to time, knowing that they were not very well off at home. She made some soup, and eat it all alone, for that scoundrel Coupeau did not return on the morrow. On the Monday he was still absent, and on the Tuesday also. The whole week went by. Ah, by Jove! if a lady had only carried him off, that would indeed have been a good piece of luck. But on the Sunday it happened that Gervaise received a printed paper, which frightened her at first, because it looked liked a communication from the commissary of police. Afterwards she became reassured; it was merely to inform her that her pig was in a fair way to croak at Sainte-Anne. The paper was worded more politely, only it amounted to the same thing. Yes, it was, indeed, a lady who had got hold of Coupeau, and her name was Sophie-Put-'em-to-Sleep, the drunkard's last good friend.

Gervaise did not disturb herself. He knew the way; he could very well get home from the asylum by himself. They had cured him there so often that they could once more do him the sorry service of putting him on his pins again. Had she not heard that very morning that for a week Coupeau had been seen as round as a ball, rolling about Belleville from one dram-shop to another in the company of My-Boots? Exactly so; and it was My-Boots, too, who stood treat. He must have hooked his missus's stocking with all the savings gained at the pretty game you know of.

Ah, they were drinking some pretty money there, capable of giving one every abominable disease imaginable! So much the better if it had given Coupeau the colic! And Gervaise was especially furious when she considered that this lousy, selfish pair had not even thought of calling for her and standing her a drink. Did ever any one hear of such a thing?—a week's booze, and not the least gallantry shown to the ladies! When one swills by oneself, one may croak by oneself, there now!

However, on the Monday, as Gervaise had a nice little meal for the evening, the remains of some beans and a pint of wine, she pretended to herself that a walk would give her an appetite. The letter from the asylum, which she had left lying on the drawers, bothered her. The snow had melted, the day was mild and grey, and on the whole fine, with just a slight keenness in, the air which was invigorating. She started at noon, for her walk was a long one. She had to cross Paris, and her shank was always lagging. With that the streets were crowded; but the people amused her; she reached her destination very pleasantly. When she had given her name, she was told a most astounding story, to the effect that Coupeau had been fished out of the river, close to the Pont-Neuf. He had jumped over the parapet, under the impression that a bearded man was barring his way. A fine jump, was it not? And as for finding out how Coupeau got to be on the Pont-Neuf, that was a matter he could not even explain himself.

One of the keepers escorted Gervaise. She was ascending a staircase, when she heard howlings which made her shiver to her very bones.

"Eh! he's playing a nice music, isn't he?" observed the keeper.

"Who is?" asked she.

"Why, your old man! He's been yelling like that ever since the day before yesterday; and he dances, you'll just see."

Ah, good heavens! what a sight! She stood as one transfixed. The cell was padded from the floor to the ceiling. On the floor there were two straw mats, one above the other; and in a corner were spread a mattress and a bolster, nothing more. Inside there, Coupeau was dancing and yelling. A regular guy of the outskirts, with his blouse in tatters and his limbs beating the air; but not a funny guy—oh, no!—a guy whose terrible capers made every hair of your head stand on end. He wore the mask of one about to die. By Jove! what a breakdown! He bumped up against the window, then retired backwards, beating time with his arms, and shaking his hands as though he were trying to wrench them off and fling them in somebody's face. One meets with jokers in the low

dancing places, who imitate that, only they imitate it badly.
One must see this drunkard's rigadoon danced if one wishes to
know what it is like when gone through in earnest. The song
also has its merits, a continuous yell worthy of carnival-time, a
mouth wide open uttering the same hoarse trombone notes for
hours together. Coupeau had the howl of a beast with a
crushed paw. Strike up, music! Gentlemen, choose your
partners!

"Good Lord! what is the matter with him? what is the
matter with him?" repeated Gervaise, seized with fear.

A house surgeon, a big fair fellow with a rosy countenance,
and wearing a white apron, was quietly sitting taking notes.
The case was a curious one; the doctor did not leave the
patient.

"Stay a while if you like," said he to the laundress; "but
keep quiet. Try and speak to him, he will not recognise you."

Coupeau, indeed, did not even appear to see his wife. She
had only had a bad view of him on entering, he was wriggling
about so much. When she looked him full in the face, she
stood aghast. Good heavens! was it possible he had a countenance like that, his eyes full of blood and his lips covered with
scabs? She would certainly never have known him. To begin
with, he was making too many grimaces, without saying why,
his mouth suddenly out of all shape, his nose curled up, his
cheeks drawn in, a perfect animal's muzzle. His skin was so
hot, the air steamed around him; and his hide was as though
varnished, covered with a heavy sweat which trickled off him.
In his mad dance, one could see all the same that he was not at
his ease, his head was heavy and his limbs ached.

Gervaise drew near to the house surgeon, who was strumming
a tune with the tips of his fingers on the back of his chair.

"I say, sir, it's serious then, this time?"

The house surgeon nodded his head without answering.

"I say, isn't he jabbering to himself? Eh! don't you hear?
what's it about?"

"About things he sees," murmured the young man. "Keep
quiet, let me listen."

Coupeau was speaking in a jerky voice. A glimmer of fun
lit up his eyes. He looked on the floor, to the right, to the
left, and turned about, as though he had been strolling in the
Bois de Vincennes, conversing with himself.

"Ah! that's nice, that's grand!—There're cottages, a regular
fair. And some jolly fine music! What a Balthazar's feast!

COUPEAU'S NEVER-ENDING DANCE IN THE PADDED ROOM OF
THE LUNATIC ASYLUM. p. 446.

They're smashing the crockery in there—Awfully swell! Now
it's being lit up; red balls in the air, and it jumps, and it flies!
Oh! oh! what a lot of lanterns in the trees!—It's confoundedly
pleasant! There's water flowing everywhere, fountains, cascades, water which sings, oh! with the voice of a chorister—
The cascades are grand!"

And he drew himself up, as though the better to hear the
delicious song of the water; he sucked in forcibly, fancying he
was drinking the fresh spray blown from the fountains. But,
little by little, his face resumed an agonised expression. Then
he crouched down, and flew quicker than ever around the walls
of the cell, uttering low menaces.

"More traps, all that!—I thought as much—Silence, you set
of swindlers! Yes, you're making a fool of me. It's for that
that you're drinking and bawling inside there with your
strumpets—I'll demolish you, you and your cottage!—Damnation! will you leave me in peace?"

He clinched his fists; then he uttered a hoarse cry, stooping
as he ran. And he stuttered, his teeth chattering with fright.

"It's so that I may kill myself. No, I won't throw myself
in!—All that water means that I've no heart. No, I won't
throw myself in!"

The cascades, which fled at his approach, advanced when he
retired. And, all on a sudden, he looked stupidly around him,
mumbling, in a voice which was scarcely audible:

"It isn't possible, they've set conjurers against me!"

"I'm off, sir, good-night!" said Gervaise to the house
surgeon. "It upsets me too much; I'll come again."

She was quite white. Coupeau was continuing his breakdown from the window to the mattress, and from the mattress
to the window, perspiring, toiling, beating the same time. Then
she hurried away. But though she scrambled down the stairs,
she still heard her husband's confounded jig until she reached
the bottom. Ah! good heavens! how pleasant it was out of
doors, one could breathe there!

That evening, all the household talked of old Coupeau's
strange illness. The Boches, who now treated the Hobbler in
a most off-hand manner, offered her, however, a drink in their
room, just to hear the details. Madame Lorilleux looked in,
and Madame Poisson also. They made endless remarks.
Boche had been acquainted with a carpenter who had gone
along the Rue Saint-Martin perfectly naked, and had died
dancing the polka; he used to drink absinthe. The ladies

wriggled with laughter, because it seemed to them very funny all the same, although rather sad. Then, as they did not quite comprehend, Gervaise pushed the people aside, and called for room; and, in the centre of the apartment, she acted Coupeau, bawling, jumping, throwing herself about with the most abominable grimaces, while the others were looking on. Yes, honour bright! it was exactly like that! Then the others expressed their amazement : it was not possible! a man could not have lasted three hours at such a game. Well! she swore it on all she held most sacred, Coupeau had been at it since the day before, thirty-six hours already. Besides, if they did not believe her, they could go and see for themselves.

Madame Lorilleux, however, declared, thank you for nothing! she had had enough of Sainte-Anne; she would even prevent Lorilleux putting a foot inside there. As to Virginie, whose shop was going from bad to worse, and who had a most funereal face, she contented herself by murmuring that life was not always gay, ah! by Jove, no! The glasses being emptied, Gervaise wished the company good-night. Directly she had left off speaking, her head assumed the crazy look of a madwoman, with her eyes wide open. No doubt she beheld her husband stepping his waltz.

On getting up the next morning, Gervaise promised herself she would not return to Sainte-Anne again. What use would it be? She did not want to go off her chump also. However, every ten minutes, she fell to musing, became absent-minded. It would be curious though, if he were still throwing his legs about. When twelve o'clock struck, she could no longer resist; she started off and did not notice how long the walk was, her brain was so full of her desire to go and the dread of what awaited her.

Oh! there was no occasion for her to ask for news. She heard Coupeau's song the moment she reached the foot of the staircase. Just the same tune, just the same dance. She might have thought herself going up again after having been down for a minute. The attendant of the day before, who was carrying some jugs of infusion along the corridor, winked his eye as he met her, by way of doing the amiable.

"Still the same, then?" said she.

"Oh! still the same!" he replied without stopping.

She entered, but she remained near the door, because there were some people with Coupeau. The fair, rosy, house surgeon was standing up, having given his chair to a bald old gentle-

man who was decorated and had a face like a martin. He was
no doubt the head doctor, for his glance was as sharp and
piercing as a gimlet. All the dealers in sudden death have a
glance like that.

Gervaise, however, had not come to look at this gentleman,
and she stood on tiptoe behind his bald pate, devouring Coupeau
with her eyes. This maniac was dancing and yelling still
louder than the day before. She remembered having seen in
former days, at the balls in mid-Lent, sturdy men from the
wash-house cut capers for a whole night ; but never, no never,
would she have imagined that a man could take pleasure in it
so long ; when she talked of pleasure, it was merely a figure of
speech, for there is no pleasure in turning somersaults in spite
of oneself, as though one had swallowed a powder magazine.
Coupeau, soaked with perspiration, smoked more, that was all.
His mouth seemed to have grown larger through force of shouting. Oh! ladies in the family way did well to keep outside.
He had walked so often from the mattress to the window, that
he had made quite a little path along the floor ; the matting
was worn away by his old shoes.

No, really, it was not a pretty sight ; and Gervaise, all in a
tremble, asked herself why she had returned. To think that
the evening before, they accused her at the Boches' of exagger-
ating the picture ! Ah ! well, she had not done half enough !
Now, she saw better how Coupeau set about it, his eyes wide
open looking into vacancy, and she would never forget it. She
overheard a few words between the house surgeon and the head
doctor. The former was giving some details of the night : her
husband had talked and thrown himself about, that was what
it amounted to. Then the bald-headed old gentleman, who
was not very polite by the way, at length appeared to become
aware of her presence ; and when the house surgeon had informed him that she was the patient's wife, he began to question
her, in the harsh manner of a commissary of police.

"Did this man's father drink ?"

"Yes, sir, just a little, like every one. He killed himself by
falling from a roof, one day when he was tipsy."

"Did his mother drink ?"

"Well ! sir, like every one else, you know, a drop here, a
drop there. Oh ! the family is very respectable ! There was
a brother who died very young in convulsions."

The doctor looked at her with his piercing eye. He resumed
in his rough voice :

" And you, do you drink ? "

Gervaise stammered, protested, and placed her hand upon her heart as though to take her solemn oath.

" You drink ! Take care, see where drink leads to. One day or other, you will die thus."

Then, she remained close to the wall. The doctor had turned his back on her. He squatted down, without troubling himself as to whether his overcoat trailed in the dust of the matting ; for a long while he studied Coupeau's trembling, waiting for its reappearance, following it with his glance. That day the legs were going in their turn, the trembling had descended from the hands to the feet ; a regular puppet with his strings being pulled, throwing his limbs about whilst the trunk of his body remained as stiff as a piece of wood. The disease increased little by little. It was like a musical box beneath the skin ; it started off every three or four seconds, and rolled along for an instant ; then it stopped, and then it started off again, just the same as the little shiver which shakes stray dogs in winter, when cold and standing in some doorway for protection. Already the middle of the body and the shoulders quivered like water on the point of boiling. It was a funny demolition all the same, going off wriggling like a girl being tickled.

Coupeau, meanwhile, was complaining in a hollow voice. He seemed to suffer a great deal more than the day before. His broken murmurs disclosed all sorts of ailments. Thousands of pins were pricking him. He felt something heavy all about his body ; some cold wet animal was crawling over his thighs and digging its fangs into his flesh. Then there were other animals sticking to his shoulders, tearing his back with their claws.

" I'm thirsty, oh ! I'm thirsty ! " groaned he continually.

The house surgeon handed him a little lemonade from a small shelf, Coupeau seized the mug in both hands, and greedily took a mouthful, spilling half the liquid over himself ; but he spat it out at once, with a furious disgust, exclaiming :

" Damnation ! it's brandy ! "

Then, on a sign from the doctor, the house surgeon tried to make him drink some water, without leaving go of the bottle. This time, he swallowed the mouthful, yelling as though he had swallowed fire.

" It's brandy, damnation ! it's brandy ! "

Since the night before, everything he had had to drink was

brandy. It redoubled his thirst, and he could no longer drink, because everything burnt him. They had brought him some broth, but they were evidently trying to poison him, for the broth smelt of "vitriol." The bread was sour and mouldy. There was nothing but poison around him. The cell stank of sulphur. He even accused persons of rubbing matches under his nose to infect him.

The doctor had risen and was listening to Coupeau, who was again beholding phantoms at mid-day. Was he not fancying that he saw cobwebs on the walls as big as the sails of a ship? Then these cobwebs became nets with meshes which grew smaller and larger, a queer sort of plaything! Black balls passed in and out of the meshes, regular jugglers' balls, at first as small as marbles, and then as big as cannon balls; and they increased and they decreased in size, just for the sake of bothering him. All on a sudden, he exclaimed:

" Oh! the rats, there're the rats, now! "

It was the balls changing into rats. These filthy animals got fatter and fatter, passed through the net, and jumped on to the mattress where they disappeared. There was also a monkey which came out of the wall, and went back into the wall, and which approached so near him each time, that he drew back through fear of having his nose bitten off. Suddenly, there was another change, the walls were probably cutting capers, for he yelled out, choking with terror and rage:

" That's it, gee up! shake me, I don't care!—Gee up! shanty! gee up! tumble down! Yes, ring the bells, you set of crows! play the organ to prevent my calling the police!— And they've put a machine behind the wall, the lousy scoundrels! I can hear it, it snorts, they're going to blow us up— Fire! damnation! fire! There's a cry of fire! there it blazes. Oh! it's getting lighter, lighter! all the sky's burning, red fires, green fires, yellow fires—Hi! help! fire! "

His cries became lost in a rattle. He now only mumbled disconnected words, foaming at the mouth, his chin wet with saliva. The doctor rubbed his nose with his finger, a movement no doubt habitual with him in the presence of serious cases. He turned to the house surgeon, and asked him in a low voice:

" And the temperature, still the hundred degrees, is it not? "

" Yes, sir."

The doctor pouted. He continued there another two

minutes, his eyes fixed on Coupeau.   Then he shrugged his
shoulders, adding :

"The same treatment, broth, milk, lemonade, and the potion
of extract of quinine.   Do not leave him, and call me if
necessary."

He went out, and Gervaise followed him, to ask him if there
was any hope.   But he walked so stiffly along the corridor,
that she did not dare approach him.   She stood rooted there a
minute, hesitating whether to return and look at her husband.
The time she had already passed there had been far from
pleasant. As she again heard him calling out that the lemonade
smelt of brandy, she hurried away, having had enough of the
performance.   In the streets, the galloping of the horses and
the noise of the vehicles made her fancy that all the inmates
of Sainte-Anne were at her heels.   And that doctor who had
threatened her !   Really, she already thought she had the
complaint.

In the Rue de la Goutte-d'Or, the Boches and the others were
naturally awaiting her.   The moment she appeared, they called
her into the doorkeepers' room.   Well ! was old Coupeau still
in the land of the living ?   Good heavens ! yes, he still lived.
Boche seemed amazed and confounded ; he had bet a bottle
that old Coupeau would not last till the evening.   What ! he
still lived !   And they all exhibited their astonishment, and
slapped their thighs.   There was a fellow who lasted !   Madame
Lorilleux reckoned up the hours : thirty-six hours and twenty-
four hours, sixty hours.   By Jove ! already sixty hours that he
had been performing with his mouth and legs !   Such a feat of
strength had never been seen before.   But Boche, who was
laughing on the wrong side of his mouth because of his bet,
questioned Gervaise with an air of doubt, asking her if she was
quite sure he had not filed off behind her back.   Oh ! no, he
had no desire to, he jumped about too much.   Then Boche, still
doubting, begged her to show them again a little how he went
on, for them to see.   Yes, yes, a little more ! the request was
general ! the company told her she would be very nice if she
would oblige, for just then two neighbours happened to be there
who had not been present the day before, and who had come
down purposely to see the performance.   The doorkeeper called
to the persons to make room, they cleared the centre of the
apartment, pushing one another with their elbows, and quivering with curiosity.   Gervaise, however, hung down her head.
Really, she was afraid of making herself ill.   Desirous though

of showing that she did not refuse for the sake of being pressed, she tried two or three little leaps; but she became quite queer, and threw herself back; on her word of honour, she was not equal to it!. There was a murmur of disappointment; it was a pity, she imitated it perfectly. However, if she could not do it, it was no use insisting! And, on Virginie returning to her shop, they forgot old Coupeau, to gossip about the Poissons and their home, a regular bear-garden now. The day before, the bailiffs had been; the policeman was about to lose his place; as for Lantier, he was now making up to the girl of the eating-house next door, a fine woman, who talked of setting up as a tripe-seller. Ah! it was amusing, everyone already beheld a tripe-seller occupying the shop; after sweeties should come something substantial. That cuckold Poisson had a funny head altogether. How, goodness gracious! could a man, whose business it was to be sharp, be such a noodle in his own home? But they suddenly stopped talking on beholding Gervaise, whom they had no longer been watching, and who was going through a portion of her performance all alone in a corner of the room, her hands and feet trembling like Coupeau's. Bravo! that was it, that was all they wanted. She stood with a bewildered look, as though just awaking from a dream. Then, she went off erect, wishing everyone good-night. She was going to try and get a little sleep.

On the morrow, the Boches saw her start off at twelve, the same as on the two previous days. They wished her a pleasant afternoon. That day the corridor at Sainte-Anne positively shook with Coupeau's yells and kicks. She had not left the stairs, when she heard him bellow:

"What a lot of bugs!—Come this way again that I may squash you!—Ah! they want to kill me! ah! the bugs!—I'm a bigger swell than the lot of you! Clear out, damnation! clear out!"

For a moment she stood panting before the door. Was he then fighting against an army? When she entered, the performance had increased and embellished. Coupeau was a raving madman, the same as one sees at the Charenton mad-house! He was throwing himself about in the centre of the cell, placing his hands everywhere, on himself, on the walls, on the floor, turning head over heels, hitting into space; and he wanted to open the window, and he hid himself, defended himself, called, answered, produced all this uproar without the least assistance, in the exasperated way of a man beset by a mob of people. Then

Gervaise understood that he fancied he was on a roof, laying down sheets of zinc. He imitated the bellows with his mouth, he moved the iron about in the fire, and knelt down so as to pass his thumb along the edges of the mat, thinking that he was soldering it. Yes, his handicraft returned to him at the moment of croaking ; and if he yelled so loud, if he fought on his roof, it was because ugly scoundrels were preventing him doing his work properly. On all the neighbouring roofs were villains mocking and tormenting him. Besides that, the jokers were letting troops of rats loose about his legs. Ah ! the filthy beasts, he saw them always ! Though he kept crushing them, bringing his foot down with all his strength, fresh strings of them continued passing, until they quite covered the roof. And there were spiders there too ! He roughly pressed his trousers against his thigh to squash some big spiders which had crept up his leg. Jove's thunder ! he would never finish his day's work, they wanted to destroy him, his employer would send him to the Mazas prison. Then, whilst making haste, he suddenly imagined he had a steam-engine in his stomach ; with his mouth wide open, he puffed out the smoke, a dense smoke which filled the cell, and found an outlet by the window ; and, bending forward, still puffing, he looked outside at the cloud of smoke as it unrolled and ascended to the sky, where it hid the sun.

"Hallo !" cried he, "there's the band of the Chaussée Cliguancourt, disguised as bears, with drums."

He remained crouching before the window, as though he had been watching a procession in a street, from some house-top.

"There's the cavalcade, lions and panthers making grimaces —there're brats dressed up as dogs and cats—there's tall Clémence, with her wig full of feathers. Ah ! by Jove ! she's turning head over heels, she's showing all she's got !—I say, ducky, let's slope—Eh ! you confounded asses, just you leave her alone !—don't fire, thunder ! don't fire—"

His voice rose, hoarse and terrified, and he stooped down quickly, saying that the police and the military were below, men who were aiming at him with rifles. In the wall, he saw the barrel of a pistol pointed at his chest. They had come to take the girl from him.

"Don't fire, damnation ! don't fire—"

Then, the houses were falling in, he imitated the cracking of a whole neighbourhood collapsing ; and all disappeared, all flew off. But he had no time to take breath, other pictures passed with extraordinary rapidity. A furious desire to speak filled his mouth full of words which he uttered without any connection, and with a gurgling sound in his throat. He continued to raise his voice.

"Hallo, it's you? Good-day!—No jokes! don't make me swallow your hair."

And he passed his hand before his face, he blew to send the hairs away. The house surgeon questioned him.

"Who is it you see?"

"My wife, of course!"

He was looking at the wall, with his back to Gervaise. The latter had a rare fright, and she examined the wall, to see if she also could not catch sight of herself there. He continued talking.

"Now, you know, none of your wheedling—I won't be tied up —Jupiter! you are smart, you have got a fine dress. Where did you get it from, cow! You've been after the men again, camel! Wait a bit and I'll do for you!—Ah! you're hiding your gentleman behind your skirts. Who is it, eh! Stoop down that I may see—Damnation it's him again!"

Taking a terrible spring, he went head first against the wall; but the padding deadened the blow. One only heard his body rebounding on to the matting, where the shock had sent him.

"Who is it you see?" repeated the house surgeon.

"The hatter! the hatter!" yelled Coupeau.

And the house surgeon questioning Gervaise, the latter stuttered without being able to answer, for this scene stirred up within her all the worries of her life. The zinc-worker thrust out his fists.

"We'll settle this between us, young 'un! It's full time I did for you! Ah! you coolly come, with that strumpet on your arm, to make a fool of me before everyone. Well! I'm going to throttle you—yes, yes, I! and without putting any gloves on either! I'll stop your swaggering.—Take that. And hit! hit! hit!"

He hit about in space. Then rage took possession of him. Having bumped against the wall in walking backwards, he thought he was being attacked behind. He turned round, and fiercely hammered away at the padding. He sprang about, jumped from one corner to another, knocked his stomach, his back, his shoulder, rolled over, and picked himself up again. His bones softened, his flesh had a sound of damp tow. And he accompanied this pretty game with atrocious threats, and

wild and guttural cries. However the battle must have been
going badly for him, for his breathing became quicker, his eyes
were starting out of his head, and he seemed little by little
to be seized with the cowardice of a child.

"Murder! murder!—Be off with you both. Oh! the brutes,
they're laughing. There she is on her back, the strumpet!
She must give in, it's settled. Ah! the brigand, he's murdering her! He's cutting off her leg with his knife. The other
leg's on the ground, the stomach's in two, it's full of blood, Oh!
my God—oh! my God—oh! my God—"

And, covered with perspiration, his hair standing on end,
looking a frightful object, he retired backwards, violently waving his arms, as though to send the abominable sight from him.
He uttered two heart-rending wails, and fell flat on his back on
the mattress, against which his heels had caught.

"He's dead, sir, he's dead!" said Gervaise, clasping her
hands.

The house surgeon had drawn near, and was pulling Coupeau
into the middle of the mattress. No, he was not dead. They
had taken his shoes off. His bare feet projected at the end,
and they were dancing all by themselves, one beside the other,
in time, a little hurried and regular dance.

Just then the head doctor entered. He had brought two of
his colleagues—one thin, the other fat, and both decorated like
himself. All three stooped down without saying a word, and
examined the man all over; then they rapidly conversed together in a low voice. They had uncovered Coupeau from his
thighs to his shoulders, and by standing on tiptoe Gervaise
could see the naked trunk spread out. Well! it was complete.
The trembling had descended from the arms and ascended from
the legs, and now the trunk itself was getting lively! The
puppet was positively wriggling its stomach about as well.
There were smiles along the ribs, a breathlessness of the bread-
basket, which seemed splitting with laughter. And everything
was moving, there was no denying it. The muscles were
dancing quadrilles, the skin was vibrating like a drum, the
hairs were bowing to each other as they waltzed. In short, it
was probably the great clear out, similar to the final gallop,
when day breaks and all the dancers hold each other by the
hand, and stamp their heels on the floor.

"He's sleeping," murmured the head doctor.

And he called the two others' attention to the man's countenance. Coupeau, his eyes closed, had little nervous twinges

which drew up all his face. He was more hideous still, thus flattened out, with his jaw projecting, and his visage deformed like a corpse's that had suffered from nightmare; but the doctors, having caught sight of the feet, went and poked their noses over them, with an air of profound interest. The feet were still dancing. Though Coupeau slept the feet danced. Oh! their owner might snore, that did not concern them, they continued their little occupation without either hurrying or slackening. Regular mechanical feet, feet which took their pleasure wherever they found it.

Gervaise, having seen the doctors place their hands on her old man, wished to feel him also. She approached gently, and laid a hand on his shoulder, and she kept it there a minute. Good heavens! whatever was taking place inside? It danced down into the very depths of the flesh, the bones themselves must have been jumping. Quiverings, undulations, coming from afar, flowed like a river beneath the skin. When she pressed a little she felt she distinguished the suffering cries of the marrow. With the naked eye one only saw the little waving motions forming dimples, like on the surface of an eddy; but inside there must have been a precious devastation going on. What confounded work, a work worthy of a mole! It was the "vitriol" of the "Assommoir" pickaxing away in there. The whole body was soaked with it, and well! the work had to be finished, crumbling up Coupeau, and carrying him off in the general and continuous trembling of the entire carcass.

The doctors had gone away. At the end of an hour Gervaise, who had remained with the house surgeon, repeated in a low voice,

"He's dead, sir—he's dead!"

But the house surgeon, who was watching the feet, shook his head. The bare feet, projecting beyond the mattress, still danced on. They were not particularly clean, and the nails were long. Several more hours passed. All on a sudden they stiffened and became motionless. Then the house surgeon turned towards Gervaise, saying,

"It's over now."

Death alone had been able to stop those feet.

When Gervaise got back to the Rue de la Goutte-d'Or, she found, at the Boches', a number of women who were cackling in excited tones. She thought they were awaiting her to have the latest news, the same as the other days.

"He's croaked," said she, quietly, as she pushed open the door, looking tired out and stupid.

But no one listened to her. The whole household was topsy-turvy. Oh! a most extraordinary story. Poisson had caught his wife with Lantier. Exact details were not known, because everyone had a different version. However, he had appeared before them just when they were not expecting him. Some further information was given which the ladies repeated to one another as they pursed their lips. A sight like that had naturally brought Poisson out of his shell. He was a regular tiger! This man, who talked but little and who always seemed to walk with a stick up his back, had begun to roar and jump about. Then nothing more had been heard. Lantier had most likely explained the matter to the husband. Anyhow, it could not last much longer; and Boche announced that the girl of the eating-house next door was for certain going to take the shop for selling tripe. That rogue of a hatter adored tripe.

On seeing Madame Lorilleux and Madame Lerat arrive, Gervaise repeated faintly:

"He's croaked. Gracious goodness! four days dancing and yelling—"

Then the two sisters could not do otherwise than pull out their handkerchiefs. Their brother had had many faults, but after all he was their brother. Boche shrugged his shoulders, and said loud enough to be heard by every one:

"Bah! it's a drunkard the less!"

From that day, as Gervaise often got a bit cracked, one of the amusements of the house was to see her imitate Coupeau. It was no longer necessary to press her, she gave the performance gratis, her hands and feet trembling as she uttered little involuntary shrieks. No doubt she had caught that at Sainte-Anne, through looking at her old man too long. But she was not lucky, it did not kill her as it did him. It went no further than making grimaces like an escaped monkey, which caused the street urchins to pelt her with cabbage stalks.

Gervaise lasted in this state several months. She fell lower and lower still, submitting to the grossest outrages, and dying of starvation a little every day. As soon as she had four sous, she drank and fought the walls. She was employed on all the dirty errands of the neighbourhood. One evening some one bet she would not eat something filthy, and she had eaten it to earn ten sous. M. Marescot had decided to turn her out of her room on the sixth floor. But, as old Bru was just about that time found dead in his hole under the staircase, the landlord had allowed her to turn into it. Now, she roosted there in

FATHER BAZOUGE LAYING GERVAISE TENDERLY IN HER COFFIN.

the place of old Bru. It was inside there, on some old straw, that her teeth chattered, whilst her stomach was empty and her bones were frozen. The earth would not have her apparently. She was becoming idiotic, she did not even think of making an end of herself by jumping out of the sixth floor window on to the pavement of the courtyard below. Death was to take her little by little, bit by bit, dragging her thus to the end through the accursed existence she had made for herself. It was never even exactly known what she did die of. There was some talk of a cold; but the truth was she died of privation, and of the filth and hardship of her spoilt life. Overgorging and dissoluteness killed her, according to the Lorilleux. One morning, as there was a bad smell in the passage, it was remembered that she had not been seen for two days, and she was discovered already green in her hole.

It happened to be old Bazouge who came with the pauper's coffin under his arm to pack her up. He was again precious drunk that day, but a jolly fellow all the same, and as lively as a cricket. When he recognised the customer he had to deal with, he uttered several philosophical reflections whilst performing his little business.

"Every one goes. There's no occasion for jostling, there's room for every one. And it's stupid being in a hurry, because one does not arrive so quick. All I want to do is to please everybody. Some will, others won't. What's the result? There's one who wouldn't, then she would. So she was made to wait. Anyhow, it's all right now, and, faith! she's earned it! Merrily O!"

And when he took hold of Gervaise in his big dirty hands he was seized with emotion, and he gently raised this woman who had had so great a longing for him. Then, as he laid her out with paternal care at the bottom of the coffin, he stuttered, between two hiccoughs:

"You know—now listen—it's me, Bibi-the-Gay, called the ladies' consoler. There, you're happy. Go by-by, my beauty!"

THE END.

42, CATHERINE STREET, STRAND,
APRIL, 1885.

VIZETELLY & CO.'S NEW BOOKS, AND NEW EDITIONS.

In Demy 8vo, cloth gilt, price 12s. 6d.

A JOURNEY DUE SOUTH;

TRAVELS IN SEARCH OF SUNSHINE.

By GEORGE AUGUSTUS SALA.

ILLUSTRATED WITH 16 FULL-PAGE ENGRAVINGS BY VARIOUS ARTISTS.

CONTENTS:—

IMPORTANT NEW WORK BY THE AUTHOR OF "SIDE LIGHTS ON ENGLISH SOCIETY."

Two Vols. large Post 8vo, attractively bound, price 25s.

UNDER THE LENS:

SOCIAL PHOTOGRAPHS.

By E. C. GRENVILLE-MURRAY.

ILLUSTRATED WITH ABOUT 300 ENGRAVINGS BY WELL-KNOWN ARTISTS.

CONTENTS OF VOL. I.

JILTS:—Mrs. Pinkerton—A Western County Belle—Zoe, Lady Tryon—An Inconsolable Jilt—A Jilted Drysalter—Love and Pickles—An Entr'acte—Mrs. Prago and Miss Daisy Caunter—A Widow with a Nice Little Estate—An Unmercenary Pair of Jilts.

ADVENTURERS AND ADVENTURESSES:—Of the Genus Generally—Matrimonial Adventurers—The Joint Stock Company Chairman—A Financial Adventurer—A Professional Greek—The Countess D'Orenbarre—Lady Goldsworth—Mirabel Hildacourse—Lily Gore—Bella Martingale—Pious Mrs. Palmhold—Mrs. Decoy—Mrs. Lawkins.

PUBLIC SCHOOLBOYS AND UNDERGRADUATES:—Drawbacks of Eton—Of Various Eton Boys—Rugby and Rugbeians—Harrow, Winchester, Westminster—Oxford Undergraduates — University Discipline—Sporting and Athletic Undergraduates—Reading and Religious Undergraduates.

CONTENTS OF VOL. II.

SPENDTHRIFTS:—Prefatory—The Gambletons—Lord Charles Intynges—Lord Luke Poer—Lord Rottenham — Lord Barker—The Marquis of Malplaquet—The Lords Lumber—Sir Calling Earley—Tommy Dabble—Dicky Duff.

HONORABLE GENTLEMEN (M.P.'s):— Preliminary — Erudite Members — Crotchety Members — Free Lances — The Irish Contingent—Very Noble M.P.'s—Money Bags—Beery M.P.'s—Workingmen M.P.'s—Party Leaders—A Seatless Member.

SOME WOMEN I HAVE KNOWN:—An Ex-Beauty—Miss Jenny—Mademoiselle Sylvie—Miss Rose—Madame de l'Esbrouffe-Tourbillon.

ROUGHS OF HIGH AND LOW DEGREE:—How Roughs are Made—The Nobleman Rough—The Foreign Garrison Rough—The Clerical Rough—The Legal Rough—Medical Roughs—The Rough Flirt—The Wife-Beating Rough—Vandal Roughs—The Tourist Rough—The Nautical Rough—The Professional Bruiser—The Low-Class Rough—Women Roughs.

"Brilliant, highly-coloured sketches, . . . contains beyond doubt some of the best writing that has come from Mr. Grenville-Murray's pen."—*St. James's Gazette.*

"Limned audaciously, unsparingly, and with much ability."—*World.*

"Distinguished by their pitiless fidelity to nature."—*Society.*

"Extremely personal. The author, brilliant as were his parts, appears to have laboured under a delusion which obliged him to mistake personal abuse for satire, and ill-nature for moral indignation."—*Athenæum.*

"Some of Mr. Murray's trenchant blows do real service to the cause of public morality and order."—*Daily Telegraph.*

"Includes unvarnished portraits of various characters who have made a flutter in recent times in this little world of ours."—*Vanity Fair.*

THE MISSES D'ORENBARE EXHIBIT THEIR AVERSION TO FAT MEN AND SMOKERS. *from* "UNDER THE LENS."

VIZETELLY'S ONE-VOLUME NOVELS.

In Crown 8vo, good readable type, and attractive binding, price 6s. each.

PRINCE SERGE PANINE.

By GEORGES OHNET.

AUTHOR OF "THE IRONMASTER."

TRANSLATED, without Abridgment, from the 110TH FRENCH EDITION.

THE CORSARS; OR, LOVE AND LUCRE.

By JOHN HILL.

AUTHOR OF "THE WATERS OF MARAH," "SALLY," &c.

MR. BUTLER'S WARD.

By MABEL ROBINSON.

COUNTESS SARAH.

By GEORGES OHNET.

AUTHOR OF "THE IRONMASTER."

TRANSLATED, WITHOUT ABRIDGMENT, FROM THE 11STH FRENCH EDITION.

BETWEEN MIDNIGHT AND DAWN.

By INA L. CASSILIS.

AUTHOR OF "SOCIETY'S QUEEN," 'STRANGELY WOOED: STRANGELY WON," &c.

THE FORKED TONGUE.

By R. LANGSTAFF DE HAVILLAND, M.A.

AUTHOR OF "KATINKA; OR, UNDER THE VENEER," "ENSLAVED," &c.

THE THREATENING EYE.

By E. F. KNIGHT.

AUTHOR OF "A CRUISE IN THE FALCON."

NUMA ROUMESTAN; OR, JOY ABROAD AND GRIEF AT HOME.

By ALPHONSE DAUDET.

TRANSLATED BY MRS. J. G. LAYARD.

"'Numa Roumestan' is a masterpiece; it is really a perfect work; it has no fault, no weakness. It is a compact and harmonious whole."—MR. HENRY JAMES.

In Crown 8vo, 450 pages, 6s.

A MUMMER'S WIFE.

A REALISTIC NOVEL. BY GEORGE MOORE.
AUTHOR OF "A MODERN LOVER."

"A striking book, different in tone from current English fiction. The woman's character is a very powerful study."—*Athenæum.*

In small 8vo, price 3s. 6d.

A MODERN LOVER.

BY GEORGE MOORE. AUTHOR OF "A MUMMER'S WIFE."

In Large Crown 8vo, beautifully printed on toned paper, and handsomely bound, with gilt edges, price 7s. 6d., suitable in every way for a present,

AN ILLUSTRATED EDITION OF

M. GEORGES OHNET'S CELEBRATED NOVEL,

THE IRONMASTER; OR, LOVE AND PRIDE.

TRANSLATED FROM THE 146th FRENCH EDITION AND CONTAINING 42 FULL-PAGE ENGRAVINGS BY FRENCH ARTISTS, PRINTED SEPARATE FROM THE TEXT.

"M. Georges Ohnet's 'Ironmaster' has proved the greatest literary success in any language of recent times, the author having already realised £12,000 from the French edition of it."

An Edition of the above Work is published without the Illustrations in small 8vo, price 3s. 6d.

Second Edition, with Frontispiece and Vignette, price 5s.

HIGH LIFE IN FRANCE UNDER THE REPUBLIC:

SOCIAL AND SATIRICAL SKETCHES IN PARIS AND THE PROVINCES.

BY E. C. GRENVILLE-MURRAY.
AUTHOR OF "SIDE LIGHTS ON ENGLISH SOCIETY," &c.

"Take this book as it stands, with the limitations imposed upon its author by circumstances, and it will be found very enjoyable. . . . , The volume is studded with shrewd observations on French life at the present day."—*Spectator.*

"A very clever and entertaining series of social and satirical sketches, almost French in their point and vivacity."—*Contemporary Review.*

In Large Post 8vo, cloth gilt, price 9s.

IMPRISONED IN A SPANISH CONVENT:

AN ENGLISH GIRL'S EXPERIENCES.
BY E. C. GRENVILLE-MURRAY.

ILLUSTRATED WITH PAGE AND OTHER ENGRAVINGS.

Fourth Edition, in Post 8vo, handsomely bound, price 7s. 6d.

SIDE-LIGHTS ON ENGLISH SOCIETY:

Sketches from Life, Social and Satirical.

By E. C. GRENVILLE-MURRAY.

ILLUSTRATED WITH NEARLY 300 CHARACTERISTIC ENGRAVINGS.

CONTENTS:

I. FLIRTS:—Born Flirts—The Flirt who has Plain Sisters—The Flirt in the London Season—The Ecclesiastical Flirt—The Regimental Flirt on Home and Foreign Service—The Town and Country House Flirt—The Seaside Flirt—The Flirt on her Travels—The Sentimental Flirt—The Studious Flirt.

II. ON HER BRITANNIC MAJESTY'S SERVICE:—Ambassadors—Envoys Extraordinary—Secretaries of Embassy—Secretaries of Legation—Attachés—Consuls-General—Consuls—Vice-Consuls—Queen's Messengers—Interpreters—Ambassadresses.

III. SEMI-DETACHED WIVES:—Authoresses and Actresses—Separated by Mutual Consent—Candidates for a Decree Nisi—A very virtuous Semi-Detached Wife—Ulysses and Penelope.

IV. NOBLE LORDS:—The Millionnaire Duke—Political Peers—Noble Old Fogies—Spiritual Peers—The Sabbatarian Peer—The Philanthropist Peer—Coaching Peers—Sporting Peers—Spendthrift Peers—Peers without Rent-rolls—Virtuoso Lords—Mad and Miserly Peers—Stock Exchange and Literary Lords.

V. YOUNG WIDOWS:—Interesting Widows—Gay Young Widows—Young Widows of Good Estate—Young Widows who take Boarders—Young Widows who want Situations—Great Men's Young Widows—Widows under a Cloud.

VI. OUR SILVERED YOUTH, OR NOBLE OLD BOYS:—Political Old Boys—Horsey Old Boys—An M. F. H.—Theatrical Old Boys—The Old Boy Cricketer—The Agricultural Old Boy—The Wicked Old Boy—The Shabby Old Boy—The Recluse Old Boy—The Clerical Old Boy—A Curiosity—An Old Courtier.

"This is a startling book. The volume is expensively and elaborately got up; the writing is bitter, unsparing, and extremely clever."—*Vanity Fair.*

"Mr. Grenville-Murray sparkles very steadily throughout the present volume, and puts to excellent use his incomparable knowledge of life and manners, of men and cities, of appearances and facts. Of his several descants upon English types, I shall only remark that they are brilliantly and dashingly written, curious as to their matter, and admirably readable."—*Truth.*

"No one can question the brilliancy of the sketches, nor affirm that 'Side-Lights' is aught but a fascinating book ...... The book is destined to make a great noise in the world."—*Whitehall Review.*

THE RICH WIDOW (reduced from the original engraving).

Second Edition, in large 8vo, handsomely bound, with gilt edges, price 10s. 6d.

PEOPLE I HAVE MET.

By E. C. GRENVILLE-MURRAY.

Illustrated with 54 tinted Page Engravings, from Designs by FRED. BARNARD.

CONTENTS :—

The Old Earl.	The Rector.	The Doctor.	The Bachelor.
The Dowager.	The Curate.	The Retired Colonel.	The Younger Son.
The Family Solicitor.	The Governess.	The Chaperon.	The Grandmother.
The College Don.	The Tutor.	The Usurer.	The Newspaper Editor.
The Rich Widow.	The Promising Son.	The Spendthrift.	The Butler.
The Ornamental Director.	The Favourite Daughter.	Le Nouveau Riche.	The Devotee.
The Old Maid.	The Squire.	The Maiden Aunt.	

"Mr. Grenville-Murray's pages sparkle with cleverness and with a shrewd wit, caustic or cynical at times, but by no means excluding a due appreciation of the softer virtues of women and the sterner excellences of men. The talent of the artist (Mr. Barnard) is akin to that of the author, and the result of the combination is a book that, once taken up, can hardly be laid down until the last page is perused."—*Spectator.*

"All are strongly accentuated portraits. 'The Promising Son' is perhaps the best, though the most melancholy of the series. From first to last, as might be expected, the book is well written."—*Standard.*

"Mr. Grenville-Murray's sketches are genuine studies, and are the best things of the kind that have been published since 'Sketches by Boz,' to which they are superior in the sense in which artistically executed character-portraits are superior to caricatures."—*St. James's Gazette.*

"All of Mr. Grenville-Murray's portraits are clever and life-like, and some of them are not unworthy of a model who was more before the author's eyes than Addison—namely Thackeray."—*Truth.*

An Edition of "PEOPLE I HAVE MET" is published in small 8vo, with Sixteen Illustrations, price 6s.

A BUCK OF THE REGENCY: *from "DUTCH PICTURES."*

"Mr. Sala's best work has in it something of Montaigne, a great deal of Charles Lamb—made deeper and broader—and not a little of Lamb's model, the accomplished and quaint Sir Thomas Browne. These 'Dutch Pictures' and 'Pictures Done With a Quill' should be placed alongside Oliver Wendell Holmes's inimitable budgets of friendly gossip and Thackeray's 'Roundabout Papers.' They display to perfection the quick eye, good taste, and ready hand of the born essayist—they are never tiresome."—*Daily Telegraph.*

In Crown 8vo, price 5s.

DUTCH PICTURES, and PICTURES DONE WITH A QUILL.

Illustrated with a Frontispiece and other Page Engravings.

FORMING THE FIRST VOLUME OF THE

CHOICER MISCELLANEOUS WORKS OF GEORGE AUGUSTUS SALA.

A SMALL NUMBER OF COPIES OF THE ABOVE WORK HAVE BEEN PRINTED IN DEMY OCTAVO, ON HAND-MADE PAPER, WITH THE ILLUSTRATIONS ON INDIA PAPER MOUNTED.

The Graphic remarks: " We have received a sumptuous new edition of Mr. G. A. Sala's well known ' Dutch Pictures.' It is printed on rough paper, and is enriched with many admirable illustrations."

Uniform with the above Volume,

UNDER THE SUN.

ESSAYS MAINLY WRITTEN IN HOT COUNTRIES,

By GEORGE AUGUSTUS SALA.

Illustrated with an etched Portrait of the Author, and various Page Engravings.

In One Volume, Demy 8vo, 560 pages, price 12s., the FIFTH EDITION *of*

AMERICA REVISITED,

From the Bay of New York to the Gulf of Mexico, and from Lake Michigan to the Pacific;

INCLUDING A SOJOURN AMONG THE MORMONS IN SALT LAKE CITY.

By GEORGE AUGUSTUS SALA.

ILLUSTRATED WITH NEARLY 400 ENGRAVINGS.

CONTENTS.

Outward Bound.
Thanksgiving Day in New York.
Transformation of New York.
All the Fun of the Fair.
A Morning with Justice.
On the Cars.
Fashion and Food in New York.
The Monumental City.
Baltimore come to Life again.
The Great Grant "Boom."
A Philadelphian Babel.
At the Continental.
Christmas and the New Year.
On to Richmond.
Still on to Richmond.

In Richmond.
Genial Richmond.
In the Tombs—and out of them.
Prosperous Augusta.
The City of many Cows.
A Pantomime in the South.
Arrogant Atlanta.
The Crescent City.
On Canal Street.
In Jackson Square.
A Southern Parliament.
Sunday in New Orleans.
The Carnival Booming.
The Carnival Booms.
Going West.

The Wonderful Prairie City.
The Home of the Setting Sun.
At Omaha.
The Road to Eldorado.
Still on the Road to Eldorado.
At Last.
Aspects of 'Frisco.
China Town.
The Drama in China Town.
Scenes in China Town.
China Town by Night.
From 'Frisco to Salt Lake City.
Down among the Mormons.
The Stock-yards of Chicago.

"It was like your imperence to come smouchin' round here, looking after de white folks' washin."

"In 'America Revisited' Mr. Sala is seen at his very best; better even than in his Paris book, more evenly genial and gay, and with a fresher subject to handle."—*World.*

"Mr. Sala's good stories lie thick as plums in a pudding throughout this handsome work."—*Pall Mall Gazette.*

"A new book of travel by Mr. Sala is sure to be welcome. He possesses the happy knack of adorning whatever he touches, and of finding something worth telling when traversing beaten ground."—*Athenæum.*

"A pleasant day may be spent with this book. Open where you will you find kindly chat and pleasant description. The illustrations are admirable."—*Vanity Fair.*

"As for the style of this entertaining and lively book, it is exactly what we should have expected. The writer is full of life, observation, and swiftness to seize upon salient and characteristic points. His description of the Chinese quarter of San Francisco may be strongly commended."—*Saturday Review.*

"This brilliant work possesses an irresistible charm, difficult to define indeed, but none the less delightful. Reading it is like listening to a good talker—the usual slightly wearisome sense of reading is effaced by the vivaciousness of the style in which the cleverest *feuilletoniste* of the day has narrated his experiences on the occasion of his last visit to America."—*Morning Post.*

"'America Revisited' is bright, lively, and amusing. We doubt whether Mr. Sala could be dull even if he tried."—*Globe.*

*Seventh Edition, in Crown 8vo, 558 pages, attractively bound, price 3s. 6d.,
or gilt at the side and with gilt edges, 5s.*

PARIS HERSELF AGAIN.

By GEORGE AUGUSTUS SALA.

WITH 350 CHARACTERISTIC ILLUSTRATIONS BY FRENCH ARTISTS.

"The author's 'round-about' chapters are as animated as they are varied and sympathetic, for few Englishmen have the French *verve* like Mr. Sala, or so light a touch on congenial subjects. He has stores of out-of-the-way information, a very many-sided gift of appreciation, with a singularly tenacious memory, and on subjects like those in his present work he is at his best."— *The Times.*

"Most amusing letters they are, with clever little pictures scattered so profusely through the solid volume that it would be difficult to prick the edges with a pin at any point without coming upon one or more. Few writers can rival Mr. Sala's fertility of illustration and ever ready command of lively comment."—*Daily News.*

"'Paris Herself Again' furnishes a happy illustration of the attractiveness of Mr. Sala's style and the fertility of his resources. For those who do and those who do not know Paris these volumes contain a fund of instruction and amusement."—*Saturday Review.*

"This book is one of the most readable that has appeared for many a day. Few Englishmen know so much of old and modern Paris as Mr. Sala. Endowed with a facility to extract humour from every phase of the world's stage, and blessed with a wondrous store of recondite lore, he outdoes himself when he deals with a city like Paris that he knows so well, and that affords such an opportunity for his pen."—*Truth.*

"'Paris Herself Again' is infinitely more amusing than most novels, and will give you information which you can turn to advantage, and innumerable anecdotes for the dinner-table and the smoking-room. There is no style so chatty and so unwearying as that of which Mr. Sala is a master."—*The World.*

THE ARRIVAL OF THE ELEVEN YOUNG MEN AT NANA'S EVENING PARTY.

In large 8vo, handsomely bound and gilt, price 7s. 6d.

A NEW ILLUSTRATED EDITION OF M. EMILE ZOLA'S REALISTIC NOVEL,

NANA.

Illustrated with upwards of 100 Engravings, nearly half of which are full-page.

TO BE FOLLOWED BY ILLUSTRATED EDITIONS OF

THE "ASSOMMOIR," PIPING HOT,

AND THE REST OF M. ZOLA'S MORE POPULAR WORKS.

In Crown 8vo, handsomely bound and gilt, price 6s., the Third and Completely Revised Edition of

THE STORY OF
THE DIAMOND NECKLACE,

COMPRISING A SKETCH OF THE LIFE OF THE COUNTESS DE LA MOTTE, PRE-
TENDED CONFIDANTE OF MARIE-ANTOINETTE, WITH PARTICULARS OF THE
CAREERS OF THE OTHER ACTORS IN THIS REMARKABLE DRAMA.

By HENRY VIZETELLY,

AUTHOR OF "BERLIN UNDER THE NEW EMPIRE," "PARIS IN PERIL," &c.

Illustrated with an Exact Representation of the Diamond Necklace, from a contemporary Drawing, and a Portrait of the Countess de la Motte, engraved on Steel.

"Mr. Vizetelly's tale has all the interest of a romance which is too strange not to be true. . . . . His summing up of the evidence, both negative and positive, which exculpates Marie-Antoinette from any complicity whatever with the scandalous intrigue in which she was represented as bearing a part, is admirable."—*Saturday Review.*

"We can, without fear of contradiction, describe Mr. Henry Vizetelly's 'Story of the Diamond Necklace' as a book of thrilling interest. He has not only executed his task with skill and faithfulness, but also with tact and delicacy."—*Standard.*

"Had the most daring of our sensational novelists put forth the present plain unvarnished statement of facts as a work of fiction, it would have been denounced as so violating all probabilities as to be a positive insult to the common sense of the reader. Yet strange, startling, incomprehensible as is the narrative which the author has here evolved, every word of it is true."—*Notes and Queries.*

In Large Crown 8vo, handsomely printed and bound, price 6s.

THE AMUSING
ADVENTURES OF GUZMAN OF ALFARAQUE.

A SPANISH NOVEL. TRANSLATED BY EDWARD LOWDELL.

ILLUSTRATED WITH HIGHLY-FINISHED ENGRAVINGS ON STEEL FROM DESIGNS BY STAHL.

"The wit, vivacity and variety of this masterpiece cannot be over-estimated."—*Morning Post.*

"A very well executed translation of a famous 'Rogue's Progress.'"—*Spectator.*

"The story is infinitely amusing, and illustrated as it is with several excellent designs on steel, it will be acceptable to a good many readers."—*Scotsman.*

In Crown 8vo, attractively bound, price 2s. 6d.

THE RED CROSS, AND OTHER STORIES.

By LUIGI.

" The short stories are the best—Luigi is in places tender and pathetic."—*Athenæum.*
" The plans of the tales are excellent. Many of the incidents are admirable, and there is a good deal of pathos in the writing."—*Scotsman.*

In Two Volumes, post 8vo, price 10s. 6d.

SOCIETY NOVELETTES.

By F. C. BURNAND, H. SAVILE CLARKE, R. E. FRANCILLON, JOSEPH HATTON, RICHARD JEFFERIES, the Author of "A French Heiress in her own Château," &c. &c.

Illustrated with numerous Page and other Engravings, from Designs by R. Caldecott, Linley Sambourne, M. E. Edwards, F. Dadd, &c.

"The reader will not be disappointed in the hopes raised by Messrs. Vizetelly's pleasing volumes. . . . There is much that is original and clever in these 'Society' tales."—*Athenæum.*
" Many of the stories are of the greatest merit; and indeed with such contributors, the reader might be sure of the unusual interest and amusement which these volumes supply."—*Daily Telegraph.*

In Crown 8vo, price 3s. 6d.

A NEW EDITION, COMPRISING MUCH ADDITIONAL MATTER, OF

IN STRANGE COMPANY.

By JAMES GREENWOOD (the "Amateur Casual").

ILLUSTRATED WITH A PORTRAIT OF THE AUTHOR, ENGRAVED ON STEEL.

In square 8vo, cloth gilt, price 3s. 6d.

LAYS OF THE SAINTLY;

OR, THE NEW GOLDEN LEGEND.

By the LONDON HERMIT (W. PARKE),

WITH HUMOROUS ILLUSTRATIONS BY J. LEITCH.

"Lovers of laughter, raillery, and things ludicrous would do well to become possessed of this volume of humorous poems levelled against the absurd though amusing superstitions of the Middle Ages."—*Newcastle Chronicle.*

In Post 8vo, price 2s. 6d.

THE CHILDISHNESS AND BRUTALITY OF THE TIME:

SOME PLAIN TRUTHS IN PLAIN LANGUAGE.

By HARGRAVE JENNINGS, Author of "The Rosicrucians," &c.

"Mr. Jennings has a knack of writing in good, racy, trenchant style. His sketch of behind the scenes of the Opera, and his story of a mutiny on board an Indiaman of the old time, are penned with surprising freshness and spirit."—*Daily News.*

In Demy 4to, handsomely printed and bound, with gilt edges, price 12s.

A HISTORY OF CHAMPAGNE;

WITH NOTES ON THE OTHER SPARKLING WINES OF FRANCE.

By HENRY VIZETELLY.

CHEVALIER OF THE ORDER OF FRANZ-JOSEF.

WINE JUROR FOR GREAT BRITAIN AT THE VIENNA AND PARIS EXHIBITIONS OF 1873 AND 1878.

Illustrated with 350 Engravings,

FROM ORIGINAL SKETCHES AND PHOTOGRAPHS, ANCIENT MSS., EARLY PRINTED BOOKS, RARE PRINTS, CARICATURES, ETC.

"A very agreeable medley of history, anecdote, geographical description, and such like matter, distinguished by an accuracy not often found in such medleys, and illustrated in the most abundant and pleasingly miscellaneous fashion."—*Daily News.*

"Mr. Henry Vizetelly's handsome book about Champagne and other sparkling wines of France is full of curious information and amusement. It should be widely read and appreciated."—*Saturday Review.*

"Mr. Henry Vizetelly has written a quarto volume on the 'History of Champagne,' in which he has collected a large number of facts, many of them very curious and interesting. Many of the woodcuts are excellent."—*Athenæum.*

In large imperial 8vo, price 6d.

THE SOCIAL ZOO;

SATIRICAL, SOCIAL, AND HUMOROUS SKETCHES BY THE BEST WRITERS.

Copiously Illustrated in Many Styles by well-known Artists.

NOW READY.

OUR GILDED YOUTH. By E. C. GRENVILLE-MURRAY——NICE GIRLS. By R. MOUNTENEY JEPHSON——NOBLE LORDS. By E. C. GRENVILLE-MURRAY ——FLIRTS. By E. C. GRENVILLE-MURRAY——OUR SILVERED YOUTH. By E. C. GRENVILLE-MURRAY——MILITARY MEN AS THEY WERE. By E. DYNE FENTON.

In double volumes, bound in scarlet cloth, price 2s. 6d. each.

NEW EDITIONS OF

GABORIAU'S SENSATIONAL NOVELS.

NOW READY

1.—THE MYSTERY OF ORCIVAL AND THE GILDED CLIQUE.
2.—LECOQ, THE DETECTIVE.
3.—DOSSIER NO. 113, AND THE LITTLE OLD MAN OF BATIG-NOLLES.
4.—THE SLAVES OF PARIS.
5.—THE LEROUGE CASE, AND OTHER PEOPLE'S MONEY.
6.—THE COUNT'S MILLIONS.   7.—THE CATASTROPHE.

Uniform with the above,

THE OLD AGE OF LECOQ, THE DETECTIVE.

By F. DU BOISGOBEY.

In Small Post 8vo, ornamental covers, 1s. each.

GABORIAU'S SENSATIONAL NOVELS.

THE FAVOURITE READING OF PRINCE BISMARCK.

> " Ah, friend, how many and many a while
> They've made the slow time fleetly flow,
> And solaced pain and charmed exile,
> Miss Braddon and Gaboriau!"
>
> *Ballade of Railway Novels in " Longman's Magazine."*

IN PERIL OF HIS LIFE.

"A story of thrilling interest and admirably translated."—*Sunday Times.*

"Hardly ever has a more ingenious circumstantial case been imagined than that which puts the hero in peril of his life, and the manner in which the proof of his innocence is finally brought about is scarcely less skilful."—*Illustrated Sporting and Dramatic News.*

THE LEROUGE CASE.

"M. Gaboriau is a skilful and brilliant writer, capable of so diverting the attention and interest of his readers that not one word or line in his book will be skipped or read carelessly."—*Hampshire Advertiser.*

OTHER PEOPLE'S MONEY.

"The interest is kept up throughout, and the story is told graphically and with a good deal of art."—*London Figaro.*

LECOQ THE DETECTIVE. Two vols.

"In the art of forging a tangled chain of complicated incidents involved and inexplicable until the last link is reached and the whole made clear, Mr. Wilkie Collins is equalled, if not excelled, by M. Gaboriau. The same skill in constructing a story is shown by both, as likewise the same ability to build up a superstructure of facts on a foundation which, sound enough in appearance, is shattered when the long-concealed touchstone of truth is at length applied to it."—*Brighton Herald.*

THE GILDED CLIQUE.

"Full of incident and instinct with life and action. Altogether this is a most fascinating book."—*Hampshire Advertiser.*

THE MYSTERY OF ORCIVAL.

"The Author keeps the interest of the reader at fever heat, and by a succession of unexpected turns and incidents, the drama is ultimately worked out to a very pleasant result. The ability displayed is unquestionable."—*Sheffield Independent.*

DOSSIER NO. 113.

"The plot is worked out with great skill, and from first to last the reader's interest is never allowed to flag."—*Dumbarton Herald.*

THE LITTLE OLD MAN OF BATIGNOLLES.

THE SLAVES OF PARIS. Two vols.

"Sensational, full of interest, cleverly conceived and wrought out with consummate skill."—*Oxford and Cambridge Journal.*

THE COUNT'S MILLIONS. Two vols.

INTRIGUES OF A FEMALE POISONER.

THE CATASTROPHE. Two vols.

/AYWARD DOSIA, & THE GENEROUS DIPLOMATIST.
By HENRY GRÉVILLE.

"As epigrammatic as anything Lord Beaconsfield has ever written."—*Hampshire Telegraph.*

A NEW LEASE OF LIFE, & SAVING A DAUGHTER'S DOWRY. By E. ABOUT.

"'A New Lease of Life' is an absorbing story, the interest of which is kept up to the very end."—*Dublin Evening Mail.*

"The story, as a flight of brilliant and eccentric imagination, is unequalled in its peculiar way."—*The Graphic.*

COLOMBA, & CARMEN. By P. MÉRIMÉE.

"The freshness and richness of 'Colomba' is quite cheering after the stereotyped three-volume novels with which our circulating libraries are crammed."—*Halifax Times.*

"'Carmen' will be welcomed by the lovers of the sprightly and tuneful opera the heroine of which Minnie Hauk made so popular. It is a bright and vivacious story."—*Life.*

A WOMAN'S DIARY, & THE LITTLE COUNTESS. By O. FEUILLET.

"Is wrought out with masterly skill and affords reading which, although of a slightly sensational kind, cannot be said to be hurtful either mentally or morally."—*Dumbarton Herald.*

BLUE-EYED META HOLDENIS, & A STROKE OF DIPLO-MACY. By V. CHERBULIEZ.

"'Blue-eyed Meta Holdenis' is a delightful tale."—*Civil Service Gazette.*

"'A Stroke of Diplomacy' is a bright vivacious story pleasantly told."—*Hampshire Advertiser.*

THE GODSON OF A MARQUIS. By A. THEURIET.

"The rustic personages, the rural scenery and life in the forest country of Argonne, are painted with the hand of a master. From the beginning to the close the interest of the story never flags."—*Life.*

THE TOWER OF PERCEMONT AND MARIANNE. By GEORGE SAND.

"George Sand has a great name, and the 'Tower of Percemont' is not unworthy of it."—*Illustrated London News.*

THE LOW-BORN LOVER'S REVENGE. By V. CHERBULIEZ.

"'The Low-born Lover's Revenge' is one of M. Cherbuliez's many exquisitely written productions. The studies of human nature under various influences, especially in the cases of the unhappy heroine and her low-born lover, are wonderfully effective."—*Illustrated London News.*

THE NOTARY'S NOSE, AND OTHER AMUSING STORIES. By E. ABOUT.

"Crisp and bright, full of movement and interest."—*Brighton Herald.*

DOCTOR CLAUDE; OR, LOVE RENDERED DESPERATE. By H. MALOT. Two vols.

"We have to appeal to our very first flight of novelists to find anything so artistic in English romance as these books."—*Dublin Evening Mail.*

THE THREE RED KNIGHTS; OR, THE BROTHERS' VENGEANCE. By P. FÉVAL.

"The one thing that strikes us in these stories is the marvellous dramatic skill of the writers."—*Sheffield Independent.*

www.ingramcontent.com/pod-product-compliance
Lightning Source LLC
Chambersburg PA
CBHW052341110726
47901CB00005B/1309